FIRE
OF
LIFE

GARY DAVID SPRINGER

Cover Artwork by
Lindsay Tiry of LT Arts
http://ltartsdesign.com

Tribal Map by
Arik Rhys Wikman

Tech Dude
Skye Bailey

Section image by www.freepik.com

For Heather and Lucy,

PREFACE

I should begin with a word of explanation.

The first chapter in this book is largely a summary of my previous work, *Phera,* self-published in 2009.

Interwoven in this summary is also a self-critique of *Phera,* a reflection born of lingering regret.

This first chapter in *Fire of Life* is intended to accommodate all readers – both those who have read *Phera* and those who have not.

If you have not read the prequel story, this chapter should bring you into the Pheran world and sketch its history in general form. You need not worry about detail.

If you have read *Phera,* this chapter should refresh and remind. Beyond that, the story of Silvarhen and the author's reflection are entirely new.

Please be patient through the early chapters in *Fire of Life.*

Trust that we climb to great heights.

N
E
W
S
ALCYANS
SEDE RIV
VARRANS
CYECU
DANVE RIVER
VARRAN
POCO
CHAUCAU
HERDERS
EBRIN RIVER
TRIB
ARIK.R.W

MEDANS
MOUNT ARRAN
MYSHENITES
TYRAENS
LYCIRA
TEKENNA
BALTHE
TORITES
LYTARR
PALE RIVER
BOKOL RIVER
ADILANS
DRAVN
BLACK RIVER
TELAND
QUORELL
PHERA

CONTENTS

I. THE FIRST VISION

"I was one of the strange faces that you saw on the Day of Contact. I was a speaker for the Pheran people. I told you of our long journey across the stars, our many achievements, our great plans for your world. You listened to my words with wonder and respect. Through my words you were filled with hope.

But I lied to you.

At first, I lied unaware that I was lying.

Later, I lied knowing well the suffering I would cause.

We did not come to you a prosperous, wise, and civilized people. We came desperate and dying. We came to take from you, not to help. We came to talk, not to listen. We came thinking only of ourselves.

Now, I will stand.

I will wander the crystal memory of my people.

Through poem, song, and story, I will speak the truth."

- Introduction of *Phera*, the confession of Silvarhen

Silvarhen was more than a speaker for the Pheran people. He was a leader, a planner, a member of the ruling elite. Through his words and actions, the dynamic of the Pheran-Human relationship was shaped. Because of his blindness and denial, the Earth was stripped.

Silvarhen's considerable role in history began in the Aquean Era, long before Pherans ever reached the Earth. From his youth in the academies off the Aquean home world, he showed the gift of rhetorical persuasion and the dangerous combination of ambition and self-righteousness. He entered the high circle of Pheran minds late in the Aquean Era by joining other young writers in a bladed criticism of the old guard of Pheran leaders. These young writers criticized the old leaders for their dull and heavy-handed methods in dealing with the Aqui. They blamed the old leaders for the constant conflict and recurring violence of the Aquean Era. They questioned the strategies of the old, but not their policies or motivation. "Our charge against the old leadership is not a moral one," Silvarhen wrote. "We believe that they acted consistently with the best interest of both the Pheran and Aquean people in mind. Survival was always the primary goal, as it should have been, as it must always be. But the old leaders failed terribly in their communication, in their lack of persuasion. They did not convince the Aqui. They did not take the time to teach."

The old leaders faded. The young rose. The young inherited the problems of the old. When the young critics became governors, their ideas were severely tested. Attempts to teach the Aqui and convince them of benevolent Pheran intention failed. The Aqui saw little difference between the old Pheran leaders and the new. The Aqui continued to reject the fundamental assumption behind Pheran policy that the Aquean home world could not be saved. They continued to resist the Pheran demands of labor and resources in the preparation for interstellar flight. "The Aqui cannot see beyond their own world," Silvarhen wrote. "We gave them dreams and visions, great works of art and detailed plans of science. They rejected every one."

The new governors blamed the failure of their persuasive strategy on some deficit in the Aquean character. They also blamed their predecessors for doing irreparable harm to Pheran credibility and reputation. Though many words were written and spoken in analysis of the problem, no Pheran governor considered the problem from the perspective of the Aqui. The Aqui were concerned with planetary problems: diminishing resources, a dying ecosystem, starvation, thirst, disease. They doubted the grand Pheran vision because it came from governors living in off-world space stations, condescending rulers who did not share in Aquean suffering.

In the final years of the Aquean Era, the Pheran governors abandoned vast regions of the planet, entire continents, and focused their attention on a few areas still rich with resources. The governors resorted to new strategies of enticement and deception to control the Aqui in these areas. They increased the number of Aquean workers allowed in the off-world stations. They exaggerated the capacity of the interstellar vessels. They fed compliant sections of the local population and starved the resistant. "Sadly, the demands of survival forced us to utilize crude methods," Silvarhen wrote. "This will not happen again."

During the long voyage to Earth, the Pheran leaders devoted themselves to the study and shaping of crystal - the encoded historical memory of their race, the vast collection of images and data, poetry and theorem, literature and event. The raw crystal of the Aquean Era (Fourth) was shaped quickly then set aside. The Thiran Era (Third) was rediscovered and praised for its achievements in biological regeneration, polydimensional mathematics, and universal mapping. The Kaetan Era (Second) was celebrated for its advances in cybernetics, life extension, sensory enhancement, and immersive art forms. And the Pheran

Era (First), deepest in memory and soul, was approached as a ground almost holy, a childhood precious and innocent. The leaders dreamed in the early days of discovery and peace on the Pheran home planet. They relived the shock and terror of the Andaran attack on the Pheran supercontinent. They savored the victory of their ancestors in the great war against Andara.

Silvarhen, in his late confessions, described the wandering and re-shaping of crystal that occured during the long voyage to Earth. "The recent past was too painful to us, too shameful," he wrote. "We had to retreat deep into the ancient past. We had to mold crystal memory into an image of ourselves that we could bear."

As they neared the Earth, the Pherans turned from dreams of the ancient past to dreams of the future. They imagined a peaceful and nurturing relationship with humans. They imagined taking humans under their wings, teaching and guiding them like wide-eyed children. They imagined a benevolent adoption filled with gratitude, love, and awe. Silvarhen helped in the forming of these dreams, but he also warned against an indulgent and non-selective sharing of knowledge. "We should not labor to teach all humanity," he wrote. "We must choose the best among them, the elite leaders of art, culture, and science. Even among this elite, we must reject those that cannot be molded, those that cannot grasp the Pheran vision. To this moldable elite, knowledge should be given incrementally, cautiously. They must prove themselves trustworthy and effective in the guidance of their people."

But a great stumbling block stood between the Pherans and their dreams. It was an old problem, ever present, never acknowledged. Pheran technology, both medical and cybernetic, allowed for the extension of life beyond centuries, into millenia. At a tremendous cost of effort and resources, the bodies of historical figures from past eras were maintained in life support. They were scientists and generals, poets and explorers, politicians and philosophers. They were symbols of Pheran strength and achievement, the pride of their race. Though their hands had become too weak to lift, though their thoughts had faded to an occasional throbbing in the virtual crystal realm, these heroes were kept alive in starlit chambers. Silvarhen, like all governors before him, accepted the necessity and sacredness of the heroes' chambers. "The chambers gave us courage," he wrote in his confessions. "We were afraid of the unknown future and the haunting past, afraid of failing as leaders of our people, afraid of the darkness and loneliness of space, afraid of the harsh surface world. And our greatest fear was dying. By keeping the chambers, we denied the reality of death. Each of us hoped to earn our own chamber before the life within us faded. Each of us hoped to hide from God in a place beyond the claim of death."

The keeping of the chambers had required a vast expenditure throughout the Eras, a burden inevitably passed down to the other races. This expenditure was ever-increasing as more chambers were added over time, and medical technology struggled to preserve the ancient, wilted bodies. By the end of the journey to Earth, the expenditure had reached the point that Pheran governors were forced to terminate cryogenic support to a fraction of their own people. Silvarhen's description of the Pherans coming to Earth "desperate and dying" was, thus, both accurate and misleading. Pheran workers had died in substantial numbers, but not from any external force or physical disease: They were killed by their own leaders.

The keeping of the chambers put the Pherans in a position of deficit and need from the beginning of their relationship with humans. This need was further compounded by the Pheran inability to survive long periods of time on the surface of Earth, and the expense of transporting resources off-world. The Pheran governors hid this need from the humans. Instead of honest and realistic communication with humans, the governors offered delusional promises. They made genuine efforts to improve living conditions on Earth, but Pheran needs always trumped human needs, and the flow of resources invariably ran skyward.

Silvarhen's historical guilt is, perhaps, greatest among all Pherans because he presumed to act as an intermediate between humankind and his people. Drawn to the center of power and attention, he had a clear view of human suffering on Earth and obstinate Pheran policy pressing down from the off-world. Adept at duplicity, he presented himself as an ally and supporter to humans, a strong executor to Pherans.

During the extensive pre-Contact planning, Silvarhen studied human culture and language while the other governors focused on science and technology. He fashioned himself by long rehearsal into the role of an old grandfather, kind and wise, patient and listening. On the Day of Contact, Silvarhen, the grandfather, proved the most accessible and convincing of all the Pheran speakers. In the early post-Contact years, he cultivated relationships with human leaders and used his influence to allow Pheran takeover of human industry, markets, and government. He gave frequent addresses to the wider population urging patience and inflating human hopes.

When the years of wild hope gave way to years of bitter disillusion, Silvarhen's assurances increasingly rang hollow, even to his closest human supporters. Like a nightmare, patterns of the old Aquean Era returned. Entire continents on Earth were abandoned to starvation, violence, and disease while regions with valuable resources were provided comfort and security. Enticement and deception were again used to prevent widespread rebellion. Throughout this long deterioration, Silvarhen listened to human complaint but did little to alter Pheran policy. He relayed earthly grievances to the off-world but did not advocate for those who suffered. His private writings from this period reveal fissures in his composure, a wounded idealism, self-absorption, and denial. "Our greatest plans and dreams are swallowed by the hard laws of the universe," he wrote. "In the end, the universe takes everything from us except the tender scrap we call survival."

Silvarhen eventually broke from the strain of his impossible position. He relinquished his role of intermediate and retreated to the off-world. He lived in isolation and self-imposed exile in the colony of Europa. Even on Europa, his guilt allowed him no peace or rest. He could not escape the human cry. "I was hourly crushed by the burden of memory," he wrote. "I built elaborate constructions of the mind to justify my actions, to deny and repress, to escape the painful truth. But each construction was brought to ash."

Silvarhen published *Phera*, with deliberate irony, on the fiftieth anniversary of the Day of Contact. Pherans were shocked by the book's introductory confession. Humans were not. Humans considered the confession long overdue. They also resented that the confessor now lived far away from the desperate mess that he had helped to create. The body of *Phera*, a 200-page poetic exploration of the roots of the Pheran people, was largely ignored by both races.

Silvarhen endured the backlash from his confession. He absorbed severe criticism from human leaders and weathered character attacks and cries of betrayal from Pheran governors. In public writings, he offered no defense. In private writings, he expressed disappointment and a diminished but lingering self-absorption. "I expected my honesty to count for something more than nothing."

Silvarhen's confession sparked violent waves of rebellion across the Earth.

Human leaders that had been used by Silvarhen now tried to use the former governor. They asked for his support in their attempt to overthrow the Pheran rulers.

Silvarhen refused. "With what will you replace them?" he asked.

The leaders responded with questions of their own. "When did you know? Why did you lie? Why do you do nothing now?"

The memory of Silvarhen would have rotted. Human-told history would have remembered him with disappointment and contempt. Pheran history would have cast him as a failure and betrayer. But Silvarhen went back. He returned to the Earth. He lived, worked, suffered, and died among humans. "I could not atone or repay," he wrote. "I could only walk beside."

Silvarhen's humbled walk quenched much of the anger against him. After his death in the Russian desert, his writings experienced a significant rediscovery. Many off-world Pherans were exposed to the horrible conditions on Earth through Silvarhen's journals. Many humans surrendered violent plans because of Silvarhen's poetry and religious writings. And *Phera*, his first work of confession long ignored, stirred to life.

Phera is a crystal journey, a dream of history. In this single book, Silvarhen attempted to capture all of the dominant tides and pivotal turnings of early Pheran history. He attempted to explore and reveal the soul of his people. From cold Europa, gazing beyond the wrecked Earth and the wasted systems of the Thiran, Kaetan, and Aquean, Silvarhen searched for answers on the small Pheran home world. Of his ancestors he asked the difficult and painful question: What went wrong?

Phera opens with the naked and poetically brief confession of Silvarhen. Hoping that the door to his personal past has closed, he enters the memory of his people.

He tells of Llarai, the Mother Poet, the woman scarred and despised by her people, the seeker that climbed the winter mountains alone in search of a life with meaning, the poet whose words and deathly ascent would form the root of the Cerran faith.

He tells of the Alcyans, a quiet and thoughtful people that whispered poetry into the soft currents of the great river. He tells of a rebellious generation that forsook their heritage and rejected the wisdom of their ancestors to search for the great river's end. He tells of the disaster at Valthan where their boats cracked like kindling against the jagged rocks and many of their people drowned.

Silvarhen, in his first steps, is both searching for light and seeking to blame. Llarai is his light, his vision of poetic beauty, his ideal of suffering and salvation. To Silvarhen, Llarai is the first light of God in history. Her words are the precious root of God's coming people, the Cerrans. The Alcyans, the river people, live a bit further from God's light. Silvarhen respects their poetry and humility, but he also magnifies the flaws of Alcyan individuals. Aton, selfish and greedy, entices the Alcyan children away from their families with false promises then works them like slaves. Atonyi, his angry son, leads the rebellion of the young and becomes as harsh a master as his father had been. Myr, the heartless daughter, manipulates the people and prods them toward the disaster at Valthan. Through his telling of the Alcyan story, Silvarhen has, consciously or unconsciously, begun to cast deep shadows onto those he considers outside the light of God.

From the ancient Pherans, Silvarhen moves to the Age of Tribes. Many historical tribes and peoples are ignored by Silvarhen. He focuses on the tribes involved in the dominant trading system of the young Pheran continent - western wood for eastern metal. In this system, the Varrans control the western forests, the Torites control the eastern mines, and the Tyraens manage all negotiation and transportation between the two. This system of trade creates a corresponding system of power cooperative with self-centeredness, competitive with interdependence. All tribes outside the power triangle of the Varran, Torite, and Tyraen are forced into secondary, subservient, and impoverishing roles.

Only the Cerran people escape this system. Inspired by the poetry of Llarai, the Cerrans leave the empty life of the central valley and journey across the eastern lowlands. They settle in small, resilient farming communities that carve hard-earned lives out of the wild. They survive flooding, drought, and disease through collective sharing and the sacrifice of individual wants for the needs of the group. The Cerrans draw inspiration for their struggle from their prophets. These lone travelers wander the eastern wild and speak with God. They write poetry of guilt, ascension, and love. Silvarhen includes several prophetic writings but lists no prophet's name. Authorship was never claimed, he implies, because the prophets selflessly spoke the word of God, because the Cerrans universally lacked the vanity and personal ambition inherent in other races. The absence of a single remarkable Cerran personality from this time period is, to Silvarhen, an indication of humility, not blandness.

The light of Silvarhen, cast soft and glowing at the feet of the Cerrans, becomes harsher and more revealing when cast upon the face of other races. The Draun are simple farmers without the Cerrans' purity of heart. Drained and exploited by the power triangle, they resist with stupid violence: riots and vandalism. They are historically significant to Silvarhen only as the mothers and fathers of the Cerran people. The Myshenites, aggressive hunters of the central valley, are also victimized by the power triangle and similarly resort to futile violence. Silvarhen downplays their long and bloody struggle against the encroaching Torite army, deeming it less courageous than the Cerran struggle against the natural wild. The Torites are a mining and building people, more advanced than the Draun farmers but similar in their low-mindedness. Silvarhen, interestingly, considers the Torites' heavy drinking and resentment of Varran intellectual achievement as noteworthy as their slaughter of the Myshenite people. When Silvarhen turns his critical eye on the Varrans, he makes his first, perhaps only, acknowledgement of cultural heterogeneity: He distinguishes between the Varran woodsmen and the Varran academics. The Varran woodsmen, bland as the Draun farmers, are used by their supposed brothers, the Varran academics, to fund the creation of the university system. Though inspired by the exciting early days of scientific discovery, the universities become cold institutions stifled by conformity. They also prove unprofitable in the short term. Varran leaders keep the universities afloat by the continued exploitation of their wooded kinsmen and by the enticement of foreign tribes into the Varran market system. Shrewd and clever, the Varran leaders even recruit the brightest young of foreign tribes, indoctrinate them with Varran ideology, and return them to their tribes to assist with Varran takeover.

And Silvarhen's harshest criticism is saved for the Tyraens. To Silvarhen, the Tyraens represent the most selfish and damaging aspects of the power system. They form the worst member of the power triangle, eventually exceeding even the Varrans in shrewdness and cruelty.

The complex origins and ancient history of the Tyraen people are glossed over by Silvarhen with the pithy summary: "The early Tyraens struggled more than any other tribe to find their place in the Pheran world." They are a lost and runtish people to Silvarhen, too soft for work in the mines and woods, too weak to hunt large game in the fields. They wander the central valley for generations without a permanent home or consistent way of life. They unknowingly plant crops on Myshenite hunting grounds and are driven from the valley into the northern hills. The Myshenite attacks in the valley are downplayed by

Silvarhen. So are the Tyraen years of suffering and struggle in the northern hills. Silvarhen describes both only to establish the deep bitterness of the Tyraens, a hardness of heart passed from old to young through lamenting song.

The embittered Tyraens return to the central valley, become masters of the financial trade game, and take economic revenge on tribes that had never harmed them. They become middlemen between the Varrans and the Torites, playing one side against the other. They become negotiators, translators, merchants, investors, transportation agents, and currency converters. Through their control of the continental market centers, they gouge their clients, bankrupt their competitors, and trample the poor to rise in power.

Silvarhen reveals his own shrewdness in his telling of early Tyraen history. His summary is structured to minimize the effect of an exceptional moment in Pheran history - the Tyraen sparing of the Myshenites. When the Myshenite hunters had been driven from the central valley by the ever-encroaching Torites, they had fled to the northern hills. In the northern hills, the Myshenites had crossed paths for a second time with the Tyraens. This time the Tyraens were stronger, the Myshenites weak and defeated. The opportunity for revenge lay wide open to the Tyraens. But the Tyraens did not take revenge. They spared the Myshenites and allowed them to pass safely to higher ground. Such an act of mercy was unprecedented in the tribal world. Considering how little time had passed since the Myshenite attack, the act was truly remarkable. Silvarhen, unmoved by the sparing, places it between two negative aspects of Tyraen history in his summary. The first is the story of Taldon, a Tyraen hero that had fought bravely in the valley but later caused the death of his own family. The second is the rise of the bitter generation of Tyraens that conquered the continental trading market. Between these two negatives, the sparing of the Myshenites loses its fair weight and resonance.

Silvarhen's summary is unbalanced and unfair, but it is not shallow. Silvarhen accurately perceives deep conflicts and contradictions in the Tyraen psyche. The sparing of the Myshenites in the hills was a genuine act of mercy, but it later became less of an example to follow, more a source of self-righteousness, preserved in poetry and song. The Tyraen heart was torn between the natural instinct for revenge and the psychological need for a positive moral self-image. Some Tyraens came to regret the sparing of the Myshenites. Others clung to it with pride.

This conflict, this tearing of the spirit, is vividly revealed in the legend of Taldon, even when told by Silvarhen. Taldon was the only Tyraen that drew enemy blood during the Myshenite attack in the valley. Because of the young Tyraen's bravery in fighting, Taldon became more respected than all the Tyraen elders. He led his people in their flight to the northern hills. But Taldon was humbled in the first northern winter. A heavy snowfall trapped Taldon and his family inside a cavern with little to eat. When the snow finally thawed, only Taldon emerged from the cave.

On the valley floor,
running past the bodies of my fallen brothers,
I had wondered,
What kind of people could kill so many strangers
with so little reason?

In the cold cavern,
staring at the bodies of my wife and son,
I had wondered,
What kind of man could take food from their mouths
to fill his own stomach?

Years later, when the wounded Myshenites entered the northern hills, the people looked to Taldon to lead them in revenge. "I killed on the valley floor and I killed in the cavern," Taldon said. "I will not kill again."

Silvarhen misses the poignancy and raw honesty of the legend. In his summary, he highlights Taldon's failure in the cavern but glides quickly over Taldon's mercy. He also fails to acknowledge an obvious fact. The legend of Taldon was kept alive by Tyraens. For several generations old Tyraens passed the legend on to young Tyraens in all its ugliness and truth. Surely, they resisted strong urges to soften the story and paint a more flattering picture of their race. Silvarhen, after lamenting that his honesty counted for nothing to his critics, counts Tyraen honesty for nothing.

The Bursting Age, a period of rapid technological advance and explosive population growth, follows the Age of Tribes. Large cities fill the central valley then overflow onto the plains of the east and west. Bridges span the widest rivers. Paved roads cover the hills and lowlands. Tunnels burrow through the stony mountains.

The old power triangle - Varran, Torite, Tyraen - leads the rapid growth and continues its dominance. Varrans lead in theoretical science; Torites lead in engineering, materials, and machinery; and Tyraens lead in management and finance. Each member of the triangle acknowledges dependence on the others but jostles and claws for supremacy.

The Shalkov Affair reveals the rivalry and flaw inherent in the power system. Silvarhen considers this conflict a pivotal and revealing moment in Pheran history. He develops this conflict and its antecedent roots in detail.

He begins with the post-tribal history of the Myshenite hunters. After the Myshenites fled to the northern hills, their society and culture underwent a radical transformation, a transfer of power from men to women. Women attained dominance over men by controlling the history taught to their children and by the arrangement of marriages. Mothers taught their sons a history that placed singular blame upon the Myshenite men for the wandering and suffering of their people. They allowed their sons wives only with the approval of all the elder women in each community. The influence of women became so strong that they were able to change the entire way of life for their people. The Myshenites became fishers of the mountain lakes.

When Torite mining towns began to appear in the mountains, the Myshenite women were not afraid of their old enemies. They purchased boats and heavy equipment from the Torites. They built towns, docks, and fisheries around the lakes. They sold fish to the Torite miners at ever-climbing prices. Through aggressive business skill, the Myshenite women hoped to dominate the Torites that had once defeated their men by arms in the open valley.

But the Torites grew more quickly than the Myshenites in the mountains. Torite mining companies banded together to bankrupt the Myshenite fisheries. The companies purchased a surplus of meat from the Draun and launched their own fishing boats onto the lakes. Demand for Myshenite fish plummeted. Desperate and overextended, the Myshenites pled for help from the leading financial manager in the region, Shalkov.

Shalkov had amassed a fortune by acting as an intermediate between the Torites and the Myshenites. The Myshenites had used Shalkov to obtain their boats, equipment, and fuel. The Torites had used Shalkov to negotiate fishing prices and handle all shipping. An intermediate would no longer be necessary, however, if the Myshenites were driven from the market. Self-interest seemed to push Shalkov toward the Myshenite side. But Shalkov was a Tyraen. The Tyraens pressured Shalkov to allow the Torite takeover; some even argued for the deployment of the Torite army into the mountains. The Tyraens, according to Silvarhen, wanted no second sparing of the Myshenites.

In the end, Shalkov hesitated, then spared. He watched the Myshenites fall toward hunger and ruin, then suddenly invested the bulk of his fortune in their rescue.

The Myshenites loved Shalkov for his action.

The Torites despised him.

The Tyraens, according to Silvarhen, reversed their position. After their initial shock faded, they praised Shalkov for his act of mercy. "Though revenge was his to take, he showed himself merciful and kind to his enemies," the Tyraens said. "He reminded his people of their great history and heritage."

Silvarhen's portrayal of the Tyraens could be dismissed, except that it holds largely true to Shalkov's own writing. Near his death, after years of suffering from an intestinal disease, Shalkov wrote a brief and self-piercing confession. In his confession, Shalkov admitted that his motives had been less than pure in the saving of the Myshenites. "I did not save the Myshenites from destruction," he wrote. "I saved my own people from the truth." Shalkov revealed this truth and explained his real motives by telling of his father.

> *When I was a boy, I watched my father. I watched him labor with his stacks of books throughout the long hours of the night. I memorized the sternness of his face, his tired but piercing eyes, his grim persistence against an unseen enemy.*
>
> *I hated the demands his strictness put upon me. I questioned the slanted history he taught and doubted the reality of the hostile forces he struggled against. I*

hated my father for many things, but I also loved him.
My blood pulled toward his strength.

After many years apart, my father came to me. I
expected bitterness from him and stern rebuke, but he
came to me with sorrow and humility.

"I was cold and hard to you," he said. "I hid my love
for you, my son."

In my father's weeping, I saw the heart of my people
laid bare. I saw the shedding of our anger, the stripping
of our self-righteousness. I saw weakness.

Silvarhen could not have missed the similarities between
Shalkov's life and his own. Both were powerful and wealthy.
Both stood between races and played a significant role in history.
Both lied, regretted, and confessed. If Silvarhen identified with
Shalkov, there is little indication of this throughout *Phera*.
Silvarhen consistently links Shalkov's honesty with Shalkov's
flaws. He does not credit Shalkov for the depth, honesty, and
insight of his confession. Again, Silvarhen holds Tyraens to a
different standard than he holds himself. Perhaps, Silvarhen saw
his own story *too* clearly in the life of Shalkov. Perhaps, he could
not bear his own reflection.

The Shalkov Affair greatly irritated the power triangle.
Determined to tighten their control of the market, each
member of the power triangle creates a more centralized form
of government. The Varrans form the Assembly, a loose council
of university chairmen that shape western policy through debate
and letter. The Torites select Generals of Industry, Army, and
State, aggressive leaders expected to pull power to the east. The
Tyraens establish a secretive and dogmatic council, the Syllvar.

In this period of centralization, Silvarhen develops a deeper
and somewhat more favorable image of the Torites. He focuses
on their first three Generals: Lyevara, Phelon, and Sal.

Lyevara, the Torite military leader, begins his career as a harsh commander in the Draun heartland. After his promotion to Army General, he leads a deployment to the northern mountains that is plagued by supply and logistical problems and over-aggressive planning. A humbled Lyevara accepts responsibility for his mistakes. He improves communication within the military, establishes a base near the mountain lakes, and softens his treatment of civilians.

Phelon begins as a poor, sixth-generation miner in the eastern mountains. Realizing that a hard life and an early death are in store for him, Phelon looks for a way out of the darkened, dust-choking mine tunnels. He becomes skilled with explosives inside the mine then learns to operate the heavy trucks and conveyor lines outside the mine. Aggressive and tireless, he is promoted to manager of the conveyor lines and leads a crew of several hundred workers. The mine closes, but Phelon, a man of sweat and calculation, becomes the first General of Industry.

The once-poor mountain miner begins his new office by touring the Pheran continent. He visits the great Varran universities and laboratories in the west. In the Torite east, he explores factories, mills, and refineries; he drives with pride the giant farming equipment built and engineered by his people. After a biting letter from the General of State, Phelon abruptly ends his touring. He heads to the far eastern plains, summons the corporate managers, and pronounces an end to "the fat days of subsidizing." The corporate managers resist his demand for the repayment of investment funds. Phelon wages a paper war against the managers with his army of accountants, bookkeepers, and lawyers. He exposes corruption in the east, brings many criminals to justice, and recovers some of the taxpayer's money. But the war exhausts Phelon. In the end, he collapses like Orwell's tired workhorse.

Sal, the first Torite General of State, was educated in a Varran university. Realizing his people's dependence on western technology, he pursues an alliance with the Varrans and plans an economic assault against the Tyraens. "The Tyraens have shrewdly and skillfully played us against the Varrans," he wrote. "If we can open dialogue with the west, if we can build a working relationship with the Varrans, we will remove the Tyraens from the center of power." Sal's plan includes the creation of non-Tyraen trading centers in the major cities of the central valley, the transition to a continental currency, and cooperative projects between western scientists and eastern technicians.

The Varran political process delays and frustrates Sal. He is denied a private meeting with the Varran Assembly then forced to defend his plan in public debates and a slow exchange of letters. Throughout the long process, Sal tries to guard the specifics of his plan, but the Tyraens are quick to realize his intentions. The Tyraen secret council pulls investment funds from several continental corporations. The market shakes in response. A furious Sal is finally given a private meeting with the Varran Assembly.

> *The Varrans deflected my anger with subtle smiles. There was satisfaction in their expressions, deep pleasure on their faces. In that moment, I realized that the long process I had endured had been a farce.*
>
> *The Varrans had wanted to attack the Tyraens as much as I did. But, first, they wanted to humble the proud Torite. After I had lost composure, once I had shown weakness in their eyes, they heard and accepted my economic plan.*

Like Phelon, Sal fights a difficult and lifelong war. He eventually achieves a continental currency, some independent trading centers, and several collaborative projects. The Varrans participate in Sal's work but carry little of the financial burden. Sal is repeatedly forced to increase taxes on the Torite worker. Near his death, Sal admits to Phelon a painful uncertainty in his life's work. "Perhaps the Tyraens are not our greatest enemy," he said.

Silvarhen moves from the Torite perspective to the Varran. He fails to mention any of the great Varran scientists and artists from this time period. He focuses, instead, on factional rivalries within the Varran Assembly.

The purist faction sought a return to the early days of discovery when knowledge was its own reward. They wanted to lessen the influence of corporate managers within the university and escape the pressure for tangible, profitable results. The purists wanted freedom in the laboratory and in the library.

The capitalizers considered the purist position unrealistic and corporate influence unavoidable. They believed that Varran technological advantage had to be accompanied by prudent and aggressive economics: the university had to enter the market. The capitalizers, disturbed by heavy Tyraen investment, argued for more Varrans to cross over into the corporate and financial world. They hoped for Varrans, not Tyraens, to manage and own the major corporations of the Pheran continent.

The pherists, smallest of the factions, were concerned by wider and deeper problems facing the Varran people. They were troubled by the inverse relationship between environmental health and population growth, the widening gap between rich and poor in the Varran cities, and the rapid depletion of resources. The pherists fought within the university to maintain the non-scientific departments and promote the teaching of the arts.

Silvarhen provides a brief summary of the conflict within the Assembly over Sal's economic plan. He condenses to a few lines an argument that that likely consumed the Assembly for many days.

The pherists question the benefit of Sal's plan to Varran society and culture.

The capitalizers support Sal and promote his plan as beneficial to Varran economic interests.

The purists reject the plan. They wear down the capitalizers with long-winded speeches and refuse to grant Sal a private hearing.

According to Silvarhen, the purists went on to frustrate Sal with letters and public debates after the early argument in the Assembly. Here, Silvarhen misses an interesting historical sidenote. The debates and letters did frustrate Sal, but they were more often capitalizer attempts to keep the plan alive than purist attempts to destroy it. Sal, accustomed to straightforward eastern ways, had failed to recognize his supporters in the Varran Assembly. Seeing only hostile resistance behind the debates and letters, he had unknowingly counted his allies as enemies. Silvarhen, ever impatient with detail, also failed to see the different and opposite intentions behind the Varran debates and letters.

Silvarhen blurs historical detail here but accurately captures the dominant tides. The capitalizers rebound after the Tyraens shake the market. They persuade the Assembly to grant Sal his private hearing and win approval for his economic plan. The purists lose the second debate but harden their position over time. They effectively undercut funding for Sal's programs and force the capitalizers to draw from their own university budgets. Varran support for the Torite plan proves to be more symbolic than substantive.

Silvarhen's blurring worsens when he moves to the Tyraen perspective. He portrays the Tyraens as a people slightly persecuted but greatly paranoid. He fails to consider how slivered Tyraen communities would naturally have felt living between the massive Varran and Torite populations. He fails to appreciate how terrifying the Varran-Torite alliance pursued by Sal would have been to the Tyraens. He does not capture the dangerous air of the times or the reasonable threat of the Torite army, the largest military force on the continent.

As with the Varrans, Silvarhen is primarily concerned with the innermost circle of political power. He focuses on the Syllvar, the high council composed of individual leaders from each Tyraen community.

Younger and more radical Tyraens take control of the Syllvar after Sal's economic plan is approved by the Varran Assembly. The young warn of impending Torite assault. Expecting siege, they stockpile weapons and supplies in the Tyraen compounds. When the Torite attack never comes, the young lose credibility.

Older and more conservative Tyraens regain control of the Syllvar. A secret meeting is held to determine a new course of action. Some members argue that the trading centers should be used as economic weapons against the Varrans and the Torites. Others argue that this would only hasten the loss of the trading centers and strengthen the east-west alliance. They argue bitterly until Davel, a quiet and thoughtful Tyraen, enters the debate.

"Where does power lie?" Davel asked.

"In the market," the Syllvar answered. "In the trading center."

"Present power lies in the trading center," Davel said. "Future power lies in the corporation. The corporation will eclipse region, race, and politics. The corporation will span the continent. The corporation will rule the future market."

"But we pulled investment in the corporations and still failed to break the alliance against us."

"Our investment was small at the time," Davel said. *"The corporations were young. There can be no doubt that the corporations will continue to grow in size and strength. Future power lies in their ownership and management. We must understand that the trading center is a battleground, not a force. We can lose the trading center and still rule the market if we control the corporation."*

The wisdom of Davel was eventually accepted.

Silvarhen's dialogue of the secret meeting is highly imaginative. He portrays the Syllvar as monolithic, paranoid, and power-craving, Davel as wise and ruthless. Though both portrayals are unrealistic, Silvarhen is more unfair to Davel.

Davel was a widely respected writer, teacher, and consultant. His friends and colleagues included leaders of every race across the continent. He was experienced in academics and industry, politics, and economy. Davel was no separatist. He predicted the rise of the corporation, but he also gave many warnings about a corporation-dominated world. He hoped that a strong continental government would one day be formed, but he doubted that a central government could ever outweigh corporate power. Given this unfortunate reality, he advised Tyraens to protect themselves by advancing within the corporate hierarchies.

Silvarhen's dialogue implies that Davel intended a self-serving corporate infiltration that would increase Tyraen power yet maintain Tyraen separatism. Davel's life and writing directly contradict this implication. Throughout his life, Davel's circle of friends and colleagues was ever-expanding. In his writing, Davel often criticized separatist views and urged Tyraens to branch out from their communities, both in their professional and personal lives.

Perhaps Silvarhen, in the interest of brevity, attempted to capture the sizeable gap between Davel's intentions and historical reality. Davel was frequently attacked and constantly resisted by conservative Tyraens. He often found himself isolated in the Syllvar and an outsider among his own people. Silvarhen is right in asserting that Tyraen separatism remained a problem; he is wrong, however, in claiming separatism to be the dominant historical trend. The Tyraen people gradually branched out from their tight communities. Increased contact with other races, though abrasive and difficult, generally softened the attitudes, widened the perspective, and lessened the fears of the Tyraen people. Most Tyraens chose assimilation over separatism.

The Cerrans also struggled with separatism. Silvarhen describes the inexorable encroachment of the Torites into Cerran lands during the Bursting Age. The Torites poured over the hills in smoky caravans of heavy machinery and equipment. They built towns and cities, factories and plants, canals and silos. The Cerrans watched their land shrink, their livestock dwindle, and their streams dry up.

Under the severe pressure of the Torite encroachment, the Cerrans split.

A fragment fled to the eastern coast, awaiting deliverance or revelation. They practiced an ascetic life, sleeping in sparse huts, fishing, and scavenging along the shore. They gazed into the ocean and whispered the poetry of Llarai and the prophets. They hoped for some new dawn to rise from the eastern waters.

The Cerrans that remained faced difficult and more complex challenges. Some resisted the trespassing Torites with community protests and hunger strikes. Others accepted training from the Torites, became skilled with heavy machinery, and hired into the large agricultural corporations. Silvarhen, tellingly, seems to favor the Cerrans that assimilated over those that resisted.

Of the Cerrans that stayed,
there were two paths chosen:
the straight and the bending.

The straight path was chosen by the purists and the separatists,
the proud and the bitter.
The straight path led to isolation, anger, and suffering.
It waited for the revenge of God.

The bending path crossed into the Torite world,
through its difficult language and complex machines.
The bending path exhausted, confused, and tore apart.
It hoped to remember.

Silvarhen's story deepens as he cuts into the Cerran heart. In his telling of the Andaran War, he will rise to his full stature. He will lay bare the Pheran spirit, lift high his vision of God, and commit his greatest sin.

The Cerrans who gazed to the east with patient longing would find no deliverance. Instead, they would see the coming of warships.

The warships came from Andara, a rocky, jungle island about one-fifth the size of the Pheran supercontinent on the opposite side of the Pheran planet. Varran planes had circled Andara and its surrounding islands many years before the Andaran attack. The Varrans had found an early-industrial civilization on the mainland and mostly primitive tribes on the surrounding islands. The Varrans, who considered aviation technology to be the measure of civilization, had been disappointed to find the Andaran skies empty. Unimpressed with the slow fleets of Andaran naval vessels, they had returned home without attempting any communication.

Andara was the island of a thousand wars. Its early history was scarred by a host of warlords and continual tribal warfare for control of the mainland. Ancient war in Andara had no negotiation, alliance, or surrender. Battles were fought to the last warrior because a quick, glorious end was preferable to humiliating capture, long torture, and slow execution. Captured workers were spared execution but not torture. Workers that survived torture were, perversely, accepted by the conquering tribe.

In the later history of Andara, one tribe attained dominance over the mainland and one family established an imperial line. The Andaran Emperors varied widely in character and competence but each extended war outward to the surrounding islands when internal problems on the mainland arose. Through the constant demands of war, the Emperors built a heavy industrial base focused on naval warfare and a society grossly unbalanced but largely compliant. Because the military capability of the surrounding island tribes was minimal, the Emperors often struggled to find new ways of prolonging conflicts. The Emperors played their own generals against one another, intentionally spread misinformation within the Andaran military, and created an atmosphere of fear and suspicion by the frequent demotion, transfer, and disappearance of military officials.

It was the manipulative methods of the Emperor that led to war with continental Phera.

A vicious general, Ciralan, was raised up by the Emperor to be used against the popular and widely respected General Ryon.

The Emperor ordered both generals to attack the island of Nyava. Ciralan was sent to land on the soft eastern beaches of Nyava, while General Ryon was sent to the rocky northern coast.

Ciralan cut a swift and bloody path to the Nyavite capital.

Ryon struggled in the steep jungle of the northern mountains.

The Nyavites fled from Ciralan into the mountains and unleashed their anger on Ryon's exhausted troops.

Ryon's forces were crushed, but the general and a few of his officers survived the fighting. They hid in a jungle ravine and radioed for help for many days. Several Andaran generals rushed their forces to Nyava to aid Ryon.

When Ryon's body was found in an area empty of Nyavites but thick with Ciralan's troops, the generals advanced on Ciralan.

The Emperor avoided disaster by ordering Ciralan to fall back to the Nyavite capital and ordering the generals to stand down until his arrival.

The generals were less than pleased when the Emperor's investigation concluded that Nyavites had killed Ryon, and they learned that Ciralan had slipped back to the eastern coast.

The Emperor executed an entire battalion of Ciralan, but the generals were still not satisfied.

Finding himself cornered and on the verge of a civil war, the Emperor loosed Ciralan upon continental Phera.

Silvarhen delves briefly into the Emperor's character. He exposes the Emperor's decision to send Ciralan to Phera as either muddled in logic or twisted in motive. If the Emperor expected Ciralan to defeat the Pherans, his decision was illogical because a victorious Ciralan would have become an even greater problem. If the Emperor expected Ciralan to be defeated by the Pherans, the Emperor would be guilty of sacrificing his own general and many thousands of his own soldiers.

Silvarhen leaves the question unanswered. He describes Ciralan's attack of continental Phera in dramatic verse.

The Andaran fleet pooled in the eastern bay. Long chains of boats, turreted and black-horned, slid up the eastern rivers.

The Andarans shelled the highways, captured bridges, and blasted small towns. They pushed all the way to Lytarr, the largest city east of the mountains.

At Lytarr, the Torite army made a stand. Their gunmen lined the riversides. Their boats blocked the river's width.

The Andarans did not flinch or hesitate. They crashed and shattered the blockade. Their soldiers waded through the bloody waters, over broken stone and twisted metal, to claim Lytarr.

On that dark day, the Torites learned that they were not soldiers but policemen, sleepy-eyed guards.

The loss of Lytarr; the defeat of the Torite army; mass slaughter, capture, and torture - all these were unimaginable to continental Pherans of this era.

Under this fierce external threat, the old rivalries of the continent were forgotten. Varran, Torite, and Tyraen leaders met together for the first time, united by their common terror.

The Pheran leaders could not imagine any path to victory over the Andarans. Defeated in mind and spirit, they proposed a negotiation with Ciralan. They hoped to use their resources as leverage to attain some kind of peaceful arrangement.

But a young Tyraen rose. Dyraveen, grandson of Davel.

Dyraveen scorned the wispy hopes of the Pheran leaders and forced them to face stark reality.

"Did the Andarans appear eager to talk when they struck Lytarr?" Dyraveen demanded. "Do they seem a civil and reasonable people? We know nothing of their history, but it is clear that they have risen from a den of murder. They are the king of the wild wolves, the blood-fanged ruler of the pack. Will the dog sit quietly and listen to our pleading? No. The dog will listen only after we have broken his every tooth and pulled his every claw."

Dyraveen chastised the leaders then prodded them to be strong and reasonable. He pointed out that the Andarans were far from their home; their war machine required constant fuel and food; their ships were strong but their army weak; and the mountains shielded the central valley.

The Pheran leaders gave Dyraveen control of the entire continent.

Dyraveen mined the rivers west of Lytarr. He surrounded the city with rows of tanks and waited the Andarans out.

When the Andarans withdrew from Lytarr and returned to their homeland, Dyraveen allowed only a brief celebration. He warned the Pheran people that the Andarans would soon return. "If we do not defeat them in their own land," he said, "they will return to ours again and again. Every city of the continent will suffer as Lytarr."

Dyraveen raised taxes across the continent, rationed the supply of food and fuel, and converted the eastern factories to the mass production of tanks, bombers, and warships.

Silvarhen is quick to pull Dyraveen from the hero's pedestal. In the years of preparation, Dyraveen commissions artists to mythologize the Pheran resistance and the Battle of Lytarr. He uses propaganda and government-sponsored media to frighten, spur, and prod the Pheran workforce. He employs manipulative psychology to present the Pheran people with "a fearsome but vulnerable enemy, a high but attainable goal." Silvarhen again casts a Tyraen as clever and shrewd.

In the years of the Pheran counterattack, Silvarhen's Dyraveen becomes ruthless, vengeful, and cruel. He knowingly sacrifices ten Pheran ships during a naval battle. He subjugates the indigenous population on the Island of Troqual and destroys their forests to build hangars and airstrips. He bombs the islands surrounding Andara, killing many tribal peoples that had been victims of the Andarans themselves. He bombs the Andaran mainland to "blood and dust."

Silvarhen's narrative of the war traces events forward in chronological order, but his portrayal of Dyraveen is entirely backward driven. His darkened image of Dyraveen is formed in postwar, bomb-stricken Andara and projected backward through all stages of the war. He allows Dyraveen no emotion, vulnerability, transformation, or regret. He does not enter the historical moment experienced by the living Pheran.

A fuller, truer image will emerge if Silvarhen's criticisms are examined more closely and the war is viewed from the perspective of Dyraveen.

Dyraveen genuinely feared the Andarans and expected a second attack on continental Phera. He prepared his people to win a war he reasonably considered inevitable. Silvarhen suggests that the war was not inevitable. He subtly casts Dyraveen as the aggressor by showing the unlikelihood of a second Andaran attack using as evidence the suicide of the vicious Andaran general, Ciralan, and the deteriorating political situation in Andara. Dyraveen was largely unaware of these developments, however.

In the early war years, Silvarhen downplays Dyraveen's vulnerability and exaggerates his power. Dyraveen suffered significant losses in early naval encounters. He was fiercely criticized by his own naval commanders for his tactical hesitancy and avoidance of battle. After his routing at the Battle of Troqual, several commanders openly defied his orders. Others attempted mutiny. Facing internal military rebellion, an extremely confident enemy, and a dangerously dissatisfied homeland, Dyraveen stood on the edge of defeat.

But Dyraveen survived. He clung to his original strategy: the aerial bombardment of the Andaran mainland. He secured the airfields on the island of Troqual and began a vicious bombing campaign of the railways, factories, crops, and cities of Andara.

Silvarhen portrays Dyraveen's bombing as simple and reckless revenge. There is some truth in this portrayal, but there is also a forgetfulness and distortion. Dyraveen focused his bombing on inland civilian targets largely because he still feared the Andaran naval fleets. Given his defeat off Troqual and the tone of war set by the Andaran torture of civilians, Dyraveen's decision to avoid naval battle and bomb the Andaran mainland is understandable.

For some of Silvarhen's criticisms, Dyraveen's actions can be partially explained but not justified.

Troqual was the only non-mountainous island within striking distance of Andara. Dyraveen forced the indigenous people onto the northwest corner of their island. Few indigenous were killed but all were herded and driven at gunpoint.

The islands surrounding Andara were bombed intermittently throughout the war. Dyraveen, ignorant of Andaran history, mistakenly assumed all tribal peoples in the east to be Andaran.

Silvarhen's account of postwar Andara is accurate and penetrating. Dyraveen, the great wartime leader, "flinched before the enormous task of reconstruction." He left the task to others and returned to the Pheran continent. But, sadly, Silvarhen says nothing of Dyraveen's later regret. As Silvarhen returned to the Earth, so Dyraveen returned to the island of Andara.

Having cast the war in broad outline, Silvarhen returns to the war's beginning.

He tells the story of five Pherans.

Dekanara was a giant Torite. Though born into a wealthy family, Dekanara chose the life of the fighter. He fought for coins and bread in the Lytarran underground. He found a home in the low and dark places, sandpits, fields, and alleys, punching, kicking, bleeding. He loved the simplicity of the fight, bone against bone, muscle against muscle, two fighters trading blows until one fighter fell. He loved the bloodrush and explosion of pain, the wildfire nerves, the brainwires arcing and crackling.

The fight lost its thrill when Dekanara left the lower fighting ranks to challenge the veterans. His mountainous size, quick hands, and explosive power were not enough to beat the veterans' experience and skill. A string of losses shook his confidence. He felt the first fading of his young body and the first sting of time.

But an old fighter, Tycee, took Dekanara under his wing. Tycee taught Dekanara the mental toughness to weather the twists and turns of the fight, the discipline to restrain emotion and wait for openings, and the creative planning to bait an opponent and think several moves ahead. He taught Dekanara to box a wrestler and wrestle a boxer. He taught Dekanara to conserve his energy until the moment of explosion, to use every part of his body for offense and defense, to protect himself until his opponent made a crucial mistake, and to finish without hesitation.

Tycee and Dekanara grappled, sparred, and trained together. Together, they made a run at the upper ranks.

Dekanara climbed. He broke his opponents apart physically and mentally. He ended the careers of good fighters.

Tycee fell. His body stopped listening to the commands of his brain. The cuts, breaks, bruises, and tears from a lifetime of fighting caught up to him.

"I should have quit years ago," Tycee said. "Now I'm all used up, no good for anything else."

Dekanara stood by his teacher and friend. He gave up the best fighting years of his life and joined the Torite army with Tycee.

They were stationed at the pier in Lytarr when the Andarans attacked.

Bullets clipped Tycee in the arm, chest, and neck. He fell onto his back and slowly bled out.

Dekanara dropped his gun, knelt, and watched his friend die.

The Andarans stormed the pier. They circled Dekanara, curious at the sight of a weeping giant.

Carrdava was a mixblood, the son of a Cerran cook and a Torite mechanic. He never met his father. He was raised by his mother in a small Cerran community outside of Lytarr. Carrdava hated the strictness and moral self-righteousness of the community. He hated the way his mother was subtly ostracized and constantly held down for her one mistake. As a young man, Carrdava drank heavily, clashed with the elders, and rejected their teaching. He was expelled from the community.

After a few stays in Lytarran jails, Carrdava met a strong Cerran woman from a different community. He married, fathered two children, and built a home for his family. Carrdava respected the Cerrans in his wife's community. He admired their hard work, eager sharing, and quiet humility. He admired their dedication to the study of Llarai and the wilderness prophets. He was accepted among them.

But the community's way of life was threatened by the Torites. The Torites continually encroached into Cerran land. Torite machinery companies built roads over Cerran grazing lands and warehouses on Cerran fields. Torite farming companies diverted the rivers, built their own waterways, and left the Cerrans with thin, drying streams. Carrdava could not understand the community's lack of resistance to the Torite aggression. "I believed in the strength of my people," he wrote, "but I did not understand why our strength could not be turned against our enemies. Surely, God hated crime. Surely, God could not bear to see a people trampled."

When Carrdava heard of the Andaran attack on Lytarr, he laughed. He celebrated when he saw Andaran cannons blast the Torite warehouse on the edge of his land.

But the cannons also shelled his community and home.

His wife and two children were killed. He was captured by their smoke-charred bodies, beaten by rifle butts, kicked by many boots.

Valas was a pure-blooded Cerran of the eastern wild.

He was marked a prophet by his mother's death during childbirth. As blood and life flowed from the mother, she pulled her child close and whispered: "May your eyes see the rising of your people."

Valas followed the path of the old prophets and poets.

He wandered the still plains of the east, the broken hills, the white-stone canyons.

He walked beneath the grey-boned trees and asked questions of God.

Why are you silent?

Why have you abandoned your people?

When will you humble the Torites and lift your people high?

When no answer to his questions came, Valas vowed not to eat or drink until he heard the voice of God.

My skin pulled tight against my bones.
My blood slowed. My vision dimmed.
I lay against a tree, cursed God, and waited to die.

I laid in weariness but could not sleep.
No voice came to me, instead a slowly rising truth.
Why did I speak for my people but suffer far from them?

Valas left the eastern wild and returned to his people.

He lived in a small village along the river. He worked beside his hungry brothers and sisters.

Valas smiled when the black Andaran boats came.

The other Cerrans fled the village, but Valas waited.

He was captured alone by the river.

Dona was a Torite, a woman, a soldier. She was young in years, but her body carried the wreckage of a long and violent life. She had been stabbed by a prisoner in a Lytarran jail, shot accidentally by a fellow soldier in the mountains, and knocked unconscious in a Draun riot. Her hip and ankle had been broken in a fall from a moving truck. Her hands, broken in fights with women and men, had unnatural bends and crooks from self-doctored casts. Dona was respected and feared by the men of her unit. Her unyielding stare and determined limp made the men uneasy. Her scarred and damaged body was fearful proof of Dona's willingness to carry a fight to the deepest places of pain.

When the Andarans attacked Lytarr, Dona's unit was positioned on a riverbank outside the city. They fired their guns at the enemy ships, but their bullets only dented the heavy, black hulls of the Andarans.

The Andaran ships shattered the Torite blockade. Their cannons blasted and sunk every Torite boat in the river. The Andarans headed into the heart of Lytarr.

Dona ran to her jeep and sped toward the city.

The Andarans shelled Lytarr, flurry upon flurry.

A building exploded above Dona, showering her jeep with brick and metal.

Her jeep spun and rolled.

Dona hung helplessly, her head above the ground, her hair in a bloody puddle.

A circle of Andaran soldiers watched her.

They laughed as her twisted arm flopped on the ground.

Dona turned her head, spit blood through cracked teeth, and reached across the ground for her pistol.

The Andarans kicked the gun away. They cut the harness.

Dona dropped, yelled in pain as her broken arm crashed against the hard ground.

The Andarans carried her away.

The Andaran ships left Lytarr and gathered in a wide bay on the eastern coast. All of the Pheran prisoners were dropped on the shore, pressed into a herd, and forced into a single line to march past the Andaran general, Ciralan.

Dekanara, Carrdava, and Valas walked by the general with their heads low and their eyes on the ground. They were taken to the cruiser in the bay.

Dona, exhausted and weak, also walked by Ciralan with her head low. But Dona, with her slinged arm, determined limp, and blood-soaked rags around her head, caught the general's attention.

Ciralan ordered her to stop.

Dona stared at the general. She spit at his Torite translator.

The general sent Dona to his own battleship.

On the cruiser, the old separating lines between the continental races disappeared. The Pherans were brought together by their fear of the Andarans and the bitter struggle for survival.

Dekanara, Carrdava, and Valas took control of the Pheran prisoners in the cold, dark hold of the cruiser. The towering arms of Dekanara received every bucket of water and bundle of food lowered into the hold. The three distributed the food and water according to need, but those that grumbled or questioned their authority received nothing. The three also controlled the distribution and use of the other valuable resources in the hold - clothing, blankets, and sources of light.

A terrible problem arose early in the voyage to Andara. Prisoners stricken by the sea fever required three times the water of other prisoners. The sick also needed many more blankets, which became contaminated once soaked with fever sweat.

The power assumed by Dekanara, Carrdava, and Valas forced the three into the heart of the problem. They tried to provide for the sick, but the draining needs of the ill weakened the rest of the prisoners and caused the fever to spread more quickly. Seeing no other solution, the three leaders decided that the sick must be killed.

Dekanara was the first to kill. He crossed the dark chamber at night, climbed on top of a sick prisoner, and wrapped his hands around the man's throat. After a short and muted struggle, Dekanara returned. "Never again," he said, trembling.

But the three killed again and again.

Valas wrote of the dark hours on the voyage:

> *In the day, I was strong. A bite of food, a taste of water, a beam of light - these were enough to give me hope and strength. But my heart shriveled in the long hours of the night. The crying of my stomach and the twisting of my thoughts led my hands to kill. I convinced myself that the killings were necessary, that the sacrifice of the fever-stricken was necessary for the group's survival. I convinced myself that the Andarans were the guilty ones. But my certainty vanished as I crossed the chamber floor, as I climbed atop my sick brother and choked his feeble breath. The Andarans were responsible for the war, for our imprisonment, for the horrible conditions we suffered by day and by night. But it was my hands around my brother's neck. May God forgive.*

On the battleship, a smaller group of Pherans suffered more than hunger, thirst, and disease.

They were tortured. They were stripped, bound, and beaten with metal rods. They were thrown into boiling vats and held under freezing water. They were electrocuted, burned with irons, and forced to crawl through feces.

Most of the Pherans broke quickly. They could find no meaning in their blinding agony, no hope in their long nightmare.

The remaining few were tortured by Ciralan himself. The general weakened the prisoners' spirit with temptation. He allowed them sweet sleep, rich foods, naked photographs, cigarettes, painkillers. Prisoners that indulged in Ciralan's pleasures soon yielded under the slightest pain.

Only Dona and Llevar, a young Cerran, refused the temptations of the general.

By the mistake of a guard, the two were allowed one night in adjoining cells.

Dona's encounter with Llevar that night forever changed her.

His eye was swollen shut, a bag of purple over a bag of black.

His skin, though blistered and swollen and scarred with many knives, showed youth in places, places smooth and hairless, soft with the glow of life.

"Dona," he said. "Dona, the beautiful."

He said my name as if he had always known me. He looked at me with a father's compassion. I felt somehow that he had seen my birth, my growth as a child, my long journey to this terrible place.

Throughout the night, he fought his pain with poetry. Slumped and shivering against the metal bars, hands shaking from hunger, unblinded eye blinking slow and heavy, he recited poems in the tongue of his people.

I did not understand the words, but I saw that they brought strength to him. The words filled, sustained, and carried him. The words lifted him above the wrecked shell of his body to a place I yearned to know.

"Teach me your poetry," I said.

He spoke of Llarai, the great mother of the Cerrans. He spoke of her suffering in the white mountains. He spoke of her splintered bones, her body torn apart by the bitter cold.

"I am Llarai," I said.

He took my hand through the bars. "Llarai cried out in her suffering," he said. "Llarai cried out to God and was answered. Llarai saw the opening of heaven."

Dona and Llevar survived Ciralan's torture and the long voyage to Andara.

In the capital, they were brought before the Emperor.

They were asked to kneel.

Both refused.

Ciralan hung himself that night in the palace courtyard.

All of the surviving Pheran prisoners from the cruiser and the battleship were taken to a remote barrack in southeastern Andara.

The barrack lay in the black hills on the edge of the Andaran jungle.

Cyrion, the commanding officer in the barrack, threw all the Pheran prisoners into the jungle except for Dona and Llevar.

Cyrion had Dona and Llevar unchained. He sat them down at a table, fed them, and offered them liquor. He told them that they would be killed that night by order of the Emperor.

Llevar ate then moved to a bunk near the window. He gazed into the jungle.

Dona drank with Cyrion.

The officer asked about the war in Phera, about Dona's life and home and family. He asked how she had not broken under torture. He said that he was sorry for what he had to do.

Dona gave short answers to Cyrion's questions, the best she could manage in his language. She did not understand much of what he said, but she sensed that he was an honest man under great pressure, a good man expected to do a terrible thing.

In the end, Cyrion could not bring himself to execute his prisoners. He drank himself to sleep that night.

Dona and Llevar left the barracks in the morning. They entered the jungle, found a deep hollow beneath an ancient tree, and rested.

The other Pherans also rested in small caves beneath the trees. They ate leaves, drank from streams, and wiped mud on themselves to drive away the clouds of insects.

The Pherans were helped by a group of Nyavites that had also been taken prisoner by the Andarans.

The Nyavites showed the Pherans how to survive in the jungle. They taught them about the jungle's many trees, plants, and animals. They taught them what would kill and what would sustain life.

The Nyavites pitied the Pherans as lost children in the wild.

The Pherans, though thankful for the Nyavites' help, feared becoming like their new friends, wild and savage.

Dekanara became weakly ill from the Nyavite diet of beetles and leaves. He persuaded Cyrion to give the prisoners a few knives and tools. The Pherans built a string of huts. They also hunted.

Dekanara, Carrdava, and Valas again took control of the Pheran prisoners. They planned rebellion and escape from the jungle. Carrdava expelled from the huts any Pherans that he considered weak. He recruited the Nyavites most violent and vengeful. Carrdava's plan was to leave the jungle, travel south beneath the mountains, and cross into the western hills. The rebels would raid small towns for food, weapons, vehicles, and fuel. They would find and free other prisoners. Once strong, they would terrorize western Andara.

Valas agreed that they should cross into the western hills. But he argued that the Andaran soldiers in the barrack should be spared because Cyrion had given them tools and knives.

Carrdava said that their only choice was to kill first, because Cyrion would hunt them down after they fled.

Dekanara took the side of Carrdava.

The Pherans waited for the right moment to strike.

Dona and Llevar rested for many days in the hollow beneath the ancient tree. They rested and healed.

Dona's first words of poetry were written.

In the darkness of the cave,
wrapped in moss warm and soft,
I broke.

The horror of Ciralan,
the long night of the voyage,
returned to me.

I rolled in nightmare.
I twisted into tears,
a child in the dark.

But I was not alone in the darkness.
Llevar suffered with me.
He brought me leaves and water.
He whispered poetry.

From the heights,

I saw Andara burning.
I saw Pheran planes fill the sky.
I felt the mountains shake and quiver,
sheets of fire through the hills.

But the hand of God traveled far.
It reached across the sea and land.
The trampled reached out to the fallen.
The despised touched their enemies with love.

Llevar left the tree. He prepared for a great journey. He invited all Pherans and Nyavites to join him. He welcomed even Cyrion, the Andaran officer.

The moment to strike came for the rebels.

On Andaran holiday – a night of eclipse - the soldiers celebrated inside the barrack.

The rebels waited outside. When the blue and silver moons touched in the night sky, the rebels attacked.

Dekanara struck down the outside guard with a knotted stick. The rebels poured into the barrack. They stabbed the sleeping Andaran soldiers with stakes and knives.

When the attack was over, Valas fled into the jungle.

The Pherans gathered all the weapons, equipment, and supplies in the barrack.

The Nyavites hung the Andaran bodies from trees.

The rebels stole the Andaran trucks, traveled south beneath the mountains, and crossed into the western hills, as Carrdava had planned.

They raided small farms for food.

The hills quickly filled with Andaran police and soldiers hunting down the rebels.

The rebels split. The Nyavites attacked a railway station. They were trapped and killed by a swarm of soldiers. The

Pherans abandoned their vehicles and headed on foot into the mountains.

After several days of chase and climb, they reached an old mine in the mountains and rested the night. Dekanara, weary and ill, could not continue in the morning.

Carrdava and the remaining Pheran rebels climbed on. They heard flurries of gunfire behind them throughout the day. Near dusk, they heard a dull and muffled explosion. Then quiet. They camped, stared into the fire, and drank to their friend.

The Andaran soldiers left the mountains when the winter rains came.

In the spring, the soldiers returned and found the Pheran bodies. They cut off the hands, heads, and feet of the rebels, put them into bags, and threw the torsos down the mountainside. Carrdava watched, helpless, hiding in a cave.

Alone, Carrdava survived three winters in the mountains. He survived to see the coming of Dyraveen's bomber legions.

Long ago, I had watched a thin trail of smoke climb
into the sky and mark the death of my brother.
Now, I watched our bombers shake the land and set
the hills afire. Now, I saw the Andarans finally repaid.

Llevar had asked Cyrion to leave his life, land, and people behind. He had told Cyrion to follow him to the island of Eskalla. He had told Cyrion to walk with God.

On the eve of the Andaran holiday, Cyrion sat alone in the barrack. The Andaran officer wrestled with the words of Llevar.

I did not understand Llevar. With a calm voice
and steady eyes, he spoke the words of a madman.
Eskalla, the land of snakes and cane, home of a
people too weak to resist even the Nyavites. Should I

deny my duty, leave everything behind, and brave the wild jungle in the ridiculous hope of reaching Eskalla?

I cursed myself for not obeying the command of the Emperor. I should have killed both prisoners that first day. I should not have listened to them. I should not have hesitated.

But Llevar had looked into my eyes. He had seen clearly my weakness, the impossibility of my position. If I had obeyed the order to kill, I would have pierced my own chest. The prisoners had not been broken. They had not brought shame to themselves. The killing of the unshamed would have been hypocrisy, murder, and disgrace.

I poured a glass of liquor but did not drink. The truth I had to face would not be numbed by alcohol. I lit a cigarette and sat in silence.

The Andaran heart is rotten. Our history is a lie. Our mind has twisted by endless war.

As a boy, I had stood at the feet of the great statues. I had adored their glory, the pride and suffering of the soldier-hero, the brilliance and fierce will of the generals. As a young man, I had read the sacred literature of the great Andaran writers, their histories of warrior and general, their carving of the same statues, their crafting of myth.

I had not questioned as a boy. I had believed because I had needed to believe.

We had fought in countless wars, but our history taught that we had never been the aggressor. I had believed this. Though being the most numerous island people, though having the largest fleets and greatest army, our victories had always come against nearly impossible odds. I had believed this, too.

I had believed because of the sad eyes of the statued soldier. The soldier had killed only after seeing many horrors. The soldier had killed only after being scarred by the atrocities of the enemy.

In Nyava, my own eyes had saddened after seeing many atrocities. Some had been committed by Nyavite hand, but many more had been committed by my own people.

I spoke against these atrocities to the commanders.

I was scolded and made to feel disloyal.

I saw more horrors and spoke to the generals.

I was transferred to the jungle.

The core is rotten.

The highest leader of Andara ordered me to kill a young man and woman that had done nothing wrong. They had been attacked in their own land. They had been captured, chained, and tortured, yet they had not broken in spirit. Even according to our twisted rule of shame, they did not deserve to die. The Emperor knew this. To avoid hypocrisy, he sent them far from the capital. He wanted their blood poured out in secret. He expected his lowly officer to kneel and to obey.

I will join Dona and the madman.

I will die in the wild. I will die by hunger, beast, or disease, not by the bullet of my own people.

Many Pherans and Nyavites followed Llevar into the jungle. Motivated by curiosity, several turned back after a single day's march. Many lasted longer, drawn by the comradery and excitement of the group. But, day by day, the followers thinned. Pherans turned back because the journey was too difficult, the goal too distant and obscure. Nyavites turned back because of Llevar's acceptance of Cyrion.

Only six remained.

Llevar.

Dona, the Torite woman.

Valas, the Cerran prophet.

Cyrion, the Andaran officer.

And Jesse and Hale, the Nyavite brothers.

The first year showed little progress. They moved their camp from time to time, but the barrack could still be seen in the distant hills.

Llevar was not concerned with the lack of progress. He learned the Andaran and Nyavite languages. He learned their history, their culture, their thought. He worked alongside the others in daily chore and joined them in explorations of the jungle.

The year was difficult. Cyrion and the Nyavite brothers shared few words. Valas stayed at the edge of the group, always silent.

In the second year, when the dry season had withered the jungle streams, Valas walked in the heat of the day, searching for water.

He collapsed in a clearing under the hot sun.

The others found him, delirious, shaking violently.

Cyrion offered him a drink from his canteen, but Valas refused.

"I am a killer," Valas said. "Let me die as I deserve."

Valas shook throughout his legs and chest. His eyes glazed over. His lips quivered, but he did not speak.

Llevar stepped forward and knelt at his side. "Relieve yourself," Llevar said. "Speak the truth and be forgiven."

"I killed a soldier in the barrack," Valas said. "I killed four men on the cruiser, two Torites, two of my own people."

"You are forgiven," Llevar said. "You are free."

The words of Llevar touched Valas like a cool mist across his skin. He sat up and drank.

When the dry season had passed, they marched east, away from the mountains, into the lower hills. They maintained a brisk pace for several weeks and covered much ground.

But when they turned to the north, they entered a series of marsh valleys thick with insects, reptiles, and disease. Their bodies weakened under dehydration, cramps, and diarrhea. Jesse and Valas contracted diseases of the stomach and intestine. Dona, Llevar, and Hale caught bone fever. Cyrion was bitten by a snake.

The travelers ground their way out of the marsh valleys and into a small range of hills. Eager to escape all places wet and low, they climbed the highest hill in the range and set their camp.

The exhausted travelers rested for several days.

"We must continue north," Llevar said.

"We should rest a few more days," Jesse said. "Then we should return to the mountains."

"Llevar is our commander," Cyrion said.

"More rest will soften, not strengthen, us," Dona said.

Jesse and Hale watched the others pack up the camp.

Valas pleaded with the Nyavites to follow Llevar, but they refused.

"What can we do?" Valas asked Llevar.

"Stay with them," Llevar said. "When they are ready, travel north to the Tallen River. Follow the river east. We will wait for you."

The Nyavites, Jesse and Hale, would regret their rebellion against Llevar. They would travel north with Valas, follow the Tallen River, and discover a wonder of God and history.

Nyava, the home of Jesse and Hale, was a black-green, tear-shaped island northwest of Andara.

The ancient Nyavites were fishers, sailors, and carvers of wood.

Countless Andaran attacks on the coast of Nyava drove the sea people inland, into the jungle and mountains.

But a few Nyavites refused to change their way of life or take up the sword in resistance. In small fishing boats, they left their coastal homes, braved the deep ocean, and sailed into the surrounding fleet of Andaran warships.

The Andarans laughed at the Nyavites and allowed them to pass, certain that the ocean would swallow their tiny boats.

But the Nyavites survived the ocean. They sailed to the shore of northeastern Andara and fished their enemy's own waters.

The Andarans, no longer laughing, chased and attacked.

The Nyavites fled up the Tallen River. They scattered and hid in the streams of the jungle.

The Andarans fired at the fishing boats, but their warships were too large to enter the narrow streams. They returned to the ocean, certain that the jungle would swallow the little fishers.

But the Nyavites survived the jungle. They fished the Tallen River and built their homes along its banks.

The Nyavites crafted a new identity as a people of the jungle but kept their history alive in story. Parents told their children the story of the Nyavite journey with pride and humor. "Your ancestors were crazy," they said. "They crossed the ocean on tiny boats, ran from the Andaran warships, and made their home in the wild jungle. The world will never see such fools again."

Jesse and Hale expected rejection and cold silence from Llevar and the others, but they were embraced.

Llevar, smiling, showed the Nyavites a boat on the Tallen's shore. It was light yet sturdy, ornate with the carvings of sun, moon, wind, and ocean.

"How did you make such a boat so quickly?" Hale asked.

Llevar laughed. "Your people made this boat," he said.

The travelers lived among the lost Nyavites for two seasons. They fished the Tallen from deck and boat. They learned to weave tapestry and cloth. They witnessed the burials, births, and weddings of the community. They learned the rich history of the river people.

At the end of the rainy season, Llevar gathered all the lost Nyavites together. He thanked them for their kindness and hospitality. He thanked them for their many stories.

Llevar then told them of Phera. He told them of the ancients, the tribes, the great mother Llarai, and the wilderness prophets. He told them of the Andaran attack on Phera. He told them of the Pherans' capture, voyage, and torture. He told of their long journey through the jungle, mountains, hills, and marsh.

"The hand of God has brought us to this place," Llevar said. "The time of God has come."

"What would God have us do?" an elder asked.

"Prepare your hearts," Llevar said. "To follow God, you must leave your home. You must leave everything behind."

"Where will our new home be?" a young Nyavite asked.

"You will have no home. You will follow the wind and sea. You will know few comforts. And your greatest joy will be found in the love of your enemies."

The Nyavites asked many more questions of Llevar.

"Why do your boats bear the carvings of ocean waves and winds?" Llevar asked. "Has any among you ever seen the ocean? Has any traveled beyond the river's end? No, the carvings are only a dream, a dream that has long slept within your people, a dream stirred by prophets and born by fools."

The calling of Llevar stirred great discussion and division among the Nyavites.

Several elders came forward and promised that their entire families would follow Llevar.

"All are welcome," Llevar said. "But each family member must make their own decision. Even the children."

"This is not right," the elders said. "You will tear families apart."

"From currents deeper than blood, God is building a new family," Llevar said.

When the elders went away confused and angry, Cyrion argued with Llevar. He said that they needed many boats, supplies, fishers, and sailors for their journey. He said that Llevar had been unwise to discourage potential followers and turn away valuable resources.

"When will you see beyond the surface of things?" Llevar asked. "Until your heart breathes, your mind will wander in fog and mist."

Less than a quarter of the lost Nyavites joined the travelers. They had only five boats.

The librans - the fools - sailed down the Tallen River. They saw the towering black canyons of the jungle, the moon-skinned snakes that ruled the night waters, and the giant rib-wing fliers that blocked the sun.

On the river journey, the librans struggled to control their boats. Changes in the wind turned and spun the boats. Drops and falls in the river were not avoided. The boatside carvings were battered and splintered.

When they reached the mouth of the delta, the librans turned their boats toward the delta banks.

"Where are you going?" Llevar asked.

"To camp on the delta," they said. "We will rest for a few days."

"No one is tired," Llevar said.

The librans nodded but kept their boats pointed toward shore. They glanced fearfully into the wide sea.

"Be strong," Llevar said. "God is with us."

The five boats entered the sea.

Four of the boats struggled but held their course.

The fifth boat swept left and right and turned in wide, erratic loops. The other boats disappeared on the horizon.

After hours of watching the Nyavite crew fight the sails, Cyrion stood up suddenly. He cursed the boatsmen, pushed them away from the mast, and strapped down all the sails. "Stop, before you kill us," he said.

Cyrion, Valas, and the Nyavites took up the oars. They rowed until their backs were soaked with sweat and their hands slipped from the oars. When night fell, they pulled their oars from the water.

"Now we drift," Cyrion said.

It was a bitter night for Cyrion.

I listened to the creaking of the boat. I felt each wave strike the hull, our helpless spin and tossing. I felt the waste of every moment, the progress of the other boats, the ever-growing space between us.

I smiled to myself. This was what Llevar wanted from me. To feel. To feel and not think. To let my heart breathe.

Llevar said that my mind wandered in fog and mist. This foggy mind had led me to recruit the elders and their families in the village. This foggy mind had warned me that our disordered crews were not ready to sail the ocean. But Llevar, with sharp and crystal thought, had known better. Llevar had turned away the elders and their families. He had watched the boatsmen struggle on the tame river then sent them charging into the wild ocean.

He was right. The crews were ready. All but one.

While the others slept, I cursed and fumed. Where

was the God of Llevar? Why had I been called and abandoned? Did my sparing of Dona and Llevar count for nothing?

When my anger passed, I sank into self-pity and despair.

In the hour before dawn, I finally slept.

I slept and dreamed.

Against the deep night, I saw the face of a woman aglow with the light of stars and moons. The face was both young and old. The face held the brightness and hunger of youth, the dignity and long-earned pain of the old. The face held defiance and peace. It was scarred yet achingly beautiful. It was beautiful because of its scars.

The eyes of the woman saw far across the sea. She waited for the boat to sail. She waited for the wind to take her hair, to end her pain and separation.

Cyrion woke and fed the others. He raised the sails.

With a bright sun, soft winds, and Cyrion's encouragement, the Nyavite crew found their confidence. They sailed all through the day.

At night, Cyrion told Valas of his dream.

"You dreamt of Llarai," Valas said. The Cerran's face saddened. "You, an Andaran, have seen Llarai."

The fifth boat caught up to the others off the northern reefs.

The librans sailed together. They smiled through the mist of breaking waves.

Two days after passing the reefs, an Andaran cruiser approached on the water.

The cruiser circled them several times. Its wake shook the smaller boats and forced them into a tight huddle. With turrets manned and guns aimed, the cruiser trolled toward them.

An officer shouted down from the side of the cruiser. "Identify yourselves," he said.

"We are fishers," Cyrion said.

"Where do you come from?" the officer said.

"We come from Andara," Cyrion said. "We are fishers."

The officer scanned the faces in the boat. "I see Nyavites among you."

"We are fishers."

The officer cursed Cyrion. He threw down a rope and ordered everyone out of the boats.

Cyrion took the rope. He turned to the others. "No one leaves the boats," he said.

Cyrion climbed.

On the side of the cruiser, he faced the officer.

"You are Andaran," the officer said.

"I was Andaran," Cyrion said. "Now, I am a follower of Llevar, a servant of God."

The officer stared at Cyrion with contempt. His eyes flashed as he recognized the posture and stare of a fellow soldier. "You are a deserter."

The officer touched his pistol to Cyrion's forehead. He fired.

Cyrion's body fell to the water.

Valas swam to the body. He wrapped his arm around its neck and drew it to the boat.

Llevar lifted the body.

The cruiser pulled away.

Llevar knelt, kissed Cyrion, and covered his body with blankets.

The librans mourned for one day. They did not eat, drink, or speak a word.

At dawn, Llevar broke the silence:

"Cyrion defied the highest orders of the land. He left everything behind to join us in our journey. Cyrion was our brother. He will be buried in Eskalla so that his walk on the other side may begin with laughter."

The indigenous of Eskalla did not see a distinction between the ancient and the present. Time was not linear or progressive in their eyes; it was circular, cyclical like the seasons. Change was unnatural in their eyes, something forced upon them with violence by the outside world. The Eskallans valued balance over conflict, organic unity over individual want, contentment over greed and craving. They felt no desire to travel the seas, no need to conquer other tribes.

The Eskallans were attacked many times throughout their history by both the Nyavites and the Andarans. But they did not view themselves as victims or a conquered people. They absorbed the raids of the Nyavites. They waited out the occupations of the Andarans. With a hope, often strained, sometimes bitter, they expected the balance and strength of the natural world to work their enemies into the ground.

The attacks of the Nyavites throughout history were short-lived bursts of rage, a frustrated and misdirected venting. The Nyavite raiders usually killed the few Eskallans that offered resistance, stole enough cane to fill their boats, then returned to their own land.

The Andarans killed in greater numbers and remained for many years. Driven by their perverse sense of honor and shame, Andaran commanders tested the Eskallan spirit with torture. The Eskallans cried out under torture but did not break like the hard-brittle Nyavites. The Eskallan face deepened to stone. Their dark eyes emptied.

The Andarans attempted and failed to implement mass-agriculture in Eskalla. Though threatened with death, the indigenous farmers clung to their traditional methods. Andaran foremen struggled with the unfamiliar terrain and obstinate workforce. Neither cruel nor sensible foremen could produce enough cane to match the cost of equipment, fuel, and transport. A transfer to Eskalla, the land of snakes and cane, became a form of punishment for Andaran soldiers.

The librans reached Eskalla and traveled west along its southern coast.

For several days, they saw only black sand, brush, and rocks along its shore.

On the southwestern tip of the island, they found a single thatch-roofed hut. They landed their boats and set up camp.

Dona and Valas walked to the hut.

Through the open door of the hut, they saw an old woman grinding meal. The woman sensed their presence but continued to work her stone pestle. When the meal was finished, she looked up at the strangers without fear or surprise. She greeted them in the Andaran tongue.

"You speak Andaran," Valas said.

"Yes," she said, staring at their faces, then their clothes. The old Nyavite patterns of their long shirts held her eyes longer than their faces.

"But you are Eskallan," Valas said.

"I am Eskallan," she said. "My son-in-law is Andaran. He hides in the back room."

"Why is he hiding?"

"Because he is a stupid man," she said. She turned toward the back room. "They are not soldiers," she yelled. "They have not come to take you away."

They heard footsteps in the back room. A pair of eyes peeked through the doorway.

The old woman stood up. "Please sit at our table," she said. "Dinner will be ready soon."

The Eskallans served them dinner. Hechel, the old woman, brought cakes of meal cooked on the fire. Cyvel, her son-in-law, brought fruit and hot tea.

Hechel was a widow. Her husband had drowned in the sea. Her four children were also dead, one by disease, one by hunger, two by the snake. Though Hechel joked harshly with her son-in-law, a deep love could be seen between them.

Cyvel, whose wife had died by the snake, had been stationed inland at an Andaran base. In the field, he had seen a beautiful Eskallan woman and had fallen in love. In the field, many years later, he had watched the same woman drop to the ground and die.

Dona told the Eskallans of the attack on Lytarr, their capture, their long journey through the Andaran jungle, and their voyage to Eskalla.

When Dona finished, the Eskallans sat back and considered.

Cyvel smoked his pipe. His face tightened, relaxed, then tightened again. He struggled to believe their story.

The dark eyes of Hechel showed both doubt and belief. Her face, though etched with the lines of time, showed no tension, rather a patient faith that time would reveal all truth.

The early days in Eskalla were disappointing to the lost Nyavites.

Llevar, interestingly, had not corrected a great misunderstanding in the Nyavite minds.

We had thought that Eskalla was the Pherans' word for ocean.

We had imagined many years of wild journey across the seas. We had hoped to taste new fish, delicious and exotic. We had dreamed of traveling to the great land of Phera.

When we learned that Eskalla was an island, we

were disappointed. Our arms tired at the oars when we saw its dead, barren coast. Our chests emptied of wind and blood. For many days we would not look at Llevar. We would not say a word to the man that had led us to this place.

But time warmed our hearts. The old woman, Hechel, welcomed us. She treated us as precious children. She taught us the Eskallan language, their history, and way of life. With the strength of a young woman, she showed us how to build homes, how to cook and gather food. She showed us how to protect ourselves from the dangers of the island - the snake, the rat, the storm. When we told her the story of our ancestors, her face glowed with smile and laughter.

Through Hechel we met many other people of the island. They, too, welcomed us. They treated us as family and friend. More than that, many fell in love and married. The fire of the skin burned between libran and Eskallan.

Llevar joined in the marriage celebrations. He shared in the joy of the people, but he also offered warning.

"Does not fire end in ash?" he said. "Only the love of God burns forever."

"But we know love," the people said.

"The love of God does not fade like the body," he said. "It grows and deepens like the oldest trees of the jungle. Its arms are ever-reaching."

In the second year on Eskalla, the unity of Llevar's followers faded, their purpose and drive dissolved.

The librans that had married built new homes across the island, had children, and settled into predictable rhythms of life. Hale also married.

Jesse and Valas, their intestinal disease reawakened, shared a hut on the southern shore far from the others.

Dona lived alone in the hills. In the morning, she took food to the old and sick of the island. In the afternoon, she gathered blueleaf, the healing plant of Eskalla. She dried the blueleaf on sun-cooked stone and tied it into bundles. At night, she joined Llevar on the mountain.

In the third year, a trio of Pheran planes passed over the island.

"We must sail to Andara," Llevar said.

They left the island in a single boat. There was Llevar, Jesse, three librans, and the Andaran deserter, Cyvel.

As they sailed Jesse looked back at the island and muttered a curse.

"We will return to Eskalla," Llevar said. "And many that abandoned the dream of God will be restored."

"Do they deserve to be?" Jesse said.

"Be honest, my friend," Llevar said. "Without the love of Valas and your brother, wouldn't you have died in the Andaran jungle?"

On a beach outside the Andaran port of Letrane, they landed and camped.

Throughout the night, they heard the deep whistle of the Pheran bombers. They watched the red-star flashes and felt the panicked shivering of the ground.

In the morning, after the bombers had fled the open sky, they entered the city. Army and fire trucks rushed through the streets. Columns of smoke rose from the burned-out shells of buildings and homes. The dead were bagged and gathered. Ash, blood, and soot were washed from the faces of the wounded.

Cyvel vented his anger and grief on the Pherans. "What kind of a people bombs cities and kills the innocent?" he said.

They worked in the city for many days. They eased the pain of burn victims with the dampened blueleaf. They took food, water, and blankets to those in need. They dug through the rubble, bandaged the wounded, and covered the dead.

When a soldier recognized them as foreigners and threatened arrest, they fled the city.

They worked in small towns around Letrane until a group of angry factory workers accused them of looting and chased them to the beach.

Exhausted, numb, and frustrated, they returned to their boats.

On the sea, Llevar encouraged the others. "Through our hands, many were helped," he said.

"We came to help them, but they treated us like criminals," Valas said.

"Their anger will pass, like that of Cyvel," Llevar said. "We have seen only the beginning of Andara's pain."

When they arrived on Eskalla, Llevar gathered all the people of the island. He told the people what they had seen in Andara.

"We saw sons without mothers and mothers without sons," he said. "We saw great buildings laid to dust, fires throughout the city, hundreds wounded, and the dead in piles."

"This is justice," an Eskallan said. "The Andarans have long earned this horror."

"I saw no justice in the attack of Lytarr, my home," Dona said. "I saw the same in the bombing of Letrane."

They returned to Andara with two boats, more workers, and piles of supplies.

The beach that had been empty on their departure was now littered with a fleet of ships, charred and wrecked.

A crowd of hungry and wounded Andarans surrounded them before they reached the first town. In a single day, their supplies were exhausted.

Llevar called Cyvel. "Return to the island," he said. "Plead for your people."

Cyvel sailed for Eskalla.

Those that stayed ventured into the city. They found no streets, only heaps of rubble. The army and fire trucks had all fled or been destroyed. The dead remained where they had fallen. The wounded crawled for shelter.

When Cyvel returned to Eskalla, he found the people gathered in mourning. A bomb had killed two men, three women, and a child.

Cyvel mourned with the Eskallans for three days. They sat together in silence around the fire.

When their mourning was finished, the old widow, Hechel, approached him.

"My son, what did you find in Letrane?" she asked.

"Blood and dust," Cyvel said.

Hechel nodded slowly. "We will help you now," she said.

In the bombing years, the followers of Llevar came to be called the *libranales*. The teaching of Llevar spread throughout the Andaran islands and the number of the libranales grew. The libranales were Pherans, Andarans, Nyavites, Eskallans, and many other tribal peoples. Their small boats delivered fish, bread, and the healing blueleaf to the devastated Andaran mainland. The libranales built a chain of refugee camps along its northern coast.

When the war ended, Dyraveen landed in the Andaran capital. He summoned the few surviving Andaran generals and commanders.

"Your people started this war," he said. "You will repay us for every bomb, bullet, and drop of fuel this war required."

Dyraveen knew that the massive war debt would be difficult to collect. He knew that a harsh Pheran leader must be chosen as governor of Andara, but he did not want the job himself or trust in the loyalty of his own military commanders.

He chose Carrdava, the escaped prisoner and lone surviving rebel.

Carrdava's first action was the liberation of all Pheran prisoners. After the prisoners had given written statements of abuses and crimes suffered, they were allowed to return to the Pheran continent. Nyavite prisoners were promised their freedom after one year of labor on the Andaran mainland.

Carrdava's next action was the punishment of the lower ranks of the Andaran military. These soldiers and officers were executed based on a single claim of abuse from a Pheran prisoner or three claims of abuse from Nyavite prisoners. Those that survived the wave of executions received life-sentences in the labor camps.

Carrdava gathered the middle and upper ranks of the Andaran military in the capital. These commanders and generals were stripped, beaten, marched through the rubble streets, then killed.

All Andaran civilians were sent to labor camps.

Carrdava considered most Andaran cities destroyed beyond repair. He focused on debt repayment through the extraction of fuel, metal, and lumber. He built labor camps around the refineries on the western coast, mines in the central mountains, and mills in the southeastern jungle. The rest of Andara was abandoned.

When the continental government was not satisfied with the production of the first year, Carrdava denied the Nyavites their promised release.

The Nyavites rebelled. Some were killed in isolated uprisings. Many escaped and fled to the north. Many Andarans also fled the labor camps to seek refuge in the north. The rescue camps of Llevar were rumored to welcome all people and overflow with fish and bread.

Furious, Carrdava flew to the north. He stormed into Llevar's camp with a squad of Pheran soldiers.

"Your camps are now closed," Carrdava said. "All Pherans will be arrested and sent back to the continent for trial. All Andarans and Nyavites will return to their labor camps or be shot."

Llevar responded with a story.

"In an island town, an old man lived who was often drunk and always angry.

"One night, in a rage, this old man killed another. He was brought before the town's judge. Now, this judge had been a good friend of the man who was killed. So, hurt and angry, the judge sentenced the murderer to death. And the killer was executed for his crime.

"Time passed on. But the judge could find no peace in his heart. So, the judge, still hurt, still angry, arrested the killer's son. And the son of the killer was executed for his father's crime.

"More years passed. But the judge, again, could find no peace. So, the judge arrested the grandson of the killer. And the blade waits now at the grandson's throat.

"Tell me, Carrdava, will the judge know peace after the boy is killed?"

Carrdava spent a few hours in the camp of Llevar. He talked and listened.

Carrdava allowed the refugee camps to remain in the north. He freed all Nyavites.

In his second year as governor, Carrdava ended the poor treatment of the Andarans. He gave them adequate food, clothing, and housing. He allowed them sufficient rest and occasional reward. As a result, morale and productivity improved. Escape attempts decreased and violent rebellion stopped completely.

Carrdava significantly improved the labor camps, but he could not meet the expectations of the continent. He resigned as governor of Andara and returned to his Pheran home.

The continental government chose to sell Andara. They sold the Andaran mainland and the surrounding islands to the highest bidding companies.

The businesses traveled east with more ships than Dyraveen's wartime fleet. They reopened the refineries, mines, and mills of Carrdava. They built new towns and cities, restored the supply of water and electricity, repaired the highways and railways, and planted new crops. They put many Andarans and Nyavites to work.

The libranale camps emptied.

An Andaran leader asked Llevar if the western corporations could be trusted.

"They did not come to help," Llevar said. "Their eyes see profits to be made and resources to be stripped. They will take what they want and leave when there is nothing left."

Valas returned to Phera to seek a cure for his disease.

The Eskallan libranales left to protect their land.

Jesse left to protect Nyava.

Dona and Llevar traveled to the mountains, to the womb of the Tallen River.

One night on their journey, Dona dreamed.

"I saw grain sprout in a field of stone," she told Llevar. "I saw a tree rise in the deepest night. The tree stilled the wind and scattered the darkness."

Llevar smiled. "Let us go to the river," he said.

Llevar baptized Dona.

Beneath the icy water, my breath was stolen.
I felt the pull of Death, its hungry cry and tireless claim.
But the hands of Llevar lifted me upward.

The surface broke.
The waters fell.
With wild breath, I entered the sky.

Dona and Llevar returned to the northern coast.

In time, they were joined by many they had loved.

Valas also returned. He came on a ship with supplies, gifts, and many brothers and sisters of Phera.

A string of villages grew on the coast. The people fished and sailed. They told stories and shared poetry in the night.

In the village of Libranale, Dona and Valas were married.

When word came that the great mother, Hechel, had died in Eskalla, Dona traveled to the island to mourn with the people.

On the journey back, Dona gave birth to a son.

I will wander the crystal memory of my people. Through poem, song, and story, I will speak the truth.

Silvarhen's crystal journey led him to a rich and beautiful vein in the history of his people.

He found the light of God in the poetry of Llarai, the story of the libran fools, and the life of Llevar.

But Silvarhen also cast shadow and darkness.

His shadow fell on the Alcyan, the Varran, the Torite, the Myshenite, the Draun, the Andaran, and the Nyavite.

His darkness fell on the Tyraen.

As Dyraveen flinched before the mammoth work of postwar rebuilding, so Silvarhen flinched before the full truth of Dyraveen and his people, the Tyraens.

II. TRIBAL MISTS

During the Bursting Age, while scientists, inventors, and engineers achieved rapid technological advance, another intellectual circle looked to the past. They were anthropologists, archaeologists, geologists, explorers, linguists, historians, and literary analysts. They searched for the origin of life on the Pheran continent.

The origin circle, forced to compete for university funding with the formidable tech circle, adopted new and creative strategies of self-promotion. They were the first academic sector to publish major works outside the university in private presses and the first to support independent documentary filmmaking. They drew the non-academic world into their search with an aggressive campaign of educational outreaches, public debates, and open-discussion forums. With most of their fields still in infancy, they borrowed the hardened logic of the philosophical sciences and the strict methodology of the physical sciences, but they kept their writings accessible and interesting to laypeople. At its best, the origin movement was a humble professor - sharing and exploring new ideas in the daytime college auditorium, volunteering nights for the teaching of children in neighborhood schools, spending every free hour outside of sleep immersed in his, or her, own field, tracing veins cautiously outward into other fields. At its worst, it was a charismatic spokesperson - widely conversant in many fields but unrooted in any single discipline, avoiding the check of peer criticism and debate, exploiting the mystery and thrill of the search into the ancient past.

The origin movement blundered in its first steps. It allowed a few leaders to sensationalize the movement by changing its publicly expressed goal from a search for the origins of life into a search for the first people. As likely predicted and intended by these leaders, the search for the first Pheran people evoked deep feelings of tribal vanity and pride. Pherans of every ethnic group followed the search hoping and believing that their ancestors would prove to be the first people. Disappointment was inevitable. Sensationalist followers were disappointed by the slowness of the scientific process, the hesitancy of scholars to provide definitive conclusions, and the ever-branching flow of newer, harder questions. Most disappointing of all to the sensationalist followers was the emerging reality that none of the presently dominant Pheran tribes would ever trace their lineage directly to the first Pheran people.

The movement survived this early blunder. Its self-interested followers fell away, but a faithful core of supporters remained. Scholars and teachers across the wide range of origin fields became more vocal and critical of their presumptive leaders. They discredited the champions of the first-people search and drove them into obscurity.

But the pendulum swung too far.

Potential leaders, good and bad, were attacked and roundly rejected; works crossing multiple fields were unfairly scrutinized and belittled.

The movement stalled, hamstrung by fear of another blunder, crippled by self-inflicted criticism.

The impasse was broken once the problem was acknowledged openly and honestly. Scholars resisted territorialism, improved communication among field colleagues, and developed many cross-field relationships. New leaders stepped forward who earned the trust of the specialists and sparked public interest without resorting to sensationalism. Many of these leaders served as faithful representatives, communicators, and advocates. A remarkable few were able to synthesize the best work across the range of origin fields, make connections unseen by field specialists, and create new lines of exploration.

Though the origin movement never found a consensus first-people, it unearthed an entire age of tribes before the Age of Tribes.

The Northern Caedans

From a wealth of clay-sealed temple records, origin scholars were able to trace in great detail the rapid rise and disastrous fall of an ancient coastal people.

The Caedans were first a modest population of fishers, planters, and weavers living in small clusters along the northern shore.

The discovery of metal pulled the Caedans into the ore-laden hills, swelled their numbers, and sparked the development of towns, farms, and mills.

The population surged again at the discovery of gems in the lower mountains.

The drive for gems split the Caedans. As they climbed and searched for treasure, they became separated by the steep veins of the mountains. They were broken into factions, clans held together primarily by material desire, not by the blood and line of family.

In the formative years of the Caedan factions, origin scholars observed several general trends: 1) an increased separation and hostility between social groups, 2) the descent of the old dominating classes - blacksmiths, engineers, stoneworkers, 3) the rise of the soldier class, and 4) a worsening struggle for the traditional classes - fishers, planters, weavers.

The old dominating classes were unable to organize and sustain the drive into the mountains. Their governing councils struggled to direct production, distribute supplies and resources, and control the broad range of Caedan workers, from coastal fishers to mountain miners. Large councils failed by inertia and indecision, small councils by instability. As the councils struggled, they increasingly called upon soldiers to enforce production quotas and maintain order. The soldier class ballooned. Eventually, the soldiers cast off the authority of the councils and attempted to govern themselves.

In the early histories of the Caedan factions, scholars observed three general patterns of development. These patterns varied in the alliances chosen or refused by the soldier class.

In S-pattern factions, the soldier class attempted to govern alone, without the aid of any ally classes. The soldiers created a gem-based currency and enforced a reasonably balanced wage system. (Blacksmiths received higher wages, likely due to the soldiers' dependence on weapons and armor.) Despite the relative fairness of the wage system, no class was pleased. Farmers considered food production to be the heart of the Caedan workforce and expected greater reward. Miners, engineers, and stoneworkers believed mountain labor to be the most difficult and resented their wage leveling with the workers of the hills and coast. Even the traditional classes, who gained from the system, complained against the soldiers. Distrusting the gem economy, they resisted work quotas, refused faster methods of production, and clung to the old ways of fishing, planting, and weaving. The soldiers, greatly frustrated, lowered the wages of every class and raised production quotas. A period of strain and tension followed. Stretched thin across the factional area, worn out by the tracking of production and the transportation of supplies, the soldiers became vulnerable. The miners turned the blacksmiths against the soldiers. After rebellions, often bloody and prolonged, the soldiers lost control. Of the four S-pattern factions, one dissolved and scattered, three were absorbed by other factions.

In SO-pattern factions, the soldiers encouraged the growth of an official class. These officials were initially charged with clerical duties, primarily the recordkeeping of production, supply, currency, and population levels. Their duties expanded over time. The officials traveled throughout the factions, gathered information directly from the Caedan workers, and bore the brunt of worker complaint. They also managed the distribution of all supplies and resources, except gems. (In some factions, the soldiers forced the expansion of duties upon the officials. In others, the expansion was initiated by the officials, either for efficiency or for positioning and power.) The officials' shouldering of the workload allowed the soldiers to impose lower wages and enforce higher production quotas. The soldier-official alliance remained intact until the late factional years. When the production of gems reached its plateau and the upward drive of the factions stalled against the mountains' heart, the soldiers struggled to maintain order. The soldiers expected the aid of their old and subservient allies. But the officials withdrew from their positions and watched the soldiers fall to violent rebellion. In two of the SO-pattern factions, the officials attempted to govern themselves and failed. In three, the officials negotiated with other factions and assisted in their own takeover.

In SPO-pattern factions, the soldier class governed with the help of the priest and official classes. An arrangement, informal yet binding, was formed early between the soldiers and the priests. Soldiers provided gems, crystals, stones, and wood for the construction of temples; priests, in turn, supported the soldiers among the people. The mountain temple became the center of religious and social life in the faction, a place of worship, rite, feasting, and ceremony. With the endorsement of the temple and the logistical support of officials, the soldiers ruled freely. They allotted the bulk of gem production to the priests, a substantial portion to themselves, a smaller portion to officials, and an occasional reward to the most productive work units of the hills and coast. They created efficient networks of supply and distribution. They built large storage systems with warehouses and silos. They managed the supply of food to keep the workers fed adequately throughout the year, lavishly at harvest feasts and wedding celebrations. In the middle years of the SPO factions, the soldier, priest, and official classes bloated while the non-governing classes experienced higher production demands and declining standards of living. The relationship between the leading and the working classes became strained, but no organized rebellion or violent uprisings split the SPOs, as they did the S and SO factions. Origin scholars concluded that this difference was due primarily to the social structure and outlet provided by the temple. "The alliance of priest and soldier publicly affirmed and displayed in temple services would have seemed quite formidable to the weary miner, farmer, or fisher," wrote one scholar. "The workers may have survived their many days of hunger and labor by dreaming of a coming celebration - a wedding feast, a child's blessing - a night when family and friends would fill the temple together. In most of the SPO factions, it was the priests that insisted upon this consolation to the workers, perhaps from compassion, perhaps from manipulation." In the late years, the SPOs absorbed the workers and gems of the failed S and SO factions. Despite the additional resources, life remained bleak for the workers of the SPOs. The governors pushed the workers into competition with neighboring SPO factions. They built larger temples and barracks, new fortresses, and great crystal towers. The factions raided one another for gems. They sent war parties to attack the barracks and temples of their rivals. When these attacks failed due to the steep and difficult terrain, fighting shifted downward to the hills. Long and costly battles were fought for the towns of the hills. With the advantage of higher ground and the help of civilians - often turned soldiers - defending forces generally prevailed in these battles. Attacking forces left the towns to burn silos, crops, and supply wagons.

Caedan civilization crumbled in a single year.

Fall attacks on food supplies left many Caedans to starve in winter. By winter's thaw, the soldiers had slaughtered nearly all of the factional herds.

In the spring, new crops were planted. Hunger pulled the priests from the mountain temples to the hills. The soldiers left the temples and mines unguarded to protect their remaining livestock and shipments of smoked fish.

In the early summer, the eruption of Mount Arran sent a massive plume of ash and cinder over the northern mountains.

By the end of the summer, the traditional classes, led by the fishers, had left the factions and migrated along the coasts; the priesthood had dissolved and scattered; and the factional soldiers had lost governing control and turned against one another.

Origin scholars analyzed the fall of the Caedans in depth.

They began with the eruption of Mount Arran. Based on the rapid splintering of the Caedans after the eruption, scholars expected to find evidence of a thick and devastating blanket of ash over Caedan lands. Volcanologists challenged these expectations, however, by predicting only a thin coating of ash, based on factors of distance, volume, and inland wind patterns. Archaeologists shook these expectations even further by terming the ashfall a mere "dusting" after numerous digs uncovered only traces of ash and cinder. Scholars were forced to reconsider the impact of Arran. Accepting that Arran's damage to the crops, structures, and health of the Caedans had been minimal, scholars explored its psychological effect. They imagined the state of the Caedan people before Arran - their emotional and physical fatigue from years of worsening conditions; their exhaustion from hunger, labor, and war; their disillusion with the governing classes, especially the priests; their fading hopes and shaken security. Perhaps, the scholars ventured, Arran's sprinkling of ash was like the soft headwind that crushed the tired runner. Another perspective was found in the writings of a low-level priest from the hills: "We were not shaken by the ash at our feet. It was the dead-grey ash of the temple that terrified us. The crystal temple that had once streamed with life and glowed with light and color, now stood bleak and bare, like a grave marking the end of our people."

Scholars then questioned the role and responsibility of the priesthood in the fall of the Caedans. Distinguishing between the low-level priests of the hill and coastal communities and the high-level priests of the mountain temples, scholars examined the relationships and actions of the priesthood throughout the factional histories. The low-level community priests supported the soldiers during the early and middle factional years. They criticized the soldiers' leadership occasionally in their private writings, but they continued to support the soldiers publicly and discourage complaint among the people. In the late factional years, as conditions dramatically worsened in the lowlands, nearly half of the priests left their communities for the newly built temples and towers of the mountains. Most of the priests that remained in their communities served quietly. An emboldened few, however, openly criticized the leadership of soldiers, officials, and their fellow priests. When the soldiers began raids and attacks on rival factions, the defiant priests condemned their greed and aggression. The people stood by the priests until their own towns were attacked, then swung abruptly to the soldiers' side. The priests suffered with the people throughout the winter and spring. After the eruption of Arran, the priests joined their people in the migration along the coast. High-level priests uniformly supported the soldiers into the late factional years. During the height of violence in the hills, a handful of the temple priests called for an end to the fighting. Soldiers responded by cutting the supply of food to the temples until the outspoken priests were silenced or exiled. The temple leadership caved to the soldiers' demands. After the hungry winter and their flight from the mountains, the temple leadership collapsed. The priests scattered and lived among the workers of the hill and coast. Most were rejected by the people and forced to beg for food. Origin scholars generally concluded that the dissolution of the priesthood was more consequence than cause in the fall of the Caedans. Wrote one spokeswoman: "With each gem accepted from the soldier's hand, the priesthood surrendered its voice and authority. Through its long silence and denial, the priesthood became a load to be carried, a bloated appendage, a mass without fiber or bone. The temple cannot be blamed for the Caedans' fall because its leadership never led."

Origin scholars turned to the traditional classes - the fishers, planters, and weavers of the coast - the first Caedans. Because literacy was the privilege of the elite, scholars could find no written historical accounts from the traditional classes. For the perspective of the traditional classes, scholars relied on the writings of priests accepted into the coastal communities. One community priest summarized the early naiveté of the traditional classes: "The soldiers learned over time that intimidation, threat, and prodding were ineffective methods in dealing with the traditional classes; these hard methods produced only silence and obstinate resistance. Much more effective was the plea of kinship, the claim of hungry, needy Caedans high on the mountain.

This worked well until the coastal workers saw the magnificent new temples and towers rising." Coastal productivity dropped sharply in the late factional years. The relationship between the soldiers and traditional classes deteriorated. When the towns of the hills were attacked, the traditional classes responded to the soldiers' calls for food and aid. They supported the people of the hills throughout the destructive fall, hungry winter, and desperate spring. The mass migration of the traditional classes occurred in the midsummer, after first harvest and the eruption of Mount Arran, before second harvest. Scholars examined the curious timing of the migration. "By leaving after first harvest, they ensured that the people of the hills would not starve," wrote one scholar. "By leaving before second harvest, they ensured that intense pressure would fall upon the already strained leadership of the soldiers."

Wary of bias and preconception, origin scholars turned to the soldiers. Scholars outlined the development of the soldier class throughout the stages of factional history: 1) Origins. Scholars noted that there was no soldier class before the discovery of gems. The soldier class began as small and lightly armed units under the command of the early councils, responsible for maintaining order, guarding the gem mines, and enforcing production quotas. Their ranks increased as the early councils struggled and failed. In the absence of civilian leadership, the soldiers assumed power. 2) Short-lived factions. In S factions, the soldier class grew to approximately one-fourth of the population. The soldiers were led by loose and shifting councils of regional commanders. Without the support of an official class, the commanders struggled to manage production and distribution. When their wage system was ill received by the people, the commanders lowered wages and raised quotas. This alienated the workers, precipitated an alliance between miners and blacksmiths, and, ultimately, led to bloody civil war. In SO factions, the soldier class swelled to nearly one-third of the population. The soldiers were led by a dense hierarchy of officers. Taking advantage of a diligent official class, the soldier class enjoyed light duties and comfortable living, particularly the officers. When gem production stalled, the exploited officials betrayed the soldiers. The hierarchy of officers proved slow and cumbersome in facing rebellion and crumbled quickly. 3) Progress and efficiency. In SPO factions, the soldier class grew steadily in number throughout the early factional years yet remained around one-tenth of the population. Leaner, better organized, supported by priests and officials, the soldiers accomplished much. They built massive storage systems and efficient distribution networks to ensure a steady food supply. They diverted and branched streams in the hills and dug wells in the lowlands to improve water access. Some soldier units even assisted in the building of the temples and civilian homes. The leadership of the soldiers headquartered in the hills. Barrack commanders maintained security and led construction projects; distribution managers orchestrated the steady flow of resources throughout the faction; interfacial officers linked with priest, official, and worker representatives. 4) Bloating, building, and arming. In the middle years, the soldiers moved their headquarters from the hills to the mountains. Reasons for the upward move likely included the soldiers' close ties to the priesthood, the prestige of living on higher ground, and the retirement of the first generation of officers. The move detached the military governors from their own soldiers and the Caedan people. The move also placed a heavy strain on the factional distribution networks and necessitated a wide recruitment of new foot-soldiers to transport goods. In the late years, the young leadership of the soldiers, eager to prove themselves and match the progress of their predecessors, drove higher into the mountains. They built new barracks, fortresses, and towers. They built temples high enough to look down on rival factions.

The leadership used pride and competition to motivate their workers. When these failed, they used fear. Workers absorbed from the failed S and SO factions were treated as servants and forced to work on the mountain construction projects. When the projects finished, the leadership transitioned to mass arms and weapons production. 5) Escalation. The third generation of military leaders inherited a tired and disillusioned workforce, a crowded factional area, an infrastructure stretched to the limit, and an army of foot-soldiers heavily armed and poorly trained. The leaders considered internal change unlikely and fighting between factions inevitable. Their early raids were cautious and exploratory. Their attacks on mountain barracks were bolder but unsuccessful. The leaders shifted forces to the hills. They decided against the committed full-scale attack of rival armies and instead allowed a few aggressive commanders to attack small towns on the factional borders. Reasons for this decision were mixed and complex, including a fear of war, a distrust of the inexperienced core of foot-soldiers, the vulnerability of dual fronts, the tactical and moral reservations of many officers, and a serious underestimating of rivals. Whatever the intentions of the military leaders, this decision weakened their authority and control. It also opened the door to total war. The aggressive commanders encountered more resistance than expected at the border towns and quickly drew their fellow commanders into the fighting. When defensive forces rallied and swarmed against them, most of the aggressive commanders, significantly outnumbered, chose to avoid direct military confrontation, split their soldiers, and carve destructive, veering paths through the enemy's civilian interior. The supporting commanders had to choose between following the aggressive units, facing the enemy army in the field, or retreating. Most chose to retreat. 6) Confusion, blood, and chaos. As movement and violence accelerated in the hills, the communication between commanders and central leadership broke down. Most commanders ignored the orders that managed to reach them and instead defended their hometowns. In the early battles, defending forces generally suffered heavy losses but outlasted attacking forces. Many defending commanders, however, were hardened by the bloodshed and sought revenge on enemy ground. They attacked the towns of their enemies, then the food supply. 7) Hunger. During the hungry winter, leaders regained some power and authority. They seized the factional herds, drove the livestock to protected higher ground, and controlled the slaughter and distribution of meat. When the herds dwindled in the spring, the foot-soldiers shook free of the leaders' authority and moved in disorganized packs to the hills and coast. Some soldier packs quartered in farming communities and directed the spring planting of crops. Other packs seized and guarded the scant supply of fish on the coast. A tenuous peace and order between packs was enforced by a handful of feared commanders. 8) Disintegration. The eruption of Arran and the dissolution of the priesthood had a marginal effect on the soldiers. The migration of the traditional classes, however, severed the remaining strands of unity between soldiers. Some of the soldiers became the guardians of small communities. Most became bandits, mercenaries, warlords, and raiders.

The Caedan farming communities struggled for several generations then died out. A faint surviving line became salt traders.

The Caedan traditional classes spread along the northern coast and returned to their old ways of fishing, planting, and weaving. They thinned in number but never died.

A small order of priests lived and worked among the fishers. They built humble shrines adorned with only stones.

<u>The Central Valley</u>

Though the central valley was the geographical spine and population heart of the ancient Pheran continent, origin scholars could find surprisingly little archaeological evidence between the eastern and the western mountains. Lamented one scholar: "The center stage of the ancients has been obscured by the mist of time, the carve of the plow, the terror of the bulldozer, and a million-footed trampling."

The origin movement, leaning heavily on the oral and written traditions of surviving tribes, pieced together a broad and partial history of the central valley.

Origin scholars believed that five powerful city-state empires (three in the east, two in the west) came to dominate the central valley at different times in ancient history. These empires were generally formed by the merging of two or three tribes; expanded through the creation of centralized institutions and the subjugation of regional tribes; weakened through infighting, corruption, and overextension; and militarily defeated by alliances of the other valley tribes. "No city-state empire was able to conquer or control all the tribes of the central valley," wrote one scholar. "The cross-valley community of tribes eventually pulled together against the rising and undeniable threat of the empire. Their delay in response likely kept the valley in an almost constant state of rebuilding and surely retarded cultural, social, and scientific development."

The western city of Pocone provided scholars the best-preserved sites in the central valley and their clearest view into ancient imperial history and dynamics.

In Pocone, origin scientists discovered evidence of a wide ring of docks on the lake, stone-terraced gardens and cascading falls in the hills, and an underground order of priests with a network of secret tunnels and hidden chambers. They also discovered a magnificent royal tomb. The tomb held the remains of a short line of kings and illustrated their accomplishments in elaborate marble carvings. According to the tomb carvings, Pocon, the first king, bearded and broad-shouldered, organized the farmlands into efficient sectors, built huge storehouses for surplus crops, amassed a great army, and drew nearby tribes into a powerful union. His sons prevailed in battle against the strongest armies of the western valley and collected tribute from all the western tribes. His grandsons defeated the strongest armies of the east. His great-grandsons died in valiant defense of Pocone.

A less flattering portrayal of the Pocon family was found in an underground cache of scrolls. Genealogical records kept by priests revealed that a different royal line, the Hols, preceded the Pocon family. The line of the Hols ended abruptly with the drowning of their king, the poisoning of their queen, and the disappearance of their princes. The priestly records also revealed that Pocon's queen, the family matriarch, had four previous marriages. Among the scrolls archaeologists found writing fragments that they attributed to the final surviving member of the Pocon family, the youngest great-grandson of Pocon:

> *In the family chamber, the name of Hol was never spoken and the Pocon ascent to power never questioned. Fathers said little to their sons. The family sickness was passed down in silence.*
>
> *Pocon raised, fed, and nurtured his beast of war. His sons unleashed it on the west, his grandsons on the east. The beast was passed down to my brothers exhausted and battered.*
>
> *My family made enemies of all in the valley. We trusted too much in fear, too little in balance and revenge.*

Origin scholars believed that recurrent war in the central valley led to a decline in agriculture. Tired of bloodshed, the heavy-booted traffic of armies over their land, and the high tributes demanded by imperial kings, many farmers migrated outward from the heart of the valley. Some returned to the old ways of hunting in the northern fields. Others became woodsmen in the thick western forests or nomadic herders in the low southwestern hills. The great cities of the western valley disappeared. The eastern cities shrunk to small mining towns, often harassed by mounted raiders of the southeastern steppes.

The Eastern Hunters

In the deep forest of the eastern mountains, archaeologists found evidence of a great hunting people.

They found bones and weapons arranged in concentric rings around the oldest trees of the forest.

The inner rings, closest to the tree, contained the bones of large animals, primarily legs of iron wolves, skulls of golden bear, and spines of scaled elk.

The outer rings contained spearheads, axeblades, and pheran bones, primarily the hands, feet, and ribs of the hunters.

Scholarly interpretation of the rings' symbolic meaning varied widely.

The trophy scholars believed the rings to be displays of hunting trophy, testaments to the hunters' strength, courage, and prowess. They interpreted the pheran ribs to be symbols of sacrifice, the life of the individual given for the survival of the group. They interpreted the pheran hands and feet to represent instruments of the hunt, weapons as potent as the hunters' spears and axes. They considered the trees significant only as convenient collection sites for the trophies.

The nature scholars believed that the trees symbolized the natural world as a source of life, a preceding force. They believed that time flowed outward in the hunters' rings. First, there was the life of plants and trees. Then animal life. Then the pheran. They believed that the hunters placed the bones of animal and pheran beneath the tree with humility and understanding.

One writer, drawing from the thought of both the trophy and the nature scholars, believed the rings to be a sacred place visited by fathers and sons before the boys' first hunt. "The father likely would not speak a word," the writer imagined. "The boy would see the bones of old hunters and be sobered to the danger of the hunt. The boy would see the bones of great beasts and know that the hunt was not impossible. And over the bones of animal and pheran, the boy would see the towering tree. In a single image, the boy would understand the way of his people, his place in the world, the power of death, and the flow of all life."

Origin scientists traced a gradual eastward migration by the hunting people, likely due to a depletion of wildlife in the mountains.

The archaeological trail ended in the eastern hills. Scholars were disappointed to find that the eastern hills had been trampled as badly as the central valley. The Torite cities had sprawled rapidly with little regard for the artifacts of the past. Cerran farmers had intentionally destroyed burial and trophy sites that they considered sacrilegious.

The only significant site of the hills was found atop a ravine at the edge of Tekenna. It was a three-layered stack of skulls packed with small rocks, soil, and ash. The skulls were all pheran.

The Tekennan discovery led to a new theory about the forest tree rings. The war scholars believed that intertribal warfare, not animal hunting, accounted for most of the pheran bones in the tree rings. They believed that competition over game, streams, and women had divided the forest people into warring tribes.

They believed that these tribes had used the ringed trees as territorial markers and warnings to their enemies.

In fertile discussion, the trophy and nature scholars conceded the possibility of division and fighting among the hunting people, but each camp still held to the core of their original theory.

All camps lamented the lack of evidence and the trampling of history.

<u>The Southeast</u>

While stopping for supplies in Lytarr, a team of origin scientists received this letter from an explorer in the southeast.

To my colleagues and friends,

From the reports out of the eastern hills, I gather that you have found little or nothing in your search for traces of the hunting people.

I remember when we stood together beneath the ancient tree in the mountains, surrounded by the hunters' fearsome work, the sea of bones and killing tools. I was silent among the bones. You were not. You chattered with great excitement. You analyzed and minced. You theorized and argued. My friends, you should have simply bowed your heads to the mystery.

The hunters will never be known, not with the clarity you desire. You curse the trampling of history and the centuries' deep shadows, but, perhaps, you should be thankful for what is hidden from you. Were the true face of the hunter to emerge from the shadows, you might recoil.

Let me offer you a new and living mystery.

Follow the Black River beyond the mill towns, through the triple gorges, beneath the crumbling white-stone archway…

The explorer promised the scientists an elaborate and breathtaking network of underground caverns and a surviving indigenous tribe living within the caverns, a diverse people skilled in fishing, hunting, mining, trapping, and planting.

The team of scientists wasted little time. They left the eastern hills the day they received the explorer's letter and journeyed to southeastern Phera.

The team kept their journey and the discovery of the cavernous tribe a secret from their colleagues in the origin community. For the better part of a year, the team enjoyed exclusive, unlimited access to the cavern system and the Adilan tribe.

The team geologist explored the cavern system. She probed the sparkling White-Crystal Chamber, the Temple Chamber with its thirteen stone columns reaching from floor to high-vaulted ceiling, and the Cataract Chamber with waters trickling down stalactites into a deep and echoless pit. With the help of young Adilan men, she mapped the system's upper levels, the many small chambers and labyrinth of interlocking tunnels.

The team linguist was thrilled to find an old Cerran missionary couple living among the Adilans. The missionaries provided an immediate gateway into the Adilan world and saved the linguist years of stumbling research. The linguist became passably conversant in the Adilan language within a year by shadowing the missionaries and bothering Adilans young and old with unrelenting questions. Based on slight differences in syntax and distinctly emerging vocabularies, the linguist categorized the Adilans into subgroups: deep cavern, river fishers, naturalist planters, hunters, and trappers.

Vail, the team anthropologist, estimated the population of the Adilans to be between 140 and 155, an exact count made impossible by the lower levels of the cavern system and the anthropologist's old knees. Vail observed a striking lack of ritual and institution among the Adilans. They had no birth celebration, no wedding ceremony, no funeral rite. They had no recognizable structures of authority or body of central leadership. Adilan marriage/coupling was loose, informal, and temporary, usually dissolving within a few years. Adilan children, not long after weaning, were given untethered freedom to explore the world within and outside the caves. Real bonding, instruction, and discipline occurred only after the child finished their years of exploring and accepted the labor and craft of their chosen subgroup, often different from the subgroup(s) of their biological parents. "Adilan identity is determined more by work than family," Vail wrote. "Beneath their loose and thinly defined family structure lies the higher value of individual freedom. Behind their seemingly detached methods of parenting lies a great respect for personal growth and development."

Other team members specialized in the various subgroups within the Adilans. The members observed and often joined their respective subgroups in daily work and routine.

The fishing subgroup was predominantly male and elderly. The old men lived alone in small cavern chambers close to the surface. They fished in the morning and evening from rock ledges along the river. In the afternoon, they talked at small fires in groups of two or three after the cooking of the day's catch.

The hunting subgroup was entirely male with a younger population and wider range of age. The hunters slept in the giant Temple Chamber. They woke in the late morning, washed in streams outside the caverns, hunted in packs until late afternoon, then gathered and ate at a large firepit outside the eastern cavern entrance. The hunters were the loudest, the most volatile and aggressive, among the Adilans.

The trapping subgroup was largely female and lived in or near the dripping Cataract Chamber. The trappers rose at first light and bathed in the cold river before the fishers lined its shore. They ate a light breakfast of nuts and smoked game then headed into the brush and woods, alone or in small groups, to check and set their traps. The trappers returned in the midafternoon, skinned and dressed their game outside the southern entrance, then ate by torchlight in the Cataract Chamber. Before an early sleep, they socialized around small fires, worked pottery, and dyed animal skins.

Though land and game were plentiful, territorial conflict between the hunters and trappers often flared. The hunters considered it their right to chase large game wherever the animal might flee. This inevitably led to the hunters' stumbling into traps and their retaliation for subsequent injuries, usually the trashing, occasionally the burning, of the Cataract Chamber. The trappers, not innocent in the conflict, tended to work their line of traps and snares gradually northward, closer to the hunters' preferred grounds. After the hunters' injury and retaliation, the trappers pulled their line south for several days then slowly, deliberately, inched north.

The planters were a healthy mix of men and women, young and old. In the winter they slept in a vertical cave. The rest of the year they lived in tents in the northwestern fields. They pruned and sculpted wildberry tangles at the edge of the woods, weeded their vegetable and fruit patches in forest clearings, and tended their experimental strips of corns and grains in the valley. The planters talked, traded, and shared with the other subgroups. They made sure that the elderly fishers were warm and well-nourished.

The Adilans of the deep caverns, all men, rarely ventured to the surface. Their skin was ever pale, damp, and stained with soot, their age impossible to fix. Called *shades* by the other Adilans, they moved like ghosts in the depths of the caverns. They mined and forged light-metal tools and weapons for the other Adilans. Their trading arrangements with the various subgroups were curiously unbalanced; the hunters were required to give about five furs per unit of metal, the trappers only two. The shades seemed to mine, forge, and trade just enough to cover their basic needs. The rest of their time was spent in individual burrowing, tunneling, and exploring. Each shade tried to carve out and expand his own vein of the cavern depths. The shade territories of crack, nook, and void were contested more fiercely than the hunters' grounds.

Word of the cavern's discovery and the team's work among the Adilans eventually leaked out.

Rhecton, origin writer and historian, prepared a summary of the team's findings for publication. He included in his summary several questions and concerns. "We are puzzled by the segregation between the Adilan subgroups and the chasm between the Adilan sexes," Rhecton wrote. "More troublesome still is the absence of collective Adilan memory, their lack of mythology, oral tradition, and history. Perhaps the answer lies in the mournful chants and echoed drums that haunt the Adilan night."

Vail, the team anthropologist, and other team members strongly objected to Rhecton's added concerns. They criticized Rhecton for premature speculation and ethnocentric projection. Rhecton withdrew his concerns.

After publication of the summary, a wave of new scientists descended on the Adilans. The original team shared their work and findings with their colleagues but restricted access within the caves, claiming that the Adilans should not be disturbed in their homes and living spaces.

The new scientists soon asked the same questions raised by Rhecton but omitted from publication. They developed several theories to explain the subgroup segregation, gender chasm, and lack of oral tradition among the Adilans. These theories included a merging of separate tribes within the caves precipitated by a season of great storms above ground, a subjugation of tribes by dominant hunters that declined under the burden of governing, and a hidden yet pervasive homosexuality and lesbianism in the dark chambers of the cavern.

All of these theories were resisted by the original team. Vail assaulted the theories in anthropological journals; the team specialists attacked the theories' proponents in argument and debate; and Rhecton responded to each theory publication with an enumeration of gaps and flaws.

The origin community, though irritated by the team's early concealment of the Adilans, respected the team's longer working experience among the Adilans and adopted a hesitant, skeptical attitude toward the newly arrived theorists.

The new scientists, blocked from investigation inside the caves, searched for evidence in the surrounding woods and hills. They found a faint archaeological trail: small and scattered pockets of bone fragments, tools, and weapon heads. Some scientists interpreted the pockets as evidence of multiple and distinct hunting groups, others as evidence of a single nomadic tribe. The origin community feared another unsolved mystery. After two years of digging and scouring in the southeast produced little new evidence, many scientists returned to their universities or left the southeast for more promising regions of the continent.

In the fourth year, a new discovery shook the origin community and reinvigorated the Adilan debate. A line of fishers was found on the southeastern coast. The Quorell lived in raised huts and fished by boat in rocky coves. Scientists that studied the fishing people were immediately struck by similarities between the Quorell and Adilan languages. The possibility of historical kinship was raised. Radical differences between the two people soon emerged, however. There were no subgroups within the Quorell, only fishers. Quorell marriage was a permanent arrangement sanctioned by elders and ceremony, binding both nuclear and extended families. Quorell parenting was strict and involved, parental discipline extending through young adulthood. The Quorell family was a tight body centered on the teachings of their elders.

It was the teachings of the elders that shook the origin community and, in the opinion of many scientists, proved an historical tie between the Quorell and the Adilans. The Quorell families gathered regularly in the homes of their elders. Their gatherings began with a dinner meal followed by a long period of meditative silence. The silence was broken sometime after nightfall by the singing of the tide songs. These songs, though having some standard elements and recurring verses, were largely an improvised and dynamic exchange between the people and their elders. The people voiced angry complaint against the pain and struggle of living; the elders prodded and encouraged. The people expressed hopes and dreams; the elders grounded. "The people rose and fell in lyric like the waves of the sea," wrote one scholar. "Again and again, their surging crest was broken against the elders' heavy sky, their fall absorbed by the elders' rigid depths." By the end of the tide songs, the people's voice had joined the elders' rhythm, a soft and steady drumming that had driven, anchored, and carried the songs from the beginning. The elders' drumming slowly faded into another period of meditative silence.

In the deep hours of the night, the elders taught and told stories. Their stories traveled backward through time, generation by generation, from parents and grandparents to distant ancestors. The stories were both deeply respectful and highly critical; examples of virtue and flaw were recounted in the life of each ancestor. Ancestors were praised for long suffering, hard work, and individual sacrifice for family and tribe; they were condemned for personal ambition, recklessness, and the neglect of their children. Four generations of the Quorell had lived on the seashore. Five generations had lived in the inland hills. At least seven generations had lived in the great cavern. "The Quorell are flower, stalk, and root," taught the elders. "We have been lifted by the sweat of our fathers and the pain of our mothers. We have been joined to Phera and bound to one another by the blood of the ancients."

According to the teachings of the elders, the Quorell were the first people to live in the great cavern. They lived and worked in the cave in peace, while many tribes of hunters fought in the hills and fields. The Quorell took pity on a small tribe of hunters being attacked by larger tribes. The Quorell brought the hunters into the safety of their caves. The hunters used the cave first for refuge then as a base to surprise, ambush, and slaughter the larger tribes. On a fiery night, the hunters seized the caves for themselves and cast many Quorell into the pit. The surviving Quorell fled into the hills. Each slain Quorell, seventeen, according to tradition, became a symbol carved into the skin of their descendants.

The origin community was taken by the Quorell. Their detailed genealogies, depth of oral tradition, and strength of family structure led many scholars to accept their historical claims. The theorists, previously received with hesitancy and skepticism by the origin community, soon advanced the argument that the great cavern of the Quorell was the same cavern presently inhabited by the Adilans. When this argument was generally accepted by the origin community, the theorists then asserted the logical conclusion to their argument: the ancestors of the Adilans had killed the ancestors of the Quorell.

While the theorists gained ground, most members of the original team to the cavern avoided the debate and continued their work quietly among the blood-charged Adilans.

Rhecton, the team historian and writer who had previously withdrawn his concerns about Adilan subgroup segregation from the team's summary, refrained from public response but corresponded privately with leading theorists. He asked many questions about the Quorell elders and their teachings. He challenged some of the theorists' assumptions but eventually accepted their core argument and conclusion. Rhecton secretly began work on a comprehensive and speculative history of the Adilans.

Vail, the team anthropologist and staunchest defender of the Adilans, followed the theorists' early work among the Quorell without public response. When the theorists made their claim that the Quorell were the first people of the cavern, Vail traveled to the southeastern coast to see the Quorell in the flesh. His trip, originally planned for ten days, extended through the summer and into the fall. During this time, he exchanged a series of letters with Rhecton.

In his early letters, Vail mocked Rhecton for his avoidance of public academic debate, his "cowering from the fray." Vail described his hosting scientists among the Quorell as friendly, accommodating, and utterly credulous. He described the Quorell people as herdish and stubborn, their elders as sullen and arrogant. Vail admitted similarities between the Adilan and Quorell languages but emphasized differences in the accounts of the various elders. "The genealogies of the elders do not match," he wrote. "Ancestors prominent in one elder's teaching are peripheral or entirely absent from another elder's account. There is a confusion of names. There is a confusion of offspring. This blurring divergence worsens as the elders travel deeper into the past and yet, somehow, we are to accept the holy number of seventeen that emerges suddenly from the fog."

Rhecton's early letters were logical and measured responses to Vail's charges against the Quorell. His counters borrowed heavily from the work of the leading theorists. He pushed Vail to accept ideas that he himself had initially resisted.

Purpose is primary, Rhecton argued. The Quorell tradition was intended to unify the strands of families that fled the cavern; to create a supportive and sustaining memory of the past girding the Quorell against an uncertain future; and to mold, harness, and channel the young. In their crafting of ancestor stories, the elders were driven by their concern for the unity and survival of the Quorell people. Secondary to the elders, but not unimportant, was a precision of name and detail. Rhecton allowed that some of the genealogical differences were best explained by the erosion of time and the subjectivity of memory. "All pheran memory is subjective," he wrote. "And the memory of families is, perhaps, the most subjective of all." Many of the differences, however, could be explained by the subtleties and quirks, little understood, in Quorell culture. Multiple names may have been used for the same ancestor depending on their stage in life or transformations of character. The stillborn may have been included in the lists of offspring recounted by female elders but omitted from the lists of male elders. Rhecton urged Vail to look deeper, beyond the apparent surface flaws of the Quorell tradition. "The psyche of the Quorell was clearly scarred by a traumatic event in their ancient history," he wrote. "Their ancestor stories contain vivid, detailed, and largely accurate descriptions of places far from the southeastern coast. Weigh the Quorell tradition against its alternatives – an imagined night of murder in the cavern, an invented history of generations in the hills. Compare the deep-veined memory of the Quorell to the amnesia of the Adilan."

By the end of Vail's summer among the Quorell, the anthropologist's views had substantially changed. He came to accept that the Quorell had lived for several generations in the southeastern hills and in the great cavern. Though he still questioned the "holy number of seventeen," he accepted that the Quorell had fled the cavern after some violent conflict, possibly with Adilan ancestors. Vail's views were likely changed more by a warming connection with the Quorell people than by any of Rhecton's arguments. The Quorell men invited Vail onto their boats for many afternoons of fishing on the sea. The Quorell girls taught Vail how to mend nets and smoke fish; Quorell boys taught him how to carve and shape wood. Families welcomed Vail at their sunset fires on the shore. "Thankfully, the Quorell are a forgiving people," he wrote. "Beneath the hard-crusted edges of an old man, they saw a friend." Vail was also welcomed into the homes of the elders for communal gatherings. He experienced firsthand the singing of the tide songs and the telling of the ancestor stories.

The songs begin with violence and end with calm. All the aches, fears, and longings of the people are poured out into the darkness. The listener is pulled by the cry of each voice, tossed by the needs and wants of each Quorell heart. The many voices of the people form a restless and lurching sea. But the dividing currents of the people are drawn together by the elders' steady rhythm and refrain. "Nothing is new," the elders sing. "The lone life dies. The people are born."

The tide songs are the wetting of the clay, the ancestor stories its molding. The elders speak the names of the ancestors as if drawing from a deep and holy well. The elders bring the ancestors to life with curious details, a limp, a stutter, the broken bend of a nose, eyes of a wildgrass fire. Once coated with flesh and flaw, the ancestors enter their days among the people. Their days are viewed in the context of the people's greater story. Every act of sacrifice and kindness is a blessing to the people, every act of selfishness a wound.

After experiencing four communal gatherings and the teaching of most living elders, Vail concluded that the Quorell tradition was based on a solid skeleton of lineage and history. To this factual skeleton, he believed, the various elders added their own creative flesh. Enhancing details were sometimes invented, liberties taken with time and place. "The world of the ancestors was sacred to the Quorell," he wrote, "but it was also a fertile ground for the imagination, a fluid soil which even the children were allowed to touch and shape."

Rhecton was greatly pleased by the changes in Vail and his deepening connection with the Quorell people. Inspired by Vail's description of the imaginative Quorell, Rhecton undertook an ambitious new project, a book encompassing the history of both the east and the southeast, a unique mixing of origin science and speculative literature. Each chapter of his book began with a summary of scientific findings and ended with imagined characters, scenes, and stories. "I will explore beyond the consensus views of the origin community, beyond even the theorists' reach," he wrote to Vail at the outset of his project. "I hope to capture the living moment experienced by the living ancient."

Rhecton began his book with the ancient hunters of the eastern mountains. Lacking the heavy weapons, experience, and tactics needed to take down large game, these early hunters survived primarily on red deer. They hunted the always shifting deer population in small and mobile packs. Without defined territories, the packs often fought and killed one another. The hunters left the bones of deer and the bodies of rival hunters strewn across the forest floor. Scavenging jackals harassed the packs of hunters. The greater beasts of land and air frequently attacked. "To the ancient hunter, there was only the moment," Rhecton wrote. "And the moment had no peace. The approach of a mist, an unfamiliar face, a paw's crackling of fallen branch, the coming of night – these were sources of terror to the ancient."

In the book, the story of Kennagel bridged from the time of packs to the time of clans.

One morning a hunter spotted a red deer across a stream.

The hunter's spear flew and struck the deer in the side.

The wounded deer fled.

The hunter waded the stream and chased. He followed the blood trail through the woods and tangles until the sun was high overhead.

The hunter found the deer dead in a clearing, already under the knife of another hunter.

The two hunters quarreled.

The first hunter was slain by the second.

The second was joined by the members of his pack.

"What happened here?" they asked.

"After I killed the deer, he tried to steal," the hunter lied.

"His pack will want revenge," they said. "We must kill them first."

The pack of the lying hunter attacked the pack of the hunter who had first speared the deer. They slaughtered the men and women. They scattered the children into the wilderness.

Many years later, a young man walked out of the night and into the circle of the killing pack's fire. He wore many hides of jackals. His skin was streaked with redleaf, blackroot, and the purpled gem of deer's liver.

He placed a bundled hide on the ground at his feet.

"I am Kennegal," he said. "Seventeen years ago, you killed my father and my mother. You also killed the men and women of my pack. You also killed my brothers and sisters by driving them into the wilderness where they soon died. And you tried to kill me as well. But I was spared by Phera. The great mother cleansed me with rain and mist. The great father warmed me in the sun. The winds of Phera carried me from safety to safety. In the day, I walked among the trees, cloaked in Phera's shadow. In the night, Phera hid me in high places, held me, wrapped me in dreams, taught me with whispers. All the hunters of the mountains are children of Phera." Kennegal opened the bundle at his feet to reveal the bones of hands and feet and ribs. "These are the bones of my father. His feet chased the swiftest beasts of the woods. His hands cast spears like fallen lightning. Within these ribs, his life burned and flowed."

"What do you want from us?" the hunters asked.

"Change," Kennegal said. "You must respect all life and never kill another hunter. You must honor the animals whose flesh sustains you and honor the hunters that fall to the beasts. The bones of both animal and hunter must be placed with respect around the oldest trees of the forest. And my father's bones will be first honored."

"All hunters kill pherans and beasts."

"Each will answer."

"To you?"

"To Creation and to the Creator."

"Take your bones and go," the hunters said.

Kennegal left the killing pack.

He returned to a place he had known as a boy, the ancient tree of his father's pack. He placed the bones of his father between the massive roots of the tree. He knelt, touched his head and hands to the tree, and prayed. Kennegal rose. He set out to share his message with all the hunters of the mountains.

Kennegal traveled the mountains for one year. He spoke to the many roaming packs of hunters. Most of the packs listened to his story but rejected his call to change. Kennegal gathered the few packs that accepted his call around the great tree. The hunters knelt and prayed to Phera. They prayed for protection, courage, and sustenance.

"The great tree will be our base and root," Kennegal said. "During the day we will hunt in the woods around the tree. Each night we will return. We will guard our territory fiercely but without killing."

Kennegal's hunters successfully guarded their new territory without killing. They drove away the roaming packs that came within a day's walk of the tree. Their hunting was sparse and difficult, however. Worn down by the guarding of a wide territory, unable to chase deer beyond its limits, the hunters killed just enough to survive through the first season. Around the great tree, the bones of fallen hunters nearly matched the bones of beasts.

"Phera is hard," the hunters said. "We will not survive another season."

"What will you do?" Kennegal asked.

The hunters said nothing to Kennegal, but night by night they slipped away into the forest.

Kennegal waited until only the faithful remained. "As our numbers have been purged," he said, "so we purge our land."

Kennegal and his people slaughtered every jackal within a day's walk of the great tree. They killed every horned cougar and iron wolf. Kennegal slew the golden bear that had taken the limbs and lives of many hunters. The people feasted on the bear and its cubs.

The purged land was a softer land.

Season by season, Kennegal's people grew, thriving in number, health, and unity. Their bone rings flowed outward from the great tree. They were the first hunters of the mountains to take down the grey-scaled elk, the first people whose elders survived to teach the young. The name of the Redleaf Clan spread throughout all the eastern mountains. Redleaf mothers gave birth with their backs resting against the great tree, their legs down its giant roots. "Life begins where Kennegal prayed," the mothers said.

When Kennegal neared the end of his days, he took a skin of water and a pouch of meat and began to walk.

"Where are you going?" his people asked.

"When I was a boy, I watched Death strike down the young suddenly and savagely," Kennegal said. "Now Death comes softly. It whispers into the ears of old men. It tricks them into a dark and endless sleep. But I will face Death walking."

Kennegal climbed high into the mountains. Alone.

In the heart of his book, Rhecton imagined a history of the hunting clans that followed, a trail to the present-day Adilans and Quorell.

After the passing of Kennegal, the example of the Redleaf Clan was followed by the other hunters of the mountains. The many small and wandering packs gradually merged into larger clans which settled down into defined territories. Each clan's territory centered around its own tree of life and bones. Like the Redleaf, the clans thrived. A peace between clans held for several generations.

The clans of the east became more numerous and prosperous than the clans of the west. The eastern clans were able to expand into the eastern hills as the red deer population migrated to lower ground. The western clans were pressed against the mountains. Unable to follow the deer without trespass, the western clans were forced to hunt the deadly bear and the elusive ram in the high mountains.

Relations between the eastern and western clans stiffened. The eastern clans were controlled by dominant families rich in furs. These families rejected the pleas of western chiefs for better territory. "Kennegal's way was established long ago," the families said. "Each clan must remain rooted to its own sacred tree. Phera will provide."

The western chiefs faced a difficult decision: the path of war or the withering path. The hunger, hardship, and fierce spirit of their people pushed the chiefs toward war. But the western clans lacked unity. Quarreling over the scarce game in the high mountains had divided the western people and sowed distrust between clans. Each western chief questioned the loyalty and motives of the other chiefs. Believing that they could be abandoned in war, each chief decided not to attack the larger clans of the east.

The hardship in the high mountains led to the first southern migration. In light but steady streams, hungry families abandoned their clans and traveled south. They followed the Black River into the game-laden hills of the southeast.

The war between east and west was precipitated unintentionally by two pherans, Tahon and Menejo.

Tahon was chief of the western Ravine Clan. As a boy he had stolen from the camp of an eastern clan and lost an eye to a guard's arrow. He had become chief at a young age and spent many years quarreling and fighting with other western chiefs over territory. Tahon outlived all his wives and children.

One morning the old chief was hunting alone. From inside a cave, his arrow flew and sent a ram tumbling down the mountainside. Tahon hurried after the ram, knife in hand. But the ram had only been grazed and unbalanced by the arrow.

When Tahon came close, the ram struck him on the hip. Tahon fell many times over rock and boulder.

Tahon survived the fall, but his hip was broken and his skull cracked.

The hip healed sooner than the mind.

Tahon was visited in dreams and visions by his dead father. His father warned of a coming attack by all the clans of the east. Convinced that this attack was imminent, Tahon took his people deeper into the mountains. He allowed only a few of his people to hunt for food. The rest labored at mining and forging. Tahon drove his weary people to produce great weapons that could resist the attack of the eastern clans. From the blood ore, they formed swords, battleaxes, and heavy spears. Tahon built a mountain stronghold high in a ravine and waited for the eastern clans to come.

In the many years of Tahon's rule before the fall, his word and order had never been questioned by the people of his clan. When the people saw their leader bloody and still on the mountainside, they trembled. Their hearts lifted in the days of his recovery, but the whispering began as Tahon shared his dreams and visions. The people followed Tahon deeper into the mountains. They endured hunger, thirst, and exhaustion to provide his weapons. Waiting was a harder test. Many guards lost their faith after a long and quiet night-watch of the empty ravine. Families snuck away at first light to travel south. Tahon limped the stronghold walls from edge to edge and told his people to be strong.

One guard, Menejo, devised his own plan during the long watch hours. Menejo had been born into the eastern Redleaf Clan and had married into the western Ravine Clan. Saddened by Tahon's decline, knowing well the prosperity of the east and the struggles of the west, Menejo determined to force conciliation upon the prosperous east.

Menejo slipped away at dawn and traveled east.

At nightfall he entered the circle of the Redleaf fire.

He placed a large bundled fur on the ground at his feet and spoke to the people of his birth clan.

"I am Menejo," he said, "child of the Redleaf, children of Kennagel. I come to you tonight your son, your brother, your friend. Too long have I been separated from my people. I come to you tonight with both an embrace and a warning." Menejo opened the bundle at his feet. He lifted a sword and a battleaxe. "The western clans have crafted many weapons such as these. There are those among them that argue for peace and those among them that urge for war. But war can be avoided. If the eastern clans will give a little land to the western clans, their hunger will be satisfied, and their anger will pass."

Menejo's father came forward and embraced his son. "Tonight, we must celebrate your return," he said. "Tomorrow we will speak of the west."

The next morning Menejo was circled by eight brothers of the Arrua family, leaders of the Redleaf. The brothers asked him many questions about the western clans, their chiefs, plans, weapons, and forging. Menejo's answers did not satisfy the brothers.

"You are lying," the eldest brother said.

"Give land to the western clans," Menejo said. "Do not curse your children and grandchildren with war."

The brothers took Menejo's weapons, tied him, and summoned his father. "Your son is lying," they said. "Find out the truth or your family will be exiled." The brothers left them.

"Did you betray your family and clan?" his father asked. "Did you come to spy for the west?"

Menejo was silent for a long while. "I did not betray you, my family in the east, or my family in the west," Menejo said. "The Redleaf have lost their way, father. You must leave the Redleaf and travel south."

"The brothers will kill you."

"Go south, my father. I will give the brothers what they want."

Menejo called for the brothers. He promised to show them the western forges if his family was spared.

The brothers agreed. They sent their three youngest with Menejo to spy on the western clans.

Menejo traveled with the three Arrua brothers to the west. He led them to the sacred tree of the Ravine Clan. The brothers cursed Menejo beneath the long-abandoned tree. "Where is your clan?" they said.

"They were here when I left," Menejo said.

The brothers beat Menejo with the bones of the sacred tree. "Stop," he said. "I lied to you. I lied."

"Where is your clan?"

"They hide in caves deep in the mountain," Menejo said.

"Show us," the brothers said.

Menejo did not answer. The brothers dragged him to a stream and held him under the water. They pulled him to the shore and beat him again with the bones of the sacred tree.

"Stop," Menejo said. "Please stop."

"Take us to your clan," the brothers said.

Menejo led the brothers higher into the mountains.

When they entered the ravine, Menejo fell to his knees and wept.

The brothers again beat Menejo. "Show us the caves," they said, "before darkness falls."

Menejo breathed. A heavy wind pushed the tears from his eyes. He looked out into the ravine and smiled. The ravine was thick with shadows.

"Let's go then," he said. "Keep your eyes low. Look for a narrow cavern mouth between two trees, one dead, one living. Also watch for the mountain cougar."

Menejo drew the brothers deep into the ravine. Many times he rushed ahead saying that he had seen the cavern mouth.

When the brothers' patience had been exhausted, they told Menejo to stop. "We rest now until morning," they said.

"Just a little farther," Menejo said.

The brothers caught Menejo by the neck and threw him to the ground. "We rest until morning," they said.

In the morning, the brothers ate and offered scraps to Menejo.

"Last meal," Menejo said.

"Show us the cave and we will let you live," the brothers said.

"*Your* last meal," Menejo said.

"Get up," the brothers said. "Let's go."

Menejo leaned back against the ravine. He rested his head against the firm stone of the mountain, closed his eyes, and prayed.

"Go home," Menejo said. "Forget my lies. Forget the west. Go home and live in peace. Search for the way of Kennagel."

The brothers looked around the ravine. They saw the stronghold of Tahon above them. The brothers drew their weapons. One held a blade to Menejo's side.

"Tahon," Menejo cried. "Tahon! The east has come."

The brothers killed Menejo.

A volley of spears from the stronghold killed two of the brothers. The third escaped.

The Redleaf soon came for revenge. The Redleaf men marched as one body into western territory and attacked the stronghold of Tahon. In one afternoon the Redleaf lost a full quarter of their number and three Arrua brothers. The surviving brothers pulled their people back from the blood-stained slope beneath the stronghold.

The Redleaf mourned their dead for one day. After their mourning, Redleaf archers encircled the stronghold and advanced to positions just beyond the range of Tahon's spears.

For many days they struck at any sign of life or movement in the stronghold.

The march of the Redleaf into the west had not gone unnoticed by the western clans. The western clans forgot their past quarrels with one another and rallied to defend Tahon's people. The western clans drove the Redleaf from their siege of the stronghold deep into the ravine.

The cornered Redleaf fought with desperate ferocity. With their backs to the mountain, aided by the narrowness of the ravine, a pocket of Redleaf survived the long day and night of relentless assault.

In the morning, the last surviving Arrua brother called for the western chiefs.

"Tahon amassed weapons of war," the brother said. "Tahon sent spies into Redleaf land. Tahon killed two of my brothers without cause or provocation. Let me face Tahon alone."

Tahon came down from the stronghold with sword and shield and killed the last brother. Tahon called his people to finish the Redleaf, but the western clans held them back.

"Enough," the western chiefs said. "Let them live."

Tahon returned to his stronghold.

The western clans gathered their dead and returned to their territories.

The Redleaf lay their dead inside caves and limped back to their eastern homes.

A season without fighting passed.

The Redleaf widows turned in bitterness against the surviving Redleaf men. "So life goes on and the dead are forgotten," the widows said.

"What can we do," the men said, "but work without rest to feed our brothers' wives."

The Redleaf widows went to all the clans of the east.

"Do the lives of our husbands, your eastern brothers, count for nothing?" they said. "Soon the western clans will come for you."

Several eastern clans believed the widows' warning. They gathered and vowed by blood to avenge the people of Kennagel.

These avenging eastern clans slaughtered the Silvermist hunters around the lakes and scattered their children throughout the mountains.

They also slaughtered the Blackvein hunters of the crags.

At the great waterfall, however, they were swarmed by a host of western clans. The avenging clans fought to break through the swarm but were turned back in battle and forced to take cover in the rocks of the falls.

By night a messenger of the avenging clans escaped. The messenger rushed east and begged the help of the other eastern clans. The eastern clans rallied and marched west.

The Battle of the Falls would last two full cycles of the emerald moon. Both east and west would be devastated by the long, chaotic, and gruesome fighting.

The avenging eastern clans were all but exterminated by the time the reinforcing clans of the east arrived. The reinforcing clans might have crushed the western forces by their greater numbers, but they reached the falls at different times and attacked the western host in separated waves, allowing the west time to recover. On entering the battle, the reinforcing clans were each dealt quick and heavy losses, their confidence and order destroyed. The western clans were worn down by the many fresh waves of eastern attackers. Their defensive front weakened from solid wall to porous shell.

The middle stages of the battle were marked by the dissolution of eastern and western unity, the splintering of all clans into disjointed packs, confusion, uncoordinated attacks, and the accidental killings of kinsmen and allies. An unspoken truce was heeded by the warring packs at sunfall each night. Wounded enemies were thrown into the great pool of the falls to drown. Fallen brothers were laid in the river to be carried away.

When starvation became a greater threat than blade or arrow, the hungry packs abandoned the battle to search for food. They left the high and barren mountains to hunt in the lower grounds of the east. Once their strength was recovered, the hunters sought revenge for their dead. The hunters fed and killed, fed and killed. Eastern Phera once again became a land without territory or honor, a land of blood and scattered bones.

Abandoned by the men during the war were the women, children, and elderly. The abandoned of east and west left their homes and journeyed south. They followed the Black River into the hills of the southeast. In the hills, they found ample game, fertile soil, and an unwelcoming population of earlier migrants.

The hunters who had fled from hunger in the western mountains before the war had settled around the choicest hunting grounds of the southeastern hills. These first settlers showed little sympathy for the women, children, and elderly that streamed into the hills fleeing from war. The first settlers drove the new migrants from the best hunting grounds.

The war widows took up planting and trapping. The old fished along the river. The fatherless young watched and waited.

When the young had reached their strength and the fathers of the first settlers had faded, the young moved. Those born of the east pushed the first settlers from the best hunting grounds to rocky places. Those born of the west killed the aged western fathers and scattered their children into the wilderness.

The Quorell, people of the cave, had watched the streams of northern migrants flow into the southeastern hills. The Quorell men were wary of the newcomers and avoided contact. The Quorell women avoided the first settlers but reached out to the widows, children, and elderly that came later. They gave food and clothing to the abandoned and guided them to the best hunting fields. When the first settlers pushed the widows from the hunting fields, the Quorell women asked their men to intervene. The men refused. The Quorell fell back from the first settlers and stayed near to the cavern.

After the first settlers had been driven from the hunting grounds, many of the newly risen young hunters looked to marry.

The young hunters born of the west asked the Quorell for their daughters.

"You killed your own fathers," the Quorell elders said. "How could we give our daughters to you?"

"Our fathers died in war in the distant mountains," the western hunters said. "They left us alone in the world when we were too small to hold a spear or shoot an arrow. We traveled to these hills with a burning in our stomachs and the hope of a life without hunger and pain. The men we killed were not our fathers, though our kinsmen by blood. These men abandoned our clans before the war. These men treated us cruelly, like strangers and beggars, when we came to the hills."

"We helped you," the Quorell said. "We gave you food and clothing. We showed you the hunting grounds."

"You did nothing when we were driven from the grounds to starve in the wilderness," the hunters said.

"You are murderers," the Quorell said. "You will not have our daughters."

The eastern hunters also asked the Quorell for their daughters.

"Marry your own," the Quorell elders said.

The Quorell remained near to the cavern, their daughters deep within. They had no further relations of any kind with the western hunters, who they considered killers. But the Quorell warmed to the eastern hunters over time. The people traded and shared with one another. Friendships were built, languages learned. The Quorell daughters were brought out of the cavern darkness.

Though many romances sparked between the Quorell daughters and the eastern hunters, few led to marriage. Romances were sometimes ended by the disapproval of the parents but more often by the unwillingness of the lovers to leave their way of life. The Quorell daughters feared the dangerous life of the open field; the hunters feared the darkness and chill of the cavern.

The western hunters resented the friendly relations between the Quorell and the eastern hunters. They remembered too well their rejection by the Quorell elders. Throughout the hills, the western packs chased and harassed the eastern packs. They attacked at the smallest provocation.

One day an eastern pack was attacked by several western packs.

The eastern pack fled and took refuge in a small cave of the Quorell.

An eastern hunter emerged from the cave to strike the killer of his brother.

The western hunters flooded into the cave.

They killed the eastern pack then went deeper to attack the Quorell.

The Quorell fled.

The cave killings and flight of the Quorell sparked a wave of retaliatory attacks by eastern packs throughout the hills. The fighting flared, smoldered, and flared again. The hunters of the hills, both eastern and western, declined steadily from violence and disorder. Their women pulled away. Motivated by both the need for safety and stability and by the stinging memory of the men's pursuit of the Quorell daughters, most of the women left the dangerous hunting grounds to live in the great cavern. They trapped and planted near to the cave. A few of the hunters left their packs and followed the women.

Rhecton ended his speculative work with character sketches of these early Adilans. He traced women self-sufficient, proud, and bitter; men tired of fighting and violence but somehow lost without it. He told of loves that burned and faded in the crystal night, of children who slept alone in the darkness and watched from shadows the sunlit work of mothers and fathers. He told of the mournful chants and ghostly echoes that drew many boys into the depths.

Rhecton emerged from his creative isolation and returned to the cavern. For days he sat along the river and watched the old Adilans fish. He watched the Adilan hunters and trappers, planters and shades.

Rhecton trusted only Vail to read his work. He sent a copy of his draft to the old anthropologist along with a short confessional letter.

> *I have no idea what I have written. History, myth, fantasy, I cannot say. I was so confident writing alone in my den. But now my work shivers in the light of day, exposed by flesh and blood. I have been humbled by the living.*

Vail received Rhecton's work at a critical time. After his breakthrough summer of living and working among the Quorell, Vail had extended his stay into the fall. In the fall, his experience continued to be rich and rewarding, his connection deepening. The old anthropologist considered spending his remaining years of life with the coastal people. But there was also the Adilans. Vail's work in the southeast had begun with the Adilans. He had spent three years among them, learning their language, studying their way of life, examining their subgroups and divisions. The ancient night of murder repelled him from the Adilans, but a sense of loyalty and unfinished work pulled him toward the cavern.

Vail read Rhecton's book by candlelight in a single night. In the morning, he gathered the Quorell elders together. He told the elders about his work with the Adilans. He told them openly about his difficult decision and asked for their counsel. "You should go to them," the elders said. "You should go and not return."

Vail left the coast. He returned to his university, wrote and published a short factual summary of his visit with the Quorell, then announced his retirement. He wrote a long and despondent letter to Rhecton. "The explorer was right," he wrote. "We should have bowed our heads to the mystery long ago."

Rhecton answered his friend reproachfully. "Ours is the study of people, not things," he wrote. "We should bow our heads to the mystery, curse the mystery, and plod on."

Though officially retired, Vail added his own chapters to Rhecton's work. He explored the Quorell tradition in all its depth, vibrancy, and richness. He described the tradition as both root and chain.

Vail joined Rhecton at the caves.

The two scientists shared their work with the Adilans.

The Adilan hunters and trappers shrugged, laughed, sneered.

The shades said nothing.

The old fishers nodded. "It is possible," they said.

The planters talked, questioned, considered.

<u>The Western Chaucau</u>

The ancient Chaucau people lived on the southern banks of the Ebrin River from mountain to sea. The Chaucau fished from shore and built homes of clay and branch. They clung to the river and likely never traveled beyond sight of its blue-green waters.

A great flooding of the Ebrin destroyed the homes of the Chaucau and drove them inland.

They fled south along the edge of the western mountains.

The fishing people made poor hunters. They foraged for food in the scrub and brush of the mountain woods. They ate nuts and berries, insects and beetles.

From the difficult Chaucau journey, a new poetry and mythology outpoured.

The first darkness hungered.
Its night burned and the Moons were born.

And the Moons hungered.
They gave birth to the Stars, their children.

And the Moons despised their children.
They drove them from the land with a fierce wind.
They scattered the Stars, their children, into the darkness.

And as the Stars were driven and scattered,
they stretched wide their arms.
They pulled Color from the darkness to clothe themselves.
They pulled Time from the emptiness to stop their flight.

And the Stars pitied the land that lived under the Moons.
They gave the children of the land the seeds of Color,
keeping only the seed of gold for themselves.

They shared with us the gift of Time,
that our hunger might have an end.

The Chaucau journeyed to the crater lakes. They fished, rested, and recovered their strength.

A fraction of the Chaucau chose to remain on the lakes and return to their old way of life. They fished from shore. They built homes of clay and branch, this time on higher ground or well beyond the water's edge. The Chaucau of the lakes survived in scattered pockets for several centuries and were eventually swallowed up by the Varrans.

But most of the Chaucau chose to continue their journey. Though the Chaucau had been a fishing people, a people of water and clay, hook and net, for generations, most rejected a return to this way of life after the flood.

Origin scholars questioned this surprising decision. Some scholars believed that the Chaucau had been traumatized by the flood and left the crater lakes because of a deep fear of all bodies of water. Others doubted that the Chaucau would have feared the small, stone-buffered, and relatively shallow lakes. One suggested another possibility: "Those that left the lakes may have found the waters, *too* calm, *too* safe. They did not seek another catastrophe or disaster like the flood. But, transformed by their journey, stirred by their poets, they now sought something more than mere survival."

The Chaucau traveled without a destination, a defined vision, or a prominent leader. They drifted along the edge of the mountains, sometimes veering west toward the coast, sometimes cutting south into the high hills. Their often-shifting direction was determined by the contours of the land, the availability of food and water, and a complex interaction between their lead explorers, poets, and the body of the people. The explorers set the pace and carved the path followed by the people. The explorers' freedom to probe the wilderness was broad but constrained. If the explorers pushed the people too hard, led them too far from food or too near to danger, the people resisted and chose their own course. If the explorers were too gentle in pace or indecisive in course, they faced the poets' criticism at the nightly fires. The poets had their own struggle. Each night the poets were expected to relieve the aches, fatigue, and hunger of the people with their words. The people needed hope and sustenance, but their arduous journey had made them cynical of the future; the people wanted a tangible fantasy, a dark road leading into light. The poets added flesh to their mythology, a host of characters pheran, bestial, and divine. The lesser poets told stories of bravado, tales of heroes overpowering the forces of nature, defying the whims of gods, and defeating the fiercest creatures of the wild. The heroes of greater works were smaller. They wrestled with complexity, fear, and limitation. Their journey was an inward struggle between the bestial and divine within themselves.

The Chaucau journey wore on.

They wavered between south and west, mountain and coast, for several years, gradually working their way to the southwestern thigh of the Pheran continent.

Their numbers thinned from frequent animal attacks, recurrent waves of disease, and winter starvation. The Chaucau could find no home of rest or safety.

Their people drifted apart.

Their poets fell silent.

The surviving Chaucau limped into the hills and lowlands beneath the mountains. They crossed into the central valley and encountered the herding peoples of the southwest. The herders, remembering their own flight from war in the valley, helped the survivors of the flood. They fed and clothed the Chaucau. They taught the Chaucau their language, their work, their way of life.

Though the Chaucau were likely saved from extinction by the help of the herders, the relationship between the two races chilled after the Chaucau population stabilized and new social structures became necessary.

The herding people considered their helping of the Chaucau an act of familial love, the deepest bond possible in herding culture. They expected no repayment from the Chaucau but assumed that intermarriage would naturally occur. When many Chaucau women refused marriage, the herders were deeply wounded and offended.

The Chaucau family had been devastated by the journey. Most families had lost two, three, even four, members; they had become a fragmented people, a tribe of lone parents, widows, and orphans. The orphans were readily adopted by the herders and absorbed into their culture. The older Chaucau resisted absorption, however. They served in the tents and fields of the herders but guarded their private hours. They learned the language and culture of the herders but maintained their identity as a unique and separate people. Wrote one scholar: "To the Chaucau, marrying meant forgetting. They had lost husbands, wives, mothers, fathers, children. They had accepted a foreign land, a new language, a way of life difficult and strange to them. They felt deep gratitude and love for the herders, but, for many Chaucau, the memory of their journey was one thing they could not share."

The adopted orphans and the Chaucau who intermarried were accepted into herder society and treated as family. Their blood and mind merged with the herding people. Their succeeding generations prospered in health and number.

The Chaucau who refused intermarriage faced a harder road. They lived outside the family tent. They labored in the pastures, shearing grounds, and slaughtering pens, fighting for a place in herder society. But the outsiders were struggling against the herding mind. The herding mind recognized in the world only family and stranger; it had no place for friend.

Origin writers offered different views on the outsiders' struggle and their place eventually reached in herder society. Some writers believed that the herding mind broadened and that the herders allowed the outsiders to become a second family, cousins accepted and respected, perhaps even loved. Other writers believed that the outsiders struggled continually against a rigid and unchanging herding mind. The outsiders' lives of labor carved for them only the place of the worker, the hired hand.

Whatever the place reached by the outsiders, their struggle was painful and long. To ease their loneliness, many of the first generation married among themselves. At nightly fires they taught their children the lyric and story born of the Chaucau journey.

The Striders

Strands of Chaucau lingered at the edges of herder society for centuries. These strands were worn thin by the struggle for survival, frayed by the pressure to join and conform. The generations of Chaucau were each pulled, torn, and tested. They survived in faint lines sustained primarily by oral tradition.

The Chaucau tradition was deepened by a rich, new vein of poetry. To the journey poetry was added the poetry of the wasteland. Lone men and women, called *striders*, left the herding grounds and journeyed for days into the vast southern wasteland. They traveled without food, shoe, or compass. They wore only a swath of cloth around their waists and carried a single skin of water around their necks. The striders believed that the pheran body was a burden to be shed. They believed that exhaustion led to clarity, pain to illumination. The striders walked into the great wasteland until their feet entered a thoughtless, flowing rhythm; until the body's cry of hunger, ache, and thirst passed from scream into silence; until words came.

The striders' poetry struggled against the structured confines of the ancient Chaucau language. To express themselves more fully, the poets stretched the syntax and grammar of the ancient tongue. They created entirely new words and added multiple, often contradictory, layers of meaning to existing words. *Chlorace* could mean molten gold, a state between states, the horizon, wings, or a secret between enemies; *rennar* to descend, to lead, to assume the debt of another; *nerrar* to ascend, to thicken with light or shadow; *vortea*, birth, the beloved, the point of fracture, the moment before death.

During their long journey, the minds of many striders returned to the ancient flood. These poets had never seen the Ebrin River, but they imagined its historic flooding as experienced by their ancestors.

Some poets, perhaps embittered by their present state of living, imagined a minor flooding and a panicked response.

> *Night river rises,*
> *creeps the shore,*
> *trickles on trickles,*
> *bubbles and yawns.*
> *In the morning,*
> *grandmother wakes*
> *and wets her ankles,*
> *grandfather takes to flight.*

Others, a cataclysm.

> *Winter fattened the calf with snowflakes wide as leaves,*
> *blankets to banks in the high places.*

Spring slit the belly with warm rains and winds.
The Ebrin swelled.
The Ebrin burst.
It swept the hills, surged the shores, and spewed over the grasslands.
Trees were snapped like infants' fingers,
boulders tossed like pebbles,
brush pulled from the ground like summer fur.
The clay homes of the Chaucau were swallowed by the water,
a swirling, vanishing stain.
In the sandy depths, the bodies settled.

The striders were also drawn to the ancient journey through the southwestern wilderness. Their wilderness poetry was stark and bleak.

Families were separated by the attacks of wild beasts.

Frostbitten fingers clawed the winter turf, digging for roots to eat.

Vacant and dull, the eyes of the diseased gazed into the sky.

Through their own wasteland journey and transcendent imagination, the striders entered the ancients' crucible of survival, the low and desperate places of the spirit faced by those ever near to pain, death, and hunger. There were few heroes to emerge.

Lagging elderly were kissed and left to die.

A son killed his father over a fallen bird.

Young lovers strangled one another for extra furs on winter nights.

The wilderness story-poem of Liis contained both tragedy and enigmatic warning.

As the old have told us,
Liis was young,
a heartbeat past the flower.

She kissed her love, her first, beneath the tree.

And
beneath the tree,
she watched the Ebrin roll proud upon its work,
the dead,
her family, her friends,
her love and hope and sun.

In the moonlight,
Liis entered the waters to join her love.

But the arms of a little girl,
her niece,
saved her,
wrapped tight around her neck,
pulled her back to the living.

Woman and child,
aunt and niece,
fled from the river.
They wandered south and west
through hills and forests,
mountains and valleys.
They scavenged like mice.

In time,
they joined another family —
a widowed man and his children.

Liis loved again.
She was given a season with her love, a winter.
Her eyes glistened in the starlight.

Her winter skin glowed like summer heat.

But her love, again, was taken,
her second by disease.

With fire,
she sent her love into the sky.
With fire,
she chased away his children.

The striders were butchers in the cold season of the year. In the killing pits, they worked, skinning, flanking, carving, tossing organs into the fire, flicking blood from their fingers.

The striders butchered the animals of the Chaucau but refused to touch the animals of the herding people. They would not speak to a man, woman, or child of the herding people.

The striders wandered between the scattered camps of the Chaucau throughout the year, sharing poems and stories at the nightly fires, avoiding other striders.

The striders never married.

Their uncut tangles of hair were pulled back and held by seared animal tendon.

The Chaucau people, mired in the daily struggle for bread and meaning, looked to the striders for more than imaginings of the past.

An early generation of striders attempted to cross and conquer the wasteland. Many of this generation hoped to find a new home for the Chaucau, a bright and virgin land far from the herding people. Others walked to pierce the mystery of life, each step a protest against the law of death and decay, their march a defiance of bloodless gods and heartless universe.

The Chaucau people watched the early striders wither in skin, crumple in bone, and dwindle in number. The Chaucau watched old poets limp into the wasteland on their final march, young poets stare silently into the fire.

Later generations of striders held a greater tolerance for pheran limitation and a deeper reverence for the wasteland. The later striders approached the heart of the wasteland with mystical fear.

The greatest of our old cursed your face and fell to your chest,
their dreams, your breath and dust.

You are reflection,
the blade that bares and strips the craving heart,
the cure of wanting and desire.

You are abyss,
untouched by the river of time,
the living ashes,
the whispering dead.

You are mystery,
shadows of the first darkness,
keeper of creation's embers,
still trembling with the pains of birth.

The mysticism of the striders left many of the Chaucau unsatisfied. The people crafted their own poetry, shorter verses of wry humor, bitter lament, ancestral cry.

Mother, why this place?
Father, why these people?

III. TYRAEN ROOTS

The Chaucau and the striders would form a great tributary – genetic, artistic, historical, and spiritual – flowing into the Tyraen.

The Tyraen would be slight of bone, narrow of frame, and lean with muscle.

The Tyraen would view, meet, and repel the world with poetry and literature. The Tyraen would dutifully preserve the work of former generations, approach these traditions with more skepticism than reverence, and create new stories and verse to be handed down, in turn. The Tyraen would demolish and build, imagine and destroy.

The Tyraen would undertake impossible tasks and plod until ruin or completion.

But, first, the Chaucau waited, still outsiders of herder society, faintly surviving pockets in the southwestern corner of the continent's central valley.

The Alcyans

The oldest Alcyans fished on the shores of the many streams and creeks feeding into the Danve River.

Over quiet centuries, the Alcyans developed skill in pottery, crafts, carpentry, and boatmaking. They drifted onto the wide first leg of the Danve. They built homes in the trees, fished from boats, and gathered in small communities.

The Danve inspired many works of poetry and meditation. The great river was a source of life to the Alcyans, an eternal and sustaining force. For the Alcyan poets, the great river taught and revealed.

The young man sees the colors of the river.
He sees the river ease at night's approach,
shards of blue and gentle silver
swallowed into black.

In the morning, he sees the river tense
at the long work ahead,
leaves of blue and green
twisted into broken sheets of gold.

The young man sees the strength of the river.
He wonders of its secret,
how even in sleeping the river moves on.

The young man will grow old.
His back will bend.
His eyes will blind.
He will stand at the river and listen.
He will understand why the river never tires.

The severe winter and warm spring that flooded the Ebrin also swelled the Danve. The banks of the Danve were steeper and rockier, however; the damage done to land less extreme. Most of the trees on the banks held root and the Alcyans simply waited in their homes for a few days or hours for the waters to subside.

The flooding of the Danve did little damage to the land, but the Alcyan spirit was still shaken, unmoored. The immutable had changed. The eternal had been marked and bound by time.

A portion of the Alcyans left their boats and towns behind and journeyed upriver. They traveled on foot to the higher streams and creeks. They fished from shore as the oldest Alcyans had done. They carved poetry into stones, genealogies onto trees. They built shrines to the river. Lyrical creativity waned among the Alcyans upriver, but these traditionalists canonized and treasured the body of ancient Alcyan poetry. The traditional Alcyans would not leave the upper streams and creeks for centuries.

Most of the Alcyans remained on the first leg of the Danve. They turned away from traditional reverence for the river and poured their energies into new directions. They designed faster boats, built bigger homes, and developed more elaborate pottery and crafts. They explored the surrounding hills and probed the Danve's second leg.

Young poets looked toward a future down the river, perhaps beyond it.

> *The river is a tree.*
> *A thousand fathers have sat at its base, searching,*
> *staring, praying.*
> *With sleepy and lowered eyes, they have watched*
> *the ground,*
> > *not knowing the heights above them.*
> > *We will brush aside their bones.*
> > *We will raise our eyes and waken.*

<u>Aton</u>

Aton was born on the river in the year of the flood. His mother drowned not long after his weaning. His father died from disease several years later.

Aton became a child of the community, fed and clothed by many, adopted by none. The boy slept alone in the woods. He disappeared into the hills for days at a time and returned only to take food from the families of the community. He hoarded the food, burying caches under rocks and bushes, hiding bundles in the highest branches of trees.

Aton, the young man, left the hills for soft-eyed Mira. He worked for Mira's father for eight years cleaning and fishing. When they had reached the age of marriage, Aton and Mira wed.

"What can I give you?" Aton asked on their first night together.

"Take me far from here," Mira said.

Aton took Mira away from her family. They moved downriver to an Alcyan town far to the west. Together they built a tree-home and a boat. They had their first child, Atonyi, a boy.

Aton seized the energy of his time, the post-flood dynamics of exploration and growth. He learned from the most experienced and skilled Alcyan fishers and boatmakers. He experimented with new types of spears, rods, and nets. He designed wider boats that could carry hundreds of fish. He traded with hunters to the north.

The children of Aton bore much of the burden of their father's dreams and hunger. While daylight held, their little hands mended nets and gutted fish; their backs carried heavy totes to shore. At night, Myr, his only daughter, worked the smokehouse; the boys, Atonyi and Atonera, drove wagons by torchlight to the hunters.

One day Atonera, the youngest, cut his hand badly while cleaning a large catch of fish. Aton saw fear and exhaustion in the boy's eyes. He watched the boy continue working with dripping hand, desperately trying to finish the catch. Aton stopped his son and called the other children together. "Though I had no childhood," Aton said, "you will." Aton no longer made the children work at night and gave them an occasional free afternoon.

Aton hired the young of other Alcyans.

He built a storehouse, lodge, and market.

His fleet of boats dominated the choicest fishing pools.

His children grew. Each passed the age of marriage without marrying.

Atonyi and Myr stirred the young that worked for their father.

"He treats you harshly because he knows that you cannot return to your parents," Atonyi said. "He despises you because you left your families. In time he will treat you even harsher."

"We will build our own boats," Myr said. "We will ride the river to its end."

For three seasons the Alcyan young worked secretly on their boats.

The Alcyan young left at midday so that all could see their going.

Aton watched his many workers and his own children drift by on the river.

Aton stared into the river until the sun sank low in the sky.

Mira, his wife, urged him to eat and come home.

"A thousand times I tried to die," Aton said. "I walked into the hills. I walked for days and days, hoping for a wild beast or gnawing hunger to end my suffering. But the beast never came. And hunger was too hard. I returned to the living, fed my greedy stomach, and cursed my weakness. One day I would have found the strength to finish. But your eyes pulled me from the hills and ended my walking. You saved me. You saved me for this."

"I only married you to leave my family," Mira said.

Journey of the Young

The Alcyan young rode the Danve west toward the distant ocean, traveling over hills and lowlands, veering between cliffs and coves.

Atonyi and Myr assumed leadership of the young rebels. Brother and sister drove the young. They woke the young before dawn to catch the day's food. They staggered crews and breaks so that the oars never stopped while the sun shone. They made the journey more flight than exploration.

At night, exhausted, the young travelers camped on riverbanks, built fires, and listened to poetry.

In the early journey, the poets shared visions of lands windless and bright, lush with plant, teeming with game.

After the first excitement faded, the poets shared simple dreams of warm homes and quiet paths, dreams of settling down.

Myr rebuked the poets. "Stop adding weight to the people's burdens," she said. "Stop sapping their strength."

"Son is harder than father," the poets said.

"Atonyi is leading us to a place greater than all your dreams."

"And daughter is colder than mother."

Myr also rebuked her younger brother, Atonera. "You are always writing but never speaking," she said. "Why don't you defend your brother?"

"If I speak, I must speak the truth," Atonera said. "If I speak the truth, my brother will hate me."

"Like the old say - The untold truth turns to lie."

Grumbling, the young followed Atonyi down the great river. Atonera said nothing. He only wrote.

There was no stopping once we entered the rocks and rapids.
There was no turning back.
A cold and twisting wind attacked us.

Many plunged into the icy water,
their boats spun like leaves,
cracked like kindling against the jagged rocks.
We could not help the fallen.
We watched them drown,
silent screams against the water's roar,
hands reaching high, grasping at the empty air.

Those that survived the rocks and rapids gathered in a cove downriver. Shivering, they cried bitter tears.

Atonyi waded into the river. He swam out, grabbed the first body floating past the cove, and carried it to shore.

Myr screamed at him. "You fool," she said. "Let the bodies pass."

Entranced, Atonyi heard nothing.

He returned to the water.

One by one, he retrieved the bodies and carried them to shore.

Each time, Myr cursed her brother and pushed the bodies out.

For many days and nights, the people stayed in the cove. They did not eat or speak. Silently, they stared into the passing water.

Atonyi finally broke the silence.

"We disgrace our dead brothers and sisters if we do not continue," Atonyi said. "We must find strength in their memory. We must continue west."

The people, no longer young, stared into the Danve.

They broke their gaze when Atonera rose to stand before them.

"We were wrong to leave our families the way we did," Atonera said. "We were wrong to disrespect our ancestors and cast aside generations of teaching. We should have listened more, spoken less. We were wrong to trust my father, a man of endless hunger. We were wrong to follow my brother, a man of equal need."

"Now, he speaks," Myr said. She gathered the remaining boats, threw them into a pile on the shore, and set them to fire. "May all the rivers of the world dry and shrivel," she said.

Myr led most of the Alcyans into the northwestern hills.

A few, including Atonera, continued down the river on foot.

Atonyi sat alone on the shore, watching the river through the flames.

<u>Atonyi</u>

In the dark of night, Atonyi waded out into the river.

"I will die as I deserve," he said.

Atonyi closed his eyes, dove beneath the water, and surrendered himself.

But the cry of his lungs was too fierce and the water too cold. Atonyi rose to the surface. He breathed and cursed.

Atonyi swam across the river to the southern shore.

He wandered the southern hills throughout the night and following day, fleeing the chill in his bones.

On the second night he spotted a sliver of firelight to the west. Weary and shivering, he walked toward the distant light. He reached the campfire near dawn.

The travelers were Bhadaan traders returning to the western coast. The traders saw Atonyi, a pale and sickly shadow, hovering around their camp as they prepared in the morning. They quenched their fire, left a few cakes of grain upon a stone, and returned to the trail.

Atonyi ate the cakes of grain and followed the traders. He followed them all the way home on their return journey. He found gifts each morning of the journey on the campfire stones – graincakes, melons, a fleece, a waterskin.

On the coast Atonyi saw the great marshy bay, the hundreds of artificial islands built from reeds, the Bhadaan long huts and animal pens on each island, the host of slender canoes gliding between islands and shore.

Atonyi lived and worked among the Bhadaan for many years.

In the early years, Atonyi slept on the shore with only his fleece to shield him from the wind and rain. He swam to the islands during the days, cleaned the animal pens of the Bhadaan, and accepted their gifts of food.

In later years, Atonyi built his own island, long hut, and canoes. He discovered shellfish in the western bay, became a wealthy trader among the Bhadaan, and accumulated stores of fleece and crystal shells. He traveled with other Bhadaan to trade with tribes in the east.

One year, Atonyi and his party explored deep in the southeast. They were captured by Oselen riders in the fissured plains between the Danve and Ebrin Rivers. Their heads were shaved, their necks tattooed. They were put to labor in the Oselen silver mines.

A war between Oselen clans broke out during Atonyi's second year in the mines. When the guards of the mine left to join the fighting, Atonyi fled for the mountains.

At the twin falls, Atonyi was again captured by Oselen riders, these of the Whitefire Clan. His forearm was branded with the sign of the Whitefire. He was driven to a northern village and put to work in the village mill.

Atonyi worked the mill season by season. He watched the number of villagers dwindle as the war between clans continued. When the mill had no grain left to grind, the slaves of the village were bound, thrown into the back of a wagon, and taken on a journey north.

"What is happening?" Atonyi asked another slave.

"The Whitefire are starving," the slave told him. "We will be traded for food."

The Whitefire took their slaves to a trading station in the foothills beneath the Danve. A line of bones and branded forearms, the slaves stood before the master of the station.

"They are a day from death," the old master said.

"They are young," the Whitefire captain said. "A few good meals and they will lift boulders."

The old master wrung his beard, grimacing, considering. "An hour from death," he said.

"Help your friends, the Whitefire," the captain said. "Many times we have given your riders safe passage. Many times we have protected your merchants."

"I know the Oselen too well," the master said. "Threats follow pleas."

"There are no threats today," the captain said. "The Whitefire will perish without your help. These slaves are the only gift we have to give our old friend, Aton."

Aton, the master, walked the line of slaves.

"I will help my friends, the Whitefire," he said.

After the Whitefire departed, Aton faced Atonyi.

"Here is Atonyi," he said, "the great traveler, the leader of the Alcyan youth, the proud rebel."

The slaves were fed and rested until their strength and flesh returned. All the slaves except Atonyi were put to work in the station. Atonyi was taken alone to a rocky field.

"The stones must be cleared from the field," his father said.

For many days Atonyi pushed, pulled, and rolled the large stones from the field. Then Atonyi carried every small stone from the field. Then Atonyi raked the pebbles from the field.

"The field must be plowed," his father said.

Atonyi plowed the field for many days.

"The field must be seeded," Aton said.

Atonyi seeded the field.

Aton ordered his son chained to a tree at the edge of the field.

"Now you will watch your seed grow, your work come to life," Aton said. "And you will see your work cut down, your life taken away."

Day by day, hour by hour, Atonyi watched the grain grow, slumped against a tree.

When the grain formed heads, his father could take no more. Aton ordered his son to be unchained, washed, and fed.

"Your debt is paid," Aton said, "your betrayal forgiven."

A horse laden with supplies and arms was brought out and given to Atonyi.

Atonyi mounted the horse. He looked to the mountains. His weary eyes sharpened.

"Thank you, Aton," he said, "great merchant, pride of the Alcyans, collector of silver and slaves."

Aton became ill soon after his son left for the mountains. His strength faded until he could no longer ride, walk, or stand. He lay a long winter, turning in his bed, torn by memory and dream.

In the spring, Aton rose from his bed. He paid every debt he owed to other merchants and canceled every debt owed to him. He gave many gifts to his workers and left the trading station to his fairest managers.

Aton gathered all his slaves together. He made each slave swear to find and help his son, Atonyi, then gave each a young horse and ample supplies.

"Will you lead us into the mountains?" they asked.

"No, I travel the Danve west," Aton said. "I search for Atonera."

Most of the freed slaves scattered in search of their own families and people.

Only the criminals and orphans crossed the mountains.

They found Atonyi walking in the hills alone, feverish and pale, mumbling of rocks and rivers.

The Cyecurans

We were born of a hard man's kindness, freed by a father's regret.
We entered the mountains as strangers.
We left as brothers and sisters, bonded by our journey.

At Cyecura we settled down, built homes, learned the land.
The world was new at Cyecura.
Orphans married.
Killers planted and farmed.
Thieves shared.

We had hoped for nothing before Cyecura.
At Cyecura everything we touched turned to life.

The freed slaves of Aton wove their way down through the hills and into the broad central valley.

Their journey ended where the four rivers broke like a shattered mirror into hundreds of glistening streams.

The vision of Cyecura drew Atonyi from his weary stupor. "A home to never leave," he said.

The freed slaves descended onto the lush floodplain. They saw small waterfowl in the streams, copses of the squat arrowleaf trees, banks of reedgrass, willowherb, and milkflower. They touched the rich, dark soil of the plain. They smelled the wild rye.

Slave became settler. The Cyecurans built homes of clay and bark thatched with reedgrass rushes. They gathered nuts, mint, seeds, and herbs. They hunted birds and trapped small game. They harvested wild rye and planted beans and corn.

The first generation of Cyecurans lived in close community. Meals were shared and resources pooled. All Cyecurans came together for building, planting, and harvesting.

The second generation flourished and branched outward from the first community.

The third generation settled to the edges of the floodplain. Some explored the central valley and made contact with the Torite miners of the eastern valley and the herders of the southwest.

The fourth generation befriended the herding tribes. The Cyecurans were given many animals in trade. The herders were given grains, produce, safe passage, and water access.

The fifth generation traded for Torite metals and tools. They designed irrigation systems across the floodplain and built silos for surplus crops. Small towns began to nucleate around the silos.

Cyecura continued to grow and thrive but subsequent generations became increasingly divided between farmers and herders. Many Cyecuran men had taken daughters of the southwestern herders in marriage and had received large herds and flocks as wedding gifts. Most of these men chose to remain in Cyecura and their livestock inevitably strayed onto farmers' fields. The wandering animals caused bitter disputes between families whose understandings of property and boundary often contradicted. Farmers added to the tension by digging canals that diverted water away from the herders' lands and onto their own fields.

Conflict was partially resolved by the building of animal pens by the herders, the improved sharing of water by the farmers, and the peacemaking interventions of family matriarchs, both herder and farmer. As family bonds and material heritage thinned over time, the trading and selling of property became more common. Herders concentrated in southern Cyecura, farmers in the north.

A People Old and New

After the first Cyecuran explorers made contact with the southwestern herders, several Chaucau left the southwest and searched for the settlement at the meeting of the four rivers. None of these Chaucau returned and the Cyecurans were forgotten for many years.

When the southwestern herders gravitated to Cyecura for trade and marriage, the Chaucau also traveled north.

The first Chaucau to live in Cyecura refrained from intermarriage. Some of the Chaucau offered their services to the Cyecuran herders inexperienced with livestock, others to Cyecuran farmers. A generation of Chaucau lived in Cyecura and served as chief hands to the dominant herding and farming families.

The next generation of Chaucau intermarried with the Cyecurans.

A new people, the Tyraens, were born.

The Tyraens, though small in number, became vital intermediates in Cyecura. They negotiated trade, facilitated transport, and mediated conflict between the north and south. They provided an interface and buffer between Cyecuran herders and farmers. With their success in trade, the Tyraens acquired key strips of land and built roads throughout Cyecura. They lived on small hybrid farms with both crops and livestock.

When the rising Cyecuran population exhausted the local supply of trees, the Tyraens established a trade relationship with Varran woodsmen and a trade route to the Varran Cradle.

The Tyraens also established trade routes to the growing Torite towns of the eastern valley.

While the eastern mining towns were young and hungry, the Tyraens pressed their advantage in trade and acquired many steel tools from the Torites. When the Torites opened trade with Draun farmers in the southeast, however, the Tyraens quickly lost their economic advantage.

To recover from their loss the Tyraens again played the role of vital intermediate, this time bridging the western valley with the east. They provided the Varran woodsmen with grains, meats, and steel tools. They provided the swelling Torite towns with lumber for the building of homes and mines. All lumber and metal was transported by Tyraen barges and wagons; all east-west trade flowed through Tyraen hands.

To understand the Tyraens one must understand the power of mothers and fathers, the burden of generations, the bitter intertwining of heritage and debt.

The first Chaucau to live in Cyecura were friendly and respectful toward the local herders and farmers. Sensing opportunity, this generation served the Cyecurans in field and pasture, butchering and shearing, planting and harvesting. They worked tirelessly for the Cyecurans and proved themselves diligent and loyal. As this generation of Chaucau approached their twilight, they passed on to their children an acceptance of the Cyecuran people and a permission to marry outside the ancient lines. With this permission, however, the older generation also passed down a measure of guilt and obligation.

Never forget that you are the first.
Remember your ancestors who fled the Ebrin flood,
their poetry born of the wilderness.
Remember the striders who broke the body's limit,
their poetry born of the wasteland.

And remember us, your mothers and fathers,
whose labor earned the respect of all Cyecura,
whose sweat carved soft ground for your feet to stand,
whose strength burned and faded for you.

Their children married Cyecurans of the north and south, farmers and herders. These last pure-blooded Chaucau married happily but never shed completely the weight of their inherited privilege. To ease their burden, they built new homes and acquired livestock.

Their children, the first Tyraens, heard often of flood and strider, of their grandparents' sacrifice and the homes built by their parents' hands. To ease their burden, they acquired land, built bridges and roads, and bred tharic for racing and draft.

Poets and Seekers

Tyraen trade arteries connected east and west and fueled an era of rapid growth and expansion throughout the central valley.

Tyraens branched out from Cyecura.

They built many towns and stations along the east-west trade routes.

They built canals linking the rivers of east and west.

To meet the demands of trade, the Tyraens divided into a wide array of new jobs and classes. They became wagon-runners, scouts, and bargers; negotiators, translators, and brokers; clerks, station owners, and stable masters.

Despite their varying trades and increased separation, the Tyraens maintained a strong cultural identity. The Tyraen young were immersed in the poetry of their Chaucau ancestors. They were told many stories and legends of the first Cyecurans.

The combined heritage of Chaucau and Cyecuran both unified and tore apart. Some Tyraens took seriously the striders' march toward truth, the tightly interwoven community of the first Cyecurans, criminal and orphan. These extreme Tyraens considered the life of trade a betrayal of their roots. They sought something higher.

A steady trickle of young seekers fled the trade towns of the central valley and journeyed into the northern hills.

Some of the seekers joined small indigenous tribes of the north.

Some became hermits in the aerie crags.

Many were drawn to Mount Arran, the great smoldering and half-spent volcano of the northern mountains. Arran's whisper of rising smoke guided the seekers through the valley and high hills. The pilgrims climbed Arran's steep walls in slow and spiral labor.

One poet received her clearest insight during the ascent.

> *Alone I had dreamed in the night's starry ache.*
> *Alone I had journeyed through valley and hill.*
> *At the mountain I walked in the footprints of others,*
> *many others,*
> *who also had dreamed*
> *and had ached.*

Other poets found their voice gazing down from Arran's cratered rim into its great steaming cauldron.

Apocalyptics imagined thick molten veins rising beneath all the Pheran land, pushing toward the surface, soon to break and consume.

Monists felt the tearing of the veil between two worlds. They saw the material fade, the spirit emerge in form, color, force, and movement. The stone spirits pulled and held. The fire spirits gnawed and tore. The winds crept toward fire then fled to sky.

Mystics saw the womb of creation.

Some poets never left the northern mountains. They lived alone in small caves and made daily pilgrimage to Mount Arran. They gathered only at the death of a fellow poet. They chanted the work of the fallen throughout the night then cast the body into Arran's fire at the first light of day.

> *Flesh to fire*
> *we fall.*
> *Our word*
> *the breath of the living.*

Other poets returned to the central valley transformed by their journey.

Vhedor

In a small eastern trade town, a Tyraen man was crushed by logs when the binding chain on a wagon snapped. Station workers cleared the timber and rushed to find the man's family.

The dying man asked first for his wife, then his brother, then his daughters. Each was held and kissed.

Finally, the man asked for his son. He grabbed his son by the neck and pulled him close. "You were named for a killer," he said.

Vhedor, the young son, worked to support his sisters and mother. He worked at the trading station for seven years, first as a messenger, then a sweeper, then loader. He remembered the words of his father every day.

When his mother remarried, he set out on a long journey across the central valley, a search for the first Vhedor. His journey would stretch from his youth into his middle years and range from the eastern hills to the western woods. His search would untangle family legend and trace family lines all the way back to the first Cyecurans and Chaucau. He would taste of the life and labor of all Tyraens.

Vhedor traveled first to the eastern foothills. He lived with many aunts and uncles strewn throughout the border towns of the hills. He worked with his uncles in Tyraen stables. He worked with his cousins in Torite forges and mills. Among his family in the east, Vhedor observed a rapid erosion of heritage and family tie. He predicted that within two or three generations the Tyraen of the eastern hills would look no different than the Torite.

Vhedor left the eastern hills for the southeastern lowlands. He found second and third cousins living around the Sedde Lakes in the wide midvalley trough. The Tyraens of the trough came together each spring to dig the Sedde canals eastward. They worked together throughout the spring and summer then drifted apart in the fall, some riding north for trade, some exploring the steppes of the southeast. Vhedor spent six years among the Tyraens of the trough. He worked alongside them in the summer heat, carving the canal walls with pick and shovel, creeping stone by stone toward the distant hills. Vhedor absorbed their poems, stories, and legends shared at the nightly fires. He crafted his own first verses.

> *In the dark and idle winter,*
> *lone Tyraens question if*
> *the canal will ever reach the east.*
> *But when they come together in the spring,*
> *when they sweat, struggle, and advance together,*
> *they have no doubt.*
> *The work will require Tyraens not yet born,*
> *but the work will be finished.*

Vhedor spent the longest portion of his journey on the east-west trade route. He traveled west town by town, season by season, staying with many distant relatives along the way. When the wagons rolled into town, he helped his family in the stables, inns, and shops. At other times he cleared brush from the trails, set guideposts, repaired wagons, and built bridges. Vhedor learned much about his family history as he traveled west. He filled his traveling journal with dense branches of genealogies. He recorded a wealth of ancestral stories and lore. He learned much but knew his journey would not be complete until he found the first Vhedor, the killer. He spent a year in the fields and stables north of Cyecura, the training and breeding grounds for most Tyraen racers. He spent another year in the lumber mills between Cyecura and the Varran woods.

Having spanned the central valley from end to end, Vhedor rested for a season. In a winter cabin, he spread wide his pages and pieced together his family story. He found that every family line across the valley could be traced to a single Tyraen family in Cyecura. The patriarch of this family had died suddenly from disease in the prime of his life. The matriarch had also fallen ill with bone fever. Before her death, she had called for each of her six children. "Others will take the valley," she had said.

The oldest brother and sister had built stables together in the fields north of Cyecura. They had traveled to Varran cities and brokered deals with Varran woodsmen.

The middle twin brothers had run wagons. They had transported barley from Cyecura, lumber to the eastern hills, steel to the west.

The youngest brother and sister had brokered deals with the Torites and served as scouts for the wagon trains in the east. The brother had drowned while working on one of the first canals.

Vhedor's mother traced back to the second twin, Vhedor's father to the youngest sister.

Every child of the matriarch had lived, worked, and died outside Cyecura.

> *The great mother knew that her children*
> *would be alone in the world.*
> *She knew that they would be vulnerable,*
> *weakened by loss,*
> *tempted to self-pity.*
> *So the great mother gave them a final gift.*
> *She gave them a blow to their pride,*
> *a spur in their ass,*
> *a blade to their heel.*

Vhedor entered Cyecura.

He learned that the matriarch was a third generation Tyraen.

He traced back to the matriarch's grandparents, the first Tyraens, and to the matriarch's great-grandparents, the last Chaucau.

The great-grandparents had left the southwestern valley, journeyed to Cyecura, and served a large family of barley farmers.

The barley farmers traced back to the youngest son of first Cyecurans, Cyla and Vhedor.

Cyla was an Oselen thief sold for grain to the old slave-master in the hills.

Vhedor was an Alcyan murderer. In his youth he had drowned another Alcyan boy in the river. Hated by his tribe, he had fled the Alcyans and wandered the hills beneath the Danve until his capture by guards of Aton. Vhedor had served as a slave of Aton for many years. In Cyecura, he had planted and farmed alongside Atonyi, the slave-master's son. The houses of Vhedor and Atonyi later split over the problem of Oselen refugees crossing into the central valley. The sons of Atonyi attacked the fleeing Oselen. The sons of Vhedor left them in peace.

Vhedor, the Tyraen, lived in Cyecura among the descendants of his namesake. He lived in a cabin on the edge of the barley fields. Three times he watched the barley planted and harvested.

Vhedor felt lost and adrift at the end of his journey. He felt tricked by his father into undertaking the long search, disappointed by what was revealed during the search, frustrated by what remained hidden. Vhedor slowly, painfully, came to realize that his father's final words were much more than trickery or manipulation.

> *He had reached across centuries and leagues,*
> *praying all on a thin thread of family legend,*
> *choosing the first father,*
> *not the greatest.*
> *With one name I was cast to the birth of my people.*
> *I was given a blow,*
> *a spur,*
> *a blade.*

Vhedor never married but fathered several children.

He traveled the valley until the day of his death.

His first journey across the valley was a gathering of poems, stories, and legends.

In his later journeys, he shared and spread. He cast many seeds.

Vhedor's own writings were few. His final verse was written to all Tyraens.

> *Sweat to blood,*
> *labor to life.*
> *We are the vein.*
> *They are the body.*

IV. FLIGHT AND RETURN

The seeds of Vhedor challenged and stirred the generation to follow.

Many Tyraen families left the east-west trade towns to farm in the fields of the northern valley.

These northern Tyraens settled in communal clusters. Like the first Cyecurans, they planted, cultivated, and harvested together; they shared meals and pooled resources.

Each sunrise the northern Tyraens meditated alone on the ancient poetry of the wilderness. They gathered each sunset to share the poetry of the wasteland.

The northern Tyraens heard rumors of war to the east.

Ancient Bloodwells

Bloodshed in the valley began long before the birth of the Tyraens.

The torch of war was passed down from each of the five empires in the ancient tribal era. Power volleyed between east and west with the rise and fall of each city-state.

The first Iron Empire rose in the east. The Torites, or mixed ones, were formed by the merging of numerous smaller tribes around the rich iron deposits deep in the eastern hills. The Torite mines grew into Torite towns; Torite towns developed into a handful of powerful cities. These cities, lacking an agricultural base, formed blackguard units to raid the farming villages of the central valley during harvest. The blackguard packs were heavily armed but slow and cumbersome. To escape the range of the Torite troops, many farming tribes migrated into the western valley; some tribes banded together to resist the raids. The hungry eastern empire declined. A branch of Torites left the eastern hills to colonize and farm the Draun heartland to the south.

The ancient Oselen Empire rose in the west. Oselen power sprang from the hoof of the sandy tharic. Oselen riders protected the valley harvests. Their mounted archers raided the eastern Torite towns. Their lancers and light cavalry slaughtered the blackguards of the eastern mines. The Torites were driven by the Oselen deep into the eastern hills, surrendering town and city until only walled Tekenna remained. The Torites held Tekenna despite repeated attacks and prolonged siege. An Oselen captain rebelled during the siege and took many riders from the eastern hills to the southeastern steppes. The remaining Oselen scattered.

The Silver Empire drew its power from the lodes of Lycira, the twin and rival city to great Tekenna. Lyciran silver purchased Tekennan bronze and iron, the surplus grains of the Draun, and livestock and horses from the west. The Silver Empire secured its trade routes with mounted patrols and guarded its caravans with pikes and crossbows. Once strong, the empire burned the stables of the valley, slaughtered the tharic broken and wild, and collected tribute from all outside Lycira. The empire waned after a failed campaign to eliminate the raiders of the southeastern steppes. The empire collapsed after a rebellion of the Tekennan iron guilds.

The Pocone Empire forced the farmers of the western valley into organized agricultural sectors. Pocon, the first king, set production quotas, determined the types of crops planted, and managed the storage of surplus. The empire's great storehouses and variety of crops minimized its dependence on any single harvest. Pocon's sons, freed from labor, attacked and subjugated the farming tribes of the midvalley. His grandsons, eager to surpass their fathers' glory, attacked the east. The east unified in defense. Tekennans, Lycirans, and Draun came together to defeat the imperial army.

The second Iron Empire was driven by the merging of old and new power in the eastern hills. Between ancient Tekenna and aged Lycira, young Balthe rose. Balthe controlled trade between the old giants and played the two against each other in negotiation. Balthe unified all Torites of the eastern hills under its council of guilds and conscripted a massive imperial army. The empire built garrisons in the Draun and along the southern trade routes. The empire burned the great storehouses built by Pocon and drained the reservoirs and canals of the central valley. When the council of Balthe dropped negotiation with its fellow Torites and simply dictated its terms, Tekenna and Lycira closed their gates to all trade. The raiders of the steppes attacked the southern garrisons and crippled the southern trade routes. Emboldened, the raiders attacked Lycira. Without aid from Balthe or Tekenna, the city fell to the raiders, its vaults of silver stripped.

The farming peoples of the central valley, tired of war and tribute, migrated outward from the heart of the valley, some to the western woods, some to the southwestern hills.

The raiders ruled the east.

Fall of the Raiders

Centuries later, a wave of diseased parasites swept across the southeastern valley and ravaged much of its animal life.

The raiders of the steppes survived the disease but lost nearly all of their tharic.

Myshe, an old raider, declared the plague to be a judgment of the winds and sky against his people. He led a handful of riders and their families into the northern valley to hunt red deer and iron wolf, never to raid again.

Other raiders foraged the steppes on foot. With the steppe fauna devastated, the foragers survived on plant stalks and worms.

Some raiders delivered themselves as slaves to the farmers of the Draun.

The Draun farmers accepted the raiders as slaves. For their many years of theft and killing in the southeast, the raiders were yoked like oxen and driven to plow.

The Second Sons

Without the attacks of the raiders, the Torites of the eastern hills slowly emerged from their centuries of fear and shadow. They built outward from Tekenna. They built new mines, new roads, new cities. They traded with the Tyraens for horses and lumber. They traded with the Draun for corn and grain.

An old Tekennan family, the Mhedaals, organized the guards of the Torite cities.

The Mhedaals also formed an army from the second-born sons of the Torite towns.

At rebuilt Lycira, the Mhedaals commissioned the army of second sons. "Take darkness to the steppes," they said. "Kill every raider, young and old, man and woman."

The second sons flooded the steppes of the southeast. Their cavaliers took down the raiders with lance and spear. Their foot-soldiers carved the fallen.

The second sons traveled to the Draun. They commanded the Draun farmers to bring forward their slaves of raider blood. The farmers refused and rallied to fight. But the slaves came forward on their own. The second sons cut down the slaves like grain beneath the scythe.

After returning to the eastern hills, the Torite army was disbanded by the Mhedaals.

The Mhedaals sent new steel plows, wagons, and reapers to placate the farmers of the Draun.

The Mhedaals built trade towns throughout the hills. They built lumber mills in the west, grain mills in the south. In the cities, they built markets, parks, and reservoirs. The resurgent empire thrived.

One problem marred the Torite prosperity. The second sons. Madness and violence followed the executioners of the raiders. The second sons were cast out, first from their homes, then from their towns, then from the parks of the cities.

The Mhedaals built a thousand-celled prison in Lycira.

When the prison overflowed, the Mhedaals commissioned a new army from the fittest of the prisoners. "Destroy the hunters of the northern valley," they said. "Their blood is Oselen. They are killers, raiders, and thieves."

The Myshenites, children and grandchildren of the hunter-prophet Myshe, routed the prisoner army in the northern fields of the valley. The Myshenite riders outmaneuvered and unmounted the Torite riders. The Myshenites drove lines through the disordered Torite ranks and scattered the timeworn second sons.

The Mhedaals sent no reinforcements or supplies to aid their defeated army.

Lost in the fields and hills, many Torite soldiers starved to death or froze, more dying after the battle than during.

A Longer War

The Mhedaal family was overthrown by an alliance of professional guilds.

The new guild government forced one-sided trade arrangements onto the Draun and rebuilt garrisons throughout the southeastern farmlands.

After the Draun rioted and burned several garrisons to the ground, the guild government turned its eye to the fertile soil of the northern valley. The government encouraged Torite families to plant crops and settle in the north. The government shifted troops from the Draun to protect the Torite settlers. Sector by sector, the Torites claimed the rich northern fields. Year by year, the Myshenites surrendered their valued hunting grounds.

A full generation of Myshenite hunters withdrew without resistance. They were the same warriors who had defeated the army of the second sons, who had watched many Torite soldiers starve to death in the fall, freeze to death in the winter.

The children of these warriors, lacking their parents' regret, resisted the encroachment of the Torites. They trampled freshly planted fields. They burned crop silos on moonlight raids and destroyed vital farm equipment. The Torite soldiers, in turn, burned Myshenite camps and killed much of the northern game.

As the conflict escalated, the settlement frontier flurried with continual chase and skirmish. Myshenite raiding parties were captured in grain fields and executed by the sword. Torite units were lured from the settlements, encircled by riders, and killed by javelin and arrow.

The strategies of the Torite commanders varied over the years. One commander built a supporting network of camps and forts throughout the north and attempted to sweep the Myshenites into the west. Another commander attacked in winter's thaw when the Myshenite horses were slowed by mud and slush. Another targeted the Myshenite women. Most commanders, sensing the steady decline in Myshenite strength and numbers, simply protected the settlers' front and let hunger serve as their greatest weapon.

With a wall of Torites to the east and the midvalley fields barren of game, the Myshenites had little choice but to search for food in the west.

The hungry Myshenites found a small community of farms in the northwestern valley. They broke into the communal storehouse and gorged on meat and grain.

The Tyraen farmers came forward with shovels and sickles to stop the plundering.

Hardened by years of trespass, fire, hunger, and blood, the Myshenite warriors showed no mercy to the Tyraen farmers. The Myshenites struck down those with weapons raised. They struck down those who stood their ground. They struck down those who ran.

A few Tyraens escaped the slaughter to warn the other farming communities of the northern valley.

The Tyraen communities fled under Myshenite spear and arrow into the high northern hills.

The Tyraens ran until darkness blinded their steps. They collapsed along a riverbank, their blood black in the moonlight.

<u>Iava</u>

In the morning sun, a young man watched his mother's shoulder swell with infection. Iava carried his mother to the river and rinsed her wounds. He laid her beneath the trees and went in search of food. When Iava returned at dusk, he found his mother slumped against a boulder on a steep hillside, her empty eyes to the south.

Iava scavenged the hills throughout the days.

By night's embers he listened to the scribes and the poets.

His anger rose as the scribes recited the ancient verses of the wilderness and the wasteland.

> *With relish they tell of the mighty Ebrin flood, the spewing of the river, the trees ripped and boulders tossed. They stir the bones of the ancients until the people choke on dust.*

His neck bristled as new poets shared their work.

> *The loudest poets are those who did not lose mothers, fathers, sisters. The longest verses come from those who stood the furthest from the killing. They imagine loss. They imagine terror. They mourn and lament the Myshenite attack, but they secretly savor the tragedy. The pain of others has paved their way into the holy canon of Tyraen poetry.*

Iava joined with other Tyraens outside the poetry circles. He spoke with men who also distrusted the poet leaders and found their lyrics hollow. He spoke with families who had been disillusioned by the years of meager harvest in the northern valley, who dreamed of their old lives in the midvalley trade towns.

*We are not farmers. We are wagon-runners, scouts,
wheelwrights, freight lifters. We are Tyraens of the trade
era, not ancient Chaucau.*

Iava joined a group of families that journeyed to Cyecura,
his first home, the birthplace of his mother, father, sister.

Angheres

Angheres had lost his wife and child many years before the
attack of the Myshenites, his young wife by a coil of tumors
around her spine, his only daughter by drowning. The Myshenite
attack woke Angheres from a night of twenty years.

Angheres built the first fire on the riverbank. He built
shelters from fallen branches. He tended to the wounded. He
held the dying.

In the daylight, Angheres carried the dead from the river to
the hilltops. He burned the bodies on altars of stone.

At dusk, Angheres called Tyraens together for the sharing of
food and poetry.

As their scavenging thinned and their hunger deepened,
the Tyraens argued fiercely over heritage, home, and the path
to survival.

One group of families rejected the Chaucau tradition, left
the north, and journeyed to Cyecura.

Another group believed the north to be the future,
themselves the true Tyraen people. This group attempted to
reclaim their old farms and restore their old communities. They
were destroyed by the Myshenites.

The remaining core of Tyraens accepted both their ancient
tradition and the end of their communal farming lives in the

northern valley. They faced an uncertain future in the northern hills and mountains.

Angheres sensed a great weight and shadow upon the people. He felt the withering of grief.

Angheres collected the ashes from the hilltop altars.
He led the people into the Seden River.
Poetry flowed from the mouth of Angheres.
Ashes fell from the hands of the people.

In the ages before
the mountains' rise
and the moons' descent,
the Ebrin nursed the ancient Chaucau.
Age by age, the Ebrin tired of her children's suckling.
She drove them from her breast
into the wilderness.
But the mother's love remained.
She reached for the Chaucau
with cooling mists and cleansing rains.
She tore herself to race alongside them in streams.
She poured herself into lakes at their feet.

The Danve carried
the children of Aton
and the Alcyan young
nearly to the sea.
At Valthan,
her patience ended.
She swallowed the young.
She spit ashore the children of Aton.
Though cursed by Atonyi,
the Danve called out to her sisters of the valley.
The four rivers rushed to Cyecura.

They plunged into rock.
They bled into a thousand streams
that Atonyi's children,
the Tyraens,
might thrive in the land.

The Seden ended our desperate flight.
She washed away our blood and tears.
She held us in the darkness.
She lifted us into new light.
The Seden will carry our dead away,
someday to return.
She will guide the living to her source.

The Tyraens climbed the Seden River.

Throughout the summer, they traveled upriver into the high hills.

In the fall, they entered the mountains. Nights of frost and days of rain embittered the people against Angheres. They questioned Angheres' quest for the source of the Seden.

Taldon, the killer of three Myshenites on the day of raid and slaughter, led most Tyraens east on a journey for Mount Arran.

Only a small fraction of the Tyraens followed Angheres all the way to the mountain streams, falls, and snowbanks that fed the Seden.

In the heart of winter, these followers of Angheres were trapped against the mountain by snowstorms.

The followers burrowed into clefts and caves.

In spring's thaw, only Lycis, the wild poetess, emerged.

<u>Lycis</u>

In the cleft of the mountain, alone with Angheres, the poetess told stories.

She told of her childhood in a midvalley trade town, of her blacksmith father and stablehand mother.

She told of the nightmarish vision that sent her from her home.

The jackals rose from deep-shadowed ravines. The jackals gathered on the hillside. They were rotting. Blood-pink flesh shriveled from the flank. Thick-muscled haunches decayed into bare, wet bone. Eyes dissolved into skulls. They were healing. White-curved fingers of ribs thickened with flesh then hide. Ears, paws, and snout returned. In constant tear between death and life, the jackals looked down on the people of the valley with envy and contempt.

Lycis fled from the midvalley.

She wandered the fields of the north. She slept by day and ran by night, her path guided by the cries of falcons in the darkness.

Lycis found the Tyraens of the northern valley.

She lived with a cluster of corn and gourd farmers for a few seasons. The farmers cut her tangles of hair and shaved her head. Lycis washed their clothes in the stream to earn bowls of sour cornpaste. She joined them only to listen to the poetry of the wilderness and the wasteland.

Again, she was shaken by a vision.

One night, exhausted from labor, she stared into the stream as the sun fell. The rush of the stream quieted. The waves flattened. The current stilled.

Dark waters climbed in the channel of the stream. A great black pool flowed outward, swallowing crop and roof and branch.

The waters rose in mist to meet the sky. The night sky sank low, stretched tight and thin across the land. Contour faded, horizon dissolved. All became a formless black.

I saw the first darkness,
before time and color,
before cause and place.
I saw the light that spanned the edgeless abyss,
the dagger-tendrilled lightning that pierced the endless void,
its thousand spines broken in flight.
I saw the agony of fire that birthed the moons and the stars.
I saw cold Phera warmed by the sparks of life.

Lycis left the corn and gourd farmers.

She joined a new community of gardeners and farmers of rye. The young women of this community brought her fresh vegetables and boiled eggs. The old women wove her shirts and blankets. Lycis slept in their gardens beneath sunflower moons. She shared her visions as the sun fell.

From girl to woman, Lycis grew. She lived among the gardeners and farmers of rye until the day of the Myshenite attack.

The attack of the Myshenites seared the poetess as much as any of her visions. She remembered the tightening circle of riders around her community, their strange whistling of signals to one another, their sudden charge upon the storehouse. She remembered the strong young men of her community rushing forward only to be cut down. She remembered an old man mangled beneath the horses, a flap of his scalp dangling down, his broken jaw twisted toward his ear. She remembered a child pierced through the neck by an arrow, his desperate gagging, his panicked eyes everywhere pleading. She remembered a woman struck in the back with a javelin, lifted high off the ground, her feet still striding through the empty air.

Lycis fled into the northern hills.

She followed the other Tyraens, a blur of shadows, climbing, plunging, veering moon to moon.

She called out to the sky. *Help us. Save us.* She listened for the cries of falcons but heard nothing.

Lycis fell to her knees on the riverbank. The tears and curses of the people drowned out the lapping of the river.

Lycis closed her eyes. The sounds of the people faded away. Lycis felt the river swell to touch her knees. She shivered. She bowed her head. She prayed for the waters to work quickly, for the formless black to claim anew.

But a fire crackled.

The warmth of Angheres drew the Tyraens together.

The light of Angheres saved the people from hopelessness and despair.

Angheres healed.

Angheres sheltered.

Angheres loved.

The poetess wept against the neck of Angheres. She held his body, long still, in the cleft of the mountain.

Taldon Scarred

From the first morning on the river, the eyes of the Tyraens followed Taldon. They saw that he was himself unwounded. They watched him kneel at the water's edge and rinse the Myshenite blood from his blade. They listened to him tell of the three riders he had killed. They waited for his word, his action, his plan.

Taldon felt the eyes upon him. He wandered the hills alone during the day. At night he sat with his wife and sons far from the poets' fire.

Taldon listened to Iava in the shadows of the fire. He agreed to join the Tyraen families leaving for Cyecura.

On their day of departure, however, Taldon remained. "We left the valley for good reason," he said.

Many young and hungry Tyraens approached Taldon. They asked him to lead an attack against the Myshenites, to reclaim their farms and avenge their dead. Taldon agreed.

But when he saw the Myshenite camps around the storehouses, Taldon abandoned the attack. "We will lose," he said.

Taldon returned to his wife and sons on the river.

The eyes of the Tyraens again fell on the young killer, this time with contempt, not expectation.

Angheres rebuked the people at the nightly fire. "Taldon is our son and brother," he said. "He burns with the blood of our ancient father, Atonyi."

When Angheres climbed to the hilltop altars, Taldon followed. Taldon gathered ash with Angheres. Taldon waded into the river with the old poet. He received the poet's verse like a father's blessing.

As the Tyraens traveled upriver throughout the summer, Taldon ventured into the aerie crags to hunt mountain goats. He brought back many skins for Angheres and the elders. He brought back many flanks of meat for the people.

In the fall, when the hard rains and mountain frost shriveled the spirit of the people, Taldon defended the vision of Angheres. "We will find the source of the Seden," he said. "We will follow Angheres to the end."

Taldon fell silent after the death of his first son.

After the death of his second son, Taldon pleaded with Angheres to leave the mountains.

"The living climb," Angheres said. "The dead descend."

In the winter, Taldon left Angheres. He led the Tyraens down from the mountains. They traveled east for Mount Arran.

The snowstorm that trapped Angheres against the mountain also trapped the Tyraens in the hills. Taldon's last son and wife starved to death in a small cave. Taldon clawed through ice to escape their bodies.

The mystics of Mount Arran found Taldon beneath the mountain, staggering and limping, mumbling of bones and ice. The mystics washed Taldon in the underground springs. They held him down and cut off his frostbitten fingers, toes, and ear.

The mystics called together hermits, monists, apocalyptics - all the poets of Mount Arran. The mountain poets searched for the followers of Taldon. They fed, washed, and clothed all those who had survived the winter.

Union and Division

Throughout the spring, the Tyraens of the valley lived with the mountain poets in their caves around Arran.

The valley Tyraens joined with the mountain Tyraens in all of their daily rituals: the climbing of Arran, the milking and butchering of herds, the study of ancient lyric at dawn, the chanting of new verse in the night.

The valley Tyraens admired the intensity and vigor of the mountain poets, their devotion to ancient roots, their striving for new branch and flower.

The mountain Tyraens respected the hard journey of the valley Tyraens, their suffering in the Myshenite attack, their loss of land and home and blood.

The Tyraens bonded into one community.

In the heat of summer, Arran trembled and churned for several days then vented a chain of ash clouds to the east. The community of Tyraens came together at the base of the mountain. Poets climbed atop boulders and shouted over the steaming fissures.

A young mystic prophesied a crumbling of the mountains, a flattening of the hills, a desolation of life, a new Pheran wasteland.

Another mystic predicted a powerful eruption, an outpouring of stone rivers, coursing fire in the Pheran veins, a rebirth of the land.

Some poets cried out for a scattering of the Tyraen seed, a thousand journeys beyond the valley and mountains to all the people of Phera.

Other poets proclaimed that they would never leave Arran – their source and center, their guide and foundation, the keeper of the fallen.

Then Lycis, the wild poetess, spoke. "What have the mountains given us but death and pain?"

A handful of Tyraens left Arran alone to scatter the seed of the word.

A fraction remained on the mountain.

Most journeyed together into the eastern hills.

Generation of the Hills

The Tyraen flock traveled to the high lakes of the eastern hills.

The Tyraens camped on the shores of the lakes. They separated each dawn to fish and hunt. They came together each night for the fire's warmth and the poets' vision.

Many speakers predicted a new and prosperous age for the Tyraen people on the high lakes.

Many poets added to the water verses of Angheres, the violent rage of the ancient western rivers finally quieted in the vast, still lakes of the east.

Words of optimism ended in the fall, however, with the discovery of small rafting clans on islands throughout the lakes. The Tyraens watched the rafters from shore for several days, each night silent at the fire. When rafters crossed the lakes waving and calling out, the Tyraens pulled away.

Only Taldon met the rafters.

The Tyraens left the lakes. They wandered the eastern hills throughout the fall and winter. They drifted apart.

A flush of births came in the new year. Babies conceived in the dark hollows of Mount Arran were born in hillside gullies and bathed in icy streams. These children, the generation of the hills, would know much hunger and disease. They would wander by tent and by cave. They would be pressed against the eastern mountains by fuming Arran and the ever-expanding Torites. They would live in fear of the Myshenite rider, the mountain's fire, and the winter's deadly blanket of snow.

Taldon the Trader

For many days Taldon had remained underground. He had stared into the springs with empty eyes. Finger tracing the void of his ear, he had cursed the mystics of the mountain.

"Why did you save me?" he said. "Now I will see their faces in every shadow. I will hear their voices through every hour of the night."

The cries of newborn calves drew Taldon from the darkness. He left the underground springs and joined the mountain poets in their milking and butchering of herds. He spoke with other

Tyraens of the valley that had also lost children and lovers in the winter snowstorm.

Taldon climbed Arran each morning and gazed to the west, searching for sign of Angheres.

When a lone traveler appeared on the horizon in early summer, Taldon rushed down the mountain and over the hills. He slowed when he saw the face of a woman inside the tattered cloak.

Taldon gave meat and milk to Lycis.

"Does Angheres live?" he asked.

"He lives in me," she said, her hand across her belly.

After the trembling and venting of Arran, many of the people asked Taldon what path to take. "Does it matter?" he said.

Taldon laughed when the poets prophesied atop the boulders. He took the hand of Lycis as she spoke. He followed her into the eastern hills.

Lycis gave birth to her first child, the daughter of Angheres, on the shore of an eastern lake. She left Taldon after a vision of the lakebeds dry as dust.

Alone, Taldon befriended the rafters. He hunted birds and fished from shore. He traded with the rafters and other small tribes of the east.

On summer journeys Taldon acquired leather and fleece, jewelry and tools, servants and horses.

After winter storms he rode into the hills to aid Tyraens sick and hungry.

<u>Mother and Daughter</u>

Lycis carried her newborn from the lakes into the hills. She washed her daughter in the cold streams. She held her daughter in the skin of a goat, nursing, kissing, whispering the words of Angheres.

Lycis disappeared many times in the childhood of Anarel, sometimes for days, sometimes for seasons.

Anarel wandered. She explored the thin veins of the hills, the streams that flowed into rivers, the rivers that forked into streams. She caught eels and rats by hand. She wove reeds through her hair. She listened at Tyraen fires and slept in the crooks of trees.

In her tenth year, Anarel saw Taldon camp with her mother. She watched her mother's belly swell.

In her twelfth year, she saw Taldon return and take away his son.

Lycis clung to Anarel after losing her son. The two wandered the hills together. Daughter filled; mother greyed.

Anarel pleaded with her mother to leave the hills.

"There is no hunger on the lakes," Anarel said, "no grinding of bones."

The eyes of Lycis darkened.

"Then let us return to the valley," Anarel said.

"Because we are Tyraen, we will never live in the comfort of the lakes," Lycis said. "When we know who we are, we will leave these empty hills."

In the warm seasons, Anarel ventured alone to the edge of the hills. She saw the spread of the Torite farms horizon to horizon. She saw clashes between the Torite troops and Myshenite riders.

In the cold seasons, Anarel held her mother deep in the cave, listening, kissing. Lycis shared the poetry of the wilderness and the wasteland, the lyric of the butchering strider and the

Cyecuran orphan. She told of her visions in the valley, the Myshenite slaughter, the Seden journey. She told of Arran and the poets of the mountain.

When Lycis burned with fever, Anarel asked of her father, Angheres.

"Your father carried the people when they had no strength," Lycis said. "He lost his mind to disease. He froze to death against the mountain."

Lycis whispered the words of Angheres until the light left her eyes.

Father, Son, Sister

Taldon traveled among the small tribes of the eastern mountains. From the tribes he gathered many orphans and outcasts by deformity. His company cleared the mountain passes of beasts and thieves. Taldon brokered peaceful trade arrangements between the mountain tribes. Throughout the spring and summer, his company guarded an unending circuit of trade caravans.

As Taldon prospered he began winter journeys into the hills to give food, skins, and herbs to suffering Tyraens. He also sought wives and husbands for the people of his company.

Some Tyraens married into Taldon's company and left the eastern hills.

Some cursed and shunned Taldon, considering his new way of life a betrayal of Tyraen roots.

Taldon asked Lycis many times to leave the hills.

"Have the hills been any kinder than the mountains?" he said. "Ride with me."

"I trust the loneliness of the hills," Lycis said.

Taldon waited until his son had been weaned. He stole Delvven while his mother bathed in the river.

Delvven grew amid his father's company of scouts, guards, and pack riders. He learned how to ride and camp, how to pack and hunt, how to read the skies for weather and negotiate with tribes. Told that Lycis had died during his birth, Delvven asked few questions about his mother. He watched the Tyraens in camp repeat their poems by dawn and dusk. He heard their stories of the Myshenite attack, the first deadly winter, and the journey east from Mount Arran.

After stealing his son, Taldon ended his winter journeys into the eastern hills. He sent servants with gifts for Lycis, but none could find her. When Taldon's company became too large to travel the mountain passes, he began small trade runs to the Torite towns beneath the mountains. He made contacts in the Torite cities of Balthe and Tekenna. Taldon made plans to move his company from the mountains to the Torite east.

While Taldon maneuvered among the Torites, Delvven traveled among the Tyraens of the hills. Though first motivated by a desire to marry, Delvven discovered the older, deeper story of his people through his travels. He learned of the Chaucau flight through the wilderness, of the striders' march into the wasteland, of the rivalry between hard Aton and rebellious Atonyi. Delvven memorized the ancient verses. He freed his horse into the hills. He lived and walked among his people.

One spring night in the hills, a Tyraen woman stared at Delvven across the fire.

"Your father is a killer and a thief," the woman said. "You were stolen from your mother."

"My mother died the night of my birth," Delvven said.

"Taldon lied to you," the woman said. "Your mother, my mother, died from fever just three years ago."

Delvven and Anarel talked through the night.

Delvven stayed with his half-sister throughout the spring and summer.

When his father came in the fall, Delvven would not return to the mountains.

"You tore me from my mother once," he said. "You will not tear me from my sister."

Legacies

After the thaw of winter, Taldon led his company down from the mountains. His company encountered the surviving Myshenites as they crossed into the valley. Defeated and weary, the Myshenites begged safe passage to the mountains. Taldon watched them pass. Barefoot children. Women with faces of cracked stone. Men missing hands, arms, legs.

The company of Taldon built a market and trading center on the northern edge of Tekenna. Taldon negotiated trade agreements between the Tekennan iron guilds and the Torite farmers of the northern valley. By wagon, cart, and dray, his company transported tools to the farmers and crops to the city.

The Taldoneans, as they came to be called, were resented by many Torites. They were blamed for every shortage of food in Tekenna and any scarcity of steel in the north. There were fights with Tekennan miners. There were fires and disappearances.

Some Taldoneans argued for a return to the eastern mountains, some for a migration west.

Taldon withstood all pressure internal and external. He held his people together in Tekenna. He kept their work flourishing, their enemies frustrated. Still haunted, Taldon labored until the day of his death.

After a handful of years together, Anarel told Delvven, her brother, to leave the hills.

"You are a trader, not a poet," she said. "Leave the hills. Return to your father. Marry. Live."

"I am a Tyraen like you," Delvven said. "I will wait for my people to rise."

"The old branch smolders. The new branch flowers. Join the living, my brother."

Delvven left Anarel. He gathered all but a few of the Tyraens remaining in the hills. The party of Delvven traveled west along the Torite frontier. Once clear of Torite settlements, they cut south into the heart of the valley. They settled around the Sedde canals. They worked for the valley Tyraens in locks and mills. After the birth of his first child, Delvven traveled to Tekenna and made peace with his father.

Anarel wandered the hills, year by year, winter to winter. The bones of the old woman stiffened. The eyes of the old woman dimmed. Anarel withdrew to the grove where her mother, Lycis, had died. Young poets brought her scraps of fish and eel. The poets circled in the grove.

"I was challenged like Vhedor," Anarel said, "my mother's words, a spur, a blade. *When we know who we are, we will leave these empty hills.* I cannot say who we are, my people. And I will never leave these hills."

Anarel waited for fever.

She spoke of death. The trailing shadow inescapable. The ever-watching, ever-waiting stranger. The breath of winter.

She spoke of the wasteland, the striders who marched into light, who pulled death near, who whispered as the fire seared.

She spoke of Cyecura, the warm and generous land, the fields risen by sweat and seed.

She spoke of the Tyraen. The trader and the poet. The labor and the word. Blood and bone. Hands and eyes.

She spoke of her mother, who loved only once, who clung to the dead in the cleft of the mountain.

And she spoke of her brother. "He left behind all that he had known to learn the story of his people," she said. "He led his people in search of home."

V. SEDENEL

The Tyraens of the midvalley received and largely rejected the story of the northern Tyraens. Their children, however, proved fertile ground. This generation absorbed the legends of Taldon, the poetry of Angheres and Lycis, and the words of Anarel. The body was shared from Tekenna to Cyecura.

When the Varran and Torite populations exploded in the Bursting Age, the thin-numbered Tyraens leaned heavily upon the northern story for identity and pride. The attack of the Myshenites, the mountain journey, the wandering years, the sparing of the Myshenites, the return to the valley - these became the central narrative of Tyraen-told history.

Though unified by their history, the Tyraens faced intense pressure in the new era. The continent was ruled by Varran ideas and Torite machines. Western cities swelled outward from the university center, dense urban rings around the ancient blackstone towers. Eastern cities spilled downward from hilltops to lowlands, a patchwork sprawl of factories, warehouses, refineries, and barracks. Both cities of west and east swallowed up small pockets of Tyraen communities. Both demanded the flow of continual resources.

Like the old wagon-runners and wheelwrights, many Tyraens became drivers, loaders, and mechanics. Other Tyraens fought for position in the emerging trade-finance market as brokers, investors, and managers. Others linked the companies of the east and west serving as mediators, translators, and negotiators.

Despite their small numbers and the strain of their diverging classes, the Tyraens came to dominate the continental trade market.

Resentment of the Tyraens deepened in the east and west.

The flux and danger of these times, the economic grappling, the darkening shadows of race – these would shape the mind of young Sedenel, the artist.

My first memories glimmer like a faint line of torches around a shadowed mountainside. The memories are unconnected fragments, mismatched parts that form no whole, shards that cut to the touch. Memories of my father are like clay earthen and dusty, or metal worn black and dull. Memories of my mother are glass sunblue, cloudgrey, bloodred.

Sedenel remembered riding through Tekenna in the back of his father's truck, pressed shoulder to shoulder with all of his stepbrothers, the oldest bleeding from the nose, crimson specks flicking across the downwind faces, drops falling then whipping sideways, caught by the breeze.

He remembered his father's warehouse, the loud echoes of joke and instruction, the workboots pounding staccato, firma trembling under the four-axled trucks, the heave and cycling of legion motors.

He remembered his father, wrists black with grease, exhausted in the late afternoon, his back to the warehouse wall, his eyes wet slits, white smoke blasting through long and narrow nose.

168

Sedenel remembered the hilltop pyres, the stone altars high above Tekenna, the air cold and crystal in his throat, helping his mother, brushing ash from the foot of the altars, pulling charred bones from the altars' mouths, spreading sticks and kindling.

He remembered nights in the catacombs, the swaying shadows of the stone arches cast by torchlight, his mother copying old poems by candlelight in the inner chambers, soft rain falling in the moon chamber, his mother breathing the words of Anarel and Lycis.

Sedenel also remembered visits with his mother to Tyraen compounds throughout Tekenna. He remembered the deep-blue suits of the trade officers, the shining, black guns of the portal guards, the strange tongues of the translators at the video screens.

In all of his early memories Sedenel could not recall a single image of his mother and father together. He remembered summers with his father, winters with his mother. There was no fall or spring in his memory, no words of anger or affection between the estranged.

Heavy blows would bring the family of Sedenel together.

Acuuran, his mother, developed a degenerative and incurable disease that attacked the joints, arteries, and muscle tissues. She was hobbled by sudden swellings of her knees and ankles, weakened by the loss of circulation and muscle until everyday chores became nearly impossible. By the time young Sedenel had whiskered and stubbled, he had assumed all of his mother's duties as pyrekeeper.

His mother's deterioration in physical health paralleled his father's decline in career and industry.

Davel, his father, had started in business with a single hay truck and a small garage. Through ten years of labor, through sweat, maneuver, and connections both Torite and Tyraen, he had built one of the leading freight distribution companies in

Tekenna. Davel sought to grow even larger when the eastern continental shelf opened to trade. He joined with several partners, all Torite, to form a new corporation aimed at controlling distribution in the virgin eastern territories.

The new corporation was successful, but Davel's company was absorbed and fragmented during the merging process. Davel was also asked by his partners to sit out negotiation meetings with Torite government contractors because of rising anti-Tyraen sentiment. Davel left the corporation within its first year. He tried to pull every resource he had contributed to the merger, but he found his old company now deeply entangled in the wider corporate body. He emerged from the split with a small fraction of his original staff and equipment.

Angry and embittered, Davel waged a pricing war against his old Torite partners. Davel fought until he had lost every worker, truck, and warehouse. Divorced by his half-Torite second wife, abandoned by his mistress, Davel returned to the Tyraen community.

Davel worked as an assistant mechanic in a small garage next to a Tyraen trading center. He slept on a cot in the loft of the garage. He wrote letters to Acuuran, not knowing that she was ill.

The heart of Acuuran softened with each letter. She told Davel of her disease. Davel pleaded with her to leave the catacombs and promised to care for her.

Acuuran and Davel moved into the Tyraen compound together.

Sedenel stayed alone in the catacombs for one year. When Acuuran wrote commanding her son to leave the pyres, Sedenel joined his mother and father.

> *Time does not flow into the future; it releases*
> *rivers from the past within us. The ancestors walk on*

in each Tyraen chest, still haunted, still hungry for the
impossible joining of trader and poet, labor and word.

After moving into the Tyraen compound, the health of Acuuran improved significantly. She was visited often by Tyraen physicians and attended daily by Tyraen nurses. She received a broader diet of vegetables and meats, potent herbal mixtures, and medicines that eased circulation and reduced swelling. Her mobility returned. She worked in the gardens of the compound, planting, watering, pruning, weeding. With the sunshine of the courtyard, the sweet return to labor, and the hand of her first love, the woman bloomed.

Accuran taught in the library at night. She recited poetry for the children to copy by candlelight. She told of the Tyraen journey in the mountains and hills, the stories of Angheres, Lycis, and Anarel.

When the children left for their homes, Acuuran met with other teachers in the upper hall. The poets, scholars, and scribes discussed fiercely. Agreement was rare.

Acuuran clashed with young poets who were not afraid to criticize or amend classical Tyraen works.

She fought with chronist historians who built their narratives upon documents, journals, and letters, rather than trusting poem and lyric.

And she argued, perhaps most bitterly, with the Taldonean historians who downplayed the contributions of Lycis and Anarel, who traced Tyraen history primarily through the life events of Taldon, who cast the patriarch as great warrior, explorer, and tradesman, the living tower and foundation of his people.

Despite her frictions with other Tyraen teachers, Acuuran never questioned her decision to live in the compound.

Davel felt differently. He missed his days alone in the small garage outside the compound. He missed the little cot and single woolen blanket; the fused smells of oil, rubber, leather, and metal always in the air; the feel of tools in the hand, their heft, their solidness, their singularity of purpose. He missed the brave and simple hunger of the working man fighting for bread, the sweet, pouring hope of the man alone fighting for love and family. In his nights of aching regret over the past, Davel vowed to seek the pure and the simple all of his remaining days.

Inside the compound Davel savored the time with his reunited family and appreciated his second chance like a criminal reprieved. He tried to take care of Acuuran as he had promised. He cooked, cleaned, and washed for the family. He pressured the doctors and nurses for new remedies. Davel taught Sedenel the basics of engines and motors. He switched to mathematics when he realized that his son had little mechanical skill.

After the health of Acuuran improved, the Tyraens of the compound expected the newcomers to enter fully into the life of the community. Davel joined the crew of craftworkers that maintained all the homes and buildings outside of the trading center. The crew favored versatility over specialization and stretched Davel beyond mechanic work to a wide variety of projects: masonry, carpentry, plumbing, painting, electrical. Used to working alone and setting his own schedule, Davel struggled to match the crews' rhythms. During breaks he watched the activity of the trading center. At night, while Acuuran argued with teachers in the upper library, Davel listened to the traders in the center lounge.

The world of Tyraen trade intrigued Davel.

He studied the various subgroups within the system, the complex dynamics of the system in motion, the unspoken rules that governed.

There were the Data Gatherers whose job was to precisely quantify all material flow and supply levels throughout the continent.

There were the Intelligence Agents who were responsible for knowing the character of all non-Tyraen leaders and players in the trade market, who mapped the hierarchies of company, guild, government, bank, and university, who wrote personality profiles, tracked career histories, and predicted future trajectories.

There were the Integrals, the absorbers of the overflowing stream of information, the dealcrafters, who identified areas of need and demand across the continent, who formed and linked malleable networking strands, who adapted the structure of the deal and the terms of trade to ever-shifting market conditions.

There were the Trade Officers, the trilingual chameleons who interfaced with Varran and Torite corporate leaders, the cunning sellers and protean talkers, who tempted, manipulated, flattered, and pacified.

There were the Disruptors, who blocked and sabotaged trade agreements made outside the Tyraen trading center, who supplied misinformation, induced material shortages, and sowed distrust between Varran and Torite leaders.

Davel left the craftworkers and joined the traders. Invaluable for his extensive experience outside the trading center, he consulted for the various subgroups.

There is the suffering of the young.
And there is the suffering of the old.
The young are wounded by their dreams.
The old are tortured by unspoken words,
unfinished labor.

Before joining the Tyraens of the compound, Sedenel had long watched his mother deteriorate in the catacombs of the hill. He had seen the disease work its patient violence upon her body, eroding tissue, hollowing bone, shriveling vein. He had seen her eyes dim and void in the candle's glow.

When the letters of Davel lifted the spirit of Acuuran and returned the life to her eyes, Sedenel would not share in her joy.

"Where was he?" Sedenel said.

"Suffering in his own way," Acuuran said.

Father and son faced each other on the day Acuuran prepared to leave the hill.

"I will not join you," Sedenel said. "I have work here."

Acuuran argued with Sedenel and pressured her son to join his family.

"Let him stay," Davel said.

Sedenel lived alone inside the hill. He served as pyrekeeper, cutting wood, receiving corpses, burning bodies.

Sedenel drew.

One of his earliest works, *Destination*, was a sketch colored only with black, white, and brown. The viewer looks down into a pit where ashes and bones have been thrown. Bladed rays of moonlight pierce the dense shadows of the pit revealing a toothless jawbone, the tail of a rat hanging from the mouth of a skull, and a dusty mound of charred vertebrae.

Sedenel filled the sketchbook, *Faces, Lives*, with hundreds of drawings of the dead received at the hill. He drew many sketches of those who had died from sickness and disease. Most of the disease sketches showed the dead resting flat upon a glassy marble, the body wrapped in translucent cloth, the lethal agent still active, visible beneath the cloth – bluegreen tumors of the stomach and lung growing like fungus, failed organs leaking streams of black and yellow poison, burst blood vessels in the heart and brain flooding purple. Sedenel drew the young, imagining who they might have become; he drew the old, imagining who they might have been. In the drawing, *Rusted Tools*, an old man sleeps with hands gnarled and arthritic resting on his chest. In the corners of the page, the man in younger years works, digging trench with pick and shovel, grinding welds, nailing trusses, setting fenceposts. In the drawing, *Second Breath*, the body of a young girl battered in an accident lies stretched across the marble. Down the long glass slashes on her arms, a blue liquid flows, shining like mercury, dissolving the blood crusts, sealing the wounds. In the deep, swollen bruises of her face, the white trails of cooling, healing fingers can be seen. Between the fractured chasm of bone in her neck, a white-hot light burns, pulls, joins. Above the body of the young girl, an older woman is seen in two opposite, symmetric profiles. One profile gazes to the left into a towering range of snow-swept mountains, her eyes set to conquer. The other profile gazes right into a wind-torn sea, her eyes at peace despite a gathering storm. Below and left the body of the young girl, two hands are entwined, bound by the cords of marriage. Below and right, an old woman walks, blind by cataracts, led by a child's hand.

In *The River of Angheres*, Sedenel painted a skyblue and swiftly flowing river, its lines of current traced in lightning white. In the upper-left corner of the painting, furthest in perspective, bodies wrapped in white cloth sink, rigid and pale, into the river. Moving diagonally down and to the right, the currents strengthen; the white cloths dissolve; the limbs are freed. Moving further, the currents branch and multiply through the silver tangles of a woman's hair. In the lower-right corner, nearest in perspective, the skin of the dead flushes with life, arms stretch wide as if in flight, eyes open and shine with reflected fire.

And Sedenel wrote.

He gathered all of the poetry and legends of the Tyraen flight, read every account of the life of Taldon, then attempted his own version of the patriarch's story.

In Sedenel's story, Taldon faced the attack of the Myshenites fearlessly. By stealth and knife, he killed three of the Myshenite riders as they searched for the Tyraen storehouse. Taldon would have fought to the end had he not stood alone against the attackers, abandoned by other Tyraens.

Taldon grieved with his people on the bank of the Seden. When others pressured him to return to the midvalley, Taldon remained committed to the original mission of the northern communities – the search for a way of life true to the ancestors. He also refused to join the Tyraens who attempted to reclaim their farms and take revenge on the Myshenites. Taldon sensed the historic moment. He knew that there was no returning to their old lives. He knew that his people had been thrust into their own wilderness and wasteland. Taldon walked the hard path of the ancestors.

Taldon loved Angheres. Humbly, he yielded to the spirit and wisdom of the older pheran. Taldon left Angheres only after many had died in the mountains, only after he had lost two of his own sons. In turning from the hopeless Seden quest, Taldon saved the Tyraens from Angheres' madness.

The hellish winter cave took from Taldon his wife and last surviving child. Numb, raw, broken, Taldon walked on.

When mystics prophesied disaster at Mount Arran, Taldon remained steadfast and clear-headed.

When poets foretold a prosperous age on the high northern lakes, Taldon countered with warning. "The future is earned," he said, "not dreamt."

Taldon forged a new Cyecura in the eastern mountains, a company of orphans, outcasts, and criminals. Taldon's company cleared passes and secured safe trading routes throughout the eastern mountains. His company drew closed tribes from their isolation and fostered peace between conflicting clans. His company prospered and grew.

Throughout his success, Taldon remembered his first people. He braved winter snowstorms to take blankets, tents, and supplies to the Tyraens of the hills.

When the Taldoneans became too numerous for the narrow mountain passes, Taldon led them down from the mountains and into the valley. On their passage they encountered the defeated Myshenites. Taldon showed mercy to his enemies.

Taldon carved a place for his children among the hard Torites.

Though Taldon died in Tekenna, his children carried his ashes deep into the northern mountains and cast them into the highest falls of the Seden, the river of Angheres.

When Sedenel joined his parents in the Tyraen compound, he read them his story of Taldon.

"Heroes are for children," his mother said.

Sedenel hid his drawings.

In his first days at the compound, Sedenel worked with the labor and maintenance crews.

Davel watched his son struggle with simple tools, confuse instructions, and tire quickly. Davel apologized to the crews. He taught Sedenel mechanics in the garage, economics in the trading center, mathematics in the library. "You can write and draw at night," his father said, "but how will you earn in the day?"

Sedenel swept floors and washed windows around the compound during the day. At night he read and sketched alone in the corners of the library.

In the library, Sedenel befriended two other young seekers, the twins, Rhoa and Enteres, sister and brother.

Together the three planned escape from the Tyraen compound. They studied to enter the Academy of Engineering in Tekenna.

When Sedenel's parents learned of his plans, his mother fought with him. "You would leave your people, your family, to live among Torites?" she said. "You must continue writing."

Sedenel sneered.

"Let him go," his father said.

Enteres passed the entrance exam on his first attempt, Rhoa on her second, Sedenel on his fifth.

When memories of the Academy are dredged, I return to the classrooms with the instructors' tranquilizing drone, the bleary-eyed transcribing students; the laboratories of the noxious fumes and flesh-burning chemicals; the testing chambers that stressed, strained, and crushed the students' finest designs of bridge and building. I see the pages filled with strange symbols and cryptic equations. I struggle to swallow, to breathe. My throat tightens, dry with dust.

The mind of Sedenel was first set to light by poetry, by the otherworldly visions of Lycis, by the dense symbolism of Anarel. Sedenel learned to think by seeing. He learned to find metaphor in the natural world, meaning beneath the skin of reality. Through the eyes of Sedenel, the outer world entered. Through his hand, he cast his own vision back into the world.

Sedenel came to mathematics much later in life, after his mind had already been shaped by poetry and painting. Ingrained with an artist's perception, he translated mathematical concepts into images.

The number line of Sedenel was a staff of sky and ground, positive numbers a brightening blue rising from the midway zero, negative numbers a darkening brown in their descent, each number a nick in the staff, each group of ten a notch. Variables were concealing shells, each letter its own texture and color. Lines were the streaks of comets. Equations were scales wavering in the breeze. The shaded sides of inequalities were marked by flames rising or falling rain. Inverses were reflections across the frozen lake.

Sedenel enjoyed the highly visual study of geometry. He enjoyed coordinate geometry which fixed every point in space by the placement of a single origin. He enjoyed areas and volumes - the slicing of the sphere into circles, the cube into squares, the cone into ellipses and parabolas. He enjoyed the symmetry, balance, and uniformity of the geometric shapes.

And Sedenel excelled in trigonometry. He solved for the missing sides and angles in all types of triangles. He used identities to reduce complex sums and quotients into single terms. Sedenel liked the rolling waves of sine and cosine, the stretch of increasing amplitude and period, the simple shifts that could transform one wave onto another. He loved how shadows could fix the height of mountains, how the positions of stars could guide voyagers from pole to pole.

Approaching calculus, Sedenel lost his certainty and his clarity of vision. Subjects clouded.

He learned how to apply the rules of logarithms, but he could never explain why the rules worked or even what a logarithm was.

His mind, firmly planted in the x-y, struggled to re-orient in the polar and the parametric systems.

The harder he pushed to understand the concepts of asymptotes, imaginary numbers, and infinity, the further he was repelled.

Entering calculus, the clouds of Sedenel thickened.

He understood continuity as the tracing curve unbroken, but the idea of diverging limits left and right abraded his instinct.

He learned how to apply the rules of differentiation and integration, but the derivation of these rules mystified him.

Equally mystifying was the summation of infinitely thin slices to find the area beneath curves and to find volumes by rotation. (If the thickness of the slices approached zero, wouldn't the number of slices approach infinity, even in a bound region?) Again, the infinite bewildered.

Through persistence and the tutoring of the twins, Sedenel learned enough calculus to eventually pass the entrance exam to the Academy of Engineering.

Sedenel struggled at the Academy from the beginning. He struggled to digest the torrent of new concepts and information. He struggled to compete with the younger Torite students who had been trained in mathematics and science since they were children.

Sedenel survived his introductory courses in chemistry, physics, geology, and differentials.

He limped through his second-year studies in forces, structures, materials, and design.

He withdrew from the Academy early in his third year.

Before the end, I drained every well within me. The well of pride. The well of fear. The well of delusion. But the hawk will never slither, the serpent never soar. I was an artist. Enteres was born for science. To him every unanswered question was a challenge, a thrill, a torment. Enteres, the young scientist, believed that all problems had solutions. And he believed that he could find every one. Rhoa was both scientist and artist. And she was neither.

The decision of the three Tyraens to enter the Academy of Engineering in Tekenna had been a serious one. The three had alienated their families and the larger Tyraen community by leaving the compound. They had also made a serious commitment to Torite institutions. Students of the Academy were given education, housing, food, and books at no personal expense. In return, they were expected to serve the Academy for at least ten years after completion of their coursework. The Academy decided the location of this service and determined the role of the graduate, from technician to field engineer to research scientist, based on skill and ability. Students failing to complete their ten years of service could expect debt incursion, blacklisting from city government and regional guilds, and even prison sentences.

At the Academy, they quickly discovered that their mathematical and scientific gifts were not as extraordinary as they had imagined. Their preparatory studies, which had seemed grueling and extensive back in the compound, seemed lax and porous after a few classes in the Academy. "What did we expect?" Enteres said. "We had no teachers, no laboratories. We taught ourselves from a handful of books."

They also discovered that their story was not entirely unique. There were a few older Tyraens from other compounds in the city. There were the children of Draun farmers who had also taught themselves from a handful of books. There were Cerrans from the southeast who had studied for years to escape their isolated communities.

The Torite students of the Academy, already enjoying the advantage of greater numbers, superior preparatory schooling, and instruction in their first language, generally left the other races to themselves. In the occasional cold glance or conversation overheard, the deeper feelings of the Torites were sometimes revealed. The Cerrans and Draun were viewed with condescension, the Tyraens with suspicion.

In the classroom, Sedenel rushed to copy every step from the board, every word from the teacher's mouth, his attention waning into sketch long before the bell. Rhoa copied steadily, pausing to write her own questions in the margins. Enteres took few notes but asked the teachers many questions.

When they all scored low to failing on the first round of exams, they met together in the library. Sedenel and Rhoa spoke in somber tones. Enteres listened, eyes low. Sedenel questioned if they belonged at the Academy. Rhoa wondered where else they could go, what kind of work they might find.

Enteres left the library. He wandered the streets of Tekenna all through the night. In the morning, he returned to the Academy with sweet Cyecuran ryebread and salted Torite coffee. "We raise our intensity," he said. "And our efficiency. We wait for our time."

By the end of their first year, Rhoa and Sedenel had climbed from the deficient tier to the lower-middle, Enteres to the upper-middle.

They faced the Academic Council for their yearly review and renewal petition. Each of their interviews turned on the question of where they hoped to be in twenty years.

Sedenel brightened a stiff and floundering interview with a joke. "In a world without differentials," he said.

Rhoa won by honesty. She admitted that she had no idea what her future held. She admitted that she was uncertain about how far she could progress in the Academy and about what field she should pursue. "Whether walking or stumbling," she said, "I will never give up."

Enteres, worn by the prodding questions of the Council, jabbed back. "In Lycira," he said. "Or Balthe. Or a city of the west."

In her second year at the Academy, Rhoa plodded through her courses in statistics, materials, structures, and forces with little interest. In her design class, however, she found radiant inspiration. All the work of calculation, graph, and equation became worthwhile to Rhoa when the final product could be seen. She reveled in the canyon-spanning bridge, the mountainous dam that tamed river into reservoir, the great city tower that pounded the heart with pride and drew the eye like stars.

While Rhoa was inspired by the grand and the sweeping, Enteres became fascinated with the extremely small. He saw the microscopic grains of metal alloys etched by acid, their crystallites lustrous with silver, blue, and gold. He studied the long polymer chains of plastics stiffened by cross-linking bonds, the ceramic-matrix composites strengthened by cross-woven fibers. He chose to specialize in materials science.

Sedenel could find nothing in his classes to interest or inspire him. He studied with the twins during the day; at night he sketched alone in his room, often drawing Rhoa. The twins questioned his work habits early in the year and pressured him to try harder. By the end of the year, however, all three of them had accepted that Sedenel would not complete the engineering program at the Academy. "You still have a little time," Enteres said. "Gain as many technical skills as you can. The Academy will find a place for you."

After completing their second year, Rhoa was accepted into the advanced architecture program, Enteres into the materials science department, and Sedenel, on a probationary basis, into the civil engineering corps. They were given a twenty-day break from course and lab work, their first extended rest since starting at the Academy.

The twins saw their Torite mother for a day in the outer city then visited their father in the Tyraen compound. They returned to the Academy early to study and prepare.

Sedenel spent all of the break with his mother and father. From early conversations cautious and awkward, the family gradually opened up to one another. His father had risen in influence within the compound and ventured beyond. He was traveling often throughout the cities of the eastern valley, building a wider base of industrial contacts outside the Tyraen community, pushing against the old Tyraen strategies of division and disruption. His mother had discovered a small group of mystics still living near Mount Arran. She visited the mountain as often as her health allowed. She listened at their cavern fires, gathering centuries of poem and legend. When asked about the Academy, Sedenel said little. His father advised him to finish his studies and pay his debt quickly. His mother, again, urged him to return to his people, to draw, to write. "The first to the mountain lived by thorn and root, sun and rain," his mother said. "They begged the fire for vision. For a few living words."

Rhoa finished the architecture program at the Academy. She worked for the city government on small projects – offices, terminals, stations – until her obligation to the Academy was fulfilled. Creatively stifled by paperwork and budget constraints, frustrated by the eastern favoring of function over artistry, Rhoa left for the west.

Enteres finished the general materials program then took additional courses in corrosion, kinetic diffusion, and thermodynamics. He contributed to several research projects at the Academy, from work on semiconductors to biomaterials to the annealing of ferrous metals. His wide range of projects was due both to avid curiosity and recurrent difficulties working with colleagues and supervisors. Enteres left the Academy before completion of his service. He joined a young aviation-materials company in Lycira.

Sedenel made a final push to break from deficiency in his third year at the Academy. When this effort failed, he stopped studying. He skipped all of his classes and labs. At midsemester he was summoned to appear before the Academic Council. Sedenel packed his books and clothes, slipped a thick sheaf of sketches beneath Rhoa's door, and headed east.

I fled from the Academy like a prisoner freed. I fled from the technical, the numerical, the sterile. But not from the Torite. Many Torites had helped me in my

*second and third years at the Academy. Torite students
had given me notes and advice; Torite teachers had
given me extensions and guidance, mercies small and
great. I was intrigued by the Torites, by their dark and
deepset eyes, their stone-hewn faces, their long pauses
before speaking, their sudden bursts of action and
decision, their distance and their hardness. Ecculus
would teach me much about the Torites. I would come
to understand a little more than nothing.*

Sedenel labored for years in the mines of the east, the
ancient source of Torite pride, strength, and power. He worked
in mines of copper, gold, iron, and aluminum. He worked in the
open-pit mines of the hills ringed by giant steps of steel-bitten
terrace. He worked in the vast underground mines gnawed from
mountainsides with more passages and tunnels than the streets
of Tekenna.

In his early work in the east, Sedenel took many service jobs
outside of the mines. He swept and mopped the mine cafeterias.
He cleaned gear in the mining supply stores. He washed clothes
in the miner laundries. For these jobs Sedenel earned a few
coins a day, a nightly bed, and all the bread and stew that he
could eat. Like his father's mechanic days, Sedenel learned to
savor the simplicity and anonymity of the free worker's life, the
untightening of the mind in the flow of labor.

Sedenel saved his coins for sketchbooks and inks. He worked
alone at night while the other workers drank. Exhausted, he drew
and wrote on the same page, combining sketch and poem into
a single descriptive. He captured the open-pit mines throbbing
like infected wounds upon the soft-tissued hills, the tiny
workers stung by gusts of pebbled winds, excavators grinding,
trucks bellowing, the sloped conveyor lines shaking worthless
dust from precious ore. He fantasized about the underground

mines he had not yet seen. In the underworld of Sedenel, thick-shouldered Torites tossed boulders from the mouths of tunnels; in stalactite chambers, green waters dripped thick as venom onto the horns of lizards; long arcs of lamplight moons coursed the blackened tunnel void, dropping, rising, veering, illuminating crystal stars of speckled ore.

Drawn to the darkness by the deep-shadowed memory of catacomb nights, Sedenel left the menial service jobs and the open-pit mines of the surface to enter the world below. He worked as a sample runner in an underground copper mine for more than a year. He learned every turn of the copper mine, every passageway and tunnel, cavern and crevice. He learned in the depths that light was more precious than breath to the drowning. He saw the miners whisper silent prayers at each shift and tremor of the mountain. He saw shrines to crushed miners in abandoned forks of the tunnel.

An old miner warned Sedenel to leave the mine. "The mountain is now more hole than stone," the miner said. "The company will never stop digging."

"Will you leave, too?" Sedenel asked.

The old miner coughed then looked away. "My family will be cared for if I die," he said.

Sedenel left the copper mine. He slipped away at night, hiding on top of an outbound supply truck. With frostbitten ears and fingers, he jumped off the truck at its first stop, a government-owned aluminum mine near Balthe.

A guard stopped Sedenel as he wandered the mining complex at dawn.

"What crew?" the guard asked.

"Day," Sedenel said.

The guard, unsatisfied, pulled out his club and cuffs.

Before the guard could arrest Sedenel, a worker from a passing crew grabbed Sedenel by the sleeve. "You're late, fool," Ecculus said, handing Sedenel a sledge.

Inside the mine, the crew put Sedenel immediately to work, hauling lumber, toting equipment, lifting braces.

"You're a framer now," Ecculus said. His crooked smile revealed three missing teeth.

As they worked together, Sedenel thanked Ecculus many times and offered assurances. "I'm no stranger to mines," Sedenel said. "And I'm no criminal."

"Your story is your story," Ecculus said with a shrug.

Rumors spread among the twelve-man framing crew about their new Tyraen member. He was said to be many things from many places — a military scientist from Tekenna, an exile of Cyecura, a thief from Balthe, a killer from Lycira.

Sedenel let the mystery remain throughout his winter with the framing crew. By the spring, having shared sweat, blood, and darkness together, Sedenel spoke openly with the others. "I am from Tekenna," he said. "I failed out of the Academy of Engineering. I am a laborer. And an artist."

The Torite crew accepted the Tyraen.

In the early summer, the crew warned Sedenel that violence was soon coming to the mine. The miners had been betrayed by their managers and bullied by the government, they said. The miners were going to take the mine. They were going to cancel old debts and set new terms of labor.

This time Sedenel ignored warning and chose to stay.

The miners seized control at the evening shift change. They swarmed the guard station and the manager hall, capturing all suits and soldiers.

Five days passed without any work being done or any word from the outside. The miners carried the tables from the cafeteria onto the hilltop overlooking the mine. They drank, smoked, and laughed under the summer moons.

The army struck at the sixth dawn.

Helicopters slashed through the mining complex, stirring and scattering the miners.

A line of trucks and jeeps pressed forward, driving the miners into the hillside.

The helicopters landed.

The line of trucks and jeeps halted.

An army general stomped to the mine entrance. He stared at the miners, shook his head, and spit. "If ore doesn't start flowing out of this mine," he shouted, "I start shooting people."

The miners met inside the first chamber. After long argument they sent their hostages deeper into the mine, posted watch at the mine entrance, and returned to work.

When the sun fell that night, the miners pushed a short line of ore-filled railcars out of the mine. They chose Ecculus and Sedenel to meet with the army general.

"Send out the managers," the general said slowly. "Then send out the soldiers. Then start your evening shift."

Ecculus gave a thin smile. He nodded toward the line of railcars. "These might be all that you get," he said.

"Then we can bury you all tonight," the general said, glaring.

"And we can bury your boys and your bosses," Ecculus said.

The miners quarreled after hearing the report of Ecculus. Some miners argued that Ecculus had taken a line too rigid and that hostages should be given up immediately. Some miners defended the hard line and pushed for continued pressure on the general. The cautious miners won out. Several hostages were surrendered. Ecculus was replaced.

Sedenel followed Ecculus into the depths of the mine. They took a dusty fork off the main tunnel, slipped through a passageway three hands wide, then crawled on their bellies through a low, damp cavern. They emerged inside a broad chamber with a trickling stream of water and a faint breeze. They spread blankets above the stream, folded jackets into pillows, and turned off their headlamps.

"Will the army attack?" Sedenel asked.

"Eventually," Ecculus said.

"Why were we chosen to meet with the general?"

"I was chosen because of my father, you because of your face."

"My face?"

"You look like a child. And you're Tyraen. We thought that they might not shoot a Tyraen."

The miners drifted to sleep.

They woke in darkness, the silence pressing hard.

"Tell me stories," Ecculus said. "Tyraen stories."

Sedenel told his friend of Taldon - the young killer of Myshenites, the survivor of harshest winter, the hunter, the trader, the leader of orphans and outcasts. He told of Atonyi - the young rebel humbled by the river, the inked and branded slave, the freed settler of Cyecura. He told of the mountain mystics and the strider wasteland. He told of the Ebrin flood and the flight of the Chaucau.

"All Tyraens know these stories?" Ecculus asked.

"Fewer and fewer," Sedenel said. "Tyraens are now ruled by the business of trade."

"Your people are masters of trade."

"And your people rule the east by muscle and machine."

The men shared what little food they had. They drank from the stream.

"Tell me stories," Sedenel said. "Torite stories."

"Torites believe that life first came from the bleeding stone," Ecculus said. "This is our oldest story."

Ecculus filled the darkness with an epic poem that he had received from his mother as a child. He drew the poem from the deepest waters of his memory, sometimes pulling word by word, sometimes pouring out whole stanzas in a single breath.

The sons of Fire ruled first over the land.
The sons burned the surface of the land to ash and dust.
The sons rushed over the land in gusts fiery and shrieking,
their flames clawing the darkness,
consuming all.

But the sons of Fire forgot
that they were carried by the Wind.
The Wind tired of the sons' rage.
The Wind tore the sons apart,
separating brother from brother,
casting each star deep into the sky
to burn alone.

And the Wind pulled the daughters of Rain from the three moons:
Silver,
Blue,
and
Green.

The daughters fell upon the land
in twisting, plunging droves,
torrent upon torrent,
rinsing pure.

"Can the Wind travel anywhere?" the daughters asked.

"I can," the Wind said.

"Then take us to the future," the daughters said.

V. SEDENEL

So, the Wind followed Time.
He watched for a single slip,
a step too slow, too fast,
the hesitation of a trailing shadow,
the impatience of a falling stone.
But Time never slipped,
not a moment forward,
not a moment backward.
Time always matched
the steady rhythm of the sun.

"Time can be tricked," the Wind said.

The Wind swept the daughters from the land.
The Wind pressed the rains into a cloud dense and dark.
The Wind drove the cloud high into the sky,
blanketing the light,
blocking the sun.

Having ever followed the steps of the sun,
Time stumbled
for an instant.

And
the Wind rushed into the future
with all his speed and strength.
For a flashing moment,
the barren land showed hills and mountains, trees and brush,
creatures that burrowed, creatures that flew,
the walking pherans.

So
the Daughters of Rain

fell hard upon the barren land for many ages,
summoning the future life.

But no life came forth from the ground.

"Perhaps the Wind was tricked," the Green Rain said. "Not Time."

"Perhaps we will die before life comes to the land," the Silver
Rain said.

But the Blue Rain,
oldest of the daughters,
passed through the soil of the ground.
She slid between the cracks of rocks,
slipped into the chambers of the deep.

The Blue Rain called out for Stone to awaken.

"I have never slept," Stone answered.

"Then sleep," she said. "Sleep and dream."
The Blue Rain dripped in the deep chambers,
slow echoes stilling the breath of Stone.
In a thousand weaving rivers,
she coursed
the age-sheared faces of Stone.
She caressed.

"Dream," the Blue Rain said. "Dream of your children."

Through the whispers of the waters,
Stone imagined the world above
with land and sky,

with sun and moons and stars.
Stone saw the life that would come from the land,
grasses and flowers,
stag and hawk and ram.
He saw the Torites of the hills,
his children.

Stone was filled with ache and longing.

"I must see my children," he said.

Stone stirred.

Blue rain fled from the depths.
She rose in mist and vapor to the sky.

Hopeful,
afraid,
she watched the trembling ground.

Stone girded his feet upon the land's foundation.
He climbed layer by layer upward,
casting boulders aside,
grinding rock into pebble,
burning,
shedding.
Stone reached for the surface,
head raised,
arms wide.

But the land resisted.
Its skin pulled tight.

The shoulders of Stone were held down,
forming hills.

The arms of Stone were driven outward,
forming mountains.

The mouth of Stone cried out in fire
at Arran.

Everywhere that Stone broke free
the Blue Rain poured.

Each wound of land bore life.

When hunger forced the men from their hidden chamber, they were quickly captured by army guards.

The guards recognized them as the first negotiators and raised their guns.

"Bloodrun," Ecculus said.

The soldiers lowered their pistols. They took Ecculus and Sedenel to the surface.

The miners squinted in the moonlight, their eyes weak from the days of darkness below ground. They were driven to the guard station and kicked to their knees in front of the general.

The sleepy eyes of the general brightened as he recognized the prisoners. He smiled and drew his pistol. "It's the bold negotiator and the silent Tyraen," the general said. "Burrowed deep, did you? Your friends gave up this morning."

Sedenel and Ecculus stared at the ground, not answering.

The general paced slow circles around his prisoners, studying, waiting.

His patience ended suddenly.

He took his gun by the barrel, clipped Sedenel behind the ear, and shoved him face-first onto the floor.

He wheeled around, struck Ecculus in the face, once, twice, a third time. The general switched his grip on the pistol, held the barrel to the temple of Ecculus.

"Bloodrun," Ecculus said through swelling lip.

The general scowled, disappointed. He lowered his pistol. "Take them to their cell," the general said.

Ecculus and Sedenel spent four days in the holding cell of the guard station. Their cell door was left open. Ecculus slept little, said little. He read many letters through narrowed eyes.

On the fifth day, Ecculus rose. "I will go to prison now," he said.

"Why?" Sedenel asked. "What does *bloodrun* mean?"

"When the father dies, the Torite son walks in his steps until he understands," Ecculus said. "My father spent half his life in mines, half in prison."

Ecculus called for the guards.

In his last year of wandering throughout the eastern hills, Sedenel experienced the crueler side of the mining world and saw the ugly face of Torite prejudice. He was beaten and robbed walking between mines. He was falsely accused of stealing, sabotaging equipment, and industrial spying. He witnessed another miner strike, this one with many wounded on both sides and several miners killed. After falling down a mine shaft and tearing tendons in his leg, he was cast aside by the mining company, abandoned like a crippled mule.

Hungry and weary, Sedenel left the mines for his family.

Before he could reach the compound, however, he was captured by an Academy debt-hunter and thrown into prison, a ten-year sentence passed.

Sedenel wrote and drew in his cell, darkened dreams and razor-clear visions freed onto page, his years of wandering captured and revealed.

In *Fighters*, an old miner pauses before entering the mouth of a wide cavern, his back turned to the viewer. The miner's right hand carries a helmet of gnawed grey plastic, many times dented and gashed. His left hand grips the handle of a pickaxe worn smooth by years of service, its wood grains stretched in parallel, black veins. The neck and back of the miner sag in a permanent, tired stoop. The bones of his shoulders poke sharply against coveralls deep-stained with mountain dust. The coverall arms have been cut at the elbows, exposing skeletal wrists, thick-palmed hands, and a bulb of forearm muscle still tight and dense. The head of the old miner turns, sunlight across cracked cheek, eyes closed, to draw a final breath of fresh and open air.

An old soldier emerges from the mouth of the cavern. The soldier presses a hand against the cavern wall for support. Legs battered by thousands of marches, he drags a metal-braced knee behind him. The other leg plants ahead, digging into the gravel, struggling for purchase, tilting dangerously inward. The soldier's club is held like a cane, ready to drop and brace at next misstep. The soldier's eyes look down in tired concentration. The soldier's nose plunges flat from the bridge then crooks left. Sunlight strikes the brow of the old soldier, sharply casting a jagged stream of scars from forehead to ear, the explosive signature of glass.

In *Superstition*, a miner's body lies beneath a pile of collapsed rock, an arm awkwardly splayed through the rubble, a leg twisted sideways, the head crushed by boulder. A group of miners has gathered in the tunnel. A friend, open-mouthed and stricken, places impotent hands on the pile of stone. A crew chief, pale and sweating, aims his lamplight high into the cavern voids, gestures for the rest of the miners to retreat down the tunnel. The miners miss the gesture of the crew chief. Their eyes are focused low on the streams of blood flowing from beneath the stone pile. They are cutting strips of cloth from their shirts. They are soaking up the blood with the strips. They are touching the red, dripping cloth to their necks and faces, tying the strips around their heads.

Sedenel drew many sketches of Ecculus, his Torite friend.

An older Ecculus is imagined in several drawings.

In *Prisoner*, Ecculus slumps against his cage, a white-fired rage in his eyes, a fist against the iron bars, a hand pushing the cell door closed. The legs of the prisoner dissolve into the shadows of the cage. The prisoner lies helpless on his back.

In *Miner*, two shifts of workers cross paths on a rain-wet, gravel hillside. The hand of Sedenel, the viewer, waves down the line of workers ascending. Ecculus, the last in line, does not see. His eyes, lightless and empty, stare only at the hard path rising.

In the *Climber* series, Ecculus is seen high on a steep mountain face, road and city far below. Breaking the ring of trees, Ecculus enters the final naked heights of rock and sky. His eyes widen, sharpen. His chest billows with long inhale. Flecks of frost shimmer in the mountain air - blue, silver, white - the high places trembling electric.

Other drawings came from memory.

Sedenel sketched Ecculus saving him from arrest on his first day at the mine, raising wooden beams upon his shoulders in the tunnels, grinning in negotiation with the hard general, sharing the oldest story of the Torites in the hidden cavern.

Sedenel clung to the thin and dwindling hope of finding his friend. He rushed to the fence at each arrival of new prisoners, scanning face to face with desperation. He begged information from every prisoner transferring in from other prisons. No one had heard of the aluminum-mine framer.

As his sentence crept on, the thoughts of Sedenel slowly turned from his friend to his father.

He realized that his own bloodrun was nearly finished.

The blade that I had long held against my father now worked against my own flesh. We had both rejected the closed Tyraen community and driven deeply into the wider Torite world. We had both been crushed and beaten. We had both failed the ones we loved. The Tyraen son now understands.

Sedenel wrote many letters to his father and mother from the Tekennan prison. His earlier letters from the years of wandering had been sporadic and brief, offering little more than assurance that he still lived. His prison letters, however, were open and raw. He asked forgiveness for the way he had left and for his long silence and disappearance. He told them in detail of his many jobs in the Torite mines. He told them about the strikes of the miners and the bloodrun of Ecculus, his friend. He admitted to hopelessness and despair. He confessed a longing to die.

"Send me drawings," his mother wrote. "Send me stories. Send every page your pen has touched."

Sedenel sent many writings and sketches to his mother, all that he had gathered in his years of mine and prison.

Acuuran, in turn, sent many scripts to her son, poetry of the Arran mystics and her own works.

"When will you visit?" Sedenel wrote.

"Soon," his mother promised.

But a year passed with only poems and letters.

When a visitor finally came to the prison, it was his father. "Your mother is sick," Davel said. "Very sick. She cannot leave the compound. She will soon die."

Davel used his connections in the city government and courts to arrange a hearing for his son.

At the hearing, Davel pushed for a settlement of five years' service to the Academy. The Academy representative accepted this offer, but the prison official refused. Davel argued fiercely with the prison official, attempting threat, counter, bluff, and plea.

Sedenel tired of the arguing. "I will serve the Academy seven years, one more than I owe," Sedenel said. "But I will see my mother first."

The court accepted the terms of Sedenel.

Mother and son met in the courtyard of the compound.

A soft rain fell as Sedenel pushed his mother's chair among the trees.

"I remember the catacombs," Sedenel said. "I remember your voice, so sharp, so strong. I remember light and dreams, the opening of worlds."

Acuuran smiled, her swollen hands shaking on the blanket. "You will climb to me," she said. "You will climb by pain and struggle, by moments and by years. I will hold your hand in the high places."

Acuuran kissed her son, pressed her final work into his hands.

The body is vessel.
The body is cage.
From our first breath
Death is at work within us,
the traveling poison,
withering skin,
crumbling bone.

Our only hope is to
fall into flame,
our spirit to rise,
our flesh to burn.

I cannot take my eyes from the fire.

The Academy trained Sedenel in advanced surveying then sold his remaining service to a utility company of the deep east.

Sedenel traveled from the central valley to the eastern shelf, from overgrown and ancient Tekenna to newborn Lytarr.

Sedenel worked for four years in the canyon country north of the burgeoning city. He surveyed for roads and electrical lines stretching out from the city into new settlement towns. He worked each day as long as there was light. He exhausted himself to forget.

Sedenel drew only a handful of sketches in his surveying years. He exchanged many letters, however, with his father and friends.

His father told him of an intensifying trade war throughout the continent. He told of a fledgling economic alliance between Varrans and Torites, the campaign of Torite industrial leaders to displace the Tyraen trading centers, and a rising fear within Tyraen communities. In his letters Davel often vented frustration with the Syllvar, the secretive council of Tyraen leaders. "The young leaders gather arms and spread paranoia," he wrote. "The old leaders believe that all problems can solved by the transfer of money. Neither understand the world beyond the compound walls."

Sedenel connected with the twins, Rhoa and Enteres, for the first time since leaving the Academy.

Enteres had left the Academy soon after a forced transfer from the materials research group into manufacturing. He had moved from Tekenna to Lycira to join an aviation-materials company. He had thrived in alloying and aerodynamics research for two years, but he had also fallen behind in his debt to the Academy. After arrest and a stay in a Tekennan jail, Enteres had agreed to a tripling of his debt in exchange for his freedom. He had moved to Balthe. He now taught mathematics and chemistry at the Balthean Academy. He also worked as an electrician, carpenter, and mechanic in Tyraen communities of the city. "The only great teacher is pain," he wrote. "The young Enteres piled mountains onto the shoulders of Enteres, the old."

Rhoa had avoided contention with the Academy. Through the aid of friendly council members and a house-painting side job, she had even paid off her debt to the Academy a few years early. Rhoa had left the eastern valley for legendary Cyecura. She had lived with cousins, worked as a blueprint proofer and coordinating assistant, and saved her money. "Join me in Cyecura," she wrote. "See the birth ground of our people."

In his fifth year at Lytarr, Sedenel was transferred from the northern canyon country to the southern agricultural fields. He surveyed land for the water canals and pipelines of a massive new irrigation system.

Sedenel did not finish the year. The new Torite irrigation system overran many small Cerran farming communities that had worked the southern fields for generations. The plotting of canal tracts through the homes of Cerran families, the carving up of another's land, allowed Sedenel no peace or rest.

He left by night for the birth ground of his people.

Cyecura contrasted sharply with the cities of the east. The eastern cities were dirty, smoky, industrial, watered by pipeline and artificial reservoir, fed through a vast arterial web of black-paved roadways. The air of Cyecura was clean and crisp, thick in spring with the pollen of crop and plant. Four natural rivers coursed into the city from the west, splitting into smaller and smaller streams as the water poured east to the valley. Towering trees lined the fields of rye, hay, and corn, shielding the rich soil from gusts of wind, obscuring the land-scar of roads. Flocks of birds filled the skies, stirred the streams and rivers. The Cyecurans tucked their farmhouses in tree thickets, their business clusters in the low-lying glens between hills. Cyecura was open, organic, vibrant with a thousand living shades of brown, green, and yellow.

Rhoa and Sedenel rented a small house together.

Rhoa painted homes during the day while Sedenel worked in the fields.

At night they explored Cyecura. They ate and drank with the people of the city.

The idyllic landscape of Cyecura belied deep-rooted rivalries among its people. Northern farmers continued a centuries-old fight over land and water with the herders of the south. The east prided themselves on being the first Cyecurans, their ancestors tracing back to the freed slaves of Aton. The west claimed an even older history, their ancestors tracing to the tribes of the four rivers and the Varrans of the mountains. Cyecurans of the inner city disparaged newcoming populations as mere appendage. Many subgroups of Cyecura without a hand in the soil – machinists, distributors, lumber workers - were excluded by the dominant farmers and pressed into isolated pockets.

Though divided by internal rivalries, Cyecurans came together quickly in defense against external threat, real or perceived. Attempts by the highland cities at political and economic union with Cyecura met with dogged resistance and inevitable defeat. Cultural and artistic tides emanating from western giant, Pocone, sank by the derision and caricature of Cyecuran landowners. Cyecurans saw themselves as the blood-pumping heart of the pheran continent, stronger in spine than the educated cities, purer than the industrial cities in river, field, and sky.

Rhoa and Sedenel hoped to receive warm greeting and familial acceptance from the Tyraens of the city. They were disappointed. The Tyraens of Cyecura knew little about the Tyraens of the central valley, even less about Tyraens of the east. Many had never heard of Taldon, Angheres, or Lycis. They denied their ancient blood ties to the Chaucau and the herders of the southwest, focusing their ancestry instead on the holy circle of first-settler matriarchs and patriarchs. Only the legends of Atonyi survived in the Cyecuran imagination.

Sedenel filled two sketchbooks with the birds, plants, crops, and trees of Cyecura.

In an untitled work, he painted the grain fields of Cyecura wide and rolling. A rain has fallen across the fields. Dampened heads of grain list groundward. Drops of rainwater slide down stems. The sky is opening, clouds scattered by gusting winds, misty blades of light shimmering down. A farmer's blurred torso rises from the grain near to the viewer. His head tilts back to catch the sun. His mouth hangs open like a nursing infant. He has no eyes or ears. Across the fields many other Cyecurans can be seen standing alone, also deaf and blind.

Rhoa and Sedenel left Cyecura for the oldest and largest city of the west, Pocone.

Rhoa loved Pocone from the first. The city would ever shine in her mind with all the brilliance she saw on first descent - the morning sun cresting the western mountains - the blackstone towers transforming yellow sunrays into auroral-misted white - the moon temples' spiral climb to the skies, their towers glistening silver, blue, and green - the university halls with oblique glass prisms atop layered pyramidal base, shimmering like mountains of perfect igneous crystal - the water canal rings separating the city into wide concentric zones, steady-flowing and sparkling, ferrying the bright-canopied worker barges, lined by lush garden and dense shrub. Her old dreams of design and architecture burned anew.

Rhoa served on the worker barges for over a year, cleaning, painting, repairing. She learned the language, flow, and geography of the city.

Rhoa began studies at the university, planning to quickly complete the advanced architecture program. Her plans changed, however, as she realized the vast chasm between eastern and western thought, between the Torite and the Varran mind. Rhoa transferred from advanced courses in architecture to introductory courses in history, art, culture, and science. She bridged west book by book.

Rhoa learned that the Varrans were first a refugee people, a forced mixing of ancient hill and river clans driven from the valley by Oselen raiders. These clans fled to the citadel crags of the western mountains after a great slaughter at the four rivers. They lived together in the mountains for three or four generations.

The Varrans named the stars. The Varrans discovered the cycles of the moons and their patterns of eclipse. The Varrans studied the rocks, minerals, and crystals of the deep mountains, imagining their formation in works of art. They walked glaciers. They explored the shallow caldera lakes and jagged lava tubes of spent volcanoes. They drained aquifer chambers by conduit and carved new networks of tunnels.

After the failed Oselen siege of Tekenna and the scattering of the riders, most of the Varrans came down from the mountains. A large Varran fragment journeyed north into the dense-wooded Cradle. The bulk of the Varran body drifted south and east, settling around the lakes of future Pocone and near deposits of gems, metals, and marble throughout the hills.

The temples rose in the early Varran settlements of lake and hill.

The Green Temple priestesses studied the varied flora of the central valley. They built great terraced gardens throughout the hills, aflame with color, lush with flower, grass, shrub, and tree. The gardens hid silent coves for meditation, sheltered rings of trees for meetings and celebrations. The botanist-priestesses crossbred plants for protection, their temples shielded by dense razorleaf shrubs and coiled tangles of caltrop vines.

The Blue Temple priests studied the flesh of all living creatures. The priests gathered animals in pens, cages, and pools outside their temples. They slaughtered and sectioned the animals in the lower levels of the temple. They examined the flesh in the upper levels, sketching, painting, sculpting models. The priests viewed the flesh in the light of fire, sun, and moons, hoping to see hidden layers of life. They believed in a perfect symmetry between the kingdoms of air and water, species of bird and fish mystically paired. They believed that all animal flesh decayed by a poison passed from mother to child in the moment of birth. They carved every female in search of the death seed.

The clerics of the Silver Temple hosted trade markets and harvest fairs in their courtyards. They developed standards of weights and measures, maintained records of land and genealogy, and settled civil disputes. They memorized codes of law and chronicles of the citadel years. Their oldest clerics, freed from ground duties, climbed the levels of the temple in a long process of renunciation. They accepted silence, isolation, hunger, and thirst. They sat in darkness for days before climbing to the final level, their first words upon seeing starlight considered sacred.

Temple affiliation divided the Varran towns of the lakes and hills.

Even under the threat of a Torite invasion, the temples failed to cooperate and raise tribute for the approaching eastern army.

The Hols, a large and wealthy family of quarry owners, saved the Varran people from Torite attack. The Hols traded their massive supply of marble for gems and livestock. They satisfied the Torite commanders with jewels, feasting, and promises of future payments. After the Torites returned to the eastern valley, the Hols claimed power in the west. They closed the markets of the Silver Temple and opened their own trading centers. They imprisoned every merchant dealing outside their centers and taxed every trade within.

The Hols reigned for three generations. They controlled mine and quarry, road and dock, academy and guild. They taxed their people heavily even after the collapse of the Torite empire. They drove the temples underground.

The Poconian kings, borrowing the methods of the Hols, secured their power base in the west and expanded east.

Pocon, first king, forced the farming tribes of the central valley into organized sectors with prescribed crops and production quotas. He poisoned and buried the wells of the deep south to force nomadic herders nearer to his capital. He conscripted a massive army from the sons of fishers, miners, and farmers, led by an officer corps of royal guards and engineers.

The sons of Pocon pushed into the eastern valley. They destroyed the mesa fortress of the Adow. They subjugated the cliff cities of the Atril.

The grandsons of Pocon routed the Lyciran army in the springtime and chased the scattered forces throughout the eastern hills into the fall. When the grandsons returned to the hills the following spring, expecting another easy victory, they were surprised and defeated by a combined force of Lycirans, Tekennans, and Draun.

The great-grandsons of Pocon faced a unified and vengeful Torite army. They were driven from the midvalley and pushed back all the way to their capital, Pocone.

The Torites, remembering the cruelty of the Oselen, ravaged the west, killing son and daughter, burning town and city.

Among contemporary Varran writers, Rhoa observed a curious range of perspectives on the age of kings.

Nostalgic writers emphasized the accomplishments of the kings and praised their organization and efficiency, their boldness and audacity. The kings were faulted only for reaching too far, dreaming too high. Nostalgic writers cast their kings against the vicious Oselen and the ancient Iron and Silver empires of the east, the Varran kings appearing as a lone countercurrent against relentless tides of outside attackers.

Temple and guild writers attempted an opposite effect by casting the Varran kings *among* the Oselen raiders and Torite generals. The Varran kings clawed to power by bleeding their own people. They spread fear and death across the valley. They perpetuated the cross-valley cycle of war and revenge, passing down to their children a legacy of blood, a land of rubble. Temple writers highlighted the kings' shameful beginnings: the Hols bowing to the Torite army, craving the power of the sword; Pocon ending the reign of the Hols in a night of thinly veiled assassination.

Academy writers shrank the Varran kings from monumental stature by contrasting them against the great creators of art and science in their time. Gau, engineer and sculptor, built the extensive canal and reservoir system that supplied Pocon's midvalley farming sectors. His refusal to design siege weaponry melted Pocon's military confidence and delayed the invasion of the east by a full generation. Atolys, scientist and mechanic, designed hundreds of watermills and windpumps throughout the western hills. In his late years, suffering from heart disease, he mapped the veins, valves, and arteries of the pheran circulation system. Opir, a mysterious underground artist claimed by every temple, coal-burned the eyes and bloodied the hands of the kings' statues throughout the capital. She imagined river wraiths - born in the white-glass night of mountain pools, cast down from highest falls, forced to join the river's moonlit flight from hill to valley, cursed to sleep by sunlight and waken, again, in mountain pool. She imagined the dark fields of heaven - wells of light overflowing, the silver fires stirred and thrown by lean-backed workers, the keepers of light long blinded.

However the kings be viewed, their reign ended abruptly and completely with the devastating vengeance of the Torite army.

The temples led the first wave of rebuilding. Before the Torite attack, the temple priests hid thousands of Pocone citizens in the underground tunnels of the capital. After the attack, the priests led the survivors above ground to bury their dead, salvage, clean, and build anew. Like the first Varran settlements, small communities formed around the temples. The temple communities lived in relative isolation for several generations. Their markets grew in size until new classes of merchants, traders, and temple officials emerged. The rising flow of trade required new roads and bridges, paid for by steep temple taxes, much of the money remaining within the temple walls.

The trade guilds led the rebuilding of the lake and hill towns. The guilds stirred resentment of the priests and moved the trading centers from the temple to the town square. The guilds reopened the old quarries and mines; built new mills, forges, granaries, and meeting halls. The guild alliance, originally financed solely by members' dues, later came to tax by bridge, dock, and gate every traveler and good.

The universities, first formed by breakaway engineering guilds, built many cities throughout the western hills and along the inner mountains. The university cities centered on the blackstone towers, symbols of the citadel years, and extended radially outward, often encircled by defensive water canals. The university governments traded with Cyecura and the Varrans of the forested Cradle. They laid heavy taxes upon the fishers of the lakes and the herders of the southwest. They played temple against guild and guild against temple.

When the Tyraens ignited cross-valley trade, regional governments formed in the west to regulate supply and strengthen the Varran negotiating position. These governments struggled to maintain the support of their constituent cities, often undermined by proudly independent universities. Hindered by poor communication and regional rivalries, they struggled to develop consistent economic strategy and coordinate maneuvers within the continental market. The regional governments were continually shifting in boundary and policy, shuffling in management.

Theories of a Varran national government were proffered only in academic circles, rarely, timidly.

Rhoa saw the Varrans as a torn people. The Varrans dreamed of the moons and stars. They longed to recapture the vitality and wonder of their citadel years. But to reach their dreams the Varrans had to work together. They had to form organized social structures, institutions inevitably sliding into corruption and wastefulness. The Varrans dreamed in starlight but walked in mud and shadow.

Torn yet striving, Rhoa thought - their works of architecture their highest achievement.

Primitive by comparison were the Tyraen compounds, edged by brick and timber walls, overlooked by dwarf towers.

Bestial were the Torite buildings, their frames exposed like skeletal ribs, their serrated rising diagonals bared like teeth.

Rhoa plunged into her advanced architecture courses.

She inspected two government towers under construction in Pocone, their twin crescents facing concave to concave, with black-green verticals tapering up, copper verticals tapering down.

She learned the synthesizing methods of obsidian glass and decorative lake coral, the design techniques of double-cladded skin and wind-cone ventilation.

She learned the Varran tricks of Light and Crystal - how the sharpest rays of sunlight could be blunted, absorbed, transmuted - how aural waves lifted blue to red from the grounds of university halls - how the moon temple orbs cast misty seas over the city.

She studied the capital tombs, the entryway spanned by a broad triangle of Poconian kings carved in marble relief, the kings climbing from the base vertices, last generation to first, Pocon towering in the center, bright fields of grain bending outward as if the king sent wind and light over the land.

She walked in the gardens of the Green Temple.

She saw the Wraith Pool sculpture, touched the bronzed hands rising out of the trembling waters.

She stood in the circles of trees where ancients had lifted their newborn into the sunlight and scattered their dead in ashes.

Rhoa kissed Sedenel in a prayer cove of the gardens. "Marry me," she said.

She wanted to marry for many reasons, none of them love. She had risen so quickly in the foreign city, from cleaner to student, from assistant to designer. She had earned an office in the glistening tower, a home overlooking the bright garden. A husband was the final piece. Rhoa had embraced everything Varran; everything Tyraen had been shed. I was her last tie to her people, her past. I was her shield against emptiness and guilt.

Sedenel shared Rhoa's early fascination with the great western city.

In his first year in Pocone, Sedenel drew thousands of sketches of the city canals, monuments, gardens, and towers. He worked the day barges with Rhoa, walked the streets at night, observing, absorbing.

In his second year in the city, Sedenel joined Rhoa at the university to study history, science, and art. He was intrigued by the Varran citadel years and the early temple artwork. He was inspired by the Varran fusing of science and mysticism, amazed that works of art could sometimes open the doors of scientific discovery, and dreaming precede learning.

Sedenel was forced to withdraw from the university before completing his first term. He had inherited a more aggressive form of the disease that had crippled and eventually killed his mother. His knees and elbows ballooned with hot fluid. His muscle tissue shriveled. His heart alternated between creeping and fluttering pace.

Rhoa argued with Sedenel to get medical help.

Sedenel resisted. "The die is already thrown," he said.

Rhoa waited. When Sedenel failed to rise from bed for three straight days, Rhoa brought a doctor to him. The doctor offered injections for the swelling, herbal supplements for tissue repair, and medication for steadying the rhythms of the heart. "More could be done in the hospital," the doctor said.

The health of Sedenel improved after the doctor's visit. He took the herbs regularly and the injections after any swelling of the joints. Sedenel refused the heart medication, however. After long argument, he confessed to Rhoa his true reason. "Between the creep and the flutter is a perfect moment," he said, "a stalling without breath or heartbeat, when numbness floods the body, when the skies pull and the ground falls away, when I hear my mother's whisper."

Sedenel wandered the streets.

He explored the outer rings of the city, neighborhoods far from the affluent university core.

He sketched the release of the water flues in the lower hills, the sunset gathering of dust-laden, sweat-soaked laborers, dipping their heads in the foamy torrent, rinsing hands and forearms, laughing, cursing, smiling.

He sketched the rare-sighted southwestern herding people, their grey-clouded eyes untrusting, their faces dark with ancient sun, moving through the streets on business errands in tight and cautious packs.

He sketched the bluepod addicts, hiding in storm drains and ravines, shaft razors behind their ears, cloth strips around their arms bled purple, young boys and girls already balding from the poison.

He sketched the tumored, the limbless, the palsied, lying on the crumbled steps of oldest temples.

In the prayer cove of the gardens, Sedenel showed Rhoa his drawings of the city. Rhoa told Sedenel of her vision for the design of her first tower. When Rhoa spoke of marriage, Sedenel looked away. "I will be dead in a year," he said.

Sedenel wandered the underground.

He explored the ancient tunnels outside the city, the chambers that had hidden the temple priests during the reign of the Hols, the catacombs that had saved thousands from the ravaging Torite army.

He met poor Varrans fleeing debt, criminals fleeing punishment.

He met painters, revolutionaries, poets.

He sketched by torch and candlelight in the underground depths.

Rhoa pressured Sedenel to complete his many unfinished canvases and show his work in university galleries.

Sedenel spent fewer and fewer nights in Rhoa's garden home. He wandered the underground and sketched.

Rhoa arranged a showing of his Cyecuran works, drawings of field and crop and tree. When interest sparked among Varran art professors, Rhoa added another set of work to the display: Sedenel's drawings from their academy days in Tekenna, hundreds of sketches of her face and form.

Sedenel heard of the showing and left Pocone.

He headed for the citadel crags of the western mountains. Jumping trucks, begging food, he reached the last town of the hills.

Sedenel walked to the crags.

He began the steep climb of the ancient Varrans.

Sedenel's heart stalled midclimb. This time no flutter came, only a faint and weakening creep. Sedenel crawled down from the mountain.

From the last hill town, he called his father.

*The compound I had fled in my youth, the people
I had rejected, received me with arms strong and wide.
The son of Acuuran was forgiven. The son of Davel was
welcomed, cared for, tended. What had I gained in all
my wandering? My eye was never satisfied. My spirit
found no rest.*

Davel brought his son back from the west.

The Tyraens of his compound comforted Sedenel but could offer no cure for his disease.

Sedenel passed in the night.

Davel gathered his son's writings, paintings, and sketches into a shrine beneath the hilltop pyres.

VI. RHOA

Rhoa had never trusted the Torite mother who had allowed her children to be taken away from her, the Tyraen father who had hesitated to touch, his hazel eyes turning from the dark eyes of his children.

In her childhood Rhoa had loved and trusted only Enteres, her brother, her twin. The twins had dreamed together in the unborn darkness, plunged together into the world of light and color. The two had shared first words, first steps, first books. They had clung together from Torite suburb to Tyraen compound. They had planned escape from the compound together, whispering in the night. Rhoa loved Enteres because they shared history, flesh, mind. She trusted her brother with the sureness of the ground that met and held her every step.

Sedenel entered her life with mystery and quaking.

She heard rumors throughout the compound of a strange boy who had lived alone in the caverns of the Tekennan hills, who had burned bodies on the hilltops in the ancient way. She watched the pale, thin boy sweep the compound halls during the day, his feet mechanically shuffling, his eyes dull and low, his arms little thicker than the handle of his broom, a blue-snaked vein down a fleshless bicep. During the day Sedenel walked the halls like a tired ghost. But at night he came alive. In a tomb-still library chamber, he devoured works of history, literature, and mythology; collections of photographs and paintings; ancient scripts of poetry. With animate eye and mind afire he pushed the books away to attack the empty page. His face transformed as he passed through each phase of drawing: breathless and wild-eyed in the early explosion of framing and casting, a tight-jawed grimace as the flesh filled, a resigned and weary scowl in the final detailing. The artist tore off sketch after sketch, never satisfied. He collapsed into sleep as if slain. In the pained struggling of Sedenel, Rhoa saw the ancient Tyraen flame still burning, from the wasteland striders to the northern wanderers. She pitied the lonely boy from the catacombs.

The twins befriended Sedenel.

The three studied, worked, and talked together into the deep hours of the night.

The twins shared their hope of attending the Academy of Engineering in Tekenna.

Sedenel shared many of his sketches and drawings.

"Join us at the Academy," Enteres said.

"I know little of mathematics," Sedenel said. "Even less of science."

Rhoa and Sedenel walked the streets of Tekenna in the early morning hours. She held his hand as they gazed across the waking city. "You will suffocate in the compound," she said.

The three prepared for the entrance examination.

Enteres led the way. He scouted and explored new subject areas; distilled whole textbook chapters to a few critical concepts; taught the others by metaphor, sample, and drill.

Rhoa absorbed her brother's teaching and tutored the always lagging Sedenel. She was often caught between her brother's drive for progress and Sedenel's resistance to scientific learning.

When Enteres fell asleep, Rhoa and Sedenel put away the science books to talk of life and art and dreams.

"The land and city could be so beautiful," Rhoa said.

"I will wound and heal my people," Sedenel said.

In the grinding first year at the Academy, Enteres pulled away from the others. Rhoa felt a sting of separation that she had never known before. She leaned on Sedenel for friendship and support.

Sedenel stared at Rhoa across the library table. When he could take no more academics, he sketched her face, her form, her eyes.

The twins found purpose and direction in their second year at the Academy, Enteres in materials science, Rhoa in architecture and design. The twins drew close once again.

Rhoa pushed Sedenel to study harder, to search patiently for his own scientific niche.

"I came here for you," Sedenel said.

In the third year, Rhoa found Sedenel alone in the hillside catacombs. He stood in a column of winter moonlight, heavy snowflakes drifting down, his hands upraised, jaw to the sky, white-iced rivers down the bare skin of his back.

When Sedenel left the Academy later in the year, Rhoa received the sheaf of drawings beneath her door like a casket. She mourned the loss of Sedenel. Turning from the sting of hope, she believed that she would never see her friend again.

Rhoa poured herself into her studies.

She climbed to the upper tier of her class, finished the architecture program a semester early, and earned a designer position within the city government.

She moved into the heart of Tekenna.

Enteres stayed on at the Academy.

After graduation he rented a room near to the campus. He spent his days in classrooms and libraries, his nights in workshops and laboratories.

Enteres sampled and explored many subsciences, but he failed to lay deeper roots or build lasting relationships in any specialty field of his own. He was impatient with less knowledgeable peers, defiant with supervisors assigning menial tasks, contemptuous of the politics of research funding.

Those he abraded eventually came together to force him out of the materials research group and into manufacturing. The ever-rolling production lines sapped the will and drained the spirit of the free-minded scientist.

Rhoa experienced her own frustrations working for the city government. City officials were continually cutting budgets, restructuring management levels, and changing design and safety requirements. Draft by draft, Rhoa's architectural plans were stripped of style, bleached of color, pared down to barest functionality. The final structures scarcely resembled her first design. Rhoa was forced to choose smaller and smaller projects to keep even modest control of her work.

Rhoa vented in poetry.

The institution feeds on the young.
It is a vast,
thousand-halled machine,
oiled by blood,
bloated with inertia,
grinding,
groaning,
sputtering on.

Enteres defied his banishment to manufacturing. He wrote to hundreds of research companies throughout the eastern valley. He traveled city to city meeting with company leaders.

Enteres received only two offers – one from an aviation-materials company in Lycira, another from an aluminum company in Tekenna.

"Stay in Tekenna," Rhoa said. "Live with me until your debt is paid."

"I hate this city," Enteres said. "The Academy can burn."

"They will come for you," Rhoa warned.

Enteres left his sister and moved to Lycira. He sent small payments to the Academy, hoping to delay the collectors.

Rhoa stayed on with the Tekennan city government. Feeling the old sting of separation, she again poured herself into her work. After meeting the demands of her city job, she assisted Academy professors with drafting and grading. She painted offices and apartments. She remodeled older homes. Rhoa plodded ahead day by day, her eyes on her steadily eroding mountain of debt.

Enteres found new life in his work at the aviation company in Lycira. Invigorated by the study of flight and aeronautics, he helped to optimize the wing and nose designs of light transport planes and to develop an improved nickel-based alloy for turbine blades. He worked for the first time with scientists from the great western universities, Varrans solid in theory and application, aggressive with imagination.

In his second year in Lycira, Enteres lapsed in his payments to the Tekennan Academy.

His old enemies at the Academy released the debt-hunters.

Enteres was captured, chained, and hauled by truck from Lycira to Tekenna.

Rhoa received a single-sentence letter from a Tekennan jail. *Save me from this pit.*

Rhoa waited several days.

When she visited the jail, she found her brother pale, bruised, and sickly thin. She remembered a young boy from the catacombs.

"Where were you?" her brother asked.

Rhoa cried. She pushed money across the table.

Her brother pushed the money back.

Enteres, weak and ill, agreed to a tripled debt in exchange for his freedom.

Turning from the sister and the company that had left him in the pit, Enteres moved to Balthe.

Rhoa plodded on, working hour to working hour.

On breaks, she wrote letters to her brother.

Before sleep, she looked at photographs of the western cities. She opened Sedenel's sheaf of drawings and stared at the girl she had been.

From the smoke, brick, and steel of dense Tekenna, Rhoa plunged into the open fields of Cyecura. She savored the bright Cyecuran sun, the pure sharp air, the wind-stirred fields of grain, the soft flowing waters of canal and stream.

Rhoa worked as an assistant to a designer of family homes and professional buildings.

She learned the basic templates of Cyecuran architecture:

- short cylindrical houses like tree trunks, their lower levels ventilated by continual breeze, rich with scent of woods and flower, their upper level above the tree line, sweeping vistas over the fields,
- crescent-shaped court and record buildings pressed into hillsides, bent around the stone contours and veins of the hills,
- squat hyperboloid towers for fuel, seed, and fertilizer,
- wheel-shaped machinery buildings with equipment hangars forming the radial spokes, service booths on the circumference, administration at the hub,
- underground helix-spired storage and distribution centers, wide-mouthed bays fanning outward at the surface.

The designer urged Rhoa to use the standard models as much as possible and warned her to expect little or no latitude from clients. "Nature is the ideal," the designer said. "The greatest architecture melts, blends, hides."

Rhoa attempted several home and building plans. Bending the classic Cyecuran models, she designed a home with ellipsoid base and wave-ridged balconies, an arched community center over a massive rock outcropping.

All of Rhoa's plans were rejected by the designer and her team. Rhoa slipped into the team's rear shadows. She took plot measurements, checked material calculations, and proofed the designs of others.

Enteres wrote from Balthe.

He reconciled with his sister.

He forgave her for the brief abandonment in Tekenna and accepted responsibility for his own mistakes. "The fall is sudden," he wrote. "The climb so slow."

Enteres told his sister about his mathematics and chemistry teaching at the Balthean Academy, his boredom with the introductory studies, his ache to return to the front lines of discovery.

He told her of the Tyraens in the city compound who had welcomed him as a stranger and had given him food and care and work. "Blood pulls strong," he wrote. "I will never forget the kindness of our people."

Exhausted by his teaching and compound labor, Enteres dreamed of joining his sister in the west. He dreamed of Varran laboratories and a life free of debt.

Sedenel returned suddenly to the twins' lives.

A stream of letters flowed into Balthe and Cyecura from distant Lytarr.

Sedenel told them of his surveying work on the far eastern shelf. He described his years in the Torite mines and in the Tekennan prison cell. He told of his mother's illness and death.

Rhoa answered every letter from Sedenel. She sent him books of western art, photographs of the Cyecuran landscape. She shared her best designs since the Academy days.

Though separated by half a continent, Rhoa and Sedenel became closer than they had ever been, easing each other's loneliness in a far and foreign place, animating roots to a long-receded past, stirring old dreams and fires.

Sedenel promised to join Rhoa as soon as his service to the Academy was complete.

Letter by letter, the two endured the separating time.

But the letters of Sedenel shortened and darkened after his transfer to the southern fields of Lytarr. The plotting of canals through Cerran farms withered his resolve. "I dread the first light of morning," he wrote. "With each family I displace, my bones ache and tremble, my stomach turns and bleeds."

Rhoa at first encouraged Sedenel to finish his term of service, fearing his return to prison.

Later, realizing the work's heavy toll, she sent money to Sedenel and urged him to abandon his service and flee Lytarr. "The west will welcome you," she wrote. "The east will forget."

Many days passed without word from Sedenel.

Rhoa waited, torn between rising hope and creeping fear.

Rhoa walked the canals on a chill fall morning. She trailed the slow, limping figure of an old man, sodden and tangled hair over his shoulders, a knotted column of beard bending at his chest, a laborer's dark-hided jacket. The man stopped on the canal bank, knelt, and pushed his hands beneath the surface. He washed his wrists, face, neck. He turned, green-fire eyes lit by the silver sun.

Rhoa smiled.

She ran to Sedenel.

By creek fire that night, Sedenel told Rhoa of his long journey west. He had traveled by road and by rail. He had ridden in the back of livestock trailers and open-bed trucks, slept against crates in uncovered freight cars, shivered in the rain and wind. He had walked long stretches of the journey.

"Why did you make the journey so hard?" Rhoa said. "I sent you money to travel well."

"I had to remember," Sedenel said.

Sedenel did little throughout the winter. He sat among the trees and drank black liquor tea. He scanned the books of Rhoa's library, smoking pipe after pipe. He sketched occasionally.

After the last winter snow, Rhoa threw out his pipe and liquor.

She shaved his head and beard in the bright spring sun.

"Time to live," she said.

Rhoa left her assistant job to paint farmhouses throughout eastern Cyecura.

She found Sedenel work in her cousins' fields, cutting weeds, moving pipes, throwing bales.

The two strengthened under sweat and sun.

Their minds hungered – Rhoa for the Varran west, Sedenel for Tyraen roots.

"Let us see where the four rivers break into a thousand streams," Sedenel said, "where the ancient Chaucau met the descendants of Atonyi."

Rhoa warned that a search for roots in Cyecura would ultimately disappoint. "Cyecura is a world unto itself," she said. "Every outward road turns back. Every inner path is rutted to the neck."

They followed the narrow canals and creeks of Cyecura westward then climbed the braided streams of the hills to the wide highland rivers. They saw the chain of midriver towers linked by steel cable, massive power turbines churning silently underwater, serpentine eddies swirling downriver. They watched the long cables sag as the fishing nets slid and filled. They saw giant hydraulic arms draw the nets from the upriver waters, pour the catch into the tanks of the tower decks, and clasp the empty nets to downriver cables. Sedenel tried to speak with the people of the western rivers but found their old Varran dialect incomprehensible. With narrowed eyes he walked the shore towns, the shadowed buildings and houses scarcely an arm's length apart, a slowly turning canopy of blue gulls over the fisheries and docks, the sun blocked by river mist and a smoke of scale and entrail.

Rhoa took Sedenel to the Bluffs of Atonyi, the legendary heights that had once revealed to the freed slaves of Aton the lush and pouring beauty of the Cyecuran floodplain. "A home to never leave," Sedenel said.

Rhoa showed Sedenel the dry and overgrazed herding lands of southern Cyecura. They saw the snow-sand bluffs and green-sage ravines fought over by the smaller clans of nomadic herders, the nomads' sharpened staves raised quickly in claim of a few clumps of grass or a finger of water, dusty carcasses of jackals lining the trickling streams. They saw the towns of the settled herders, strips of clay-brick houses stretched along the receding tails of dying rivers, the air of the towns thick with manure and fly and deafening bellow, animal flanks hung from poles between the houses, butchers' feet sinking in oil-red blood pools. Rhoa and Sedenel stopped beneath a hilltop burial site. Sedenel sketched the graves - small domes of pitch-stained ribs, animal and pheran. Old herders climbed to shout curses at the Tyraens. Young herders slung stones and chased them from the hill. "Father, why these people?" Sedenel said.

Rhoa and Sedenel wandered east, then north. They drank in the mill taverns with drivers, mechanics, and operators. They ate at the smoke pits and bread wagons of the landless farmhands. They joined the harvest bonfires of prominent Cyecuran families, skyward flames drawing guests from near and distant fields.

When asked of origins and race, most Cyecurans told of the Alcyan river people beyond the mountains and the first community of freed slaves led by Atonyi.

Many Cyecurans could trace their lineage back to the first settlers and describe in rich detail the fields, trees, and streams of their ancestors' first settlement. Many treasured the relics of ancestors, talismans clutched in times of sickness.

When asked of blood ties with the southern herders, the Cyecurans bristled.

When asked of Tyraen blood and heritage, they denied any bond.

"But the Tyraens were born in Cyecura," Sedenel said.

"The Tyraens were not the first to the land," the Cyecurans said. "They came late and left long ago."

Rhoa and Sedenel returned to their cottage.

Sedenel painted the rain-soaked grain fields of Cyecura, the eyeless and earless people.

"If the roots lay rotted," Sedenel said, "how long will the tree live?"

"There are many worlds beyond the Tyraen," Rhoa said. "Raise your eyes."

Rhoa prepared to leave Cyecura.

Sedenel delayed and resisted. He walked alone in the fields around their cottage. He sipped black tea and drew quick sketches of brush and weeds.

Backpack ready, Rhoa confronted Sedenel. "You will live, work, and die in Cyecura then?" she said.

Sedenel closed his sketchbook. He followed Rhoa in silence.

They left Cyecura in the predawn chill and darkness.

Their aircraft climbed to the soft, wind-shielded void beneath the shoulders of the western mountains. They flew southward as the first rays of sun burned away the mountainside haze and lit the knife-edged ridgelines.

Before light reached the inner valley, they veered east, away from the mountains.

As light touched land, Pocone spread wide before them.

Visions of the great western city swept over Rhoa in waves, a chain of vivid and searing images, each image drawn, held, and savored until the next achingly called.

The Silver Temples crowned the thin-forested western hills, their lower levels open and bright with courtyard markets, their upper levels windowless and dark-celled, their final level free to sky, shimmering by elevated ring of white crystals.

From palisade cliffs the Blue Temples overlooked the windswept southern lakes, rock-carved stairs leading from water's edge to temple wall. Long bracing timbers, notched like vertebrae, curved like spines, reached from the temple wall to the temple tower. Beneath the timber-spine circle lay shadowed pens and cages, shallow pools, giant stone sculptures of wing and fin. Ivythorn crept in green-black tangles up the timbers, wrapped the tower sides, disappeared in slitted blood drains. The sky-piercing towers seemed the horns of great underground beasts wresting free, their sides tight sinews of greystone spiraling upward, etched by patterns of feather and scale, separated by curling blue crystal.

The ancient Green Temples nestled against the steepest hillsides, their walls blanketed by thick moss and spiked vine, their gates shielded by dense ring of trees and web of interwoven branches. The newer Green Temples lined the canal rings of inner Pocone, their grounds bright with floral gardens and fine-sculpted shrubs, their towers clad in rust-black stone, shimmering with lines of green crystal, a veined network like the roots of some unseen cosmic tree. A single tower had no veined roots on its sides, instead topped by a massive crystal orb, a green and yellow sun. In the veering cracks and twisting voids of the crystal, Rhoa saw the stormy boil of the star.

Pocone glistened under the radiant glow of temple crystal.

From temple gardens, lush green rivers flowed across the city, streams of hedge and tree and fern.

Rhoa noticed that the Varrans hid their roads beneath twinned rows of the wide-maned lake trees, their communal living clusters beneath huddles of black-ribbed highland trees.

From the city's green sea rose mountainous buildings of university, guild, and government. The great buildings of Pocone revealed no skeletal framework, no supporting beams or vertical columns, no seams between levels. Their outer surface was not the gemstone crystal of the temples but the igneous crystal of the deep burning mountains - glassy black obsidian, silver-mirrored galena, iridescent quartz. The surface appeared fluid, gently shifting with wind and light, lakes of mercury amid the clouds.

Around the buildings stretched long coral sculptures, bloodred scoria bursting from the ground, jagged lava channels coursing through the air, skin of blistered ember.

Pocone lifted Rhoa beyond her body, beyond her world.

The lucent glow of crystal starlight.

The skyborn metal lakes.

The coral fire unleashed.

Rhoa felt herself a trespasser of sacred ground, a privileged witness to the mystery of creation.

As their aircraft descended, Rhoa watched Sedenel, his forehead pressed to the window, his eyes flickering bright with visions of the city, his fingers twitching against his thumb, gripping for brush or pen.

Sedenel turned from the window. He smiled at Rhoa with the eyes of a child.

And Rhoa loved Sedenel. And Rhoa loved Pocone.

When their aircraft landed, they walked together through the streets and gardens of the city. They walked beneath the great temples and towers they had seen from the sky.

After three days without sleep, they rented a traveler's room in the ferry station.

They slept and dreamed in each other's arms.

Rhoa and Sedenel found work on the city canals. They hauled boxes and stacked crates on freighting ships. They swept and cleaned the passenger ferries.

The Tyraens learned the language of the city from the cleaners and loaders they worked alongside. They slipped among the Varran passenger crowds to eavesdrop, study posture and gesture, observe dynamics.

Rhoa and Sedenel survived on short naps, scraps of food, and the adrenaline of discovery.

On their hours free from work, they explored Pocone.

They scouted the outer zones of the city then pressed deep into the university core.

Rhoa stood beneath the black crystal seas of the academic halls. "The mystery will be laid bare," she said.

Back in the traveler's room, in the weary and candle-blurred hours of the night, Sedenel sketched and painted.

Rhoa covered their walls with maps of Pocone. She marked the travels of each day. She tacked hundreds of notes and photographs.

Rhoa taped pictures of the three moons to their ceiling.

There were Varran astronomical maps labelling the many craters, mounts, valles, and dune seas of the moons.

And Varran artistic drawings,

A vast rock chasm falling sheer into shadowed abyss,

A silver-sanded moon tempest turned by white-arced lightning,

Fields of crumbling blue-tinged mineral flakes, boulders of prismatic green,

Mountain faces sheared by worming fissures, diagonal strata plunging underground.

In their second year in Pocone, Rhoa and Sedenel rented a small student pod and began introductory courses at the university.

From sunrise to noon each day they absorbed lectures in the academic halls.

They read in library towers and garden coves throughout the afternoon.

They talked at night in their darkened pod until exhaustion overcame them.

In their late hour talks, the two shared discoveries, formed ideas, asked questions, and, often, clashed.

In his narrative of Varran history, Sedenel drew sharp distinction between the citadel generations and all Varrans before and after.

The ancient hill and river clans of the western valley were simple fishers and hunters, limited in skill, lacking in curiosity and drive. The attacks of Oselen riders forced the insulated clans into the broader world. By common terror and flight, they were pressed together; by long journey to the mountains, the many scattered clans became a single unified tribe.

From the citadel heights the young Varrans gazed across the wide central valley. The camps of the murderous Oselen appeared as tiny fecal insect piles, the Oselen riders as burrowing fleas on the green-fur valley floor. The young Varrans turned their eyes to the mountains. To the stars.

The citadel generations lived in days of grace, safe from sword and arrow, free to explore highest mountain and deepest cave. The citadel Varrans plunged from aerie falls to misted pools, their blood and minds awakened by the breath-stealing chill of wind and water. The Varrans climbed the cruelest peaks of the western range, the frost-slain left to rest on high stone ledges, their cloaks staked to summit by prevailing climbers. The Varrans delved deep underground, exploring vast cavern systems, crawling lava channel and aquifer tube, wading subterranean stream. The Varrans gathered thousands of minerals and rocks, fascinated by the intense forces of pressure and heat, by chemical transformation and slow, grinding time. The Varrans discovered the blood-twin planets, the galaxy's emerald tail, the three moons' cycles of eclipse and occultation.

Sedenel viewed the citadel years as a brief yet brilliant flame in history's long night. The ages that followed would strive and labor but never fully recapture the purity, the intensity, and the thrill of the mountain years. The greatest accomplishments of Temple, Guild, and University would be but dim reflections of that first fire.

Many times Sedenel pulled discussions with Rhoa back to the unforced migration of the citadel Varrans down from the mountains. He traced all historical failings of the Varran people in later ages back to this decision. He dreamed of a great people who never left the mountains, who understood stars' burning and galaxies' turn, whose moonlit eyes saw clearly from creation's first light to time's end.

But Rhoa deemed the citadel years more stepping-stone than pinnacle.

She saw the Varrans of the mountains as lost refugees, rugged explorers, curious hunters. Their language was primitive, their understanding of the natural world more religion than science. They lived by tent and cave and built no lasting settlements. Their numbers thinned with each generation.

The greatest legacy of the citadel Varrans lay in their hunger to live, to see, to know.

The last citadel generation hungered as deeply as any that came before them. But this generation also understood that the mountains held no future for the Varran people. Their people could thrive only by returning to the wide and fertile central valley. Only in the City could their dreams live.

From the beginning, the Varrans were a torn people. They were pulled apart by their need to explore, stretched thin across the western range, their greatest seekers called to climb alone. Their fascination with the heavens drew mystics to long wandering, bore divisive cults fixated on Moon or Star or Sun.

In young Pocone, the temples strained to meet the needs of the growing settlements. The temples were expected to provide protective guard for the people, fair markets for trade, courts and laws, sanctuaries and libraries. Under these new and heavy burdens, the temples struggled to advance their own spiritual and intellectual pursuits - their explorations of the plant and animal worlds, the celestial realm, the kingdoms of the dead.

The Silver Temples accepted the people's call to organize and to govern. They fragmented internally to match the multifarious demands. Only their elderly and retired were freed to pursue the non-pragmatic.

The Blue Temples resisted civic burdens and the rising Silver influence. They were slowly driven from the hills to the lakes of Pocone. They studied the mysteries of the flesh, cracking the doors to biology, anatomy, and medicine, bearing the Symbic religion.

The Green Temples conceded the hilltops to the Silver towers but claimed the hillsides with tree, brush, and fern. They avoided civic duties except for the performing of ceremony rites and seasonal invocations.

The Varrans suffered long for the temples' failure to unify against the Torites.

Under the hard rule of the Hol family, many were enslaved, imprisoned, disappeared.

Under the line of Poconian kings, many were conscripted into the king's army and slaughtered in the east.

The Varrans felt the full wrath of the second Iron Empire. The hills of Pocone were scorched by fire, its buildings battered into dust, its wild grass soaked with the people's blood. Many drowned in the lakes, fleeing from the sword; many fell in the hills, cut down by cavalry.

The Varran remnant waited in the dark chambers of the underground. They heard distant cries. They coughed and choked in the smoky air. They waited for screams in the tunnels, the flash of fire, the glint of steel.

But the remnant survived.

They crawled forth from the rubble to build anew.

This was the defining moment in Varran history, Rhoa argued, the deep forging of the Varran spirit. The remnant had stood on the lightless brink of annihilation. They had hoped through the long and terrible night. They had seized life when surrounded by death.

From remnant's fragile seed the great city grew.

The moon temples fueled the early rebuilding from small colonies to trade-linked villages. The temples cleared roads, dug wells, built bridges and gates.

The trade and artisan guilds pulled the swelling villages together into organized towns. The guilds paved roads, opened mines and quarries, built forges, mills, and granaries.

The university governments raised the blackstone towers and prism-topped pyramids of the city core. The universities diverted lakes and dug the canal rings of the city. The universities regulated and taxed the barge-driven flow of trade throughout Pocone.

In their late-hour discussions, Sedenel often favored the temples and guilds over the universities.

"Are you still haunted by the Torite Academy?" Rhoa said. "Does the east still shape your mind?"

Rhoa recognized a greater complexity in the historical roles of Temple, Guild, and University. In their respective ages of dominance, each institution served as a powerful centralizing force among the Varran people. Each harnessed labor into great projects, improved trade and commerce, and widened the city's cultural and political reach.

The eventual excesses of the dominant were countered and foiled by rival institutions, the bloated and powerful cut down by sharper, leaner forces.

The Varrans feared kings.

The people accepted, often effected, the frequent and sudden toppling of leaders, the swallowing of movements.

Seeking peace and security, the Varrans churned and boiled the seas.

The students' late-night talks ended with the onset of Sedenel's disease.

Rhoa watched helplessly as Sedenel was crippled by the flared swelling of his joints and the slow shriveling of his tissue. Between her classes she brought food and books to his bed. She researched Varran medical treatments for his condition.

Sedenel shivered in the night. "This is what my mother carried," he said.

After her introductory courses had been completed and Sedenel's health had been improved by treatment, Rhoa pressed forward into the advanced architecture and design program at the university.

She excelled in the engineering courses, her technical foundation solid from her years at the Tekennan Academy.

She struggled, however, in her artistic design courses. On individual design projects, her work was graded poorly and criticized for being stiff and self-conscious. On teamed studio projects, the younger Varran students dismissed her creative input and limited her role to proofing and safety calculations. Less than fluent in the western tongue, Rhoa often failed to communicate her thoughts clearly and to keep pace with quick-turning arguments and discussions. She felt herself silenced, pushed into the shadows, just as happened in Cyecura.

Rhoa found little support from Sedenel. The sickly artist had withdrawn from all classes at the university to explore the dark corners of the city. He disappeared for days at a time. He returned to their pod sullen and haggard. He ate and slept, then left again.

Rhoa called Enteres, her brother.

"We have ever walked between worlds," Enteres said. "Find allies, sister. No one can stand alone."

In the second half of the program, Rhoa found a powerful ally, a precious friend.

Young Sedenel had entered the life of Rhoa like a trembling quake.

Cyadae came like a thunderous seastorm.

Cyadae was a visiting speaker at the university, an expert in the chemical synthesis of glass and crystal. She had the wide, flat nose of the coastal people, their dwarfish height, pale hair, scaled skin. Her gnarled fingers clenched and twisted as she spoke. Her eyes closed when she searched for words. As she built to each point, her voice groaned low like an ancient tree tested by gale. Reaching her point, her voice broke sharp and rich like timber cracking.

"When I was young," she said, "my mother sailed to the great islands of the world. Eskalla. Nyava. Andara. Troqual. But I was too soft of stomach for the oceans, too fragile of mind. While my mother wandered the seas, I stayed alone on the northern shore. Alone, I lived in the driftwood tower. I remember the waves' echo through the tower, a constant womblike throbbing. I remember the dense coastal clouds, blunting sunlight into dim shadow, blurring moonlight into haze. And I remember the night, the cold and black and endless night.

"I was saved from madness by a single box my mother left me.

"There were photographs in the box, hundreds of pictures from my mother's journeys. My young eyes soaked every picture of every detail. I saw the rust-skinned islanders, their sharp-bladed cheekbones, their neck-slit tattoos, their black and silver-flecked eyes. I saw the jagged blood reefs, islander bones swaying with the tide, caught in the red coral teeth. I saw Andaran warships bearing down on the scouts and fishers of the open sea, towering over the smaller vessels, a wall of black-green armor and spiked turrets blocking the sky. I saw the fork-tailed serpents of the deep, their green eyes glowing underwater, their patchwork sides a scaled illusion of smaller fish. I saw the acid falls of Troqual, the rocks beneath a tortured press of pore-eaten torsos and shriveling limbs. I saw the family tombs of the Nyavites carved into the steep mountainsides, their cavernous mouths narrow, white slits above the jungle, radiant marble arches etched blue and black with ancestral name and symbol. I saw the night weddings of the Eskallans, their still lakes set afire, flaring purple, gold, and red, a host of burning baskets gently drifting.

"The world of the far islands fascinated, terrified, thrilled me. Many days the islands carried me away in dreams. Many nights the islands seized me in nightmares. I might have given myself to the islands, poured all of my loneliness, hunger, and hope into the island world. But it was my mother's world. It was the world claimed by the woman who had left me.

"Beneath the photographs there were rough drawings from my mother's hand, sketches of my father, uncle, and brothers. The men built their first boat in the harbor. The men sailed the coastline, wind in their hair. The men gazed into the black, churning storm off the coast. I ached for the men. My father. My uncle. My brothers. I wailed against the storm that had taken them from me. But theirs, too, was another world, a place I had no part of.

"Beneath the drawings there was a collection of many sea maps, from ancient age to present day. These maps charted the greatest journeys of coastal sailors throughout our history and revealed the world as seen in each era. In the newest maps, the world was completely sectioned and gridded, its tides and currents charted, every island claimed, every ocean well-grooved with passageways. The ancient maps, in contrast, held shroud and mystery. The vast central valley was hidden behind a dense wall of mountains and trees. The cliffs and bays of the northern coast were drawn in accurate detail, but only a handful of small, rocky isles dotted the northern seas. The known world of the ancients was no more than a narrow shore of stone beneath a slender crescent of water. All else was the alluring unknown, a sweeping oceanic frontier without edge or limit, a place of danger, mist, and possibility.

"Looking at the maps, I felt the age-enduring strength of my people, our cursed drive. We were explorers, wanderers, seekers. The near and the familiar oppressed us. The distant called by night and by day. Looking at the maps, I understood my mother for the first time. I felt closer to her than ever. And a thousand seas apart.

"Beneath the photographs, beneath the drawings, beneath the maps, I found a treasury of books.

"The books of my childhood, the books of the north, had been collections of old coastal legends and sea lyrics. These rough books had been iron-punched and bound together by fishhooks bent into rings. Their covers had been cut from the sides of northern whales, the hides sliced thin and singed by fire, channeled with blue capillary veins as wide as fingers. The pages had been handwritten by harbor priests and village elders, green-black ink on bleached reed paper. Year by year, I had tired of the timeworn songs and stories. The legends of the coast seemed more and more the fantasies of old men, the lyrics a numb and sleepy chanting.

"But the books my mother left me were from a different realm. The Varran books were tucked inside smooth synthetic-leather sheaths, metallic-hued, with crystal symbols of moon, tree, and water impressed upon the hide. The covers of the books blazed with rich and vibrant color. I saw the silver-blue eyes of the Varran, their great city glowing blue, red, and green in the night, their gardens throbbing with the golden blossom of plant and flower. I saw the dark mountains that bore them hovering high above the white-stranded clouds. The pages of the books were a lightly grained parchment, pale yellow, with thin-ridged pores like the skin of some undiscovered race. Viewed from certain angles, under certain qualities of lights, silver-laced profiles of character and author emerged from the page. In most of the Varran books, only the pages of the right side contained the author's text, the left side blank for reader's notes.

"For days I studied the covers and illustrations of the books, imagining the secrets and wonders hidden from me in the text of the inland tongue. Again, I was torn by the near and the far, tortured by the distant beloved. But this time my mother bridged the painful distance. In a crimson sheath, I found a classic book of translation between the coastal and the inland languages. I would wear this book to tatters with many readings and continual reference. I found a binder full of handwritten notes by my mother: lists of common verbs and nouns, guidelines for grammar and tenses, samples of line translations. I would study these notes until the ink blurred illegible. And I found still greater gifts.

"My mother, in shrewd and loving wisdom, had written many notes in the margins of the pages, questions admitting her own ignorance, accepting her limits, tempting and daring me to surpass.

"My mother, woman of the coast, explorer of the seas, had studied for years to learn the language of a valley she would never travel to.

"My mother had stretched herself upon hard stone that her daughter might step softly.

"I read of the Varran obsession with flight, their historic passes over the Torite cities of the eastern valley, their triumphant circling of the Pheran coast and the far Andaran islands. I read of the ancient gliders in the deep mountains, their wooden bracers, twine bindings, and black tarpaulin wings, a small and cultic circle surviving to this day, still seen floating dark from aerie ledge to white snow basin.

"I read of the great engineer and artist, Gau, who irrigated Pocon's midvalley farm sectors but refused the king's demand for weaponry of war. I saw the body sculptures of his youth, delicate and graceful carvings of feminine beauty, the elegant curves of the woman shaped like the smooth, bending flow of water. I saw the landform sculptures of his maturity; his hands shattered by the king's hammer; his work achieved not by gentle fingers but by hard knuckles, elbow, palm, and fist; the canyons and valleys of his landscapes dug by bone; the hills and rivers worn into contour by the burning glide of his skin, his callouses working the land like wind and rain.

"I read of mysterious Opir - painter, sculptor, poet, insurgent - an underground artist with a body of work so dense and varied that many scholars considered it the work of three creative minds. Opir desecrated the king's statues with symbols of blood and blindness. She sculpted the river wraiths of the mountain pools, trapped eternal, cursed to follow the water's flight each rising moon. She gathered circles of crystals – amethyst, emerald, opal - upon the hillsides, giant teeth-like shards with tiny voids of frozen air, silver-webbed cracks writhing for surface.

"Opir glimpsed the mythic, the heavenly, the many worlds unseen.

"She wrote of the Four Suns, first mothers, who had looked down upon their cold unborn waiting in the depths of the lakes.

Three mothers plunged through sky and water
to breathe life into their children.

The children fed.

The three mothers hollowed,
faded from sun to moon.

The children raced from pool to sky.
They looked with pity on their spent-shell mothers,
Silver, Blue, and Green.

The children turned to the last sun shining,
the fourth mother who had never left her proudest height.

The children closed their eyes,
smiling,

under the golden,
the warm,
the bright.

"Whether three artists or one, Opir set my mind free in fluid dreaming.

"She opened my eyes to the dizzying heights of imagination and the unbounded range of possibility.

"She taught that the natural world can be seen and shaped by those with vision.

"I read of Atolys, scientist and mechanic, designer of many capstans, water pumps, and windmills. His work stretched from hill to valley, drawing farmers into community, empowering laborers. In his later years, fettered by illness, Atolys turned his ravenous mind to the exploration of the pheran body. He discovered and named each bone of the body, classified the organs by tissue and function, and mapped the major veins and arteries of the circulation system. Atolys found the anatomical world to surpass the mechanical in richness and complexity. He believed that the inorganic would succeed only by imitation of the organic.

"I read of Varran architecture, studied the ancient stonework temples, the great towers of the reconstruction era, the iron guild arenas, the glass-crystal university halls.

"I read of Varran chemistry, studied the cores mysteriously bound, the teardrop orbitals and the spherical energy rings, the electron flow that feeds all transformation.

"And in my studies an idea was born, a dream.

"I wanted to dissolve the separating line between the organic and the inorganic.

"I wanted to create a living glass, a breathing crystal skin for a new generation of Varran towers."

Rhoa thanked Cyadae after the lecture.

The two women talked through the night in the empty hall.

"Finish your coursework and projects quickly," Cyadae said. "Then work with me."

Rhoa surged with hope and confidence after her encounter with Cyadae.

She asked questions of her professors and challenged her opponents on the design teams. She earned an internship with the city government inspecting foundation ballasters. She completed her advanced courses and drafted designs of her own tower.

Rhoa wept when Cyadae offered her a new job and home.

"We were both called to the great city from afar," Cyadae said. "We both know well the suffering of the foreigner."

In a prayer cove of the gardens, Rhoa pleaded with Sedenel to show his artwork to the public, to take his medications consistently, to seize life, life with her.

"Your eyes look to the high city," Sedenel said, "to the shiny towers of the empty sky. My eyes are drawn to the low city, to the underground, to the true face of Pocone."

"Low city, high city," Rhoa said, "both are beautiful. Make the upper world see what you have seen."

In winter, Rhoa found Sedenel collapsed against her door, covered in snow, frostbitten in face and hands. She carried him inside. She stripped him and bathed him.

She watched him through the night, sweating, shivering, mumbling mystic verse.

Rhoa shed her robe.

"Live," she said, climbing on top of him. "Live, live, *live*."

VII. THE AVIET AND THE UNDERGROUND

Rhoa named her son, Dyraveen, combining the Varran words for Sea and Light.

She lay with her child in the nightly blue-green darkness of their bedroom, their sleepy eyes on the wide, oval skylight, the night sky fluid with moons' marine glow, brilliant by slew of white-torched stars. On bright days they walked in the radiant shadow of the Sun Orb, bathing in the honey-heat light, their skin opening, soaking, breathing, the smile of the child capturing mother. She held her child in deep garden prayer coves, telling him stories of his father. She walked with him through the tree circles, pressing his hand to the guardians' coarse ribs. Rhoa lifted Dyraveen onto her shoulders, high atop the pyramids of the university, the glory of Pocone spinning beneath them. "The world waits to be taken," she said. "The world waits for the fierce and the dreaming."

In the years between the child and the man, consumed by the monumental work of her first tower, Rhoa surrendered care of Dyraveen to his godmother, Cyadae, and to a host of personal tutors. Though absent from the daily life of her son, Rhoa guided the education of her son strictly and purposefully.

Dyraveen learned to speak, read, and write the dominant languages of the central valley – Varran, Torite, and Tyraen.

He studied the histories of the three great peoples – the Varran awakening in the western mountains, the fall of their kings, the rise of their city; the forging of the Torite in the deep mines of the eastern hills; the long Tyraen journey from flooding river to valley floor.

He studied the highest arts of the three peoples – Varran painting and architecture, Torite sculpture, Tyraen poetry.

"Language is the breath of the people," Rhoa said, "history their story, art their cry. The roots, the trunk, the branches."

Dyraveen studied mathematics. He learned the weight of numbers, the patterned flow of functions, the patient rules of statistics and probability.

He studied elemental and organic chemistry; biology from cell to system; the physics of energy and motion; the pherology of climate, core, and mantle.

"Mathematics is the faithful ground," Rhoa said, "each science a piercing tower to the sky."

Dyraveen failed his first entrance examination to the university.

He failed his second.

And his third.

"You are afraid to fail," Rhoa said. "You are afraid to disappoint."

Dyraveen shook his head. "My nerves are strong," he said.

"Then what?" Rhoa said. "Then why do you fail and fail and fail?"

Dyraveen looked away. "To my eyes," he said, "the university is prison."

Rhoa released the tutors. She gave her son a winter's break from his studies.

When Dyraveen returned in the spring, Rhoa arranged a series of internships throughout the city. She hoped to engage her son with active work of the hands rather than the dry and abstract learning of textbooks. She hoped to spark some deep-lain fire of genetic gift.

Dyraveen worked at a crystal and glass synthesizing plant. He cleaned condenser tanks, torch-hued panes, and edged by laser.

Dyraveen worked in a metallurgy laboratory. He fractured steel and aluminum alloys. He tested for sheer, creep, and corrosion.

Dyraveen worked on the construction of a latticed dome over a medical center. He surveyed for the positions of juncture plates. At dome's peak he secured the safety cords for the welders and gunners. From dome's base he climbed with packs of rod and bolt.

Dyraveen quit each job before completion.

After the third internship, his mother cancelled all remaining.

Dyraveen slept by day.

At night, he ran. He ran by tunnel from the university center to the edge of Pocone. He ran until the tunnel climbed onto the moonlit valley floor. He ran to the east until his legs and lungs could take no more. Defeated in flesh, he turned back for Pocone.

Rhoa watched her son sleep and sleep.

She watched him leave at night and return near dawn, his face sunken, his skin pale red, his eyes distant and lifeless.

"The high city was opened to you," she said, "*every* door. Now you will walk paths dark and lonely. Just as he did."

Cyadae held Rhoa when her blood and water poured. She pulled the child through, rinsed him clean, and rubbed his skin with salt in the coastal way. Cyadae stayed with mother and child through the night. She watched the mother slump back, exhausted near to death, eyes vacant, faint breath through an open mouth. She watched the child nursing with greedy desperation, pulling at hair and breast, draining the mother of life. "This is the way," Cyadae said.

In the early years of the child, Cyadae slowed and tired. She traveled less throughout the central valley, gave fewer talks at western universities and eastern academies, and published only a handful of technical essays. She released control of her synthesizing plants to younger managers, keeping only her personal laboratory. She lost connection with the innovative lead in her field.

Cyadae poured her diminishing energies into the career of Rhoa. She introduced Rhoa to a wide range of contacts throughout the city and secured funding for her early projects. She pushed and guided Rhoa's first tower design through the many layers of university screening. She gave her best assistants to Rhoa and recruited a strong team of industrial managers for the tower's construction.

When Rhoa had risen in stature and firmly established herself, Cyadae shifted her care and attention to the boy.

Cyadae cooked for Dyraveen, clothed him, and tended him in sickness.

She taught him to read, write, and speak the languages of the valley.

She led him through the city, libraries to gardens, exploring tunnels and canals.

She directed his tutoring.

With fascination and fear, Cyadae watched the shaping of Dyraveen's mind, the forming of his character.

Thin-framed and shorter than the boys his age, Dyraveen was knocked down on the sporting fields, thrown easily from the center of play. He remembered the boys that hit him, waited until they were distracted and exposed, then threw all his weight at their knees or ankles. Cyadae pulled Dyraveen from the sporting fields after a shattered nose.

On their walks through city gardens, Dyraveen paid little attention to girls his age. His eyes followed older students, young women of the university, tall Varrans with long, dark hair tied in bright cords of green and silver. He watched the women with awe and craving.

The worlds of gambling and gaming at the Titan Stone enthralled Dyraveen even more than the beautiful women of the gardens. He slipped inside the sunset huddles of poor laborers gambling their day's wages. He saw the faces of the losers struck pale and hollow, the winners' short-lived flush of confidence and overwhelming urge for higher stakes, both captured by the thrill and terror of the spinning die. Banned by his mother from the gambling pits, Dyraveen climbed to the lower coves of the mount where players gathered for games of strategy and mind. He learned the flat games quickly and dominated the circles of young and casual players within a season. Dyraveen climbed higher on the mount to challenge the advanced players and learn the more complex Varran games. He learned games with many dimensions and levels, vast and varied terrain, and pieces that evolved by experience and transformed in ability. The older players handed Dyraveen loss after loss in the upper coves, but the boy absorbed the strengths of his opponents; he expanded and adapted his strategies; he developed a small arsenal of defensive and aggressive tactics. With a handful of wins and a year's experience, Dyraveen ascended to the highest cove of the mount to play the most challenging of all Varran games – Aviet.

In the daylit hours, the Aviet cove lay quiet and empty, the game-space a still forest of tall iron needles rising from stone. As dusk settled in shadow, the spectators poured into the cove, the crowds soon filling the floor, many climbing high onto overlooking rocks. The crowds waited in silence as the night deepened. When the iron needles disappeared, melting into the darkness, the game began. The Aviet sphere came suddenly to life with streams of brilliant color. Shimmering gemstone pieces branched out from the six poles of the globe. Silica blue. Greenleaf jade. Red sunstone. Silvered diamond. Golden beryl. Rainbowed ammolite. In bright, tendrilled webs the players advanced into the core of the sphere. The gemstone networks twisted into white-arced collision, stronger lines deepening in root and surging ahead, the weaker severed and absorbed. From six to one the players fell, most by the cutting of their arteries and total absorption, a few by the rising of an enemy's star too near to their pole. The game ended with the Aviet sphere entirely filled by one color, a gemmed sun blazing in the cove, columns of scintillating light cast high over the city.

Aviet became an obsession for young Dyraveen.

Cyadae studied the game with her godson. With the help of old colleagues, she researched the game's principles of energy and movement, the many techniques of building and disruption. Cyadae cleared out her laboratory and built a large replica of the Aviet sphere. She played countless matches with Dyraveen in their afternoons together. At night they watched the masters of Aviet clash in the great sphere. They walked the tunnels home and talked of the games until the sun broke.

In their training sessions, Cyadae drilled Dyraveen on the fundamentals of the game. She held little back in their practice matches, trusting loss as greatest teacher, working to ingrain in the young mind the deep-lying principles of the Aviet world. "Each game piece is a kernel of star," she said. "Joined together, the pieces multiply in brightness and power but diminish in length of life. The piece moved too quickly will flare and burn out. The piece long separated will die in the void. Build your network strong and lean. Never branch without purpose. Once in the core, feed or perish."

Dyraveen listened to the instruction of Cyadae and absorbed the deep fundamentals of the Aviet.

In their match play, however, he resisted the conventional; he experimented with wild and unorthodox maneuvers, determined to find exceptions to the rule.

Told by Cyadae that a single trunk from the home pole was most efficient and secure, Dyraveen tried a dual-branched opening and a twisting, triple-stalked weave.

Told by Cyadae that attacks were best concentrated at a single point of weakness, Dyraveen struck along wide stretches with many slashing tentacles.

After repeated failures Dyraveen shifted his attention from the early stages of the game to the middle and closing rounds. Finding the intricate tactics of core-fighting too tedious and grinding, Dyraveen focused on the explosive and high-risk technique of star-rising. He studied the technique perfectly timed and executed by Aviet masters – the sudden break and scatter of deepest vein, the meteoric flight of sparks through enemy's defenses, the birth of star at sparks' regather, the enemy's pole engulfed by swelling light.

Star-rising, swift and elegant under the masters' hands, proved nearly impossible for Dyraveen to execute against Cyadae. His breaking veins were anticipated, their thrust blunted by defensive wedges and deflected wide of the pole. The sparks he gathered were often too few to light the star. The rare stars he ignited were too weak to consume the pole, collapsing quickly after momentary flash.

"Fundamentals first," Cyadae said. "You must dominate the core before you threaten the base of the enemy."

Dyraveen practiced his core-fighting in long sparring sessions with Cyadae. He learned to shift weight subtly within his networks, to feint and unbalance his opponent, to conceal strength and distract with movement. He imitated his godmother's style of aggressive defense – continual harassment of the enemy's building, sudden flooding attacks at arterial nodes, elusive branching and flowering when outnumbered followed by swift reform and counter.

With improved core-fighting Dyraveen saw new lanes of attack open deep in the enemy's third.

He forced Cyadae into wild and rapid-paced matches, winning one in three, losing from impatience and overextension.

Cyadae arranged a meeting with a veteran of the Aviet, the chemist and composer, Edden.

She showed Edden her laboratory overtaken by the Aviet replica.

She introduced her godson and urged Edden to accept him as an assistant and page.

Edden walked the needled forest of their Aviet. He touched up and down the thin metal rods, slipped gemstone pieces in and out of the shallow-cupped holders.

"He is young," Edden said. "Very young for the Aviet."

"He is quick of hand and sharp of mind," Cyadae said.

"Better than you?" Edden asked.

"He has beaten me," Cyadae said. "Many times."

Edden glanced at the boy and grinned. "He is too short to reach the high poles," he said.

"There are footstools, no?"

Edden left the speared forest, shaking his head. "I have many pages waiting for time in the sphere," he said. "Older pages. Experienced pages."

"I understand," Cyadae said. "His star will rise by the teaching of another."

The veteran frowned at Cyadae. He looked at the boy. "Why do you play?" he asked.

Dyraveen stood to face Edden, the boy's head lower than the man's chest. "The Aviet lights the world," he said. "Should

I chase balls around fields with the simian boys? Blind myself with library tomes? No, I was born for the great sphere."

Dyraveen served as second page to Edden for three full years. During this term of service, he was not allowed once inside the great sphere. He remained at the pole during all of Edden's matches, his only duty to distribute gemstones to the first pages between turns. He was permitted to listen without speaking at team discussions. He sometimes ran for food and drinks.

Cyadae feared that Dyraveen's lowly duties and lack of playing time might quench his fervor for the game. She saw the pain in his eyes when the first pages left him behind and entered the sphere. She watched him sitting alone in Edden's command chair long after match's end, the morning sun across his face as he replayed the game in his mind from beginning to end.

"Your time is soon coming," Cyadae said. "Remember the ache of watching."

In Dyraveen's fourth year of service to Edden, the master warmed to the student. Edden freed Dyraveen of his lesser duties and allowed him beside the commander's chair. He talked to Dyraveen during lulls in the game, offered instruction and insight, asked opinions, tested. He sent Dyraveen into the sphere on short missions. He listened to Dyraveen's reports back at the pole. In desperate moments of the game, he sent Dyraveen in full circuit of the Aviet, hoping for fresh perspective.

After a string of embarrassing defeats and early exits from the game, Edden gathered his team together in the noontime cove. The team sat in long silence on the ground of the empty Aviet. They watched the thin-bladed shadows of the rods tremble over their skin as they waited for Edden to speak.

"Why do we lose?" the master asked, finally.

The page of pole, the page of core, the page of star, and all the pages of branch answered. Each of them gave a technical response. Each suggested tactical changes in their region of the sphere.

Edden listened to each of the pages in turn, then looked to Dyraveen. "And what do you say?" he asked.

"The truth?" Dyraveen asked. Edden inhaled, nodded.

"You have lost your nerve," Dyraveen said. "You hesitate and waver. You hope only to survive into the later rounds."

"Are you ready to command?" Edden said. "To clash with the masters? To execute with a thousand eyes upon you?"

"You are my commander," Dyraveen said. "You are my teacher."

Edden withdrew from the Aviet for several weeks.

He retreated with Dyraveen to the laboratory of Cyadae.

The two sparred in the Aviet replica. They experimented with new formations.

Cyadae joined them for full matches. She fell in the middle rounds by swarm of Edden or Dyraveen's star. Student and teacher battled into the late rounds, their blows and wounds a frenzy of alternating color, the student collapsing in the rapidly shifting lights of the final turns.

"Why do I lose?" Dyraveen asked.

"You are planting in winter," Edden said, "burrowing in spring. The changing lights of the late game have a cycle that must be joined, a rhythm that must be entered. Each type of light holds unique opportunity, danger, and limitation. Each is its own season."

Edden served as Lightmaster in scrimmage between Dyraveen and Cyadae. By rings of electric torch, he demonstrated the many lights of the Aviet and their effect on each gemstone and pole.

Dyraveen watched the steady-flamed lights that halved strength and doubled movement, the throbbing flames that affected the reverse.

He studied the pale lights that cloaked and camouflaged,

The piercing lights that magnified weaknesses from pole to tip,

The lights of inversion that brightened void and darkened gem,

The white-lightning quakes that swallowed thin branches into black.

Dyraveen entered the rhythms of the Aviet.

He learned to anticipate each changing light; to weather the advantage of adversary; to plan long, bide patiently, and harvest in season.

When Cyadae could provide little challenge for Dyraveen, Edden returned to the pole. The teacher was many times overpowered by the student.

"Good, very good," Edden said. "But the six-poled match is very different from the dual."

Edden summoned his team of pages and released all but three. The remaining pages joined them for full matches at the replica.

Dyraveen struggled in the early six-player matches. His preferred technique of star-rising became even harder to execute in the crowded sphere, each attempt exposing himself to base attacks from multiple enemies. The three pages seized every opportunity to weaken Dyraveen, often combining forces, attacking in waves. Edden garnered strength while Dyraveen was occupied by defense, his network whittled into ribbons. Edden sprung from solid base to consume the weaker players one by one.

"Replace Cyadae with another page," Dyraveen said. "Then I could face five alone instead of only four."

"The same can happen in the great sphere," Edden said.

When Dyraveen vented his frustrations to Cyadae, his godmother offered no sympathy.

"All is mind and calculation to you," she said. "Of course the other pages resent you. You trod upon their backs to climb above them. And now you are shocked that they smile at your humbling."

"I cannot win against four," Dyraveen said.

"Then open your eyes to character, personality, emotion," she said. "Ask yourself what really motivates the players of the game."

Dyraveen thought carefully before answering. "Fear," he said. "Ego. Insecurity. Shame."

"Yes, shame," Cyadae said. "The first to leave the game is stung and shamed before all the others."

In the next three matches, Dyraveen built his networks dense and tight. He crept slowly from his base, letting Edden take the core. He waited patiently for the pages to move against him. When the first page came within striking distance, Dyraveen exploded. He slashed the outer branches of the page's network with tendrilled storm. He severed the inner limbs and split the trunk. Before help could arrive in force, Dyraveen had fully engulfed the base of the brazen page.

In consecutive matches each of the pages was crushed by Dyraveen in the early rounds.

Each learned to keep their distance.

The games opened up for Dyraveen. When the pages gave up trying to surround and finish him early, Dyraveen was able to build solid networks from base to core and survive into the middle rounds. Having learned the danger of alliance in the six-player Aviet, he experimented with a less aggressive style based on positioning. He avoided full engagement with opponents, instead using probe, bluff, and skirmish to drive the pages into Edden's territory. His networks thickened and spread while Edden's stunted branches struggled to enter the core. Dyraveen took out Cyadae early. He distracted Edden with feinting baseward stabs and eliminated the pages one by one. In the late rounds, he used each change of light to strengthen his advantage. He savored his victory by fully surrounding his opponent and watching the master writhe helpless.

"I understand now," Dyraveen said, exulting to his godmother. "I can control the herd."

"Control yourself," Cyadae said.

Rhoa met with Cyadae, concerned with her son's development, fearful of his obsession with the Aviet.

Cyadae answered the mother's questions bluntly.

"A dangerous thing has happened," Cyadae said. "Brilliant at the game, Dyraveen sees himself already the equal of great scientists and artists. He believes, with patience, he will rule them all."

"And in his tutoring and studies?" Rhoa asked.

"He does just enough to avoid punishment," Cyadae said. "When he can fly in the starry Aviet, why crawl in the library tomb?"

Rhoa went to the Titan Stone to see Edden's return to the great sphere, Dyraveen serving as lone page and co-commander.

She watched her son meet with Edden at their base. She saw him lead discussions of strategy with the master, hold his own in vigorous debate. She saw his eyes burn with focused intensity as he watched the moves of opposing players. She saw him slip through the needled forest with swiftness and agility, his hands a whirling flash of gemstone fire.

When red gems filled the great sphere and the night sky glowed crimson and gold, Rhoa rushed to her son.

"My warrior of light," Rhoa said, smiling and laughing.

"This is my world," Dyraveen said.

The next day Cyadae waited hours for Dyraveen, alone in the study. When afternoon turned to evening, she woke him in his room and summoned him to tutoring. Dyraveen scowled. He grabbed coat and bread and left for the Aviet.

Dyraveen returned home the next morning. He mumbled and cursed, his face livid with anger. "Alliances again," he said, "fucking alliances."

He looked to Cyadae, but the old woman ignored him.

In the afternoon, Dyraveen came early to his tutoring session. He listened closely to Cyadae's teaching and asked many questions. He worked quietly on his own.

"Enough pretending," Cyadae said. "You want me to explain your loss."

"Yes, second mother," Dyraveen said.

He described his match at the Aviet the previous night, his strategy, the moves of the other players, the shifts and turns of the game.

"Again, it was a humbling," Cyadae said. "You caught the veterans by surprise your first night back. The second night they showed your win a fluke."

"But it wasn't a fluke," Dyraveen said.

"It will be if you lose again."

Dyraveen grimaced. "Then we are back to the replica," he said, "four or five against one. And the masters of the great sphere cannot be intimidated, manipulated like the pages."

"Of course they can," Cyadae said. "The doubt you sowed in their minds on that first night will settle deep and last long."

"So they really fear me?"

"As much as you fear them."

"One on one, I can beat any player alive."

"Perhaps, but would you play in smaller coves?" Cyadae said. "Would you give up the spectacle and the thrill, the glory of the great sphere?"

"To stand in the winner's light is to feel the stars' first breath, to see the fires of creation," Dyraveen said. "And losing is dying."

In the sixteenth year of Dyraveen, the climb of the Titan Stone became too difficult and painful for Cyadae, her feet and knees embrittled. Cyadae moved into the home of Rhoa. She tutored Dyraveen each morning in preparation for his university testing. She sat with him on the deck on sunny afternoons and listened to his stories of the Aviet. She drank with Rhoa in the moonlight.

"If he fails his testing, I will take away his beloved game," Rhoa said.

"And he will hate you for long and bitter years," Cyadae said. "The Aviet has sparked his confidence and stirred his dreams. Let him have his season."

"It is a game," Rhoa said. "It is a hobby of great minds, a diversion, not their life's work."

"Give him his moment," Cyadae said. "He will not thrive in university."

"He will thrive when his distractions end."

In the seventeenth year of Dyraveen, Cyadae suffered cancer and a stroke.

Dyraveen quit the Aviet.

He pushed the chair of Cyadae through the sweetest gardens of Pocone.

When the end approached, Rhoa drove Cyadae to the northern coast.

She kissed her in the ocean breezes.

She held her when the long night fell.

The loss of Cyadae cast a deep and lingering shadow over the life of Dyraveen.

His academic studies stalled without the guidance of Cyadae. Missing the rough-timbered voice of his greatest teacher, Dyraveen battled and resisted the university tutors. He failed his entrance testing again and again.

During the winter's break his mother allowed him, Dyraveen returned to the Titan Stone. He walked the empty and snow-swept Aviet. He walked the needled forest bare of gemstones, the rods a lightless black save for blue-white specks of frost. Dyraveen retreated to the laboratory of Cyadae. Alone by the replica, he read many of the books and journals she had written throughout her long life. He learned of her younger years on the northern coast, her painful solitude, and the bright kindling of her dreams. He learned of her early days of poverty and struggle in Pocone, her wide-swathed education, her arduous climb into scientific circles. And he learned of her revolutionary advances in the field of crystal synthesis, many of her techniques still a mystery to rival manufacturers.

"And she left highest Pocone to teach an ignorant, spoiled boy," Dyraveen said.

"Not a boy," Rhoa said. "A son."

Dyraveen took work at the synthesizing plant designed and built by Cyadae in the years of her prime. Through his work at the plant he hoped to glimpse the scientific genius of Cyadae, to pay tribute to his teacher, to atone.

Because of his small size, Dyraveen was first put to work rappelling into slender flue pillars and crawling inside narrow condenser tanks. The work was hot and cramped, worsened by his heavy chemical suit. His goggles fogged from the damp heat. Sweat soaked his back, dripped from his gloves. He fought for air through his respirator mask, resisting panic.

After a few weeks of cleaning, Dyraveen welcomed a transfer from the maintenance division to finishing. He worked on a four-member crew that tempered, cut, and hued green-crystal temple panes. He was allowed only to lift and secure the panes during his first hundred days. When finally handed the torch, he melted his first pane and blackened his second. He gave up the torch by end of shift. Dyraveen also failed with the laser. His edging was careful and precise but too slow for the pacing of the team. He returned to lifting and securing after a few days' trial.

The finishing managers passed Dyraveen on to other divisions. He became a floater, a substitute, each day thrown into a different crew, each day forced to learn all rules anew.

Always bearing the disadvantage of the newcomer, Dyraveen survived by shadowing and blending, by avoiding dangerous and complex tasks, by working simple chores without rest or complaint.

Dyraveen became skilled at reading personalities. He learned to quickly assess the hierarchy and dynamics of a group. He learned to stay near to the powerful and the respected, to distance himself from grumblers and agitators.

Rhoa fought with her son to leave the plant. "Without roots you cannot learn," she said. "You blow around the plant like a leaf in the wind."

"I am learning all the time," Dyraveen said.

"You scrub tubes and mop floors. You hand tools to technicians."

"Still, I am learning."

"Learning what?"

"The mind of the worker. The pain of hard labor."

"Your days are burning by," Rhoa said. "You could still become a great scientist, a great artist. Not a servant."

Dyraveen would not leave the plant to please his mother. He stayed on into his second year.

By the second year, Dyraveen had walked every tunnel, bridge, and chamber of the plant. He had worked on every crew. Dyraveen tired of the heavy heat and noxious odors. He tired of the glaring management problems unresolved and the verbal abuse inevitably dumped upon the lowest worker. When his uncle, Enteres, called to offer an internship at a friend's laboratory, Dyraveen eagerly accepted.

The friend of Enteres gave Dyraveen freedom to roam and observe all stations at the metallurgy complex.

Dyraveen walked the lines of crucible and foundry. He saw the hellish furnaces glowing white and red, the molten metals pouring orange, space and light warped by the intense heat. The foundry's hot and suffocating air took Dyraveen back to the flues and tanks of the chemical plant. He walked the foundry lines once and never returned.

Dyraveen found the metallography lab quiet and still save for the droning spin of polishing wheels. Sleepy, young technicians held alloy samples to the wheels. They said nothing when questioned, their tired eyes locked in the wheel's endless turn.

He found a more animate crew in the destructive testing lab. The breaker techs gathered before each trial to share predictions and debate. They called out like arena fans as graph and data emerged. Early failures silenced and scattered the group; strong performances invigorated the team and sparked flurries of fresh activity. Dyraveen watched the breaker techs load the aluminum, steel, and titanium alloys until failure. He saw the alloys punctured by diamond, fractured by leaded club, exposed to acids, caustics, and steams.

The results of the destructive testing passed to the engineers and scientists of the microscope lab. With optical and electron scopes, they explored the alloy microstructures, seeking to explain performance through features of grain, boundary, dislocation, and inclusion. Scientists who varied in interpretation often sparred around the electron scopes, their hands in fervent gesture across the screened images, their voices low but sharp with condescension. Dyraveen struggled to follow much of the scientists' debates. The alloy surfaces so replete in detail to the scientists' eyes seemed to Dyraveen the strange landscapes of crystal-scaled moons; the grain boundaries seemed the edges of massive continental plates, etched by slow-quenched vulcan fires.

Dyraveen found the politics and power struggles of the laboratory complex more interesting than the scientific research.

By permission of the lab director, Dyraveen sat in on meetings of every level at the central tower of the complex. He observed all-staff assemblies, project meetings, safety and standard reviews, and peer group gatherings of technicians, engineers, scientists, and managers.

Despite the high levels of skill and education throughout the staff, Dyraveen noticed a clear tribalism between groups that would surface in moments of pressure and conflict. A peer group torn by rivalry and infighting would suddenly form a unified front when threatened by external forces, bitter rivals joining in defense against outsiders. Highest management allowed, sometimes even encouraged, these protective tribal associations. "Standing alone, the worker is insecure and frightened, cornered they become desperate and dangerous," the lab director confided to Dyraveen. "But the tribe saves the individual. And the individual will sacrifice greatly for the tribe."

Dyraveen learned much from the director, Brellen.

In meetings small and large, Brellen always listened first and spoke last, his listening patient and intent, his words few and final.

Brellen treated his body of staff as both organism and machine. Acutely aware of personality, he shuffled workers between teams to regulate stress throughout the lab, sometimes lowering tensions, sometimes deliberately fanning the flames. By induced cycles of intensifying pressure and brief release, he drove his staff beyond old limits, drained every well of ability and resource. In his people he nurtured a champion's confidence and pride, a challenger's grudge at being under-respected.

Brellen knew the informal communication networks of the lab and could accurately predict the flow of information worker to worker. To carefully chosen sources he would let slip tantalizing news of the broader industry: the plans and maneuvers of rival western companies, power shifts within the western universities, collaborative negotiations with companies of the east. The rumor leaks of the director created a sense of mystery and excitement throughout the complex; they gave context and meaning to the daily struggles of his workers.

"And when some rumors prove false?" Dyraveen asked.

"They are yesterday's rumors," Brellen said, "quickly forgotten in today's fresh drama."

Dyraveen pressed Brellen to share his knowledge of the broader industry, to reveal the true dynamics between east and west.

"Our company is young and vulnerable," Brellen said. "We hope to supply light alloys to the west and steels to the east. But Varrans are skeptical of any science done outside the university. And Torites have worked steel since tribal days."

"You will face steep walls," Dyraveen said.

"Yet the need is there. The west dreams of space and flight, but the Varran lacks the light metals required by jet and rocket. The east wants to lay buildings as great as mountains, but there are tricks of alloying and manufacturing that the Torite has still to learn."

"And my uncle?"

"For our plan to work, Enteres must overcome the old powers of Tekenna; I must deceive the academic lords of Pocone; and the great Davel must be moved in spirit."

"Davel?"

"Your grandfather, the old giant. Nothing is built in this world without Tyraen money."

Dyraveen studied closely the moves of Brellen in the academic and industrial worlds outside the laboratory.

Brellen enticed key university officials into endorsement with promises of credit inclusion on the ambitious Moonlance projects. "By century's end your work could touch on every moon," he said.

He hired Tyraen trade agents to gather intelligence on the aviation and aerospace companies of the west. He targeted small and hungry companies, young project managers with loose ties to the university. With several contracts secured, momentum building, he turned his attention to larger companies and deeper purses. By exaggerating his production capability, he entered the race for a massive materials contract with a leading aeronautical company. Through inside information he undercut the competition and won the full contract.

"How will you deliver?" Dyraveen asked.

"The science is there," Brellen said. "Now we need the ore and the factories. Now your uncle, Enteres, must move mountains."

Brellen traveled east to Balthe to meet with Enteres, accompanied by Dyraveen.

The three shared drinks in the private garden of Enteres.

When Brellen turned to business and told of the massive contract, the face of Enteres darkened. His head sunk low.

"We can never fulfill," Enteres said. "You have ruined us."

"I promised you the laboratory and the contracts," Brellen said. "I delivered you the laboratory and the contracts."

"We can never meet those numbers," Enteres said. "Every company east and west will hear when we fall short."

"You promised me production," Brellen said, leaning forward. "*Deliver* production."

Brellen returned to Pocone.

Dyraveen spent a day with his uncle walking the streets of Balthe. They visited the Tyraen compound that had welcomed Enteres after his release from jail. They flew by compound plane over the great cities of the east.

Late at night they drank together in the garden.

"He will use you," Enteres said. "For information. For leverage."

"No, he is teaching me," Dyraveen said, "grooming me."

"You are still young, Dyraveen. Leave Pocone. Come to Balthe."

"Yes. Good. I can help you here."

"My nephew, my blood, you must first finish your education," Enteres said. "Live with me in Balthe. Complete your studies at the academy here. Then we can speak of science and work."

Dyraveen left his uncle and returned to Pocone.

He stayed at home for several days, ignoring the messages of Brellen.

When Dyraveen returned to the laboratory, Brellen summoned him immediately to the central tower.

The two stared across the director's table, each trying to read the other.

Brellen broke the silence first. He asked how Dyraveen liked the east. He joked of the soot-stained air and the crag-faced Torite women.

Dyraveen shrugged, said little.

"You think I was too hard on your uncle," Brellen said, nodding slowly. "You think I set him up for failure."

"Did you?" Dyraveen said.

"You underestimate Enteres. He is fierce and brilliant with his back to the wall."

"And it was you who cornered him. Now he will have to beg for help from old Davel."

"We knew this moment would come from the very beginning."

"And yet the timing was yours alone."

The two men glared across the table.

"Davel will help the friend of his son," Brellen said. "Enteres will rise to the great challenge. But what about you, young Dyraveen? Why are you in Pocone, not Balthe?"

"My home is here."

"But your uncle has so much work ahead. The project of a lifetime. Why didn't he ask for your help?"

"He did. He asked me to stay in Balthe with him."

"To stay and work?" Brellen pressed, his eyes narrowing, flickering.

"He asked me to stay with him," Dyraveen said. He hesitated before his next words, weighing the lie, choosing truth. "Not for work, but school."

Brellen gave a loosened smile. "Perhaps, you should return to school," he said. "The uneducated are never taken seriously in this field."

"I might," Dyraveen said. "I might also visit my grandfather, Davel, with words of warning."

Dyraveen wandered Pocone for days.

He rode the city canals, walked its gardens, climbed its towers.

From silver temple peak, he gazed across Pocone, the greatest city of the west, lush with gardens, brilliant with crystal, its life flowing into the university center, the mountainous core dwarfing all outer, lesser, rings.

When Dyraveen returned home, his mother was waiting. She held a letter from Enteres.

"Your uncle, again, offered you his home," she said. "You could explore the city through the spring, start classes in the summer."

"No," Dyraveen said. "No classes."

"Then you will work."

"Yes, I will work."

"And time will burn on."

On Dyraveen's first day at the dome, the labor chief looked down at him with a hard, appraising eye. The chief squinted and grimaced as he took in Dyraveen's thin frame and fleshless arms, his soft, uncalloused hands.

"Are you good with numbers?" the chief asked.

Dyraveen nodded, shrugged.

"Help the surveyors," the chief said.

The surveyors made Dyraveen pack their equipment around the complex. He built scaffolding for them, clamped surveying rods to railings, and logged juncture positions.

Dyraveen liked the work. It was active, simple, precise. His tasks alternated between the mental and the physical. Time passed quickly between breaks.

After a season with the surveying crew, Dyraveen was offered permanent work, an apprenticeship, a chance to learn all the surveying equipment and advanced techniques.

But Dyraveen declined.

He asked the labor chief to be a runner instead.

"Are you crazy?" the chief said. "Surveying is soft work with big pay. Running is hard. And dangerous."

"I don't want soft work," Dyraveen said. "I don't care about money."

"Only the rich," the chief said, rolling his eyes. "I'll start you on the platforms."

From the top of the dome, Dyraveen secured safety cords for the welders and gunners working their way up the sides. He kept their cords untangled, watched by binoculars for any problems, and recorded progress by blueprint and chart.

After a season on the platforms, Dyraveen joined the runners.

The runners were unskilled laborers, mostly young immigrants from poor towns of the coast. They were paid by weight to deliver supplies to the gunners bolting plates and the welders tacking beams on the sides of the dome. They were offered safety harnesses and cords for the climb, but most runners worked without these, the harnesses restrictive, the cords too easy to catch and entangle. The fastest runners used short ropes and grappling hooks to climb the slanted beams; they walked the horizontal stretches with no protection at all.

Dyraveen started with cord and harness. He became comfortable with the weight of the backpack. He learned the dome's pattern of trapezoid and triangle. His arms and legs strengthened, thickened.

After a few weeks, he gave up the thick safety cord for the lighter rope.

He crept in his early climbs. Experienced runners led the way and left hooks behind for him. He always kept an additional vertical safety rope attached to his belt.

Little by little, Dyraveen improved.

He learned to block out all sound, to bring all light into focus on the beam at his feet, to think no more than one step ahead, to live breath by breath.

Dyraveen gave up the safety rope.

He climbed as the fastest runners did, one rope on slants, nothing in the flats.

For ten days Dyraveen climbed the dome safely with the best of the runners.

On the eleventh day, the runner below him fell. Distracted, Dyraveen also fell. He caught himself on the beam with one arm. His free hand clawed the air. His feet kicked desperately to wrap around the beam.

Dyraveen clasped hands.

He swung his legs high and locked his feet together.

He stared into the empty sky until another runner reached him.

Dyraveen had said nothing of his climbing to his mother.

When he quit his job after his near-fall at the dome, Rhoa did not speak to him for days.

Dyraveen began to run at night.

He ran away from the city. He ran from glorious Pocone, the pride of the west, his mother's temple, his wound and cage.

He escaped Pocone by tunneled road. His burning lungs and aching legs were forgotten the moment he emerged from the blackened tunnel into the radiant moonlight of the valley. The moons cast upon the valley grasses a soft and glowing silver. An emerald sea undulated over the land. The cool valley winds pushed sweat through his hair.

He ran for Tekenna, driven by visions of father and grandfather.

Finite is the distance to home. Finite.

And the will can conquer all in time.

But the will of Dyraveen failed. His legs could not conquer the wide valley. Flesh bowed to pain.

Dyraveen slept through his days.

He dreamed of his hazel-eyed people in the east, his grandfather's legend, his father's art.

And he dreamed of the cold beam and empty sky, his weakening hold on life, the death that waited on a single slip.

When Rhoa spoke to him of the high city and his father's descent, Dyraveen left his mother's house.

Dyraveen returned to the Titan Stone. He slept by day in caves of the mount. At night he climbed to the Aviet cove. He watched the games from the edge of the crowd. He recognized only a few of the pages working light in the needled forest. Players he had once beaten now reigned.

Dyraveen came down from the mount to join the laborers of the gambling pits. He threw dice and played cards. He drank late into the night then staggered back to cave.

266

When his money ran low and his clothes stank of rot, Dyraveen left the Titan Stone. He headed to the water flues of the outer city. He dove into the sunset flood with the workers of the hills.

Dyraveen wandered the city's edge.

He saw the slaughtering fields of herders, their curved blades glistening in the sun, hideless carcasses strung from trees.

He saw the addict dens of shed and cellar, the bluepod presses of abandoned warehouse, thieves' hands dangling from portal chains.

He saw the city graveyards, the crystal spires of the rich, the shallow trenches of the poor.

He saw the prison pits, guarded by black-masked riflemen, oil barrels burning, capstan pulleys lowering rations, raising lifeless bodies.

At the edge of Pocone, Dyraveen met many travelers, some fleeing to the city, some fleeing from.

At nightly fires, he heard talk of the city's underground, a place of criminal and artist, a shadowed land whose depths shone true against the lie of high Pocone.

Dyraveen wandered fire to fire.

When he found a small group of musicians heading for the underground, he followed behind them.

He trailed them over fields of brush, into a grove of wild nut trees.

The grove thickened.

He lost sight of the group.

He walked in circles in the heart of the trees.

An arm wrapped suddenly around his chest. A knife blade pressed to his neck. The musicians stepped out from the shadows of the trees.

"Who are you?" they asked.

"A traveler," he said.

Dyraveen was shoved to the ground, kicked by boot. Each of the musicians drew knives, crept forward.

"My father was a painter of the underground," Dyraveen said, hands raised. "I wanted to see."

The musicians held their ground, knives high. "What was his name?" they asked.

"Sedenel," he said.

A hand reached for Dyraveen, pulled him to his feet, brushed leaves from his back.

The musicians led him out of the tree grove.

They walked together through the fields of abandoned herding grounds.

They passed through broken-fenced pens and roofless shearing flats.

From a toolshed's trapdoor, they entered the underground, their gemstone chains lighting the darkness.

Dyraveen entered last. He followed behind Ottea, the one who had held a knife to his neck. Ottea called back to Dyraveen as they worked their way down.

"This wing was carved by priests of the Blue Temple," Ottea said. "Before the first kings."

They crawled on their stomachs through a narrow, twisting tunnel. Every body-length they passed a grooved ring carved into the tunnel stone.

"This is the great worm," Ottea said, "designed to cripple the armor-bearing."

The narrow tunnel climbed steeply then dropped into a wide chamber. Flat boulders ringed a dribbling fountain. Everyone stood and stretched their legs. The musicians drank from the fountain, smoked, and stared at Dyraveen.

Dyraveen drank and sat with Ottea.

"I am sorry for the knife and boot," Ottea said. "There are debt-hunters. Police. Vandals. Robbers of art and gem."

From the fountain chamber, they entered a wider, smoother tunnel. They were able to walk, rather than crawl. They passed through stretches of carved serpent scale and avian feather.

"The snake rules the descending tunnel," Ottea said, "the bird rules the rising."

The tunnel opened into a giant, plumed chamber. Massive, tree-like pillars circled the plume. Water dripped from the chamber ceiling, streaked the pillars in jagged rivulet. A green-mottled fungus wrapped around the pillars, its spotted colonies rising from the floor.

Ottea sidestepped the fungus, covered his head from the dripping water. "We are almost there," he said.

They entered a long, flat tunnel without scale or feather.

They walked into the stone-carved rays of a moon on tunnel's ceiling.

They passed beneath the moon, radiant with copper flake, misted bright with blue-specked minerals.

They followed the moon rays outward until the rays thinned and disappeared.

In a distant chamber, they saw flickers of firelight. Drumbeats gently shook the cavern walls. Voices passed through the tunnel, a wordless song, hollowed by distance, distorted by echo of cavern voids.

As they neared the light, the sounds of different drums could be distinguished within the song. Smaller drums beat rapid and light - a fierce and unrelenting rain. Heavy drums pounded slow and strong, their beat jarring, lingering in the bones. And many voices could be heard. A choral host of masculine voices blended together, filled the body of the sound, matched the rapid-paced rhythms of the smaller drums. *Derre, derre, derre,* they sang, their powerful voices breaking by end of chorus into a sharp and anguished cry. At longest interval, in the wake of the deepest drums, a feminine voice pierced the air. *Telle, telle,* she cried, drowning out every drum and singer. Her voice quivered as she stretched the words beyond breath. She sang like the blind calling for light, the fallen pleading for life.

Dyraveen followed the others into the song chamber. They sat in furthest ring around the fire. They took up small drums of animal hide and horns of ram. They joined the great circle in masculine chorus.

Dyraveen soon fell asleep, his dreams haunted by woman's voice. *Telle, telle.*

When he woke from his dreaming, the fire had died; the music had ended.

Some slept in tight huddles against the cold.

Some talked in small circles, their faces cast in light of gem.

Dyraveen slipped into the circles. He shared nuts and dried meat from his pack. He accepted smokes and drinks. When questioned about his life, Dyraveen answered bluntly, simply.

"By blood, I am Tyraen and Torite," he said. "My father, a painter of the underground, is dead, fallen to disease before my birth. My mother is a designer of towers, a lord of the university, a queen of the high city. I was tutored and groomed to follow after her, but I fled from her world. Instead, I played the Aviet sphere. I worked in plant and laboratory. I labored with the real builders of the city."

The people of the underground accepted Dyraveen.

In the gemmed twilight, the long and unbroken cavern night, the cavers told him stories of their own lives.

He met highborn Varrans of the city who had clashed with old powers at the university. He met deserting soldiers of the Torite army, salt-runners of the southern wasteland, climbers and guides of the deep western mountains, fishers of the great western rivers. He learned that most of the people only visited the underground for short periods; they returned often to the surface for work and supplies. Only the greatest of artists lived underground for whole seasons and years. The purest artists lived in chambers far from the others, crafting poem, lyric, painting, and sculpture alone in cavern shrine, returning only for a rare night of song and fire.

Dyraveen learned that his father had been an artist of the deep caverns. Many had heard of him, but few had seen his work.

"I saw sketches in the catacombs of the Green Temple," Ottea said. "Some said they were the work of a citadel cleric. Some said Sedenel."

"And the woman?" Dyraveen said. "The singer?"

"She buries herself deep in the stalax."

Dyraveen filled his flask of water, borrowed a chain of glowing opal, and headed into the stalactite forest.

He crawled in the slippery gaps between the giant stone trunks.

He climbed the webbed veins of the shorter columns and plunged into the shadows beyond.

Dyraveen drove deep into the forest of stone. When his flask of water ran dry, he sucked the dripping rock. He licked crumbs from his empty pouches of food.

Dyraveen slipped and fell from a steep stalactite vein. His leg twisted beneath him. He slumped against the column, knee throbbing, weak from thirst and hunger.

He took the opal chain from his neck and tossed it high onto the column's web, hoping to send light wide throughout the cavern.

The chain landed on column's vein, bounced, turned, and slid down the other side.

Dyraveen lay in shrouded darkness.

He hoped to sleep until help came, but there was no sleeping against the stone, no rest from the burning of his throat and stomach.

He shifted and turned, never beyond pain.

The dome came back to him, the cold iron beam, the empty sky above, the agony and death waiting below.

He weighed sudden death against slow death - a moment of absolute terror against a slow, grinding fade.

He chose neither.

Telle, telle, he cried out.

He thought of Cyadae who had loved and hoped and waited.

Telle, telle.

He thought of his mother who had clutched and poured and prodded.

Telle, telle.

He thought of his father who had wandered lost and suffered long, whose trail of work his own son had abandoned for voice and form of woman.

Telle, telle.

And he thought of himself.

The boy who had considered the wide world no more difficult or complex than the Aviet sphere.

The boy who had spurned highest privilege and education, who had quit every job and failed in every field.

The boy who would die alone on cavern floor.

Telle, telle.

Dyraveen bent his knee, stretched and bent, stretched and bent.

Telle, telle.

He remembered spinning round and round atop the pyramid, the dizzy city reeling beneath them, his mother's arms an anchor strong.

Telle, telle.

He remembered the face of Cyadae under Aviet light.

When he had shocked the masters, her old eyes had glistened wild.

When he had taken her hand for the champion's walk, she had smiled like a little girl.

Telle, telle, telle.

Dyraveen wept.

Telle.

The chill of the stone traveled deep.

He curled into a ball.

He rocked and shivered.

His tired muscles clenched, tightened, cramped.

He prayed to God.

He cursed God.

He prayed to God.

Dyraveen sat up.

He bent and stretched his knee, bent and stretched, bent and stretched.

He dug both heels into the ground and drove upward with his legs.

His hands gripped strong on the stony column.

He climbed, ignoring the stabbing ache of his knee. He jumped and pulled himself atop the column's vein. From height of vein, he saw an emerald light approaching through the forest.

Iprana helped Dyraveen to her chamber.

She gave him food, water, and blanket. She cut a strip of cloth from her robe and tied it around his knee. She studied him in the torchlight. "Why are you here?" she said.

"I heard you sing at the fire," Dyraveen said. "Your voice has haunted me since."

The eyes of Iprana narrowed. "Why were you shouting the name of Telle?"

"It was the only word I heard you sing at the fire. Who is Telle?"

Iprana walked to the mouth of her chamber. She stared into the stone forest, eyes dark. "I will take you back soon," she said.

Dyraveen limped to the cavern mouth. He leaned his shoulder against cold chamber wall, rested his knee upon stone shelf. "Who is Telle?" he asked again.

Iprana turned from the stalax. Her hard eyes softened as she stared into the face of Dyraveen. "Telle was my friend," she said. "We rode the Danve together from ocean coast to western mountain. We walked together from Cyecura to Pocone. We climbed the citadel crags together; hand in hand, we dove from white-crystal falls. Together, we explored the deepest tunnels of the underground. Together, we shared songs in the long, unbroken night; against her sweet-bladed voice, my own seemed the groaning of beast. Telle was my friend."

"She has fallen?"

"A miners' explosion," Iprana said. "A cavern collapse. The song you heard was mourning tribute."

"And Derre?"

"Her brother. Also fallen."

Dyraveen limped back to his cloak and blanket. "I will not say her name again," he said. "I will rest an hour. Then leave you in peace."

Iprana stood long at the cavern mouth, staring into the stalax, humming softly.

She turned from the stalax, crossed the cave to stand above him.

Iprana took two dried leaves from a glass vial. She placed the larger leaf beneath her tongue and offered the smaller down.

Dyraveen stared at the four-lobed leaf. It had sharp-horned teeth around the edges, an unnatural sprinkling of pale yellow dots, purple capillaries.

"The butterfly leaf," she said, swallowing.

Dyraveen took the leaf and held it by stem.

Iprana extinguished the chamber torch.

She walked the ring of chamber's edge, lighting candles in small hollows.

She pulled the chain from Dyraveen's neck, split it with a heavy stone, and gathered the opals into her arms. She drifted slow and light throughout the chamber, dropping gemstones along her path.

She returned to Dyraveen and pulled her blanket close to his.

Dyraveen slipped the leaf under his tongue. He felt the leaf's sharp teeth open his gums.

"Push down," Iprana said. "Deeper blood, deeper journey."

He pushed down with his tongue until he tasted blood. His gums burned. He gagged on the bitter leaf, slowly dissolving.

Iprana covered his mouth with her hand. "Swallow," she said.

Dyraveen swallowed.

Iprana's hand slipped from his mouth, rested on his chest.

Nausea rose in his stomach.

His heartbeat quickened.

His skin flushed.

Dyraveen closed his eyes and focused only on his breathing. In by nose, out by mouth. In, out. Slow, slow, slower.

When his blood and stomach had settled, he turned to watch her.

Iprana gazed into the trembling lights and shadows of the cavern ceiling. Her head moved as if she followed the flight of unseen birds. Her eyes shifted in and out of focus. Her silver-green pupils bled into darkened iris.

Dyraveen lay back and peered into the chamber heights.

He saw candlelight rise in red-gold tides from all corners of the chamber. The tides of light washed over the jagged ceiling stone in slow, wind-rippled waves. Many waves disappeared in the shadows of porous void. Others joined in strength to light and magnify protruding stone.

Dyraveen stared longer.

The black voids darkened, turned in slow rotation.

Goldentail fires swirled around the stony bulges, rotating counter to the voids.

The voids quickened in turn, widened, drained all light from enveloped stone and shadow.

The fires swelled, brightened; silver-forked flames spun in raging circle.

Realms of void and fire touched.

Black claws scattered invading flame.

Bright swords slashed front of darkness.

Dyraveen closed his eyes. He heard the fire's violent crackling, the rushing winds of the void.

The laugh of Iprana silenced flame and abyss.

She stood, smiling, at his feet, an opal glowing in each hand. She wove the gemstones through the air in loop and swirl, bleeding rainbows, trailing frosted light.

She dropped the stones, shed her robe, and slipped inside his blanket.

Dyraveen stayed in the shadowy chamber of Iprana until his beard fell heavy upon his chest. They lived together through the long cavern night, surviving on fountain's water, scraps of dried meat, and stalks of summer grass. They warmed themselves by sex and blanket.

Iprana paced the cavern floor and practiced lyric.

Dyraveen watched Iprana.

He slept and dreamed, dreamed and slept.

When their food ran low and hunger burned, Dyraveen argued with Iprana to leave the stalax. "We are weakening here, slowly dying," he said. "Come with me to the catacombs. I must find the work of my father."

Iprana shook her head and looked away. "And I must make her tribute perfect," she said.

"Then you will die alone in darkened hole."

"Darkness waits for all of us," she said. "We are given only the breath for one short and final cry into the void."

"And we are given love."

Dyraveen emerged from the underground to find the moonlit hills covered with heavy snow. The reflections of the moons across the snowdrifts blinded his cave-weakened eyes. He trudged and stumbled through the shin-deep powder, blinking long, squinting moonlight into haze.

Dyraveen drifted over hill and field in search of travelers' fire. He walked until the silver moon fell beneath the mountain ridge. He walked until the green moon disappeared in the distant lights of Pocone. He walked through the night, shaking, shivering, knowing that to stop was to die. Drained of all strength, he followed the piercing winds, unable to turn or to face them.

As dawn broke, the bitter winds drove Dyraveen down a hillside gully.

The gully flattened then opened into an abandoned stone quarry.

He crouched behind the rusted shell of an old bulldozer, waiting for a break in the wind. When the gusts waned and powder settled from the air, he looked across the quarry. A green and black lake, partly frozen, lay in the quarry's pit. Terraced ledges ringed the quarry in long, contoured waves. Steep conveyors stretched from quarry floor to central tower.

A breath before the wind returned, Dyraveen spotted two details in the view that stopped his heart. Black iron wolves approached on the terraces. Smoke wafted from a glassless window of the tower.

He ran for the closest conveyor.

Wolves baying near, Dyraveen leaped onto the line. He slipped at first step on the conveyor snow. He tumbled back to the ground.

Dyraveen rolled to his feet, ran to the conveyor's base, and hurled himself back onto the line. He climbed the line, carefully this time, crawling by hands and feet, keeping his weight low.

As he climbed he saw the wolfpack lunge onto the conveyor beneath him. Most of the wolves slipped and fell back. Three landed steady and climbed strong.

Dyraveen flipped onto his back. He held onto the conveyor with both hands and kicked at the snarling wolves.

The black wolves dodged and pounced, ducked and nipped.

The silver-streaked leader of the wolves caught the pant leg of Dyraveen in his mouth, twisted side to side until the cloth shredded.

Dyraveen kicked at the leader. His boot glanced off the wolf's side. He slid lower down the line, three wolves snapping at his waist.

A clap of thunder shook the quarry.

The lead wolf spun circles in the air and crashed to the ground.

Thunder struck again. Again.

Another wolf dropped limp.

Another spun and fell.

Dyraveen kicked the blooded head by his feet.

The last wolf fell from conveyor.

Dyraveen rolled onto his stomach.

He crawled to tower.

When he reached the conveyor's end, a gloved hand gripped his shoulder and pulled him onto the platform.

Dyraveen brushed snow from his chest, wiped blood from his boots. He looked up at the man who had saved him.

The man had dark-slitted eyes, stooped shoulders, a long jawbone and pointed jaw. From his belt hung a knife, radio, and pistol. He patted Dyraveen for weapons, lifted his sleeves, felt his arms. "You look like an addict," the gunman said, searching the arms for bluepod slits. "A few steps from the grave."

Dyraveen pulled his arms away. "I was underground for weeks," he said, "in the caverns of the Blue Temple."

"Are you a drummer? a singer?"

Dyraveen shook his head, rolled down his sleeves. "No, I search for the artwork of my father," he said. "He was a painter of the underground."

"You found his work?"

"No, but I learned that some of his sketches might lie in catacombs of the Green Temple."

"And now you travel without money, without food, without weapons, without friends."

"I travel with purpose. It is more than many have."

The gunman sneered, laughed, eyed Dyraveen. "I am Cirico," he said. "I, too, travel with purpose. I flee for my life. I pray for the mercy of the Council of Thieves."

Cirico led Dyraveen to his fire inside the quarry tower.

While Dyraveen warmed himself over the flames, Cirico cut strips of meat from a smoked and spitted flank.

"If we had time," Cirico said, handing strips, "we would feast on iron wolf tonight."

Dyraveen sucked the meat, saliva dripping from his mouth. He gnashed and swallowed, gnashed and swallowed. When he had finished every strip, he fell onto his back and closed his eyes. He licked his gums for residue of smoke. His tongue probed for scraps between his teeth.

Dyraveen felt a wet cloth press upon his shins, a flare of pain between feet and knees.

Cirico stood over him, grinning, an alcohol-soaked rag in his hands. "Pay now or pay later," Cirico said.

After Cirico finished, Dyraveen curled his body around the fire. He inched closer and closer to the red-black coals. When the heat singed his cloak, he slid back. He savored the sweet numbness that spread beneath his skin. He crept forward, again.

"When the wind stops, we run," Cirico said. "We flee for the catacombs."

Dyraveen already dreamed.

He lay in the stalax forest. Gusts of icy air passed over him. Crystal mists coated the trees, silver specks of frost glistening upon the dull grey stone.

The seeds of frost grew into pebbles.

The pebbles grew to gemstones.

The winds died.

Lights of the Aviet swept over the stalax forest.

The cavern floor turned gold and red from sunstone beryl, a molten sea gently rippling.

Alternating swirls of blue and green wrapped around the stalac pillars, rising from pools of mixed silica and jade.

Shimmering diamonds dissolved the jagged coves of cavern ceiling, receded by swords of light into the blackened depths of star.

A boot touched his back.

Ammolite clouds lit the lower skies, their ether rainbows turning.

A hand shook his shoulder.

The Aviet lights dimmed to grey.

Get up. The winds have died.

The stalac pillars melted into the ground, shriveled into the ceiling.

Dyraveen got up and followed Cirico to the tower platform. They slid down the steepest conveyor. They walked to the edge of the quarry, clinging to the shadows of the lowest terrace.

They traveled over the hills toward the western mountains. They ran when exposed in the open fields, walked when covered by trees. They used shallow streams to break their tracks, jumping rock to rock. Each time they rested, Cirico checked the radio for chatter. He studied the movements of the clouds, his grimace deepening as the sun sank lower in the sky.

They drove deeper into the hills. There were fewer trees and fewer streams. The ground hardened into broken boulders and fissured slabs.

When they spotted a hilltop windmill, Cirico managed a thin smile.

They climbed to the summit and caught their breath beneath the nine-vaned mill.

Cirico pointed to the south, to a lone river weaving through the stony hills. "That leads to the underground gate," he said. "Not far from here."

His smile disappeared when he looked back to the north. Quadtrackers searched the hills, their headlights bobbing, slashing left and right.

"You continue on," Dyraveen said. "I will turn back north and lead them away."

Cirico shook his head, scowling. "These aren't police guards who will question and imprison you," he said. "These are guild assassins who will torture and kill. Hide here in the mill, my friend. Wait until this is finished."

Dyraveen looked back to the north. He watched the hunters' lights draw nearer.

"I have a runner's chance," Cirico said. "More than I deserve."

"And I have a debt of life," Dyraveen said. "More than I can pay."

The two rushed down the hillside.

Cirico led the way over the rock-strewn terrain. Dyraveen followed, his legs burning and bleeding.

When they reached the river, they looked back. Headlights glowed on both sides of the windmill. A searchlight swept from windmill's base.

Cirico cursed and drew his pistol.

They ran upriver, weaving between the boulders of the shore, ducking low when the searchlight passed.

Shadows deepened with the setting sun.

They stumbled over loose rocks.

They slipped on the snow-covered ice.

Cirico drew a small flashlight. He quickened his pace.

Dyraveen followed the thin blade of light bobbing through the rocks and shadows. He felt the searchlight catch his shoulders, pass by, then return.

Cirico disappeared at the side of a waterfall feeding the river.

Dyraveen crouched. He reached from boulder to boulder in the darkness. The searchlight caught his head. A motor revved high.

"Here," Cirico said. "Here."

Dyraveen crawled toward the falls. He saw a pinprick of light beneath the crashing water. The light flickered across his eyes then circled a narrow ledge beneath the falls.

Dyraveen followed the light to the ledge. Torrents of water passed over him. A dribbling rain settled his hair, soaked his beard. The hands of Cirico, again, pulled him to safety.

Underneath the river, they took three breaths' rest then headed into a narrow tunnel steeply falling. They slid down mud and pebble drifts, their hands grasping for hold on rock clefts above them.

Dyraveen crashed into Cirico at slope's bottom.

Cirico braced himself with one hand against the ceiling. With a forearm, he deflected Dyraveen aside.

Cirico pivoted backward. He leaned against the tunnel side, a thigh and elbow carrying his weight. Hand to his pistol, he looked back to the tunnel's mouth.

"Will they follow us here?" Dyraveen whispered.

"They might," Cirico said. "They could also bury us by bomb."

They pressed deeper.

The tunnel flattened into a long stretch. Its sides fanned slowly outward, drifting further and further apart until no edge or wall could be seen.

They advanced carefully into the great chamber, their footing tested by winding crevice and slick stone. The boulders they passed were sharply cut and damp with droplets. As the flashlight passed over the rocks, it left behind streaks of glowing minerals, red-blue stars. The stars flashed an iridescent blue when first struck by light, formed crimson halos in their peak, then slowly dimmed and hollowed. Water dripped from thousands of stone fingers high above. The many echoes of the drops swallowed their footsteps, disoriented, nauseated like the sea.

They followed a line of metal stakes that wove throughout the chamber, thin stakes reaching high, holding battered helmets, blood-stained boots, uniforms slashed by knife and riddled by bullet.

Between the stakes Dyraveen caught glimpses of company emblems cut from the helms of ships, the mangled gears of heavy machinery, charred quadtracker doors with guild insignia. He saw open-cut geodes with hundreds of pheran teeth strewn between the crystal buds.

"Trophies," Cirico said. "Warnings."

The spaces between stakes lengthened. Helmets, boots, and uniforms were replaced by oblate gemstones. Under the light of

Cirico, the fist-sized gems came to life. The gems glowed a bright and embered orange, burning slow like furnace coals.

They followed the ember lights until they reached the edge of a wide circle, the ground inside cleared of all boulders and rocks, the core mottled and stained with pools dark violet.

Cirico stopped at circle's edge. He turned off his flashlight. He laid down his jacket, knife, and pistol. He walked to the center of the circle and knelt on the bare stone. Dyraveen knelt beside him.

The two waited.

They stared down the lines of their long-stretched shadows.

They watched as the ember slowly faded and their shadows blurred into the black-grey stone.

When darkness settled, Cirico prayed with desperate breath. He spread himself across the stone.

Dyraveen raised his gaze. Still kneeling, he searched for any trace of light or color in the cavern depths. His eyes widened, strained, tired.

The circle suddenly blazed with rays of blinding orange.

Dyraveen covered his eyes. He bent low to the ground. He listened to footsteps approach on all sides.

"A killer asks for mercy," Cirico cried out. "A killer begs for life."

Dyraveen, though shaking, stood. Through squinted eyes he glimpsed the back of Cirico, drenched in sweat, white cloth darkened grey. He turned around, head low, to see the feet of the enclosing circle, four pairs booted, three pairs bare.

"What killer?" a Varran voice said, his mountain accent slow and sharp.

"Cirico, assassin of the Stone Guild."

"Who have you killed?"

"Keepers of the southern locks. Guards of the arc bridges. Officials of every rival guild in the city. Assassins, many."

"And now *you* are hunted. And now *you* ask for mercy."

When his eyes adjusted to the light, Dyraveen looked around at the faces of the circle.

There were three tribal Iccin, barefoot, clay-skinned, bronze eyes haloed blue, a shimmering blade in each hand.

There were two Artauk, broad-shouldered, towering, hairless of face and scalp, hided gloves wrapped around the gnarled heads of staves.

There were two Varrans, their knotted hair down their backs, a raised hand with long pistol, a lowered hand carrying rope.

Eyes turned to Dyraveen.

"And you who stand?"

"I am not a killer or a criminal," Dyraveen said. "I am the son of a painter, Sedenel. His work lies somewhere in this cave."

"Why do you travel with a killer?"

"He saved my life from pack of black wolves. Cirico fed and healed and guided me."

The Varrans holstered their pistols. They tied the hands of Cirico and Dyraveen. "The Council will soon meet along the underground river," they said. "You can tell your stories to the hundreds."

The Varrans led the way from empty circle into a maze of fissured rock plates. They walked, climbed, and crawled in the narrow cracks between the giant slabs of stone. Their path veered and switched, rose and fell. Handicapped by the rope, Dyraveen bruised his knees and bloodied his elbows.

They dropped into a lens-shaped crevice and slid down rounded tube through several dips and bends.

The smooth tunnel flattened then forked in triple tunnel.

The Iccin took the left passage, the Artauk took the right.

The Varrans led their prisoners straight.

As they walked Dyraveen noticed a faint light rising on the tunnel floor, a misty silver and blue, the soft glimmering of moons. He heard echoes of waterfall, currents breaking over stone, the churn of whirlpool and eddy. Emerald light shafts spun and twisted across the ceiling as the tunnel widened into cavern mouth.

They emerged at the base of an alcove, a giant thumbnail carved from wall of steel-grey rock, its tip disappearing in the high-vaulted darkness.

As they crossed the alcove bay, two other coves emerged on each side, the Iccin left, the Artauk right.

Together, the three bays formed a wedge-shaped beach along the river.

On the left side of the beach there were scattered pockets of domed tents, a few Iccin sharpening blades by whetstone block.

A wide hexagonal firepit dominated the middle of the beach. Some Varrans slept by blanket outside the pit; some drummed softly at pit's edge; a few hauled ash by bucket from the unlit center.

In the right bay, the Artauk rested against stone altars, solitary giants of moonpale skin, their dreams adrift in waters' rhythm.

One of the Varran guards broke away to the Iccin tents. The remaining guard led the prisoners around the firepit, down to the water's edge. He chained the prisoners to a brick-shaped boulder, their ropes exchanged for manacles. The guard tested the chains then turned for the firepit.

Dyraveen gazed across the river, each bend and fall of water caught in emerald and silver light. He looked high above to the moonlight pouring through jagged surface rift.

Cirico and Dyraveen leaned against each other.

"This is good," Cirico said. "Many are killed in the barren circle."

Cirico slept within a few breaths.

Dyraveen saw tails of streaked serpents gliding among the river waves. He remembered the warmth of the quarry tower, the sweet dripping meat, the radiant lights of the Aviet sweeping dead stone.

He slept through day.

And night.

And day again.

He woke on the third night, shaking from hunger.

Cirico sat atop the boulder, chains coiled loosely around his wrists, dead eyes upon the river. His eyes sharpened at the slide of Dyraveen's chain. He threw the sagging chain behind him as Dyraveen climbed on top of the boulder.

The two prisoners sat, shoulder to shoulder, listening to the river's steady flow.

"In the barren circle, it was not the fear of blade or bullet that crushed me," Cirico said. "It was the darkness, the lifeless void. On my knees, I saw clearly the abyss that waits. For me. For all. I saw the night without dawn. I heard the cries of the slain."

"Your slain?" Dyraveen said. "Your victims?"

Cirico slumped forward. He closed his eyes, covered his ears with manacle, and ground into his temples with metal edge.

Dyraveen crawled down from the boulder. He lay huddled against the stone, hoping to sleep and dream.

But aching bones and burning stomach kept him on the wakeful ground, the pain of flesh holding mind from flight.

He stared at a small patch of light on the boulder's side, an ice-silver moonray glancing his hip, casting a wide-arched crescent near to his chest. He studied each grain of stone caught in the light, each ridge and valley of the surface, each mineral speck and pore.

Dyraveen almost slept.

But the trembling of Cirico, the rattling of chains, the cursing and sobbing, allowed Dyraveen no rest.

Too weak to rise, Dyraveen watched the boulder's side.

The silver moonlight slowly faded in hue. The kingdoms of light disappeared beneath blanket of grey-shadowed cloud.

Finite is the time until dawn. Finite.

The boulder blackened.

Cirico wept and shook.

Cyadae smiled under the Aviet stars, the bright gems freed from rod to wander sky.

Across boulder and cave, a faint light spread.

Cyadae.

Cirico whispered. Name after name.

Remember me.

The morning light burned.

The crystal-blue river pounded rapids and shore.

Remember me, Cyadae. Raise me into your skies.

There were voices on the river. Many voices.

Dyraveen sat up, the spell of half-dreams broken.

He stood, walked to the limit of his chain, and gazed up the river.

The Iccin floated down - three, four, five in a line, straddling bundles of thin logs strapped together, crossed blades over their backs. Some floats wove deftly between the river rocks, their paddles digging into turns, jets of water fanned aside. Other floats bounced from rock to rock, the paddleless riders leaning away from oncoming stone, laughing between collisions.

The Iccin rafters veered toward the firepit as they passed Dyraveen. They landed on a wide, flat strip of shore. A few of the rafts missed the bank, the riders forced to dive and swim.

The Iccin drew their blades and slashed the float straps. They hoisted the logs onto their shoulders and carried them from shore to firepit.

The Iccin of the tents emerged with axe and hatchet. The logs were cut and split, a fire started, spits raised.

The reunited Iccin turned to the crowd of Varrans watching around the pit. They called for meat and drink.

The Varran hosts brought flasks and canteens to the Iccin. They pulled trapped serpents from a bank of shallow pools. They cut the serpents' heads and slit their bellies. They coiled and tied the dripping bodies around the spits.

As if drawn by the sweet smoke, the Artauk soon arrived.

The giants swam upriver, slicing through the strong current with relentless, deep-carved strokes, their bare heads blinding under shafts of morning light.

The taller, leaner Artauk women beat their men to shore. On the bank they brushed the water from each other's backs, pressed close for warmth, and waited.

The Artauk men emerged from the water, chests heaving, stumbling like newborns, their wide bodies many times bitten by fish and eel.

The women rubbed oil into the cuts of the men.

The Iccin and Varrans surrounded the Artauk.

The three tribes embraced.

They ate and drank around the fire.

"At sunset they will take us to the fire and question us," Cirico said. "Whatever they ask, you do not know me. I am a stranger you followed out of curiosity. Nothing more."

A young Iccin girl wandered over to the boulder of chains, two stakes of meat in her hands. "For strength to face the many," she said, holding out the meat.

"Hunger purifies," Cirico said, refusing.

Dyraveen took both stakes and kissed the hand of the Iccin girl.

Dyraveen had studied the history and legends of the underground in his childhood tutoring. He remembered many stories of the Thieves.

The Thieves' first council had been born during the ancient reign of the Hol family.

Leaders of the early temples, driven underground by Hol persecution, had hidden deep in the caverns of the hills. The temple leaders, once intense rivals in market, art, and culture, had joined together in desperate struggle against the imperial family.

The leaders drew in all groups disaffected - the scattered priests and clerics, the small tribes displaced by Hol expansion, the young left fatherless by Hol assassination and imprisonment. All were given sanctuary and voice in the underground.

The first Thieves explored and mapped the vast cavern systems of the hills.

Escape routes were planned, linking tunnels carved, surface entrances trapped and hidden.

The Thieves trained together in deep chambers. They struck the surface world in lightning raids, ambushing royal guards, stealing precious supplies.

The Hols sent several war parties into the underground. None returned.

The Poconian kings employed a wider variety of methods throughout their reign. Rivers were diverted by royal engineers to flood whole underground sections. Entrances were crushed by siegecraft, tunnels collapsed. Raiders were captured and tortured above ground. Bounties were offered on Council leaders. Informants were bribed and threatened, a stream of spies released.

There were full battles fought in torchlit chamber.

There were long nights of massacre and betrayal.

At lowest ebb and weakest hour, the Thieves could not muster a single raiding party. The Council separated to ensure survival, each member scattering, burrowing deep.

In the early Poconian years, the underground Thieves may have been saved by the underground artists. Opir's desecration of the kings' monuments - the bloodied hands, the coal-burned eyes, the hollowed, neutered organs – sounded an echoed battlecry throughout the city. The boldness of Opir invigorated rebellion. Her defiance transformed many citizens from sympathetic observers to active supporters of the underground. Her graphic symbols resonated in the Varran mind for centuries.

As the kings weakened generation by generation, the underground strengthened.

The massive royal armies that had shaken the hills on their departure for the Torite east returned to the western valley in broken, limping strands.

The Thieves emerged from the darkness. They secured their cavern networks then moved above ground. They claimed mines, quarries, granaries, depots. Their patrols controlled the hills outside the city. The hunted turned to hunters. Their raiding parties struck deep into the city itself, avoiding only the royal palace.

When the vengeful Torite army burned its path across the central valley, the officers of the western army abandoned the royal palace and sought the protection of the underground.

At cavern mouth the Council of Thieves listened to the officers' request for sanctuary.

"Alone, you will find no entrance here," the Thieves said. "But the officer who gathers his soldiers, who leads a hundred citizens from doomed city into these hills, who lays down all weapons and vendetta at cavern mouth – that officer will be welcomed into the underground."

Many officers gathered soldiers and citizens.

Many thousands were saved in the underground.

The survivors emerged from the caverns into a charred and empty world. The line of kings was dead, the royal palace razed. The terrace gardens of the city were scorched, tree and flower burned to root, rainbowed flora deadened black. The temples and towers of the city lay in flattened rubble, the people's homes reduced to ash. Bodies floated in the lakes, corpses strewn through dusty street and silent hill.

Faced with this devastation, this work of death and fire, the people trembled. Centuries of building and labor had been swallowed by the eastern flame. Whole ancestral lines had been erased by the Torite rage.

The survivors walked a new and groundless world.

For courage, for footing, they looked back to the ancient world.

They chose to return to the sacred faiths of the moon temples.

In the horrible days of waiting underground, the people had visited shrines of the temple artists. They had found shelter in the catacombs carved by temple acolytes. They had knelt beneath the paintings and statues of Opir. They had been comforted in their terror.

The Thieves watched the people reclaim the city, rebuild the wondrous towers, and forget who had saved them.

The Thieves remained in the underground. They ended their surface raids and learned to fish the underground streams. They absorbed the indigenous tribes forced from hill and mountain homeland. They guarded the deep-cavern treasures of shrine and gem. They offered sanctuary to wandering artists and repentant criminals.

The Thieves survived, age to age, a slender fragment.

The new city rose.

First, by Temple.

Then, Guild.

Then, University.

The Thieves survived each reign of influence and power. In every age the underground drew into its depths the boldest minds, the fiercest poets and painters, the most cursed of killers.

So told the lore of the Thieves.

As the last glow of sunlight faded from the ceiling fissures, Dyraveen feared the distance between legend and truth.

The prisoners were unchained from the rock.

They were led through the altars of the Artauk, ringed by red coals, bitter-pitched leaves smoldering in their basins.

They were made to sit on one of the six ledges surrounding the firepit.

An Artauk giant threw buckets of sand into the fire. By staff he separated the logs still burning. He tamped the logs, stripping embers, casting sparks into the air.

Dyraveen noticed other prisoners on the ledges around the firepit, small huddles of two, three, four, eyes low, faces drawn.

The Thieves quieted.

The fall of the river once again sounded across the chamber.

The dying fire crackled.

A torch was lit at each corner of the hexagon.

Six Thieves entered the pit – one Artauk, two Iccin, three Varrans. The Council.

The rest of the Thieves pressed forward to line the six ledges. The Thieves loomed high above the prisoners. Wide Artauk shadows cloaked three or four down the line. The sharp-boned Varrans cast angular shadows of nose and jaw, their wrists thin black swords parrying light. Iccin faces slipped in and out of the splintered torchlight, their blue-bronzed eyes flashing out of the darkness.

The Council chose to hear the easy cases first. An older thief had returned after traveling to the city for the funeral of his mother. A poet, two sculptors, and a musician asked permission to work in the lower vaults. A young sister and brother sought refuge after the killing of their parents in guild wars. Each of these prisoners was heard quickly and welcomed out of the pit.

As the cases increased in complexity, the Council turned more and more to the body of Thieves for testimony and opinion. Thieves jumped down from the ledges to question the prisoners of the firepit. The Artauk of the Council called out the Thieves' questions and the prisoners' answers for all in the chamber to hear.

A pherologist requesting escort into the vaults to take rock and mineral samples was subjected to intense questioning because of suspected ties to guild and university officials. The scientist weathered the interrogation with calm expression and measured voice. He acknowledged university sponsorship of his work and admitted family ties to the Machine Guild. He denied connection of any kind, however, to the Miners' Guild, to gem-hunters, or to prospectors of precious metals. The Thieves remained unmoved until the pherologist spoke of his work. The scientist came alive with animate gesture, frequent smile, and a teacher's passion as he described the specimens that he hoped to find in the deep vaults. He was lifted from the pit and granted Iccin escorts.

A filmmaker and a photographer followed, choosing to be heard together, accepting common verdict. The artists asked entrance into the catacombs to photograph the oldest temple relics and the hidden works of Opir. They also asked to film a season of war in the deep mountains.

"The people of the city know little about the fighting in the mountains," the filmmaker said. "They hear only the complaints of the miners, the loggers, the mill workers. Let us tell your story."

The Thieves rejected both requests.

The Varran leaders of the underground attacked the Varran artists of the city. "The art of the underground will never be sold," the leaders said, "never scattered in the wind for all to see.

The artwork of the ages waits for true seekers, for those willing to leave everything behind and brave the darkest descent. Those unwilling are unworthy. As for the war, those who want to know already know. The rest are accomplice."

"You turn allies into enemies," the photographer said.

As the filmmaker and photographer left the pit, the lone Artauk of the Council came to Dyraveen. He stooped low to speak into Dyraveen's ear, green-rivered veins across his bare scalp. "Walk the pit," the giant said.

Dyraveen walked the edge of the firepit. He passed beneath each ledge, the eyes of every Thief upon him.

He stopped in front of Cirico.

The Council circled around them.

"We will be heard together," Dyraveen said.

Cirico stood up and stepped away. "We are strangers," Cirico said. "I will be heard alone."

The Council watched the two prisoners with interest. They turned to Dyraveen.

"Why do you stand with a killer?" they asked.

"Killer to you, savior to me," Dyraveen said. "I live because of this man's mercy. He will live because of yours."

The Council separated the two prisoners.

Cirico was made to kneel at the ledge, Dyraveen to stand in the fire's ashes.

Dyraveen told the Council all that he had heard about his father. He asked to see any of Sedenel's paintings or sketches in the catacombs. Again, he pled for Cirico.

The Artauk called out to the body of Thieves for anyone who knew of the artist, Sedenel.

Throughout the crowd, Thieves' eyes sharpened with recognition; heads nodded.

An old Iccin man stepped down slowly from the ledges. He walked across the pit with a determined plodding, his bare, grey-dusted feet flattening ash and ember. The old man entered the circle of the Council. He spoke to Dyraveen then turned his left ear close to listen. "I am Iddir," the old man said. You say you are the son of Sedenel? Convince me your words are true?"

"He was a Tyraen of pure blood," Dyraveen said. "Born of the east. Hobbled by disease."

Iddir squinted, a web of lines pulling tight to the corner of his eye. "Where did the disease strike?" the old man asked.

"Joints, tissues, heart," Dyraveen said. "He died soon after he left the underground."

Iddir turned to the Council. "I will take the bearded boy to the place I remember," he said.

Dyraveen, now guest, not prisoner, followed Iddir out of the pit. He stopped on the ledge. He turned back to watch the trial of Cirico.

"Turn away," the old man said. "Come with me. Some will die in the pit tonight."

"He is my friend," Dyraveen said, refusing to leave.

Cirico faced the body of Thieves from his knees. The guild assassin confessed to many crimes and many killings.

"Name your victims," the leaders said.

Cirico named the victims he could remember, his voice trailing into whisper.

"Name their children," the leaders said.

Cirico's head slipped low, his jaw a blade into his chest. Eyes closed, breath faint, the killer trembled. "I do not know their children," Cirico said.

The Council walked away from Cirico. They climbed onto the ledges to join the body of Thieves. All eyes glared down into the pit. Staves were raised, blades unsheathed, pistols unholstered.

Cirico raised his head, opened his eyes. The sight of the crowds' weapons stoked his courage. Cirico climbed to his feet. He circled the Thieves' pit, glaring defiantly at his accusers. "Am

I the only killer in this chamber?" Cirico shouted. "Do I walk among the pure? the innocent? the bloodless? No, Thieves, you are mired and stained, just as I am."

The Council stepped back into the pit.

A Varran leader walked toward Cirico, pistol in hand. "And what do you want from the underground?" the leader said. "What do you ask of the Thieves?"

"I ask for sanctuary," Cirico said. "Protection."

"You would become one of us?"

"Yes, I would defend the underground. I would fight for the Thieves."

"You would become our killer? our assassin?"

"No, I would guard your caves. I would protect your people."

The leader raised his pistol, muzzle to the chest of Cirico. "Choose now," the leader said. "Servant or Soldier."

Cirico breathed deep. He looked high to the cavern ceiling, to the misty light slipping through the jagged wounds of stone. "Servant," he said. "I have seen too much killing."

The leader looked around the pit, first to the faces of the Council, then to the body of Thieves. He lowered his pistol. "You will work in the vaults," the leader said. "You will build shrines for each of your victims. In one year's time, you will return to this chamber and face the Council again."

Cirico climbed from the pit. He disappeared into the body of Thieves.

Iddir touched the arm of Dyraveen and motioned to leave.

Dyraveen nodded at the old man, but he turned back to the pit at the sound of loud shouting. He watched the next prisoner dragged and kicked into the ash. He saw Thieves pour down from the ledges and surround the prisoner.

The Artauk of the Council raised his hands and shouted.

The crowd fell back.

The Artauk grabbed the fallen prisoner by the hair and pulled him from the ground. The Artauk turned the prisoner's head into the torchlight, his face gashed and swollen, blood and spit dribbling onto his chest.

"Our brother, Ferros, once shared our journeys and battles above ground, our long night below," the Artauk said. "But Ferros, our brother, was captured by the guilds in the mountains. And in their camps, Ferros died, our brother broken by torture and labor." The Artauk shoved the face of the prisoner into the ash. "And this shell, this reptile, this shit, returned to us to spy and to betray. His new masters now wait, impatient for his word."

The prisoner lifted his face from the ashes.

The crowd of Thieves surged forward. Staves rose and fell. Pistols sparked and split the air. Blades slashed low in silver crescent.

Dyraveen looked to Iddir.

"Now we will go?" the old man said.

Iddir led Dyraveen along the river.

The shouts and cries of the pit faded into the surge and crash of the river. The torches' throb vanished in the glare of moonlight beneath the surface fissures. A last flurry of gunshots echoed faintly like boot-loosened pebbles down a mountainside.

The river dipped, curved, and dipped again.

They walked steep banks of stone along the river, hand-carved trails slick and narrow.

Dyraveen kept his eyes from the icy river, concentrating instead on every step and handhold, each shift of weight and change of slope. He struggled to keep up with the old man. He slipped and stumbled. He bruised his knees, ass, elbows. He opened both hands with cuts. Twice, he nearly fell into the waters.

The old Iccin plodded forward with slow and measured steps. He touched the bank wall with an occasional finger to steady or gently push off. The rest of the time his gnarled, veiny legs kept near-perfect balance, his bare feet somehow holding firm on the slippery rock.

Iddir kept the same sure pace regardless of the trail's switch or dive. Dyraveen crept through sharp corners. He slid and crawled through steep drops.

Dyraveen lost sight of the old man.

The trail leveled.

Then widened.

Dyraveen passed beneath a line of massive greystone towers. White mists circled slowly around their peaks. Veering cracks rose from the ground to split their bases. From their sides great rock slabs and shelves had fallen, like frost-pierced leaves from winter tree.

"The Widow Towers," Iddir said, stepping out from shadow. "They climbed toward the sky in their youth but never reached the sun. Now, time takes everything. They wither and crumble. They wait for final collapse. They dream of places never seen, faces ever fading."

Iddir walked on.

Before the last tower, the old man stopped and wrapped his eyes in strip of cloth. "The light is coming," he said.

Dyraveen ripped cloth from the waist of his shirt and tied it over his eyes. Stumbling forward, he followed the dim, blurred shadow of his guide.

They clung to the tower's side as they walked, fingertips trailing over coarse stone grain.

When they rounded the fullest width of tower, white-fired rays of light slashed over them. They turned their heads to the ground but even the cavern floor blazed bright.

Dyraveen touched his hand to the back of Iddir, closed his eyes, and followed blindly. He felt hard-frozen raindrops sink into his hair, flakes of wet snow melt into his beard. His eyes watered, the white light burning even through the cloth. He heard birds above. He smelled sweet vine and tree.

Iddir whistled in signal.

Others whistled back from perches high and low.

Iddir called out a few words in the tongue of the Iccin.

The guards laughed.

Dyraveen took his hand from the back of Iddir. He followed the old man by the sound of his hoarse and labored breath. As he probed forward, Dyraveen eased his squinting. Little by little, he opened his eyes beneath the cloth. He raised his head skyward to glimpse the outline of an enormous white star, crust of land collapsed into broad-mouthed pit. His eyes traced groundward from the starry pit, down sharp columns of silver light, over razor-cleft rock face and thick-shadowed voids, through gusted tides of falling snow and flocks of birds fleeing vine to vine. He inhaled deep and long.

Iddir stopped and looked back. "Do you miss the surface world?" he said. "Now is the time to turn around."

Dyraveen took a last breath of the open air. He wiped the melted snow from his brow and eyes. "I have already walked the caverns of the Blue Temple," Dyraveen said. "I have heard the great singers and drummers of the deep. I have wandered the stalax forest. I know well the long night of the underground."

"You know too much, my bearded friend," Iddir said, laughing. "What is left for you to see or do?"

Dyraveen followed the old man away from the stinging light of the open pit.

They trailed the river as it plummeted into the darkness.

They took the cloth from their eyes as the last light of the surface disappeared.

Dyraveen pulled the opal chain from under his shirt.

Iddir drew a talisman of bronze and jadestone.

Dyraveen's opal cast a sphere of blue-pearl light ahead of him, rainbowed spectra bending, blurring, turning within the seablue cloud.

The jadestone of Iddir filled the wide cavern chamber with brilliant emerald light. It penetrated deepest shadow, illuminated from floor to ceiling, cast in clear outline the small bubbles of the river, the pebbles of the trail, the cavities of ceiling arch.

The light of Dyraveen melted into the light of Iddir. Emerald dissolved blue. Jadestone swallowed opal. The rainbow pools dimmed and paled, rare glimmers of fresh color breaking free from the sea of green.

"Your stone is powerful," Dyraveen said.

"Yours is weak," Iddir said. "It was made by imitators, by the untrained."

"There is an art to the gems and crystals?"

"An art from the first days. The line of the Blue Temple makers died out long ago. Our line survives by a thinning strand."

"Will I see crystalmakers in the catacombs?"

"There are makers in the catacombs," Iddir said. "But you will not see."

They crossed the river at a bridge of fallen limestone plate.

The river split around a mammoth septum of contoured blackstone.

The trail dropped.

The river forked again.

And again.

They followed a weakened, shallow stream.

The stream pooled on a hilltop slope. It dripped from the summit into terraces ringed by amber-crusted walls. It trickled over the mineral walls to fill pools no deeper than a boot sole. Webs of red-coral algae branched to surface through the thinnest waters of each marbled terrace.

Iddir led the way down the hillside. He stepped through deepest waters, carefully avoiding the coral webs. "Follow my steps," he said. "The makers use the red fiber."

They traced slow steps down the hillside, terrace to terrace, until they reached a dry and flattened stretch.

They approached a wide-spanning portal - an X-shaped void in the rock wall, hand-carved wing tips reaching high, slashing tail fins dipping low.

Iddir stopped before crossing through the portal. With a stabling hand to the stone, he coughed up bloody phlegm.

"These are the catacombs carved by the ancient clerics of the Blue Temple, protected by the Thieves' brethren since the first days of Pocone," Iddir said. He spit a red, clinging trail from his lip. "You are a boy, Dyraveen. Only by the blood of your father are you allowed within."

Dyraveen bowed his head.

They crossed the portal of the catacombs.

They followed the tunnel down. The carved wings stretched, snapped, and lifted high. The lower fins swayed in and out, whipping suddenly, darting forward.

Wing and fin sped downward.

The tunnel narrowed.

Fish and bird merged into single beast.

The tunnel opened at the foot of the catacomb mount.

They entered a chamber broader and deeper than any Dyraveen had yet seen.

The steep hillside climbed ring by ring toward the surface. The mount vanished into a skyward cloud of misted shadow and glowing mineral.

The surface of each ring was carved by different flesh of animal. Fur. Scale. Feather. Hide.

Many caverns opened across the rings of the mount, their mouths marked by gemstone script - sapphire blue, blooded pearl, amethyst star - with letters of the first tongue, symbols of the ancient temple.

Chains hung from the mouths of many caverns, gliding over the roughhewn blackstone, hanging down the hillside all the way to chamber floor.

Iddir walked tired to the lowest ring of the mount.

He entered a cavern marked with a single blue crescent over the mouth.

Inside, he knelt at a small fountain pool. He drank long then leaned back against the cavern wall.

"Your name," Iddir said.

"Dyraveen."

"Bring me the bones, Dyraveen," he said, looking deeper into the cavern, breathing heavy through an open mouth.

After a drink at the fountain, Dyraveen headed into the cavern to search. He found circular stone tables, dark-stained with layers of dried blood and fine-dusted ash. He found fang of serpent, wing of hawk, tail of lizard.

Iddir nodded when Dyraveen presented the bones. The old man took a flask from his waist, poured oil over the bones, and lit them on the ground. The bones burned slow, a dim purple flame spiraling through the bits of flesh remaining. When the fire died and the bones lay charred and bare, Iddir ate. He finished wing and fang then offered tail.

Dyraveen, famished, bit the tail. His tooth cracked. He spit up splinters of bone.

Iddir took the tail. He ground the bones to powder in his back teeth. He swallowed.

"Rest a moment, my friend," Iddir said. "The climb to the shrine is long."

Iddir slumped against the rim of the pool. He slept instantly, head upon stone.

Dyraveen curled in the open tunnel. In the endless night, he dreamed of his mother's eyes glowing fierce against the sky of Pocone. He dreamed of his father limping cavern to cavern.

When Dyraveen woke, he found Iddir still slumped against the rock, his eyes a wet sliver of bronze.

"I remember your father," Iddir said. The old man spoke slowly. He drew his breath like muddied water from deepened well. "He was sickly and thin. Like you. When his knees swelled, he would sit at the edge of the river. He would hold his legs under the icy water until his hands trembled, until his chest heaved. In the coves, he sketched the giants, the Iccin, sculptors, poets. His words were always few, his eyes tired but piercing. He was allowed in every shrine and chamber of the underground except for the caves of the makers. I saw only his sketches, but others spoke of his paintings. Your father was admired as an artist, respected as a man."

"Where are his paintings?" Dyraveen asked. "Where are his sketches?"

"He was too weak to climb far. Maybe the third ring, maybe the second." Iddir took the talisman from his neck and held it out. "Take this. If you are questioned, say that Iddir, your guide, now dreams within the mountain."

Dyraveen stared at the talisman. "I have light," he said. "Get up. Let's go."

Iddir's arm dropped and fell against the cavern floor. He released the talisman. His arm slid across the rock, back into the cradle of his chest. His eyes closed, the sliver of bronze extinguished.

"My breath returns to sky," the Iccin said. "My flesh returns to stone."

Dyraveen hid the talisman inside his pocket, the opal chain inside his shirt.

He sat quietly in the darkness of the chamber.

When Iddir gasped for air, Dyraveen took out his canteen. He poured water into the old man's throat until the body lay still.

Dyraveen lived on the mount.

He caught lizards and snakes by hand and cooked them in the oil of Iddir.

He stashed his boots and jacket, cut his ragged pants above the knee, his shirt beneath the shoulder.

He walked and climbed with bare feet like the Iccin.

Dyraveen explored the catacomb tunnels of the lowest hillside ring, the hallways once packed by the huddled refugees of ancient Pocone. Inside these oldest networks, he found pottery shards, dusty scrolls, broken tool fragments, and rusted-out cauldrons. He found no paintings, no sketches.

In the caverns of the second ring, Dyraveen found life-size sculptures of bestial hybrids, unnatural mixings of land, sea, and sky creatures, mythology and science stirred in delirium.

On the third ring, he found pits of musicians' fires. He found sketches strewn throughout the chambers, the parchments lead-blurred and moisture-warped, the unsigned, untitled drawings covered with dead flies and excrement of rat. He found canvas paintings hole-pocked and bleached of color. He found thin traces of powder paintings on cavern walls and ceiling. None of these rotting works were signed by the artist, Sedenel.

Dyraveen stashed away the talisman and opal chain.

He learned to see in darkness and deep shadow.

He crawled like a reptile among the boulders and crevices of the mountain's base.

Gaunt of flesh, blackened of skin, he studied all other creatures.

Dyraveen watched every spark of light and step of movement across the mountain.

He saw artists come and go from the middle rings.

He saw Iccin couples enter the caverns beneath the mountain's shoulders, hand in hand, hip to hip.

He saw the young children of the giants left alone on the cavern floor, Artauk boys and girls racing to the summit, one falling to his death.

And he saw the light of the makers, a distant throb and flicker of crimson-purple fire on mountain's highest pyramid.

Dyraveen waited until makers came down from the heights. He watched the stout, black-hooded workers descend by iron chain to the cavern ground, plunging faster than any artist, Iccin, or Artauk. He held his breath while they made their way through the field of broken boulders, their line passing by him close enough to touch.

The crystal-makers left the great chamber for the terraced pools of coral.

Dyraveen ran to the mount. He climbed by longest chain.

He passed quickly through the wide and familiar lower levels.

In the steepening middle levels, his pace weakened, ring by ring.

By the high, stone pyramid of summit, his calves and forearms burned with exhaustion; sweat dripped steady from his chin; blisters flared and broke across his palms. He climbed the outcropped shoulders at pyramid's base then ducked into the mouth of nearest cavern.

Safe within the mouth, Dyraveen collapsed.

He lay on his back.

He breathed.

He gazed long into the faint, glowing mist beyond the summit.

To sleep is to die.

Dyraveen pushed for the summit without the safety of the chain. He dug his hands into the barbs and vanes of the rock-carved feathers. He worked his feet along the feathers' slanted shafts.

Dyraveen never glanced down the mount to see his progress. Or up to see the height remaining. He never turned to glimpse the brilliant gems embedded in the stone.

Dyraveen thought only one move ahead. He focused only on the grip of rock around each toe, each finger. All of the giant mount, the underground, the world, shrunk into the tiny span between his arms.

With each breath of mountain drawn, he took death inside him.

With each breath expelled, he claimed life.

Dyraveen followed the column of light fallen from highest cavern. The early light fell still and faint, an indigo muted by distance and distortion.

The column brightened with the upward climb. Indigo separated into overlapping clouds of blue, green, and red. The clouds churned as if heated by strongest currents of star.

By mountaintop the twisting fires of light - topaz, turquoise, violet, ruby - blinded Dyraveen.

He closed his eyes. He walked the last feathered shaft until his hands touched the loose pebbles of the cavern floor. He climbed into the cavern's mouth. He slumped against the cavern wall.

Dyraveen held his mind to single track. *I will see the secrets of the makers. I will see and I will leave. I will see and I will leave.*

He stood and turned his back to the inner cavern. He blinked in flutters. He forced his eyes wider and wider. He held his eyes open longer and longer, until the scorching fire no longer stung.

Dyraveen stared out from the mountain. The makers' light washed over him, warmed his neck and shoulders. The crimson light caught trails of mist and wisps of dust in the heights beyond the mountain. The light illumined the distant walls of scaled stalactite. Dark clouds moved through the fiery glow - the shadows of head and hands.

Dyraveen drew the knife of Iddir from his waist and turned to face the inner cavern. He crept forward, one hand blocking light, the other pointing blade.

The fire raged inside the chamber, rays of white-bladed light slashing and searing.

Dyraveen peered into the shadows.

He saw one head, two arms…

Was the maker facing toward him? or away?

He saw each hand moving, each hand holding…

Weapons? or tools?

The white light dimmed suddenly to blue.

The shadow faced him.

Staff in left hand.

Sword in right.

Dyraveen struck, jabbing forward with his blade. The knife ripped cloth.

Dyraveen stepped forward, stabbed again. The knife sunk to bone.

The sword slashed for neck. Dyraveen ducked low.

Dyraveen stabbed again.

Again.

Again.

Staff and sword dropped to floor. The weight of shadow crashed against him. Dyraveen pushed the body away.

Shaking, he turned toward the inner chamber, blade raised, hand dripping. He searched the chamber for other shadows, other makers.

The cavern chamber was deep and wide.

He saw teardrop mineral torches…

Racks of strange tools – slender rakes, heavy pestles, curved trowels, tined claws.

Marble basins storing powders, liquids, mosses, lichen.

Small pools of silver oil, a green mist rising from the surface, a milky vapor falling.

Blunted cones of interwoven coral, surrounded by curved mirrors of amber-tinted glass.

Vertical looms of crystal strand, shimmering with heat, shifting in color red-to-violet, sweating drops of golden mercury.

Dyraveen found no other makers in the cavern.

He dropped his blade and ran.

Dyraveen descended iron chain to mountain's base.

He hid in bouldered field. He burrowed into hole.

Sleepless, trembling, he waited until the line of makers returned.

When every maker had crossed the field, climbed their chain, and disappeared into their cavern, young Dyraveen fled for the river.

Dyraveen stood alone on the river shore.

The water sped by in streaking currents green and silver, its deep rush echoing wall to wall.

His eyes followed the river downstream to the black horizon. The cavern ceiling pulled tight to the river surface. The space of air above the water disappeared. Dyraveen imagined drowning. He imagined suffocation. He imagined the rib-crushing press of the water, his bones being hurled against mountain rock, the fading of all light, the opening black.

Dyraveen looked upriver toward the Thieves' great meeting chamber. He remembered the face of Ferros - the Thief turned traitor - slick with blood, spit, and sweat, the eyes pleading for bullet's mercy. He remembered Cirico in the barren circle, prostrate on the stone, breathless, the hard killer shivering with fear. He remembered the assassin chained at the boulder, cursing, sobbing, naming victim after victim, his shoulders slumping, his voice weakening into whisper. And he remembered Cirico at his firepit trial before all the Thieves, the moment after his sentencing, a long and sweet breath taken, his face softening with relief, something close to peace.

Upstream, Dyraveen faced the justice, the wrath, of the Thieves.

Downstream, he faced implacable Nature; he required the mercy of fierce and heartless forces.

Young Dyraveen gazed long into the river.

In the end, he borrowed from the strength of Cirico.

He journeyed upstream.

Dyraveen walked beneath the blinding light of the pit before the Widow Towers. He waited for the high-perched guards to signal one another. He waited for arrow's whistle or pistol's crack. He heard only the winged flutter of crows and gulls.

He passed Artauk along the corridors of the towers, but none stopped him.

He passed Iccin along the river's slopes, but none said a word.

Dyraveen followed the rising glow of the moons into the great meeting chamber.

He sat atop the boulder of manacle and chain. He waited for questioners, accusers, executioners. He waited two days. Three days. Four.

Out of the darkness, a face from another life appeared.

Edden. The old master of the Aviet. His teacher, rival, friend.

Dyraveen drew his blade and held it high.

Edden brushed the blade aside. He looked down at Dyraveen with saddened eyes. "Your mother sent me," Edden said. "It's time to go."

Back in the city, Dyraveen drank and ate with Edden. He accepted new clothes but refused to cut his beard or hair.

Dyraveen met with his mother in a prayer cove of the city gardens.

Rhoa gripped the hand of her son. She felt his rough-hided palm, his fingers without flesh, the sharp bones of his wrist. Rhoa remembered the Tyraen compound of her youth, a boy, pale and gaunt, sweeping silent through the halls. Rhoa let go of her son's hand. She looked away. "You live," she said.

"I searched the underground," Dyraveen said. "For the paintings of my father."

"What did you find?"

"Only shreds and scraps in old caves."

"Shreds and scraps?" his mother said, a wry smile twisting. She lifted a long cylinder wrapped in grey cloth from the ground at her feet. She touched the leather straps binding the roll together. "Was it worth it, my son? the long journey down? the wasted years?"

"I learned much of life and death," Dyraveen said. "I learned that darkness waits for all of us, that every breath is borrowed, that the future dims and the past haunts."

Rhoa searched the eyes of her son, probing for depth. Her wry smile faded. She held out the cylinder to Dyraveen.

"The work of your father," Rhoa said. "Hundreds of sketches. Sixteen canvases."

Dyraveen stared at the cylinder. On its end he saw the thick and weathered edges of many canvases, plastic-shielded papers wrapped in tight circles, thick as a fist. "You kept these from me?" he said.

"You were a boy," Rhoa said. "Now you are a man."

Dyraveen took the roll into his arms. He held it close to his chest. He felt the soft threads of the wrapping cloth, the knots of leather strap.

"There is more I kept from you," Rhoa said. From within her cloak she pulled out an envelope and leather pouch. "Cyadae left an inheritance for you, a gift for the man she would never see. And from the east your grandfather wrote. He is Davel, the father of your father, Sedenel."

Dyraveen studied the pouch, thick and bulging, the envelope, worn and thin.

"Take them," Rhoa said, pushing both into his hand. "Now, you are free, my son. Now, there is nothing to bind you to your home."

Dyraveen kissed his mother.

Rhoa touched his hand and turned away. "Go east," she said. "See the pyres of your father, the lowly birthplace of your mother. Meet Davel, the great Tyraen flame."

VIII. LAST DAYS OF DAVEL

The leaders came to the eastern hills in the moonless hour of the night.

Tiny specks of red and blue light approached the hills from all corners of the valley. The dim specks opened, brightened, grew. The dots stretched into pale and hollow rings, throbbing faint through the black-dusted valley winds.

At the edge of the hills, the lights turned south, tracing slowly across the horizon, looping around the heart of the range.

At the great southern gorge, the aircraft banked sharply into the long channel climbing back to the highlands. The tricopters opened their full beams to bare the channel under green and silver light, exposing a stream of broken-toothed boulders and the winding grooves of ice-worn glacial crawl.

The aircraft crept north.

The craft followed the channel to its end on a plateau shelf.

One by one, the tricopters landed. The broad shelf filled with whirring, ghost-white blades.

The silver beams died. The white blades locked still. People spilled down from circular hatches.

Assistants, pilots, and crew set their camp against the eastern wall, wedging tarped rods between boulders, bracing against the strong-gusted winds.

The leaders ran to the western edge.

They wormed below through slitted pores.

They walked silently through spiral tunnel driving deep.

They descended, blind in the darkness, stumbling, bumping, gripping arms and grasping stone.

When the tunnel opened into a flamelit hall, the leaders circled around a boulder topped by a beaming oil lantern. Into hand-carved shelves around the stone, the leaders dropped shoes, watches, rings, and chains. They emptied their pockets. They shed their coats, pants, shirts.

The leaders left the boulder and walked deeper into the chamber. At a wide spring basin, they shed the last of their clothes. They dove into the icy water of the pool.

Naked and shivering, they rose on the pool's far side. On the bank, they took up rough canvas shorts and tunics. A few found torches and flasks of oil along the walls.

Old Davel emerged from the flame-spun shadows of the chamber. He gathered the shed undergarments of the leaders, carried them back to the boulder shelf, and laid them down.

Davel returned to the hall's end. He passed through the leaders, his eyes low, his breathing deep and slow like river's turn.

The cragged voice of the old man broke the long quiet of the chamber. "The soul hides," Davel said.

"Beneath many skins," the leaders answered, heads bowed.

Davel led the trembling huddle out of the hall and into the mine.

They walked the empty vaults and rubble tunnels of an old silver mine long depleted. Their bare feet bruised upon the rusted heads of pick and shovel and the rotted ties of rail tracks. They paused to kneel at shrines to fallen miners.

In a deep corner of the silver mine, they entered by trapdoor into a vertical tunnel. They climbed by steel-spiked footholds and half-moons chiseled into the amber stone. The strong-drawn breath of Davel filled the narrow tunnel.

The leaders joined the rhythm of the old man's breathing. They matched his every inhale, every exhale, each pause and surge. They followed, hold for hold, his upward climb.

But the old man slowed in the upper reaches of the tunnel.

His pauses lengthened.

His drives and stretches faltered.

On final step, his legs quivered; his foot slipped from the spike. He was saved from fall by the climber below.

The leaders circled around Davel in the cavern at tunnel's end. They studied the face of the century-old Tyraen. They saw his pale-blooded skin, his desperate breath through gaping mouth, his eyes glassy and confused.

Every hand reached out to help.

The old man stared at the hands reaching down. He stared at the faces above. "I can finish," he said, rising on his own strength.

The others parted, opening a path to the lead. They waited.

"I will follow now," Davel said.

The group marched on, Davel at the rear.

They tracked the tunnel to a massive plate of blue-grey stone. They slid beneath the plate then traced upward through fissures in the rock. With shoulders turned, they slipped through narrow cracks. They knelt and crawled through flattened crevice.

The slender cracks widened.

The air dampened and warmed.

Breezes passed over them, traces of open sky and molten fire.

They followed the plate to its edge where it butted against another giant slab of blue-grey stone, both plates rising after collision. They walked freely in the wide pocket below the plates, the line of climbers gathering into close circle. Near to their goal, their steps quickened.

The plate lines melted into black stone.

An ashen gust drove sweat over skin.

The cavern opened into sky above, abyss below.

The leaders took their seats on the boulders of the ledge. They looked upward to the mouth of the great pit, over the pocked and blistered blackstone, into the white-silver sun. They held out their hands to savor the light of the higher world.

The voice of Davel called over the heated winds. "The first fire reigns below," he said.

The leaders looked downward into the pit, along silver-bladed sun rays blunted into shadow, beyond fallen drifts of rain burned to mist, into the fearsome depths. They gazed long into the churn and quiver of the molten darkness, a breathing sea of coal and ember stirred by redfire slither.

The leaders sat, weary from their journey, weak with thirst and hunger, a step away from oblivion and death. The leaders were no longer confident and self-assured. They were no longer powerful with wealth and resource, the highly honored of their field and office. They were helpless animals. They were the smallest of creatures tucked in stone nest, desperate with craving, terrified of height and depth.

Old Davel stared into the deep.

His memories stirred in the bloodburn glow of the ancient fire. He traveled over days, seasons, years, to the first time he had seen the great pit.

He had trembled like a child on the ledge.

Behind him, the old cavern mystics had called out. *Be strong. Do not turn away.*

He had crawled to the edge on his knees, laid flat upon his stomach, wrapped his arms tightly around the boulder. He had stared into the deep, still trembling.

Again, the mystics spoke. *This is the first fire. From its breath, the moons and stars. From its shedden ash, our days.*

316

Davel had seen no fear in the eyes of the mystics. The old wanderers had looked into the depths with hope and expectation. The first light still lived, they believed. The sparks of creation still burned beneath the land. On a day soon coming, the thin shell of the land would melt by risen fire. And the night-weakened sky would burn and glow eternal.

In the years of his prime, Davel had returned each summer. He had followed his mystic guides through the vast, tunneled webs of the eastern hills. He had wandered old mines and ancient strongholds, white rivers underground and black-crystal vulcan channels. He had learned the pebbled markings of the mystics — directions to trail and water, warnings of shifting rock and tunnel collapse. In hidden chambers he had seen their ochre-slashed paintings of flame and wind; their grey-carved symbols of ribbed moons, burning branches, and slender, marrowless bones.

The mystics had accepted Davel as a respected visitor to the hills but had denied him entrance to the sacred burial coves and witness to the Blue Fire rite.

They had pressed Davel to choose between the airy kingdoms and the underworld.

"Your world is dying," they had said. "All of its wealth is melting away, all its power fading."

Standing before the great pit, consumed by awe of the ancient fire, Davel had believed. And he had doubted. In the fire's trance, he had sensed a power older than the deep-rooted Tyraens, his people. He had glimpsed a strength greater than the mammoth Torite machine that ruled the east, a vision more radiant than the Varran starlit dreams. There was some force of creation beyond principle of science. There was some truth alive before first breath of time, some will that would stretch into eternity untainted and undying. But was the mystics' fire this force, this truth, this will? The mystics claimed to understand the deepest currents of time, but pain of flesh made them impatient for the coming future. They hoped for fire to end the present age, fire to sweep the land, fire to transform the faithful. They imagined that, somehow, finest creation would emerge from greatest destruction. The contradiction tore.

When the mystics had realized that Davel would never completely forsake the land above, they had pulled away from him. Their faces had hardened, their eyes deadened. They had crossed the underground river while he slept and vanished into the shadows.

Davel had spent years away from the caverns.

He had traveled the continent.

He had busied himself with books and letters.

And each summer away the ache inside him had worsened.

He had missed the heavy quiet of the depths, the sweet fading of surface fears and worries, the dream-like clarity of mind, the thrill of first step into undiscovered chamber.

Davel had returned to the caverns with a small group of friends. He had led his friends on a short and slow-paced journey. He had realized that his friends needed more than time away from their cities, more than exercise and peace. They needed to be humbled. They needed to be stripped of mask and artifice. They needed to feel want and pain and fear – the smallness of the creature.

The next summer Davel had led his friends on a longer, steeper journey into the underworld. He had challenged, spurred, and prodded. His friends had complained much in the early hours, but by journey's end they had come to understand.

Year by year, the group had grown. Torites and Varrans had been added to the first circle of Tyraens, leaders of industry, government, and finance, the many friends of Davel.

All submitted to the journey.

All were stripped and reborn.

But, now, the old guide could no longer climb. His body had spoken, the stark refusal of the flesh. He would not see the pit again.

Davel stared into the fires of the deep.

The young leaders looked high to the silver sun.

The leaders spoke of the future - the harvesting and mining of the continental wings, the opening of trade with many islands.

The old man remembered. He remembered the dead eyes and hard faces of the cavern mystics, the wet-blooded bones of rats and serpents strewn around him as he slept.

The leaders looked to Davel, waiting for words from their teacher.

Davel said nothing.

The leaders looked away, their faces long with sorrow, their eyes quick with calculation.

Davel returned to Tekenna.

He stayed throughout the remaining summer in the Tyraen compound of his first wife, Acuuran.

Old friends of the compound brought meals to his chamber, delivered letters, and shared books and journals of the wider continent.

Old enemies criticized and maligned him in the compound halls, hoping to draw him into debate in the trading center.

He worked alone in the gardens of the compound, weeding, pruning, planting.

At the burial shrine of Acuuran, he carved poetry of Lycis into the black marble arcs.

In the winter, he returned to his cottage beneath the stone bluff at the edge of the city. He cut and burned the overgrown tangles of brush and weeds. He swept thorns from the paths. He chopped firewood.

By first snow, the piles of letters poured over his desk and onto the floor.

By second snow, the messengers and assistants came. They followed him on the paths. They asked him for his testimony before councils, his sponsorship of projects, his endorsement of books, his appearance at summits and meetings around the continent. He declined all.

On a windy morning, crossing the frozen pond to gather wood, Davel slipped. His knee twisted. His head struck ice. He shivered and moaned, half-conscious, until his third wife found him just before nightfall.

The rest of the winter passed as a long and sleepless nightmare to Davel. His head pounded like rack of needles driven through his skull. His knee ached when he lay still, flared with pain at any movement. Rare moments of comfort were interrupted by doctors' hands; his sweetest rest ended by the loud voices of wife and children. No layers of blankets could warm him; he sweat and shivered through day and night.

A vision broke sharply through the fevered haze. An old man's beard on a young man's face. Tyraen eyes like glowing hazel candlelit. The long, thin hair of the Varran; the black leather braids of the Torite miner. It was the face of his first son, long dead.

He touched the face. "Sedenel," he said.

The head shook. "No, I am Dyraveen."

In the flush of spring, the fevers of Davel lifted; his knee settled into joint; his burning skull numbed and cooled. A cough still lingered in his throat, his chest tight with fluid.

The sons and daughters of third wife helped him along the paths, his arms across their shoulders.

The son of Sedenel watched, apart, beneath the trees.

By summer, Davel could walk by staff. He thanked his wife, his friends, his children and grandchildren. Then he asked them all to leave, only Dyraveen to stay.

When all were gone, Davel forced a promise from his grandson. "Next time I fall," Davel said, "let me lie."

The heat of summer could not clear the fluid from the old man's chest. He coughed and choked through the warm, clear nights.

Dyraveen helped until he could take no more.

He bathed and dressed his grandfather. He pushed his chair from the cottage and lifted him into the truck seat.

As the engine started, shaking fingers gripped his arm.

"No hospital, no doctors," Davel said in fierce whisper. "Take me to the pyres."

Old Davel knelt at the altar high on the hill. He gripped the horns of the altar. He pressed his forehead to the encasing ribs of goat on the altar sides. He stooped even lower and touched the ash of the ground, ran his hands through the bodies thousand.

Dyraveen knelt beside his grandfather. He felt the windworn grooves of the altar horns, stared at the blackened tips of pheran bones above the altar basin.

"The stories of my childhood return to me," Davel said, dusted ash falling through his fingers, "the heritage I scorned as a boy."

"My father worked here?" Dyraveen said.

Davel nodded, rising to one knee. "He lived with Acuuran in the catacombs below," the old man said.

The two climbed down the hillside.

They walked to the entrance of the catacombs.

They shook the locked gate. They called out, waited. The old man coughed and spit.

A hooded shrine guard stepped from the shadows into the light. The guard pulled back her hood. She looked first at the old man, then the young.

"This is Dyraveen," the old man said. "He is my grandson. He is the son of Sedenel."

The woman pressed close, her nose through the bars of the gate. She studied Dyraveen, his face, his hair, his eyes. "You are the son of Sedenel?" she said.

"Yes, his only son," Dyraveen said. "I come from the west. I bring many drawings of my father."

When young Dyraveen presented the cylinder of drawings, the guard fell back. She stared at the roll, her mouth slipping open, her eyes wide and bright. "These were painted by your father in the years of Pocone?"

"Yes," Dyraveen answered, "Pocone and Cyecura."

The guard opened the gate.

She kissed the son and father of Sedenel then led them both inside.

She brought them flat squares of bread, honeyed meat, and tall cups of moss liquor.

She shouted at another guard to spread word.

As the afternoon sun fell, the catacombs filled with a crowd of both Torites and Tyraens. The many shrine guards gathered. Then the cultics. Then poets, sculptors, painters, writers. Then miners and convicts.

When all had shared bread, meat, and liquor, the shrine guards led Davel and Dyraveen into the chamber of scrolls.

The father and the son of Sedenel were given seats of honor on the stone dais in the library center. Around them spanned an arc of Sedenel's work from Cyecura and Pocone. Sketches and drawings covered a dozen broad tables, black inks and silver leads on parchments faded brown to white. Painted canvases, finished and unfinished, filled between and behind the tables, raised by easel and shielded by glass.

Dyraveen, having already memorized every work in the cylinder on the long train ride east, watched the reactions of the crowd as they passed from table to table. He listened to the conversations of those who honored and loved the father he had never known.

Sedenel's early sketches of Rhoa, dominating more than half of the library tables, disappointed many in the crowd. The artists of the crowd found these works one-dimensional, immature in technique, and shallow in theme. The shrine guards passed over the sketches of Rhoa quickly, disappointed as much by their quantity as their quality, surprised that the legendary painter would have drawn the same girl hundreds of times. The cultics scorned the early works and looked away, some suggesting forgery, unable to imagine that great Sedenel had ever been stricken by boyish love. Only the hardened miners and convicts enjoyed the sketches. They stared long into the soft, young eyes of Rhoa.

The works of Cyecura elicited warmer response. The artists complimented rich detail in plant and animal life, complex movements of wind and water, sharpened brushwork. Many in the crowd lingered before the painting of the eyeless and earless in the rain-dampened grain fields.

The faces in the crowd came alive as they entered the final display section – the works of Pocone. All were enthralled by the sketches and paintings of the great western city. The face of convict and miner animated with curiosity. The eyes of the artists, cultics, and guards widened, then dampened, as if in witness of some celestial birth.

Dyraveen and Davel left the chamber of scrolls.

They walked to the shrine of Sedenel. They lit an arc of candles and sipped liquor in the shadows.

They stared into the painting of the river, where the white-clothed dead sank deep, then rose by silver currents, reflected fire in their eyes.

"Your father saw other worlds," Davel said. "He dreamed beyond the flesh."

"He was cut down at quarter-life," Dyraveen said. "He wandered and suffered alone."

"Sedenel was not born for home and peace," the old man said. "He was a painter. He was a Tyraen." Davel, weary, sat down on the stone floor, slumped against the wall. "Find blankets," he said. "And more liquor."

Grandson and grandfather drank deep into the night.

They talked of many things.

Davel told stories of his son. He told of Sedenel's part in the miners' strike, his courage before the prison officials, his travels from Lytarr to Pocone.

Dyraveen told of the Aviet lights, the underground of Pocone, the singer he had loved, the maker he had killed.

"My father was a painter of legend," Dyraveen said. "My uncle is a master of science. And my mother is gifted in science *and* art. Talent overflowed in their generation. In mine it dried to dust."

"But you bear the mark of Taldon," Davel said.

"What mark?"

"You will live as the patriarch lived, blessed and cursed, seized by history's fierce waters, the pride and shame of your people."

Dyraveen woke early the next morning. He drove into Tekenna. He found medicines for Davel and returned to the catacombs before the old man had risen. He crushed a tablet into powder and stirred it into tea.

Visitors flocked to the catacombs for many days. Dyraveen helped the guards prepare food and drink each morning. He guided the visitors through the catacombs and protected the works of art throughout the afternoon. When cool night fell, he climbed with Davel to the hilltop pyres. They talked in the moonlight and slept in altar's shadow.

In these last days of summer, Davel slipped deeper into memory. His mind returned again and again to the long, diseased suffering of his wife and son. "Are we ruined by sickness," he said, "or are we formed?"

By early fall, the throat and chest of Davel had cleared of all infection. He walked through the hills without resting. He ate and drank with pleasure.

Davel knelt once more at the altar of his son. He looked skyward, hands raised. "To all of my blessings a little time has been added," he said. "A final flush of life."

Davel and Dyraveen thanked the guards of the catacombs and shrine.

"Keep all of my father's works," Dyraveen said. "Protect them from thieves. Share with any who seek."

The shrine guards bowed their heads to the son and father of Sedenel.

They woke hours before dawn. They took to the air as the emerald moon slipped beneath the cloud-darkened hills. They crested the eastern hills then plunged through swirling fog toward the valley floor. Twisting tails of mist flashed blue and red, their writhing captured by the tricopter lights.

The fog disappeared. The central valley opened wide before them. They crossed amber-lit freight roads and goldrail shuttle lines, slender black rivers and stone-edged canals. The trade towns passed beneath them, following road, river, and canal, tight clusters of fuel towers, machinery tents, and domed inns.

The mists of the valley thinned.

A gold and purple flame stretched the edge of land and sky.

They entered the southern wasteland just as the first rays of morning sunlight touched the valley floor. The sun struck the sharp ridges of the wasteland plates. The grey-sand quartz flashed brilliant. The plates flared with sun's reflection, a vast sea of gently swaying leaves, their edges burning.

As the sun rose higher, the wasteland dimmed from blinding gold and white to pale clay brown and faded grey. They scanned the wasteland in all directions but saw nothing. No stream or pond of water. No slope or bend of land. No sign of life – pheran, plant, or animal. All was flat, still, and dry. All was dead.

Dyraveen shivered.

"Tomb of the striders," Davel said. "Birth of the word."

The pilot veered east, out of the wasteland.

Red brush and yellow grass emerged from the sandy soil.

The land climbed by winding chains of low-mounded hills, separated by steep ravine.

The land abruptly flattened onto a wide and green plateau.

"The steppes," Davel said. "Ancient den of the Oselen rider."

The pilot banked to the southeast, toward ocean shore.

Grass and brush disappeared.

Smooth plateau roughened into black rock crag.

Axe-beaked gulls reared and plunged to water.

When the boundless sea spanned horizon to horizon, Dyraveen, again, shivered in fear of the infinite.

The pilot banked to the east, dropped low, and followed tight the ragged southern shore.

The mist of ocean breakers wetted the clear belly of the craft.

"Higher, *higher*," Davel said, gripping his harness.

The tricopter climbed and pulled away from the rocky coastline.

The waves crashed soft beneath them.

The dark coast receded.

The deep waters sprawled blue and black.

Over the dark sea, Dyraveen told his grandfather of Cyadae's years on the northern coast. He told of her great loneliness breached by her love of Varran learning.

The old man smiled. "The name of Cyadae is known even in the east," Davel said. "Her work with crystals mystified the eastern academies for years. Her theories of diffusion and the bridge phases seemed sorcery in their eyes. But none could deny that the crystal, somehow, breathed."

The pilot turned back to the coast.

They saw the offshore power plants, the floating turbine bridges, the quarter-circle rings of tidal towers.

They saw the salt cliffs, the slitted caverns gouged by wave, the sheared facets damp with green mineral, the stone pillars twisted and crumbling.

They saw indigenous fishers swim to timbered columns, crawl the radial planks, stand and spear fish too broad to hoist alone.

At midday sun, the pilot slashed inland.

The tricopter cruised over shallow marshlands of crimson reed and crawling blue moss.

It split the triple gorges of the Black River, stirred dust-pebble clouds from the narrow canyon walls.

It crossed the barren foothills beneath the eastern mountains.

Then the eastern shelf opened clear before them - the flat continental third that stretched from mountains to sea. Though less developed and lighter in population than the central valley, the eastern shelf throbbed with activity and labor. Thick-dusted mists swirled over quarries of marble, rock, and mineral, the hard crust uprooted by diamond-spear splitters, hydraulic claws, and steel-fanged dozers. Massive, triple-tiered freight trackers crept the gravel roads between town and quarry. A steady flow of green-black cylinder barges cruised the rivers west, entered the locks at mountains' feet, and climbed the elevators to highest station. Discs and tillers churned the blue-clay soil of the fields; rotary swathers cut the hays and grains; arc-blade harvesters lifted beans, tubers, and melons onto rolling belts.

The buildings of the countryside were scattered – lone machinery hangars, riverside loading and processing plants, storage depots at cropfields' corner.

The homes of the countryside seemed too few for the legion of workers across the shelf. Circles of laborer tents surrounded low-lying ponds. Narrow, brown-brick halls paralleled irrigation canals. Gold-veined marble portals glistened from hillock slope.

The towns of the east were oblong, small, and loosely bound. Most had barracks, parts yard, fight pit, and fuel tower.

"Your father surveyed these lands after prison," Davel said. "He fled for Cyecura when the work became crime."

"What crime?" Dyraveen said.

"The Cerrans were pushed to the sea."

The tricopter looped around Lytarr, greatest city of the eastern shelf. Wide, arterial freightways radiated outward from the city's core, fanned and multiplied into lighter branches, then stretched like razored wire into all territories of the east. A dozen rock and steel arch bridges spanned the severing Pale River and connected the upper city to the lower. Tankers, trawlers, and reefer boats climbed west from sea to city to feed the barge armada mountain-bound. Crowded trading centers and bustling markets ringed the artificial bays at each corner of the city river.

Dyraveen gazed into the heart of the city. He stared long into the prominent, white-domed buildings, edged with crimson marble, sectioned by open spiral stair. "Government headquarters?" Dyraveen said.

Davel shook his head. "There is no government in the east," the old man said. "There are no courts, no councils."

"Then there is chaos," Dyraveen said.

"No, the keepers rule," Davel said. "They are governor, judge, and soldier. They gather companies around them. In the city, they clash by word. In the country, by bullet."

The pilot turned toward the mountains as the sun sank low.

As they headed home to Tekenna, the mind of Dyraveen burned with image and possibility, his eyes wide to see, his breath to swallow all.

Davel, worn by the day's long journey, slumped against the porthole and closed his eyes. His tired breath wetted clouds across the cool glass, gone by next inhale.

They returned to the cottage beneath the bluff.

Throughout the fall and winter, Davel summoned many friends and leaders from across the central valley to meet with young Dyraveen. "The last of my blood and spirit flows through him," Davel said, hands upon his grandson.

Davel rested. He read old Tyraen legends under the trees. He climbed the bluff each sunrise. At sunset, he recited the treasured lyrics of Acuuran, his wife - the ancient poetry she had memorized as a child and whispered as prayer through her anguished passing.

Dyraveen traveled throughout the eastern hills, through the cities of Tekenna, Lycira, and Balthe. Guided by the friends of his grandfather, he toured academies and compounds, factories and plants, halls of finance, trade, and government.

In summer's first heat, the two walked together along the moss-scented trails around the cottage.

"Many eyes followed me in the cities," Dyraveen said.

"Word has spread," Davel said. "I am slipping from this world. You are rising."

"Some looked at me with fear, some with contempt, some hope. Every word spoken to me was a test, a challenge, even from your friends."

"The ground is shifting. Friends and enemies alike wait to see how the mountains will settle."

"Why would strangers despise me? Why would any fear or hope in my rising?"

The old man sat down on a tree stump. He rested his staff against his shoulder, gathered his breath. "I had no special talent, no gifts beyond the ordinary," Davel said. "I dealt openly and honestly with all people. I befriended Torites and Tyraens, Varrans and Draun. I listened to all. It was the poverty of my youth that made me strong. I learned to live on almost nothing, to pour myself into any job, no matter how menial. I learned to be thankful for every drink of water, every meal, every breath. And it was my poverty that made me free. I lived simply, humbly, debtless. I wanted nothing. My travels ranged the continent from shelf to shelf. My friendships stretched wide through industry, government, academy, and university. Beholden to no one, free from institutional clutch, I always spoke the cold, bare truth. I became counselor and friend to many."

"But Tyraens saw you as a traitor for leaving the compound."

"Some, yes, the hard and the fearful. A younger Davel saw them as enemy and battled them fiercely in letter and debate. An older Davel merely ignored them and searched out the free-minded within the tribe."

"The Syllvar barred you many times from their council."

"And many times asked me to return."

"What did you fight for?"

"We wanted to bury separatism. We wanted to transform the tribal mind. We wanted to end the eternal trade wars that impoverished the many and empowered the worst."

"And what did you achieve?"

"Alternatives to rutted paths. A quiet rebellion. A thousand bridges of spirit and mind. A tenth of what we dreamed."

"So now the hard and the fearful will attack me, remembering your work."

The old man leaned forward, pulled against his staff, and climbed slowly to his feet. "It is likely," Davel said.

Dyraveen followed his grandfather, a steadying hand against his side. "The central valley is stagnant and ingrown," the young man said. "Its arrogance will lead to rot."

"You want the eastern shelf," Davel said. "You want the wild frontier."

"I want to live free. Like you."

"I will write the keeper, Rael."

Dyraveen traveled to Lytarr.

He met the keeper, Rael, in a stairway of his low-domed headquarters.

Rael read the letter of Davel quickly. He smoked, answered several calls on his radio, then turned the volume low. He read the letter again.

"Ancient Davel," the keeper said, folding the letter and handing it back. "The untouchable teacher. The man of shadow and whisper. The peasant sought by kings." The black and deep-set eyes of Rael narrowed. The lines of his sun-weathered brow widened. "We were beaten at the summer conclave, chopped down at the knees by the western keepers."

"Davel was very ill," Dyraveen said. "He could not travel."

"Our support from the valley was called into question. A single note from him might have saved us."

"My grandfather came near to death," Dyraveen said, matching the cold stare of the Torite. "What was lost at the conclave?"

"Our southern lock. Two mineral roads. A power plant in the north."

"Can they be regained?" Rael looked away, grimaced, exhaled tired and slow. His glare faded as he looked across Lytarr from the open stairwell. "So why does a bearded Tyraen from western Pocone travel all the way to the eastern shelf?" Rael said.

"To see," Dyraveen said. "To learn."

"Are you a writer?"

"No."

"A student? An academic?"

Dyraveen shook his head.

"A trader?"

"I told you," Dyraveen said, "I came to learn. I have seen the valley. Now I wish to see the frontier."

The eyes of the Torite again narrowed. "You want a holiday tour of the eastern frontier?" Rael said.

Dyraveen took a step toward the wide-shouldered Torite. "I will soon take up the mantle of my grandfather," he said, unblinking. "I have studied under finest tutors. I have worked in crystal plants and metal labs. I have climbed the iron skeletons of city tower. I have beaten the sharpest minds of the university at the Titan Stone. I have withstood trial before the Council of Thieves and survived a year in the underground caverns of Pocone. I have killed and I have watched men die. Find work for me, my friend. I will long remember every kindness shown."

Torite and Tyraen stared at one another.

Rael moved first. He drank from his canteen then held it out to Dyraveen.

"Does anyone know you here in Lytarr?" Rael asked.

Dyraveen shook his head and drank.

"Then you are a trade agent from the western valley," Rael said. "You represent investor bands from Cyecura and Pocone. Follow me closely. Speak to me in a mixture of tongues."

For several days Dyraveen followed the keeper around the headquarters. He pretended to take notes, make calls, perform calculations. He feigned argument with Rael, a struggle to translate Varran and Tyraen words into Torite.

Alone with Dyraveen, the keeper smiled. "You are gifted with the lie," Rael said. "All of the officers believed."

"I am tired of being a prop," Dyraveen said. "When can I start real work?"

"You don't understand, my friend. You are most valuable to me as a mysterious Tyraen, as a promise of wealth and resource from the western valley."

"But it is a lie."

"I was beaten by lies at the summer conclave. Now I will paint perceptions with truer color."

Rael took to the road with a small armada of trucks, jeeps, and tanks, three copters circling above. His cavalcade cruised the busiest arteries of southern Lytarr. They commandeered and blocked a bridge to the north until their passing. They surrounded a blue-marbled trading center on the northern riverbank. They idled and revved their engines for almost an hour, until all business inside the center stopped and the head officials came out to greet Rael.

The keeper and his armed flock entered the trading center. They took prime seats around the trading circle and sent their agents into the pit.

Rael summoned Dyraveen to his side. "We visit a keeper next," he said, his hand shielding mouth to ear. "Dialla will want to speak with you. She studied in the west."

After the agents finished their trading in the pit, Rael's troop returned to the road.

They crossed the northern half of the city, traveling west to east. They cruised by utility plants, construction sites, and a string of keepers' domes.

After the last dome, they parked around a flat-topped, grassless hill.

They joined Dialla's troop around a cluster of smoking grills. The two troops mixed, shared fish, smoked, drank.

Rael led Dyraveen into the open tent of Dialla. The tall and slender keeper worked over a table of maps, charts, and reports, the papers held down by rifle shells. Her bare arms were red with sunburn, her nose and forehead white-blistered. She motioned her guests to stools, noticed their eyes upon her skin. "We chased pod-runners for three days across the northern dunes," she said in explanation. "I lost my helmet in first skirmish."

"Did you catch them?" Rael asked.

Dialla nodded behind her. They saw three men and a girl chained to the back of a supply truck. The runners leaned low against the truck, clinging to shadow, hiding from sun. Their clothes were ripped and torn, their skin flame-red, their lips cracked, scabbed, and bleeding.

"What will you do with them?" Rael said.

Dialla shrugged. "They're addicts," she said. "They'll be chewing off their own arms soon."

Rael tilted his head to Dialla then took his stool.

Dyraveen remained standing. "Their supply lines trace back to Pocone?" he said.

Dialla studied the newcomer. "Probably," she said, "somewhere in the outer city."

"I walked the outer city," Dyraveen said. "I saw the rotting addict dens, the press houses hung with severed hands."

"The western soldiers do nothing?" Rael said.

"In Pocone, university soldiers care only about university grounds," Dyraveen said, "and guild soldiers care only about guild money. The regional government feeds upon itself, imploding every year. Local officials keep water flowing and the city core clean, nothing more. So the edge of Pocone festers."

Dialla nodded, smiled slightly.

Dyraveen tilted his head respectfully, shook her hand, and took his stool.

"This is Dyraveen, the investor I told you about," Rael said. "He comes with deep pockets."

"My friend exaggerates," Dyraveen said. "I have come to see the eastern frontier. I have some friends who would also travel east. If opportunity presents."

"There are few Tyraens in the west," Dialla said. "I saw no compounds in any western city."

"My mother fled from a Tekennan compound to study in Pocone," Dyraveen said. "She is an architect and designer of city towers, a Varran in heart and mind."

"And you? Are you Varran or Tyraen in heart and mind?"

"Neither. Both. I struggle to carve my own path."

"A path that left your mother far behind."

"Does not every child resist the world thrust upon them?"

The two keepers exchanged glances.

"You talk like a mystic," Dialla said. "There are no mystics on the frontier, only workers and soldiers."

"I am my father's son."

"And what is he?"

"My father is dead. He studied at Tekennan academy. He mapped and surveyed Lytarr when the city was young. He was a pyrekeeper, a miner, a prisoner, an artist."

"Dyraveen has made his bloodrun across the valley," Rael said. "He has walked the steps of his father."

"So your heart and mind are Torite as well," Dialla said. She sat up, leaned closer to the young Tyraen. "You are every man. And no man. Like water that creeps, lower and lower. And bends to the shape of every vessel."

The two keepers watched the Tyraen for reaction.

Dyraveen parted his lips in half-smile. "I will leave the keepers to their business," he said, rising from his stool.

"Stay," Dialla said. "Listen. Learn what you can."

"Stay, stay," Rael said. "Take down numbers for me."

The keepers dove into rapid conversation, a mix of friendly banter, storytelling, and subtle negotiation.

Rael offered to purge the northern black dunes of all podrunners.

Dialla declined, saying any purge would be futile as long as the bluepods grew wild through the coastal marsh. "We only chased those four runners because they stole one of our trucks," she said.

The keepers traded stories about blundering young recruits: a driver who lodged a freight tracker of grains in an open pipeline canal, a sleepwalking cook who wandered unaware into rival headquarters, a duct worker who lost two fingers to a ventilating fan, a mechanic who pissed himself when his wrench touched terminals across a motorcycle battery.

The keepers asked permission for movements through the other's territory, always granted.

They exchanged workers and equipment. A paving crew, excavator, and crane for Dialla. A fuel tanker, two medics, ten guards, and ammunition for Rael.

They shared rumors and news. A rift among the western keepers over refinery control. A push at the coming winter conclave for collective management of all mountain locks.

Another delay in the mountain tunnel project because of flagging support from the cities of the valley. Another breakdown in trade negotiations with the far Andaran islands.

Dialla warned Rael of encroachments on both flanks of his northern territory – gravelers to the west, the burgeoning and unruly town of Meadonne to the east.

At this word, Rael stiffened. The meeting ended soon after.

Rael stormed from the tent. He crumpled and tossed the page of numbers handed to him by Dyraveen. His officers, seeing the look in his eyes, shouted for all soldiers to return their trucks.

They drove through the night. Dyraveen dozed against the window. Rael seethed behind the wheel.

The clenched jaw and gritted teeth of the keeper relaxed in the last hour before dawn. He cracked his window. The cool night wind whistled through the cab, a hint of grain in the air.

"You know who are the wisest of all people?" Rael said. "Fishers. They live far from the struggle and pain of the land. They lose themselves like babies in the throb of the great blue womb. They dream through their lives, unafraid."

First sun lit up a powdered web of dust and slashing rubber tracks across the roadway. One swath of road lay gashed, chunks of asphalt strewn, deep lines carving to the soil.

Rael took up his radio and ordered the pilots to probe east and west.

He stopped his truck at the break in the road.

The troop stopped with him, their engines idling, all waiting anxiously for pilots' report.

"There are stripped hillsides to the east," a pilot said, breaking the radio silence. "No vehicles in sight."

"I see gravel trucks in the west," another said, "a line of them dumping into a double-tiered tracker. I see loaders working the hillside bank."

The news settled over the troop.

Everyone waited for the keeper's word.

"Torch the loaders and the tracker," Rael said. "Steal the trucks. No blood, no bodies."

The jeeps tore off-road.

The trucks followed.

Then the tanks.

After rounding a redstone butte, the gravelers appeared across a shallow-trenched valley, gutted bare by thousands of loader passes.

The jeeps headed straight for the gravelers working the far hillside.

The trucks looped around both sides of the hill, blocking escape.

The tanks entered their range of fire, stopped, and aimed.

"Five strikes," Rael said.

Five times the ground shook; the air split; rock and dirt launched skyward.

The gravelers abandoned their vehicles and rushed to higher ground.

Rael waited until all the graveler guards and drivers were safe on the hilltop. "Light up the loaders," he said.

A loading tractor crumpled like tin. Another flipped, the cab crushed into the ground. Others twisted and spun, black smoke pouring from shattered engine blocks.

"Bury the tracker," Rael said.

The glass of the tracker's cab erupted into a fine-sharded mist. The posts of the first tier splintered. The second tier fell. The massive circular cams on the tracker's side disappeared into gritty, blue-grey clouds. The giant belt slipped from its grooves and crashed to the ground, a mangled, lifeless snake.

Rael jumped out of his truck and climbed onto its hood, rifle in hand. Breathless, euphoric, his wide eyes surveyed the wreckage of the valley. He ordered his copters, tanks, and jeeps back to the road. He sent soldiers from open-bed trucks to steal the gravelers' rigs.

The keeper stood triumphantly atop his truck. Last to leave, he raised his fist for each passing jeep and truck. The soldiers roared.

Back on the road, the exhilarated flush of Rael cooled. His face tightened; a burn scar on his neck stretched long. His mouth and lips moved in muted argument with unseen critic. He smoked to pack's end.

"There will be payback?" Dyraveen ventured.

"What else could I do?" Rael said. "They crossed *my* road. They stole *my* gravel."

"Why steal rocks at all?"

"Gravel is worth as much as fuel, lumber, and iron on the frontier. Gravel paves roads. Roads claim territory."

"But wide claim spreads your forces thin. Your borders are too long to guard or defend."

"So the keeper relies on reputation, threat, fear."

"Is this game or war?"

"A war restrained. A vicious game."

"And the strong always win," Dyraveen said.

The keeper scowled. "We aren't bullies on a playground," Rael said. "The violent will always gather the young around them. But warlords will always be servants to those more clever, more cruel." Rael stopped the truck. "Drive," he said, crawling into the backseat.

Dyraveen drove through the afternoon while Rael slept.

In the early evening, the troop reached a small guard station. They washed and drank from hoses. They refueled, ate beans from tins, and traded guards with the station.

When soldiers began to doze off, the keeper stood on the table. "We drive all night to Meadonne," Rael announced. "Switch drivers on the hour."

The soldiers trudged back to their vehicles.

Three lieutenants joined the keeper in his truck. When Dyraveen reached for the door, Rael motioned him away.

Dyraveen turned to find a ride. The jeeps were already down the road, the trucks already climbing through lower gears. He headed toward the tanks, but their hatches quickly closed. He ran for the last remaining vehicle – a tricopter in the field.

Dyraveen waved his arms as he ran.

The pilot kicked the three rotor blades to life, pretending not to see.

Dyraveen shouted and waved.

The pilot opened his door just enough to talk.

"Let me on," Dyraveen yelled, a hand on the glass. "Keeper's order."

The pilot frowned but opened the door.

They climbed into the night sky.

Out of the station, the caravan of Rael turned to the right, following a narrow crossroad. The pilot passed over the caravan and accelerated east. Another copter cruised parallel. White lights swept the barren fields rushing by beneath them.

The pilot relaxed in the open skies. He held out a flask and gestured to the empty front seat.

Dyraveen climbed to the front. He took a sip from the flask, gagged, and handed it back.

"Draun weed tea," the pilot said, grinning through chipped tooth. "The churning of your stomach will keep you awake."

The pilot, Del, talked deep into the night. He had grown up in a small mountain town and moved to Lytarr as a boy. He had worked as field hand, sprayer, trucker, and tractor mechanic before his recruitment by Rael. In the keeper's service, he had rebuilt motors for ten years, manned crane for twelve, flown for six. He hoped to retire from service soon. He hoped to move to the valley and grow orchards. He asked Dyraveen about the Varrans of the west, especially the women.

"Varran women have eyes like the moons," Dyraveen said. "They are singers, painters, sculptors. They are elegant and slender. Their hair is dark and tied by silver cord. They are quick to kiss but slow to love. They move like little birds."

Del fell silent, his eyes soft and bright with western dreams.

Dyraveen crawled into the back.

He pulled his hood and slept.

Dyraveen woke from the steep tilt of the copter, his head pressed against the window glass.

When the pilot finished the sharp bank, Dyraveen crawled into the front seat. He squinted in the morning sunlight. He watched Rael's armada pass close below, its dust plumes drawn by blades' turn into greycloud, slashing tongues.

Del pointed down the roadway to a dark spot on the horizon. "Meadonne," he said. "Another splinter in Rael's eye."

"What's in the town?"

"A nickel mine already peaked. A parts warehouse for the outer territories. The tail of an unfinished water pipeline."

"And the people?"

Del rubbed his eyes, sipped his weed tea. "A headache from the beginning," he said. "They used our roads but fought our taxes. They expected water, power, and fuel for almost nothing."

"Rael's patience is running thin?"

"He's threatened to tear up his roads, plug his wells, take back his generators."

"Would he?"

Del cracked his neck, leaned back, considered. "Probably not," he said. "But Rael makes most decisions in the moment. Swift and sudden."

The pilot halved the throttle as they approached the north-south freightway. Before they crossed the road, they passed over a village of canvas tents and makeshift box homes of particle board and tin sheet, ringed by wooden outhouses. A row of large plastic cisterns raised on concrete blocks stretched along the roadside shoulder. All of the cisterns stood dry except for one, its line of bony old men and barefoot children winding throughout the village.

Del shook his head as the village passed. "Not good," he said.

After crossing the freightway, the pilot circled slowly around the edges of Meadonne, pointing out its industries and sections. Near to the road, they passed over the pink-eel farm, a fenced-off grid of square pools walled by concrete. High-booted farmers waded through the shallow waters, pouring out buckets of powdered feed, spearing and netting their slippery crop. "Wild pink-eel are delicious," Del said. "But those taste like gum and rubber." Through the heart of the town, they passed over the wide-gouged pit of the nickel mine, the equipment hangars, the grills and bread wagons, the yards and warehouses of heavy machinery parts. On the eastern edge of the town, they saw the hanging rows of the fine-meshed fogcatchers and the tail of the water pipeline headed toward the sea. On the north side, they saw the half-ring chains of worker lodges, single-storied, black-bricked, with shower tanks and smoke pits in their open core.

The radio crackled live with the keeper's voice. "Send out the smoke," Rael said. "Meet on the freightway."

Del cut across the town. He launched two rounds of gas cannisters from the underbelly of the tricopter. Powdered comets red and orange crossed the sky of Meadonne.

"Confrontation time," Del said, heading for the road.

Within an hour the people of the town and village had gathered on the freightway, converging in a dense crowd around the truck of Rael. The keeper and his three lieutenants stood in the truck bed high above the crowd. Below them stood the miners, farmers, mechanics, cooks, and builders of the town. The backs of the workers were dark with sweat, bright with powdered dust. Their hands had streaks of oil and grease, smears of paint, crusted layers of dirt; cuts, bruises, callouses, and blisters; lines like cracked stone. The workers pressed toward the truck, their expressions agitated, defensive, defiant. The old men and women of the tent village hung at the edge of the crowd, their faces etched and hard. Children slipped through gaps in the crowd, begging, stealing.

The crowd waited.

The keeper called out for Dyraveen.

The lone Tyraen, a full head shorter than most in the crowd, worked his way to the truck. The lieutenants pulled him out of the throng and lifted him onto the tailgate. Rael gave Dyraveen an exaggerated nod of respect and a long, solid grip of both hands before starting.

First, the keeper's guards stationed in Meadonne were called upon to report. The guards, clipboards in hand, shouted out the names of every vehicle owner behind on their road taxes, every shop, home, and lodge behind on their power or water payments. The guards reported on generators damaged by customer overload, on water pipes crushed and electrical wires severed by reckless digging. They reported the beating and exile of three rapists. They named two truck thieves executed by bullet, and a killer executed by blade of victim's brother.

"All payments and taxes are due by sunset," Rael said. "For those who fall short, their vehicles will be taken, their water and power cut off."

Many workers cried out in complaint against this year's rise in tax and water rates.

"More freight traffic means more road maintenance," Rael responded. "You demanded more water this year, so we were forced to drill two new wells."

"Soon we won't need your wells," a farmer said.

"Our water will flow from the desalting plant on the sea," a builder said.

"And you will carry the pipeline costs for many years," Rael said. "I warned you about trusting the keepers of the coast."

"All keepers are thieves," a miner cried out. The section of miners around him yelled and cheered.

Rael motioned to guards on both sides of the crowd. His soldiers pushed into the crowd, surrounded the miners, and forced them closer to the keeper's truck.

"You miners live in the past," Rael said, "the distant past."

"We named this town," the miners said. "We built this town."

"You built nothing," Rael said, jumping down from the truck bed. "Others built. You dug nickel from the ground. You lived like princes in the early days. You strutted. You softened. You expected to be kings."

"Our fathers bled and sweat in Meadonne," the miners said, "while you stole and bribed in Lytarr."

Rael, enraged, pushed into the heart of the miners. "Your fathers?" he shouted. "You call on the name of your fathers? the men who thirst and starve on the other side of the road? the men driven from town to live in tents and boxes?"

The miners fell silent.

"Many on the frontier have no fathers," Rael said. "Yours fed and clothed you. They taught you tool and trade."

The eyes of the miners looked to their foreman.

The foreman stepped forward to face Rael. He raised his arms with open hands. "What are we to do with them?" the foreman said. "They are too weak for hard labor, worthless by first break. If we let their shaking hands run loaders or conveyors, our production crawls. If we give them drills or carts, people get hurt."

"Then let them keep books, log inventory and hours, track production," Rael said. "Let them maintain equipment. Let them train recruits. Let them visit and learn from other mines."

The foreman shook his head at each suggestion. "They will only slow us down," he said, scowling at the keeper. "You know nothing about mining."

Rael returned to his truck. He spoke to his lieutenants, loud enough for the miners to hear. "Find Ekken among the old men," he said. "And bring the prisoner wagon around."

The lieutenants signaled to officers. The officers rushed to obey.

The foreman stood his ground, some miners drawing close to him, others backing away. The miners who stayed close slipped hands inside their jackets, unstrapped holsters.

"You're finished here," Rael said. "I'll drop you and your followers anywhere you want between here and Lytarr. Anywhere *outside* my territory."

The foreman stared down the lines of soldiers on each side. His hand came empty from his jacket. "What about our trucks, our tools, our clothes?"

"You can take your tools and clothes," Rael said. "The trucks you forfeit."

The crowd of workers parted for the wagon.

The wagon's gate was lowered.

The foremen and his followers climbed in the back.

The wagon pulled away.

The old miner, Ekken, approached the truck.

The keeper jumped down, embraced him, waved his hand for the other miners to come close.

"This is your crew now," Rael said. "This is your crew to teach, to guide, to manage. The mine is yours, Ekken, as it was years ago."

Ekken breathed hoarsely, trembled slightly through the shoulders. He looked over the younger miners. He gazed across the crowd at all the workers of Meadonnne, beyond them to the homeless old. Then he turned to the keeper, shaking his head. "Amed, the Draun bull, is a better miner than me, a stronger leader, too," he said. "Give Amed the mine. And if the great bull would let me assist him in any way, I would, gladly, thankfully."

The keeper, smiling with pride, clasped the shoulder of the man, He called the Draun forward and shook his hand. "The mine is yours, Amed," the keeper said. "And Ekken is your second."

Rael called upon all farmers, mechanics, cooks, and builders to find homes and work for the old. He sent his medics through the crowd for evaluation of the elderly. He promised to take all the sick and disabled back to Lytarr for better care. "The rest must have a place among the working," he said.

Rael ordered the gathering of all children. Some children came to the keeper without resistance, others were dragged by soldiers, pulled by shirt and hair. Rael, the keeper, called out to all the people of Meadonne. "Look long at your future," he said. "These will rule when you become too weak to stand. Mothers, fathers, claim your children. Know that you will share each sentence for their crimes." Many of the children were claimed by workers in the crowd. The orphans that remained were pushed into a huddle at the feet of the keeper. Rael spoke to the orphans in a lowered voice that only they could hear. "The frontier has no place for thieves," he said. "The lazy starve and die. You have one day to prove yourselves to me, to show some spark of life."

By keeper's command the gravel trucks were started, rakes and shovels retrieved.

The lieutenants pulled Dyraveen to the fore.

"You have until sunset to pay all bills and taxes," Rael said to the workers. "Settle your debts to me with Dyraveen, the young Tyraen. He comes from Pocone with great dreams for the eastern territories. He plans voyages of trade to Andara and Troqual. He plans cities of the eastern shelf to dwarf the outpost of Lytarr. Dyraveen, the Tyraen, is merciful and fair, but lie to him and he will take everything you own."

The keeper took up shovel and led the orphans off the freightway into the town. They followed behind the trucks, spreading gravel, filling potholes, smoothing the town roads.

The crowd of Torite workers stared at Dyraveen, alone in the truck bed.

"I will set up table between the worker lodges," Dyraveen said. "Bring all documents and contracts with you. Have money in hand."

As the crowd left the freightway, Dyraveen rushed to find the guards of the town.

From morning to evening, Dyraveen listened to the people of Meadonne and rendered decisions on their accounts. As the workers told their stories, he watched their eyes and faces closely, but he looked more often to the guards of the town. When the guards received a worker with grimace or scowl, Dyraveen added penalties, seized vehicles, and cut power; when the guards showed respect, he extended deadlines and lowered fees. Dyraveen halved the debts of the mine to aid the newly appointed managers, Amed and Ekken. He negotiated and compromised with the eel farmers - lower water rates, higher power. Five times he rejected low payment offers from the owners of the parts yard, their full taxes finally surrendered at sunset. When the pipeline foreman claimed to own fewer trucks than counted by the guards, Dyraveen sent soldiers to take back the generators of Rael. The foreman gave in.

After closing all accounts, Dyraveen found Rael in the shower tank of a worker's lodge. He held up a bulging sack of credits for the keeper to see, too heavy for a single hand to lift.

Rael glanced at the sack. He kicked off his boots, stripped down. "Give me the numbers," he said.

"I made a summary sheet for you," Dyraveen said, setting down the sack, pulling a folded sheet from his pocket.

The keeper shook his head under the cold stream of water, dark rivers dripping from his hair. "Give me the numbers," he said again.

While the keeper rinsed, Dyraveen summarized the town's accounts, all of his decisions from the long day.

Rael dried himself and dressed. He looked over the wall of the shower tank to check on three children standing by his truck, two boys, one girl. "The generators will probably be ruined by the next time we come," he said. "They'll wear them down to shit, remembering your face."

"Then they can pay for every one they break."

"And I'll have to ship more all the way from Lytarr," Rael said, stepping from the tank. "You were probably too hard on the parts mechanics, too soft on the farmers."

"When did I claim to be a brilliant frontier-town negotiator?" Dyraveen said.

Rael grinned. "Walk with us," he said, motioning Dyraveen to follow.

The keeper walked to the three children by his truck. He looked down at them, saying nothing. The kids squirmed under the weight of his stare.

"Can we eat?" the girl asked, pulling on his arm. "Can we shower?"

Rael pushed his lips out, shook his head. "Follow me," he said.

They walked toward another worker's lodge. The smell of fresh meat floated to them on the evening breeze. They saw the other orphans of the town at a ring of tables around a flaming grill. They saw clean-showered children biting meat from the bone, sipping ice water and fruit juice, smiling, laughing.

Rael stopped. He held back the three. The three watched the others eat from a short and agonizing distance.

"What do you feel?" the keeper asked.

The three did not answer. Mouths open, eyes wide, they stared at the others.

"What do you feel as you watch the others eat?" the keeper asked. "Jealousy? Pain? Rage? Get used to it. You will know this feeling again and again and again."

"Why them?" the smaller boy asked. "Why not us?"

"Because they worked," Rael said. "They fought for better life. They sweat and struggled."

"We worked," the larger boy protested. "We worked all day."

Rael spit. "You worked when you saw me watching," he said. "The rest of the time you did nothing. You were worthless. You made the others carry you."

"We shoveled," the girl said. "We raked."

"You failed the others," Rael said. "You think only of yourselves."

The three orphans shook.

"The people of the town don't want you," Rael said. "I have no place for the lazy and the selfish. Where will you go?"

Bitter tears fell from the eyes of the three.

"You spit on my offer to help you," Rael said.

"No, no," the three said. "We worked."

The scene began to wear on Dyraveen, tired from the day. "Stop lying," he told the children. "Plead for second chance."

Dyraveen did not wait for the children's response. He headed for the showers and the grill.

Later that night, back in the keeper's truck, Rael woke Dyraveen from sleep.

"Never ruin the moment of choice," the keeper said. "It is the time when the weak first stand."

"Those children will grow to be thieves and killers," Dyraveen said, pushing away the keeper's arm. "Why did you waste your time?"

"Two might turn away but one might live," Rael said. "You are not God."

"Was there a god in the village of tents and boxes?" Dyraveen said. He cracked his window to the night air whistling and pulled his hood.

When the troop arrived at the keeper's headquarters in Lytarr, Rael gave all soldiers, officers, and lieutenants from the northern journey two days leave from duty. He trudged, tired and sore, toward the dome. A small mob of assistants poured from the stairwell with questions and papers for Rael. The keeper looked back and called out to Dyraveen. "Find me tonight," Rael said. "We will talk and drink."

Dyraveen slept through the day in an old machine shop in the headquarters' basement.

He woke up ravenous sometime in the night.

He raided the officer's kitchen for food.

He ate fruit and eggs in the dark cafeteria.

A flashlight passed over him, clicked off. Heavy bootsteps approached. "Have you slept yet?" Rael asked.

"Since we got back," Dyraveen said. He finished his plate, pushed it away. "And you?"

The keeper shook his head, rubbed the thick, black whiskers of his jaw. "Much happened in Lytarr while we were gone," he said. The keeper sat down at the table, double-tapped a globe light into life. He slid a bladder hide of liquor down to Dyraveen.

The Tyraen drank, eyed the weary Torite, drank again, then returned the hide. "You live on adrenaline, anger, and thrill," Dyraveen said. "Coming down must be hard."

"There is no down, no rest," Rael said. "The demands of the keeper never end."

"Of course you have no rest," Dyraveen said. "An assistant in your headquarters cannot order paper without your approval. A soldier in your army cannot take a piss without your permission."

Rael paused, the hide at his lips. "Say what you have to say, Tyraen," he said, drinking deep.

"Delegate. Let go of absolute control."

"Go on, grandson of Davel, go on."

"Your forces are spread too thin. Your territories stretch too wide."

"And what can be done?"

"Gather all of the honorable keepers like Dialla. Trade lands and resources. Consolidate into tighter regions."

Rael dimmed the globe light. He smoked in long draws, the redcoal tip lighting the shadows. He finished the cigarette, finished the bladder, shivered. He slung a second hide from his back to his chest. "Fresh drink for fresh blood," he said, sliding the new hide to Dyraveen. "My friend, you may be right about delegation and control. You may be right. But, as for the rest, you are wrong. This era of the frontier is all about expansion and claim. Every keeper is spread thin. Every keeper pushes from the stripped and overrun core to the rich and virgin outlands. Any who remained near to Lytarr would soon be swallowed. And your idea to trade lands with other keepers is impossible and naïve. There are no honorable keepers. Even Dialla has undercut and deceived me at times in our long history."

Dyraveen drank. "Is all governing just a squabble?" he said.

Rael laughed, rose to his feet, unsteady. "Perhaps, but our squabbling in Meadonne gave work and shelter to the old," the keeper said. "Every mouth must be fed. Every voice should be heard."

Dyraveen tossed back the hide. "No more," he said. "Please, no more."

They stumbled together through the halls, bumping shoulders, bumping walls.

They pissed on tanks in the hangar. They threw knives at fruit trees in the garden. They wrestled in the sand pit, the strong keeper winning twice by pin, the quick Tyraen winning once by choke. They lit and stoked the outside grill, flames singeing the beard of Dyraveen.

Rael shot and cooked a white crow. Dyraveen puked. They ate the bird. Dyraveen puked again.

The Tyraen curled up beneath the grill and closed his eyes.

"You were right," Rael said. He pulled on the arm of Dyraveen. "Get up, my friend. Tonight, we sleep in the copter. Tomorrow, we fish on the ocean shore."

"Fuck off," Dyraveen whispered, a finger to his lips.

Rael hoisted the limp Tyraen onto his shoulders. He carried him back to the hangar. He set him inside the copter, covered him with jacket.

"Tomorrow, we fish," Rael said, dozing in the pilot seat.

By dawn of the following day, the keeper had taken to the sky.

By noon, they fished on the eastern ocean shore.

They stripped off their shirts, waded into the sea, and cast lines for an hour.

Without a bite or nibble on the shore, they walked into the delta marsh.

They speared red snakes, lizards, and flat fish.

They ate by fire at sunset.

"Stay on the frontier," Rael said. "Work with me."

Dyraveen smiled, nodded. "As soon as my grandfather passes, I will join you," he said. "Let me fly on the way back to Lytarr."

When Dyraveen returned to Tekenna, he found only the third wife of Davel in his grandfather's cottage beneath the bluff. Embra, the old woman, stood at the kitchen table. She sorted through tall stacks of papers, books, and photographs, throwing some to the ground, gathering others into bags.

"Where is my grandfather?" Dyraveen asked.

The old woman glanced at him, returned to her sorting. "My husband was left alone," she said.

"Where is Davel now?"

"He was left alone with no one to help him, no one to hear his cries."

Dyraveen breathed deep. "Where is my grandfather? Tell me."

The old woman stopped sorting. She glared with piercing eyes, violet and golden. "You left him alone," she said. "You were the precious one he chose to keep. We were the ones he sent away."

"Please, where is my grandfather? Where is your husband?"

"All winter and spring you wouldn't look at us. You hardly said two words."

"I was quiet with respect."

"You glowed so proud when you were chosen."

"He pities me, the fatherless."

Embra sat down at the table. "Davel lives," she said. "I found him here, weak with fever, vomiting on the floor. Now he recovers safely at my cabin."

Dyraveen helped Embra sort through the stacks of the table.

When she had finished sorting, he carried her bags to the trunk of her car.

He waited at the passenger door.

The motor turned.

The motor idled.

Embra unlocked the door.

Dyraveen found his grandfather in a wheelchair on the cabin's porch, his eyes on the setting sun, his legs wrapped by blanket.

When Dyraveen touched his grandfather's shoulder, the old man's head turned slowly around. His dull eyes struggled to focus on the face before him. Across his lap, his fleshless wrist appeared like palest sword.

"What happened?" Dyraveen asked.

The eyes of Davel cleared. He smiled weakly. "Food poisoning," the old man said. "Some meat I ate. Raw in the middle. A stupid mistake."

"Are you getting better?"

"Little by little. I need to eat. But everything burns."

Davel dozed off as the hills darkened.

Embra came to the porch. She took the wheelchair in hand and nodded toward a small shed beside the cabin. "You can sleep in there," she said.

Throughout the summer's strongest heat, old Davel gradually recovered. His appetite and energy improved. He walked with lengthening stride. His clarity of mind returned. His flesh thickened. Color returned to his skin.

When Davel learned that his grandson slept in the shed, he confronted his wife. "I told him to explore the frontier," he said. "You can hate me for my foolishness but leave young Dyraveen alone."

Dyraveen declined when invited by Davel and Embra to sleep inside the cabin. "Thank you, but the shed is luxury enough," he said. "I spent a hundred nights on cavern floors. I slept in trucks and copters on the frontier. In summer past, we slept on open hillcrest against horned altar."

On warm summer nights, grandson and grandfather sipped iced maple liquor together on the porch.

Dyraveen told his grandfather of everything that he had heard and seen on the eastern frontier.

Davel listened long, nodding occasionally. "Will you carve your place on the hard frontier?" the old man asked.

"I will return to work with Rael, the keeper," Dyraveen said, "but it is difficult to imagine a future there. Everything in the east seems shifting and uncertain. The Torites are strange and rough."

"The Torites of the frontier will test you, just like the Tyraens of the compound. Work hard and you will earn their respect. Stay close to Rael. You will learn much from him."

Prodded by his wife, Davel began work on a final publication – an exhaustive collection of his writings, from youth to present day, each prefaced by sober reflection and assessment.

Davel fought to exclude his lesser works. "They make me cringe," he said. "My skin crawls when I read them."

Embra fought to include. "Your entire life and career were built on the bare truth," she said. "Let the readers decide for themselves. Let them see your growth, your flaws, your glories."

Husband and wife battled each day over text and preface.

The cabin raged with argument, seethed in silence.

A weary armistice fell each day with the setting sun, a kiss and embrace shared between the spent warriors.

Dyraveen treasured the nights with his grandfather, but the slow days drained him. He read books and journals until the pages blurred. He walked the trails of the hills until his feet ached and blistered.

Bored and lonely, Dyraveen made plans to return to the eastern shelf.

But the children of Embra arrived midsummer for reunion.

Cydir, the first and oldest son, came from Pocone.

Adee and Elee, the daughters, came together from Lycira.

Toch, the third son, came from prison.

Youngest Oson, came from hospital.

From the stories of the children, Dyraveen filled the outline of the mother's life. From the color of their eyes, he traced her path, lover to lover, across the continent.

Embra, herself, carried the stout legs and violet eyes of the reclusive fishing tribes from the high mountain lakes. As a young girl, she had followed a Varran anthropologist from her mountain village to great Pocone. She had studied five years in his academy, borne his child in the third year, Cydir, the blue-eyed. Embra assisted an origin research team in a project among the herding people of the southwest. She stayed behind in the southwestern hills long after the team left. By shepherd man she bore her first daughter, Adee, brown-skinned, bright-eyed. She studied sculpture in Lycira, dark-eyed Elee the seed of Torite teacher. After a visit to her old village, she lingered in the mountains among the Myshenite fishery towns, the black-eyed Toch a seed of village elder. And hazel-eyed Oson was born in Tekenna, the crippled son of Davel.

Dyraveen bonded first with Toch, the giant Myshenite recently freed. The unlikely pair rode together through the black hills north of the city. They shared the tall motorcycle of Toch, Dyraveen a dwarf against the titan's back, his legs reaching halfway to the ground. They rolled and smoked dry leaf. They hunted wild dogs by pistol. Dyraveen never asked the crimes of the convict. He told his new friend of the wild and lawless frontier.

Dyraveen expected no connection with Cydir, the Varran chemist from Pocone. But Cydir was curious and humble. When he learned that Dyraveen was the son of Rhoa and the nephew of Enteres, he beamed with deference and respect. "Your mother stands among the greatest architects and designers of the continent," Cydir said. "Your uncle leads the daring Moonlance projects."

The daughters, at first cold and guarded, slowly warmed to Dyraveen. Both skilled and creative photographers, they shared old collections of their work. They described their latest project – a visual comparison of the elders and children of all non-industrial tribes throughout the continent. Their mother managed the project, arranged each tribal expedition, and edited all photographs and captions before inclusion.

Oson, the crippled and crutched, the final child of Embra and Davel, avoided Dyraveen for days.

When Dyraveen cornered him and forced conversation, Oson vented.

"Don't ask me about my legs," Oson said. "At the cottage you wouldn't even at look me."

"I felt like I didn't belong among your family then," Dyraveen said.

"You don't belong among my family. You stole Davel from us when he was weak and sick."

"I stole nothing," Dyraveen said. "If you have issue with your father, speak to him."

Embra and Davel shared only their morning meal with the family. The rest of the day they worked alone inside the cabin, debating and contending over final book.

Dyraveen flew the children of Embra by tricopter throughout the eastern hills and valley. Only Oson remained at the cabin.

When they flew to the eastern mountains a second time, the sisters convinced Oson to join.

Dyraveen cruised over the villages of the mountain lakes – the birth-ground of their mother, Embra.

He headed south, weaving gently between the highest peaks of the range.

At the first lock station, he landed.

The family stood together on stone ledge, gazing down from mountains to coast, across the vast eastern shelf.

"There's nothing there," Oson said.

"The future is there," Dyraveen said. "The city of Lytarr explodes. The small towns swell. The barges run the rivers night and day. There are trading centers, mines, quarries, farms, plants, refineries."

"And there is good work for newcomers?" Toch asked.

"Most frontier jobs pay twice the valley rate," Dyraveen said. "There are no guilds to appease. There is but one tax for the keeper."

"When will trade open with the islands?" Cydir asked.

"Who knows," Dyraveen said. "Troqual has little interest. Nyava will only deal in their own ports. Andara verges on civil war."

The sisters, Adee and Elee, took photos.

On the ride home, Toch asked to join Dyraveen when he returned to Lytarr. Cydir promised to visit the eastern shelf on his next break from teaching and research. The sisters hoped to photograph the people and the landscape of the frontier as soon as they finished their latest project. Even Oson mentioned a possible visit if his next surgery went well.

Back at the cabin, alone with his grandfather, Dyraveen inquired about progress on his book.

"The nightmare continues," Davel said.

"Are you half-finished?" Dyraveen pressed. "Near to the end?"

"Alone, I would have finished weeks ago with a book of fifty pages. Under the slave-master's hand, I will finish in the winter or spring with a book of three-thousand."

"But Embra is right, the full truth must be told. History will lay us all bare beneath the knife."

"But why carve myself? Why not savor my final days?"

"Because you pity the young who walk behind."

Davel refilled their glasses, stared into the eyes of young Dyraveen. "You want to return to the frontier," he said. "The cabin bores you."

"I would only leave with your understanding."

"I understand completely," Davel said, a wide grin quickly fading. "The cabin drains me as well. Go to the frontier, my blood. Chase your dreams. And your demons."

"If you are sick, I will return. A single call. A single letter."

"Go," Davel said.

Toch said nothing on the flight through the mountains. He stared tensely into the stony heights, clenched and unclenched his jaw, tapped his teeth.

"A new beginning," Dyraveen said as they dropped from the mountains onto the wide frontier shelf.

"I hate starting over," Toch said. "Traps wait. Dangers hide. The wolves always challenge. The jackals circle round."

"The keeper is a friend. We come by his offer of work."

"*You* come by his offer."

"He needs good workers badly," Dyraveen said. "I'll vouch for you."

Toch nodded, felt the wiry stubble of his cheek.

"He'll ask about your experience," Dyraveen said, "your history."

"I'll tell the truth," Toch said. "Don't worry."

When they arrived in Lytarr, they met the keeper at his headquarters. The three shared a smoke together in the sand pit where Dyraveen and Rael had wrestled drunk.

"This is Toch," Dyraveen said. "He is friend and family."

The dark eyes of Rael looked up to Toch, down to Dyraveen. He laughed, little clouds of smoke escaping from his mouth. "Family?" he said. "You two couldn't be any further apart."

"Fool, we are family by marriage," Dyraveen said. "His mother. My grandfather."

Rael studied the giant, noticed the long jaw, sharp-bladed cheekbones, eyes even darker than the Torite. "You are Myshenite," he said.

"Half-Myshenite," Toch said, "but I was raised in Tekenna."

"What did you do in Tekenna?"

"A few trade schools. A few jobs."

"What trades?"

"Mostly metal work, grinding, cutting, welding."

"We need welders," Rael said. "Are you ready to work?"

Toch tossed his cigarette into the sand. "I need to tell you, I've been in prison," he said. "Two years. Some shorter stays in jails before that."

Rael stared up at the friend of Dyraveen, rolled his cigarette between his fingers. "For?"

"Fighting."

"Only fighting?"

"I never ran pod, never killed, never stole, never raped. Only fighting."

Rael shrugged, tossed his cigarette. "Half my officers have been in jail," he said, "and nearly all my workers. The frontier forgets old crimes. For new crimes, it kills."

Toch exhaled, a burden lifted.

While Toch welded in the armory, Dyraveen and Rael met in the keeper's office.

Dyraveen explained that the health of his grandfather had improved and that he could likely stay on the frontier for several seasons.

Rael admitted that he had followed Dyraveen's advice. He had expanded the duties of those beneath him, added new levels of both officers and workers, and created a more graduated hierarchy of support.

"I have also traded with many keepers since you were here," Rael said. "Properties, crews, equipment, commodities."

"You're consolidating," Dyraveen said.

"More than that," Rael said. "Ties of trade, bonds of contract, shared resources, overlapping personnel – all these will make the community of keepers hesitate."

"Hesitate to do what?" Dyraveen asked.

"To ally against me," Rael said. "I'm going to war with the keeper, Chirilech."

Rael explained.

Chirilech owned the trespassing fleet of gravelers, its trucks taken by Rael, its loaders and tracker torched.

In response to response, Chirilech had ripped and plowed a long section of Rael's freightway. He had burned two guard stations of Rael. He had captured, and possibly killed, twenty soldiers.

Rael described an orchestration of maneuvers with tall Dialla, the woman keeper. He had made no immediate retaliation against Chirilech. He had detoured his trucks to the eastern freightway passing through Meadonne and abandoned the guard stations burned. Dialla had taken over all of his territories bordering Chirilech. She had repaired the freightway, rebuilt the guard stations, and started construction on a new trading depot. Rael, meanwhile, had taken over her fields of redgrain to the southwest of the freightway.

"You're feigning retreat," Dyraveen said.

"The back foot plants before the hardest punch flies," Rael said. "Each fall Chirilech and his officers hunt birds in the scrubland trees. They hunt for days. They drink to collapse every night. They are guarded only by a handful of soldiers stretched thin around the ring of trees. The soldiers are jealous of the party inside, numbed to outside attack by frequent hunter fire."

"But the canyons separate the scrubland trees from the redgrain fields," Dyraveen said.

"The whitestone canyons are impassable for heavy vehicles," Rael said, "but little trackers can get through even in mud, rain, and snow."

"Only a small force could get through," Dyraveen said, "likely even fewer than the guns of Chirilech."

"We would accept odds much worse than those to avenge our twenty lost," the Torite said, chin high.

"But you don't know for certain that they are dead. They could be prisoners."

"Either way, Chirilech and his officers must be executed. His forces will flee at the news. Our soldiers, if living, will be freed. And I will take all that was his."

"And his friends and allies?"

"He has no friends and few allies. Most in the region will celebrate his death."

"And your new allies, the keepers that you once told me could not be trusted?"

"I had no choice. I avoided the liars, the snakes, the spineless. I cultivated ties with only the most solid and proven keepers of the frontier. I chose the firmest ground."

"And Dialla?"

"If Dialla stays with us, we will succeed."

"She could ruin you with a single word."

"My friend, she is the firmest ground."

The two spent hours poring over maps of terrain.

Rael defended his strategy and plan of attack.

Dyraveen probed, tested, and challenged.

Hard questions abraded Rael. Soft questions enraged him.

The two argued until their eyes blurred, their stomachs growled, and their throats groaned hoarse.

They left the keeper's office before dinner to check on Toch's progress.

In the armory, Rael pulled the welding supervisor aside for a few words before approaching Toch.

They found the giant leaning against the front armor-plate of a tank. His hands and forearms showed blister burns where his undersized jacket sleeves ran short. Sweat dripping from his chin, breath labored, he wiped the steamy fog from the inside of his helmet. His head barely lifted when the keeper came close.

Rael inspected the welds across the front plate. He ran his fingers down the wide gaps, touched the thick metal drips and globs. Rael handed a water bottle to Toch. "That might be the worst welding I've ever seen," Rael said.

Toch glanced up at the keeper. He opened the bottle, poured water into his mouth, swirled, and spit. "I can't see inside the helmet," Toch said. He tilted the bottle high, finished it in three gulps. He stretched his bare-skinned forearm in front of the keeper. "I can't work in a child's jacket."

"Even so," Rael said. He picked up a hammer and struck along the weld lines. The gaps widened even further. Chunks of black slag fell to the ground. "The worst I've seen," he repeated.

"I can grind smooth and tight," Toch said, grabbing the keeper's arm. "I can cut anything - metal, wood, plastic, concrete. I can lift anything - pipes, rods, blocks, pallets."

"You're not built for machine or mechanic work. We have forklifts for heavy lifting."

Toch looked at Dyraveen with pleading eyes.

Dyraveen glared at Rael.

The keeper stepped close to the giant, stretched an arm across his shoulders. "My friend, you were made for one thing," Rael said.

Toch looked away, slipped the arm, shook his head. "No," he said, "I won't fight anymore."

Rael grabbed Toch by the neck, pulled him close, whispered low. "What sent you to prison in the valley will make you a king on the frontier," he said. "Here, fighters reign."

Toch looked to Dyraveen.

Dyraveen nodded.

Toch shook the keeper's hand.

"Your training will start tomorrow," Rael said, smiling. "You will be a fighter and a soldier."

Toch, exhausted, leaned against the tank.

"Let me train with him," Dyraveen said.

"You, my friend, will never be a soldier," Rael said, "or a fighter."

"Did I ask to be?" Dyraveen said. "Let me learn the basic skills. Let me taste what every young officer and soldier endures."

"Good," the keeper said, "this is good."

Toch and Dyraveen woke each morning in darkness.

They jogged one hundred times around the dome.

They carried concrete blocks down the hill. They carried concrete blocks up the hill.

They dug trenches. They buried trenches.

They built walls of stones. They tore down walls of stones.

They ate breakfast.

They strapped full packs and marched along the river until the great city disappeared on the horizon.

They used maps and scopes to find targets throughout the stony plains.

After reaching the final goal, they rushed back to Lytarr, trackers chasing, bullets ripping at their heels.

They ate lunch.

They learned to fire pistols, rifles, machine-guns.

They learned to drive cycles, jeeps, trucks, trackers.

They learned the coded languages of the keeper.

They learned defensive and attack formations.

Chained naked beneath water flues, they suffered quizzes, a rubber bullet for each wrong answer.

They ate dinner.

They jogged one hundred times around the dome.

They carried concrete blocks down the hill. They carried concrete blocks up the hill.

They dug trenches. They buried trenches.

They built walls of stone. They tore down walls of stone.

They shared one glass of liquor.

They shared one cigarette.

They slept.

Dyraveen and Toch helped each other. When one had nothing left to give, the other stepped in to carry two packs, two blocks, to dig or build at twice the pace. Together, they learned the details of every vehicle and firearm, every code and formation. They failed together, sharing bullets and bruises. They succeeded together, a look and a touch between brothers.

One morning they were woken by the keeper himself, instead of the training officer.

"It's time," Rael said. "Chirilech's gone hunting."

The war party, forty strong, met at dawn in the keeper's dome for briefing and assignments.

By midday all of the party had been airlifted to an equipment hangar at the edge of Dialla's redgrain fields. They ate in the hangar, received more detailed instructions, then waited for the afternoon sun to fall.

Toch, a support gunner in the third tracker, dozed throughout the afternoon, the tracker's belt his pillow.

Dyraveen, backup driver for the rear medic tracker, could not rest. He sat at the officer's table with his ear to the radio and scanned frequency by frequency for enemy chatter. He cycled once through all the frequencies but found only static, hum, and drone.

When he began a second cycle, Rael grabbed him by the shirt and took him outside the hangar. The keeper lit a cigarette and stashed away his pack, not offering to share.

"Most fights are won or lost before the first blow," Rael said. "The winners stay calm and focused. The losers are crippled by their own nerves."

"So?" Dyraveen said.

"So leaving the fucking radio alone," Rael said. "We don't need the added noise and tension in the hangar. Every fighter is preparing in their own way."

Head low, Dyraveen nodded apology.

Rael offered out his pack. "Dialla will be here soon," the keeper said. "Come to the meeting when I signal you for water."

"Like a servant boy."

"No, fool," Rael said, lighting Dyraveen. "Do you know a better way to get you into the keepers' meeting without pissing off the officers who've served me twenty years?"

When the small plane arrived, the two keepers met inside the wide hangar door, Dialla in sun, Rael in shadow.

An officer of Dialla's troop came forward, spoke to the keepers briefly, then returned to the plane.

Rael signaled.

Dyraveen hurried to the keepers, handed each a bottle. Seeing the hard eyes of Dialla and the clenched jaw of Rael, the young Tyraen turned to go. But Rael stopped him with two fingers on the arm.

"Tell him," Rael said. He stared into the northern canyons, his eyes dark slits.

"Why is he here?" Dialla asked.

"Because he's not an investor," Rael said. "He's the grandson of Davel."

For an instant, the mouth of Dialla slipped open; her eyes widened; she fell back a half-step. But the veteran keeper regained her mask of composure quickly. "The blood of Davel," she said, licking top lip. "I was right – you are the creeping water."

"Forgive the deception," Rael said. "I had to test him. I had to see how he handled himself."

The keepers drank their waters.

They smoked with Dyraveen.

"Circumstances have changed," Dialla said. "Some within the troop of Chirilech have said that your soldiers are still alive."

"Not some," Rael said. "Only two. Her lieutenant's cousin. And a mason that has floated between six or seven keepers."

"So the mason's word is worthless," Dyraveen said. "What reason do we have to believe the cousin?"

"The cousin says that the prisoners labor on a gourd farm in the north, a farm I know exists," Dialla said. "He also says that Chirilech would negotiate, if carefully approached."

"Didn't Chirilech give up the right to negotiate when he tore up our road, burned down our stations, and attacked our guards?" Dyraveen said.

Dialla tossed her cigarette, turned from Dyraveen to Rael. "If your soldiers were killed at their stations, then few will question this ambush in the trees," she said. "But if your soldiers were only taken prisoner, most will see your attack an assassination."

"What are you asking me to do?" Rael said. "Wait a day? Wait a year? Do you think you can talk Chirilech into releasing the prisoners? Do you think you can turn his troop against him?"

"I don't know," Dialla said, "but does every officer in his troop deserve to die while hunting birds?"

"Our target is the keeper," Rael said. "I will spare as many of his officers as I can."

"I stretch to cover you in this, my brother," Dialla said. "I stretch, exposed."

"If condemned at winter conclave, I will bear the punishment alone," Rael said. "You knew nothing of my plans. You traded territories with another keeper. That is all."

Dialla stared down at young Dyraveen. "And what do you say, blood of Davel?" she asked. "Will your grandfather be proud of this killing in the trees?"

Dyraveen matched her stare but did not answer.

The keepers shook hands, came close together. Dialla whispered to Rael. Rael whispered back.

Dialla turned for her plane.

The kill party of Rael rode through the night.

The keeper led the way through the winding canyons. He gunned his tracker over the flat and smooth stretches, crawled up and down the rocky slopes.

They rode without headlights for most of the night, guided by the blue and silver half-moons.

Deep in the night, headwinds stirred.

Thick clouds blocked the moons.

A haze of rain and sleet fell steady.

The ice-crusted ground halved their progress. The trackers slid sideways and stalled in deep-puddled ruts, belts smoking. Several had to be pushed by their riders onto drier ground.

The party reached the end of the canyons a full hour behind schedule. They skipped their meal, sipped from canteens, and smoked a quick cigarette as the morning sun broke on the horizon.

The shadows of the needle trees fell long and dark across the icy ground.

"We enter the trees on foot in V-formation," Rael said, "two wings, two pincers closing on the hunters' cabins. We hesitate to kill all but Chirilech."

The party entered the trees, radios low, rifles drawn. Their two wings stretched out through the grey-misted rain. They wove between blue-shadowed thickets of needle trees. They stepped carefully over frosted stones, hard-frozen grass and dirt.

By keeper's command, the wings narrowed; the pincers closed on the columns of smoke over the hunters' cabins.

A shot rang out suddenly. Somewhere between the wings.

The officers of Rael dropped to the ground, took cover.

Another shot.

Another.

The officers waited, peering through rifle sights into the trees.

A hunter emerged from the mist. More hunters. Four of them, all armed, none Chirilech.

Rael split his party - those north of the hunters pushed on for the cabins; those south held their positions.

In the south, Toch and the keeper circled behind the hunters, blocking their retreat.

An officer called out to the hunters to lay down their guns.

The hunters fired and ran. They entered the sights of the keeper, unaware.

Rael dropped three with three shots.

Toch missed badly, then nicked the shoulder, then pierced the neck.

"Finish them by knife," Rael commanded the giant, running north.

In the north, they surrounded the cabins.

The smallest officer snuck close, tossed two smoke grenades into the cabins, three explosives into the cluster of trucks.

Hunters poured, barefoot and groggy, from the doors of the cabins.

The officers of Rael held their fire, waiting for the rival keeper.

Over the radio, a lieutenant's voice: "Red shirt. Grey shorts."

Red-shirted Chirilech ran for the trucks, fired his pistol blindly into the trees.

A bullet clipped his thigh.

He spun.

Bullets ripped his arm, chest, face, gut.

He fell.

The officers of Chirilech tossed their weapons and laid facedown on the cold ground, hands behind their heads.

When Rael reached the cabins, he saw first to the care of his own wounded, then to the wounded of the enemy. The fallen officers of the enemy were covered with blankets respectfully, their comrades allowed to pray and bury. Only the body of Chirilech was treated with contempt – burned to ash, gathered into buckets, and thrown among a heap of rotting birdskins.

While his officers ate and drank, Rael spoke to the prisoners.

"I am sorry for your dead and wounded," Rael said. "I came only for Chirilech. I came only to restore honor to my troop. The territory of the dead keeper is now mine. My roads. My plants. My mills. My quarries. All of the workers will stay with me. All of the soldiers will go. You officers will be freed in Lytarr, safe and untouched. I ask only two things of you. First, to know the fate of my captured guards. Second, for your word of submission to be passed on to those beneath you."

With one hand Rael held out his radio to the enemy officers; the other held a pistol, muzzle tapping at his knee.

Dyraveen had entered the trees in the rear of the formation, his only assignment to protect the two medics of the party.

The thin hands of Dyraveen trembled against the cold barrel of his rifle. His oversized helmet slopped side to side with each marching step. He stumbled over the icy rocks and frozen grass, fell against trees.

Dyraveen pushed forward to join the ring of snipers around the four hunters.

When the hunters refused surrender and opened fire, a bullet struck the tree by his head. Bark and splinters flew. The hard, shredded wood ripped skin from his temple to his ear.

Dyraveen dropped, rolled, and curled.

He blinked and breathed. He blinked and breathed.

The medic checked his eye, treated the wound with ointment and wrap.

Dyraveen spit and cursed through the antiseptic sting. He got up slowly.

He ran after the rest of the party.

He reached the bodies of the hunters just as Toch, the giant, finished his work of blade - four hearts stabbed to the hilt.

Toch looked up, red blood dripping from his black gloves. And Dyraveen knew that Toch had earned his time in prison by harder crimes than fighting.

They covered the bodies with blankets.

A trio of explosions shook the ground. Hot waves rippled through the cold mists. A rapid flurry of shots followed.

They rushed to the cabins, but the fight was already finished. Chirilech was dead. His officers lay prone and unarmed. Black smoke drifted from the cabin doors and windows. Orange flames climbed through the shattered windshields of the trucks.

Later, after the fires had died out, Dyraveen approached the keeper's circle around a cabin table. The Torites looked up from their maps and saw the bandaged Tyraen. Some grinned, some laughed.

"This happens when I put you in the rear?" Rael said. "What would happen if I put you in the front?"

A few days later, Dyraveen returned to the central valley.

Through the friends and contacts of his grandfather, he recruited many soldiers, mechanics, laborers, and technicians to the eastern shelf. He solidified the funding networks of Rael and found several new investors. He bought weapons, ammunition, tanks, and planes.

On his last day in Tekenna, he visited his grandfather.

He found Davel at the cabin, sipping maple liquor, watching the winter sunset from the patio table.

Dyraveen touched his shoulder, sat down beside him.

"My grandson returns from the wild frontier," the old man said, smiling, holding out his cup. "Drink with me, grandson. The book is finished."

Dyraveen drank the last of the liquor. "Fly with me, grandfather," he said. "I have a new plane."

The winter conclave was held south of Lytarr in a flat span of land between an unfinished laboratory complex and the syrup-slow Bokol River.

Between complex and river lay the wrecked memory of a failed canal project, thirty years abandoned. There were overrun trenches, support mounds split and caved. There were stagnant and murky pools between broken-gated locks. There were the brown-rusted frames of old dozers, a massive, nose-blade plow sunk deep into the soil like a crashed and wingless plane.

The Torite workers of the eastern shelf loved to tell stories of the failed Varran project. The team of western scientists had come to the eastern shelf with grand visions. The canal diverted from the Bokol would support a growing community of researchers and artists. They would launch rockets beyond the clouds. They would harness abundant energy from compost slews, catalyzed by river fungus. They would breed hybrid species of lizard, fish, bird, and plant. They would grow boneless meats, pitless fruits, grains more head than stalk, hays more leaf than stem.

But the dreamers had failed. Their best designs had been crushed by the deep, slow waters of the Bokol. Their funding and support from the valley had dried up not long after the pouring of their laboratory foundation. The westerners had fled the east with only debt and shame to carry home.

The soldiers of the eastern shelf enjoyed these stories as much as the workers. The arrogant and high-minded scientists had been defeated by the simplest of elements, the crudest of forces. The soft westerners had been turned and scattered by the rugged eastern frontier. The people of the rock had prevailed over the people of the moons, Torites over Varrans.

Over the last thirty years, the keepers had held more conclave meetings at the unfinished canal site than at any other location.

Landing pads for the tricopters had been cleared. A fire pit had been dug, two rings of marble blocks laid around the pit. Iron stands had been set outside the rings for barrels of liquor and pots of stew. A wide patch of grass for fighting had been kept and tended.

The rules of the conclave had developed over the years. No radios or weapons beyond the landing pad. No second officers within the inner marble ring without summons. No fights beyond the patch of grass. No fights continued after word of submission.

The order of the conclave had been settled: Talks of territory and trade until midday. Fiercest quarrels through the afternoon. Settlements and verdicts at sunfall. Fire and drink all night.

In his first conclave, Dyraveen would see many rules broken, convention thrown aside.

Rael caused the first stir. While all of the other keepers arrived by small tricopter, Rael landed in his new transport plane, a four-engine turboprop, red and silver. He also brought two Tyraens to the meeting, Dyraveen and Davel.

All eyes watched the Tyraens as they took their seats. All keepers and seconds fell quiet.

Dialla, the slender keeper, made her way through the crowd. She shook hands with Rael. She nodded to Dyraveen. She leaned down to embrace Davel.

"You should have sent your grandson to me," she said, standing up, still holding the old man's hands. "I could have taught him to do more than shoot pistols and drive trucks. Perhaps, he learns too quickly, though. Perhaps, he soars too high."

The old man stared into the dark eyes of Dialla. He smiled faintly, released her hand. "As did I in my youth," he said. "As did you."

"Fools that we were," she said. "Thank you for coming, old father. Your voice still thunders from shore to shore."

Many keepers and seconds crossed the circle to pay their respects to Davel.

Others glared and looked away.

By midmorning, the seconds had quieted and taken their seats in the outer ring; the keepers had gathered around the pit and lit the fire.

As the conclave began, the talks immediately flared into confrontation.

Five keepers from the north stepped to the center. They stood together, their backs to the fire, and called out for Rael.

"You cannot kill another keeper," their bald spokesman shouted. "You cannot ambush, slaughter, and steal."

Rael stepped forward and walked within arm's reach of the spokesman. "The dead keeper stole from me again and again," Rael said. "He wrecked my roads. He burned my buildings to the ground. He attacked twenty of my guards."

"Your guards were not killed," the bald one said. "The twenty were found alive."

"They were found hungry, weak, and sick," Rael said. "If I had not acted, Chirilech would have worked and starved to death."

"Again, your guards were found alive."

"I protected my people. I protected my ground."

"You killed by deception. You stole from the dead."

Rael and the bald keeper turned from one another. They walked throughout the inner circle, appealing, reasoning, persuading. The bald keeper warned of dark days to come if this murder went unpunished, a flood of violence not seen on the frontier since the last generation. Rael reminded the keepers of his many years of fair, honest, and peaceful trading throughout the east. He claimed to have no choice but self-defense in the quarrel with Chirilech, no desire to expand in the future beyond his present holdings.

The body of keepers split roughly into thirds: those for Rael, those against, and those unconvinced by either side.

It was agreed by all to settle the matter at the end of the day.

Other arguments and quarrels broke out.

Dialla challenged the keepers of the black dunes to close the well-trafficked routes of the pod-runners. She suggested that the outward flow of pod matched the inward flow of bribe.

The refinery keepers were criticized for unstable fuel supply and arbitrary price spikes.

The lock keepers were attacked for long delays at the mountain elevators and heavy river traffic.

The coastal keepers were faulted for the breakdown in trade talks with Andara and Troqual.

Before any of these matters could be settled, a trio of jet planes was spotted over the western mountains. The jets descended onto the eastern shelf and followed the Bokol River.

The keepers took their seats around the marble ring. Most smoked alone, quietly, eyes low.

"Who is this?" Dyraveen asked.

"The Torite generals," Davel said, "the governors of the valley."

"What do they want?"

"Money, I would guess," Davel said.

Rael signaled to Dyraveen.

Dyraveen signaled to their plane. The ramp of the plane lowered. Toch, the giant, walked down the ramp with a barrel of liquor across his shoulders. A pair of officers followed behind him, carrying a large pot of stew. Three soldiers came with a barrel of water.

All the keepers and seconds of the conclave drank together while the pot of stew was boiled. They finished their stew as the trio of jets touched down on the wildgrass plain.

"This is our meeting," Rael called out. "And our frontier."

First, soldiers poured out from the wide-bellied jets, holsters at their hips, their dark boots shining, their uniforms coal-black, their rank and honors stitched in silver from cuff to shoulder. Next, a thinner stream of guards and mercenaries spilled down, machine guns strapped, their boots mud-brown, their pants and jackets an unmatched range of blues and greens. Then came the aides and staff, unarmed, carrying pads and cases, their shoulders wrapped in fleece, their feet in low-cut leather. And last, the three generals came, their uniforms dead-black, their gold-stitched honors glowing over chest and sleeve, their faces stern and biting.

The horde of the generals headed straight for the keepers' fire, expecting the easterners to fall back.

But the wall of keepers held firm. Led by Dialla and Rael, they stood tall on the marble blocks of the outer ring, unmoved, unflinching. Anyone who tried to climb through was pushed down by firm, unfisted hands. A handful of soldiers that tried to outflank and sneak behind the arced wall were cut off by Toch, the Myshenite's heavy steps and hard stare enough to stop the soldiers where they stood.

When the horde abruptly halted at the wall, the generals pushed their way to the front. Two of the generals were very young, one was very old.

The young generals faced off with Dialla and Rael. They shouted for the keepers to move. They threw out insults, threats, and warnings. They demanded to be paid for the keepers' debts.

Having weathered the generals' early flush of rage and bluster, Dialla answered calmly. "This is the keepers' circle," she said. "We allow no weapons beyond the planes. We allow no fights outside the grass."

The generals again shouted their demand for payment.

"Take your weapons back to your planes," Dialla said. "Then we will talk about debts."

The young generals shouted once more for payment.

Dialla shook her head slowly, pointed to the jets.

The young generals looked down the lines of their troop, all eyes upon them, anxious and expectant. Their faces reddened. They clenched and unclenched their fists, glared at the keepers, unstrapped their holsters.

Rael called out to the old general standing behind them. "General Piron," he said, "how many times have we welcomed you to these conclaves as our guest? twenty? thirty? But today your people come without word, without invitation, armed to the teeth, charging like bulls. And you stand there silent while these young dogs foam and snarl."

Piron, the old general, nodded sadly. He walked forward, splitting the young generals, nudging them back.

Rael stepped down from the marble to meet him.

The two shook hands.

Piron gripped the forearm of Rael, pulled him close, spoke low into his ear. "The boys are new to power," he said, "terrified by the pressure. Both lost their fathers in the summer. Forgive me, Rael. I have allowed too much."

"Forgiven and forgotten, my old friend," Rael said. "When you return from the planes, we will have hot stew and cold liquor waiting for you."

Piron turned and shouted for all weapons to be returned to the planes.

Rael shouted for a feast to be prepared.

While the troops of the valley mixed with the troops of the frontier, the oldest men at the conclave, Piron and Davel, were sent into the inner circle for negotiations.

After an hour by the fire, the Torite and Tyraen finally compromised on terms of repayment.

Their proposal was rejected by both sides.

The old men were sent back to the fire.

Once.

Twice.

Three times.

Four.

Davel, coughing and shivering, cast his papers into the fire after the fifth rejection. He disappeared into the white-flaked wind.

Dyraveen was sent to the fire.

He was met by the young general, Sethe.

"Enough bickering," Sethe said, sipping his liquor. "We have carried the mountain tunnel project from the beginning. Now it is your turn to bear the load."

Dyraveen sat down, leaned back against the marble shelf, lit a cigarette. "You planned the project without a word from the keepers," he said. "Now, when you need money, you speak to them like partners."

"The project will benefit all," Sethe said. "All should pay."

"Did you share the cost of the mountain locks?" Dyraveen said. "Have you paved a single road east of the mountains?"

Sethe finished his liquor, tossed his cup, and towered over Dyraveen. "Brothers or enemies," Sethe said. "This is your choice."

Dyraveen crushed his cigarette, shook his head. "Fool," he said, "you have treated us as servants, not brothers. Humble yourself quickly or you will soon face your troop without a coin in your hand."

The young general left the ring.

Dyraveen threw fresh logs into the pit. He stood on the marble shelf and stared patiently into the fire.

Sethe returned with two cups of liquor. He offered Dyraveen the first.

By nightfall, all business had been finished, all quarrels ended.

The night stretched on.

Dyraveen drank with many. Rael. Dialla. Keepers. Seconds. Mercenaries. Soldiers.

He passed out next to the fire.

Deep in the night, strong hands shook him from sleep. The giant knelt beside him. "Davel is sick," Toch said, "very sick."

Embra would not speak to Toch and Dyraveen at the hospital. She would not even look in their direction. She would not allow them one step inside the room of her husband.

For many days they waited in the halls, begging information from Embra's other children, from nurses, medics, cleaners.

When they learned that Davel's infection had spread from his lungs into his lower organs, they defied their exile. They entered his room and demanded their time. "Give us our last goodbye," Dyraveen said.

Embra released her husband's hand. She took up her bag and left the room.

Davel lay still in the bed. He was bundled to his chin with blankets. His eyes were a thin, yellow crescent. Sweat dripped from the wet cloth across his forehead, ran down his cheeks, soaked the top blanket. His catheter bag bulged with more blood than urine.

Dyraveen, trembling, walked to the window.

Toch removed the wet cloth from the forehead of Davel. He wiped his face with fresh towel, pressed it to his hair. Toch held a cup of ice water to his lips.

The old man sipped. His fingers slid into the stone-knuckled valleys of the giant's hand. "More than a killer, you are," Davel said. "You must become."

Toch left the room.

Dyraveen stayed at the window, his head sinking lower.

Davel raised his hand, called for his grandson.

Still shaking, Dyraveen breathed deep. He turned from the window and came to the bed. He looked into the eyes of his grandfather, saw the spark of life still burning.

Davel took both hands of his grandson into his grip. "My blood, my blood," he said. "What you desire will destroy you. What you scorn will save."

Davel let go.

He leaned back.

He closed his eyes.

He drew long breath.

"I cannot take my eyes from the fire," he said, cracked lips risen into smile.

IX. DYRAVEEN RISES

Eleven years after the death of Davel, the frontier keepers again gathered south of Lytarr, between the Bokol River and the abandoned research complex, in the marble rings of the still-unfinished canal. But this time there were no negotiations with hot stew, no celebrations with moss liquor. A first wave of keepers arrived by air, their tricopter windshields cracked by bullet and singed by flame, wounded soldiers and officers slumped together in the backseat, bloody arms splayed across bare shoulders. The trucks came later, speeding through the wild grass, jarred by rut and hole, the wounded in the bed huddled by the tailgate, the dead pressed and piled against the cab.

The many dead were laid outside the marble rings and covered. When blankets ran out, shirts and jackets were used, then brush, then tufts of grass soon blown away.

The wounded were screened and sorted by medics at the edge of the marble – the gravely wounded sent to doctor's care in the inner circle, the seriously wounded tended to by nurses in the outer ring, the rest sent away with bandages, splints, and peroxide.

Outside the marble, few words were spoken. Some of the survivors slumped against truck tires, staring into ground or sky. Some lay on their backs in the dirty road, groaning, cursing, sobbing. Others walked through the grass in wide and aimless loops, mumbling incoherent.

Rael straddled the outer ring, staring blankly down at the marble between his knees.

Dialla screamed beside him as the medics forced her dislocated shoulder into joint.

Rael stared on, unaware. Blood dripped steadily from his charred and lobeless ear onto his leg. Once or twice an hour, he would touch his red-soaked pants, each time surprised, confused.

Only Dyraveen moved with purpose outside the ring. He gathered canteens from the dead and gave water to all who would drink. He ran supplies from the trucks and copters to the medics. He worked the radio, summoning help from every town of the eastern shelf, every city of the central valley. Before nightfall he had organized their retreat to the shelter of the old Varran laboratories.

Dyraveen saved when all seemed lost.

The keepers and soldiers of the frontier would long remember his ferocity in the hard days after their defeat. They would forgive his late arrival to Lytarr, his safe watching of the battle from the dunes outside the city.

Dyraveen sent Dialla by copter to the north. Together, they directed the reinforcements that came in from the towns of the frontier. They dropped hundreds of mined explosives into the river west of Lytarr. They surrounded the city with a tightening ring of tanks, trucks, and small artillery. Their foot soldiers drove the looting Andarans back to their warships.

Surprised by the mines, harassed by tank and artillery fire, the warships pulled anchor and fled for the ocean.

Dyraveen allowed no celebration. His copters followed the warships all the way to the sea. His planes tracked them into the ocean, then patrolled the coasts.

Dyraveen built rocket silos in the stone cliffs of the bay. He mounted artillery in concrete bunkers along the river east of Lytarr.

Imminent return, he said again and again in meetings. *We must prepare for their imminent return.*

The generosity and support of the frontier people exceeded Dyraveen's highest expectations. Rivalries between keepers, troops, towns, and companies dissolved in the wake of the Andaran attack. Freight trackers arrived daily in Lytarr, packed with food and supplies. Trucks poured into the city, crammed with volunteers of all trades, eager to rebuild. The poor laborers of the frontier tent camps, sensing opportunity, offered themselves to Dyraveen, ready to fight.

But the rest of the continent disappointed.

The Torite generals of the eastern valley, still bitter over the costly mountain-tunnel project, sent just two planes, three medical teams, and fifty soldiers.

The Varran governors of the western valley, skeptical of Dyraveen's battle account and of a naval attack so far inland, sent one bus of doctors, soldiers, and officials.

The Tyraens of the trading centers sent only intelligence agents.

The Tyraens of the eastern compounds, remembering the life of Davel, sent four trucks of food and medicine.

The fishing towns of the western shelf sent five boats, loaded with shellfish harvested on their coastline journey east.

Dyraveen, enraged, accepted only the gifts of the western fishers and the compound Tyraens.

He loaded the rest of the visitors – soldiers, doctors, officials, agents – into the dusty bed of a gravel truck. He dumped them all at river's edge in the heart of Lytarr. "Walk the city," Dyraveen said. "See the work of the Andarans."

The visitors walked from the bridgeless river to the dunes outside the city. They walked by flattened keepers' domes, warehouses gutted by fire, buildings crushed into shard and rubble. They saw scorched jeeps and crippled tanks. They passed by overcrowded medical tents, supply trucks swarmed by mob, dirty bathers in the puddle of a mainline break. Followed by wild dogs, they rushed through blackened fields of bodies undiscovered.

After nightfall, the visitors headed for a hilltop lit by bonfire.

The guards of Dyraveen met them at tables with warm stew and cold liquor.

"Remember what you have seen," the guards said. "Remember us when you go home."

After the visitors left, Dyraveen went further to stir continental sympathies. He employed his stepsisters, Adee and Elee, to photograph the devastation of Lytarr then arranged public exhibitions of their photos in every city across the continent. Dyraveen commissioned artists of his father's cult to dramatize the battle in graphic paintings, and writers to tell stories of the surviving and the fallen. He hired sculptors to carve monuments throughout the city – concentric arcs of silver, black, and crimson marble illumined at night by brilliant censer fire.

Dyraveen and Dialla spoke to massive crowds throughout the central valley. Dialla described the Andaran attack, the vicious fighting in Lytarr, the agonizing loss of the city and its heroic retaking. She told of innocent thousands captured by the Andarans and taken prisoner to their mainland. Dyraveen spoke of the dark-shadowed future. He warned that the Andarans would soon strike again. He warned that their first attack had only been a test, a cautious probing. He warned that the entire

Pheran coast lay vulnerable to naval attack, the interior ripe for army pillage.

Dyraveen summoned hundreds of leaders to continental conclave.

He flew the leaders deep into the southern wasteland.

They stayed in tents outside an old mine of mineral salts.

"We must taste the captivity of our brothers and sisters across the sea," Dyraveen said. "They cannot be forgotten."

Dyraveen let the deep quiet of the wasteland settle upon the leaders. He let the glaring sun exhaust them. He let their hunger bite, their thirst reduce. He sat among them, day by day, shedding cloth, shedding mask.

On the morning of the fourth day, Dialla opened the well. They drank from trough on hands and knees.

On the evening of the fourth day, Dialla dropped rations to the ground. They ate by tongue, no spoon or fork. They swallowed beans whole and licked the tin for hours.

At dawn of the fifth day, Dyraveen woke the leaders. He walked with them, arm in arm, into the lowest terrace of the mine. They surrounded a pit of coals.

"Have we tasted the pain of the prisoner?" he said.

The leaders nodded, eyes dull, heads dipped low and weary.

Dyraveen tossed a burning branch into the pit. A pool of yellow fire poured outward from the branch, fed by the oil-soaked coals. The servants of Dyraveen carried stew pots to the pit, handed canteens to the leaders.

After all had eaten, Dyraveen called the leaders into the open tent.

Together, they planned the continent's defense.

Toch stood high in the torchlit prison chamber, one arm cast in plaster, his neck covered with layered gauzes, dribbling red and yellow. With his good arm, he grabbed the pulley's hanging chain. He looked to Dyraveen for sign.

Dyraveen nodded toward the ceiling.

Toch pulled. The line of prisoners lurched upward. Their bare feet dangled above the stone floor. They spun helplessly, drifting in and out of flames' shadow, their weary eyes half-closed.

"Which one raped in Lytarr?" Dyraveen asked the guard.

The guard pointed.

Dyraveen shoved a piss-soaked cloth into the rapist's mouth, shot him in the belly.

Dyraveen walked the line of prisoners, rapping pistol on his thigh. "Who will answer my questions?" he said. "Who will eat and drink and live?"

The translator relayed to the prisoners.

The prisoners cried out, ten voices whimpering and barking at once.

Toch walked the line.

The prisoners quieted.

Only the rapists' muffled cries sounded throughout the chamber.

Dyraveen shot the rapist through the temple. The limp body swung away, swung back, sprayed blood across the shooter's chest.

The prisoners, again, cried out.

Toch shot the loudest through the heart.

The chamber quieted.

Dyraveen waited to speak until the bullet's echo faded under the sharp tapping of his bootsteps. "Who will answer questions?" he said softly. "Who will eat and drink and live?"

Uncle and nephew met in the heart of Pocone, on the highest balcony of the Moonlance Tower.

Dyraveen stared, unblinking, across the table.

Enteres stared, disbelieving, at the sheet of paper in his hands.

"This is what I need," Dyraveen said. "This will win the war."

"This is fantasy," Enteres said, pushing the sheet away.

"I need missiles to reach the enemy mainland," Dyraveen said, pushing the sheet back. "I need warships to match the Andarans in speed and power. I need bombers and fighters with global range."

Enteres glanced again at the dates and the numbers on the sheet. Shaking his head, he turned away. He stared into the wide city below. "Impossible," he said. "Even if the technologies can be developed, there isn't enough time for production."

"You have troves and troves of money," Dyraveen said. "You have an army of staff. You control every factory, plant, and laboratory on the continent. Your authority as General of Science is second only to my own."

"And I give it all back to you," Enteres said. "I never asked for any of this."

"Do you think we are up against a problem of numbers and theory?" Dyraveen said. "This is about *survival*. The Andarans will destroy us." Dyraveen walked to the edge of balcony, waved his arm across the city. "All this can be burned in a day."

"I'm not your man," Enteres said. "Use your old friend, Brellen. You two have much in common."

"Brellen is a whore," Dyraveen said, sitting down. "Fulfill your duty, my uncle. For the people."

The nephew smoked.

The uncle drank.

"It can't be done," Enteres said. "Find someone else."

"I understand," Dyraveen said. "The burden frightens. We all carry burdens. You should also know, my blood, that this is the only project of the continent. Moonlance is dead."

The inner circle of planners met in the home of old Davel, the cottage beneath the bluff.

They talked from midday deep into the night, their table strewn with maps, reports, and aerial photos, the old cottage stale with dust and smoke.

After second stew, Dyraveen opened the windows, poured fresh drinks, and paced the room. "So what do we know for certain?" he asked.

Dialla, leaning back, gave a wry smile. "For certain?" she said. "Nothing. Every report we receive about Andara is contradicted by the next."

Oson sat forward in his wheelchair. "So is our intelligence shit," he said, "or is Andara in chaos?"

"The Emperor is the highest leader in Andara," Toch said, "but his power might be more symbol than strength. Beneath him are powerful generals competing for control of the mainland ports and the outer islands. The prisoners we questioned named seven of these generals on the mainland. All named Ciralan the one who attacked Lytarr."

"Did Ciralan act by orders of the Premier?" Dialla asked. "With the help of other generals? Alone?"

"We don't know for sure," Toch said. "The prisoners spoke only of Ciralan, the vicious, the mad."

Dyraveen cut off the giant before he could say more. "Regardless how the war began," Dyraveen said, "the Andarans will undoubtedly stand together now until its end. The question is, where will they strike next?"

Rael stood up, collected all the aerial photographs from the table, arranged them by date from one end of the table to the other. He walked the table slowly, returned to the beginning, and walked again. He sat down, lit a smoke. "I don't see it," Rael said. "There are no warships on our coast. Only barges and fishers on the open seas."

"We've spotted more than forty warships throughout the outer islands, twice as many around the mainland," Dyraveen said.

"So why do they wait?" Rael asked. "Why no attack since Lytarr?"

The planners debated several explanations for the long period of Andaran inaction, none completely satisfying.

The attack of Ciralan appeared to lack the support of every other Andaran general. But would he have to dared to drive so deeply into the greater Pheran continent without some measure of support from his homeland? Would his soldiers have followed him to farthest sea on such a reckless mission?

Whatever support Ciralan may have counted upon had utterly failed to come through. Alone, he had followed the river west. Alone, he had battled for the city. Alone, he had been repelled from land and banished to the sea.

Had Ciralan been condemned by his fellow generals on his return to the mainland? Had he been shamed and stripped?

Or did he now boast of Lytarr's destruction, promise easy conquest of the continent, and mobilize even greater forces of invasion?

The planners argued until dawn.

When Dyraveen saw the glow of sunrise on the horizon, he ended the meeting.

"We plan for the worst," he said.

In the southern dunes, Dyraveen watched the runners struggle up and down the white-sanded slopes. He watched Dialla pull away from the pack, the young recruits unable to match her fierce, long-legged strides. Trying to keep up, some of the runners stumbled and rolled down the dunes; some knelt in the sand and puked.

Dyraveen stepped out of his tracker and walked to the transport truck. He slammed his fist on the hood. The dozing guard in the cab jerked alert. "Back to base," Dyraveen said.

The truck pulled away. Only Dyraveen and his tracker remained on the gravel road at dunes' edge.

Dialla crested the final hill, her hair dark and heavy with sweat. She shortened her stride, slowed her pace. She walked to the road, her head tilted back, eyes closed, chest heaving.

Her face whitened when she saw the Continental Commander. "What happened?" she said. "Have we been attacked?"

Dyraveen handed her a water, shook his head.

Dialla leaned against the tracker, sipped. She watched the pack of recruits pour over the final hill.

Dyraveen raised a towel. He wiped Dialla over her face, neck, chest.

When the recruits came near, Dyraveen pulled a water cooler from the tracker's cab and tossed it into the sand. "One bottle each," he said. "Then march to base. Together."

He waited until all the recruits had finished their water then threw the cooler into the tracker.

The recruits started for base in a loose huddle.

As they marched, Dyraveen idled the tracker alongside them. "Tighter," he yelled. "Faster."

The recruits pulled together, doubled their pace.

Dyraveen sped away on the gravel road. "How soft are they?" he asked.

Dialla breathed deeply, savored the rush of cool air over her skin. "They're just kids from the valley," she said. "Just kids."

Back at the base, Dialla showered, ate dinner, then joined the Commander on the roof.

They watched the red-hazed sunset.

They watched the moons climb and brighten.

"You're bone-tired," Dyraveen said. "Take a few days."

"I can't," Dialla said. "Too much quiet takes me back to Lytarr."

"Then fly away with me," Dyraveen said. "We can disappear in the western mountains. We can swim in lakes as still as glass. We can sleep by star and fire."

"The king dreams," she said with thin and tired smile.

When the night winds surged across the roof, they headed below to the Commander's chamber. They sipped maple liquor. They stared at the world map across the wall, its seas storming by the flickering twist of oil-lamp flame, its islands slipping in and out of bloodred shadows.

The lamp ran dry of oil late in the night.

Dyraveen carried Dialla to his bed, covered her with blanket, watched her sleep.

In his second year of power, Dyraveen encountered much resistance across the continent. The memory of Lytarr had faded in civilian minds. The Andarans had not struck again. There had been no imminent return.

Continental taxes went unpaid, rules of rationing ignored. Less than half of the continental leaders returned to Dyraveen's wasteland conclave. Many of the new soldier recruits abandoned their coastal posts and fled for inland homes.

"The heart of the resistance is in Pocone," Dialla said. "Your birthplace rejects you."

Dyraveen wrote his mother.

She received him in an unfinished university hall, its bare trusses streaked by white slush of birdshit and rain, iron rods protruding from concrete footers unpoured.

"Your latest work?" Dyraveen said.

"A small project," Rhoa said, "stopped by the forced shortages."

Dyraveen kissed her. "You will finish," he said. "When the war is over."

"What war?" she said, leaning away. "From all reports Andara fights only with itself."

The mother and son stood together after years apart. Each stared into the fierce-lit eyes of the other. Each saw a face both familiar and new.

"How long has it been? four years? five?" Rhoa said. "Not one letter from you in all this time. Not one call. And now, suddenly, you are here."

"Yes, I have long been away," Dyraveen said. "I had to walk in the steps of my father. I had to see my grandfather in his last days."

"You had to find your place among the criminals and soldiers in the east."

"Yes, I had to earn the respect of all on the frontier - keepers, officers, soldiers, farmers, builders, mechanics. Do you think this was easy? I was a lone Tyraen in a sea of Torites, a soft westerner in the hard east, a dwarf among giants."

"And yet you climbed so high, so quickly."

"How did you climb, mother? How did a young Tyraen girl from a small Tekennan compound come to build the greatest towers of Pocone?"

"I worked. I struggled. I suffered."

"As have I."

"I explored all ages and hours of history. I pursued the highest concepts of art and science."

"I sweat and bled. I learned the fear of the animal. I held the dying as they passed."

"And are you more than animal, Commander? You threaten and bark like a thug. You take what you want like a thief. You walk with a killer's eyes."

"I adorn this armor for a short time. Only to survive."

Rhoa grabbed her son by the neck, pulled him close, wept against his cheek.

"Your father came to me in the winter," she said. "He sweat and shivered under final fever. He trembled like a newborn desperate to return."

Dyraveen wept. And trembled.

Rhoa took her son into her home for days.

Dyraveen told his mother of Sedenel's shrine beneath the pyres, the many who came to see her lover's work. And he told of old Davel's last days, his final, piercing words. "None saw clearer," Rhoa said.

Rhoa brought her son and brother together.

Dyraveen begged forgiveness for his earlier disrespect.

Enteres accepted and drank with his nephew.

The three talked deep into the night.

Again and again, Dyraveen asked of Pocone.

Dyraveen walked the university halls without uniform, guards, or pistol. He talked to many teachers and researchers, many scientists and artists. He asked questions. He listened long.

With the help of his mother and uncle, the higher places opened for him. He was allowed into directors' meetings, private assemblies, planning sessions. He was invited to tower feasts and balcony parties. His circle of Varran supporters widened.

At an exhibit of sculpture and painting, a black-robed Varran stepped forward to block the path of Dyraveen. The Varran stared down with widening smile and unbelieving eyes. He shook the hand of the Tyraen, clapped his shoulder.

It was Brellen. The old partner and colleague of his uncle. The lab director Dyraveen had studied under years ago.

"It is you," Brellen said. "Though I've heard your name spoken a thousand times, I couldn't bring myself to believe."

"Believe what?" Dyraveen said.

"That my old student had traveled so far. That the wide-eyed boy who once wandered my laboratory halls is now a commander of the frontier."

"*The* Commander," Dyraveen said, "of the continent."

Brellen smiled, gave a quick, dismissive wave of his hand. "You don't control much beyond the frontier, though, do you?"

Dyraveen walked on through the exhibit. He circled slowly around a stone replica of the citadel mount, the first home and refuge of the Varran people. The mount appeared the billowed chest of rising giant, its grey-rock ribs twisted to breaking, stretched to bursting, the jagged rib ends stabbing through.

Brellen followed closely. He leaned into Dyraveen, pressing his shoulder against the smaller man's throat. "I know what you're doing," Brellen said in a low voice.

"And what is that?" Dyraveen said.

"Feigning humility. Begging university favor. Pretending to be Varran."

Dyraveen moved on. He stopped before a massive bulb of shimmering, black crystal. Cavernous pores marred the bulb's smooth skin. Blue crystals flowed smoothly into the bulb like subterranean streams. Red crystals shot outward like lava's boiling or blood's arterial spray.

"It won't work," Brellen said, still following. "All of the friendly Varran faces will harden the moment you speak of taxes and rations."

Dyraveen nodded with a thin smile. "Let me guess your next words, Brellen," he said. "Only you can deliver the support of Pocone. Only you can persuade the Varran elite."

"Blood is the strongest of forces, young commander, especially in times of war. Varrans will never accept a Tyraen ruler, no matter the danger."

Dyraveen entered a cove of paintings brilliant with celestial light. The burning gold of star's first fire. The silver, blue, and emerald of young moons' rising. The misty, white halo of galaxy's slow turn.

Brellen pressed closer, whispered fiercely: "I understand the mind of my people. You need me. You will not rule without me."

"Do you understand the Varran?" Dyraveen said. "The Varran is a stargazer. The Varran is a dreamer. And the Varran is proud, very proud."

"Without me, they will reject you. Again and again."

"Have you not heard? I am bringing the Moonlance project back. Varran rockets will soon land on every moon. The Varran people will be the first to space. The great Varrans will walk through the heavens and stand among the gods."

Dyraveen abandoned his highly unpopular food-rationing programs. He closely monitored the supply levels of critical materials – fuels, metals, chemicals, munitions – throughout the continent but allowed their free sale and movement.

Dyraveen restored his uncle to the lead of the Moonlance project. Together, they pushed the project ahead, Enteres handling the technical challenges, Dyraveen stirring public interest and securing funds. They launched trial rockets over Pocone that deafened the people, shook the city towers, and soared beyond highest cloud. Huge rocket models were placed along the city canals for the workers to see each day. Visionary paintings of the three moons were reprinted and hung in classrooms, restaurants, homes, and halls. Triple-crescent symbols appeared everywhere throughout the city, from terminal walls to pyramid face to high-flying banners. From the robed scientists in university towers to the laborers rinsing sweat in lowest flues, the city came together to support the daring project.

The Commander followed each rocket launch with a modest increase of taxes. He reached a three-tenths rate without protest from the citizens.

Dyraveen secretly siphoned money from the Moonlance project to his war effort.

Enteres, with a team of top aeronautical engineers, experimented with designs for long-range bombers, heavy bicopters, and fighter planes. After three generations of models, they succeeded in meeting all of Dyraveen's specifications except range.

"The fighters would be as slow as copters if we built them with global range," Enteres said. "The bombers would look like blimps."

"Nothing can be done?" Dyraveen said.

"Given the power and accuracy of Andaran cannons, no."

"Then shift from research to manufacturing. We need hundreds of the attack and transport copters, thousands of the bombers and fighters."

For the design of his naval warships Dyraveen assembled a team of Tekennan engineers, coastal fishers, and ocean traders. When the team factions clashed and came up with radically diverging ship designs, Dyraveen took them to a warehouse in Lytarr. He showed them the remains of Andaran warships dredged from the river.

"The Andarans have fought at sea for centuries," Dyraveen said. "We will steal from their experience. Imitate their basic designs. Aim only for small improvements."

When the replicated warships of the team survived drills and storm at sea, Dyraveen authorized their mass-production.

The inner circle of planners met once more at the cottage of old Davel. They estimated the cost of factory conversions and the production of Dyraveen's massive air and naval fleets. They calculated the incoming taxes from the continent.

"Double," Oson said. "Your projected costs are twice your tax revenues."

The planners argued for hours over how to bridge the gap. Most of the planners focused on higher taxes for the Varrans, Cyecurans, and coastal towns.

"There is a way to save money for the east and the west, the frontiers and the coasts," Dyraveen said, "a way to turn a sharp-thorned problem into a rich, unending fountain."

The planners sneered, poured new drinks, lit new cigarettes.

"Bluepod," Dyraveen said. "We seize all the pod fields of coast and swamp. We harvest, alter, synthesize, distribute. We profit."

"Turn the whole continent into addicts?" Dialla said.

"No, we don't sell pure pod. Our chemists dilute the raw harvest into milder forms. They develop pod to kill pain, pod for dream state, pod for adrenaline surge, pod for healing."

"The science is there?" Rael said.

"It will be. We have the best minds of the continent."

"And the runners?" Toch said. "The addicts? The pressers?"

"If we can't take out the drug cults and gangs, what chance do we have against the Andarans?" Dyraveen said. "Consider it hard training for our soft recruits. A prelude to war."

While the chemists hit the labs, the soldiers took to the field.

Rael led an early morning attack on the pod farms along the northeastern coast. His plan was to trap the pod farmers between a line of paratroopers on land and a ring of warships at sea, the farmers surrendering without bloodshed. But the warships came too close to shore. The ships' overanxious gunners disobeyed orders to fire only at fleeing drug boats. They shelled and battered the drug farms before the troopers could form their line. The pod farmers, heavily armed and desperate, fled by land. They crashed and split the troopers. They separated into dozens of bands and ran for the dunes. The troopers chased. The dead fell from both sides. Rael ordered his soldiers to take cover. He led the dive of the attack copters. The copters unleashed, shredding any who still ran, leaving no wounded. Rael landed his copter back at the pod farms. Enraged, he radioed to the ships for all captains and gunners to report on shore. When he heard that three captains had grounded their vessels on reefs, he broke his radio into pieces.

Dialla faced her own difficulties on the opposite side of the continent. Her infantry bogged down in the swamplands of the western shelf. Her planes and copters were rendered virtually useless by the thick ocean mists, grounded except for the rare hour of clear sky. Her armored boats were too slow to catch the darting drug skimmers, too heavy to enter narrow channels. After losing several vessels and patrols, Dialla changed her strategy from capture to siege. She pulled her boats from the mire. Her troops fell back to dry ground and circled the swampland with trenches and tanks. Her attack copters picked off all traffic between swamp and mountain, while her fighter planes cleared from swamp to sea. Dialla trucked small-rocket batteries to the edge of the marshes. At every break in the coastal mist she filled the sky with missiles, the batteries launching north to south, then back again. Dialla ordered all those fleeing the swamp to be captured, not killed. From starving addicts she learned the safe paths to the pod farms by open stream and solid ground. Dialla took the entire swamp with ten light boats, two-hundred troops, and one windless, sunny hour.

Before his clearing of outer Pocone, Dyraveen pulled Toch aside.

"Tell me about the pod addicts," Dyraveen said. "Is there any hope for their recovery? for normal life?"

"Maybe one in six will beat the disease," Toch said. "The rest will relapse again and again. They will lie, steal, and kill as long as they have breath."

"Should I let the five go free to save the one?"

"Yes, because we cannot tell the one from the five," Toch said, a wet light of fear in his eyes. "Because we have killed too many already. And we will kill many more before the end."

Dyraveen instructed his soldiers to shoot only the armed, the dealers, the runners. The addicts were to be unharmed.

On the morning of the clearing, the Commander waited alone in his truck at the abandoned stone quarry. He held the radio to his ear, scanned frequency by frequency, cycle after cycle.

Toch returned at midday with his squad, silent and weary.

The squad smoked. Then drank. Then smoked again. Then stared into the quiet sky.

"What happened?" Dyraveen said.

"Every pod house is cleared, every press destroyed," Toch said. He dipped a cloth into the open cooler, washed the crimson-streaked sweat from his hands, face, neck.

"And the addicts?"

"Most of them ran for the caves. They hid in the underground."

"The rest?"

Toch grimaced, looked away. "When your soldiers saw one of their own wounded," he said, "instincts took over, distinctions blurred. You cannot ask for more from those who wade in blood."

After a long day of surprise inspections in the factories of Tekenna, Dyraveen retreated to the old cottage for rest. Five drinks deep, he watched a truck speed toward him on the gravel road. The truck stopped at the edge of the trees, its trail of dust continuing on. From the white-dust cloud emerged the angry faces of the young Torite Generals, Sethe and Lacan.

The generals stomped to the patio stairs, stopped halfway to the top, and yelled at the Commander in his chair.

Sethe and Lacan took turns shouting their complaints against Dyraveen. They shouted until the shadows fell long across the deck and the insects swarmed over the streams.

When they had tired themselves, Dyraveen lit the torches around the deck. He poured three fresh drinks and motioned to the generals. "Why are you standing down there?" he said. "Come to the table. Rest your feet. Drink with me."

The three sat down together.

The Commander waited until the generals had each enjoyed a drink and a smoke.

"The inspections were routine, my friends," Dyraveen said. "They are not a sign of suspicion or mistrust. I make them everywhere I go."

"Why won't you admit it?" Sethe said. "The keepers of the frontier are favored over the generals of the valley."

"My friends, you are still generals of the continental army," Dyraveen said, "the same rank as Dialla and Rael."

"But they fight in the field while we sweat in factories," Lacan said.

"And your work is more important," Dyraveen said. "You build the fleets that will defeat the Andarans and win the war. They only clean up criminals and filth."

"What about our officers and mercenaries?" Sethe said. "They have all been passed over for promotions."

"We are simply behind on paperwork," Dyraveen said. "Their promotions are soon coming. And greater pay as well."

"When?" Sethe demanded.

"A few days," Dyraveen said. "Be patient, my friend. My territory stretches from coast to coast. The entire system must be remade."

Dyraveen lit fresh smokes for the generals, poured fresh drinks.

The generals put their feet up, leaned back in their chairs.

"Are you really Torites?" the Commander said, grinning wide. "Are you really soldiers? Then drink with me tonight."

The three never made it inside the cottage. They slept in their chairs, their jackets for pillows, empty glasses in their laps.

With the harsh morning sun came the sound of Oson's crutches through the gravel.

He climbed each stair step in four movements – right crutch, left crutch, right foot, left foot.

At the top of the stairs, Oson breathed heavy, sweat dripping. He pushed over a chair with his crutch.

The generals groaned.

The Commander fell from his chair, rolled, and drew his pistol, eyes wide and bleary.

"Answer your radios next time, you fucks," Oson said.

Dyraveen holstered his pistol. He reached for his jacket, balled it back into a pillow, and turned onto his side.

Oson leaned against the railing, pulled his forearms from the crutch's soft-padded grips, and retrieved his backpack. "You're needed in Pocone, High Commander," Oson said. "We have a prisoner for you."

Dyraveen rolled onto his back, covered his eyes from the sun. "An Andaran?" he asked.

"Worse," Oson said. He tossed a thick book onto Dyraveen's chest. "A photographer."

Dyraveen raised the book. He scanned the cover, a black-and-white photograph. He saw a pod house in flames. One body slumped in the doorway, blood dribbling from the neck. Three bodies lay still in the grass outside - two young girls, one man, no weapons in hand. A soldier on the deck stared into the hills, oblivious to the dead at his feet. Smoke poured in dark clouds from the burning roof. A blackened arm reached for sky, surrounded by fire. *Dyraveen's Trail*, the book's title.

Grava, the photographer and prisoner, had the dark-clay skin and bronze-blue eyes of the Iccin. Her long hair was tied with silver cord in the Varran way. Her cheek and neck bore the black-pocked scars of childhood disease. Through rips and tears in her shirt, Dyraveen saw rock-bladed dagger tattoos over her fleshless ribs.

Grava had refused food and water. She had sat stone-faced and silent through all of the officers' questions. She had spoken only to ask the condition of the soldier she had stabbed during her capture.

Grava had also refused the plate and bottle offered by Dyraveen. But her hard face had loosened upon seeing the Continental Commander in her small cell. She had smiled like a child with a secret.

Dyraveen had asked many questions of the prisoner. Do you know who I am? Do you know why you are here? Who helped you on this book? Who knows of its existence?

But Grava had only smiled.

Impatient, Dyraveen had lifted her book high, slammed it onto the table.

The Iccin woman had laughed.

Now, Dyraveen, uncomfortable, unnerved by the woman's cold eyes, reversed his strategy. He apologized to Grava for the guards' rough treatment. He took off her handcuffs. He offered her a cigarette and lighter.

"I ordered my soldiers to kill only the makers and dealers of bluepod," Dyraveen said. "No addicts were to be touched."

Grava scowled at the Commander's outreached hands. She pushed her chair back from the table. She stretched her arms and legs, cracked her neck.

Dyraveen leaned against the cell door, lit the cigarette. "My soldiers were under intense pressure that day," he said. "Ten were wounded. They did the best they could."

Grava finally spoke, her voice soft and low. "You killed at least fifty addicts," she said. "You killed twelve artists of the underground, far from any pod house."

"There was chaos that day. My soldiers were fired upon from every direction."

"My brother, the painter, the drummer, the father of two, was shot while walking in the fields."

Grava stood.

Dyraveen drew his pistol. "I am sorry for your brother," the Commander said. "I have also lost many in this war."

Grava took a step toward the door.

Dyraveen raised his pistol to her chest.

"You don't understand," Grava said. "The underground knows all, remembers all."

The hand of Dyraveen trembled; the barrel shook. "My father, the painter, lived in the underground," he said. "I lived in the underground."

"I know," she said. "I was there. I saw you stand with Cirico. I saw you face the Council of Thieves."

Dyraveen's arm dropped limp. His pistol fell to floor.

"Do you not remember your history, Commander?" Grava said, taking another step. "The underground was born fighting tyrants. The underground survived every war of king and empire. Again and again, we rebuilt the wasted land."

"I fight for the underground," Dyraveen pleaded. "I fight for all of Phera."

"The wind whispers in the underground," Grava said. "The truth breathes."

Dyraveen slid to the floor.

"You left the Council with the old guide, Iddir," the woman said. "Then Iddir was found dead."

Dyraveen shouted for the guard.

"Many saw you leave the catacombs," the woman said. "Then the maker was found dead."

The guard burst in, club ready.

"Do not touch her," Dyraveen said. "She goes free."

Dyraveen surrendered himself on a cold, bright morning. The second snow of winter blanketed the hills outside Pocone. Gusts of wind stripped the hilltop drifts, launched white plumes high into the sky, far across the gullies.

The Artauk giants stood at the cavern entrance like stone towers. Their hands rested on the heads of wooden staves taller than any Varran, Torite, or Tyraen. Strips of blue cloth covered their eyes.

Dyraveen stripped down in the back of the transport wagon. He took off soldier's boots and Commander's jacket. He laid down pistol, belt, and wallet. He shed pants, socks, and shirt. Shivering, he stared at the giants.

"How long shall we wait for you?" Dialla asked.

"One year," Dyraveen said. "If I have not risen from the underground in one year, assume that I am dead. Do not waste any time or resources to look for me. Attack Andara as soon as you are ready."

"You leave your labor unfinished," Rael said.

"The war can be won with or without me," Dyraveen said. "I will rise from the darkness reborn. Or I will die as I deserve."

"You trust too much in me," Toch said. "I cannot take your place."

"Many stand with you," Dyraveen said. "Many will help."

The three embraced Dyraveen.

Then he was gone.

Barefoot, he ran through the snow.

In the cavern mouth, the Artauk tied him to a staff by his hands, feet, and waist. They carried him into the tunnel like hunters' slain game.

A cry rang out in the tunnel.

A crowd rushed near.

A hail of stones struck Dyraveen. Then fists.

Even the giants were caught up in the mob's fierce press. The two Artauk carrying Dyraveen spun sideways in the tunnel. One lost his grip on the staff. Dyraveen dropped, headfirst, toward the ground.

The mob kicked and kneed his sides, stomped down at his face.

The giants rallied. They pushed back the crowd. They lifted Dyraveen high into the air. They turned into a narrow passage.

The mob's cry faded.

In a high, slivered cleft, Dyraveen faced the Council of Thieves. He knelt in firepit ash, head low. The long shadows of Varrans, Iccin, and Artauk buried him in darkness.

The questioning of the judges began.

"Did you kill old Iddir?"

"No. Yes. He was ready to die, to dream within the mountain. He could not walk. He could not rise. When his lungs failed, I poured water into his throat. To hasten the end."

"And the crystal maker? How did he die?"

"I climbed to his chamber. I had to see the living crystal. I had to know the makers' secret. He came at me with staff and sword. I stabbed. Again. Again."

"You trespassed?"

"Yes."

"You trampled sacred ground?"

"Yes."

"You killed the maker?"

"Yes."

"And Dyraveen, High Commander, what have you brought to the west?"

"I have stirred the pride of the west. I have invigorated Pocone."

"You have manipulated."

"Varrans will soon walk the skin of every moon."

"And your bombers and warships pour from eastern factory by western coin."

"All must contribute to the continent's defense."

"But your war is not defense, High Commander. It is revenge for Lytarr. It is opportunity for you to seize power."

"Yes. It is both. And more."

"And your bloody pod campaigns? What have they achieved?"

"We burned the leeches from the body. We stopped the cancer's spread."

"Now you are the cancer, Dyraveen. You spread the same poison in wider branch."

"We spread medicine."

"You spread drugs to pay for your war."

"We spread medicine."

"And the twelve artists that were killed in the hills?"

"I know nothing of the twelve. My orders were not followed."

"And the western mountains that have run with blood since your command? The mining companies that have killed by explosion and flood? The timber mills built upon the bones of Artauk and Iccin?"

"I know nothing of this."

"Nothing? With every speech you gave in high Pocone, the miners and the millers drove deeper into our heart."

"I know nothing of this."

"Nothing, High Commander? You know nothing of the continent you rule?"

Dyraveen breathed deeply, raised his eyes to the Council. He struggled to his feet with gritted teeth. "Announce your judgment then," Dyraveen said, "the sentence settled long ago."

The Council of Thieves spoke among themselves in a strange, mixed tongue.

Achlora novol, the two Iccin said, again and again, throughout their arguments.

Each of the three Varrans spoke at length. Each ended their words the same. *Achlora novol.*

The Artauk giant looked down at Dyraveen. *Achlora novol.*

A Varran stepped to Dyraveen, pronounced the Council's judgment.

"For the great light you have stolen from the world, you will live in darkness," she said. "For the many lives you have taken, you will soon die. Dyraveen, you will be caged in a lightless tomb of stone, your escape blocked by iron stakes and boulder, a mountain of rock between you and the world you once ruled. *Achlora novol.* The living death. Nothing can save you now but the hand of God."

The legs of Dyraveen buckled. He dropped to one knee, a hand in the ash.

"For the sake of your father, Sedenel, the painter, you will be given one crystal of light," she said. "For your freeing of Grava, you will be given two more."

As the iron stakes pounded, Dyraveen moved quickly. He laid his first crystal at the tomb's entrance. By the crystal's blue light, he climbed the steepest face of rock within the tomb. At the top of the face, he laid his second crystal. He raised the third crystal high to see the nooks and contours of the cavern ceiling. He followed the cavern's bend until it looped back to another rock face, gentler in slope than the first. He dropped the last crystal. Scanning high and low, he followed the softer slope back to tomb's entrance. That was it. That was the full length, width, and depth of his new world.

Before panic could seize him, he bent his thoughts toward hope. He had expected a coffin, a quick and suffocating death. But the tomb was large. And in its size, there was promise.

Dyraveen climbed the steep face again, this time noticing each foothold and handhold.

At the top of the face, he felt the angled surfaces of the rock, noted several different textures, several different pores and grains.

Around the cavern's high bends, he found a dribbling of water in three places.

Down the soft slope, he saw patches of brown fungus, the droppings of lizard, worm, and rat.

He climbed again.

And again.

By his fifth circling of the tomb, the crystals of light had dimmed to half-strength.

By tenth circle, he climbed in total darkness, the path memorized by his hands and feet, cemented in his mind.

By twentieth circle, he knew the pebbles, sand, and moisture under every touch and hold.

Dyraveen lost count of his circles through the tomb. Tired and weak, he rested against the massive stone that trapped him, the boulder that had taken the strength of five Artauk to lift.

He dozed. He dreamed. Still climbing on. Still walking. Still trapped in endless circle like the river wraiths of Opir.

Ravenous and thirsty, Dyraveen woke from his restless sleep.

He sucked dripping water from cracks in the wall. He licked wet stones.

He ate small worms from a handful of wet soil. He gagged on the swallowing, but the worms settled in his stomach without nausea or fever. Dyraveen decided to live on worms rather than risking the diseases of the uncooked rat. He would try to catch the lizard only in greatest desperation because of the low odds of success and the danger of falling during chase.

Dyraveen gathered every handful of soil in the tomb. He gently placed each handful in a tub-shaped void on the upper terrace. With a stone saucer he carried water from the dribbling cracks to his bed of worms. With a flat-edged stone he scrapped fungus from the floor and sprinkled it over the soil.

Dyraveen slept beside his little farm. He dreamed of grill and smoke and dripping flanks of meat.

When he woke from long rest, he drank greedily and ate sparingly.

A fear of permanent blindness gripped his thoughts. He found sharp and heavy stones throughout the tomb. He pounded the rock around the widest drinking crack. He raked up and down the slit. He pounded again. He raked again. He pounded. He raked. His hands bruised. He raked. His fingers bled. He raked.

A single drop of light-glistened water fell through.

He leaned into the wall, conformed his body to its ridges and valleys, twisted himself awkwardly to get closer to the drop.

His eyes feasted.

He stared at the drop until he could see all colors radiating from the speck of white light.

He watched his exhaled breath ripple over the water's skin.

As he breathed in, he watched the turning of oceans.

Dyraveen attacked the rock with all his strength.

Finite is the distance to surface, finite the length of stone.

He had always relied on willpower and cunning. He had always probed opponents for flaws, pounced upon slightest opening, smallest weakness.

But the rock gave little. One more drop of light. Maybe two.

The intense labor stoked his hunger. Reckless, he gorged on his farm of worms. He ate all of the fat worms in the center. He left only the meatless newborns around the edges.

Sober and regretful, Dyraveen yielded to the hard mountain. He abandoned his drive for light. He stirred, watered, and fertilized the farm. He nibbled only to kill the pangs of hunger, never indulging in a full worm.

Dyraveen shifted his focus from light and vision to other senses.

With his ears and hands to the rock, he felt a distant tapping, steady and faint vibrations, rare tremblings. His heart pounded at the discovery. Miners. This was the work of miners. The sharp tapping was the work of picks, the dull tapping the work of hydraulic hammers. The steady vibrations came from rolling conveyors and the slide of railcars. The tremblings were explosions, shifts, collapses. He was no longer alone in the dark.

Dyraveen formed other connections with the world beyond the tomb. He found small vents and holes between stone slabs. His skin sensitized to the faintest breeze, the slightest change in temperature. He tracked the passage of days and nights by the air's warming and cooling. By common breath he joined with the caves beyond the tomb, with the skies beyond the caves.

As his supply of worms ran dangerously low, he conserved his energy, limited his movement. He stayed on the upper terrace, never venturing below. He worked his arms and legs just enough to avoid cramping. He drank from one crack, listened at one hole. As his strength of flesh diminished, he depended more and more on his mind's ability to roam.

Dyraveen relived old matches of the Aviet.

He remembered the stories of Cyadae, his second mother.

He remembered the songs of Iprana, his first love.

He remembered the passing of old Davel.

He remembered Pocone, Tekenna, Lytarr.

He remembered Dialla, Toch, Rael.

But all of these memories slipped away. The images blurred in detail, distorted in form, faded in resonance and color. The past of Dyraveen receded like ship's departed shore. All hope of future shriveled back into the present void.

Dyraveen pissed and shit where he lay.

Rats chewed his feet, nibbled his sides, ventured closer and closer to his face.

Gunfire.

Loud. Close. Much nearer than the work of the miners.

Several flurries of gunshots. Back and forth.

Many voices. Shouting.

Then a long, fierce exchange.

Then a few scattered shots.

Then, nothing. The silent dark returned.

Dyraveen brushed the rats away. He grabbed the tomb wall, pulled his torso above his sleeping legs, and crawled to the nearest vent. He shouted for help.

He propped himself against the wall, pulled up his knees, bent his feet. The dead flesh of his thighs ached, clenched, throbbed. He bent his feet further and further, wiggled his toes. Slowly, the blood flowed down.

He drank.

He ate.

He stood.

For three days, Dyraveen shouted into the vents and holes. He beat heavy stones against the wall, sometimes in precise code, sometimes desperate rage. No sound was heard from the world above.

On the fourth day, the stone suddenly cried out.

Thunder shivered through the rock.

The ground swayed weak as water.

Jagged cracks snaked across the tomb walls. Wide fissures streaked plate to plate. Blinding swords of light slashed through the air.

Dyraveen rushed for highest corner. He ripped the tattered cloth from his waist, tore a strip least soiled, and tied it over his eyes. He curled into a ball, covered his head, and waited.

When the settling came, the terrible grinding of rock upon rock deafened.

The wall above the gentle slope collapsed. Boulders rushed down. Huge plate fragments burst through, crashed into the tomb's entrance. The tomb blazed with crystal light. Dyraveen listened helplessly as the stream of falling rock continued to pour into the tomb, climbing higher and higher on the slope. The tomb filled nearly to the top.

When the stream of rock ceased flowing, Dyraveen walked toward the void of light, his back to the length of wall still standing. He reached his hand into the void, groped for solid hold.

But smaller rocks poured down, thick streams of gravel, dirt, and pebbles. Dust and grit clouded the air.

Then water exploded through every gap of stone and showered down in jets and mists.

A huge cone formed in the void above, a twisting liquid funnel, blasting smaller rocks aside, turning boulders.

Dyraveen watched the dark water below him climb, a muddy, rising tide.

But the water above subsided.

The water below drained down.

Dyraveen climbed toward light. He slid between boulders. He crawled up muddy ramps and slithered over plates on his belly.

When he reached a wide and open space, he filled his lungs with sweet, new air. He climbed onto a ground solid and level.

Boots tromped toward him. A beam of electric light burned his eyes. A Varran voice called out. "Who are you?"

Dyraveen turned his head from the light.

"*Who are you?*" the Varran shouted. A bullet entered chamber.

"I am Dyraveen."

The Varran laughed, spit. The butt of his pistol cracked Dyraveen above the ear.

Dyraveen dropped.

The Varran dragged Dyraveen to a muddy pool by his thick-matted hair, shoved his head under the dirty water, held him down with both hands.

Dyraveen spun and twisted out of the Varran's grip. He rolled across the puddle. He staggered to his feet and ran.

Still blinded, Dyraveen crashed against the tunnel wall. He fell to the ground. This time he had no strength to rise. He lay still, moaning, waiting for the end.

The Varran walked slowly toward him.

Three shots rang out.

Four.

Five.

The body of the Varran dropped.

Dyraveen heard Iccin talking. And Artauk.

Among the voices of the underground soldiers, Dyraveen recognized one he had not heard in many years. It was the guild assassin, the penitent killer, Cirico.

The underground soldiers circled around him.

The soldiers stared at the Tyraen – filthy with blood and grime, naked except for the cloth strip over his eyes, emaciated with jutting bones and skin-stretched hollows, infected welts from feet to chest.

"Why did you come back?" Cirico said quietly, kneeling down. "Why?"

"Because I saw the maker," Dyraveen said. "Every night, every dream."

Cirico handed his canteen, nodded with understanding, then spoke to the other soldiers. "Achlora novol," he said. "Dyraveen."

Some raised weapons and stared, unbelieving.

Some fell back in terror of the dead.

Cirico threw Dyraveen over his shoulder and carried him down the tunnel.

As they approached the underground camp, more and more soldiers followed, talking loudly, spreading word.

By the time Cirico set him down before the Council of Thieves, hundreds had gathered around them.

Cirico reported to the Council in the Iccin tongue. He answered several questions then stepped back.

"Can you see?" It was the voice of the woman again. The Varran.

"I see outlines," Dyraveen said, "shades of fire."

"You have survived the living death," she said.

"I was only freed by the miners' explosion," Dyraveen said.

"You endured two seasons in the tomb. You survived quake and flood. You rose from the depths."

"Did I bring the maker back from the darkness? I fought only for my own survival. I thought only of my own life, as I have always done."

"If you were freed into the world above, what would you do?"

"When I said before that I did not know the crimes of the miners and the millers, I was not lying."

"And now?"

"Now, I know. Now, they will learn consequence."

The Council of Thieves freed Dyraveen.

Cirico would guide him to the surface.

Messages were sent to Dialla.

Cirico stayed through the night in the moonlit cavern mouth.

Dyraveen untied the cloth strip behind his head and threw it aside. He opened his eyes slowly in the harsh blue and silver light. "What happened in the vaults, my friend?" he asked.

Cirico gazed squint-eyed across the hills toward Pocone. "I built shrines," he said. "Many shrines."

"You found peace?" Dyraveen asked.

"*Peace?*" Cirico said the word with both yearning and contempt. "There is no peace below ground. There is no peace above."

"Is your debt to the underground now paid?"

"Yes, I am a free soldier."

"Then return with me to the city. I have great plans in store."

"You plan revenge on the miners. You want an executioner."

"No, I want your testimony, your guidance, your insight. I am ignorant of the history."

"If I leave the underground, I will be seen as a deserter. If I return to the city, my old enemies will come for me."

"Trust me, my friend. The page is turning. The miners and the guilds will soon fall. The underground will rise."

"Tyraen, you dream like a madman. You leap from grave to sky."

"Why not? The world belongs to the fierce and the cunning."

For the rest of the night, Dyraveen sipped water and nibbled dry eel.

Cirico looked from dark cave to distant city, the burden of choice heavy in his eyes.

The morning sun rose. Even its shadows stung their eyes.

They heard the attack copters land, four, maybe five.

They squinted to see a tall woman and giant cross the field.

Toch embraced Dyraveen. The Myshenite threw his own jacket over his friend's shoulders. The jacket covered all but Dyraveen's skeletal face and feet.

Dialla stared down at Dyraveen with open mouth. She brushed the knotted hair from his eyes. She kissed his cheek.

"Walk behind us," Toch said. "Your officers and soldiers can't see you like this."

Dyraveen handed the jacket back. He nudged his friends aside. "Let them see," he said. "I will soon recover."

"What about him?" Dialla said, looking back at Cirico.

Dyraveen walked to Cirico, put a hand to his shoulder, and led him from the cavern.

"This is Cirico," Dyraveen said. "He saved my life many times in the underground and in the hills. Cirico is crucial to our next campaign."

The troops of Dyraveen seized every mine and mill outside of Pocone.

He executed the explosive crews that had killed by flood and burial, and the death squads that had terrorized cave and mountain. He hung their bodies over cliffs by iron chains.

The workers were forced into huddles and stripped of their tools and boots.

"Enough killing," Cirico whispered to Dyraveen. "But know that some of these will always seek revenge."

Dyraveen separated the work crews. By transport planes he scattered the workers throughout the factories of the eastern valley.

In the blackened shell of a burned pod house, Dyraveen met with guild leaders and the owners of the mines and mills.

The Continental Commander spoke first to the guild leaders.

"The time of the guilds has passed," Dyraveen said. "You will no longer employ soldiers and assassins. You will no longer extort workers and bribe officials. Your sole duty now is to supply labor for the war effort. Fail in this duty and you will be replaced. Stray from this realm and I will take everything from you, as I already took your workers to the east."

Dyraveen then spoke to the owners of the mines and the mills.

"Your equipment, trucks, and workers now belong to the war effort," he said. "Your mines, your mills, your stolen land, have all been returned to the Iccin and Artauk. Find work in the city, if you can, but do not return to the hills or mountains."

Some of the owners protested, saying that they had no idea about the killing of the Iccin and Artauk.

"How could you not have known?" Dyraveen said. "I should have hanged you all from cliffs."

Other owners warned of their connections in high Pocone. They threatened retaliation from powerful investors in the east.

"If true, your supporters will be very disappointed in you," Dyraveen said. "Your stupidity and cruelty have cost them dearly."

When the owners left, Dyraveen summoned Oson. The Commander sent Oson to find out how deep and high the support of the owners truly reached.

A few days later, Oson reported back.

"One mine owner has several university friends, a few in the biochemistry wing, a few in architecture," Oson said.

"How high in biochem?" Dyraveen asked. "Any links with pod research?"

"Only teachers, low level," Oson said. "No ties to pod."

"Compensate him," Dyraveen said. "A fifth of what we took."

"A lumber mill owner has a partner who runs several power plants in the city, two fisheries, and a major grain distribution center outside Cyecura."

"Give him half."

"Another mill owner has family serving in the Water Guild and high-ranking friends in the Stone Guild."

"Where was his mill?"

"Deep in the mountains. On old Artauk land."

"Give him nothing. Place him on our list of enemies to be watched."

"That list is growing fast," Oson said. "Our internal security forces are stretched thinner and thinner."

"Help is coming," Dyraveen said. "What about the owners' claim of investors in the east? Was this bluff?"

"Far from it. The financial web is tangled and shadowed, but many threads connect the mine and mill owners with the Tyraens of Lycira. The compound investors of the eastern valley can easily say that they were unaware of the small-scale conflicts in the western mountains."

"They sponsored criminals. They partnered with thieves."

"You understand how the continent works, don't you? A third of your money is tied to Tyraen compounds."

"The world is changing. To win our war, we must create a new dynamic; we must carve a fresh path."

"And what is the first step on this path?"

"You will lead negotiations in Lycira. You will draw the Tyraens out of their compounds and into the war effort."

"By what incentives?"

"Many prime leadership roles lie unfilled in domestic production and in all branches of the military. When Andara is defeated, the opportunities for trade and development throughout the islands will be unprecedented in pheran history. Convince them that the future is all sunlight and open doors."

"And will their losses from the mills and mines be compensated?"

"They will be partially compensated, this time only. In the future, they will receive nothing for criminal ventures."

"Give me numbers for negotiation."

"Open at one-quarter. Stand like stone at one-half."

"Anything else, Commander?"

"I will have some old friends and allies of Davel waiting for you in Lycira," Dyraveen said. "And Toch should accompany you as well."

At the mention of his brother, Oson shook his head, frowning. "Let my brother stay," Oson said. "We clashed many times in your absence."

"Toch is a general."

"And I am a half-breed cripple," Oson said, taking up his crutches. "My brother may be vicious in the field, but he stumbles and limps in all other duties. He hesitates before decisions and second-guesses after. He cannot follow rapid conversation or subtle verbal sparring. He divides the world into clear, unshifting camps of allies and adversaries. He believes every word spoken by friends and imagines only malice and deceit from all others."

"Enough," Dyraveen said, "Toch will work with me. But listen well to the friends long faithful to your father. They will save you from many traps and blunders."

The underground received Dyraveen in a colossal, ark-shaped chamber deep in the hills. No trials had ever been held in this chamber, only celebrations of new birth, first climb, last love, and enemy defeat.

Blue and silver moonlight slipped through cracks in the rocky ceiling. Crescent pits of red coals followed the curve of chamber side. The sweet smoke of grilled eel wafted through the air in swirls of green haze. Hand-carved water canals wove across the stone floor like serpents intertwined. Fibrous corals crimson, gold, and violet swayed in soft currents.

The overflowing crowd of the ark chamber exceeded even the great gathering at the river he had witnessed years ago.

The people parted for Dyraveen.

No stones were thrown this time. No kicks. No staves.

The three Varrans of the Council walked behind him, the lone Artauk ahead, the two Iccin on his side.

When they reached the central platform, the Artauk giant lifted Dyraveen by the waist and set him down on the raised stone.

Dyraveen turned a long, slow circle on the platform. He gazed across the crowd, taking in faces, eyes, expressions, every detail he could store and treasure.

He saw the undying pride of the people. He saw the wounded strain of those cast down, thrown aside, forgotten, despised. And he saw a burning hope for future days, a cautious faith in him who had survived the living death.

The sea of faces exhilarated Dyraveen. The moment seized and overwhelmed.

Dyraveen spoke to the crowd of his thankfulness for breath and light, for forgiveness undeserved.

He shared his vision of coming days, his dreams for the people of the underground.

"I have brushed your enemies from hill and mountain," he said. "I have cleared your path to highest climb. The world now waits for you to lead.

"The voices of the ancients call out across the ages, reminding you of debt and duty. Your ancestors defied every king and tyrant. They turned back invasions of the imperial army. They survived unending raid, attack, and siege. The cry of Opir, the rebel artist, shook city, throne, and sky.

"When the eastern army ravaged the west, the underground saved the Varran people. When fire swept the world, your ancestors trod upon the flames.

"And now is your time to save and to lead. History waits for you to fill the unwritten page, to do what has never been done, to live what has only been dreamed.

"The underground will rise. The sleeping world will waken to our thunderous march out of the depths. The underground will bring all Phera together, east and west. The underground will lead the war against the Andarans."

The Council of Thieves joined Dyraveen on the platform.

Each member spoke at length in support of Dyraveen's dreams, in defense of his war.

The leaders assured the people that the shrines and treasures of the underground would remain protected throughout the war.

The leaders argued that leaving the underground for the surface world would not be a betrayal of their ancient roots but, rather, an imitation of their ancestors' highest example, the crowning fulfillment of centuries' struggle.

The people feasted in celebration of history's new dawn.

At the end of the feast, the Council led the people on a final journey to the deepest shrines and treasures of the underground.

Then Dyraveen led them up from the darkness.

In the first year of the new dawn, most of the Artauk stayed near to the underground. They patrolled the mountains, hills, and caves by a rotating guard set to rhythms of the three moons' rising. Some joined the Varran strike teams in the city that raided guilds for weapons, eliminated assassins still active, and uprooted new networks of drugs and weapons. A few Artauk trained in the wasteland for Dyraveen's elite forces.

The Varrans traveled far. Painters and sculptors of the underground connected with artists of the western universities. They enthralled many with samples of their work and tales of subterranean shrines. Musicians wandered city to city through the central valley. They gathered in dark garages, empty lots, and open fields to play through the night and day, welcoming any with skilled instrument, strong voice, or passionate ear. Many Varrans of the underground took leadership roles in civilian production and resource management. An equal number joined the officer corps of the continental army.

The Iccin followed Dyraveen to an instruction center deep in the southern wasteland. They received training in advanced weaponry, navigation, communications, and linguistics. They followed the Commander on strider marches into the wasteland, long days and nights without food or sleep. The dead were swallowed by the sand and wind. The survivors joined Dyraveen's elite - the shadow forces - free to move anywhere on the continent, silent killers slipping between the forces of land, sea, and sky, reporting all to their Commander.

On first day's push into the wasteland, Dyraveen led the party south.

Throughout the long night, the lights of the training center shrunk from a shimmering, red-gold moon into a distant, pinprick star.

By the morning of the second day, the base had completely vanished from the horizon.

The wasteland stretched infinite in all directions.

Dyraveen continued south. The Iccin striders followed close.

On the second night, Dyraveen bent their path to the east and north. They entered a dry, scaled sea. Emerald moonlight etched the white-cracked flakes of the wasteland skin. The striders lost themselves in the sound of the flakes' crumbling, their thirst and hunger dulled by sweet rhythm. Each member attuned to the steps of all the others.

On the third morning, they glimpsed a sliver of red-gold light on the horizon, a puff of grey smoke. Dyraveen led them away from the light. They saw nothing the rest of the day. The skin of the wasteland gradually softened into sands and dust.

The wind came hard on the third night. Sand-bitten gusts whipped across their bare and sunburned skin, tossed and staggered them.

Dyraveen shouted for the Iccin to lock arms. He set a path directly into the wind. The Iccin striders marched as one body through the night.

On the fourth day, the sun rose fierce.

Gusts turned to gales.

Blinded by wind and sun, weary to the edge of death, the line of striders broke.

Dyraveen shouted over the wind. Some of the striders followed the Commander's voice. Others drifted off alone.

By early afternoon, the winds had died. The training center appeared across the dust-hazed plain, its camps and buildings clear.

Dyraveen allowed the survivors to head for base, all save one.

The Commander faced off with Adan, the strongest of the young Iccin. He stared into the boy's bright eyes with contempt.

"You rode my heels in the wasteland," Dyraveen said. "You grumbled against me in the day. You cursed me in the night."

"No one grumbled," Adan said. "No one cursed. We all followed our Commander."

"You grumbled. You cursed. And in the day, you pushed the pace. You tried to break me."

"No, Commander."

"Then march with me."

The soldier and Commander headed back into the wasteland.

Adan tried to slow their pace and bend their path back toward camp.

But Dyraveen only walked faster. He forced their course away from camp, deeper and deeper into the heart of the wasteland.

"Turn back, Commander," Adan said. "Your strength is fading."

"You will break like glass before night falls," Dyraveen said.

Adan followed in silence.

When the bloodred sun melted black on the horizon, young Adan still marched strong and steady.

But older Dyraveen hobbled on stiffening legs. He stumbled side to side. His glassy eyes wandered sky to ground, unfocused.

"The wall," Adan said. "Your body fails you."

Dyraveen dropped to one knee.

The Iccin grabbed the small Tyraen, threw him over his shoulders, and turned for camp.

Adan carried his Commander through the night.

He saw the pinprick star of camplight grow on the horizon.

He watched the light spin red and gold.

Adan fell at dawn, still far from the base. He lay on his back, eyes closed, coughing, choking on blood and dust.

Dyraveen crawled to Adan. He poured the last of his water into the Iccin's mouth. He kissed his cheek and gripped his hand. "You are the strongest of your people," Dyraveen said. "Walk with me, my friend."

The Commander pulled the soldier to his feet.

Together, they marched for camp.

Dyraveen showered with Adan under the water tower.

When they sat down with the surviving Iccin in the medics' tent, their legs cramped, then clenched, then spasmed violently. They leaned against the tent pole, arm in arm. They sipped fluids and swallowed salt tablets. When one dozed off, the other shook and woke.

Their spasms worsened.

Other Iccin helped them back to the water tower. They held their heads under the ice-cold stream. The cold penetrated, soothed.

Dyraveen and Adan were led between tent and tower.

Adan fell into deepest sleep on a medic cot.

Dyraveen, standing, sucked a paste of fruit and protein. He watched bubbles of red and blue light approach in the eastern sky.

The Commander walked out of camp, climbed to the top of a dune.

Many lights approached.

From north.

And east.

And west.

The generals and leaders gathered around the wheelchair of Oson before entering the camp.

The huddle passed by Dyraveen on the trail without a word, without a nod or smile.

They took over the Commander's tent. They pushed his papers from the table. They lit cigarettes, flicked ash onto the clothes strewn across the ground.

Dyraveen sat down at the table, barefoot, shirtless, a pistol in his lap, a cup of ice in hand. He touched ice to his blistered forehead, held it to his reddened, peeling neck. "Say what you have to say," Dyraveen said, looking around the circle.

Oson sneered, incredulous. "We came to hear *you* speak," Oson said. "We came to hear you explain your long absence… before we strip you of command."

"I have no need to defend myself," Dyraveen said. "I have labored without rest for our cause."

"Commander, do you know anything about the state of your continent?" Oson said. "Do you know that the latest Moonlance rocket has crashed in the sea? Do you know that a third of your pod trucks are hijacked in the western mountains? Do you know that riots, strikes, and sabotage have cut the production of the eastern factories in half? Do you know that Cyecura refuses to pay taxes? Do you know that Toch was mobbed and stabbed at the flues of Pocone? Do you know that Dialla's plane was shot down crossing the Ebrin River? Do you know that Rael has survived assassination attacks at sea and in the cities of Tekenna and Lytarr? Do you know that millions across Phera believe you dead? Dyraveen, my brother, do you know any of this?"

With each of Oson's questions the head of Dyraveen had sunk lower and lower.

He stood up suddenly, set his pistol on the table, and shouted for Cirico to bring steaks, bread, and liquor.

"Forgive me, my friends," Dyraveen said. "Every general will be heard tonight. Every leader will tell their story."

Late in the night, when everyone had spoken, when all had eaten their fill and shared black liquor, Dyraveen faced his comrades.

"Forgive me for my absence, brothers, sisters," Dyraveen said, "but I have led ten parties into the wasteland."

"Are you a marching trainer or the leader of the continent?" Rael said.

"I raised the underground," Dyraveen said. "I joined the Varrans of the depths with the Varrans of the surface world, the high city and the low. I brought the Iccin and Artauk into the continental army."

"And this mixing has caused chaos," Toch said.

"When in history has the mixing of races been smooth and easy?" Dyraveen said.

"The underground is a distraction from our goal, a derailment," Oson said. "Our sole purpose is to defeat the Andarans. First, we must regain control of our own continent. Then we must build a unified military, a consistent core of top leadership, a sound strategy of war. But tonight there is only one question that we must answer. Is Dyraveen the one to lead us, or should we seek another?"

Dyraveen, legs cramping, walked slowly around the table. "You have forgotten the prisoners, Oson, the hundreds captured in Lytarr at first attack," Dyraveen said. "They are the reason we push for Andara."

"Of course," Oson said.

"And you misunderstand many things, my brother," Dyraveen said, passing Oson, gripping his shoulder. "The continent has torn itself apart in a few weeks of my absence. And your solution is to *strip* my power?"

"I only meant to prod you into return," Oson said. "You cannot lead the continent from this wasteland camp."

"I will return," Dyraveen said. "And order will be restored to the continent."

"How?" Rael said. "Your name is not enough."

"Our military will be unified by fear of the shadow forces," Dyraveen said.

"You mean by terror," Rael said.

"Respect, fear, terror – call it what you will," Dyraveen said, "but it will save us. Fear and terror are the currencies of our trade. The absence of terror led to your assassination attacks. A lack of fear and respect led to Toch's stabbing, Dialla's crash, the strikes, the riots, the hijackings."

"And your Iccin killers will terrify all of Phera?" Dialla questioned.

"No, the elite forces of the underground - Artauk, Varran, Iccin - will purify our military ranks," Dyraveen said. "They will eliminate corruption, treason, and betrayal. They will restore discipline, trust, and loyalty. The purged continental army will easily clean up the lingering fragments of the guilds and the drug-runners."

"Easily?" Sethe said.

"We have lacked coordination and cohesion," Dyraveen said. "Many feet out of rhythm, many hands working alone. This is my fault. Completely. But now, brothers, sisters, we will reclaim our land."

"Your disappearance buried us," Oson said. "Now we climb from deepest pit."

"My friends, I do not regret my journeys into the wasteland and the underworld," Dyraveen said. "For I have learned what decides every struggle and determines every end. It is the force of will. It is a resolve fearsome and bitter. Only this will win our war."

Seven Iccin scouted the western mountains on foot. Two were killed by packs of pod thieves and raiders. But the rest returned and provided the locations of a dozen camps.

Dyraveen unleashed his attack in the killing hour - the predawn dark. His bombers shelled the campsites in wave upon wave. Boulders jarred from the mountainsides rolled and crashed. Burning tree towers stretched high into the blue-violet sky. Attack copters shredded any who fled from the blazing trees.

The fires spread throughout the forest, smoldering in patches of dewy grass.

Dyraveen let the fires burn themselves out, destroying the mountain cover.

By afternoon, a strong western wind had scattered most of the smoke and haze. He sent in two divisions of the continental army to finish any survivors still hiding in caves.

After his sweep of the western mountains, Dyraveen extended the territory of the rotating Artauk guard to cover all of the mountain roads and passes.

The Commander left Dialla once more in control of the western continental shelf, responsible for protecting the rivers and coasts and securing the flow of raw pod from marsh to mountain.

Dyraveen then traveled to Pocone.

He visited his mother briefly.

He met with his uncle, Enteres, to discuss the future of the Moonlance project.

"What happened with the last rocket?" Dyraveen asked.

"We made design changes too close to the launch date," Enteres said. "We rushed the engineers and exhausted the technicians. Corners were cut, standards broken, lies told."

"My mother has told me many stories of your academy days. She said that you carried her through every course. She said that you saved my father time after time. You challenged renowned teachers and held your own against the highest officials. The other students feared you."

"You have come to take Moonlance away from me."

"I have come to free you from tedious accounting, endless paperwork, and petty squabbles. Return to real science, my uncle. Leave the details to lesser minds like me."

"Who will replace me?"

"You choose your replacement. You choose your new role. If you see fit, change the structure from top to bottom. All is in your hands."

"Only I must be removed from the lead."

"My blood, I can offer you no more. How many great minds would kill for these luxuries?"

Enteres assumed the role of lead materials scientist. He named his replacement, a manager known for dogged loyalty, military precision, and ruthless maneuver.

While still in the city, Dyraveen learned of a parasitic disease spreading through the prison pits outside Pocone.

He toured the pits with a team of medics. He found the disease active in half of the pits, rampant in a quarter.

"Can the afflicted be saved?" Dyraveen asked.

"At significant expense and risk to staff, it is possible for the recently infected to be saved," the chief medic said. "But those infected for more than five days have never recovered."

"Tell me of the disease and its symptoms."

"It travels by leeching mites too small to see. After first bite the skin flushes, itches, and burns with hives. Then a day of vomiting and diarrhea. Then a day of deep ache and stabbing pain throughout the bones. Then a day of fever, confusion, and failing breath."

"How does the end come?"

"Some pass suddenly by heart or liver failure. Some suffocate slowly by the collapse of the lungs. But most die by the bursting of blood vessels and the drifting of blood to the skin, red-black welts covering from feet to forehead."

Dyraveen and Toch stared long into the pits. They saw the infected in all stages of the disease. They saw the uninfected hiding in the furthest corners. Dyraveen and Toch gagged on the stench of rotting flesh. They covered their ears against the moan and howl of the dying.

Hands shaking, the general and Commander smoked by their truck.

"We could save the uninfected," Dyraveen said. "We could lift them from the pits."

"Then the mites would travel to the medics," Toch said. "Then the disease would spread into Pocone."

"Didn't you once persuade me to spare all the pod addicts for the one in six that might overcome?" Dyraveen said.

"I did," Toch said. "And now these pits overflow with those addicts spared."

None were saved from the infected pits. The Commander lowered pallets of food, water, and blankets. He also dropped bundles of knives and poisoned bluepod strips. Prisoners, sick and well, cut open their skin, tied the strips, and lay back in euphoric relief. By the time the blue strips bled purple, all prisoners were dead. Dozers buried the prisoners, filled the pits to the surface with dirt and rocks.

Dyraveen then circled the dozers around each of the pits uninfected by the mite disease. With the dozer buckets full and raised to dump, the Commander shouted down to the prisoners. "A plague has swept the prison pits," he said. "We cannot risk the disease spreading to the city." Dyraveen watched the prisoners as the weight of this final sentence settled upon them, dust spilling from the buckets. The prisoners looked away from the sunlight, heads low. "But you are the lucky ones, untouched by the disease. A narrow path to life and freedom lies open for you. If you prove yourself strong and faithful for one full year, all of your past crimes will be forgotten. A season marching in the southern wasteland. A season moving gravel in the western hills. A season building ships and planes in the eastern factories. And a season sailing in the continental fleet. Endure each of these and you will be set free. Stray from the narrow path and you will die."

The prisoners climbed by ropes lowered into the pits.

At Iccin gunpoint they piled into the back of freight trucks bound for the southern wasteland.

Dyraveen sent Toch and his unit of fellow Myshenite soldiers along with the prisoners.

"I trained the Iccin and Artauk," the Commander said. "Now you can make something of the Varran criminals."

"Most will be worthless," Toch said.

"Then break and bury them," Dyraveen said. "But the good must be refined."

Dyraveen left Pocone.

He traveled to Cyecura.

On a bridge of the four rivers, he met with Aen, an infantry officer from Cyecura.

"Why do your people refuse to pay their war taxes?" Dyraveen asked.

"They see it as a war of the east, a Torite war," Aen said.

"Would they support a Varran war?"

"No, they would also resist any effort led by Pocone and the Varrans of the university. The Cyecurans see themselves as a people completely unique to history, neither Torite nor Varran. They believe in the strength of blood and family, in ancestral lines as old as the rivers. They believe in self-sufficiency and independence."

"And denial. And backwardness."

"The Cyecuran would remind that you are the one asking for their help. They have never asked for yours."

"The little island of Cyecura needs to feel the waves of the broader world."

"Your maneuvers must be surgical," the officer said. "And swift."

"Where do I target?" Dyraveen asked.

"Shake the ground they consider immovable," the officer said. "Take down one of the oldest families, a line powerful and resented."

In a sweeping, nighttime raid, troops arrested over fifty members of the Delton family, owners of rich farmlands in the north and east, notorious for stealing water. The troops captured family members from the newly married young to oldest patriarch and matriarch, sparing none from chains and blindfold.

Dyraveen held the Deltons in an empty grain silo for three days, letting word spread throughout Cyecura.

On the fourth day, other Delton members brought half-payment for the family's tax debt.

The Commander refused to accept the partial payment.

On the fifth day, they brought full payment.

Dyraveen, again, refused.

On the fifth day, they brought twice the original debt.

Dyraveen took their money. He loaded the Deltons onto trucks and had them tossed like garbage across the city.

Taxes quickly poured in from all parts of Cyecura.

Violence also increased throughout the region.

Other land-owning families were attacked. Hostages were taken, equipment vandalized and stolen.

The richest families hired many mercenaries from Tekenna and Pocone.

The Cyecuran night, once still and quiet, now rang out with gunshots. The Cyecuran sky glowed red with scattered fires.

Dyraveen promoted Aen to leading officer of the region. He supplied him with one-hundred troops, ten trucks, two copters, and a tank. "I will send more troops in time," Dyraveen said, "but the invasion of Andara has highest priority."

"How can I possibly control this vast, ignited territory with one-hundred troops?" Aen said.

"You don't have to govern the region," Dyraveen said. "You only have to collect taxes and keep Cyecura from total implosion."

"The mercenaries will soon outnumber us four-to-one."

"Then divide and conquer. Play the rival families against each other. Stir up herders against farmers, mechanics against operators, men against women, plants against animals. I don't really care how you do it."

"My stature in the community will plummet with each lie I tell."

"The herd is moved by fear, not reason. The flock turns only by prod and by pain. My friend, these are the games of power. Sword and honey. Masks upon masks. Truth wrapped in lies. This is the way we lead a continent to war."

Aen refused the promotion.

Dyraveen demoted Aen to guard and arranged his transfer to an isolated coastal station.

Aen left the continental army. He returned to his family in Cyecura and farmed redgrain with his brothers.

The Continental Commander traveled east.

He hosted a gathering of Tyraen leaders at his grandfather's cottage outside Tekenna.

The leaders pressed Dyraveen for assurances of victory against Andara and guarantees of postwar land and trading rights.

"Every coin given beyond the war tax is recorded," Dyraveen said, "and will be rewarded many times over after the war."

The Commander also toured factories in the eastern hills.

He met privately with Sethe, the Torite General of Industry.

"Has there been any unrest among the factory workers since my return?" Dyraveen asked.

"Very little," Sethe said. "The worst agitators have all been arrested. Production levels are climbing back to peak."

Dyraveen praised his general, rewarded him with a few days' rest, and hinted at a possible transfer from the central valley to the invading fleet.

The Continental Commander flew to the eastern shelf.

He found that Lytarr had fully recovered from the Andaran attack, even grown beyond its old limits. New shipyards lined the Pale River. Factories, plants, and mills sprawled inland. Continual streams of cargo trucks flowed in and out of the city on widened freightways. Barges cruised the western river. Warships patrolled the eastern river to the sea.

Dyraveen followed the river all the way to the delta port.

He left his tricopter on the ocean docks and braved the misty gusts outside.

He watched the warships drill at sea.

When gales slashed across the white-chopped waters, the ships returned to port.

Rael ran across the dock to meet Dyraveen behind the shielding copter.

"Is the fleet ready?" Dyraveen asked, handing his general a lit cigarette.

Rael turned away from the wind, inhaled slowly. "This fleet might not survive a fishing trip," Rael said, his dark eyes worn, smoke from his nostrils whipped toward land.

A few days later, they were joined on the seaside cliffs by Dialla and Oson.

The leaders met together under the camouflaged blue glass of a sentry shell, shadows of clouds drifting overhead.

"Where do we stand?" Dyraveen asked.

"Individually, our ships can perform simple maneuvers on days of fair weather," Rael said. "Can the fleet survive the island storms? Can they attack and defend in unison? Can they hold their line under fire? I have doubts, aching doubts."

"A year of drilling and we can only stop and turn in still waters?" Dyraveen said.

"Phera had no navy a year ago," Rael said. "We copied the design of one wrecked ship a hundred times over. We trained crews that had never even seen the ocean. We brought in fishing captains from the north coast and captured pirates from the poles."

"Fucking pirates?" Dyraveen said.

"The pirates are the best captains and sailors we have," Rael said.

Dyraveen stared into the wide sky. "Pirates captain our ships," he said, shaking his head.

"Given his resources," Oson said, "given the frantic rush to war and the ridiculous expectations of his Commander, Rael has done a tremendous job."

"We face a deficit of centuries in naval experience," Dialla said. "We pay a heavy price for the arrogance of our ancestors who thought the world beyond their shores of no importance."

"I meant no slight to Rael," Dyraveen said. "But the question remains: When will our fleet be ready to invade?"

"The pirates have no love for the Andarans," Rael said, "but they have rivalries among themselves, long and bitter histories I cannot begin to untangle. They are quiet and deferential in conversation, but what they will do in battle is impossible to tell."

"And the fishing captains?" Dyraveen asked.

"Their loyalty is greater," Rael said, "but their tactical skill is much weaker, their nerve under fire entirely untested."

"Who do we trust then?" Dyraveen asked. "Inexperienced fishers or ruthless pirates?"

"Our air power is supreme," Oson said.

"But the Andaran mainland lies beyond the range of our bombers and our fighters," Dyraveen said.

"We only need to take one island halfway to Andara," Oson said. "One island we can use as base, airfield, and fuel stop."

"Troqual," Dyraveen said. "If our warships can reach Troqual, our bombers can pound Andara into dust."

Dialla stretched a map across the floor.

The leaders knelt and studied the map, their minds racing with possibility.

The continental armada gathered into position in the delta waters east of Lytarr.

The warships circled the fuel and supply vessels in protective rings.

Dyraveen sailed to the lead of the central vanguard. Rael led the right wing, Dialla the left.

"Stay in tight formation," Dyraveen ordered his captains. "Do not veer from course for any reason. Do not stop until you reach the shores of Troqual. Protect the supply ships at all costs."

The armada sailed forth.

For two days and nights, Dyraveen could not sleep, could not take his eyes from the sea. He worked the radio constantly, checking on each copter scout, checking with Dialla and Rael, checking with every captain of every vessel. But the sea was calm and still.

On the third day, clouds blocked the sun. Winds rose quickly from the south. A storm rushed over the armada, forcing all copters back to ship.

Fearful of reefs, Dyraveen halved the speed of his fleet.

When rain and lightning came fierce in the night, he halved their speed again.

Reports of near collisions between ships poured in. Dyraveen ordered the fleet to scatter wide until the storm passed.

The storm lingered throughout their fourth day at sea.

On the fourth night, the winds calmed, the rains ceased, and moonlight broke through the thinning clouds. The widespread armada crept back into formation.

The Commander called each ship of the vanguard. A full tenth of his captains did not respond.

Dialla and Rael called to report even greater losses.

"Switch to code," Dyraveen said.

The leaders switched to a coded language they had created prior to departure. (The code was based on the letters of the Artauk alphabet and the difference between two numerical sequences, one of diverging spiral, another of cyclical wave. Varran techs translated each message, character by character, ended by the speaker's name.)

Desertion claimed as many as the storm. Dialla.

Same on right wing. Rael.

Who deserted? Fishers or pirates? Dyraveen.
Pirates. Dialla.
Pirates. Rael.
Say nothing. Dyraveen.
The Commander addressed the full armada on open radio.

"By ill fate the storm has taken a few of our sister vessels," Dyraveen said. "But we sail on. Troqual is near, very near."

They sailed full speed through the fifth day and the sixth.

At sunset of the seventh day, the scouts reported a spot of land on the horizon.

By emerald midmoon they had reached Troqual.

The supply ships landed on the beaches, dropped ramp, and began unloading.

Transport copters shuttled soldiers from the boat decks to the sand.

Offshore, the warships linked to the tankers and refueled.

When Dyraveen came ashore, he found a group of soldiers celebrating and drinking.

"Jackals," he shouted, shattering their bottle against a dozer hull. "Do you think that we are safe now? Until the airstrips are cleared and our planes have landed, we are entirely exposed."

Dyraveen sent three warships back to the continent to rally the legions of bombers and fighter planes.

The soldiers worked through the night. They unloaded equipment and supplies. They began to carve an inland path through the brush.

The soldiers' progress through the dense and tangled brush was painfully slow. By sunrise they had not even reached the first hilltop.

Dyraveen released his soldiers back to the beach for a drink and a bite of breakfast.

The leaders met inside the belly of a transport copter, a map of Troqual across the floor.

Rael leaned back against the glass, set down his hatchet and machete. Pooled sweat darkened his shirt from neck to chest. Drops fell steady from his lobeless ear. "The bushes and vines are tougher than leather," Rael said. "I saw thorns the size of fists, weeds over my head. And we haven't even reached the trees yet."

"We don't have time for this," Dialla said. She knelt and studied the island map. She pointed to a clearing on the eastern side. "We should airlift here. The upward grade will shorten the planes' distance to stop. We can build ramps down to the southern canyons and hangars against the canyon walls, tucked from view."

Dyraveen glanced at the map, frowned with irritation, and looked away. "East means closer to Andara, closer to detection," the Commander said. "There are other clearings in the west that we should try."

Dialla and Rael studied the western side of the island on the map. Finished, the generals shared a glance and shook their heads.

"No, the eastern clearing would require less work," Rael said.

"It would allow more lanes, more room to turn," Dialla said. "It would provide better cover."

"Why are we still talking about the east?" Dyraveen said, glaring, spitting. "We have planned for the west from the beginning."

"And now we've seen the land up close," Rael said. "The eastern site is best."

"You lean west to ease your nerves," Dialla said. "Exhaustion and fear twist your judgment."

Dyraveen fumed. He stomped across the map that his generals knelt to see. His muddy boot covered the eastern side of the island. "Your counsel has been heard and rejected, generals," he said through gritted teeth. "Your Commander has decided that his forces will land in the west."

Rael left the copter.

Dialla set a food tin, canteen, and pack of cigarettes in front of Dyraveen. She gripped his shoulder and pulled him close. "You haven't slept in days," she said. "Eat, drink, smoke, rest." She dug her thumb into his throat. "And never turn on me again."

Dyraveen fell asleep in the back of the transport copter.

Iccin guards surrounded him inside and out.

The Generals, Dialla and Rael, mobilized the troops for an airlift to the eastern clearing.

The airlift was successful.

Thousands of soldiers, several cargo cubes of heavy equipment, and many tons of supplies were flown over the dense jungle of the eastern island and dropped into the canyon clearing chosen by Dialla.

The villages in the area were emptied by soldier squads. The indigenous were driven at gunpoint to the northwestern corner of the island, their fields and homes burned.

Plows and dozers cleared the landing strips and built massive ramps of dirt and stone down to the canyon walls.

Conveyors and drills excavated the deep holes for the hangars' corner and support posts.

Cranes steadied the posts for concrete pouring, set the crossbeams and trusses into place.

The work continued without break by rotating shifts and nighttime floodlights.

Dyraveen, rested and recovered, coordinated the work closely with his generals. When the hangars and the airstrips neared completion after five days' work, the leaders shifted their attention from the airstrips to the problem of the pirates.

Rumors of the pirates' desertions at sea had spread throughout the ranks of the continental soldiers. Worsening suspicion and resentment, the pirates had proven to be slow and inefficient workers on the land.

The soldiers had pressured the generals to discipline the pirates.

The pirates had asked, again and again, to be returned to their ships, their work efforts declining even further.

All of the leaders wanted to discipline the pirate workers severely and to somehow sift the loyal pirate captains from the disloyal. But the leaders also recognized their dependence on the pirates' experience at sea and the significant manpower of the pirate sailors. The generals feared a total desertion in battle.

After long debate among the generals, Dyraveen summoned two warship captains from the fleet, one fisher, one pirate, both trusted by Rael.

Dyraveen questioned the fisher captain first. "Could the pirate captains be replaced by continental fishers?" he asked.

"Some might be replaced but not all," the fisher captain said. "Before the war, most fishers worked their coastlines on small trawlers and skiffs. The pirates were born to bigger ships and deeper waters."

"Could the pirate sailors and deckhands be replaced?" Dyraveen asked.

"No," the fisher said, "the fleet is too large, the workload enormous."

Dyraveen swore the fisher captain to secrecy.

The pirate captain, Nur, was next questioned.

"Why did so many pirates desert the fleet during the storm?" Dyraveen demanded.

"Most pirates are loyal only to their ship," Nur said. "All other bonds are superficial."

"What if we separated and mixed the crews?" Dyraveen asked. "Could we force a wider allegiance?"

"I do not think so," Nur said. "There would be breakdown. There would be chaos."

"You push us toward hard decisions against your people," Dyraveen said, "violent and final decisions."

"Pirates are not a race," Nur said. "We are mongrels and dregs, the outcasts of a thousand islands. We crawl for crumbs from the banquet table. We hide and wait through the long polar night. At sign of prey, we slither between the mountains of ice and strike like phantoms. Pirates have no history, no future. We wait to sleep eternal in the coldest, blackest sea."

As the leaders absorbed the words of Nur, they realized their great error. The pirates would never hold formation under attack, never submit fully to continental authority, never join, in truth, the continental fleet.

Together, Dyraveen and his generals chose the path of lowest risk.

Continental forces were given every warship that they could handle on their own without the help of pirates.

The pirates were freed from all labor on the island.

Nur gathered the few pirates willing to join the continental fleet and leave their old lives behind.

The rest returned to ships of pirate captain and pirate crew.

Dyraveen and Nur spoke to each of these ships before their release from service.

"Remember that you will always have allies, friends, and brothers on the Pheran continent," Dyraveen said. "Remember that the Andarans have always hunted and despised you."

"Raid every shore of Andara," Nur said. "Terrorize every port and fleet."

The continental leaders flew to the western coast of Troqual.

They inspected the docks and piers built by General Sethe.

Satisfied with the construction, they all shared a drink and a smoke under a warship's shadow.

"We have been lucky so far, my friends," Dyraveen said. "Our preparations on the island are almost complete and we have seen just one Andaran ship. Our planes should soon arrive."

"That single ship could return with hundreds more," Rael said. "Its course changed abruptly after it rounded the southern tip."

"We enter a new phase of war," Dyraveen said, nodding at his general's words. "The long buildup is over. Now we must fight."

"How will we divide command between land, air, and sea?" Dialla asked.

"General Sethe will command the docks and piers built by his own hand," Dyraveen said. "He will organize, receive, and safeguard all transport to and from the continent. He will manage all off-shore refueling and dry-dock repairs during battle."

General Sethe nodded.

"Dialla will control all the hangars and airstrips in the eastern jungle," Dyraveen said. "She will direct the air attacks that break Andara's spine."

Dialla nodded.

"Rael, our best at sea, will lead the continental fleet," Dyraveen said. "And Nur, the pirate captain, will be his second."

Rael nodded.

"And I will lead the scouts," Dyraveen said, "the eyes of the fleet, the copter squads that watch the seas for first sign of Andarans."

The leaders drank in heavy silence, knowing that they might never meet again.

When the first continental fighter squadrons appeared in the western sky, the sailor crews rushed to the top decks of the warships. They cheered as the planes passed overhead, the troops' cry traveling ship to ship across the bay.

Soldiers rushed onto the docks and piers, shouting, jumping, waving.

The continental forces slept well that night, dreaming of the voyage home.

The next morning a patrol copter disappeared off the eastern shore.

At midday another patrol disappeared.

Then another.

Rael led the heart of the continental fleet into the eastern waters.

Dyraveen took to air.

He probed cautiously outward from the island in widening half-circles.

On his second turn, he spotted a black speck on the eastern horizon.

On third turn, he recognized the hull of a ship.

On fourth, he saw a lead line of Andaran warships, another line behind, deeper lines blurring into dark shadow.

Dyraveen swung back toward the island, plunged low to the water, rode upon the waves' mist back to shore.

He landed in a southern cove.

The Commander sent warning throughout the continental forces.

He sent orders to Rael.

Lead Andarans south. Distract from island. Scatter. Evade. Delay. Dyraveen.

Dyraveen listened by radio to the First Battle of Troqual.

He heard the rising fear in the voices of the continental captains as the enemy ships bore down upon them. He heard their panic as the Andarans opened fire.

Rael's order to scatter was not followed by all in the fleet. Many captains returned fire and clustered together for protection. These defensive clusters were surrounded by the Andarans and picked apart by revolving circle of enemy ships, slipping in and out of range. Black-grey smoke spewed skyward as the first Pheran ships sank to the depths.

The surviving continental warships fled to the south and southwest.

The Andaran horde pursued at full speed, turrets blasting.

A black haze thickened in the southern sky.

Help now. Send planes. Rael.

Three new squadrons landed. Refueling. Ready soon. Dialla.

Send now. Rael.

Denied. Dyraveen.

Send all. Send now. Rael.

Denied. Dyraveen.

Ships sinking. Soldiers drowning. Rael.

Scatter wide. Fleet will survive. Dyraveen.

Send all planes. Send now. Rael.

Denied. Airstrips must stay hidden. Key to war. Dyraveen.

Fleet sinking. Soldiers drowning. Send all planes. Send now. Rael.

Denied. Dyraveen.

Dialla, send all planes. Dialla, please send now. Rael.

Denied. Commander.

Dyraveen, trembling, walked the cove, his eyes on the southern sky.

The black haze climbed, swallowed the sun, darkened the sea and land.

Troqual lay still and quiet, no planes in air.

The naval chase continued for days in the ocean south of Troqual.

The continental fleet, though battered and halved on the first day of fighting, managed to stretch the enemy fleet across the wide sea, to fragment and separate the Andarans, to frustrate and elude their hunters.

The Andarans used maneuvers of flank, weave, and cross.

The Pherans, absorbing occasional strikes, streaked south, leading the Andarans further and further from Troqual, deeper and deeper into their fuel reserves.

The Andarans turned back before the Black Reefs.

Rael and Nur gathered the surviving fleet. The Pherans abandoned their most damaged warships, consolidated their crews onto the safest vessels, then began the long journey back to Troqual.

After the disastrous first day of battle, Dyraveen fled to the airfields of Dialla.

Once landed, Dialla immediately surrounded the Commander with a circle of armed guards. She led him quickly behind the hangars and hid him inside an underground storage cellar.

"Do you save me from my enemies," Dyraveen said, "or deliver me into their hands?"

Dialla glared at the Commander from the doorway. "You fool, my fate is tied to yours," she said. "We live or die by the same gamble."

"So why am I trapped in a cellar?" Dyraveen said.

"To buy you time while the shock of first defeat passes over your troops," Dialla said. "To protect you when the soldiers' rage demands a target."

"Each squadron landed on Troqual is a victory for us. Soon we will have a knife at the Andarans' throat."

Dialla pointed to the radios. "Call your giants," she said. "Call your shadow killers. Perhaps we can survive a few more days."

After the early routing of the continental fleet, General Sethe watched dozens of wounded Pheran vessels creep across the southern sea, bleeding fuel and oil, trailing smoke, sinking slowly beneath the tide.

Only a handful of ships reached the western bay of Troqual, each beyond repair, each abandoned. Sailors dove for the rescue rafts as the last edge of deck slipped underwater.

During the days of chase that followed, General Sethe listened helplessly to the radio as continental vessels were hit again and again by Andaran cannons. At night he sent his transports to search for survivors. The transports returned with some living sailors but many more pale and bloated corpses. The docks of the western bay filled with the dead. Medics moved among the bodies, tagging, recording, wrapping in black tarp. Shell-shocked sailors wandered the piers, feverish with dehydration, their ears still ringing, their eyes still wild with confusion and fear.

General Sethe watched the fighter and bomber legions pass over the western bay, squadron by squadron, day by day, none ever leaving the airfields. He called Dyraveen many times. He called Dialla. Neither answered.

Sethe sent a unit of his best fighting soldiers to the eastern airfields with clear instructions. "Get the planes into the air, every fighter, every bomber," he said. "All means are acceptable. You travel with the full authority of Generals Sethe and Rael."

The underground defenders answered Dyraveen's call.

The scattered Artauk gathered quickly in protection of Dialla. The giants followed the general everywhere she moved throughout the airbase. Three guards flanked each side, two guards ahead, two behind, dozens more scouting and patrolling the surrounding area.

The Iccin shadow forces slipped quietly throughout the barracks and hangars of the airbase. They eavesdropped among the pilots, soldiers, and techs.

The Iccin pulled Dyraveen from the storage cellar. "It is too dangerous here," they said. "The air is thick with plots and whispers. Many soldiers have come from the western docks to stir up rebellion."

"We cannot leave Dialla," Dyraveen said.

"Your presence here only endangers her more," the Iccin said. "In the soldiers' eyes, Dialla is guilty only of blind loyalty to her Commander. But you are seen as planner, killer, and betrayer."

Dyraveen listened. He agreed to hide in the canyons south of the airfields. He took a small contingent of Iccin guards but ordered the rest to serve Dialla.

Dialla sensed the rising tension throughout the air base. She felt the hard eyes upon her wherever she walked. She watched the newcomers from the docks mix among her troops, pressuring, persuading, turning her own against her.

General Dialla summoned all forces to an assembly inside her largest hangar.

She waited to speak until the troops took one knee beneath the massive hangar arch.

She stood alone before the continental forces, her back exposed to the fields and barracks, no Artauk guard in sight.

"I was wounded at Lytarr, where this war began," Dialla said, her sharp voice booming wall to wall. "I drove the Andarans from our land with tanks and mines. I cleared western Phera of all pod farms and all pod-runners. And with the Continental Commander and his generals, I have planned every stage of this war.

"A strategy was formed by the continental leaders before the fleet's long journey east. It was a path to victory, costly but secure, agreed upon by all. I have remained faithful to that strategy throughout this war. Other generals have fallen short, panicked under grief and pressure. These generals have sent their soldiers on futile and destructive missions."

Voices rose among the troops.

A ring of Artauk stepped forward from the shadows of the hangar.

"All dissent ends tonight," Dialla said. "Only pilots will remain on my base. All others will return to the western docks."

The general turned and gestured, two fingers tapping toward the ground. Outside the hangar, transport planes lowered their ramps. Artauk gunners ambled down.

The dense crowd rose to their feet. They pressed together as the giants neared. Many soldiers in the crowd stared beyond the general, expectant, hopeful.

A shot rang out in the fields. Another above the barracks. A flurry inside. Another in the fields.

Dialla flinched, closed her eyes, slowly breathed.

A soldier's body was thrown down from the barrack roof.

Through barrack windows, the Iccin climbed.

From the shadows of the distant fields, other Iccin moved into the light, their hands dark with blood.

The Artauk prodded the troops ahead.

"Only pilots will remain," Dialla said.

The tide of the war turned in the days that followed.

The Andaran fleet, low on fuel and supplies, returned to their mainland. After brief stops at port, most of their fleet sailed north to chase pirates raiding off the coast of nearby Nyava. Only a fraction sailed back to Troqual. Having defeated the Pherans so resolutely at sea, the Andarans saw no threat from the continental forces.

The remaining Pheran fleet docked safely in the western bay. General Sethe repaired and refueled the battle-worn vessels. General Rael raised medical tents for the wounded and arranged first transports of the fallen back to the continent. The restored Pheran fleet resumed patrols around the island.

Dyraveen and Dialla directed several bombing runs across the Andaran mainland. The bombing severed Andaran rails and freightways, pounded the inland cities, and destroyed many factories, plants, and mills. The Commander sent word of each successful run throughout the continental fleet and army, detailing the Andaran losses, invigorating his troops.

Dyraveen sent planes for Sethe and Rael.

The two generals faced their Commander alone, unarmed, in a quiet hangar.

Dyraveen embraced Rael. "I am sorry, my friend," the Commander said. "We heard every strike against your ships but could not reveal our position."

Rael, head down, teeth gritted, nudged Dyraveen away.

"Sail east," Dyraveen said. "A thousand planes will swarm your next encounter."

Rael dipped his head slightly, stepped away.

Dyraveen turned to Sethe. He circled the Torite general slowly, his eyes afire. "When this war is over, you will face me again," Dyraveen said. "You will be fully repaid for ordering the death of Dialla."

Dyraveen woke Dialla before first light. He flew her by copter to the top of the canyons. Together, they watched the sunrise. The shadows of the jungle trees slashed black across the white-grey barrack roofs. The first bomber squadrons of the day took to the air, their cockpit glass reflecting gold on the deep bank east, caught in the bright morning rays.

"Force of will," Dyraveen said. "A fearsome resolve." He smiled at Dialla, leaned against her. "And you were the strongest of us all."

Dialla stepped away. "I have not slept one peaceful hour since this war began," she said. "I dream of worlds even worse than this we know. I hear the cry of ghosts and the scream of demons. I see the dead that cannot die."

"Nerves," Dyraveen said. "Exhaustion."

"The bombing of the cities must stop, Dyraveen."

"Andara will be bombed. Land and shore. Soldier and worker. We must break the Andaran will. We must expose our own to lowest risk."

"We can win the war without burning hospitals, homes, and schools."

"Our bombers strike factories, plants, mills, refineries."

"You drop a thousand bombs to ensure that two will reach your target."

"Have you forgotten Lytarr? the hands and tongues cut from our men? the raped girls tossed into flood drains like garbage?"

"And what of the Andaran children born into fire and ash? Will their rage not burn as purely as your own? Think beyond the moment, Dyraveen. Think of centuries and generations. Your slaughter will likely trap the continent and islands in endless war."

"I will end the war that the islands started. I will ensure that our continent never stands so weak again."

The dark eyes of Dialla widened. "Your righteous posture is a lie," she said. "You don't fight for the Pheran continent, for love of the Torite, the Varran, the Tyraen. Even your hatred of the Andaran is forced. This war is merely cloak and shield for you in another struggle."

Dyraveen lit a cigarette. He stared into the airfields as the second squadron launched. "If you have lost your will, I must replace you," he said. "I will send you back to the continent. You can chase pod-runners until you recover your nerve."

"I have no will to fight *your* war, to bomb cities and burn towns."

"Then you will be replaced. Others will lead."

"How many times have Rael and I saved you? Do you have other friends, Dyraveen? Does anyone trust you now?"

"It is sad that you would come so far, Dialla, yet fail so close to the end."

"You will stand alone now," Dialla said. "Alone with demons and doubt."

Dialla traveled home. She returned to her mother, brother, and daughter in Tekenna. She ignored the messages of the Continental Commander.

Dyraveen escalated his bombing campaign. He pounded the Andaran capital and the great port cities of the coast. He struck towns and villages of the surrounding islands, Nyava and Eskalla.

Rael led the continental fleet into the Second Battle of Troqual, this time supported by Dyraveen's aerial legions.

Rael split the enemy fleet on first attack.

The Andaran ships scattered.

Pirates chased.

X. THE DEPTHS OF DEKANE

The continent celebrated first at Lytarr.

Passenger ferries floated downriver from the mountain locks, every seat filled with workers of the central valley, latecomers straddling the outer rails. Cargo barges cruised behind, loaded with cubes of food and drink, tight-shouldered droves atop the cabin roofs, welcomed stowaways filling the lanes. These river boats docked in the western trading centers. Passengers soon poured out from the centers with bottles, gifts, and banners in hand. The workers of the valley spread down both sides of the river. They lined every bridge.

The workers of the frontier poured into the city by road and by freightway. They crammed into dozer cabs, tractor buckets, truck beds soldier and civilian. They climbed piles of gravel and ore in the back of dump-trucks. They slipped between the tiers of the mammoth freight trackers and sprawled on top of fruit bins. Heavy vehicles parked in the open fields of the outer city. Lighter trucks pushed into the city until blocked by the swelling pedestrian throng.

The huge crowds cheered as tricopters circled the heart of the city, launching canisters of bright, swirling gas - yellow, purple, green, red.

Fighter planes circled high above the tricopters, their grey bellies dark against white cloud.

Bombers cruised silently in widest loop and deepest sky.

At the warships' first arrival, the crowds' roar swept across the city in a rising wave from the eastern turrets to the western piers.

The crowd pressed toward the water, the young short lifted high onto shoulders.

Soldiers waved and shouted from the warship decks. A few jumped and swam.

The skies filled with transport copters shuttling the soldiers from the warship decks to the keepers' domes.

The crowds thinned along the river.

Around the domes, the grills were lit and the ice tubs filled.

Soldiers rushed from the copter pads to kiss, to hug, to hold.

The celebration of Lytarr continued long into the night. Bright with pallet bonfires and volleyed flares across the river, the city raged to forget its former desolation.

At second midmoon, the forces of Dyraveen moved from the central bridge. His caravan of trucks, jeeps, and tanks cruised slowly east across the city, parting the crowds, knocking abandoned vehicles aside. Many followed the caravan, whispering of Dyraveen's wartime clash with the Generals Sethe and Rael.

The Commander stopped at the dome of Dialla. He sent messengers inside with his finest trophies of war: the jeweled scepter of ancient Nyavite kings, the platinum cords of the Andaran Emperor, the noose used by Ciralan in the palace gardens.

Dialla sent back every gift. And she sent a note. *I came only to honor the fallen and embrace true friend.*

While Dyraveen waited outside, hoping for change of heart, word of his movements spread throughout the city.

Generals Sethe and Rael gathered their own forces and crossed the river. They surrounded the underground troops of the Continental Commander.

Unarmed, alone, each of the leaders marched out from their troops. They faced each other across a smoldering bed of coals.

Rael spoke first. "The war is over, Commander," he said. "The time of heat and blood has passed. We must forgive."

"Forgive?" Dyraveen said, handing fresh bottle to Rael. "Your sailors' eyes are blades. They wait for first chance to kill me."

Rael opened the bottle, drank deep, and handed to Sethe. "You see the eyes of the fallen, Dyraveen, not the living," Rael said. "Your conscience tortures."

"Would we celebrate this night if I had wavered in strategy?" Dyraveen said. "No, my friend, we would now rot if I had listened to your pleas."

"Who can say what might have happened?" Rael said. "Who can guess how many lives we might have saved?"

General Sethe drank deep then held out the bottle for Dyraveen.

The Commander scowled at Sethe and spit into the fire. Artauk and Iccin emerged from the red-flickered shadows.

"The war vendettas must be forgotten," Sethe said, the bottle shaking in his hand. "The momentary errors must be forgiven."

Dyraveen raised a fist to hold back his troops. He glanced at the closed gate of Dialla's dome.

"Dialla must claim her own revenge against her assassins," Dyraveen said. "As for me, I will not forget those who melted under pressure; I will not forgive those who withered in their resolve. You, Sethe, will live in fear of your Commander's fury. And I will live in terror of the fallen, the many thousands burned and drowned."

The forces of Dyraveen left the city at dawn.

They traveled to the central valley, to the eastern hills of Tekenna.

They found the cottage of Davel burned to the ground, the surrounding fields charred and treeless.

"A message," Dyraveen said.

"The fire is many days old," his lieutenants said, "probably the work of young vandals."

Dyraveen camped his forces at the hill of his father's shrine. He waited for reports from the eastern cities.

"Generals Sethe and Rael celebrated in Tekenna," the returning scouts said. "Then Balthe. Then Lycira."

"To great crowds?" Dyraveen asked.

"The crowds were large," the scouts said, "but many asked of you."

The eyes of Dyraveen fell low. "The old prejudice returns," he said. "Now that they are safe from the islanders, the Torites shake free of the Tyraen."

The lieutenants pleaded with Dyraveen to make appearances in the eastern cities. "Your absence will be seen as flight," they said. "The confidence of your enemies will swell."

"We have no home in the east," Dyraveen said.

Dyraveen spoke to the shrine guards at the gate. He offered the platinum cords and the jeweled scepter as donations to the shrine. "The son of Sedenel has defended the continent and crushed the invading islanders," he said. "Let my trophies lay beside my father's works."

The shrine guards refused the offerings. "These are works of war and killing," the guards said. "Not treasures of art and spirit."

Dyraveen seethed. He cursed and threatened.

The shrine guards disappeared inside the dark hill.

For several nights, Dyraveen slept against the hilltop altar.

Each day, his soldiers begged permission to kill the guards and take the shrine.

But Dyraveen would not give it.

The soldiers also pleaded to march through cities of the east or west.

"We have one home," Dyraveen said. "The underground."

The forces of Dyraveen traveled west to Pocone.

They camped around the Titan Stone.

Gamblers fled from the Artauk patrols.

Players, young and old, left their games at sight of the Iccin.

Dyraveen slept alone in the high Aviet cove.

On the fourth day in Pocone, a few visitors arrived.

Enteres, his uncle, brought photos of the latest Moonlance rocket. "We launch for the Emerald Moon in twenty days," Enteres said.

"And will Pocone receive her astronauts as coldly as her soldiers?" Dyraveen asked.

"The people wait for tower march," Enteres said, "for sleek bombers in the sky, for chain of ferries in the shimmering canal."

"The Varrans dream of moons and heavens," Dyraveen said, "not the legions slain at sea."

Rhoa, his mother, also visited.

"Your war is won," she said. "What part will you play in the coming age of peace?"

"There is no peace above ground," he said. "There is no peace below."

Later, Oson entered the Aviet, a single cane his aid.

"You walk now, brother," Dyraveen said.

"And you now hide," Oson said. "The continent waits, restless, for her Commander to lead."

"The continent is yours to carry," Dyraveen said.

Oson laughed. "Do your greedy eyes look beyond the land and the sea?" he said. "Do you plan to steal the glory of the Moonlance?"

"No, the moons are empty rock to me," Dyraveen said. "My uncle will have his long-earned triumph."

Oson held a hand to Aviet's needle. "A new Dyraveen shies from spotlight," he said with wry smile. "A new Dyraveen runs from power."

"My journey dwarfs your own," Dyraveen said. "I have lived longer, traveled farther, driven deeper. I have seen that all the world's drama is farce; all the posturing of the feared and the strong is a lie. The core rots, my jealous brother. Our many loud and foolish words cannot stay the executioner's blade."

Dyraveen left Pocone.

He sat for days in the mouth of the underground cavern.

He received the cold rebuke of the Council of Thieves – Varran, Iccin, and Artauk.

You pulled our people from their home.

You promised grandest future.

You wander dumb and blind.

Others whispered in deep chambers.

Dyraveen fled by night.

He headed east through the hills, searching for southbound freightway.

Fearful that he was being followed, he hid in a canyon cove, pistol drawn.

While he waited, shivering, a long blade slid across his chest from behind. A strong hand gripped his forearm. In the pause between breaths, his pistol was gone.

Dyraveen spun, drew the knife from his waist. He faced the tip of a short sword at his throat, the muzzle of his own gun at his chest. He faced Adan, the young Iccin he had once challenged in the wasteland.

Dyraveen lowered his blade.

Adan lowered the pistol, slipped it inside his belt, kept his sword raised high.

"Why do you follow?" Dyraveen asked.

"To confirm your suicide," Adan said. "To hasten and encourage."

Dyraveen nodded, took one step back, then two, then three.

"Give me time," Dyraveen said. "Let me see Toch, the Myshenite, before I die."

The blade of Adan crept forward, turned slowly in the blue and emerald light, then slid back into the shadows.

Dyraveen ran.

He wove between the bushes of scrub and sage.

He crossed the pebbled beds of shallow streams.

He climbed in sideward bounds the steep ravines then slid down falling slopes.

His throat dried, cracked, bled.

His legs ached, burned.

His lungs cried out.

He remembered long-tunneled runs from Pocone to the valley floor, the boy's pain dissolved by moonlit sea of grass.

At sight of the freightway, Dyraveen untied the cords of his hair – the interwoven black and crimson cords of military commander, the blue cord of the Iccin, the green cord of the Artauk, the Varran silver.

Dyraveen tossed the cords under shrubs, along with his military coat. He sharpened his knife by whetstone then began to cut. His beard floated to the ground in fist-sized clumps. His hair fell in long tangles bonded by season's paste of sweat and grime. Dyraveen drew the hood of his laborer's jacket and walked to the wide-graveled shoulder of the freightway. He followed the road south.

A hard morning rain soaked him.

Heavy tankers, loggers, and army trucks rushed by, their thunderous wake sending gravel into the air, jarring Dyraveen, lifting him from the ground, rattling his bones and teeth.

Cycles streaked by, whistling in approach, bellowing away.

Trackers cruised by, the drivers slowing to pass, the riders yelling at Dyraveen, tossing garbage.

Dyraveen marched along the freightway deep into the afternoon. He reached a fueling station near sunset. He leaned against a tree, sipped water from his canteen, and watched the copters launch and land at distant pad.

Dyraveen flew deep into the moonlit wasteland.

When the fighter planes of Toch bulleted streams of red-fire warning overhead, Dyraveen took his stolen tricopter to the ground. He shed his jacket, tossed his blade, and waited.

The fighter planes circled twice then turned and faded into the grey southern skies.

Several jeeps approached over the hills, their spotlights weaving over the dunes, closer and closer.

Dyraveen stepped down, hands raised.

The prisoner was stripped of boots, belt, and jacket.

Blindfolded, he was driven to the training camp.

He was thrown to the bottom of an empty fuel silo.

The night guards interrogated the prisoner. Laughter, piss, and spit poured down with each claim of Dyraveen.

You say you are Toch's friend?

You are the general's half-brother?

No, his step-brother?

You demand to see him now?

Or what, little Tyraen?

Or what?

The prisoner pulled his shirt over his ears and curled against the wall.

When the morning guard replaced the night troops, new voices laughed; fresh piss and spit rained down.

The prisoner said nothing.

The silo hatch closed.

Dyraveen endured five shifts of guard before the face of Toch appeared in blinding light.

The general allowed Dyraveen twice as many days to recover as he had spent inside the silo.

Clean by a dozen showers, his head and face shaved to the skin, Dyraveen walked the line of kneeling guards.

The camp guards stared down into the sand. They stirred against their chains of wrist and ankle. Their chests heaved with panicked breath. Their sweat-drenched shirts clung to their skin.

Dyraveen saw that they were young. He saw that their skin was soft, unlined, unscarred, flush with rosy blood.

"Say the word, Commander," Toch said. Behind him stood the rest of his troops, an eager, sneering mob of older soldiers, hard killers from both sides of the pod wars, their pistols raised for execution.

"Let them wait in pits and silos," Dyraveen said. "Show me your work since the war began, my brother."

They flew beyond the barren wasteland.

In the western mountains, Toch showed Dyraveen smuggler passes stopped by boulders, trails blocked by felled trees piled into walls.

Along the southern shore, between cliff and reef, they saw the wreckage of pirate vessels, small ships capsized, grounded, scorched by rocket fire.

Over steppe towns in the southern hills, Toch pointed to illegal pod labs burned to the ground; the warehouses of stolen munitions and machinery, the thieves hung from crossbeams.

Over the Draun heartland, they crossed the dry water canals of tax-refusing farmers; the aqueducts of rebellious communities missing whole sections, concrete pillars crumbled by mortar fire.

Dyraveen said few words during the trip.

When they returned to the camp that night, he declined smoke and liquor in the general's tent. He turned his chair to face the wasteland. His eyes searched the horizon as last sun fell.

"My work disappoints you," Toch said. "Not all can seize the helm of mighty fleets. Not all can ride the wind with bomber legions."

"When I left the continent, none ranked higher than you, my brother," Dyraveen said.

"You left me behind, brother," Toch said. "You left me in this godforsaken wasteland with the lowest of Varran criminals. You left me to chase highest fame and glory for yourself."

"I trusted all of Phera to your protection," Dyraveen said.

"No, you trusted the wasteland to me, the continent to Oson."

"You understand nothing, Toch."

"I understand that the war is over. The door has closed. My chance to fight was taken from me."

"Fool, listen," Dyraveen said. "I have little time left. The hunters will soon come for me."

"What hunters?" Toch said.

Dyraveen left the tent. He scanned the horizon of the darkening wasteland.

Toch followed, hand to holster.

"Understand that those who left for war are not we who have returned," Dyraveen said. "For my hard and stupid words, Dialla will never speak to me again. Rael will never forgive the mass slaughter that I allowed at sea. And Sethe will try to kill me here just as he did at the island of Troqual."

"But the people of the underground will protect you," Toch said.

"No, for shame and bitter disillusion, they hate me most of all. The Iccin will come first. Adan pitied me once, but he will not spare again."

"No one will harm you here."

"Do I deserve peace and safety, brother? Do I deserve long life and health? No, the cry of the fallen must soon be answered."

They returned to the tent.

They drank together deep into the night.

Toch mumbled of horrors seen in Tekennan prison. He told of a son who had drowned on mountain lake. He remembered Davel's last hours and the words that still haunted.

Dyraveen spoke of the underground trial of Cirico. He told of the breathless moment when the assassin defied the entire body of Thieves, when the accused took low his judges.

In the morning, Dyraveen freed the young guards who had abused him.

He kissed the giant, Toch, and boarded seabound plane.

The frantic wartime development of the mid-ocean island of Troqual had only accelerated in the days of peace.

At the eastern airbase, the dirt and gravel runways had been paved; new towers and hangars had been raised; the soldiers' barracks had been converted into workers' quarters; and a central hub for landing and receiving had been nearly completed.

At the western port, a slew of massive new cranes had been added; transfer yards had doubled and tripled in size. Refineries had been built for Andaran tar, processing plants for Eskallan bitter cane, desiccating plants for Nyavite roots and spices.

Dyraveen traveled from base to port in the cold underbelly of a cargo plane. He curled around a wide spool of electrical cable, shivering, his back to tool-chest iron.

Once landed, he helped the friends of Toch unload their cargo.

He thanked them, declined the gun, radio, and money that they offered, then said goodbye.

Dyraveen walked the bustling docks of the western port.

Bald-shaven, clothed in the frayed black canvas of a Torite miner, Dyraveen moved through the crowds unnoticed, unrecognized. He read faces and expressions. He eavesdropped on arguments and exchanges. He watched the patterned flows, the friction and jostling between groups, the dynamics of power throughout the docks.

The gold-cord continental officers of Oson, always flanked by battery of armed guards, controlled the highest-valued resources of the docks: the cranes and the fuel tankers. They decided whose loads moved and whose loads sat; whose boats refueled, whose boats waited. The gold-cords also inspected the shipments of weapons and ammunition to the occupying security forces of the islands. They took inventory of the precious metals, artifacts, and gems taken from the island capitals.

The steel-cord officers of Sethe assigned the nurse and medic crews to departing ships. By armored shuttles they escorted white-robed Varran scientists and blue-helmeted Torite engineers to the copter pads. By open-aired trackers they took the surveying crews, drill teams, and utility techs to the cargo plane runways.

The red-cord officers of Rael manned the caravan-guarding warships with sailors and gunners. They found passages on military and civilian vessels for the thousands of mercenary troops bound for the Andaran labor camps - the future slave-masters of the conquered islanders. The highest officers of Rael directed the ceremonial transfer of the remains of continental sailors, soldiers, and pilots.

Between the uniformed officers, private labor recruiters waved company banners in the air. They called out the names of workers already committed to long tours. They shouted out generous terms and pay rates to entice the uncommitted.

Contracts were quickly signed, lines of laborers pushed onto departing ships.

Dyraveen sensed a wild and surging optimism in the air, a dizzying greed.

Andara lies ripe, the recruiters shouted.

The first fare best.

Seize the continent's great reward.

Dyraveen turned from the company banners. He nudged away the mining recruiters, pushed their contracts from his face.

Dyraveen drifted from the heart of the docks.

He passed a string of crutched and wheelchaired veterans fishing from the pier, a team of Draun prospectors sharing lunch on the hood of their jeep, a caged detention center for indigenous Troqual.

From bridged overpass he gazed to the inland east.

Smoke rose green and black from the mountain jungle. Lines of pyrotechs worked upward from charred riverbanks. Their flamethrowers slowly swept the dense trees, vines, and brush in red-glowing arcs. The jungle turned in ruby boil.

On the graveled northeastern freightway, he saw a pipe truck overturn on a steep bend. Traffic slowed in both directions. The line of idling vehicles stretched backward from the spill until a three-tiered logging tracker broke through the knot. The massive tracker crushed the strewn pipes, spewed ribbons of shredded aluminum aside, then cruised around the bend. The driver of the overturned truck, nearly killed by the tracker, limped on foot to higher ground. The stream of heavy freight rolled on.

While Dyraveen watched the rising clouds of jungle fire, a military truck passed under the bridge. The corner of his eye caught stony brows and hided gloves, clay-colored skin and bronze-blue eyes. He could not stop from turning, staring. There were three Artauk sitting in the bed of the truck, four Iccin standing against the cab. They were heading to the fires, heavy suits at their feet, gas cannisters stacked high. Dyraveen recognized them. They had saved Dialla from the attack of Sethe. They had shielded her in the hangar, gutted her assassins in the barracks and fields.

Dyraveen stretched his hand in furtive wave.

One Iccin noticed, a woman, a rock-blade tattoo at her throat. The fingers of her left hand opened slightly. Her eyes narrowed in the sun.

Dyraveen returned to the docks.

He sat on the fender of a broken-down jeep. He sipped water from his canteen. He watched the crowds come and go. He watched the ships slip in and out of the black-watered harbor. The sun was setting, fading under dark horizon of thickening clouds. A misty rain drizzled. He had no place to sleep. He was hungry, always hungry. He was alone, always alone.

A language was spoken near to him, a tongue that stirred deepest memories, sweet and cutting. It was the language of the coastal people, the northern seafarers. It was the tongue of Cyadae, his second mother.

Dyraveen left the broken-down jeep and followed the two voices. He could discern only occasional words between the two women, names and places easy to recognize, simple phrases.

He followed closer.

The white-haired coastal women turned, eyed him with suspicion, pressed their shoulders close together. They spoke to him in Torite.

"What do you want?" the older woman said.

"Who are you?" said the younger.

Dyraveen spoke to them in the coastal language, long unpracticed. "My mother is from coast, my second mother," he said. "Cyadae her name. Meces her town. I hear your voices. I hear your language. Clear. Beautiful. Very clear. Very beautiful."

The coastal women took his hands, ended his awkward struggle for words.

"Torite," they said, smiling, "speak to us in Torite."

Dyraveen nodded his head respectfully to both women. "Please tell me of your journey here," he said in smooth, flowing Torite. "Please tell me of your home. Please sit with me on the pier, if you have time."

They were aunt and niece, Ibyr and Vanon, both born near to Meces.

They were volunteer translators heading to Andara.

Before the war, they had sailed throughout the islands many times selling special baits and lures to deep-sea fishers. They had become fluent in Andaran, conversant in many other islander languages.

They were traveling to a city in the southeastern jungle of the Andaran mainland.

"Relentless bombing decimated the city's population, wrecked its mineral mines, took out power, water, sewer," Vanon said.

"Now, pressure mounts on the gold-cords for production," Ibyr said. "Prisoners escape and resist. Diseases spread. Supplies dwindle."

"Why go to such a place?" Dyraveen asked. "Why volunteer?"

"Without translators Andara would have no voice," young Vanon said.

"But the Andarans should pay for the war that they started," Dyraveen said. "Is this not fair and reasonable?"

The pale skin of Ibyr reddened. "Do you think miners in the deep Andaran jungle ordered the attack of Ciralan on distant Pheran shore?" the aunt demanded. "Do you think it was the Andaran worker who plotted in palace halls? who stirred rivalries among the generals? who stoked fear and terror throughout the capital for centuries?"

"Continentals know nothing of island history," Vanon said. "Our leaders knew so little that they bombed the island of Nyava, the fiercest of Andara's enemies. They even struck Eskalla, the greatest victim of Andara's crimes."

Dyraveen started to speak but his voice trailed away. His head slowly turned and fell.

Aunt and niece shared a look.

"Come with us," Vanon said. "Let us learn together."

Ibyr pulled a yellow jacket from her bag, TRANSLATOR stitched in blue letters over the back. "You can be our assistant," she said, "our secretary and recorder."

Dyraveen stared at the jacket, inhaled slowly. "I will work near to you in the southern jungle," he said, rising to his feet. "I will work as a miner."

By the time of their arrival, all recovery and salvage efforts within the city of Dekane had been abandoned. The few buildings with partial walls still standing, those furthest from the ash-blackened bomb craters, had long been stripped of all metal, plastic, glass, and rubber. Severed water pipes poked through the scorched ground in slanted, bone-dry quills. Through the hills of powdered grey brick, the concrete sewer lines lay in broken segments, dark filth burned down every crack. Putrid fumes of the unrecovered dead still wafted through cracks in the dusty rubble.

At the height of the nightly bombings, when the city's fiery glow had hidden starlight and swallowed moons, many of the Andarans had fled to the river. They had dived beneath its cooling, quieting waters. They had floated downstream, hanging onto raft or boat or branch. They had passed small fishing towns, smoldering and empty. They had traveled all the way to the ocean, only to be captured in the barren, thousand-cratered seaport of Acrois.

Others had fled into the jungle. They had hunted birds by rifle, net-fished streams, and looted gourd and nut farms. These refugees of the city had stumbled through the danger-ridden wild. Some of the refugees had fallen by poison and venom: the bite of the ribbon-snake, the sting of the stag-lizard's tail, the claw of the fore-limbed eel. Some had fallen by predator attack: blood-seeking flocks of raptor-bats, howl-summoned swarms of green-copper pond dragons, dense clouds of skin-boring locusts. Some had died from crippling thirst and slow hunger, by moth-spread virus and parasitic flea. Only the fiercest few had driven deeper into the forested mountains, striving for the vulcan peaks of the far southeast, seeking in desperation the ancient temples of the skin monks.

Most of the surviving refugees had lingered near to the city, afraid of deeper journey, waiting to see what forces of land and sea would follow the hell-borne continental bombers. By radio they had learned of the Emperor's surrender in the capital, the mass executions of all ranks of Andaran military officers, and the indeterminant labor sentence imposed on all Andaran civilians.

For several days, the Andarans had seen no sign of the Pherans.

Then, one clear morning, hundreds of fighter planes and attack copters had poured down from the capital, following the rivers, lighting the jungle with bullets, rockets, and shells. The continental pilots, annoyed at missing the first celebrations back home, had rushed south through the jungle to the seaport of Acrois, ignoring orders to corral the Andaran refugees in their cities. The continental gunners, sensing their last chance for action and thrill, had emptied every round and chamber on their way to the sea.

The Andarans, mostly unharmed by the reckless firing, had watched the continental ground forces arrive throughout the afternoon by transport planes and supply ships. They had seen great confusion among the arriving soldiers who found the cities empty. They had watched heated arguments between officers of the red and steel cords.

The Andarans had hoped that these new forces would continue to the sea, just as the fighters and copters had done.

But these Pherans had remained.

They had broken from camp at first light and entered the jungle.

They had tracked, chased, and hunted down most of the refugees within a few days.

They had forced the last holdouts back into the cities by dumping spent oil and pesticides into the streams.

In Dekane, on the west side of the river, the red-cord officers of Rael had built the razor-wired, close-kenneled cells for the Andaran prisoners and the open-kenneled housing for the continental laborers.

On the east side of the river, the steel-cord officers of Sethe had built the command center above the mineral mine; set up the private tents of the engineers, translators, and techs near the evaporation ponds; and paved the runway and receiving pad for the supply planes.

Working at gunpoint, the Andaran prisoners had cleared the collapsed tunnels of the upper mine and replaced its damaged framing section by section. They had worked steadily and safely under the supervision of the red-cords.

Then the gold-cords arrived. These officers of Oson brought the first wave of continental laborers and tech crews with them. The gold-cords chastised the officers of Sethe and Rael for their lack of progress, ordered their demotion from mine supervision to guard patrol, and announced a twenty-day deadline for full production at the mine.

The soldiers of Rael – veterans of the pod wars, survivors of the hellish naval slaughter off Troqual – laughed at the latecomers and bureaucrats of Oson. The red-cords seized the planes of the gold-cords and flew for home.

The steel-cords of Sethe tried to reason with the gold-cords. They warned of the mine's fragile depths, of volatile relations with the Andaran prisoners, and a crippling fever spreading among the continentals.

"We have medics, engineers, and translators now," the gold-cords said. "There will be no more excuses. Oson demands full production."

The steel-cords seized the boats on the river. They sailed south to Acrois. Then home to the continent.

The gold-cords reported these desertions to their commanders in Troqual. They requested fresh soldiers and mercenaries, new mining equipment, and more generators.

The Andaran prisoners, sensing opportunity and weakness, made their move before the reinforcements arrived.

At the peak of the silver moon, they climbed through an opening cut in the overhead fence. They threw towels over the razor-wire and jumped to ground.

They killed the first guard silently by knife.

But the second guard spotted the towel-wrapped wire, fired several alerting rounds into the night sky, and ran for the river's bridge.

A prisoner shot down the second guard with the gun of the first. He shouted for the other prisoners to run and took a sniping position near the bridge.

Before the sniper was taken out and the kennels secured, more than half of the Andarans had escaped into the jungle.

In response to the rebellion, the gold-cords tripled the kennel guard and kept the remaining Andarans penned for days without food.

They sent two retrieval teams into the jungle. One team never returned; the other team limped back to camp empty-handed, ill with fever, their faces swollen red and plump with insect bites.

The gold-cords worked the continental laborers day and night to clear the lower mine.

A tunnel collapsed.

Three laborers died.

The twenty-day deadline passed.

Ibyr and Vanon arrived the day that the prisoners were finally fed. The coastal women were taken directly to the prisoners' gate and asked to translate before the rations were delivered.

Turce, the gold-cord commander, a stocky Draun with burn-scarred neck, spoke to the Andaran crowd pressed tightly against the chain-link cage.

"Every bite of food from our hand is a gift," Turce said, "every drink of water a kindness."

Ibyr and Vanon stared at the commander, the hard eyes of the soldiers around him, the haggard faces of the prisoners inside the cage.

Ibyr, the older, translated his words. She spoke in a flat voice, without emphasis or cadence.

The eyes of the prisoners lit up at the sound of their own language spoken fluently by foreign lips. They pressed even closer against the cage. Prisoner hands stretched through the chain-link wall; fingers reached. Many Andaran voices spoke at once.

My husband coughs blood.

My father's heart fails.

My daughter trembles from hunger. Her eyes roll back.

A toothless elder gripped the fence with both hands, rattled chain and post. *Why are we who stayed behind punished for those who escaped?*

Two men stood naked, apart from the crowd, their emaciated ribs like clawing fingers. *Kill us now, you beasts. Kill us here, you devils.*

"What are they saying, translator?" Turce demanded. "Will they now submit?"

"I will tell you what they said after the medics have examined them," Ibyr said. "After they have received adequate food and water."

Vanon, the younger, called out for the medics.

Several grey-shirts came forward to the gate.

The commander, scowling, unlocked the chains.

Later that day, when the trees stretched in long shadow, Ibyr and Vanon were summoned to the command tent. They were made to wait behind armed guard while Turce met first with fellow gold-cords, then engineers, then labor crew leads, then medics.

By the time the women were allowed inside the tent, the sun had set and lanterns had been lit throughout the camp. Turce sat alone at the end of the table, drained, slouched, his uniform unbuttoned, his undershirt sweat-salted white. In front of him sprawled maps of the mine, equipment diagrams, an unsheathed knife, inventory sheets, blood-stained laborer cords, personnel rosters, a pistol with loose shells, and a bag of dried, purple leaves. Turce, too tired to focus his eyes, pulled a clump of leaves from the bag, filled his pipe, and tamped it. After third inhale from the pipe, his eyes sharpened. He straightened in his chair. He stared at the women through thinning clouds of crimson smoke.

"Apologies," he said, bowing his head toward each woman. "Many apologies. To you, Ibyr. To you, Vanon. You were thrown straight into the fire. Without warning. Without instruction.

Without bearings. My deepest apologies, again, to you." Turce finished his pipe bowl, tapped ash to the ground, and tucked a fresh leaf under his tongue. "We have all inherited deepest shit from those who came before us. I arrived here on the day that two-thirds of our soldiers and officers deserted, stole every plane and boat. The next night hundreds of prisoners escaped and two of my guards were killed. By second week, I had lost five soldiers to the jungle, four officers to fever, and three laborers to the mine."

"But why punish the prisoners left behind?" Vanon said.

"Every Andaran in the cages must have known about the plan to kill the guards," Turce said. "Not one of them offered us warning. Every prisoner would have escaped if more guards had not arrived."

"As would any prisoner in any cell," Vanon said.

Turce grinned, eyes narrow, a round mole stretching oval on his cheek. "These prisoners of Dekane have stolen, wrecked, and sabotaged everything their hands have touched," he said. "The latest tunnel collapse came either from their negligence or malice." Turce lifted the blood-stained laborer cords from the table, tossed them closer to the women. "None are innocent here."

Young Vanon folded the laborer cords, placed them side by side.

Old Ibyr glared across the table, her white-black eyes burning. "And the war, commander," she said, "when does it end? What slender thread of light will you offer the Andaran people?"

"That is why I called you here," Turce said, leaning forward. "I understand that islanders and continentals must share a common future. I understand that life comes from hope. And death from despair."

Turce pressed leaves inside each cheek then offered the open bag to Ibyr and Vanon. The younger woman sniffed the bag and shook her head. The older inhaled deeply and placed two leaves beneath her tongue.

"Changes are coming," the commander said. "I plan to break from the hard methods of those before me. The Andarans who prove themselves worthy of trust will be moved from the kennels into private tents. So will the best of the continental laborers."

"And the sick?" Ibyr said.

"The weak and the ill will be taken to a medical camp west of the city," Turce said. "No matter their race."

"And the thousand mercenaries soon to land?" Vanon said. "They will be disciplined and restrained?"

"My officers distribute every ration tin and water bottle in the region," Turce said. "The cruel mercenary will go thirsty in the sun. The lazy worker, Pheran or Andaran, will go hungry night and day."

"So simple," Ibyr said. "So easy."

"Shit clings," Turce said, "but I will pull Dekane from the mire."

"And what do you want from us, commander?" Vanon said.

"I want you to help the Andarans," he said. "I want you to walk among them, to listen, to learn. Help me find their hardest workers. Help me find the educated, the skilled, the open-minded."

"You want traitors and informants, no?" Ibyr said.

"I want to build from nothing," Turce said. "I want to save any who would be saved."

"Then prove your words," Vanon said, "day after day."

The translators left the command tent brushing insects from their eyes.

The commander slumped back, dozed with open mouth, red spit pooling.

Dyraveen landed in Dekane a few hours before sunrise with the last troop of continental laborers from Troqual. The troop stumbled in the darkness through the overcrowded kennels, stepping on the arms and legs of sleeping workers, tripping over loose boots and mounds of dirty clothes. The only open space that they could find was the narrow lane in front of the outhouse sheds. They drew their hoods, slipped their hands inside their jackets, and leaned back against the kennel fence.

The laborers rested in silence, weary from their long journey, but few among them could sleep. When the cold night winds tore through the kennels, the laborers shivered and groaned. When the winds eased, the stench of the sheds enveloped, penetrated thickest cloth and canvas.

An hour before sunrise, as Dyraveen lingered on the edge of first dream, the crew leads crossed the kennels with flashlights sweeping, searching. Once their lights settled on the new troop, the leads rushed through the maze of kennels, eager for first shot at fresh blood.

The leads shined their lights over the bodies and into the faces of the new laborers. They fired a barrage of questions at the half-sleeping workers. *How many years underground? Any injuries? Can you frame? Can you drill? Are you strong? Can you load? Can you weld?* The leads quickly claimed the most experienced and skilled for their own crews.

Dyraveen spoke Varran to the Torite leads, Torite to the Varran.

The leads passed him by.

He slipped into dream. Away from the kennel. Away from the jungle. Over the dark seas.

A boot to the ribs woke him.

He rolled away from the blow instinctively, shielded his head, pulled back his hood to see.

The sun was up.

480

The kennels were empty.

A black-vested mercenary loomed over him. "Don't ever make me fetch you from the pens again," the mercenary said, tapping his hardwood club against the fence.

Dyraveen tossed his jacket, tied his boots, and stood. He matched the mercenary's stare, memorizing face and eyes.

Before the guard could swing the club, Dyraveen turned for the kennel gate. He ignored the curses and threats shouted after him.

Dyraveen jogged across the river bridge, his eyes low to avoid the questioning glare of the guards in slow patrol.

On the long, rubble-strewn path to the mine, he ran when jeeps and trackers passed by, walked when none could see.

Dyraveen found much argument and disorder outside the mine. Around a log-sized, disassembled drill, a pair of gold-cords shouted at mechanics rifling through tool chests and engineers hiding behind manuals. Beneath a triage tent, medics argued with guards over the beds of pale, shivering workers and prisoners in chairs, bruised and bloody. A line of trackers hauling debris out of the mine blocked a line of trucks delivering lumber for framing; stones were thrown by both crews, pounding tracker cabs. Teams of mercenaries heading into the jungle fought with supply officers over fresh pallets of food and water received at the copter pad.

Dyraveen spotted a front-load tracker refueling at a tank near the receiving pad. While the crew lead pumped fuel, the workers leaned back in the giant bucket, passing a canteen, sharing a cigarette, joking and laughing. He saw a Tyraen among them, a woman with lean legs dangling and mismatched boots.

Dyraveen ran to the crew lead, dipped his head respectfully, smiled. "The gold-cord sent me," he said, pointing back toward the mine. He took the fuel nozzle into hand, motioned the lead away. "Have a drink. Have a smoke."

The lead stepped back, blew dust from his glasses, took a drink, eyed the newcomer.

Dyraveen finished fueling then jumped into the bucket with the others.

The lead glanced back toward the mine then fired up the tracker.

The crew was tasked with the clearing of the future potassium-salt evaporation ponds and the building of ringed dikes down the ponds' terraced descent.

The Varran lead drove the tracker. He pushed rocks and rubble across the first pond to the edge of the dike. Dyraveen and the rest of the workers levered the heavier stones into line, shoveled smaller rocks into the gaps between boulders, then troweled concrete into every open space.

The small crew took few breaks. But they worked without urgency or care.

No one spoke to Dyraveen until last smoke. The lead shared a cigarette, introduced himself and his crew, and offered warning.

"You're working too hard," the lead said. "You won't last. This is an easy surface job, no pressure, no eyes, soft and safe. We're going to milk this as long as we can. The miserable work will come soon enough."

Dyraveen nodded, passed the cigarette, looked back at their slow progress on the pond dike. "The ponds are necessary, no?" he said. "The dikes must hold."

Mazan, the Tyraen woman, pointed toward a field against the jungle's edge. The field was completely empty except for a few marking stakes in the ground. "That is our processing plant," she said, "the great feeder to our ponds."

"Turce is a fool," the lead said. "The plant will never be finished. He will end up shipping all the ore to Troqual for processing. Most of the leads doubt that he will even get the mine up and running again."

Dyraveen stared at the empty field. The name of *Turce* lingered in his mind, stirred old memories of the eastern frontier. He remembered a Draun recruit, homesick, soft, broken in training. And he remembered a drunken night when harder Torite recruits, laughing, held his neck against an open flame.

Back in the pens, Dyraveen moved from the narrow outhouse lane to the wide, clean kennel of his adoptive crew. Mazan gave him a blanket, some socks, and a half-pack of cigarettes. The lead handed him a rat-tail file sharpened to razor point and placed him in the entrance to their kennel territory. "No one comes in," the lead said. "Guard the boots and the tool-belts. Dump the piss-bucket once a night."

Three days later, the pond crew finished the first dike wall.

Before they could start the second wall, a gold-cord officer waved them off and summoned them to the supply pad. He pointed to crates of newly arrived mining equipment: helmets, gloves, picks, shovels.

"Two of your crew will stay on the surface to finish the second wall," the officer said. "The rest will go underground."

All eyes of the crew looked to their lead, each member hoping for the surface work.

The lead looked at each of his workers, cracked his knuckles, weighed his decision.

"I go under," he said, "with the heart of my crew. The newest workers, the two Tyraens, will stay above ground. To build their strength. To soon relieve."

The crew members nodded their acceptance.

"What level?" the lead called after the gold-cord.

"Seven," the officer said. "All the way down."

The faces of the crew paled. Eyes wettened. Shoulders slumped. Heads sank groundward.

The lead breathed deep of the outside air, mouthed a prayer, then walked for the mine.

The heart of his crew followed in silence.

The two Tyraens hurried to work in the second pond.

Mazan drove the tracker. She pushed rocks small and large to the edge of the new dike wall.

Dyraveen leveraged the boulders into line by iron rod. He shoveled loose debris into the gaps.

The Tyraens drank water only when the jungle heat blurred ground and sky. They shared two cigarettes all day, four tins of rations.

They worked until the sun fell and the dike wall disappeared in thick shadow.

They slept against the tracker, shoulder to shoulder, one blanket.

"We wake at first light," Mazan said, passing the day's last cigarette. "We finish tomorrow."

"Why do we rush?" Dyraveen asked, inhaling sweet and slow.

"We rush to help our brothers," Mazan said. "Crew is the only family here."

"The underground is hard?" he said.

"I spent a few days in the third level," she said. "One of our crew disappeared in an abandoned vein. I saw an Andaran prisoner crippled by beam collapse, shot and buried by mercenary guards. I saw a young Myshenite miner snap in the long night, swing his axe at the Torite lead."

"Still, you hurry to return," Dyraveen said. He tossed the cigarette, slumped against her, spent.

"For crew," Mazan said, "for family."

The Andaran mine at Dekane delved deeper underground than any continental mines or caverns. For most of the miners, it was a full day's journey from cavern mouth to drilling front.

Dyraveen and Mazan rode the tailgate of an overloaded supply truck through the busy upper chambers. They shouted at the driver each time boxes spilled over the sides. They jumped down and rushed to save the boxes from the crush of tracker steel.

After countless tunnel forks, bends, and switchbacks, they arrived at a small transfer station on the third level.

The Tyraens carried the supplies box by box from the truck onto a handful of trackers.

Behind the trackers, a group of Varran mercenaries and miners watched the Tyraens work, none offering to help. The mercenaries passed around a bag of leaves, joking, spitting, laughing.

When the Tyraens finished unloading the truck's supplies, they looked for seats on the trackers. The Varran miners blocked their path; the mercenaries pushed them away. "We're full," the mercenaries said. "Catch the next caravan down."

The unloaded truck disappeared into a surface-bound tunnel.

The engines of the trackers growled to life. The trackers crept forward, fell into line.

"When will that be?" Mazan shouted.

The Varrans shrugged, grinned. "Today, tomorrow," they said, pulling away from the station, "who can say?"

Anxious to relieve their crew brothers, afraid of becoming lost in the maze of tunnels or struck by oncoming vehicles, the Tyraens had little choice but to chase after the Varrans on foot.

The trackers accelerated. When the caravan caught full stride, its dusty wake blinded and choked. The runners fell back. They donned safety glasses and wrapped their faces in thin-meshed cloth. They jogged at the edge of the caravan's cloud all way down to the fifth level.

Nauseous, exhausted, gasping for air through sweat-soaked masks, the Tyraens stopped to rest at another transfer station. They found a shadowed corner, sat down against the cavern wall, and collapsed against each other. They dozed as the caravan traveled on.

A deep moaning of rock woke them. The stone wall trembled, rattled their teeth.

Someone whistled across the platform.

Glaring, red truck lights emerged in the widest tunnel of the down-bound junction.

A mechanic whistled across the platform. A Varran. "Sleepers and stragglers are beaten," he called out. "Over here."

A six-axle truck pulled into the station, a massive stone drill chained to its open bed.

The Tyraens hurried toward the mechanic along the shadowed chamber wall.

Another truck pulled in, huge conveyor sections chained.

The Tyraens helped the mechanic with his welding. Dyraveen took up gloves and rotated the cracked axle slowly. Mazan swept the path between the gas cylinders and the welder, tossing metal scraps into buckets.

A smaller truck arrived with gold-cords, techs, and mercenaries packed into its waist-walled trailer. The continentals jumped the trailer walls, walked the platform, stretching legs, cracking necks. Cigarettes were lit, bags of leaves passed around.

A gold-cord yelled at a huddle of smoking techs to tighten the binding chains on the drill; another ordered the mercenaries to piss in side chambers, not on the platform.

The rest of the officers followed their commander to the mechanic's table. They pushed aside tools, spread maps of the mine, and argued over the width of passes in the lowest levels.

Turce, the commander, packed leaves beneath his tongue. He studied the maps carefully, listened closely to all sides in the officers' debate. When he had heard enough, he waved the gold-cords silent and pointed on the map.

"We cross here," Turce said. "We don't have time for rolling and winching through the old tunnels. We drive all the way down. We widen the new tunnels. The miners will frame. The slaves will pick and grind. The mercenaries will inspire."

While the gold-cords delivered new orders across the platform, the commander remained at the table. He glanced at the mechanic. He eyed Dyraveen and Mazan, took a step toward them, started to speak.

The mechanic ignited the welder, drowned out the commander with a crackling shower of sparks.

Turce frowned, spit stems, walked closer.

The mechanic paused in his welding, adjusted his gloves, shifted his footing.

Again, the commander tried to speak to the Tyraens.

Again, the mechanic welded, white sparks spraying over the commander's boots.

The commander glared into the mirrored welding visor. He spit on the axle by the mechanic's hand. The saliva bubbled, boiled.

The mechanic worked on, focused only on the axle, pretending not to see.

The platform emptied. The continentals piled back into their trucks, officers first, then mercenaries, then techs. Turce took the wheel of the supply truck. He led the way into the middle tunnel of the down-bound junction. The big trucks followed slowly, shifting first to second gear as they disappeared into the tunnel, the grind of transmission echoing long throughout the station chamber.

The mechanic tossed his gloves, stripped his visor, wiped sweat from his eyes. Staring after the trucks, he sipped water on a stool.

The Tyraens thanked the Varran for his help, bowed their heads, clasped his hands.

The mechanic shared his water. "A bottle of water a day for the underground worker," he said, shaking his head. "Two for the guard who watches the worker. Three for the officer who watches the guard."

"Our crew is at the front," Mazan said, "seventh level."

"Don't worry," the mechanic said, "a stream of trackers will soon arrive. The gold-cords always travel with overflowing supplies."

The mechanic returned to his work. He told the Tyraens to rest, but both refused. Instead, they organized all the loose tracker parts across the platform and the scattered tools across the tables. They wiped clean the grimy cabinet bins, blasted platform dust in lower ground by air compressor, and replaced the well-worn chains and hooks of the motor hoists.

When the supply caravan arrived, Dyraveen and Mazan claimed standing positions on the back of a loaded tracker.

The Varran mechanic called out to them from the platform. He tossed a sheathed knife to Dyraveen, a ration tin to Mazan. "Remember the sun," he said.

The caravan entered the left tunnel of the down-bound junction.

The jagged, pale-grey walls of the cavern flashed by under the tracker lights.

The whirring slide and rhythmic bite of the tracker belt tranquilized the weary Tyraens.

Dyraveen cut strips of twine from a spool in the back of the tracker cab. They leaned against the cab posts, tied their waists to the frame, and closed their eyes.

At sharp turns in the tunnel, their heads struck the posts; at sudden stops, their faces slammed against the back of the driver's chair.

Dozing in the rare, smooth stretches, their feet slipped from the narrow step; their shins clipped metal edge; their waist-skin flared with the cinch and burn of twine; their feet dangled over rushing gravel, caught in the lights of trailing tracker.

Twice, Dyraveen pulled a sleeping Mazan back to the cab.

Twice, Mazan lifted Dyraveen.

The tunnel abruptly fanned into an immense chamber, the dried bed of an ancient mineral lake, now the base camp to the seventh mining level of Dekane.

The caravan of supply trackers cruised through the center of the chamber, the lowest depths of the ancient lake.

The caravan climbed from lake bottom, broke from single-file line into wings, and cruised to the supply center.

Twine cut, Dyraveen and Mazan helped unload the trackers.

They walked through the base camp searching for their crew.

Twice through the conveyor assembly pads, the tents and the pens, the fields of spare parts and broken-down equipment, the stacks of iron braces and fresh-cut lumber, and the coned hills of dumped rock, they saw no one from their crew.

"They must be frontline," Mazan said.

Leaving the base camp, they followed a team of drilling techs into a wide, descending passageway.

The loud droning of the camp's generators faded as they made their way down to the front. Angry voices shouted commands; grinders whistled shrill; sledges pounded wood and stone.

They found their crew raking and shoveling loose rock into a tracker's rear bucket, struggling to match the driver's pace.

Dyraveen and Mazan grabbed shovels and jumped to the lead.

The crew looked up. Wide smiles broke across their tired faces, streaked with dirt and sweat.

The Tyraens kept the lead until their backs tightened, their legs cramped, and their arms gave out.

Two others took the lead, freshest muscles to the fore.

Then another change.

Then another.

The changes of the crew became more frequent, their breath thinner, their muscles fainter.

When a hydraulic hose burst on the tracker, the crew fell back against the cavern wall. They sank slowly to their knees. With brightened eyes and smiles of relief, they watched the dark oil shower over the dusty ground.

The bucket floated down.

The driver killed the engine, pulled the ruptured hose, and headed for base camp.

The crew caught their breath, shared water, passed ration tins around.

Before the replacement hose arrived, the tunnel lights flickered three times. A message was shouted crew to crew down the tunnel. *The drill is stuck. Everyone to the central pass.*

The continental laborers marched up the tunnel clinging to the right wall. On the left marched the Andaran prisoners, even more filthy, haggard, and worn. A line of mercenaries separated the two, spurring both ahead by machine-gun muzzle.

Dyraveen climbed the tunnel staring only at the heels of Mazan. He matched her strides, followed her steps. Every third stride he claimed a sweet moment of rest, a long, savored blinking at lung's release.

When Mazan stumbled, Dyraveen reached out to steady her.

As her strides shortened and her strength faded, he tried to waken her with the language of their people, the Tyraens.

He encouraged her in the Tyraen dialect of the eastern valley. She said nothing.

He called out to her in the western dialect.

"Older," Mazan whispered hoarsely. "Chaucau."

Dyraveen dredged deepest memory. He returned to his childhood in Pocone, to nights of shimmering emerald, blue, and silver under the crystal skylight, to the ancient poetry spoken by his mother. He remembered the first myth of the wandering Chaucau.

"*The first darkness hungered,*" Dyraveen said. "*Its night burned and the Moons were born.*"

"*And the Moons hungered,*" Mazan said. "*They gave birth to the Stars, their children.*"

The steps of Mazan lightened; her stride lengthened strong. She finished the ancient lyric of the Chaucau then asked Dyraveen for more. "Younger," she said. "Striders."

Dyraveen breathed deeply, struggling to match her new pace. "*Out of the wasteland – our life,*" he said, closing distance. "*Out of the void – our word.*"

Mazan stepped away from the wall. She passed slower miners, passed mercenaries and techs. "*The strider never tires,*" she said loudly, her voice turning heads. "*The strider never dies.*"

"Never tire, never die," Dyraveen said. He matched the pace of Mazan, his eyes on her heels.

The Tyraens were among the first to reach the central pass. They stared at the giant truck and drill caught between the cavern walls. They listened to the commands of Turce passed down from the officers to the techs and the mercenaries. They grabbed new tools from open crate.

Dyraveen pulled Mazan away from the drill. "The closest workers will be worked the hardest," he said.

Mazan shook her arm free. She shouted and waved to their crew down the tunnel. Glaring at the officers, she walked toward the truck, pick in left hand, sledge in right.

When their crew gathered in front of the truck, a Torite officer came to direct them. "Show me good progress and I'll get you some water," the officer said, patting shoulders, "great progress and I'll get you some food and leaves. Make the commander smile and I'll get you a day's rest."

The officer set up floodlights. He drove an iron stake into the ground separating their work zone from the Andaran gang behind them.

The crew attacked the stone cavern with picks and sledges. Their flurried blows rang out in the narrow tunnel, bounding wall to wall, the legion echoes deafening. Rock chips flew, stinging bare arms and faces, drawing blood. The air thickened with dust. Dark clouds swirled around the workers, settling in pauses, churning frantic with each strike.

The crew lead stepped back and stared at the ground around him. Despite all their noise and effort, little stone had fallen, no heavy chunks, no thick flakes, only scattered chips and pebbles.

The lead summoned Dyraveen. "Find hammers and chisels," the lead said. "Quickly."

When Dyraveen returned with a full wheelbarrow, the crew switched tools.

A phero-tech ran to them during the change. He pointed at faint, porous lines weaving over the cavern walls. "Follow the soft mauxite," the tech said. "Chisel around the plate lines. Hammer the loosened plates to the ground."

The lead nodded, dipped his head to the tech, touched his shoulder.

With the new technique, heavy plate fragments soon crashed to the cavern floor. Half of the crew dropped hammer and chisel to haul away the piling rock, two workers shoveling and tossing into the wheelbarrows, two running loads to the tracker. At the wall, three workers chiseled plates loose while the sledge-wielding lead shattered plates free, gauged the height and depth of cut, and directed the chiseler's path.

After a few tracker loads had been removed, the lead asked the officer for water for his crew.

The officer, frowning, tossed two bottles.

"Eight workers, two waters?" the lead said.

"Turce isn't happy with you," the officer said. He pointed behind them to the work zone of the prisoners. The Andaran miners had covered almost twice the area. Their walls were cut smooth and even like building tile.

While his crew drank, the lead studied the Andarans. They used wider chisels, smaller hammers. They worked the wall like ravenous, nibbling rats.

"No food, no energy," the lead said.

"Everyone's hungry," the officer said. "Catch up to the Andarans. *Soon.*"

When the officer headed down the tunnel, the lead addressed his tired crew. The workers expected good news and praise. They dreamed of full stomachs, cool blankets, quiet sleep in distant chambers.

"The gold-cord said no more water," the lead said. "No food until we pass the prisoner crew."

The continentals stared with disbelief down the long, smooth walls of the Andarans. They looked over their own progress, shorter, rougher, then stared into the dirt.

The lead rapped his sledge against the ground until every worker looked up. "Don't worry about the Andarans' progress," he said. "Those miners have been working these tunnels, this kind of rock, all their lives. And don't worry about the gold-cords, either. They can bluff, lie, fuss, and scream. Doesn't matter. We only have to survive. All the rest is a mountain of shit on their shoulders. If we never quit working, my friends, we leave these islands rich. We go home free and strong."

The crew went back to work. They moved without urgency, steady and slow.

A crowd of officers gathered behind them. The gold-cords took turns shouting threats at the workers.

"No food, no energy," the lead said.

Mercenaries followed. They jabbed the workers with gun barrels, spit on their sleeves, screamed into their ears.

"No food, no energy," the lead said.

Turce suddenly stepped out from the crowd and pointed down the tunnel with his pistol. "Bring up the Andarans," he shouted. "Get these fucks out of my sight."

The crew dropped their tools.

They marched down the tunnel, two guards prodding at their backs.

The endless night wore on for all of the miners at the pass. The workers chipped away mindlessly at the grey, ungiving mountain. They hauled away load after load of heavy stone, but the tunnel walls seemed only to draw inward.

When the commander's cry signaled change, the crews trudged up the tunnel to higher work zone. Only the failing top crew marched down the tunnel, their heads low, their eyes dull and spent.

The worker's hands that chiseled the stony walls trembled with hunger.

The fingers that gripped the sharp rock cracked and bled.

Back muscles clenched and burned.

Legs cramped stubborn.

The workers hoped that visible progress might appease the officers and earn them some food and rest. But the officers only became more impatient and excited as the drill crept down the tunnel.

Turce led the truck forward with slow curlings of his fingers. By the lean of his upraised pistol barrel, he guided the driver's steering; his eyes flicked rapidly, left and right, gauging clearance on each side.

When the truck advanced steadily and smoothly, the commander backtracked with wide smile. He slugged from canteen, packed more leaves against his gums, and worked his tongue across his lips.

But when the tunnel pinched too narrow or the driver swung too wide, the mournful groan of metal upon rock brought fury to the commander's face. He screamed at the clumsy driver, the officers sighting along the walls, the techs observing, the careless miners, the lazy guards.

Three times the work crews cycled up and down the tunnel. But the drill gained only a few truck-lengths into the pass.

On the fourth cycle, Turce pushed a frantic, doubled pace.

Order dissolved.

Bodies shut down.

Spirits broke.

Sent from the top by officer's boot, Dyraveen and Mazan walked the length of the pass. They saw the work crews separated and scattered, the Pherans and Andarans thoroughly mixed, islanders working alongside continentals. They saw laborers collapse. They saw mercenaries come to blows with other mercenaries over supply pallets. They saw one officer pistol-whip another to steal a bag of leaves. They saw a tech struck unconscious by a pivoting tracker, a protesting medic chained and gagged.

By the middle of the pass, Dyraveen and Mazan realized that they walked alone. Their crew was gone. No guard prodded at their back.

They walked the final stretch of the pass, stopped at the last floodlight.

Below them the tunnel darkened, widened, emptied.

Above lay chaos and pain, blinding light and raucous sound, a world unhinged.

They leaned against the wall, breathed weakly through open mouths, and stared down into the darkness.

"I saw side tunnels on the march here," Dyraveen said. "Hidden nooks and chambers."

"We could rest in the shadows," Mazan said. "We could return to help when this storm has passed."

"We'll catch our breath, then go," Dyraveen said.

They rested against the wall, heads hung low, eyes on the ground. They saw the powdered webs of tracker lines. Crushed plastic bottles, crumpled tins. A thick sprinkling of stone flakes. A pickaxe with loosened head. A sledgeless hammer.

From inside his shirt, Dyraveen pulled out a canteen. "Stolen from the medic's pack," he said, offering first drink to Mazan.

The Tyraens finished the water together. One sip to rinse dirt, sweat, and blood from the mouth. One long drink down the dusty throat.

Mazan pulled a ration tin from her belt and held it out. "The mechanic's gift," she said, "the Varran's kindness."

The tin was empty save for five red-purple leaves.

Dyraveen put two leaves on his tongue, left three for Mazan.

The Tyraens closed their eyes. They felt the sweet water quench and soothe their stomachs. They felt the leaves burn their tongues like a hundred pricks of needle. Their heads lightened. Their vision sharpened. A deep chill branched outward from their spine, loosening clenched tissue, numbing their aches and pains.

They opened their eyes.

"How can we leave them?" Dyraveen said.

Mazan, nodding, took up the wooden sledge handle lying on the ground. "For crew," she said, "for family."

Dyraveen jammed the pickaxe into a shoulder-high crevice on the wall. He pushed and pulled, working the handle through the eye, freeing the thick wooden stock.

Mazan ran to the first floodlight. She shattered it with one swing.

Dyraveen passed her. He shattered the next light. And the next.

As shadows thickened in the lower pass, the miners along the walls stopped to stare.

Mercenaries charged into the darkness.

The miners heard the crack of wood, the snap of bone.

Again.

Again.

The two Tyraens sprung from the shadows, their wooden clubs dark with blood.

Mazan called out in continental tongues, Dyraveen in rough Andaran. *The workers take the cavern. The workers take the cavern. Now!*

The miners moved.

They followed the two Tyraens up the tunnel.

They shattered lights.

They slipped among the shadows.

With hammers, picks, and shovels, they struck down officers and guards.

By the sharp bend of the middle pass, the miners had seized four trackers, many rifles and pistols, and a pallet of supplies. The mercenaries had managed just a few short bursts of fire; only a handful of miners had been wounded.

The miners swarmed the pallet.

They pushed and clawed for the bottles and tins.

Mazan separated fighting workers with her dark-blooded sledge.

Dyraveen pushed back the continentals with his wooden stock, now splintered on both ends. "Let the islanders drink first," he shouted. "The Andarans have been treated worst of all."

The continentals yielded. They waited anxiously, eyes on the water cases, inching forward.

The islanders tipped their heads to Dyraveen. They tossed bottles to the continental workers before taking their own.

All of the miners ate together beside the line of trackers. They stared ahead to the light at tunnel's bend. They listened to the loud-echoed clamor of stone and chisel, the angry shouting of officers and guards.

Dyraveen threw aside his splintered stock. He touched the pistols inside his shirt. The numbing leaves had faded in their strength. The pain had returned to every cut and bruise, the weariness to flesh and bone. Along with the pain, came a sobering fear. Their flush of rage had cast the miners into deepest waters. They were trapped between the base camp and the drill. They had killed and wounded enough that peace or truce would be impossible. They stood on empty pallet, miles from the sun. But death waited, too, on the upward path, the charge of war. They could not surprise every mercenary in the long, straight stretch to the drill. Many guns would be raised, many clips emptied in the narrow pass, a rain of bullets sparing few. Dyraveen found himself, again, in the maker's chamber. Again, the trespasser. Again, the killer doomed to flee.

"Give me one-hundred breaths," Dyraveen said to Mazan. "Then come by shield of tracker, every gun firing."

Dyraveen righted an overturned wheelbarrow.

He threw in two shovels and pushed the wheelbarrow around the bend.

The light of the upper stretch blinded at first. Head down, he wove between officers and guards, between piles of rock and collapsed miners, the lone wheel bouncing over stones, shovels rattling.

No one questioned the slender, filthy miner.

No one stopped the little Tyraen.

Dyraveen joined the first crew at the top of the pass.

He shoveled loose rock into the wheelbarrow. His eyes scouted wide with each throw.

He whispered the count of breaths.

Eighty-five.

Ninety.

Ninety-five.

At the first sound of fire down the tunnel, Dyraveen dropped his shovel and pushed the nearby miners to the ground.

The huddle of gold-cords around Turce quickly broke. The officers rushed down the tunnel, guns raised.

Dyraveen slipped behind the commander. By handful of hair and cord, he pulled him to the ground. He buried his pistol in the chest of Turce. Fired twice.

Drawing second pistol, he turned back to the truck. Riddled the windshield with twin-streamed bullets.

He climbed onto the hood.

Lizard-crawled.

Reached through the crumbling glass.

Pulled the dead driver out by ear and collar.

Dyraveen slid inside the cab.

He pressed the gas pedal to the floor.

The truck lurched forward.

Screaming metal and grinding rock turned the heads of the officers and guards down the tunnel. Distracted, trapped, unnerved, their ranks were cut to pieces by the miners of Mazan.

The truck trampled bodies, bounded high and low.

Dyraveen whipped the steering wheel right, covered his eyes from the rain of glass, covered his ears from metal shriek.

Tunnel by tunnel, level by level, the workers claimed the mine in fighting sporadic but vicious.

When the rebel workers emerged from the depths armed and prevailing, the remaining officers and mercenaries of Dekane surrounded the mine.

Both sides shielded themselves by wall of trucks, jeeps, and trackers.

The translators, Ibyr and Vanon, ran to the mine with a message from the officers. In the half-shadowed cavern mouth, the women met with rebel leaders.

"The officers promise amnesty for all continental miners," young Vanon said. "But they demand the surrender of all arms and an immediate return to work."

"And what did they promise us?" the Andaran miners asked.

"Little," Vanon said. "They made no guarantees of life or safety for the islanders. They claimed that only the Andaran leaders behind the uprising would be punished."

"So we are solely blamed?" the Andarans said.

"Yes," Vanon said, "in the eyes of the Pheran officers."

Quarreling broke out between the rebel leaders. The Andarans, fearful and suspicious, pleaded for rejection of the gold-cords' partial amnesty. They argued for an all-out, pre-emptive attack. But the Pherans promoted counter-offer, cautious planning, short rest, and healing. Tensions and voices rose. The rebel leaders shouted back and forth, speaking over one another, Ibyr and Vanon struggling to translate.

A hammer beat the ground as they argued, first tapping, then pounding.

The miners looked down to see the two workers that had sparked the rebellion by shattering the lights. The two Tyraens sat on the stone floor, their backs to the cavern wall. The woman slumped still against the man, her face buried in his shoulder, a shattered arm bent awkwardly in her lap, her hair soaked with blood. The man looked up with one good eye, the other covered by swollen, purple sack. Metal shrapnel had sliced open his forehead, now wrapped with crimson-stained cloth. Flying glass had shredded his neck and arms. A ricocheted bullet had opened his shoulder. A dark-oiled mix of sweat, grime, and blood coated his skin.

"The officers lie," Dyraveen said, the hammer dropping from his hand. "Some of the gold-cords survived the seventh level. Some saw the drill wrecked and useless. They will kill us all when they get the chance."

Old Ibyr walked forward. She recognized the voice, remembered the lone miner that she had met many days ago on the docks of Troqual. "The gold-cords care only about production, my friend," Ibyr said. "Why would they kill their own workers?"

The miners followed Ibyr, knelt around the Tyraens.

Dyraveen stared up at the old woman. Thinnest smile split his lips at the sight of her pale-white hair, the sharp-graveled sound of her voice. "The mercenaries live for blood and pride," Dyraveen said. "When they see their many dead and wounded, they will defy the officers' orders. They will take their revenge against us."

"Mercenaries care about money," Ibyr said. "If they break from the gold-cords, they will forfeit all wages."

"The heart rules the mind," Dyraveen said. "The moment blinds."

"There is a better way, a higher path," Ibyr said. "Let medics treat the wounded of both sides. Let all the dead be honored - buried in peace, freed to the river, or burned on hilltop pyre. Young Tyraen, you will learn that the fiercest hate can be quenched by shared suffering, the widest division bridged by common wound."

"Kind woman," Dyraveen said, "you know nothing of war." He turned to Mazan, kissed her lips, and laid her gently on her side. A bullet-hole above her eye dribbled dark blood. Dyraveen climbed to his feet, a steadying hand to the wall. "Many planes and copters surely pour down from the capital as we speak. Our only hope is to cripple our enemy's resolve. Let the mercenaries see their own wounded moaning, sobbing, screaming. Let the officers see piles of cords stained red. Let the dead be dropped in mangled heaps. Then we will move. Then we will finish. There is no other way. You cannot hope in the slave-master's mercy."

"And should you win your ruthless war, where will you go?" young Vanon demanded, joining her aunt. "Upriver? downriver? into the deepest jungle?"

"Survival first," Dyraveen said. "Survival only."

"You follow oldest path of brutes and fools," Ibyr said.

"You are right, great woman," Dyraveen said. "I hide from the light. I slither to live. I delay my inescapable doom."

"Let us start with one step," Vanon said. "Release their worst wounded. Receive medics to treat your own."

The rebel leaders accepted Vanon's proposal. They released two trucks of wounded from the mine. They received two teams of medics with bandages, kits, and supplies.

Dyraveen set afire the body of Mazan on the hillside above the mine. A medic stitched and wrapped his wounds while he stared into the flames.

Other miners burned their fallen.

When the fires smoldered, Andaran rebels came to Dyraveen, speaking through a sea merchant versed in Torite.

"We trust no officers, no mercenaries," they said. "We will never return to cages."

"What lies east of Dekane?" Dyraveen asked.

"A few trails, a few villages, a few farms."

"And beyond?"

"The jungle and the mountains. The old world."

Ibyr convinced many continental miners to lay down their arms and cross over.

Vanon arranged a midway meeting between Dyraveen and the new commanding officer.

The two leaders stepped out, unarmed, from their walls of trucks, jeeps, and trackers.

They shook hands in the open field.

The new commander, an older Varran, scanned the miners' wall, counting guns, counting faces.

Dyraveen, likewise, surveyed the lower wall. He judged their forces roughly equal.

Vanon offered leaves to the leaders.

Both accepted.

The Varran and the Tyraen stared at one another, eyes hard, assessing, judging, planning.

The new commander saw a small and beaten man before him, an uneducated laborer, a poor but tough Tyraen of the eastern valley. The commander spoke to him in a crude Tyraen, the withered fruit of a brief study in his youth. "We want you weapons," the commander said in a loud, slow voice, like a parent to a child. "Now you weapons give. Where? How?"

Dyraveen grinned, spit stems at the commander's feet, answered in slow Tyraen. "Our weapons keep," he said. "Your mine closed."

The commander's face reddened, then darkened. He glanced back and forth between Dyraveen and Vanon, unsure if he had understood the rebel's words correctly, hoping he had not. "Rebellion finishes," the commander said. "Total. Always."

When Dyraveen saw Vanon ready to interrupt, he addressed the commander in the Varran of high Pocone. "Can you speak your own language?" he said, loudly, slowly. "You speak Tyraen like an infant at play."

Blood drained from the commander's face. He stared down at the Tyraen, speechless, fists clenching and unclenching.

Vanon stepped between the two leaders. She glared at Dyraveen with tired eyes. "The new commander is nothing like the old," she said. "He is willing to listen. He is willing to make changes."

"Then let us start again," Dyraveen said, switching to the Torite tongue of the eastern valley. "We are the miners who have overthrown you. We are the slaves now freed. You negotiate only for the return of your dead and your wounded. You guarantee our safe journey from Dekane in exchange."

"I hold back a thousand killers ready to avenge," the commander said in Varran, nudging the translator aside. "Thousands more will soon arrive by plane and boat. Return all our wounded and captive now and your rebels will live, Pheran and Andaran. I can promise nothing more."

Dyraveen nodded, eyes low. "Let me speak to my people," he said.

As Dyraveen returned to the mine, Vanon followed.

"You cannot expect the commander to forget his hundreds killed and wounded," she said. "The memory of the rebellion will long burn."

"Let the slave-masters sting and ache. Let them fear the slave who rises."

"Turce is dead, my friend. A new Dekane is possible."

When Dyraveen crossed the miners' wall, he sent Vanon away and called out for the Andarans and the translating sea merchant. After a brief meeting, the Andarans split their forces – half remained on guard at the wall, half rushed into the mine on trackers.

Dyraveen, shaking, ate two rations and drank two waters.

He shared cigarettes and leaves with the continental miners behind a lumber truck.

"Choose your side now and forever," Dyraveen said to the Varran and Torite workers. "Return to chains or march free with me into the mountains."

"We don't know you," the workers said. "Tell us what you are planning. Convince us. Assure us."

"I am Dyraveen, the son of Sedenel and Rhoa, the grandson of Davel. The great Andaran mainland was defeated by my merciless bombing campaign. The war was won by my knowing sacrifice of a hundred continental ships, ten-thousand sailors burned and drowned. After the war, I scorned celebration and praise. Haunted by the fallen, I fled to the underworld of Pocone. Hunted by my own, I fled from the underworld. I came to Andara to suffer long. To atone somehow in smallest part. And to die unknown."

"Your words do not inspire," the workers said.

"Why did you raise picks and shovels against the guards in the depths?" Dyraveen said. "Why did you run breathless for the golden sun and open sky?"

The workers shot back with many questions of their own.

"Will you return all of their prisoners and wounded?"

"What will you do when their reinforcements arrive?"

"How will you break through the officers' wall?"

"Where will you go in the mountains?"

Dyraveen did not answer.

He watched as many continental miners crossed over to the other side. Hands in the air, they ran across the open hillside.

Emboldened by the defections, the officers pressed their wall of vehicles closer to the mine.

The new commander stepped out from the wall with several mercenary captains on each side. Guns strapped across their backs, pistols at their waist, they shouted for Dyraveen.

Dyraveen, alone, came down.

The short Tyraen faced the line of towering Varrans and Torites, their eyes narrow with contempt, their faces hard and unbelieving.

"So you are the great Dyraveen, the highest general, ruler of the continent, conqueror of Andara?" the commander said. "I saw the real Dyraveen before the war at a factory in Tekenna, then again at a shipyard in Lytarr. He had a thick beard down his chest and hair even longer, both tied in many-corded honor. The real Dyraveen is dead. He was killed soon after the war in an ambush underground, betrayed by the Artauk and the Iccin. You are not a general or a soldier. You are a poor Tyraen of the eastern valley."

"Believe what you want," Dyraveen said. "I did not reveal myself to frighten my enemies but to be truthful with my fellow workers."

"So you lied," a mercenary said, "you are just a miner."

"Believe what you want," Dyraveen said, "call me what you will. Whoever I am, I hold your remaining prisoners and wounded."

"My offer still stands," the commander said. "Release them all now and your rebels will live."

Dyraveen turned back to the rebel wall, raised his fist, and whistled. Two jeeps pulled out from the wall, opening a lane. A truck came through the opening and cruised down the hillside, its open trailer packed with wounded officers and guards.

The lower wall opened. Medics rushed onto the trailer.

"And the prisoners?" the commander said.

"You will receive no prisoners today," Dyraveen said.

"Give us our prisoners," the commander said, stepping closer.

"I told you that the mine is closed," Dyraveen said. "No slave will ever work its tunnels again. Leave Dekane now. In peace."

"Give us our prisoners or we will take them."

"Ride the river to the sea, commander. Catch the next ship home. Forget this place. We will leave your prisoners in the first mountain village, safe and unharmed."

The mercenary captains turned for their wall and shouted for all gunners and drivers to make ready.

"This is your last chance," the commander said, glancing fearfully at the captains. "Please, please take it."

"The mine is closed," Dyraveen said. "Its timbers now burn. Its bones shrivel and snap."

"There wasn't time," the commander said. With paling face, he watched a line of trackers emerge from the mouth of the mine.

"Enough to light the upper levels," Dyraveen said. "To soak the beams with fuel and oil."

The commander cursed as he saw the last of the rebel trackers pour out from the mine, behind them the first wisps of smoke.

"And soon the explosives will begin," Dyraveen said.

"We will start over," the commander said, eyes panicked and wild. "We will rebuild."

"You will remove one crumbled mountain, stone by stone, only to find another, and another," Dyraveen said. "And at the very bottom, should you endure, you will find only a broken drill and a crushed conveyor line. The mine is closed, commander. Leave Andara. Take your killers with you."

The ground trembled.

Smoke poured thick into the sky.

The ground shook in violent, lurching spasm.

Rocks bounced down the hillside.

Gravel slid.

Rebels and guards stumbled.

The commander ran to a disappearing wall, vehicles speeding for the river, gunners fleeing downhill. He jumped onto the back of a retreating jeep.

Only a few teams of mercenaries remained. These vengeful guards took aim at the rebel trucks cruising down the hill. But when they saw their own tied to the grills, they, too, turned and fled.

A small medic wagon followed the rebels. In the back rode Ibyr, Vanon, and a handful of techs, linking arms, keeping low.

The Andarans led the rebel caravan through the first hills of the jungle.

The trees and brush quickly thickened. The road soon narrowed into a single-file trail.

When the trail wove between two rocky hillsides, the rebels lodged their largest truck sideways in the gap, blocking all pursuing vehicles, forcing any mercenary hunters onto foot.

A tricopter passed over them, hovered briefly, then continued east, no rockets launched, no shells fired.

The escaped rebels stopped to rest at an abandoned farm. They ate from wild fruit trees and overgrown tangles of nuts and gourds. They drank and filled their canteens from sap-lined cisterns of hollowed tree stumps. Weary to the bone, they fell asleep under the setting sun.

Dyraveen, sleepless, patrolled the farm throughout the night. Again, he was the wraith forbidden rest, condemned to endless circle and deepest shadow.

The mine still trapped.

The mine still pained.

He heard the hundred-picked striking of stone, the sharp-echoed ring of hammer and chisel, the shrill whirring of the trackers, the guards' bursts of rage.

He remembered Turce in the pass, the commander who had slapped water bottles from tired workers' hands, dug his thumb into the driver's throat, and kicked collapsed miners from the trackers' path. And he remembered Turce before the war, the young Draun recruit who had held his neck with both hands on the barrack floor, crying without sound, the Torites above him sparking lighters.

He saw Mazan in the sun and breeze of the cavern mouth, her body slack and still, her eye a lifeless void beneath the bullet-hole. And he saw Mazan in the depths, her body electric as she raised and swung the sledge, her eyes afire as she shattered first light.

Whistles.

He heard whistles.

One whistle inside the farmhouse.

Two, three, four outside the farm in the trees.

Whistles long and short. Some rising in pitch, some falling.

It was a code. A Torite military code he had learned from Rael years ago.

Prisoners safe? From outside the farm, to the west.

Yes. From inside the farm.

Guards? From outside the farm, north.

Sleeping. From inside.

All? Outside, south.

One patrol. One. Inside.

Dyraveen slipped inside the farmhouse. He walked to the prisoners chained at the post. He held his pistol to the temple of the whistling mercenary, put a finger to his lips.

The whistles from the trees came closer.

Attack?

Now?

Answer.

Answer.

Dyraveen whistled back. *Guards moving. Many. Go.*

The mercenary at the post opened his mouth to shout.

Dyraveen stuffed his pistol into the mercenary's mouth. He pushed the barrel deeper until the mercenary gagged and whimpered.

The whistles came faint, receding into the trees.

Tomorrow.

Dawn.

Be ready.

When first sun reached the jungle floor, the three mercenary teams advanced from the north, west, and south.

The rebels, hiding from lowest bush to highest tree, let the mercenaries push all the way to the farmhouse before opening fire.

Eight mercenaries fell.

Three surrendered.

A handful escaped.

The rebels chained the new prisoners alongside the old.

They headed deeper into the jungle, higher into the mountains.

The Andarans, close to eighty in number, continued to lead the caravan on their second day of travel.

The Pherans, only twelve, yielded to the mainland natives.

By late morning, the bends and dips of the winding trails became too severe for the heavy trucks. Frames bottomed out on protruding stone; wheels slid sideways down crumbling dirt banks; axles cracked by the twist and tilt of root-gnarled slopes.

By midday, the trail vanished completely and the jeeps bogged down on a muddy, pitted hillside.

By late afternoon, even the trackers spun helplessly in a marshy ravine.

With the day's last light, the rebels loaded their packs with all the supplies that they could carry. They climbed on foot to the treeless ridgeline at the top of the steep ravine.

The rebels dropped their packs and stripped their sweat-drenched jackets. They gazed across the long valley on the other side of the ridge, then beyond the valley to the distant vulcan peaks. The jungle of the waiting valley appeared even denser in brush, vine, and tree than the rugged hills they had already crossed. The faraway peaks appeared as little more than grey-gold pebbles caught between the darkening sky and land.

The travelers drank their canteens dry then ate with open mouths, their breath still rushed and heavy. Clouds of red flies swarmed their steaming necks and foreheads. Sharp-toothed moths nibbled at patches of open skin. Hands that wiped sweat turned up black with gnats, green with thrips.

An argument flared among the Andarans.

Some shouted complaint, shook their heads in frustration, and pointed east toward the distant mountains.

Others stood to face them, matched their cries, and gestured west toward the river, south toward the sea.

Dyraveen nudged old Ibyr for translation.

'We come from the city,' the short mechanic said. 'What do we know of life in the jungle?'

'Our food will not last us halfway across the valley,' the limping woman said.

'What will we find at the temples?' the sling-armed official said. 'A few monks? Scrolls we cannot read, plants we cannot eat, beasts we cannot kill?'

'You will be captured if you turn back for the river,' the twice-shot miner said, 'if not in Dekane, then in some smaller town or village.'

'Better to die a pilgrim than a scavenger,' the fevered woman said. 'Perhaps the old world can save the new.'

Ibyr, falling behind the rapid exchanges, gave up translating for Dyraveen. She listened until the argument died out then paraphrased for the Tyraen.

"Many hesitate to commit to the mountain journey," Ibyr said. "They see nothing but pain and death on the long pilgrimage to the temples."

"They would return to the slavery of the mine?" Dyraveen said.

"No, they see a wiser path along the lower river, toward the sea," Ibyr said. "There are many abandoned farms and ranches, many empty villages and towns. They will flee inland or downriver if continental forces draw near. Prisoners escaped from other labor camps might be found. A resistance might even be formed."

"And the others?"

"The others have seen the pillars of their world collapse, their homeland scorched, stripped, and overrun by enemies. They hope for a return to ancient glory. They seek a source of power greater than flesh and blood."

"This is a dream borne of history or myth?"

"Both. Neither. More. You ask a foolish question."

The Andarans piled dead trees and lit a great fire to drive away the insects.

Tents were pitched, boots scraped of mud, damp clothes laid across boulders to dry.

Vanon and the medics came forward to stand together on a raised slab of stone. The chief medic, a Varran woman, called out to all continentals. Vanon translated for the Andarans.

"As you weigh your decision tonight, there is another issue to take into account – the sick and the wounded," the chief medic said. "Many survived today's long travel only by the help of the jeeps and the trackers. On foot, they will suffer and lag. There are countless injuries and illnesses among you. Sprained ankles and swollen knees that cannot take a half-day's march. Concussions still dangerous, internal organs still bleeding. Viruses. Fevers. Bullets and shrapnel still lodged. Hundreds of open cuts at risk of infection. Malnutrition. Dehydration."

"What do you advise?" the twice-shot miner asked. "Mountain or river?"

"Some of you have no hope of either without rest, care, and healing," the medic said. "For disease, if pressed, I would say that the jungle holds the greater risk, though the river carries its own host of pathogens, known and unknown."

"And which do you choose?"

"I stay with the sickest."

While many Pherans and Andarans talked around the fire, Dyraveen unpacked his tent. He cleared the ground around him. He staked three corners of the base. Weak and shivering, he could not stake the fourth. He lay on the hard ground, backpack for a pillow, faces lost in the fire's haze, voices drowned by roar and crackle.

Dyraveen vomited through the night – a sudden, violent heaving that scorched his throat and seized his every muscle. After each purging he lay on his back with timid breath and slitted eyes, desperate to sleep, sweat pouring through his hot-chill skin, the nausea already burning anew.

When the bright morning sun struck the ridge, Dyraveen crawled from the fire to his unfinished tent. He drew his hood, pulled the tent canvas over his shoulders, and collapsed against his backpack.

A cool wind swept the ridgeline, dried the sweat of his back to salted crust, and muffled the sounds of those already packing.

The fever subsided.

For a precious hour, he slept.

A medic shook him awake, wiped his face, held a hand to his forehead, and forced him to drink water.

Dyraveen, bleary-eyed, looked around the camp. The fire smoldered in pink coal. Only a half-dozen tents remained on the ridge. A handful of tired, slow-moving Pherans gathered dirty clothes into sacks, took inventory of supplies, and stacked dead branches by the fire.

"The rebels have separated," Dyraveen said.

The medic nodded, handed a fresh canteen.

"Did more choose river or mountain?" Dyraveen asked.

"Only ten marched into the jungle," the medic said. "Forty turned back for the river. Thirty stayed on the ridge to heal."

"And the coastal women? the translators?"

"Both stayed. The younger searches for food and water. The older tries to free a tracker back in the ravine."

"Good," Dyraveen said, managing a weak smile.

While Dyraveen drank from his canteen, the medic pitched his tent in a shaded cove near to the fire.

The medic held him up as he pissed down the slope, stripped his damp and filthy clothes, and brought him clean shorts and blanket.

"Sleep if you can," the medic said. "The worst is still to come."

Dyraveen lay down in his tent. He watched insect shadows against the nylon skin – dragon-wasps crawling loops and circles, giant moths burying eggs along the seam lines, red flies flocking streaks of vomit down the tent flap.

"Start the fire," Dyraveen yelled out.

No one outside answered.

Dyraveen tried to sleep but terrible cramps wrenched his abdomen and sides. Stabbing pains struck unpredictably up and down his spine. The burning nausea returned.

He slapped the tent skin, sent the insects into frenzy.

"Light the fire," he shouted.

"The heat of the day is coming," Vanon answered from outside. "You will sweat and burn."

"Start the fucking fire," he screamed.

Dyraveen rolled in pain until hot-gusted smoke drove the insects away.

He ripped open the tent flap, stumbled through the door, then puked on all fours. He dry-heaved, vomited black, then dry-heaved more.

He pissed over the ridge, a dark, dribbling syrup of blood and urine. He staggered back to his tent.

Dyraveen suffered through the long afternoon, a blinding headache behind both eyes.

He woke in the night, shivering under his blanket, his legs slick with sweat.

The old woman sat beside him.

"Just breathe," Ibyr said, a light hand on his chest. "The end will come when it comes."

On the fourth day at the ridge, all the birds of the jungle disappeared from the sky. A thick tide of dark, purple-laced clouds rolled in from the south. Gusts of wind ripped leaves from the trees, turned tents, sent bottles, tins, and socks through the air. Lightning bridged from jungle to sky in jagged, silver branches, the afterglow a brilliant golden-green. Thunder bellowed, first deep and low, then piercing. The clouds opened. Grey waters poured down in steely mists and slashing torrents. The pounding of raindrops on ridgestone swallowed all sound.

Dyraveen emerged from his tent. Like an age-stiffened old man, he walked slowly along the ridge, a deep breath and long pause between each step. His skeletal wrists braced against boulders as each gust of wind unbalanced.

He climbed to the highest rock. He stripped his shirt, stained with days of sweat and filth, baggy against his jutting bones. He sat on the edge of sky, face to the wind, eyes closed, smiling as the rains washed him clean. He ran his hands through the knots and tangles of his hair. He felt his beard, once again thick and strong.

When the rain faded into drizzle and a sword of light pierced through the thinning clouds, Ibyr and Vanon climbed the rock to sit with Dyraveen. Their eyes were dark and heavy, their faces drained.

"I live," he said.

"You survived the fever of the flea," young Vanon said. "You were lucky."

Dyraveen looked down to the rain-drenched camp. Throughout the tents he saw no sign of life or movement.

"Many died from the fever," Vanon said. "Many died from old-wound infections and the virus of the moth."

"How many survived?" Dyraveen asked.

"Only two remain in camp," Vanon said. "A Varran medic. And a Torite miner."

"The rest were taken by disease?"

"No, there were many survivors, over half of our number. But yesterday these turned back for the river. They had seen too many faces pale, dug too many graves."

"And you," Dyraveen said, "where will you go?"

Old Ibyr gazed east across the valley.

"To the mountains," young Vanon said. "We have seen the river, no?"

"Let me walk with you," Dyraveen said. "Let me die on my feet. Not my back."

XI. SKIN

They followed in the tracks of the ten rebels before them, path by path, campsite to campsite, matching the progress of each day.

These ten pilgrims had clung to the ridgeline in their first three days of slow travel, never venturing deep into the jungle, always camping on safer, higher ground.

On the fourth day, perhaps more confident, perhaps desperate with thirst, these first pilgrims had come down from the ridgeline and cut across the valley floor, stopping at the first stream.

They had traveled upstream for several days in search of food. They had hooked fish and eels. They had shot birds of every kind from the trees. They had burned wide patches of undergrowth to smoke out all things living.

Three of the pilgrims had died by a marshy sidepool. Wide-pawed scavengers had dragged the bodies from shallow graves on the bank. All had been consumed but clumps of hair and meatless bones.

The surviving pilgrims had fled from the stream.

They had backtracked for a half-day.

Then turned abruptly for the ridgeline.

Then camped one night without a fire.

Then fled in seven directions, seven short trails ending in blood, hair, and bones.

Dyraveen and the second pilgrims stayed at the last campsite. They stared into the fire as the night settled dark through the trees, distant howls and cries across the jungle.

"They made blunder after blunder," Dyraveen said. "They traveled too slow at the start, lingered too long on the trafficked stream. They buried when they should have burned. They lost their nerve at first casualty and panicked at next encounter."

"Encounter with what?" the Torite miner said. "Pond dragons? Pack of jackals? Jungle tribe?"

"We prepare for all possibilities," Dyraveen said. "We stay together."

"They were strong and rugged Andarans in their own land," the Varran medic said. "How will a smaller, weaker group of Pherans survive?"

"They were fools," Vanon said. "They tried to shoot and burn, slash and trample their way through the jungle."

"They fought against the forest," Ibyr said. "They wasted their strength in search of meat."

The last mountain pilgrims struck out at first light.

This time they set their own pace and chose their own path, led by Ibyr.

The old woman avoided the insect-ridden ponds, creeks, and marshes as much as possible. She gave wide berth to the towering crown trees with teeming ribbon snakes curled around the high-gnarled roots. She stopped and backtracked at sight of the deep vulcan trenches, their dark shadows hiding stag-lizard rock dens and the magma-voided lairs of the raptor-bat clans.

Ibyr and the pilgrims left all birds and beasts alone.

They sought instead the purple-veined lotus, the tall blue fern, goldfeather moss, and webbed lichen. They gathered fresh rainwater from the basin of the upturned lotus. They chewed the starchy, filling stalks of the blue fern and sucked on the stomach-soothing leaflets. Tufts of goldfeather moss boiled into a rich, brothy soup. The webbed lichen, pressed together and held to flame, caramelized into a sweet-sour fiber. Between breaks and meals, they tucked numbing red leaves under their tongues.

The pilgrims made their way slowly across the valley. By Ibyr's lead they moved with discipline and patience, caution and foresight.

Advancing or retreating, they never broke formation.

Never forced progress, regardless their frustration.

Never entered new territory without routes of escape.

Never carried less than a full day's supplies.

Their skin toughened.

Their flesh thickened, rounding over sharp bone.

Their lungs acclimated to the damp air.

Even the dizzying heat of day and unrelenting insects bothered them less and less.

As they entered the heart of the valley, they caught glimpses. They saw wide eyes peering out from under fronds and bushes; long-fingered hands in branches' crook; slender feet leaping from sun to shadow.

Day by day, the children came closer. They ran ahead of the pilgrims and climbed trees to watch the strange travelers pass below. The boys hung from the lower branches, their legs swinging high, feet dangling. The girls climbed higher to straddle the thinner branches, arched by their weight, bobbing precariously.

The children hid and tossed stones into the bushes around the travelers. When the high-strung pilgrims jumped from softest rustle or ducked from smallest bird, the children laughed, whistled, and drummed sticks against rocks.

When old Ibyr almost stepped into a den of grey boars, the children sprung from their hiding places waving and shouting.

On a morning of sudden storm and torrential rain, the children led the way to a dry space beneath an ochre-maned tier tree. The travelers sat down on moss-covered rocks and watched the mud streams flow by. The children stood at the edge of the rain and watched the mountains silver-lit by barbs and spears of lightning. Many glances passed between the two groups, but few words were spoken.

The Torite miner tapped the arm of Vanon. "Why don't you speak with them?" he asked. "They are Andaran, no? Blood-circled grey eyes. Long neck, long jaw. Dark hair like steel bristles."

"These are the first Andarans, an older people of the mountains and jungle," Vanon said. "I speak the much younger Andaran tongue of the capital and the coasts."

"But both are Andaran," the miner said, "like parent and child, no?"

"The younger people broke away from the elder tribes more than seven-hundred years ago," Vanon said. "The break was violent, long, and final – a bitter civil war. The people who left never returned. The tribes who stayed never forgot. So we were told by fishers of the coast."

"Then the ten miners were doomed before they entered the jungle?"

"The miners were likely doomed more by their burning of land and killing of birds than by any ancestral rivalry."

At the peak of the storm, the children stripped. Onto the moss they threw their brightly dyed flaxen overshirts, their finely woven undergarments, their strapped pouches, sheathed knives, and pendant chains of iron, bronze, and jade. The naked children ran out from the tree and dove face-first into the rushing streams of mud. They slid, spun, and tumbled down the hill. At the bottom they crashed into bushes, leaped to their feet, then ran breathless back to the top, spitting dirt and smiling wide.

When the storm rolled west, the children rinsed themselves beneath the dripping manes of the tier tree. Tired from their play, they dressed quickly then collapsed onto the bed of moss, their limbs entangled, their bodies close like canine litter.

While the children napped into the afternoon, the travelers bored. They left the maned tree and climbed to drier ground, avoiding the washed-out lanes and slick canals left by the storm.

Old Ibyr found a high trail weaving south and west toward the mountains, a path more worn and trafficked than any they had walked since the hills of Dekane.

The pilgrims followed the trail slowly. They savored each step of the wide-groomed path. No boot-gripping knots of ivy. No skin-raking branches. No waist-high brush to wade against. No thorns or thistles. From pruned bushes they tasted bittersweet berries, thick-skinned and chewy as the flesh of birds. They walked along garden strips of serpentine red gourds and teardrop blue melons. They passed through rowless orchards of pink-flowered fruit trees and nut trees shedding woodfur husks, dropping honeyed kernels.

The pack of children caught up as they neared a toolshed thatched with feather grass and marsh reed. With little beads of sweat dripping from their flushed cheeks to heaving chests, the children stopped and circled in front of the travelers. They stared anxiously down the trail and beyond the shed. Relieved to see no others, they grabbed the pilgrims by the arm and led them on.

The trail descended into a deep, slitted gorge.

The ground dried and hardened.

Flat fields of purple scoria and crimson pumice replaced the thick-brushed jungle floor.

The trees gave way to white, polygonal columns of basalt.

They glimpsed the strange and shining city of Ocossae. It was a city without streets, without buildings, without power. It had no metal, wood, or plastic anywhere to be seen. It was a titan heart of glassy black obsidian and scarlet ivy, arterial paths glimmering silver in the sun.

The children guided the pilgrims to a cluster of five tents and sat them down on rocky stools. Finding baskets in the shadows of the tents, the children served the pilgrims fresh melons, roasted nuts, and honeyed moss.

At a distant whistle, the children dropped their baskets and ran for the city.

They passed a man and woman at the entrance to the city, a wide-fanned ramp of green and blue stone.

Arm in arm, the man and woman walked slowly to the tents. He was young, a whale-tooth chain around his neck, his face and arms rough with purple burn scars. She was old, her long hair tied by reeds and eel-skin, a line of pink-red scars starting beneath her throat, disappearing beneath her shirt of woven flax.

The old woman touched her lips with both hands and raised her arms in greeting. She addressed the pilgrims in the ancient tongue of the jungle and mountains.

With restrained excitement in his voice, the young man translated fluently into the Andaran of the capital and coasts.

Old Ibyr bowed her head.

The two women gripped hands, kissed.

Vanon whispered to Dyraveen and the other pilgrims. "The tents and baskets are gifts," she said. "Oduir, the mother of the city, welcomes us to the gorge. She will return tonight with the monks and elders to share with us the story of Ocassae. We are to wait outside the city. We are not to leave the tents."

Oduir, the skin-bound city mother, and Efed, the war-burned coastal fisher, left the pilgrims from Dekane to rest. They disappeared into the sun-glistened silver of Ocossae.

Stories flowed deep into the night from the monks and elders around the fire. When the storytellers differed in detail or account, they looked to the city mother for resolution. With slight tilting of her head, subtle tightening of cheek or mouth, the mother guided and shaped the history unfolding, her eyes never leaving the fire.

The foundation of Ocossae was poured a full millennium before the bitter splitting of the Andarans.

According to temple tradition, three of the great southeastern volcanoes erupted in a single year.

Ulek – the lofty and treeless peak – blocked the sun with its dark clouds of ash and coated the vast jungle with its black-grey powder like snow.

Tep – the wide-crescented mount half-spent in primeval age – spewed golden lava over its sides, melted its own walls, and flooded the lower valley with rivers of fire.

And Aedor – the stony king, the central root and deepest stake of all the range – erupted with such violence and power that lesser mountains crumbled in its wake, boulders were thrown beyond the western river, and the boiling underworld sea broke through the jungle floor in red-scorched rifts and steaming fissures.

By year's end every temple of the mountains had been crushed by boulders and levelled by quakes. The villages of the mountains had been swallowed by avalanche, fire, and ash. And the villages of the jungle had also been ravaged, all abandoned.

Terrified and reeling, the survivors fled the valley.

It was the skin monks – lowest-ranking of all the temple orders – who saved and led in the year of disaster. The skin monks tracked down lost stragglers and merged the scattered packs of refugees. The monks gathered the surviving Andarans in the hills of Dekane along the western river. They found shelter in the caverns of the hills. They bridged old rivalries, ended long-standing feuds and quarrels, and unified the many tribes to forage, fish, and hunt together. They built the stone-fire circle where all could nightly share and heal.

On a night of blue eclipse, a new ritual was born.

Before the year of disaster, the skin monks had gathered in servant pairs and flayed by knife their partner's shoulder. They had cut small patches of skin from the forearm of each tribal member, then grafted the patches onto their partner's opened shoulder by paste of oil, yolk, and lichen. In burnt offering, the mountain gods had received the skin of the monk.

But in the hills of Dekane, the monks stood without partner before the fire. Each raised the dagger alone and flayed own chest, strip by strip, neck to belly. The dagger then passed around the circle to all Andarans, members of every tribe, to cut a single strip. Sharing wine and tears, the people held their strips to the monks' chests. And each accepted skin, in turn. The mountain gods received nothing.

The skin-bonded Andarans returned to the valley.

Trusting no longer in wood and clay, the Andarans carved new homes from stony bluffs facing north and west, away from the mountains. To help the jungle heal, they branched the wide rivers into many smaller streams and spread the deep lake waters by radial canals. They swept the ash-covered roots of the yellowing crown trees, rinsed the scaled pores of the sagging lizard palms, and brushed the tier trees' withering manes. They grew fertilizing mosses, lichen, and fungi on damp stream banks and transplanted these widely throughout the forest.

The jungle recovered.

By the fading of the refugee generation, the land was richer in plant and animal life than ever before.

The villages of succeeding generations crept slowly across the valley floor, nearer and nearer to the mountains. The Andarans built stone ramparts on the hills above their homes. They built low-domed temples and bronze-gilded towers defiantly facing the heart of the mountains.

Quiet centuries passed.

With no eruptions.

With quakes faint and rare.

With Ulek's breath grey-spun slivers lost in the clouds.

With Tep cold and still.

And Aedor silent.

The quiet centuries tested the skin monks. The vast and numerous Andaran people could no longer be gathered in one place; one ritual could no longer bind all tribes together and commission the lifelong service of every monk.

The refugee generation had been few in number. They had been devastated by shared terror, bonded by common loss. Given what the refugees had seen and suffered in the year of disaster, the ritual of flaying was natural and unforced, a symbol drawing from great depths of experience, the expression and release of pain as much as its source.

The generations that followed listened long to the monks' poetry, the lyrics of the refugees, the legends of the survivors. The Andaran people accepted this heritage with honor and pride; any who did not were viewed with suspicion and distrust. But the later Andarans viewed the flaying of skin as an ancestor ritual, not their own. Over time the ritual was watered down. Smaller knives were used, smaller patches taken from the back, calf, thigh. More wine was consumed before and after cutting. Children were excluded, large families represented by one or two members. Grafting was skipped - the long touching through pain. The ritual was mimed without cutting, bloodless pastes rubbed over the heart.

Other erosions followed.

The monks, once loyal to a single community for life, wandered village to village throughout the jungle, many moving as often as the changing of the seasons.

The monks, once celibate or committed to single mate, took many lovers across the valley. Male monks left villages as soon as the bellies of their lovers bulged. Female monks gave birth in the mountains, weaned quickly, and abandoned their young in village gardens.

When fighting broke out between growers, hunters, and fishers, the monks advocated for none; their voices were not heard.

When violence consumed the valley and jackals fattened on the dead, when families were torn apart and many fled to the river or mountains, the monks hid from danger. They crawled the jungle brush and wrapped themselves in ivy tangles. They burrowed like rodents under the ferns. Some tossed their priestly medallions and attempted disguise.

Ocassa, the first great mother, lost her entire family – husband, daughter, and son - to the fighting.

The tier tree of their family was climbed, ropes dropped, the bodies raised high.

Ocassa grieved beneath the tree for days with the people of her village.

When the life of her family had passed on to the birds of the sky, Ocassa lit a great fire. She raised a dagger to her chest when the sun fell low.

"The Andarans are lost," she said to her people. "We wander blind and guideless. We teach our children nothing. We maim and kill our own." Ocassa stripped her robe. She cut the cloth of her undershirt from neck to breast. "We have forgotten that all love begins with pain. For the wounds and struggles my husband shared with me, for single hour by his side, I would crawl from here to the sea. I would plunge from Aedor's peak to Aedor's fire to heal the wounds of my beloved daughter. I would give my eyes for my son to see again, my every bone that he might breathe once more. For I was joined to my children by the agony of birth. It is the mother's searing pain that bridges the worlds of the unborn and the living, that wrests eternity to single moment, that lays the heavens bare. There is no stronger bond than shared pain. And no greater love than the hand that willingly cuts."

Ocassa sliced to first bone below her neck. She turned the blade under the skin. She flayed to top of breast. She sliced again, turned again, flayed again.

The people of her village rushed forward. They rubbed her open chest with oil, yolk, and lichen. They took up knives. They matched each strip of her skin with patches of their own.

Hands to chests, the great mother and her people shared wine and tears.

After all had recovered from the ritual, Ocassa led her people from their hillside village, forsaking revenge on the killers of her family. They traveled toward the mountains, away from coveted streams and blood-stained clearings. Ocassa followed nests. She found the hanging clay and snakeskin orbs of the scythe-billed raptors; the cornice nests of the ghost osprey, braced by lizard bones, lined by hide and fur; the lofty tree hollows of the spear-tailed condor, the sandbar domes of the green-throat ravens, the mud tunnels of the yellow waxwings.

Ocassa taught the children the cries and songs of each sacred bird.

She told myths of the jungle.

"Remember that all life came by the talons of the ribwings, the first birds of creation, born of the Silver Moon," Ocassa said. "The Blue Moon gifted water to the great void, but the empty seas sank lifeless. The Emerald Moon gifted stone, but the land stretched barren, flat, and grey. The first birds fell from the silver light. They crashed into the land, raked claws across the hard ground, and broke through the stony crust. The first birds soared, reared, and crashed again. They gashed valleys and ravines; hills and mountains piled in their wake. The pale ribwings slashed and tore the land until their talons dripped with water, until the lakes swelled and the rivers rushed, and first green crept across the grey."

Ocassa led her tribe to the edge of a deep, slitted gorge. From end to end, fine-meshed nets spanned the narrow chasm. Hundreds of small birds fluttered helplessly in the tight webs, their frantic writhing only tightening the strings around their necks. Thousands more hung dead, their beaks gaped wide, necks limp, heads lolled groundward.

The people lifted the stakes around the gorge and pulled the nets from the chasm. They carefully cut free the trapped birds. Heads bowed, they burned the dead.

While most set up camp at the gorge, Ocassa and a handful of her best trackers found the camp of the netter tribe. The trackers sliced the back of their hands, dribbled trails of blood toward the netter's camp, then climbed high trees. With snarl and howl, the jackals came in the deep night. Furious to find the bodiless trails, the jackals raided the camp. The netters scattered into the darkness.

The next morning Ocassa was lowered by rope into the gorge.

"What do you see?" her people called down. Long, torch-bearing arms reached deep into the chasm. Wide eyes stared down.

"Melted stone," Ocassa said, "the blood of Aedor turned to crystal. I see heavy columns of stone like thick-poled branches. I see purple rock blistered by the heat of the depths, red stone boiled." Ocassa called out for more rope. She worked her way toward the narrowing core. She slipped between tight columns, wormed through twisting voids. When all gaps closed, she scraped the stone by knife. "The dark stone shines brightly," she said. "Like ice-captured stars. Like moons reflected on black sea."

The Ocassans slaughtered the lizards of the deep gorge. They widened the top of the chasm and dug ramps down to the canyon floor on both ends. They hauled loose dirt out by baskets and rollers, chiseled around the columns of basalt, and hammered the porous scoria and light pumice into small fragments. They carved tunneled stairs to the jungle from a giant bank of brown-spice granite. They paved fanned entrance to the city with blue-copper gravel and tiles of green-quartz porphyry. They designed cistern funnels, looped aqueducts, drainage tracks, fountains, and pools. They opened the obsidian core to the sky.

Word of the Ocassan project spread throughout the jungle. Curious Andarans from all corners of the valley traveled to see the city born of Aedor's blood, to meet the legendary mother and her people bound by ancient ritual revived. Many family clans sent gifts of kinship and respect; many tribes sent tools, supplies, and workers to aid in the great labor.

But the Ocassans tired of the outsiders' increasing presence in their city and lengthening stays. Tents packed the narrow gorge. Thickening crowds slowed progress, added to the noise and confusion. Strange faces moved freely through the city; strange voices spoke in meetings, presuming to offer guidance.

With simmering frustration, the first Ocassans visited the tent of the mother and voiced their complaint.

"The outsiders' chests are soft and smooth, their virgin skin uncut," the Ocassans said. "Let them return to their own homes and villages. Let them build their own city far from here."

Ocassa answered, "Should sister and brother treat their cousins with contempt?"

"But they have endured no ritual," the Ocassans said. "They have shared no bond of pain with their own people, as we have suffered with you."

Ocassa walked the jungle alone for days.

When she returned from the jungle, she gathered everyone together at the fanned entrance to the city. She moved slowly through the overflowing crowd. She kissed the workers, wiped the sweat of every brow.

The great mother stood on granite slab and spoke.

"People of my blood and dream, people of my skin - We have grown too quickly in our childish zeal. We have rushed the flow of life and prodded nature. We have thought too highly of ourselves. In truth, we are a towering tree of shallow roots, trembling in the breeze, groaning in the wind. Without hardest test and deepest pruning, our strength will pass like a summer rainstorm. Love gives all, my people. And Love asks all. No wall will ever cage this city. No gatekeeper will ever turn away the refugee, deny haven to the lost, or refuse the traveler rest. But the heart of the city is sacred. There will be high sanctuaries open only to the long-purified and the life-committed. There will be worship and ritual chambers sealed for all but the skin-bound and the branded. Even in death, the tepid shall not see such places."

A new line of skin monks was trained. The monks were broken by many days of isolation, thirst, and hunger. In total darkness they received the mother's teaching. Their skin was cut from chest and back, as many strips as they could bear, the people's hands upon them.

Other lines were also trained and commissioned by the people. Stone-sculptors, forgers, and smiths received the branded scar of glowing iron and obsidian upon their necks. Planters and gardeners endured long days tied to poles around the gorge's rim, naked to the burning sun and insects' feeding. Guards and rangers were exiled from the city until their return with wineskin of seawater, fang of the gold-quilled serpent, and feather of the aerie stone-hawk.

Ocossan fellowship deepened.

The watching crowds pulled back, thinned, then disappeared completely.

The great mother and her generation never finished their homes inside the obsidian heart but lived all their days in tents among the scoria and basalt.

Before her passing, the great mother walked with the young sculptor, Halah, through the open channels of obsidian. They touched the uncut banks of stone, gazed long across the unformed body.

"What would you do," the mother asked, "were every hand and tool of the city yours to command?"

"I would fall to the ground," Halah said. "I would long weep, unworthy."

"And what would you carve from the titan's heart?" the mother asked.

The young girl glowed.

She pulled Ocassa along the stone banks, her free hand pointing, waving, gesturing wild, her fevered words overflowing.

"On the heart's edge, I would carve the bending trunks of many trees, their fingered branches reaching for the sky," Halah said. "Above the forest, great wings would stretch in wide and daunting span, a dwarfing shadow cast; or rise and swell in the mighty-billowed pause before swift stroke. Beneath the forest would lie a coral mesh of star and teardrop voids, tunnels curved like twisting worms, sanctuary coves nestled and soundless, vented plumes of spiral stair. And in the core every servant of the city would find a home – a podded cell for private den; a high-vaulted communal chamber shared with those of the same skill and craft; and a wide-veined web of corridors linking all chambers together in common flow and rhythm."

"And all would be made from lifeless stone?" the mother asked.

"Stone lives at the touch of sculptor's hand," Halah said. "But, no, many plants of the jungle would fill my city. Clover tassels flowered brilliant azure, gold, and violet would hang in the corridors and tunnels. Whorls of scarlet ivy would coil the trees and wrap the coral mesh. Berry-laden vines would sprawl the rounded walls of cell and chamber."

"And for light in the dark hours?"

"Thin troughs of torchmoss filament and powdered blue algae dribbled with rainwater."

Ocassa stopped walking and nudged away the girl's hand. "And should your young vision prove impossible to realize?" she asked.

"I would labor on. I would dream anew."

"And should the work stretch into centuries? your days end with little progress?"

"Then, great mother, I would mourn."

When the women emerged from the unformed banks, Ocassa stripped her cloak and laid her mantle across the shoulders of Halah.

"Tomorrow, your skin will be cut, your heart opened to the people," Ocassa said. "For one full year, you are not to touch obsidian. You will, instead, listen to the many dreams of others."

And so the mantle passed, mother to mother, across the generations, from Ocassa to Oduir.

The monks and elders followed Oduir back into the city.

Only Efed, the burn-scarred coastal fisher, remained with the pilgrims at their tents. Exhausted from his hours of translation, the young Andaran stared with glazed eyes into the dying embers of the fire.

The pilgrims also stared into the coals, each silent with their own thoughts, the stories of Ocassae slowly taking root.

The emerald moon slipped beneath the high gorge wall.

The silver moon followed, all still quiet around the firepit.

At the blue midmoon, old Ibyr left the circle to walk the gorge alone. The Torite miner and the Varran medic retired to their tents.

Efed moved closer to Dyraveen and Vanon. He shared his flask of melon liquor and passed a pouch of red leaves. Tongues stinging, spines numb, the three watched old Ibyr walk among the deep, blue shadows of the gorge.

"You come from the continent," Efed said. "You are Pherans."

"Yes, I am from the northern coast, a fisher and a sailor like you," Vanon said. She looked to Dyraveen. "He is from the central valley. He is a miner. A Tyraen."

"Why did you come to Andara?" Efed asked.

"We worked in Dekane," young Vanon said. "But there was an uprising in the mine, a violent rebellion. Many were killed, many wounded. We fled through the jungle and wandered here, guided by the children."

Efed studied the profile of Dyraveen in the moonlight. "You are scarred like a soldier," he said.

"I am a miner," Dyraveen said, leaning away. "I was caught in the fighting at Dekane."

Efed finished his flask and looked to the sea-colored moon. "I, too, was caught," he said. "At the bombing of Acrois."

"The bombing was fierce?" Dyraveen asked, eyes on the ground.

"Fierce, no," Efed said. "It was a storm of demons, the devil's feasting." The young fisher rubbed the raw, coarse skin of his forearms, ran fingers over the blistered ridges of his cheek. "I remember the morning clear and bright in the harbor," he said. "The waking sun had just driven away the last of the night mists.

The sea breeze wafted over the deck soft as a child's breath. A string of tankers had just docked; three eelers headed for the reefs, two ferries for the islands, a whaler for the pole. We saw the planes in the sky but could not hear them, only the waves against our hull. They were so small in the sky, like a flock of tiny gulls. How could we have known?

"When the bellies opened and the grey rain fell, we were not afraid. We knew that the imperial warships cruised the western bay while we fished in the east. All of us gathered on the deck, lit cigarettes, and stared to the west. We hoped for the warships to scatter from the bombs, to leave us in peace, at long last. We dreamed of our coastline open and free.

"But the grey rain spread as it fell. Wider. Wider. We feared for the docks. We feared for the city. Then, suddenly, we feared for ourselves.

"The western bay erupted first. The warships' long cannons blasted into the sky in desperate flurries. But the cannons quieted as the hailstorm of bombs found its home. Black clouds poured from the ship decks. The battered command towers leaned and fell askew.

"Then the bombs struck the city. Everywhere. At once. Great buildings crumbled into showers of brick and dust. The timbers of the pier splintered. The docks and markets crashed. All turned to smoke and flame across the port.

"And then the sea was not the sea. Water shot to sky. Waves surged and crashed in chaos. The surface boiled white and blue. Ferries crashed against the island cliffs; eelers lurched and capsized; bombarded tankers sank in orange-fumed blazes. The whole fishing fleet of the eastern bay disintegrated into scorched debris, bodies flailing wild or floating lifeless.

"We waited for our turn.

"Some knelt and covered their ears from the roar.

"Some stared, paralyzed, into the sky.

"Some ran and plunged beneath the water.

"I crawled into the tank and hid among the fish.

"One explosion launched me forward.

"Another hurled me back.

"The tank rolled.

"The tank fell.

"The tank walls crumpled and split.

"Then a flash of heat.

"Then a long and aching darkness.

"I woke in the night, ears ringing, head pounding, nauseous, stretched belly-down over a floating deck bench, a dead man's arm across my back.

"My legs trembled and seized from the piercing chill of the ocean. But my arms burned hot and raw even under the cold waters. I raised them into the moonlight. Unbelieving, I saw my swollen skin near to bursting, blisters climbing blisters, the dribbling streams of pus and blood. I smelled the melted skin of my own face. At high salted wave, I felt the nerve-torched scream, the blinding agony of flesh boiled out.

"What could I do? I climbed the back of the dead man who had saved me. I kicked and paddled for the city."

Dyraveen left the circle. He passed old Ibyr and vanished into the night.

"Your friend has also survived bombing?" Efed asked.

"He was more than a spectator to the killings at the mine," Vanon said. "And more than a miner during the war. What happened in Acrois?"

"I buried the man who had saved me," Efed said. "I scavenged the city for days. Many survivors shared with me, but many others chased, beat, and stole. I slept among the forest graves outside the city until the scouts of Ocasse found me."

"Oduir sent rescuers to Acrois?" Vanon asked.

"Throughout the bombings Oduir sent scouts all along the southern coast and the western river, even to the eastern crags and the northern marshlands," Efed said. "Her rangers packed in for the wounded all the healing oils, leaves, and pastes that they could carry. They guided packs of refugees through the jungle, some to the mountain temples, some to Ocassae." Efed closed his eyes, smiling, savoring. "I will never forget the first taste of blueleaf, chilling throat to stomach, numbing from marrow to pore."

"Forgive the Pherans," Vanon said. "Forgive my people."

For weeks the continental pilgrims worked with the Ocossans outside the city, retiring each night to the tents. Inside the gorge they leveled ground, edged the pumice and scoria pathways, and repaired the drainage canals. They pulled and burned weeds and cut the wild flax by sickle. Outside the gorge they tended the lichen farm, moss gardens, worm beds, and flower colonies.

Each day, more and more Ocossans came out from the city to join them. Each night, the crowds around the fire grew.

After a night of heavy rains and strong winds through the gorge, the city mother appeared in the morning with warm broth and clothes freshly washed.

"Tonight you will sleep in Ocossae," she said.

After work that day, Oduir led the pilgrims into the city and gave them beds of feather moss in lung-shaped chambers. Only Dyraveen stayed in his tent outside the city.

Over the cold season of misty nights and ice-crystal dews, many friendships formed and deepened between the pilgrims, the Ocossans, and the war-rescued Andarans. The pilgrims progressed from routine chores and simple labor to specialized training.

The Varran medic learned the richly varied flora of the jungle from the Ocossan herbalists and healers. In the slit-vented collection chamber, with tools of basin, flask, hearth, and filter, the Varran learned separation techniques for acids and oils, extraction methods for barks, seeds, and roots, and dessication by furnace, salt, and air.

The Torite miner cast, forged, and sharpened tools with the Ocossan metalsmiths. He learned from the stone-sculptors the soft knapping strokes of wooden punch and antler tine. Inside the city core, he polished the obsidian contours of chamber, cove, and tunnel. Outside, he cleaned to glistening the stony trees of Halah's forest; he climbed the mighty-billowed wings, wiped the feather shafts of dust and grime, and marked by silver oil the parallel barbs of feathers' vane.

Vanon absorbed the older Andaran tongue by spreading herself in widest range across the Ocossan people, by engaging in conversation with everyone from fading elder to freshest child, by careful listening, dogged plodding, and stumbling first attempts. She trained among many cooks: soup-makers, juicers, grillers of red gourds, butchers of lizard, smokers of eel. She experimented with the cross-breeding florists. With the weavers she gathered reeds, spun flax, and worked small looms. Once comfortable in the ancient tongue, Vanon spent her mornings in the jungle with Efed and the other Andaran fishers of the coast. The deep-sea sailors tried their hand at the fishing of pond and stream. Having no luck with salamander and skink bait, they turned to the Ocossans for help. "Are you fishing for whales in the knee-high creeks?" the jungle fishers laughed. "Think smaller. Eels lose their minds for wasp heads. Anything with fins will swallow a female blue moth." Guided by the Ocossans, they hiked to a wide floodplain of looping streams, rocky chutes, and oxbow pools. They camped on the sandy banks for days.

They caught their fill of tender eel each morning, razorfish and spotted rays each night.

Ibyr sometimes worked with her niece, Vanon, in the cooking and weaving chambers of the lower city. More often, however, she walked the open sky-rings with Oduir and talked for hours with the city mother in the sanctuaries of higher Ocassae. The two older women were drawn together. Each saw in the other a great depth of experience, a fierce spirit, a rich compassion balanced by hard-earned wisdom.

But it was their stark differences that stoked their mutual curiosity and fueled their early conversations, assisted by Efed's translation.

Ibyr was a continental, a sailor of many seas.

Oduir was an islander, a native of the inland jungle.

Ibyr was a wanderer free and unfettered, her only tie to niece companion.

Oduir was a queen bonded by ritual of skin to all her people, connected by historical root to every Ocassan generation, by spiritual legacy to every city mother of the past.

Ibyr was an experienced lover, in her younger days a sampler of many coastlines' skin.

Oduir was a lifelong celibate, not by vow or sense of duty, but by fiery ambition - a shrewd decision in her youth.

"No kisses in the dark?" Ibyr asked, unbelieving. "No warm bodies for cold nights?"

"I was chosen as a girl, my skinny legs still growing," Oduir said. "For a full year I was taught in the crown sanctuary. I learned the chronicles of the elders, the lyrics of the monks, the secrets of the mothers. I understood nothing then, perhaps the smallest leaf of smallest tier. But one truth struck me by year's end, a truth hard and bitter, glorious and blinding: The greatest artists and leaders walked alone. The greatest mothers never married."

"But the city was born by the first mother's pain," Ibyr said, "her loss of husband, daughter, and son."

"And that pain opened her heart to *all* the people, lifted her to highest love," Oduir said. "Why return to lower rung?"

Ibyr described the great cities of the continent: Tekenna, Pocone, Lytarr.

She told of the sea…its churning, windclash storms that turned day to night, white lightning over jagged waves of black… the mysterious pirates of the upper pole, their docks of floating stone, their winter shelters high on crystal berg…the frost coral webbing of the lower pole, thick-arched strands dipping in and out of the icy water, a creeping glacial filament horizon to horizon, violet and green under night mists, golden blue in the sun.

And Ibyr described the great islands: Eskalla, Nyava, Troqual.

"It is a strange world," Oduir said. "How small you must feel in the open voids. How lonely."

The city mother offered solace, home, and rest to the wanderer. She promised unbroken fellowship and the abiding love of family.

"Long years turn every home to cage," Ibyr said. "Great work remains beyond the jungle in the world still wounded."

By the end of the cold season, Ibyr had become fluent in the older Andaran tongue, Oduir in the new.

The city mother shared scouting reports of the west and south. The western river now teemed with flurried droves of boats and planes, from the capital to the sea. Great ships filled the harbor of Acrois, shuttling hundreds onto shore each day.

"The Pherans rebuild quickly," Oduir said. "I fear they will be slow to leave."

"The war debt looms and greed abounds," Ibyr said.

"The Andarans in hiding along the sea and the river will be forced to flee," Oduir said. "We must prepare the city for the coming wave of refugees. We must send many to help and guide them."

Dyraveen never entered the city for work, or meal, or sleep.

When the continentals advanced to specialty training, Dyraveen joined the guards outside the city – all Ocossans, no survivors of Acrois among them, no one burned by Pheran bombs.

On first day Dyraveen surrendered his pistols to the guards. They tossed the guns and ammunition like garbage into a pit at gorge's end. The bullets disappeared into a sharp-pointed mound of rifles and machine-guns. On top he recognized weapons of the ten Andaran rebels first to the valley.

"Guns are like screams in the jungle," a guard said, "calling out to every beast and killer."

Dyraveen trained with the long bow for ranged attack; with twin daggers for close brush-fighting and silent ambush; with the bladed cane for balance on steep terrain, probing shadowed ground, and halting charged attack. He learned to send and receive messages over wide distances by the wren-like calling of the reed whistle. He learned to climb the highest tree and rest in tightest crook, eyes half-open, ears attuned to every creature. He learned the precious arbor nooks which hid the red and blue leaves.

The guards tested him with solo night patrols around the gorge.

When Dyraveen alone repelled a pack of jackals, the guards led him on a five-day hike into the jungle.

Each night they assigned Dyraveen the longest watch. Each day they pushed a pace more dangerous and grueling, through denser brush and rougher ground.

By the fifth night, Dyraveen - bruised, stiff, parched, sore - dozed off as he stared into the fire. His head leaned low. The bow slipped from his hands. Weary eyelids closed on weary eyes.

At the cry of a falcon, he awoke.

His weapons were gone, the fire dead, two moons risen.

Many stared down at him. Guards. Scouts. Rangers. A forest of long necks, tall canes, and moonlit blades.

A barefoot ranger with skin-flayed ribs stepped forward. "You slept," the ranger said. "What if all at the fire had slept like you?"

"We might never have awakened," Dyraveen said, eyes low, kneeling before the crowd.

"Yes, never," the ranger said. "We were told that you have will. We were told that you are clever."

"I have done my best to learn from the guards," Dyraveen said. "They have done their best to teach me."

"Yet you slept," the ranger said. "Yet you put their lives in danger."

"I plead for more time," Dyraveen said. "To strengthen. To learn."

Many voices spoke at once, angry, impatient, untrusting.

The circle tightened.

"Why do you shun our city?" the ranger demanded, holding the others back. "Why do you hide from Oduir?"

"I do not hide from the city or her mother," Dyraveen said, standing to face the crowd. "I avoid only the wounded of Acrois. To forget the war. To live."

"There are rumors that you fought in the war against Andara. A flyer, some say. A sailor, others."

"Worse. Much worse."

"What then?"

"I was Commander. Continental Commander. The highest leader of the land."

A guard spit into his hair, a scout across his cheek.

The rib-flayed ranger waved back the crowd.

In swift and shadowed blur, the ranger took Dyraveen by the throat. He choked with gritted teeth. The ranger expected squirming and handfighting from the small continental, but Dyraveen pulled the ranger closer by the sheath around his neck. The two spun, jostling for better grip and leverage, choking and clawing.

Dyraveen stumbled first, an ankle caught on edge of stone.

The ranger landed on top, knife already drawn.

Dyraveen lay still on his back. He gasped for air. He closed his eyes. Helpless, he waited.

The ranger coughed, spit blood, breathed deep. He looked to the faces of the watching crowd.

"You bombed plants, forges, mills," the ranger said. "Then you bombed homes. Then you bombed hospitals. Then you bombed schools."

"I deserve to die," Dyraveen said.

"No, you deserve to live," the ranger said. "To live and to see."

The ranger sheathed his knife.

After the first thaw of the warm season, all of the Ocossan scouts and rangers led search parties into the jungle, toward the western river and southern sea, accompanied by monks, healers, and the Andarans rescued in first mission.

The rest of the city prepared. Hundreds of tents were pitched in the gorge. Aqueducts were diverted and bathing chambers carved from the walls of the gorge. Great stores of provisions were gathered: fish and eel, gourds and melons, mosses and lichen, red and blue leaves. Many new blankets were woven, many clothes sewn.

Dyraveen hauled stones from the gorge. Alone, he worked each day from sunrise to sunset, ever plodding, ever climbing, his long beard pale with dust, his green eyes lifeless. Dyraveen drank from puddles. He ate the pitied scraps of stem, bone, and rind left by other workers. Alone, he slept each night outside the city, his hood drawn, his back to the cold column of basalt.

When the search parties returned with hundreds of refugees, Dyraveen fled. He hid in a mossy garden above the gorge, beneath a planter's pole overtaken by ivy. He watched the newcomers... Those wounded by metal shrapnel. Those maimed by falling brick. Those burned by first explosion and sweeping fire. Those without memory. Without arms. Without legs. The blinded. The deafened. The orphaned.

Though Dyraveen prayed for strength day after day, he could not bring himself to take a single step beyond the garden.

After anguished weeks alone, he called out one morning for Ibyr and Vanon. He shouted across the gorge until his throat stung raw.

The coastal women, aunt and niece, found him sitting beneath the planter's pole, a dagger in his lap. He had pulled the ivy from the overhanging rod. Dark sweat coursed his sunken cheeks. His skin-taut ribs stretched scarcely wider than his beard, pulled even tighter by each exhaling breath.

"Why do you call us from our labor?" Vanon asked, kicking tangled leaves aside.

"Your crimes have eaten you to bone," old Ibyr said. "You turn suicide from act to state."

"I ask you, friends, a weighty favor," Dyraveen whispered hoarsely. "I ask a solemn vow."

Vanon offered a pouch of seeds and leaves, Ibyr a flask of water.

"Eat, you fool," Vanon said. "Drink, please drink."

Dyraveen scorned the offerings but gripped both arms extended. "This night I will satisfy justice," he said. "This night I reach for mercy."

Old Ibyr stared at the dagger. She poured water into her hand, wiped the forehead of the gaunt Tyraen. "We will help you," she said.

"Return to me tonight after the lighting of Oduir's fire," Dyraveen said. "Should my strength fail at sunset, finish the work that remains."

"We will," Vanon said.

After the day's long labor, after cold bath and rich meal, fires were lit throughout the gorge. The people came together, Ocossans of the ancient world, Andarans of the new. Liquor was passed, leaves shared, stories told.

The coastal women climbed from gorge's floor to rim. They walked to the garden by the light of the silver moon and the fires' red-quiver glow.

They found Dyraveen on his knees, slumped and trembling against the pole, his beard and hair freshly shaven. The arms of Dyraveen dangled limply at his sides. His slender neck arched. His head sagged low, chin tucked to chest. He breathed in groans and whimpers.

Vanon gasped.

A dark circle surrounded him, a puddle lapping at his toes.

Blood splattered his wrists, soaked his thighs, ran steady from his open-flayed chest, dribbling, dripping, streaming.

His first work had been even, sharp, and clean - paper-thin strips cut from throat to chest in long, straight columns. But a shaking and fearful hand had worked the ribs. The unsteady knife had gouged and skimmed over the ribs, sometimes cutting to the bone, sometimes leaving untouched patches and hanging flaps of skin. The last work of the knife across the belly appeared drunken. Dyraveen had slashed with desperation, cuts into cuts, slices diagonal and crosswise, taken by both hands. Blood darkened every swollen lip. Like creeping river over rocks, blood oozed from the shredded mesh of tissue.

Young Vanon poured water into the mouth of Dyraveen, pressed leaves beneath his tongue. When she raised a flask of healing oil, Ibyr stayed her hand.

"First, our vow," Ibyr said.

Vanon lifted Dyraveen and held him.

Old Ibyr rinsed the dagger clean. With strokes firm and swift, she pared the ribs of skin remaining. She edged the bloody mesh of belly. Gripping upper corner, she sliced the skin from tissue, pulling gently, peeling down.

Dyraveen's mouth opened into muted scream, clear spit dripping. He turned and twisted without force, moaning weakly through the nose.

The wretched work finished, Ibyr threw the dagger into the jungle trees. They laid Dyraveen on his back, washed his torso clean with water, then rubbed the healing oil, neck to waist.

Dyraveen gazed into the silver moon, his eyes a wet and brilliant hazel. Through rattling teeth and shivering jaw, he smiled faintly. He waved the women near. "Take my skin to Oduir's fire," he whispered. "Show to all my depth of sorrow, the blade-cut proof of my regret. Bring back any soul willing to bond with me. Or throw my skin to flame."

At the fire of the city mother, Ibyr climbed an overlooking column of basalt. Vanon threw water from clay jars over the blazing cone of branches. Steam hissed. The inner coals crackled. The crowd looked to Vanon, then to Ibyr.

Standing atop the basalt, Ibyr reached into the dark-stained satchel slung around her neck.

She raised her hands toward the sky, rivulets of blood coursing down her wrists.

She called out to the war-scarred Andarans, to the gracious Ocossan hosts, and to the beloved city mother, her friend.

"I raise for you the skin of Dyraveen, the Tyraen, cut from throat to waist, flayed by his own hand until his flesh could bear no more," Old Ibyr said. "Dyraveen carved in humble imitation of the highest Ocossan ritual. His blade was driven by fiercest regret for his crimes in days of war, by deepest sorrow for all Andarans wounded. He opened his body in the hope of your swift healing. He survived such agony by the dream of new life for all in the jungle…and forgiveness for himself."

The fire slowly returned to its former strength while the words of Ibyr settled.

The other firepits throughout the gorge were abandoned. The smaller crowds flocked to Oduir's fire.

When the city mother rose to her feet, the people stood. The dense and swollen throng parted as Oduir made her way around the fire. The great mother, moving slowly, looked into the eyes of all her children. She took into her heart every wound and scar and burn.

At the base of the column, Oduir called out to Ibyr: "Come down, sister," she said.

The throng pressed even closer as Ibyr climbed down and Oduir waited.

The monks of the city pushed back the crowd.

The elders formed an arm-locked ring around the two women.

Oduir touched the blood-streaked hands of Ibyr. She stared at the satchel, dark and dripping. "How can we forgive this killer of thousands?" the mother said. She wiped the traces of Dyraveen's blood from her hands. "How could we share skin with this great destroyer? this lord of fire and death?"

"What more can he do to prove his sorrow and regret?" Ibyr asked. "He lingers in death's shadow as we speak. Tomorrow's sun he may not see."

"He dares to use our ritual of love and bonding to force his own ends?"

"He hopes in the legend of Ocassa, the first mother, who did not seek revenge upon the killers of her own family, who opened her heart to all people."

"To *her* people."

"And through all the city mothers, all Ocossan generations, this love has stretched no wider? Did you not forgive the younger Andarans whose ancestors fought your own centuries ago? Is this crowd around us not proof of ever-reaching love?"

The city mother looked to the faces of the monks and elders around her. "We will never share skin with Dyraveen, the killer," she cried out for all to hear.

Old Ibyr cast the satchel into the fire.

The skin of Dyraveen was quickly lost to smoke and sky.

The coastal women stayed with Dyraveen in the garden throughout the night. They forced him to drink water, rubbed his exposed flesh with herbal pastes and healing oils, and kept fresh leaves beneath his tongue.

Numb and weary, the three dozed off near dawn, leaning together, their backs to the planter's pole.

When they woke in the harsh morning light, they were surrounded by a small crowd: the Torite mechanic, the Varran medic, Efed the fisher, the rib-flayed ranger, two monks, an elder, and Oduir.

The city mother, squinting in the sun, stared down at Dyraveen, her face, at once, hardened by revulsion and contempt, softened by compassion.

She dropped a backpack laden with supplies at his feet.

"A final gift," Oduir said. "You are forgiven for your crimes, Tyraen, but you may not stay here any longer. You are not safe among Andarans. You are not safe among Ocossans. The ranger will guide you to the mountains. He will speak to the stone monks of Tep on your behalf. More than this, I cannot offer."

The ranger motioned Dyraveen to his feet.

Dyraveen, groaning, rose. He walked on weakest legs into the jungle.

Vanon followed, the pack across her shoulders.

As Old Ibyr passed, Oduir took her arm. "You choose the cursed path?" the mother said. "You scorn family and home for lonely, bitter road."

"To rest is to die, great mother," Old Ibyr said. "I stretch my final days by the grinding of my bones."

The two women embraced. And parted.

On the early trail, the ranger, not pleased with his assignment, showed little patience with the slow-marching coastal women, and scarce sympathy for the crawling, self-wounded Tyraen. He glared at the women each time they stopped to trade the heavy pack. He snapped at Dyraveen each time he dozed on breaks or stalled on the path, wiping sweat, re-tying boots, adjusting bandages.

But the heart of the ranger opened when he saw Dyraveen take up the heavy pack after their lunch of honeyed moss.

Dyraveen, teeth gritted, marched through the hottest part of the day. He took no breaks to eat or drink. He bore the pack alone. On steep climbs his unsteady knees quivered in struggle. On downhill stretches he braced himself by double cane, still falling more than once. Hour by hour, sweat and blood seeped through his bandage wraps. Crimson oil spotted his shirt. Wet spots widened into dark rings.

When Dyraveen broke from the trail, dropped the pack, and spun in confused circles, the ranger threw him over his shoulder and ran to the closest stream.

The ranger held him in the current, water to their necks.

"Drink, brother," the ranger said, an arm around his waist. "Drink your fill."

On the streambank the women took control. They stripped Dyraveen of his soaked and filthy clothes. They dried him, laid him down, and raised his feet. They applied oils and yolks to stop the bleeding of his chest, rooted balms to numb and heal.

"Were you trying to kill him, ranger?" Vanon said.

"He took up the pack himself," the ranger said. "He refused to trade each time I offered."

"You couldn't allow him one day to recover from his carving?"

"I, too, have been skinned," the ranger said. "There is no escaping from the pain, moving or still, resting or running. Distraction is the only hope, to pull the mind from body, as by new march and trail."

Old Ibyr covered Dyraveen with a blanket. "We march no more today," she said, pulling the tent from the pack.

In the sunless chill before dawn, atop a mossy boulder, the ranger shared his pipe and name with the skin-flayed continental. "Asceres," he said, "oldest ranger of Ocossae."

Dyraveen inhaled deeply from the redleaf pipe. He exhaled through his nose, twin columns of smoke rising over the jungle trees, melting into the stars. "The oldest is young," he said.

"The trail is hard, the virgin wild even harder."

"What claims most lives in the jungle?"

"The thousand poisons of the slithering and the crawling. Diseases of the wind and river. Paralyzing hunger. Delirium and thirst."

"Yet you would never leave."

Asceres nodded, waved his hand across a purple and red fan of light on the horizon, the first touch of morning sun. A lone condor glided beneath the white-laced bank of rolling mists and vapor trails. Raptor mates at play circled, chased, and fled above the mane trees. Seaborn clouds broke high over the mountains, their hanging raindrops flashing silver over the downhill slopes. The rich green of the jungle emerged from the dark valley. "I saw the great capital in his prime before the war, and the fleets of Acrois, her bay churned white with traffic," Asceres said. "I saw only spot and blemish, my friend, chaos and confusion."

Dyraveen tapped the pipe against the boulder and packed fresh leaves. He yielded first smoke to the ranger. "The cities of the continent are no greater," Dyraveen said. "They are loud and dirty. You cannot breathe. You cannot move. A pair of trees is called a park and people crowd for glimpse."

Asceres laughed, clouds slipping from his mouth. "There is no wilderness remaining?" the ranger said. "All is trampled, lifeless ground?"

"The greatest wonders lie below," Dyraveen said, exhaling. "There are hidden kingdoms in the depths - underworld rivers, forests of living stone, tunnels spiral and twisting, vast chambers aglow by mineral, gem, and crystal. There are strange tribes of the darkness — fearsome giants, slender shades, thieves and outcasts, painters and musicians."

The blood-grey eyes of the Ocossan widened with stream of visions. "You saw these places?" Asceres said. "You walked the underworld?"

"Yes. Many years ago."

"And did the people of the underground join you in the war?"

"Before their leader failed them, they proved to be fearless warriors of the land, sea, and air. They were the greatest of allies, the truest of friends. Their loyalty was fierce, pure, and unbounded."

The ranger studied the eyes of Dyraveen. He stashed his pipe, drank deep from his canteen, and climbed down from the boulder. "Forward, we march," Asceres said, looking to the trail. "Ever forward."

The travelers broke camp after dividing up the supplies of the heavy pack.

Throughout the early morning, they marched in short line together, three strides between them, the ranger in the lead, Dyraveen at rear. The ranger set a slow and cautious pace, often looking back. The women stopped and checked on Dyraveen at each misstep he made, every crack of branch or slide of pebbles.

At first break Dyraveen vented his frustrations. "For fucksake, march strong," he said. "I understand well that the goal must be reached, and part must yield to whole. If I fall behind, my friends, keep going. If I struggle, let me struggle. Alone. In peace. Without your condescending eyes."

The ranger doubled his pace.

Young Vanon, near to her limit, kept Asceres within view.

Old Ibyr fell behind her niece as the jungle warmed. She rubbed her hip and limped on swollen knee.

Dyraveen marched on Ibyr's heels for most of the morning. But his raw flesh burned and throbbed as the day wore on. The rub of bandage felt like flame. The drip of sweat stung like acid. From his knees he watched the limping old woman disappear down the trail.

By the time Dyraveen caught up to the others, they had all finished a lunch of grilled lizard, washed in the stream, and shared a pipe.

The other travelers watched him slump against a tree. Sweat dripped from his sunburned brow. He clenched his teeth and closed his eyes, his face both flush with rage and close to tears.

Vanon set gourd and lizard in his lap.

Asceres left a handful of leaves.

Ibyr touched his head. "We can change your bandages," she said. "We can rub fresh pastes and oils."

Dyraveen held her hand but shook his head. "Only at the end of day, mother," he said. "I must earn your care."

"Love is choice, not labor."

The ranger and the coastal women continued down the trail. They hid at the first bend and looked back. When Dyraveen ate and drank, they shared a smile. When Dyraveen rose to his feet, they hurried down the trail.

Though the afternoon heat was strong, the jungle sky clouded over, soft rains fell, and cooling breezes stirred the air.

Dyraveen, refreshed, encouraged, pushed ahead.

Asceres, patient, held back at half-march.

The Tyraen caught up.

The four travelers walked the trail together once again, a stride apart in narrow stretches, side by side in treeless clearings.

As they made their way along the southern trail, the foothills of Tep emerged between forest and mountain. Ancient rivers of lava, hardened bloodred, black, and rusty, flowed between the rocky hills. The rivers traced back to the wide-crescent mouth of Tep, to the melted breaches of the mountain wall, to its fanged towers still crumbling slow.

Inspired by their progress, the travelers drove hard toward the mountain throughout the afternoon and into the evening.

They pushed until the last rays of sun caught the dark, snaking cracks of the stone towers and the melted tongues of rivers' turn.

By the light of moons and fire, they pulled off the bandages of Dyraveen. The soaked cloth smelled of carcass and grave. Clouded streams of pus oozed freely from his chest - green, yellow, black. Sweat dripped steady from his forehead. Rivulets coursed his shivering back.

"Keep him awake," the ranger said. "Keep him alive." Knife drawn, Asceres ran into the off-trail brush.

The women stripped their cloaks and covered the slick back of Dyraveen.

They gave him water to drink.

He vomited foam.

They held back his arms when he scratched and ripped at his chest.

After a long struggle, Dyraveen fell back, limp and exhausted.

He gazed into the three-mooned sky as if seeing it for the first time, pained and confused like a newborn child.

He tried to sleep.

The women shook him.

He cursed and spit.

The women forced red leaves into his mouth.

Asceres returned with lizard hides over his shoulder, both of his hands bloody, his arms and face raked by many claws.

He cut the soft inner lining from the hides. He laid each across the skinless chest of Dyraveen.

The ranger kissed him, slipped a scabbard between his teeth. Dyraveen bit down.

"The sealing will hurt more than the flaying," Asceres said. The ranger pulled a thick, burning branch from the fire. "But you will survive, my friend. Just as I did. Just as every ancestor before us."

The travelers reached the mountain a few days later. They found no monks inside the wide mouth of Tep, but a handful of Andarans washed themselves in a shallow rainpool.

The Andarans called out to the newcomers from the jungle and rushed to meet them. The Andarans moved awkwardly, too weak to take full strides. Their narrow frames were fleshless, their lips bloodless, their skin a pale and jaundiced yellow.

Asceres raised his cane to keep them at a distance. He studied each for signs of disease. "Who are you?" the ranger asked. "Where do you come from?"

"We are survivors of the Pheran bombings," the tallest answered. "Two of us are from the western river, two from Acrois."

"How did you come to the mountain?"

"We were led here by scouts and monks. But both abandoned us before the cold season. The scouts left us for their mother's city, the monks for higher ground."

"The stone monks should have stayed and helped you."

"We followed the monks deeper into the mountains, but we could not keep up. Many survivors disappeared in the aerie mists. Some were hurt by falling stones from above, some by collapsing trails and rockslides under their feet. One was crippled in a deep ravine, killed by hand of mercy. But the stone monks would not turn back. They told us to return to Tep, to scavenge and hunt, to drink from pools. We watched them climb away from us, higher and higher into the steep mountains. They tossed metal rods scorched by lightning down the mountainsides and moved unstricken poles to greater heights. Across the wide range, they played some game of territory, flags, and triangles. The losers howled across the voids like wounded cubs. The winners lit fires in the mouths of caverns and branded themselves by obsidian shard."

The eyes of Asceres fell low. "Forgive us," he said, lowering his cane. "We trusted the stone monks to guide and protect you. We did not know."

Young Vanon stepped forward. "Are any of you sick or fevered?" she asked.

"We are weak, tired, and hungry," the tall Andaran said. "We throw up most of the insects that we catch. We shit mud. We shiver through the night. But, no, we are not sick."

The travelers from the jungle opened their packs and shared all that they had with the Andarans.

The Andarans, restored to life, searched the mountain throughout the day for other survivors.

By nightfall nearly thirty Andaran survivors had gathered at the fire. They ate the seeds, moss, and nuts collected in the hills by the coastal women. Arguing, elbowing, they fought for the roasted flanks of a ram killed by Asceres in the crags.

When the ranger apologized to all survivors for the stone monks' failure and offered them guided passage to Ocossae or Mount Aedor, the Andarans were lukewarm in response. Despite his promise of abundant gardens, fresh streams, and beautiful stonework in the mother's city, they had no desire to travel deeper into the jungle and farther from the coast. His descriptions of mammoth Aedor and the community of temple monks also failed to inspire; the survivors remembered too well their struggles and losses in the high mountains.

"We are people of the sea and river," Atai, the tall Andaran, said. "Your dizzying peaks terrify us. Your thick jungle air feels like sap on our skin; it chokes our throats like hot-boiled sweat."

"The body and mind adjust in time," young Vanon said. "The first days are the hardest."

"Every day has been miserable for us since the continentals came," Atai said.

"But the jungle and the mountains are the only places safe from Pheran capture," Vanon said.

"No, there are many small islands off the southern coast," Atai said. "And there is the whole eastern peninsula."

"I will take you to the pass between Tep and Aedor," the ranger said. "On the backside of the mountains you can see the southern coast all the way to Acrois. And you can see the eastern peninsula to its furthermost tip. From there all refugees may choose their own path."

After a day of planning and gathering supplies, the travelers set off on their journey.

They entered a range of pale, dusted foothills. They climbed by the trenched faults and rock-strewn draws between ridges. They followed the contoured folds of gneiss, alternating bands amber and white, coursing to higher ground in stony waves. They avoided the goldthorn brambles and stem-nettled sage.

The Andaran refugees, still weak from seasons' hunger, moved timidly. Their fearful eyes flitted from dark crevice to shadowed void. They stayed in close huddle, their hands gripping the shoulders and wrists of those around them. They plodded ahead with the hesitation of the blind.

Asceres, bored by the crawling pace, broke from the draws and trenches to hunt.

Vanon, though likewise bored, followed behind the refugee huddle with her limping aunt and dead-eyed Dyraveen, arms held tightly to his chest.

The travelers camped their first night at the top of the foothills.

In the early twilight, a lone tricopter passed high above them, its red and silver lights flickering between the clouds.

On the second day of the journey, a greener valley before them, the refugees relaxed their guard and spread out from their tight-huddled core. They released their neighbors' hands and found walking sticks beneath the trees. They talked of the islands and peninsula. They dreamed of better days.

Old Ibyr struggled far behind. Her knee swelled until the sack of fluid sloshed from side to side with each step taken. The skin pores stretched to breaking.

By midday, she was finished.

She lay down on a patch of grass and slipped her pack under her knee. She blocked the sun with one arm; the other, fisted, beat the ground.

Vanon shouted for Asceres.

The ranger found old Ibyr sweating and trembling, a long knife to her knee. Asceres took the blade from her hand. He ran his finger gently around the swelling until he touched a speck of scab, a tiny puncture.

The refugees circled.

Some turned away when blood and fluid gushed from the ranger's lancing.

Some pressed closer as Asceres teased out a golden sliver of bone from the punctured speck.

"You knelt on shedded quill," Asceres said. He rinsed the leg clean and rubbed paste into the knee. He carried Ibyr into the shade, pressed a full pouch of leaves into her hand, then turned to the refugees. "She will heal quickly, perhaps in a day, but you should march on. Follow the valley to the mineral springs. Turn…"

"No," Atai interrupted, "we will stay with you."

The ranger and the refugees shared water, meal, and leaves.

Old Ibyr rested through the lunch break with Dyraveen and Vanon at her side. She shifted uncomfortably, groaned at each new stab of pain, brushed and swatted at the gnat cloud in her face.

When the ranger came to check on her, she rose and walked to meet him.

"Let's go," she said. "I can march."

"Rest," he said, "rest a day, at least."

"I cannot sleep," she said. "And it will hurt the same whether I walk, run, or lie."

The ranger yielded the lead to the old woman.

The refugees followed in loose company, held together by the loud tapping of Ibyr's cane on hardened ground.

Ibyr tested her knee by lengthening strides. When the knee held strong, she pushed herself harder and harder, until the numbing throb of adrenaline matched her aching pain.

The travelers marched in silence through the afternoon heat.

Behind them, Tep receded. Its fanged towers slowly fell from the white-hazed sky, melting into the stony, grey horizon.

Ahead, Aedor emerged from a bedded sea of lesser peaks. The ancient king of the southeastern mountains was a mammoth pyramid with rings of mist and shrouded crown, a mighty fortress many times shaken by quake and breached by fire from within, a continent and range unto himself.

Mile by mile, the rifts between the mountain veins widened.

The jagged fissures of the slopes branched and darkened.

The cliffs etched sharply under ages' scarring of wind and rain.

The king transformed under the falling sun. Like a faceted jewel turned before candle, his many faces passed from sunlit glory to fading shadow.

At last break Asceres pointed to the thin vapors rising from the springs of the valley. "With a hard push we could reach the springs by dark and sleep in sheltered cove," he said. "Or we can camp here tonight in the open valley and reach the springs midmorning. The choice is yours, great mother."

"We push," Ibyr said, rubbing fresh oil into her knee. "But you must lead."

The travelers reached the springs just after sunset. They lit fires in the rock basins. They soaked long in the steaming pools, dozing shoulder to shoulder.

Only Dyraveen did not strip and bathe. He sat apart from the others, washed his hands in the pools' overflow, ran wet fingers through his matted hair and tangled beard.

Too exhausted to pitch tents, the travelers collapsed in blankets against the cove walls.

The anguished cries of stone-hawks kept the ranger from sleep.

Red and silver tricopter lights reflected across the pools.

The rising emerald moon revealed the broad belly of a transport plane.

Five days later, drained by hunger and long march, the Andaran refugees looked down from rock ledges on the backside of the mountains. They gazed all the way to the sea. Their hopeful eyes searched the coastline for any territory free from the Pherans, any open bay, any patch of ground, any island speck. Their frightened eyes searched and searched. The cold, biting sea winds chilled to their skin. The eastern sky darkened with coming storm.

Acrois was no longer a flattened grave of ash and dust. Hangars, docks, and warehouses had been built; labor camps walled; roads and runways paved; foundations poured for worker lodges, processing plants, mills, and refineries. Incoming supply ships surrounded the pier cranes in crowded half-circle rings. Outgoing tankers and cargo vessels left the port in steady stream, traveling west to Nyava or Troqual, east to the continent.

Carriers cruised up and down the coast launching tricopters and scouting planes on inland surveys.

Tech crews assembled banks of wave turbines inside sand and boulder levees.

Eelers and trawlers worked the dark waters between islands.

Even the rocky and treeless eastern peninsula bustled with Pheran activity. From high-fenced pits continental guards led teams of ankle-chained islanders to dig and to sample.

Sharpshooter towers surrounded promising quarry sites where hundreds of Andarans swung sledge and hauled stones.

The refugees said nothing as they watched.

They sat down on the ledges.

They searched for any speck, any patch, any bay.

A colder wind carried first drops of rain.

The storm crept closer.

Atai jumped to his feet suddenly. He passed the binoculars, pointed to an island near the peninsula's first bend. "Every ship avoids it, even the smallest trawler," he said. "The island must have reefs, sharp rocks, shallow banks. We would be safe there."

The refugees crowded around Atai.

As the binoculars passed from hand to hand, the voices rose in wild and contagious excitement.

They would slip behind the hills and avoid the crowded shore.

They would cut across the peninsula before first quarry.

They would wait for an opening between ships.

They would swim for the island, holding nothing back.

On the island they would find shelter beneath the trees, beds of downy moss, birds and fish and game.

No Pheran plane could land on the small and rocky island.

No Pheran ship would risk grounding.

The ranger took the binoculars in hand. He peered down the shoreline all the way to the peninsula. He studied the island carefully, the surrounding seas, the movements of the ships, the gathering storm.

"Most of you will die," Asceres said. "I doubt that two will reach the island."

Atai pulled the binoculars from his hand. "What do you know of the sea, jungle ranger?" he said.

"Will you swim untouched through the reefs?" Asceres said. "Will you slip unseen under the lights of every continental ship and plane? Will the coming storm veer around you or open perfect lane? Will the ocean warm for you and the sun wait patiently until you reach dry ground?"

"We thank you, friend, for your guidance through the mountains," Atai said. "But now we will return to our world. And you to yours."

While the ranger pleaded with the refugees to leave the coast and join him in the mother's city, Dyraveen stepped between them. He took the binoculars into hand, studied the island, the coast, the coming storm. Dyraveen pulled the ranger away. "Let the refugees go," he said. "They have more courage than you or I will ever know."

Before the Andarans left for the island, Ibyr and Vanon gave them every scrap of food in their packs.

When they had gone, Asceres turned on Dyraveen. "You know that they will die," the ranger said. "You know that they are doomed."

"The refugees were doomed from war's first bomb," Dyraveen said.

The four travelers sucked on the last of their red leaves and watched the refugees weave their way through the high-bouldered hills. The refugees disappeared in the dark crags leading onto the peninsula.

Gusting winds pelted the travelers with gritty sand, sharp bits of rock, and thick drops of rain.

Surging waves broke white against the rocks of the coast, topping the Pheran dikes.

Lightning flashed over the sea.

The fishing boats pulled their nets and traps and headed full speed for Acrois.

The carriers followed close behind, their planes and copters cruising parallel along the coast.

Ibyr and Vanon staked shielding tarps in a narrow cleft of the hillside. They huddled together and shouted for the men to join them.

Dyraveen started toward the cleft but stopped at the cry of the ranger.

"There," Asceres said, raising his arm. "They have entered the water."

Dyraveen fought the wind to stand at Asceres' side. He leaned into the ranger, wrapped a bracing arm across his shoulders, and listened with closed eyes.

"They struggle against the wind and the waves," Asceres said. "They strive forward, forward, forward. They are fewer now."

A sudden gust swept the rock ledge, buckled and spun them, sent the binoculars from the ranger's hand.

Asceres crawled to retrieve, wiped the lenses, and took a final look to sea. "A tall man stands on island shore," he said. "He waves and screams for those still crossing. He wades to his neck and stretches his arm."

For three full days, the travelers were pinned against the hillside by the storm, trapped inside the narrow cleft by vicious winds and relentless rain. Their tarps were ripped and shredded, their packs and blankets drenched, their clothes soaked to the skin. None could stop trembling from bitter chill and burning hunger. None could sleep a restful hour.

On the fourth day, when the dark-knotted storm clouds finally scattered, the travelers crawled out from the narrow crevice to soak up light and breathe the open air. They tried to stand on the rocky ledge, but each fell back to ground, weakened, stiff, and cramped.

On hands and knees, Old Ibyr vomited red.

Young Vanon wheezed through labored breath and coughed up green.

Pale Dyraveen lay still, sweating fevered streams.

Asceres, kneeling, swept his arm across the ledge to gather worms flooded from their holes. He chewed fiercely, swallowed quickly, spit dirt and pebbles from his teeth. The ranger drank from his canteen then struggled to his feet. He walked a slow circle, one stubborn leg, one quivering step at a time.

Asceres helped the others to their feet, held them steady through first steps.

From ledge's end the travelers surveyed the sea. A small caravan of fishing ships from Acrois headed for the peninsula. Tricopter blades spun to life on a carrier's full deck. Scouting planes passed up and down the coast.

The travelers stared at the island of the refugees, wondering, hoping.

"We must find heat and shelter while there is light," Asceres said. "One more night of freezing winds might finish us all."

"Where can we go?" Dyraveen asked.

"There is another spring at Aedor's knees," the ranger said, "with rich waters known for healing. It is a steep climb from here, a hard march even in fair weather and good health. But we would likely find other travelers there, monks and rangers of our sister tribes."

"Then we must follow the example of the refugees," Ibyr said, "who reached for thinnest hope, fearless and defiant."

The travelers wrung their clothes and climbed for the mountain king.

By late afternoon, they had covered less than half of the distance to the healing spring.

They drank and filled their canteens at a storm-flooded pool.

Dyraveen held his head under the falls, washed the white-salted grit from his face.

Ibyr and Vanon rested together under a tree, the aunt's head on niece's shoulder.

Asceres climbed high above the falls. On a twin-crested butte split like hoof, the ranger crawled through a narrow tunnel to face the mountain king. Eyes closed, hand to sky, Asceres prayed.

He scanned the feet of Aedor – deep-shadowed ravines, quake-split mounts fallen into jagged hills, skewed rock plates protruding from the ground, limestone spires rain-burned into razored curves. He looked for any sign of life, any movement, any prey that might be taken.

The ranger saw only birds in the sky, sacred and untouchable.

A pair of stone-hawks slowly ascended the mountain's lower rings of mist.

Raptor hunting packs slashed along forested strips of tree and brush.

A lone condor plunged from brightest mountain face. It passed the climbing hawks and banked toward sea. It crossed a widening column of silver-white smoke and disappeared in the blackened foothills.

Asceres traced the column of smoke down to a tiny point of orange-blue flame in the trough of a deep ravine. Landmark to landmark, he memorized the path from butte to fire. He shouted for the others.

The ailing continentals drained the last of their strength in the race against darkness. Fear of the cold night lengthened their strides. Hope of the warm fire deadened their pain. There was no continent or island, no coast or sea. Even the mountains fell away. Their whole world shrank to the single column of smoke over the ravine.

When the column dissolved into the thick shadows of dusk, they lowered their eyes to the shoulders of the tireless ranger.

When dark night swallowed the ranger, they followed the sound of his steps, the shifting tumble of rocks, the grinding of pebbles underfoot.

Staggering and stumbling, they followed Asceres until a flaming halo crowned the ranger, and a crackling fire swallowed all sound.

A young face emerged from the flames. An islander. But not Andaran. Green-inked snake scales covered his neck and forearms. Opposing serpent fangs arched from shoulder to elbow, carved by heated dagger. He was Eskallan.

Asceres raised his cane, pointed its blade toward the boy's chest.

The Eskallan studied the ranger and the sick travelers limping to his side. He dropped his scabbard and showed his empty hands. He tossed fresh branches onto the fire, dug through his pack, and offered pouches of seeds and nuts. He pointed to a spitted haunch roasting over the fire.

The ranger held the others back. He asked the boy many questions in the old Andaran tongue.

The boy, confused, said nothing.

The ranger questioned in the younger tongue.

"I come from the north," the boy answered. "I come from the libran camps."

The ranger lowered his cane.

The travelers devoured the nuts and seeds. They sat down around the fire and stared open-mouthed at the roasting haunch.

The Eskallan lifted the spit and cut thick, dripping pieces into their hands, keeping only the bone for himself. He snapped the bone, sucked the marrow.

The travelers bowed their heads and thanked him.

They asked him many questions.

But the boy lowered his hood and stared silently into the fire.

In the morning, he was gone.

On the early march to the spring, Dyraveen asked the ranger about the librans.

"Many stories have passed down from our sister tribes in the eastern jungle," Asceres said. "In the early war, a band of Pheran captives – continentals sentenced to death by the Andaran Emperor – escaped from their prison camp and fled into the swamplands. They vanished for several seasons then suddenly appeared on the Tallen River rowing wooden boats with the lost Nyavites, a tribe secluded in the marsh since ancient days. They rowed their small boats all the way to the northern coast. Then they opened their sails and entered the sea. Over many journeys they became the librans - the fools – dodgers of warships and planes, smugglers of the healing blueleaf from Eskalla, saviors to the Andarans of the northern coast battered by Pheran bombs. When the war ended, the librans built camps along the coastline where all were welcome to heal, to work, to help."

"This sounds like fantasy and dream," Dyraveen said.

"I did not see the camps myself, but I know many who did. For a time, the libran fools brought together islanders and continentals, Nyavites and Eskallans, even your Torites, your Varrans, your Tyraens."

"For a time?"

"Few travelers speak of the camps anymore. Most of the libran leaders have died or fled to other islands. The short-lived bond between the Pheran and the Andaran has been severed, the line between victor and victim restored."

A fresh rain fell midday, but the travelers had already reached the spring. They soaked in the warm and healing water, raindrops on their brows, until the sky cleared hours later.

While Asceres hunted stag and ram, the others piled branches high.

They laid a ring of stones.

They set stakes, whittled spits.

They lit the fire.

From boulder tops they scanned the rugged hills.

The ranger came first, dark hooves across his chest, horns above his head.

The Eskallan boy followed close behind, hindquarters on his shoulder, bright drops of blood streaking down his cheek.

Then others came. Barefoot scouts, scabbards dangling from their necks. Fur-clad archers. Spearmen tall and fleshless. Tatter-cloaked monks. Tribal mothers, their long hair wrapped in glowing snakeskins.

Asceres skinned and quartered the ram.

He pulled Dyraveen and the coastal women aside. "Listen well tonight but do not speak," he said. "Offer the mothers first portions."

The three continentals served the crowd of islanders.

The islanders stared at the ghost-white hair of Ibyr and Vanon. They hesitated to eat the meat cut by the hand of the small Tyraen.

"These are friends," Asceres said. "They have learned our language. They have served the great mother in Ocossae. The women are translators, volunteers, great fishers and sailors of the sea. The man, once a soldier, has atoned by a flaying even deeper than my own."

The islanders ate.

Red leaves were shared, pipes lit.

The mothers stood to speak. Each shared her fears of the growing Pheran presence in the jungle – more planes, more roads, more mines and mills. A mother whose village had been raided and burned was welcomed into the camp of another. A mother who had lost prime hunting grounds to Pheran roads was given new territory deeper in the jungle. The oldest mother offered prayer.

All the mothers sat.

Scouts of different tribes shared their reports and warned of areas dangerous for capture, trails well known to the enemy.

The tree monks promised to confront the stone monks of the mountains.

Asceres offered sanctuary in Ocossae to any in need. "At first light I will fly for home," he said. "I will share with Oduir every word spoken here tonight."

The oldest mother blessed every tribe.

Skins of melon wine were passed.

Cloaks and furs were shed, weary bodies dipped into the soothing springs.

Asceres found old Ibyr and young Vanon at the water's edge. "Come with me tomorrow," Asceres pleaded. "Return to the great mother's arms."

"We will," Ibyr said. "I am tired of wandering. I am ready for home. And rest."

Asceres found Dyraveen at the fire with the Eskallan boy. "Come with me tomorrow," Asceres said. "I will speak to Oduir for you. Her heart will have softened by now, her anger passed."

Dyraveen gripped the hand of the ranger, touched his shoulder. "No, my brother, I must journey on," he said. "We search for the first libran, the lord of the fools."

XII. CREA

Ikhil, the young Eskallan, had already traveled the entire length of the Tallen River, from the northern seashore delta to the high mountain lakes and falls. He had found no trail of Llevar anywhere on the river, no trace of the missing libran lord.

Ikhil had wandered the eastern jungle and befriended the oldest forest tribes. He had joined their scouts on survey missions, their rangers on long marches. He had hunted and foraged with the monks of canyon, stone, and tree. But no one had seen the tatter-cloaked Cerran.

"Where do we search?" Dyraveen asked.

"If he still lives, he must have returned to the swamplands," Ikhil said.

Ikhil led the way through the bog rushes, the blackpeat fen, and the mired clay.

Following the driest ground and widest view, they drove toward the north and the east. They made their best progress in the cool rise of the morning sun and the evening's slow fade. They marched in silence through the triple-mooned night. In the stifling afternoon heat, they dozed against tree trunks.

The swamplands revealed new wonders and terrors to Dyraveen. Finger-winged salamanders flew from pond to pool, catching small birds at arches' peak. Tufts of creeping reed moss surrounded and swallowed whole colonies, nests, and hives.

Pincer-tailed shadow vipers blinded grey boars to feast on tongue and colon chain.

They spotted clay-skinned hermits crawling the wild sedge for rats and locusts, and tall tribal rafters who fished only by the light of the blue and silver moons, who traveled den to den only under the green-cloaked mists of dawn.

Under hanging ivy tangles and washed-out tree roots, they hid from Pheran transport planes and prospecting tricopters.

Ikhil's frustration worsened as the days and nights passed by without any sign of Llevar.

His mood swung between aching sorrow and sullen rage, his marching pace from sprint to crawl.

He took wild and unnecessary risks: catching snakes by the hand in the tall brush, taunting razor-fanged lizards with his staff, abandoning safe ground to wade through murky waters.

Against the tree, waiting for moons' rise, Dyraveen questioned the boy, trying to understand. "Why do you search for him?" Dyraveen asked.

Ikhil told of their first meeting. "He came out of the summer's greatest storm," Ikhil said. "He floated onto the Eskallan shore in a battered and sailless boat, its mast splintered into kindling. His clothes were shredded, his skin torn raw by the wicked gusts, blistered red and white by the hot ocean sun. Where he was not blistered, he was bruised purple and black with heavy welts. Llevar lay slumped on his side, eyes closed. Only his lips moved, dry-parched and pale, mouthing a poem of Cerran tongue. We doubted that he would live through the night. But in the morning he rose before any in our village. He burned his wrecked vessel. He walked the hills of our shore and gathered blueleaf into bundles. Curious and unbelieving, we watched him pack all of our skiffs inside the cove, the bundles rising to his knees before midday. '*Sail with me,*' he called out. '*Andara groans for healing.*'"

"You followed a stranger into the sea?"

"How could we not? He had crossed the wide ocean alone and endured its cruelest storm. He had taken death deep into his bones. Yet still he burned with life."

Dyraveen asked more questions of Ikhil, but the boy fell silent, his head low, hood drawn.

Days later, they stopped together on the bank of the Tallen River, the swamplands behind them.

The Eskallan gripped the hand of the Tyraen then pointed his staff down the river, toward the sea.

"Follow the river," Ikhil said. "It will soon bend to the north in its final crook. Turn west at the seashore deltas. Follow the coast. In any libran tent, you will find friends. Search the voids of the red-iron cliffs. And if the cliffs are empty, search the open bays ringed by the branchless timber."

"And if the bays are empty?" Dyraveen asked.

"Then turn inland before the port of Letrane. Search the winding paths of the cable-vined woods."

"And if no libran remains in the woods?"

"Then all is lost."

"And you, young friend? Where do you travel?"

"To the final ground unsearched. The saltlands."

"But nothing lives in the saltlands. Not a flower grows, they say, not an insect flies."

"Yes," Ikhil said, nodding, turning. "This is my final march."

The Eskallan headed east.

He crossed a field of yellow brush and rising stone.

He climbed a flat-bouldered hilltop then disappeared down shadowed ridge.

Dyraveen walked to the Tallen.

He plunged into the cool river, felt the water rinse scales of sweat from his back, soften his hard-crusted hair.

On shore, he filled his waterskins.

He fished and set a fire.

Deep in the night, sleepless, he left his camp to follow the trail of Ikhil.

His tracks passed up and down the rocky hills beneath the coast. The young boy had chosen the hardest climb, summit to summit, rather than the longer, gentler weave between slopes. He had rested only once against a crumbling butte.

Dyraveen followed the trail through night and day and night, again.

As the morning sun rose on the second day, the trail veered from summit climb toward lower ground. The distance between steps lengthened. The walking stride stretched suddenly into a ground-closing charge.

Large pawprints fled down the hillside, the dry-pebbled ground raked by arcs of claw.

In a sage clearing, the feet and paws circled, dug, slid, tore – a scene of chaotic grappling recorded in the sand.

Bright drops of blood spotted the pale green brush.

Dyraveen, staff raised, knife drawn, followed both blood-streaked trails from the clearing. He found their end in cavern mouth.

Ikhil lay back against the stone wall, his tattooed arm and shoulder shredded raw, his forehead slashed and opened, blood dribbling down, pooling in the sockets of his eyes.

A silver-crowned cougar lay with her back to him, her neck fur wet, a dark puddle bent to the curve of her tail.

"Why?" Dyraveen said. He knelt, rinsed, stitched, and bandaged. "There is easier prey, my friend."

"I did not kill from hunger," Ikhil said. He wiped the blood from his eyes, blinked.

"What then? Do you take life to blunt the sharp edge of death? Do you rage at the lord who left you behind?"

"Dragon-chest, you know nothing of my lord. And it was your people, Pheran, who flooded our lands with death."

Dyraveen walked to the cougar. He felt the dark-wetted fur of her throat. He touched her silver crown from skull to spine. He covered chipped fangs by torn flap of cheek.

Against her belly, Dyraveen saw two cubs suckling at empty teats.

He took one of the cubs into his arms. He placed the other in the lap of Ikhil.

"My friend, what do we have but the breath inside us?" Dyraveen said. "I have nowhere left to run, no people, no home. I carry nothing with me but the memory of my crimes. And the only light in my world - my thin and fading hope - is your story of a man who crossed the sea alone, who loved enemies and strangers."

They found one set of bare footprints heading into the saltlands. None leaving.

They stood at the great rift.

A steep slope descended from the mainland plate down to the saltland shelf.

To the edge of the sky stretched the saltlands - an endless duned plane of black dust and pale crystal, ceaselessly stirred by winds from the sea, a thousand times flooded in aeons past.

Dyraveen and Ikhil gave the last of their water to the cubs, tucked them to chest, and climbed down the slope.

By their third step in the windblown sand, the trail of the lone traveler was lost, a crumbling print of heel their final sign.

The two seekers shared a glance, breathed deeply, then entered the saltlands.

They followed the daylit shell of the emerald moon.

They walked the valleys between salt dunes. They avoided the foot-swallowing hillsides, clung to the dark, chewed rock of lowest ground.

The cubs cried until freed to run. They wove between legs, chased, and tumbled.

The emerald moon slipped under the blue horizon.

Spent, the cubs slept inside carriers' shirts.

An ocean breeze whipped into gale. The sky darkened with black dust. The crystal dunes churned. Peak turned to valley, valley to peak.

The seekers wandered blind. They staggered, feet wide, arms stretched, screaming themselves hoarse to stay near.

When night fell, the wind slowed.

Then died.

A wall of stone faced them – the edge of the rift.

Dyraveen sat down with his back to the wall. He rested his head against the hard stone, rubbed the crown of the pup at his chest, soft silver in the moonlight. The cub moaned through faint breath, eyes closed in dream.

Ikhil dropped his cub to the sand and turned from the wall. He ripped the snake-eye gemstone from his neck. He tore his hided vest into rags. He cried into the wasteland that had repelled them.

"Rest a moment," Dyraveen said. "Pray. Call on the name of Llevar. We have nothing else."

Ikhil ran into the crystal dunes.

Dyraveen took the dropped cub by the neck. He cradled brother and sister together in his arms. He joined them in dream.

Dyraveen woke on his feet, marching, marching, the sea moon towering high above, the night sky fathomless with starblue waters.

The hungry cubs wailed against his chest.

Dyraveen ran.

The wasteland stirred with breeze.

Then gusts.

Then gale.

He rested at the sunlit rift wall, his back to the warm stone.

Brother clawed into his chest. Sister bit into his scars.

Dyraveen ran into the bright sands.

Again, the wind turned back.

With a hand to the cool stone wall, he prayed.

He walked into the darkened wasteland, the cubs quiet at his chest.

Again, the wind rose.

Finished, Dyraveen lay in the sand, his eyes to the sky, the cubs cold against his ribs, the red sun blistering.

Strong hands lifted.

He rode the air above the moonlit sand.

"Four times you were warned by the wind," his carrier said, "four times saved."

Dyraveen felt for his cubs. They were gone.

"This is not your place," the carrier said. "This is not your time."

Against the rift wall, he was placed.

A curled horn of pearl was pressed to his lips.

"Drink," the carrier said.

Dyraveen sipped. He took the horn into his hands, raised it high, swallowed deep.

"Wash yourself," the carrier said. "The horn will not run dry."

Dyraveen poured water through his hair, over his face, down his back and chest. He drank again. He washed again. He drank and washed. The eyes of Dyraveen sharpened. He stared at the giant above him.

Taller than any Myshenite or Artauk, the carrier blocked the moons of the night sky, his shadow cavernous and deep. The skin of his bare cheek, caught in the emerald light, showed both the strong, flushed blood of the newborn and the pale, cragged lines of the elder. His eye, struck by silver, glistened like white lightning over glass-calm lake. His slightest shifts of frame and muscle turned with the quiet power of storming ocean wave.

The giant reached down with one hand open. The snow-crowned cubs lay still upon his stony palm, their fur sunken and dry, bones sharp, eyes hollow.

"Pour over them," the carrier said. "They will awaken."

Dyraveen held up the horn. He soaked the cubs until milk-crystal water dripped through the giant's fingers. The fur of the cubs thickened and filled. On their backs they squirmed and pawed at the air. Rolling, they lapped from the white pools of the palm. The brother cub leapt to Dyraveen's shoulder, the sister to his feet.

"Now you must leave," the giant said. "The moons will soon drain."

"The Eskallan, my friend," Dyraveen said. "Where is Ikhil?"

"I saw him fall to the salt," the giant said. "He did not rise."

"Please let me go to Ikhil. I will heal him with this water."

The long face of the giant hardened. "No," the giant said. "He died with rage. He did not pray like you."

"But he is young, very young."

"There is no time. Obdiel gathers the wind as we speak. The hour of Llevar has come."

The giant took the cubs into his left hand, Dyraveen into his right. He climbed the rift wall in three lunging strides and placed them on the mainland plate.

The amber-eyed cubs sat down on the ledge. They stared into the distant mountains. Deepest memories stirred of cavern, sage, and mother. They rushed into the hills together. They chased and fled, fled and chased.

Dyraveen turned back for the saltlands, a foot down the slope. "If you will not save my friend," he shouted at the giant, arms raised, "I will."

The giant blocked the ledge. "It cannot be done," he said. "Water will not raise a pheran."

"He left his homeland to follow Llevar. He searched to the end of his flesh."

"Then know that Ikhil will be called again one day. But not in this land."

Dyraveen sat down on the ledge. He stared beyond the giant into the sea of dead crystal.

The giant descended the rift. From saltland floor he shouted a final warning: "Skinned one, do not return to the wasteland this long night. What you see will blind your eyes. What you hear will deafen."

The lone giant entered the dunes with long and hurried stride.

He halted at the sight of his brethren - a ring of fellow titans spreading outward from the wasteland heart. He joined their silent march to the saltland edge.

The line of giants stretched thin along the great rift. Each titan took his position along the wall, still as statue, a muted sentry.

Then the land paled.

Stars dimmed. Stars hollowed.

The emerald moon shriveled into a sliver of grey.

The silver moon darkened into an ashen husk.

The sea moon withered dead and dry.

A speck of fire flickered deep in the wasteland. Wind rushed upward from the ground. Streams of crystal flooded the sky.

The speck burned brighter, swaying free like candle's flame. Its red glow cast a titan's shadow long across the land. The arms of Obdiel wove black through the fiery air. He tamed the wild winds, each broken, held, and released by his mighty hand.

A cloud of crystal spun, fed by Obdiel, turned by slashing gusts of fire.

The cloud swelled with black dust, thickened with rains of salt, rushed in veering spiral for the saltlands' edge.

The titans moved. They knelt with anguished grimace. Their outstretched arms drew deep from the lowest vaults of air. With cry and fury, they raised the land to sky. Their knees buckled. Their shoulders trembled under the great weight.

The sands of the titans were swept into the turning cloud of Obdiel.

Their burden briefly lifted, the giants wove winds together like the cords of a rope. They hurled the winds upward. The unraveling gusts scorched the night air and sent sanded waves deep into the sky.

The wasteland vanished behind a clouded wall of dust and crystal.

The giants slowed in their weaving.

The wall crept by in languid turn.

With closed eyes, heads low, the titans worked long breezes.

The great cloud settled just above their shoulders.

Then the beasts of other worlds came to the edge of the rift, fearful creatures from ages older than the saltland flooding. From his knees, Dyraveen watched their slow-falling breath of misted ice, the rise and wander of scalding smoke. He saw spurred wings, spiked tails, razor-ribbed tusks, blood-wetted snouts, scales that glowed like embered coal, flanks of armor pierced and battered, horned crowns chipped and gangrene. He heard screeches and howls, bloodthirsty snarling, the grinding of jaws, the legion striking of hoof upon stone, the pleading wail of the long ravenous.

The beasts rushed over Dyraveen and sped down the steep-sloped rift.

As the last of the creatures neared, Dyraveen rose quickly, gripped its wing, and jumped across its back.

The creature reared, turned back its head, and snapped with bladed beak.

Dyraveen dug his fingers into its ear and ripped its head around.

The creature let its rider stay.

With one snap of its wings, they flew through the white crystal haze of the cloud's underbelly.

The sand-stripped ground passed beneath them, a dark bedrock bitten into jagged pocks and disk-shaped pores by ages' slow corrosion.

They overtook the beasts of land.

They chased the other fliers.

A dragon of mirrored scales led all creatures. With a thunderous crack of its tail, the dragon ended all jostling and race behind it.

The lesser flying beasts fell back and settled in its wake.

Into the wasteland they followed, their eyes on the reflected crystal of the dragon's back, the fluid silver of its flank.

A fiery light spread on the dragon's breast.

The sword of Obdiel.

The dragon flinched, a shiver through the tail, a backstroke of wing.

Then, with a piercing cry, the dragon plunged.

The titan braced, words of prayer pouring from his mouth. The blade of Obdiel waited still in the saltland air, red flames flowing hilt to tip.

The dragon raised talon and cracked tail.

But in the final breath before their clash, the dragon turned, the titan's eyes too sure.

The dragon shrieked as it passed. The silver eyes of the dragon locked on the ground behind the titan, narrowing over the small and tatter-cloaked figure stretched upon the stone.

The titan shielded Llevar. Then drove the dragon toward the sea.

The mirrored dragon landed on distant plain - a speck of reflected fire on the black bedrock.

Behind, the beasts of land caught up to the beasts of air.

The massive horde crept forward, their fearful eyes following the titan's burning blade.

The beasts halted when Obdiel ended his pursuit of the dragon. Holding their line, they growled through dripping fangs. They glared at the giant's back through a thickening rain of salt and dust.

But Obdiel did not turn back to save Llevar. He wove his blade through the air in wide, swirling arcs to summon strongest winds. With a tortured cry he released his gusts into the sky and raised the sinking cloud.

The crystal rain lifted.

The horde advanced, their tender prey exposed.

The winged fell first upon Llevar. Their talons stripped his ragged cloak and opened the bare skin of his back. In frenzied circle, they pecked out bites of flesh. With twist and jerk of beak, they pulled long strips.

The beasts of land crashed into the winged circle with ravenous fury. Heavy antlers swept aside the fliers; powerful tusks gored any slow to retreat. The landed beasts poured by droves into the opened space.

Lanced horns pierced the sides of the Cerran.

Sharp hooves trampled.

Crushing fangs snapped ribs, caved skull, pulled limbs from torso.

The horde separated into smaller circles as the fiercest beasts claimed choicest pieces.

The lesser beasts lapped from shallow pools, licked drops from the stone, sucked on dampened bits of hair and cloak.

Dyraveen had not witnessed the slaughter from a distance. When his winged beast had swooped to strip the last cloak tatter, Dyraveen had dropped down close enough to touch Llevar. He had seen the lean-muscled back slashed by many talons. He had seen scars of knife and branding iron shredded into pulp - old wounds hidden by the new. When his beast had peeled off a strip of scalp, he had seen the white-blue edge of skull. Tossed from the back of his beast, he had watched the horns pierce and the hooves trample. He had slipped on the slick-blooded rock, seen an arm pulled from socket, a foot swallowed whole. He had crawled on his belly to escape the gore. Even clear of the fray, he could not look away from the work of the horde. He gazed on as the beasts finished each bite of flesh, every shard of bone.

The beasts grew restless after the last drops of blood had been licked from the stone. They caught the scent of Dyraveen. They spotted him just outside their circle. The landed beasts crept toward him. The winged beasts took to air.

Still paralyzed by shock and fear, Dyraveen watched the horde's approach, his knives undrawn, hands trembling at his sides.

A wave of heat struck his back.

Light flared red around him.

The hand of the titan wrapped around Dyraveen, lifted him easily from the ground.

"Why are you here, skinned one?" Obdiel said, his voice like highest waters fallen deep. "Were you not warned?"

Obdiel rushed into the horde of beasts approaching. His sword slashed high and low, each stroke trailed by blazing fire.

Dyraveen covered his face from the light and the heat.

He heard the horde fall back from the titan's blade, beasts trampled, a fleeing stampede toward the sea.

Uncovering his eyes, Dyraveen watched the last beast vanish under a white crystal rain.

The titan sheathed his sword.

Obdiel turned to speak, but his head whipped suddenly away. He dropped to one knee. He released Dyraveen. A weakened hand raised his sword halfway from its sheath.

When the head of Obdiel turned, Dyraveen saw deep, clawed gashes across the giant's face. He saw a tail's wicked slice across his neck.

The dragon cried in the sky, a taunting laugh.

The dragon circled, lower, lower.

They were saved by the sinking cloud, hidden by the downpour of salt and dust.

Dyraveen knelt at the giant's lips.

"The rift," Obdiel said in thin whisper. "The titans. Bring."

Dyraveen ran from the saltland heart. This time he was carried by the wind, not repelled. His feet scarcely touched the ground. The thick-dusted air parted before him.

At the rift, he faced the line of giants, still weaving breezes.

"The dragon struck," he screamed. "Obdiel fell."

The titans charged as one toward the sea.

Dyraveen, breathless, turned.

He followed in a giant's path, twenty strides to one.

But the falling sands soon blinded. His feet sunk deep. And gales, fiercely risen, resisted every step.

Dyraveen crawled.

Dyraveen watched the titans from afar.

Their circle slowly shrank as one by one they knelt alongside Obdiel and bade farewell - a parting touch of the shoulder, a bow of the head, a kiss.

Each titan walked alone toward the sea, head hung low in shadow.

The last giant of the circle received the blade of Obdiel and long instruction. The succeeding titan walked away from the sea. He walked straight to Dyraveen atop the distant dune. He looked down with eyes of burning sunset, the sword of Obdiel held tightly to his chest.

"You will go to him now," the successor said. "Obdiel has asked to spend his final hours with you."

"I deserve punishment, not honor," Dyraveen said. "Obdiel would live if I had heeded warning."

"Yes, skinned one, he would live if not for you."

Dyraveen crossed the dunes under stars still dim, moons still pale and ashen.

He circled behind Obdiel. He approached slowly to spy the wounds of the seated giant. Grey-oiled blood fell in thick drops from his forehead to his knee. Black blood flowed in steady stream from the deep slash of his neck, thickened like sap down his chest, clotted like rust over his belly.

Dyraveen dropped to his knees when the head of the titan turned. He pressed his face into the sand when the weak, slitted eyes of the titan fell upon him.

"Get up," Obdiel said. "Am I the Eternal?"

Dyraveen stood to face the giant. The two creatures stared long at one another. Dyraveen breathed in tiny gusts, Obdiel in thinning breeze.

"Could water heal?" Dyraveen said, his words outpouring. "Could prayer and pleading?"

"The First has spoken," Obdiel said. "I will die in these sands."

"Speak again to your god, great titan. Let my life be traded for your own."

"You know nothing of God, skinned one. You understand neither life nor death."

Dyraveen sat down at the foot of the giant. "Then teach me, I beg," Dyraveen said, eyes low. "Explain to me what I have seen here. Tell me of your people."

The giant drew long breath from the open sky.

"The titans are servants of the Ever-Reaching," Obdiel said. "We were saved from a world of crumbling moons and melting rains, our home a wind-lashed, pitted mountain with needled spires climbing far beyond the clouds. Pulled from our dying world, we vowed to serve the Highest wherever sent, whatever commanded. We were creators in some worlds, destroyers in others. We learned from the oldest angels of first paradise. We battled the demons of first rebellion. We were given great weapons, powers, and gifts. But never immortality. We were punished and rewarded, tested and rebuked. Some died in deserts, forests, caverns, seas. Some streaked between the stars. Task by task, our rank has dwindled."

"And in the saltlands?"

"We were to block by crystal clouds the suffering of Llevar. Your world was not to see."

"Why the suffering of Llevar? Why the loosing of the demon horde?"

"Those were beasts, not demons, animal creatures the same as you or I. They were gathered from many ages and many worlds. They were caged and starved by the titans, surrendered to the dragon by Lord's command."

"The dragon is more than beast?"

"I have fought the dragon on a thousand fields. Many blows we have traded, many wounds we have carved. Aeon after aeon, I have waited for the perfect moment, for the chance to kill, at last. I have long prayed, skinned one. And I have long pleaded. But the Merciful has never freed my hand or the killing stroke revealed. And now I will die. And the dragon live on." The titan closed his eyes and drew hard breath. His lips moved in silence. He raised his head. "Blind, so blind," the titan said. "His is the greater work. Llevar accepted the full suffering of the creature — its burning thirst and hunger, its smallness, loneliness, and pain. More than that, he bore the sharp-toothed fury of the hunter, the helpless agony of prey; he traded purest light of heaven to see this hideous inversion of first intent; he stretched himself bare upon the cold and savage law of the wilderness condemning all creation to endless civil war. Llevar ended. Llevar bridged. Llevar freed."

"But he is dead."

"The spirit bursts the skin."

"And you are dying."

"I will not fall beyond the blooded love of God. His love like fire spans to every world, merges every age. Her love unending shatters cage and opens grave."

"How can I believe in a god I saw trampled, torn, and chewed?"

"When the watching stars breathe anew; when the moons flush and burn with many colors; when order breaks and time twists strangely – these are signs of early stirring. Do not be afraid, my friend. You already trespass beyond any before you."

The titan drifted in mind. His eyes moved throughout the empty skies. He whispered poetry of the wind-lashed mountain, titans' oldest song. A hand to his neck, a fist on the ground, he called out to Father, Mother, Daughter, Son.

When Obdiel fell back, the wasteland trembled.

Dyraveen climbed. He closed the mouth and eyes. He slept against the giant's shoulder.

The beasts plodded across the wasteland. Their hooves dragged slowly through the sand. Their horns and tusks sagged low. Weary flying beasts stumbled awkwardly afoot. The land beasts rested long between each stride, their hides cracked and bleeding from the salted winds. Sharp bones pressed under their fur half-shed.

With his heel Dyraveen dug a shallow trench around the fallen titan. He untied the scabbards from his neck and cast his knives aside.

He knelt before the trench.

"Let the creatures' thirst be quenched," Dyraveen prayed.

The beasts came near.

Dyraveen reached into the trench. A shivering chill traveled through his arms. The salt melted clear under his hands. Gentle waves flowed outward from his touch. Prismed waters coursed the trench, filled the ring like trough. The animals drank long and deep, the level never falling.

"God, my God," Dyraveen prayed, "free the beasts from chain of hunger."

The trench water thickened into a golden syrup. From specks of bubble in the honeyed current, crystal fibers radiated and branched like snowflakes forming. The animals ate.

"Loving God," Dyraveen said, "open the eyes of the beasts. Let them see beyond the moment. Deepen their memory. Loosen their tongues. Let every ancestor race through their blood. Let ancient dreaming pour into their future. Let hope burn wild."

Weakened by his own hunger, Dyraveen ate of the crystalled honey.

Dyraveen walked the trench.

Around the circle, the winged beasts cried out to one another. Their first cries rang out harsh and shrill, short bursts of single-noted squawking. But the fliers soon drew from deeper vaults of wind. Their voices stretched and softened into widely varied pitch. Their words flowed with nuanced cadence, with subtle emphasis and pause, with personality and humor.

The winged beasts took to air. Flying high in spiral flock, they called out into the deepest reaches of the night sky. Answered by an unseen host, they climbed beyond the moons.

A hard rain fell from the empty sky, a rain of seeds not water, dampened grains pale grey.

The seeds blanketed the wasteland.

Slender stalks of bone sprouted from the ground like fields of wild rye.

A viscous, blue marrow overflowed from the hollow of the stalks, dribbled down the sides, fueled the rapid growth.

The stalks grew into shoots and saplings, thickened into noded culm.

The bone trunks curved and twisted as they climbed, intertwined like ivy.

The beasts of the land stomped the twisting trees that pressed nearer and nearer. With eyes of fear and wonder, the beasts retreated behind the trenched ring. Outside the ring, the grey forest climbed above their tallest.

Blue marrow seeped through the nodes, congealed a glassy violet.

Corals green and amber multiplied in the narrow voids between the bone trees.

Dyraveen turned from the forest to see that no grains had sprouted within his circle. The seeds fallen upon the ground had hardened into a plane of smooth black pearl. Over the fallen titan, a veil of shimmering quartz now lay, its threads as thick as chains.

The beasts reared and bellowed.

Again, the waters changed, this time gold to silver. The surface of the waters pulled tight. The current accelerated under cancelling mists of frost and steam. A river of mercury overflowed its banks.

Cautiously, the beasts of land dipped tusk and horn into the silver. Upon first touch the silver set and hardened like steel. The beasts stepped into the river to dip talons, claws, and hooves. They sprung from the river to batter the trees. Bone nodes shattered upon collision. Violet glass flew in sharded spray. Tangled clusters of trees crashed to the ground. Finally sated of hunger and thirst, eager to be free, the wild beasts attacked their skeletal cage. They carved lanes through the forest. They cleared fields, deepened valleys, rounded hillsides.

Dyraveen uncovered his ears as the loud cracking of bone receded over the hills. In the wake of the beasts, he watched the quiet work of the soft-tissued corals. Amber coral spread among the lower layers, dissolved bone trunks and violet shards, dried and hardened when none remained. Green coral bonded with the amber, swallowed the splintered bones of upper layer, formed mosses, ferns, and grass.

"They have sculpted their own land," Dyraveen said with a smile.

The beasts grazed.

They called out to one another across the greening hills. From self-assertive bellow, their voices wandered over many timbres, each sound tested, held, and savored by long breath. The beasts blended and layered their calls. They echoed neighbor's cry. They imitated and adapted. Each shaped by new creation the form of rich, collective song.

Dense winged droves fell from the sky to join the beasts of land.

Together they sculpted, fed, and sang.

Dyraveen dozed to their voices, slept within their song.

In dream, he understood their newborn language. He heard their stories of ancestor and origin. He saw the many worlds from which they came.

The land was bare and dark around him. The grasses had been pulled by root, the sands by wind far blown. No living creature walked or flew.

The black rock below him mirrored the starless sky above.

Two moons – emerald and silver – had already died.

And the moon of sea was dying.

It bled into its center, pale blue sands pulled from opposing crescents.

The crescents turned.

The crescents thinned.

Dyraveen called out into the blackening sky. "Let the darkness be my home," he shouted. "But call the titan to your side."

The last glimmer of the crescents lit the titan's empty bed, the veil of white quartz flat upon black pearl.

The darkness settled deep around him.

Achlora novol. The living death. He was again blinded by the darkness, again hungry, thirsty, weary, scared. Would he live by worms again? by the lick of dampened stone? Would he lie in his own filth again, waiting for some miracle of flood?

In the long, moonless night, he had lost his bearings, forgotten the direction of the rift and the sea.

He could exhaust himself in aimless running.

He could lie upon the rock, conserving strength but stoking hunger.

Or he could walk to stretch his time, to quiet the cry of his flesh.

Dyraveen shed his boots long worn, his shriveled waterskins, his shirt more holes than cloth.

He walked through the wasteland once more.

The eyes of Dyraveen searched high and low, straining, craving. But he could not find a single ray of light, a change of hue, a shadow's promise.

He closed his eyes.

He listened.

At first, he heard only the soft touch of his bare feet upon the stone.

But his ears slowly sharpened. He heard his own breath like the rushing of wind. He heard the grinding of his knees, little bones creaking in his toes. He heard pebbles kicked ahead, two bounces, three, sometimes four.

He felt soft, curling breezes work through his beard. Under his feet, he felt grains of sand, hairs of beast, flecks of bone, powdered clod.

Dyraveen prayed.

"I thank you, God, for the freedom to walk," he said. "Even should I perish in this endless wasteland; it is better than a suffocating tomb of stone."

As he marched on, Dyraveen pondered all that he had seen in the wasteland...

The sudden rising gales that had four times refused him.

The titan who had carried him under the red-blister sun.

The paling of the moons and the stars.

The crystal clouds raised by the titans and cast into the sky.

The slaughter of Llevar.

The wounding of Obdiel and his final hours.

The honeyed feeding of the beasts and the violent carving of their land.

"I have seen unbearable terrors and wonders that none will believe," Dyraveen said. "But all is loss if Llevar yet hides his face from me."

Dyraveen marched until his back seized with cramps and his shoulders sagged low.

"All will be loss."

He trembled weakly through his arms and legs.

He stumbled side to side.

"Llevar, Llevar."

He dropped to one knee. Again. Again.

"Lord, let me live to witness your fiery rising, your thunderous return."

Dyraveen felt the brief glide of a toe. A small drop of water on the dry rock. The pressed drop spread.

He lengthened his stride. Doubled his pace.

He felt more drops under his feet.

Then puddles.

Then pools.

Dyraveen ran to return to dry ground, but the waters climbed everywhere that he stepped.

He waded until the waters rose above his neck.

He swam until his arms gave out, until his legs lost all feeling. Dyraveen floated.

The waters beneath him deepened, chilled.

He shivered in the cold sea.

"Rise, Lord, rise."

A warm current brushed his back. A crisp breeze dried the skin of his face.

The sea stirred to life.

Her waters swelled and broke.

Her powerful waves lifted and drove him.

Sharp crosswinds turned him at the crest of each wave, whistled over him on waves' descent.

Dyraveen struck something hard. He pushed against it with his legs, but the waters spun him around. He landed on top. It was solid like wood, round and thick like the trunk of a young tree. But he felt a gentle bend in its arch. On its surface he felt no bark or culm, instead smooth bone and withered sinew.

Each rising wave lifted him high above the sea. He wrapped himself around the huge bone, locking hands to keep from falling. At each wave's trough, he held his breath as the bone crashed beneath the water.

The wind slowly shifted, turning crosswind to headwind, calming the waves of the sea.

The arched bone settled into a gentle bobbing, dipping only his feet underwater.

Dyraveen rested, caught his breath, braced himself for another change of wind or lurching wave.

But the sea calmed.

Waves flattened.

Breezes ceased.

Then a streak of blue fire suddenly flared.

The long-tailed light climbed from lowest horizon to highest sky.

The light plunged like meteor into the sea.

Dyraveen turned away from the light; even its watered reflection blinded and stung.

He heard something approach over the still sea, water dripping loudly with each step.

The blinding fire transformed.

Dyraveen slowly opened his eyes.

The world was now lit blue and white - the afterglow of lightning.

Dyraveen saw that the bone he clung to was only one of many, a single rib of a giant cage. Above him, sunken patches of mirrored scales draped a long, curved spine.

A voice like mount-rending quake called out,

Are you the skinned one?

"Yes, I am Dyraveen of Phera," he answered. "Who are you?"

A feminine figure moved over the waters, even larger than a titan, a mix of beast and angel, her four paws unsinking, her four wings gilled and feathered, her forearms gauntleted with blazing ice-blue sapphire, her lean flanks alive and turning with the crater seas of many moons.

I am Crea, a servant of the Changing and Unchanged. I am a keeper of winds, a visitor of dreams, a mother of seven moons, a friend to Daavo, Tsiol, and Odyr.

Dyraveen looked away from her dark, unbounded eyes. His chest opened to a rich and fertile air. "Are you the slayer of the dragon?" he asked.

With a flick of her sapphire wrists, Crea snapped the dragon's neck. She tossed aside the spine. She lifted Dyraveen into the skull through empty socket.

The mirrored dragon? No, my friend. The old shadow starved himself. He hid from the Mother's face in lowest abyss. He wasted away to scale and bone, spurning Father's open hand. The titans hurled his body here.

"I saw the wounding of Obdiel, the greatest titan," Dyraveen said. "I stayed at his side through his final hours."

Yes, I was told.

Dyraveen watched the dragon's tail sink beneath the water, a single ripple sent. "The titan died to save me," Dyraveen whispered low.

As you will live and die to save many others. This is the passing of love. This is the price.

"But my debt is too great. It crushes. It buries."

Raise your head, little Dyraveen. From the fields of Heaven, I was sent to you. I am to carry you to the hanging lakes. Through the bridging, black waters, I am to show you many worlds, barren and fruitful, fallen and risen.

By two-thumbed paw, Crea raised the dragon's skull close to her dark eyes.

Leave this skull in flight and you will die, my friend.

Crea tied the skull around her neck by silver chain.

Then leaped.

Then flew.

Wind roared through the dragon's teeth and drove Dyraveen deep inside the skull. He hid himself in the cavity of the ear, still wet with rotting flesh. Through eye's open socket, he peered into the passing skies.

With a few strokes of wing, they entered a grey haze smelling of iron forge and smoldered fire. They climbed through streaming trails of wispy vapor – azure, bronze, ochre. The steamed breath of Crea blasted counter to the streams, the white spray flaring quickly, whipping backward.

The grey haze blackened. Bright, olivine eyes coursed by. With each wing-stroke, the glimmering corona blurred to swath of emerald and gold. Silver-flamed burrs sparked from the eyes' trailing shadows, spiraled quickly to their death. Inside opalescent nebula, smaller plumes of violet and pink reverse-imploded from billowed cloud to slender blade.

Crea groaned from her labor. Rivers of sweat darkened the fur of her neck.

The sky thickened with crimson dust. A gritty rain pelted the dragon's skull. With gust upon gust, the rain grinded the bone bare and stripped the last patches of scale and flesh. Dyraveen turned his back to the sharp, stinging dust, climbed from the open ear, and conformed himself to the cheekbone's inner curve.

Pocketed voids slashed black through the crimson haze like wounds inverted.

The dark voids widened. The red haze thinned and cleared. A last tail lashed against the dragon's skull, clung to the dampened fur of Crea's neck.

The sky emptied of all light. Even the ice-blue glow of Crea dimmed into a weakened grey.

Then, suddenly, they broke through into a windless, soundless space.

Crea folded her wings, stretched her paws.

The air around them crackled wild. Silver currents arced and raced.

Crea prayed by muted cry.

The currents paled to blue, bent themselves to revolution.

A sphere surrounded.

Dyraveen watched the silver chain go slack; serpentine waves pulsed through the links with each beat of Crea's heart.

The pulsing slowed.

Crea closed her eyes.

The skull of the dragon slowly turned. The jaw slipped open. Through rings of shattered teeth, Dyraveen watched the sphere of blue light tighten, shrink, collapse.

White-blue currents forked across the brow of Crea, writhed jagged down her spine.

Crea mouthed a prayer. Her eyes opened. She twisted and quivered through her frame like a hound shaking water. The currents fell away, replaced by a softer, brighter light.

Dyraveen crawled to the dragon's eye.

Around them spun a vast filament web, glistening at bright junctions, dim through slender-threaded branch. The filament glowed with the same blazing sapphire as Crea's gauntlets; its color shifted like the mooned seas of her flanks.

The Blackstrom Hollow - the great lobe borne by titans' rage, time enchained, and fire's seed turned out.

Dyraveen pulled himself through the dragon's eye, his shoulders beyond the skull, his legs below.

Open-mouthed, he gazed across the vast web. His wild eyes probed to the depths where myriad thread melted into white-rain halo.

"It has no end," he said. "The web goes on forever."

Restrain your wanting eyes.

Dyraveen lowered himself into the safety of the inner skull.

"This is the universe," he cried out, already climbing. "This is all."

This is part.

"Impossible," Dyraveen said, an arm and shoulder through. "What can be added to the infinite?"

The Blackstrom is one lobe of many.

"You have seen the others?" Dyraveen said, his waist above the skull.

No, I am bounded by the Hollow. But the Unbounded sometimes stumbles - a story goes too far; names and places slip; precious hints beam bright.

Crea dipped her wings sharply.

Dyraveen flew back inside the skull.

"The Almighty stumbles," Dyraveen said, crawling high again, "the infinite multiplies – this is a dizzying madness."

Should God diminish? Or your mind stretch?

"Closer, closer," Dyraveen said. "The specks of silver, blue, and gold bloom to brilliant clouds. The clouds turn with majesty and power. It is a chaos reined, a birthing fire, an unbroken glory. Take me to the heart, my friend. Show me every light of every thread."

The rider would kill his ride. My friend, the Hollow cannot be spanned by flight of demon, beast, or angel; in a thousand lives, I could not travel half its width. But the Mystery hung dark waters in the void, to bridge from world to world.

Crea veered from the dazzling lights of the web toward darkest void.

Dyraveen saw that the void was not empty. Dark waters trembled like desert's heat upon horizon, a black-green oil throbbing clear, a fluid skinned.

Brace yourself, pheran. Cover now or you will die. And when the water strikes, do not let your breath escape you.

Dyraveen glanced to Crea's eye.

He rushed across the skull and burrowed against the cheekbone's curve.

He listened to the whipping crack of Crea's wings, her taxed and gusting breath. She surged with ever-rising power. Faster. Faster.

Crea tucked her wings against her flanks.

The water struck like wall of stone.

Dyraveen launched across the skull; his legs whipped round; his head swung toward bone.

But the water already rushed to fill.

A wave slapped against his face. Another crashed his side. Another swallowed whole.

A half-breath of air escaped his mouth, the bubbles quickly lost.

Dyraveen pulled himself by the teeth of the dragon. He slipped into the tongue's recess, cupped his hands against the jawbone, and guarded his breath in sheltered globe.

Crea showed Dyraveen many barren worlds…

Thin-aired worlds battered by primeval shower, pale-dusted, flat, scarred by pock and crater.

Dense-clouded worlds, bright and groundless, churning with wind, seething with storm.

Rocky worlds of rugged, grey-brown mountains, scabrous ranges edged by darkened chasma.

Not a plant grew in the barren worlds. Not a bird flew.

"Life is precious," Dyraveen said. "Life is rare."

They followed Aode, an outcast moon stripped from its home by nova winds. Spinning chaotic, Aode was hurtled into the outer reaches of a cloudburst nebula, cyan and marine. Nebular tides of dust, gas, and rock scorched the surface of Aode, eroded her crust, and plowed deep furrows. A comet drawn to a bank of newborn stars in the nebula passed near to Aode. The comet's long tail lashed the moon with streams of daggered ice.

Aode had begun her journey as a smooth, near-perfect sphere, a faithful follower for aeons, locked in routine orbit. But the outcast moon speeding toward the heart of the nebula had been grinded into oblong shape, carved by gritted waves into a jagged and porous coral. The young and unscarred Aode had been lifeless. But the hard-traveled older moon pulsed with new creation. The penetrating ice of the comet's tail freed frozen gases and carbonaceous compounds long trapped beneath Aode's crust. Organic microbes spread through the deep pores and grooves of the coral. Warmed by slew of newborn stars, fed by mineral and melting ice, microbes crawled from darkness to light, transformed into lichen, algae, and fungus. Slender roots probed the surface. First shoots sprouted. Seeded spores drifted far.

But the surface heated and burned as the stars approached. The roots and sprouts retreated to the darkness. The last of the deep ice melted. Water vaporized, climbed from pores, and drifted into space – a bleeding silver trail.

"Will God intervene?"

From the beginning, the Father has guided; the Mother has held.

"How?"

The Creator sent first spark. The Kind nudged and encouraged. The Strong prodded. The great Protector shielded. The Patient waited. The Dreamer hoped. And Love, many times, carried.

"But the little moon will burn. Aode's seed will die."

You see only the approaching stars. Would you avoid all loss and pain?

"I think of Mother's grief and Father's sorrow."

Aode will live on, in this life or the greater age to come, should death be called to bridge. The Father does not abandon. The Mother does not forget. But you must understand, my friend, that the child cries out to God from both sides. The child suffering in this life screams for momentary pain to end. But the child in Heaven – lavish with sinew, radiant with scar – pleads for God to do nothing.

They passed between the landless planet, Endrel, and her swiftly revolving moon. The high-tide seas of Endrel, though lit by morning sun, revealed only soft-rippled waves and wandering mists. But as they traveled nearer to the sun, farther from the moon, the seas came alive in form and color. The low-tide waters receded to expose bright-spired forests and sprawling reefs. As Crea swooped and glided slow, the spires differentiated into vibrant swirls of yellow, red, and green; the spires were not tree or stone but colonies of sea moss slow climbing toward the sun. The reefs likewise strove for sun; but their tongued branches widened and flattened instead of climbing high. Evaporating seadrops glistened in warmed vesicles. The dead-grey branches of the reefs flushed and throbbed; the pale tongues brightened red, pink, and purple. Reef and spire basked.

"A beautiful kingdom."

The trigs have yet to feed.

The trigs emerged in legion: small shelled creatures with triangular carapace and three tentacled arms. They climbed the sea moss spires in communal rhythm of grasp and spin, their strokes of arm synchronized, their shells rotating with shared direction and speed. When the last climber reached the spire peak, the trigs stopped as one body, twined their arms together, and fed.

"The trigs rule the seas?"

The upper waters, yes. They will soon dominate the lower as well. They will learn to trap and ambush their hunters in the deep coral nooks. They will carve dens to protect their young and their old. By graft and splice, they will build the first reef islands of Endrel. They will enter their season of fire.

"A time of great growth?"

And danger. With every gift the trigs seize, they will sow another curse. When they sense the infinite stretch of time, they will twist their memory and fear the unknown future. Their higher forms of language will lead to more lying and deception. The arms that build and heal will also steal and kill.

"But the door once opened cannot be closed. These must be the growing pains of every people."

Yes, skinned one, you understand much.

"And the Mother endures our awkward stumbling. The Father forgives his crawling, babbling children."

No, my friend, you understand nothing. Your growth is God's joy. And the creature is damned by its lies, not its limits.

In the Keicen system, they traveled outward from the twin stars, beyond the twelve inner planets and their thirty moons, all lifeless.

They circled the mammoth thirteenth planet: a clouded, blue-gold giant orbited by one flat belt of rock and two smaller rings askew.

Crea hovered above the equator, a wingstroke beyond the belt's reach. Rock fragments sheared, chipped, and splintered rushed beneath them, held to arc by planet's pull. Huge boulders tumbled and spun; their valleys swept by parallax shadows of the twin starlight.

Dyraveen searched the shifting cloudbanks and wavering skin of the thirteenth planet. He spotted many moons traversing the planet's bright surface, dark flecks crawling the vaporous seas of gold and blue.

"Which moon holds life?"

None of these. We wait for Oro, the world of ice and steam, the smallest moon of all.

Dyraveen watched the curved edge of the planet where void met light in gentle turn. A lone bright speck flickered in the darkness, swung around the planet's bend, and disappeared into a lake of swirling gold.

There.

With a sudden snap of wing, Crea passed over the rocky belt. She dipped below the smaller rings then plunged toward the planet's heart.

As they neared the surface, the curved horizons of the thirteenth planet blurred into a swollen haze of grey. The gaseous seas churned with whirling green vortices, sparks of cloud-veiled lightning, and the collision of counter-spinning storms.

Brace yourself, friend.

Dyraveen stretched himself prone and gripped the dragon's teeth.

Crea sharply veered.

Dyraveen gritted his teeth as fierce inertia drove bone against bone.

The pressure lessened as Crea leveled into a gentler glide.

Dyraveen crawled forward.

He peered through the dragon's mouth.

The moon that had appeared a tiny speck when viewed from beyond the rock belt now loomed large before them.

Oro was a massive ball of fissured ice; a bloodshot eye of Varran blue and rusty vein; a chaotic terrain of jagged ridges, pitted fields, and canted striae.

"Oro is rougher than an elder's skin."

An ocean rages below, three times pressed - boiled by molten core, crushed by icy shell, racked by giant's pull. The fevered sea currents rise to soften, to melt, to separate crust by fault and chasm. Hardened by the frigid air, the ice plates grind, crack, and fracture. Oro is continually torn between thaw and freeze, scab and blister.

Crea curved her flight to the surface.

She rode the winds over a plain of blue ice.

The plain abruptly dropped into a winding rift of ruddy slush and floating bergs. The air above the watered rift crackled with frost and steam. Dark, red bubbles boiled to the surface, burst from freezing caps.

"What creatures can survive these extremes?"

Only the sails, the riders of the lava streams. But this rift is too tame for their flights.

Crea turned from the rift onto a broad field of cracked and shifting ice. She climbed and circled high above the field. Her dark eyes scanned. Her nostrils twitched and quivered.

When a red glow spread beneath the ice, Crea swooped low.

The ice cleared and thinned. Rusty waters seeped through cracks. Red fumes wafted.

But a bitter wind swept the field. The red fumes curled, shriveled, and fell like sands of blood. The rusty waters froze; cracks sealed. The ice layer hardened and thickened.

A flock of strange spinning creatures ascended from the depths with great speed and force, bright streaks of lucent silver.

The sails crashed into the ice.

The ice held.

The stunned creatures flailed at the ungiving crust with radial wings.

The sails tired. Their flailing slowed. One by one, they sank into the depths.

Crea looked away, her dark eyes narrow.

Some choose a timid path - a storm too small, a jet too weak.

Crea flew in silence across many rifts and fields, ridges and valleys. She traveled to the shadowed lands beyond the direct sunlight of the twin stars and the planet's full glow.

Crea roved the dark lands, looping pole to pole, searching for sign of fire beneath the ice.

Dyraveen, shivering from the cold air, crawled nearer to Crea, deeper inside her warm and shielding halo. He slid into the dragon's ear and burrowed against her fur. He listened to the strong throbbing of her heart, felt each breath rise and fall. Across her glowing flank, he traced the bend of the white shores, the drift of the blue-cratered seas.

Oro burns.

Dyraveen rushed to the mouth of the dragon.

The shadowed fields blushed crimson beneath them.

Fiery clouds billowed under the ice. The clouds swelled outward. The ice trembled and groaned.

Molten geysers shattered the frozen crust like thin, brittle glass. The geysers shot deep into the sky, trailed by icy shards and crystal spray.

Crea swerved between the shooting geysers, tucked her wing to miss a frost-slivered rain.

The ice beneath them boiled red with frothy plumes of ferrous lava.

The tortured air hissed and crackled.

The lava hardened into isles of rust. The blistered skin smoked in the cold air. The embers paled.

And now, the sails.

Silver light flared between the isles.

The sails burst into the sky through the low-lying mists of smoke and steam.

They dried themselves by rapid spinning, by the torsion of short, tight-coiled spines and the whirl of radial arms.

At the peak of flight, around spine's lowest bend, the wide, tendrilled arms of each sail stretched flat and fused into a common sheet, a circular cape suspended by breeze.

The sails hovered. Their shining underbellies rotated slowly, smoothly, turned by the gentle twist of higher arms unfused. Their topskins, dark with marine microbes gathered on ascent, opened to secreting ducts and crescent pores.

As the sails fed, their topskins cleared and brightened.

Sated and clean, the sails converged on the stony isles, gliding by the tilt of unfused arms and the lean of coiled spine.

The lowest sails spread themselves upon the rock.

The higher flocks descended to form protective shells above the isles. Hovering by slightest spin, they deflected cold winds from the isles and held the warmth of lower layers.

"What are they doing?"

Shielding the newborn. They will not leave the isles until each young seed has tasted the open air of sky and entered the warmer seas. The highest sails will hover in the cold air until their breath sets stubborn and their blood turns to ice. They will fall frozen into the sea before they abandon any seed of their people.

"They are a great race. I pray that they will soon enter their season of fire."

They have already passed their season of fire and climbed on to higher places.

"But they are simple creatures."

You think that the sails are mindless because you see no pheran skull? What pheran would suffer and die for the child of another? For every color that your eye can see, the sail can feel ten-thousand hues. The ridges of their skin can sense a gust of wind from ocean's heart. Could you hear the sailsongs of the deep, your dreams would burn, your spirit shed. Could you once ride the tip of molten storm, you would never leave their world.

"I judged without knowledge."

A high sail crashed into the ruddy waters.

Crea dipped low, snapped her wings, and circled the isles of the newborn.

She called out to the sails with a thunderous cry, a fearsome plea that scattered mists and stirred the waters.

The sails answered by wind softly turned, capes' gentle whirring. Their shared, unbroken breath settled the mists, calmed the waters. Their upper arms wove through the air in strengthening waves. Isle by isle, tendril by tendril, the sails harmonized their waves' rising and falling. Their deepening roar swallowed Crea's fierce cry.

The isles glistened silver – scintillating novas in a bloodred sea.

Crea turned for sky.

I am tired, my friend.

Crea glided through the deep voids with a rare snap of wing.

From the hanging waters, they emerged on a moon of stony, deep-furrowed hills and blue-crystal haze glimmering gold.

Crea lay down in a steep and shadowed ravine.

Now I will rest upon my daughter's strong shoulders. And you will travel her skin. Ponder all that you have seen, my friend. You will soon return to your own world.

Dyraveen walked.

Thirsty, he lapped from the potholes of dried streambeds.

Hungry, he chewed on stalks of tawny grass.

Dyraveen prayed.

When Dyraveen returned to the ravine, he found Crea on her side, weakly breathing.

He pushed, pulled, and wrestled the heavy chain from her neck, link by link, sweating, groaning.

Dyraveen circled the travelworn skull of the dragon. He touched its balding grooves and jagged cracks. By a few sharp strikes of boulder spall, he split the skull in two.

You will brave the harsh void unprotected?

"I lighten the burden of my friend," Dyraveen said. "I trust the Overflowing for miracle anew."

Dyraveen worked on. He shattered the halves of the skull into smaller and smaller fragments. He threw the scraps and shards down the steep ravine.

And why do you bother with the bones of the dead?

"For Obdiel, the titan."

Obdiel has climbed on. Obdiel has crossed over. The titan is free.

"I cannot forget the beast that killed him, the mirrored one circling, taunting, in the sky."

Obdiel walks with the Breath and the Fire.

"Still, I cannot forget."

You remember the blooded neck, but you forget the empty veil, white upon black, quartz upon pearl.

"I remember both, my friend. The veil sparks hope. The blood stokes rage."

For all your pain, skinned one, you have no patience. No trust of flowing time. No faith in God. You have nursed too long on sudden violence.

Dyraveen sat down on a curl of chain links near to her eye.

"Teach then, Crea. I will hear your words and I will weigh them."

Crea rolled from her side.

She stretched her long legs.

Her eyes of night looked down.

Listen well, Dyraveen. I will tell you of Daavo, Tsiol, and Odyr.

Daavo sprang from the hard ground of Adlan, a hot and rocky planet circling dangerously near to her star, a timid pup on mother's heels.

Adlan bore no life for aeons.

Her young skin festered with thick, seeping lava and blistered into half-shelled domes many times melted and re-formed by fresh outpouring. Her young skies filled with a leaden, yellow-grey fog, smoky and sulfurous, obscuring the broad sun, trapping the heat in stifled layers.

Adlan aged.

Her crust thickened into mammoth plates of super-hardened stone. The dense plates resisted the upward press of the underground molten seas. Trapped heat warped the plates, sheared and twisted chasma, and drove the long-chained rupe cliffs high. But the plates held back the molten seas. The old lava domes lay dormant. Only water reached the surface – springs of vented steam. The smoky skies of Adlan cleared. Her surface cooled.

The Seed poured into the springs. Deep pools brightened with bacteria purple, gold, and green. Algae bloomed in hyphae webs and floating islands. Slime crept from pool to pool.

The Blood overflowed. Across the steam-sprayed rock stretched lichen tufts, fungi shelves, and wooly mold. Spongy mosses dissolved the dampened soot, leached minerals from stone, and formed fertile basins of peat. From the peat climbed spiny grass, grey fern, and spiked sedge. Gnats and aphids nibbled through the marsh. Beetles swam and flew.

The life of Adlan burned by many flames but all were fueled and sustained by the deep spring pools. No plant or fungus could survive apart from the fresh vented waters; no insect could travel far from its den of shaded mire. By mother's withering heat, the daughter's growth was stalled, her life constrained to isolated swamp oases, separated by vast stretches of dry and rugged stone.

The Peace savored every pool and breath of vapor, every blade, leaf, root, and wing.

The Fire prodded, tested, searched.

The bridging race of Adlan would not rise from the surface swamps but from the fevered underworld.

Their ancestors fed on the algae-eating worms of the surface pools. Era by era, they adapted to the near boiling water jets. They dove to deeper and deeper hollows to feast on sulfite molds, pleuro slugs, and polypore combs. The bravest, on water's cooled recession, plunged to glimpse caverns of crystal and mist.

By daring generations and agelong struggle, many new species evolved in the underworld...

The kirs. Flat ribboned eels who clung to rocks' curve and fed by bevy of small mouths on barnacles' soft kernel.

The pons. Large, hollow-tubed worms with long outer cilia for swimming and turning, viscid inner cilia for the gathering of waterborne microbes.

The torches. Thin conical floaters with soft-tissued core wrapped by thick bristles, the tips glowing red with rising temperatures, gold with falling waters.

The forms. Shapeshifting colonies of millions of starry cells, their nerves linked by synapse cables radial and elastic, their form in constant flux — in safe and vibrant waters, swelling into tunnel-wide clouds; shuddering and spiraling in extreme heat; in predatory danger, separating into fine-haired chains, scattering, and rejoining...

Every creature of the deep was tended, loved, and carried by the Mother.

Only the lengae received the Father's sparked touch. The Father sculpted their soma sleek and lean to pierce the water like tip of spear. He bent their mouths full circle, split their tongues, and multiplied armed tentacles above and below. He insulated their mantles, vented their muscles by vapor ducts, and eased their respiration by funnel and siphon. He gave them mucal pheromone glands to mark by oiled streaks the surest routes through rock tunnel mazes. He opened their ears to a language of pulses and clicks.

The lengae mapped the steam-gnawed roots of the springs, the feeding hollows, the crystal caves only glimpsed by their ancestors.

The lengae settled in the vast, shallow-laked caverns of the underworld. They diverted caustic vents and dammed pools too alkaline or acidic. They linked the many habitable lakes by channel and canal. They cleared the underwater valleys, carved nests from banks of sylvanite and quartz, and sectioned dens by rings of slate. They farmed lagoons of algae, fish, and worms. Above the water, the lengae cultivated fungal gardens on misty sills. They recorded the symbols of their ancestral lines on the smooth facets of calcite pillars. They raised their dead high onto amethyst altars overlooking the lakes.

By light of Vision, the lengae entered a blessed age.

They ordered time by the natural rhythms of the lakes — their hour fixed by the periodic venting of steam, their day by the cycling of water temperatures, their year by the growth of stalagmites.

They classified the elements of their world, the diverse minerals that formed their rocks, the teeming microbes of their waters, the many forms of gem and crystal.

After much crossbreeding and alteration, they blanketed the lakebeds with a rich variety of marine ferns, feathered seaweed, and grassy corals, rich producers of oxygen and nitrogen.

They explored the underworld beyond the lakes, braving sludge ponds and trickling streams, venturing further and further onto ground. Adapting to longer periods out of the water, the skin of their mantles opened to amphibious pore and wrinkled into folds. Their five eyes widened ovate and sunk nearer to the skin. Their upper arms lengthened for the gripping of stalactites. Their lower arms shortened for finer movements and tool manipulation.

Their quest for knowledge fiercely burned, but the lengae matured to treasure wonder as well, to leave some mysteries unprobed, some beauties undissected. They marveled at the electric mists drawn from the lake at coolest hour to shroud the blue-salt pillars; the splintered cleavage of the cragstone walls whose spindly fibers twisted toward the milk of fern, away from heated touch; the lenses - wispy skins of cartilage — that fed on algal dross, swelled by tented steam, and floated up to highest cavern airs. The lengae left uncut the translucent emeralds found with captured fossils. In clearest pools they ringed the fossils with phosphorescent pearls. They gazed long, dreaming hours into the marine blurred shadows of shell, spine, wing, and tail.

At the height of the lengan blessed age, I was summoned to the fields of Heaven.

The Eternal revealed to me many visions of the downward journey of the lengae, from the spring pools to the cavernous lakes, from the surface of Adlan to her unfathomed depths.

The Proud shared the long and determined struggle of the lengae, their bursts of rapid growth, their elegant evolution, burning spirit, and untamed mind.

"Among the lengae you will find Daavo, a healer who travels lake to lake, accepting no reward," God said. "You will terrify him with visions of rising lava, crumbling rock, and scorching steam."

I obeyed.

Daavo, trembling, called out to God.

And God comforted, assured, instructed.

Daavo visited the lengae of every lake in the underworld.

"The rock beneath us has weakened age by age," Daavo said. "In our short days, we will see the stone give way, the deep fire freed, the lakes burned to mist, and the caverns flooded."

His warning delivered, Daavo set to work, alone, at first. He explored the old lava tubes above the lakes. He blocked by boulders the tubes that ended in voids or narrowed impassable; by the streak of golden sulfides he marked those that climbed to wider channels. Daavo pushed higher and higher. He trained his mind for steepest climb. He acclimated to the air of rarefied steam, adjusted to life out of water.

By dreams of brilliant light, I called him to the surface world.

Daavo climbed to channel's end.

He emerged from the half-shelled lava dome into the wide night sky of Adlan. He watched the drifting banks of thick-misted clouds. He peered beyond to the shimmering stars. A light rain fell.

In the early dawn, Daavo saw the many springs across the skin of Adlan.

"Your people will one day bridge to every spring you see here and bask in every pool," God said. "Now return to the underworld. Prepare the lengae. Guide them. Teach."

Daavo descended.

He traveled the lakes of the underworld once more.

He told of the strange surface lands with dazzling sun and boundless skies. He challenged his people to train for the steep and rugged climb, to prepare for the long skyward journey. He reasoned, urged, and begged.

Most of the lengae, seeing still no sign of the deep fire freed, continued with their lives unchanged.

But many believed. They heard compassion in the voice of Daavo. They saw in his eyes the light of the stars.

The climbing lengae trained with Daavo in the lower tubes and channels of his vertical trail.

The climbers returned to their own lakes. Boulder by boulder, they cleared their own paths. Tunnel by tunnel, they pushed for the Adlan sky.

While the climbers struggled through choking airs and stony labyrinths, the lengae who remained in the underworld lakes watched their waters closely. They observed an undeniable swelling of the lakes, a steady rise in water temperatures, an increased flow of steam and caustics, a stunting of stalagmite growth.

The unmooring of their oldest standards of time unnerved the lengae. The unprecedented disruption of perennial cycles opened many eyes and ears.

On his final journey through the underworld, Daavo encouraged.

"A slivered hour remains," he said. "Train with the climbers. Prepare for long journey. Pray to the One who calls us home."

Most lengae of the underworld listened to Daavo. They trained in the tunnels over their lakes. They gathered supplies. They prayed.

But the climbing veterans were less than welcoming toward these newcomers.

The veterans complained to Daavo through messenger chain. They asked permission to leave the newcomers behind. They asked to continue their own climbing and finish their mapping of the upper channels. They promised to return and help the newcomers after all veterans had seen the surface world.

Daavo refused their request.

"Many times the lengae of the underworld have helped us, many times fed and equipped," Daavo said. "Do you resent them for their late arrival? Do you expect a greater reward for yourselves in the world above? Know that the newcomers will suffocate in narrow tunnels and fall from sheer-walled flues. And your only reward will be survival, long haunted by their cries."

By sting of Daavo's words, the veteran hearts were changed. They trained with the newcomers in the lower tunnels over the lakes. They patiently taught their lengae brothers and sisters and shared all that they knew of climbing. With fear and compassion, they watched the newcomers struggle, weak of arm, faint of breath.

On fire's eve, the Near transformed me.

I coursed as tails of glowing smoke across the lakes of the underworld to frighten the lingering into flight – to save any who would yet be saved.

As I ascended the tunnels, I cooled into a dampened mist. I blanketed the anxious lengae above. I summoned all into a sweet sleep, their flesh forgotten, wrapped in purest silence, drifting in the stillness between stars.

The Mighty held back the deep fire until Adlan shivered through her core. When no more time could be given to the lengae, the Grieved released the churning seas.

Sulfurous steam exploded through the lake vents. Streams of black smoke scorched the cavern ceilings. Stalactites melted into stubs.

Magma flooded the chambers in scalding torrents. White swallowed red as the blood-crusted skin melted under fresh outpour. The lakes boiled and hissed. The underworld trembled and groaned. A shrieking vapor sped through every higher passage, crack, and tunnel.

The lengae fled.

And the Spirit burned fiercer than the fire.

Daavo calmed, directed, guided.

The veterans shielded slow climbers from blasts of steam. They lifted the weak and carried the faint. They stretched themselves across crumbling paths.

When the long journey of the lengae ended, they gazed from domes of rock into the Adlan night. They breathed the open air beneath the sapphire stars. They saw the spring pools glitter blue and green.

From the bright pools of Adlan, I followed the Winged beyond galaxies' soft glow, between the slender threads of the Blackstrom web, into the starless void.

I was young then, very young.

Terrified of the empty abyss, I chased after my Shelter.

I begged to return to the worlds of sound, form, and color.

But the Lord, silent, led me deeper into the darkness.

He hid the hanging waters from my eyes.

By fearsome wake he drew me beyond the stars' last glimmer.

All was drained by black.

"Why do you fear, child?" the Lord asked.

"Because there is no light here," I answered. "Because there is no life."

"But I am here."

And then I understood. The Highest wanted to share with me. Not the terror of the void. But the joy of first creation.

By summon, bend, and warp of light, the Infinite reversed the outward flow of time, cast ripples back to center.

The emptiness around us filled with writhing heat.

The darkness blinded by eye of seething fire.

Fevered waves exploded.

We rode the stellar winds.

We pulled from dawning tide.

The Humble spun great stars and planets.

And I formed seven moons, my children.

Age by age, I nurtured the seven moons, my children. My winds blew meteors astray. I stoked their cores, stirred their mantles, plowed their crusts. I spread damp mists and cast soft dews. I carved by ice and rain.

But no moon yielded any higher, lasting life. Like piercing thorn, I remembered great Daavo and the glory of the lengae. My young heart hardened.

I questioned God, embittered. "Seven children, seven stillborn," I said.

"Each of your creations is beautiful," God answered, "each entirely unique."

"Yet all are lifeless after ages' care."

"Let the roots deepen, my friend. The stems may yet climb, the petals still burst."

"May? What greater care can I give? How many ages must I wait?"

"This is love, Crea. The mother hopes against reason. The father waits, helpless. And a seed is only a seed."

I was sent far away from my children to swiftly spinning Octuel, a cold and arid planet distant to his star.

From high above Octuel, his surface appeared a flat, smooth plain of dimly faded brown.

Flying nearer, the brown separated into shades of pale bronze, bone grey, and ashen silver; the plains wrinkled into serpentine-ridged hills and deep, winding gorges.

On the ground, I touched his dry, clay skin. I felt his lashing, powdered gusts. I shivered in his shadows. I thought that no life could survive in a place so windworn, cold, and dry.

But I discovered many clever forms of life on Octuel - lizards that warmed themselves at the foci of wide parabolic pits; beetles that leaned into the early morning gales to gather tiny water droplets down their long-grooved wings; flat worms that tunneled through butte towers to drape themselves in the afternoon sun, mine damp mineral streaks, and nest in warm-wrapped huddles through the night.

And I saw the magnificent sun griffins whose continual migration kept them always in the light.

The griffins dozed on warmlit, claystone arches. Their wide-curved wings draped the arches, golden-feathered wingtips reaching nearly to the ground. Their long and muscled feline tails coiled loosely around the arches' crests; the tails' diamond-vaned ends dangled free in the wind. Their slender ears of midnight blue tucked against their snow-white crests. Their beaks hung low like rusted visors.

As soon as they felt the cold touch of night, the griffins sprang from their arches to chase the sun.

Heading into the wind, they tucked themselves into sharp arrows, propelled by spiral whips of tail and tight wing flutters, keeping low to sheltered ridgeline.

Sailing with strong gusts, they stretched their wings wide, ballooned above the hills, and steered through rushing skies by turn of beak or ruddered tail.

Thirsty, they veered toward the summer pole to rake ice from frozen cliff walls.

Hungry, they snatched by talon sunning worms and lizards.

The griffins flew across Octuel's broad chest from touch of night to edge of dawn.

Then they dozed on claystone arches.

"It is time, my friend," God said. "The griffins should no longer be silent. You must free their tongue."

"Who am I, Lord? How can I give voice to the griffins?"

"Since the first of wing dove from clay ridge, their cry has been stored, aching and burning. By dream of star birth, you will summon them into the highest skies. In ether chase, may they call out."

The Power stopped the turn of Octuel.

The Gentle cast long sleep upon the griffins.

And I, by sweeping vision, took them into the heart of a starcloud coalescing. They rode the searing gas streams nearer and nearer to the core, their wingtips lit by furnace glow. The griffins were crushed by the weight of the massive cloud, blinded by the spark of star's first fire, deafened by fusion's thunderous quake.

Outward, they launched.

Tumbling and reeling, they passed from densest heat to coldest void.

Across the void, I appeared to the stricken flock, my mooncast flank their brightest light.

Flying near, I called out in the tongues of many creatures, many worlds. "Speak, my friends, speak," I cried.

My cries woke the griffins back on the sunlit arches of Octuel.

The griffins shook the strange dream from their eyes.

They followed me above the vicious surface winds and into the high still airs.

The sheer climb drained them.

They groaned through every flutter of wing and whip of tail.

Some of the griffins, fearful of the dark voids above, abandoned their chase.

But others climbed on. They gasped the thin air through widening beaks. They jostled for glimpse of my eyes.

"Speak, sisters, speak," I called again.

The chasing griffins moaned but spoke no words.

I ended our grueling ascent.

I veered from the bright-lit solar cone above Octuel toward his darkened side below.

Through shadowed airs we raced.

The griffins pressed by desperate flutters, but I pulled away by wingstrokes powerful and deep.

I hoped for mighty cry from the griffins. I prayed for language to be born, first words to split the skies. But the griffins fell away in the darkness. Lone fliers turned back for warmth and sun. Paired couples turned for ground.

Entering the darkest quarter, I thought that all had surrendered the chase. Yet two still pursued - a mother and daughter. They struggled far behind me, spent and weary, gliding long between weak flutters.

The Knowing whispered to me: "Faster, Crea, faster."

I hesitated, my eyes on the slow and fading griffins.

"Faster, Crea."

I obeyed.

With all my strength, I flew for the sun.

I rounded Octuel.

I passed from shadow to light.

I looked back to the void.

And in the waiting, I was tested. Did I still hope? Did I believe? I watched for the griffins, aching, afraid. No eyes flashed out of the void. No flurry of wings or stretch of talon. The void lay quiet. The void lay still.

But the voice of the daughter suddenly pierced the air. Her cry seized and tore me. It was a wail of grief. It was a raging scream against all hunger and cold, all darkness and dying. It was a plea to live, the prayer of generations.

Alone, the daughter emerged from the void.

I called to her. I flew to her. "Tsiol," I said. "You will be Tsiol, the first to speak, the highest of griffins."

We glided together into the light.

Tsiol sang tribute for her fallen mother.

I sang prayer for seven children.

Tsiol, the first, returned to her people to teach and to share.

Transformed to wind, I passed among the griffins.

I heard the people answer Tsiol, their tongues finally freed, their voices louder than the fiercest gales of Octuel. All sang for Tsiol's mother.

And the Wild raced beside me among the arches, our currents intertwined.

"You must return now," the Patient said. "I have heard strange stories of your seven moons.

"A serpent halves itself on mid-air strike.

"A golden grass sweeps the lands, dissolving by summit rain, descending alluvial fan and re-forming.

"Blue pedes build bridges over the glaciers, raise temples of ice, and carve tunneled kingdoms underground.

"Star-limbed climbers sculpt hybrid trees by graft, bow, and weave; they shelter lofty dens by branch-vine canopy, sloped and sagging by weight of fruit.

"And, in shadowed sea caves, great chrysalide hang. Their clear skin throbs orange and crimson, cracked by horns and tail. Ptero wings stretch slow."

Ages later, when my early joy of mothering had long faded, when my seven children grieved me and my highest species failed, the Wise lifted me into the falls of Heaven.

I swam the many-colored waters. The healing traveled deep.

I bowed my head beneath the highest fall. The crashing torrents emptied every cumbrous thought, swallowed every fear and worry.

In dreaming pools, I drifted days, my eyes on wandering suns.

The Giving walked with me along the shore.

"It is time, my friend," God said. "I must take the flesh once more."

I pled for a final chance to reach my children.

"It is time," God said. "Your creatures cling to ways of blood. The highest gorge and trample."

I begged for one more generation. I named many races of the Hollow who had turned their path before the Spirit's tearing.

"It is time," God said. "No one loves beyond their own."

Silent, I stared into the golden mists of the shore.

The words of God struck deep.

The truth settled heavy upon me.

Without perfect light, my children would never see these waters.

Without purest love, my spirit, my blood, my life would die forever.

"Come with me while the way is prepared," God said. "I will show you a place unlike any other."

The Highest guided me to Tane, a world of chaos and extreme.

Tane, the dark planet, lurched and wobbled through his steep eccentric orbit.

Across his rocky skin, snaking tails of grey mist twisted and slashed. Banks of silver haze pitched and rolled to clashing tides. Clouds formed suddenly in open airs, burst by lightning, and blackened on descent.

The fierce winds of Tane rivalled Octuel in strength. Frosted gusts like winter wraiths drove me side to side, seized me, wrenched me, hurled me. When the gusts stalled, I plunged toward the rocky spires of Tane. But hot thermals rose from deep molten stirrings; the bellowed rushes caught and lifted.

In a single glance across Tane's sky, I saw whirlpools of falling rain, plumes of risen steam, slanted columns of green sleet, and a swarm of purple hailstones, hovering lost like queenless flock.

The Lord, as thread of light, descended.

By prayer, I turned to second thread.

We lit the stone needle spires piercing deep into the sky. The wind-swayed towers bent and thickened as we fell. The towers multiplied at their bases like myriad tree roots. Beneath us stretched a vast rock webbing, a wide-pored lattice of green-black shale and rusty gypsum, a boundless skeleton of thin and gnarled ribs. Tane was a world of interwoven land and sky, a planet without ground.

The Curious throbbed with lucent energy, branched from single thread of light, and rushed among the pores, probing, searching.

Signs appeared across the dampened arms of shale and gypsum - the stretch and curl of elbowed antennae; red-glass worm tails wrapped and coiled; dracon flaps unfurled to glide.

"Follow me," the Proud said.

Deeper and deeper we plunged.

Behind, the storming skies of Tane receded. Broad patches of rain, sleet, and hail shriveled into specks of grey.

Below, the rock lattice tightened and condensed. The many stone ribs blurred into a single mass of bone.

Wondrous colonies emerged among the aerate rock — the communal farms of many species.

Each colony we saw was sheltered by the complex webs of purple spinneret ants. Crowning layers of spiraled netting deflected downward winds and gathered dribbling rains onto wide loops and irrigating drip lines. Finer capillary meshes rounded its flanks, blunting lateral gusts, absorbing aeroplankton. An inverted cone of thick-spun radial strands shielded its underside from rising blasts of steam, diverting heat outward and away.

The wildly varying species tended vertical crops. Mantids with sharp-spined forelegs combed and harvested overhanging tangles of red moss. White basilisks weeded the honeydew columns of mold and mildew. Candle wasps glowed in coves of blue lichen. Long spirulae mollusks twined down arches of wet algae-coated rock, fertilizing by saliva. Bronze vipers plowed fresh stone by the sand, grind, and scrape of their keel-scaled bellies.

Teeming teardrop aphids climbed the fine-veined meshes of the colony flanks and swallowed the plankton slurry. At meshes' end, abdomens swollen and bulging, the aphids secreted a hardening foam into the mouths of titan beetles. The beetles, by mandibles tined and rounded, worked the foam into waxen balls. They built twisting bridges across the stone's wide pores, open nests of ovoid cells, looping tubes and ducts, ringed balcony canals.

By medium of corpse and molting, artists worked between the colonies.

The artists, teams of every species, harnessed the strongest winds of Tane and magnified his dimmest light.

Wide lenses spanned the voids of stone – thin, thousand-eyed sculptures of hollowed thorax, shedded snakeskin, translucent wing. The lenses caught each ray of fallen sun to cast a deep marine glow across the colonies, a sharp and fluid turning, emerald, purple, bronze, and amber. The living worked by ancestors' light.

Over stone ribs' bend, artists set long chains of empty beetle shells, sealed by aphid wax, narrowing shell by shell. These formed great horns to channel gusts through reeds of lizard fin and out of slitted tails. The tunneled gales roared upon release, whistling fierce through shifting scales, drowning out all other winds. The manifold roar of the horns echoed through the voids, fusing fuller, dulled by stone collisions into a gentler, richer sound. By colonies' web, the roar had softened into the quiet hum of deepest space.

"Look," God said, "a seeker starts her journey."

An alder fly entered the heart of her colony.

From vaulted sanctuary she took into her forelegs a shard of bloodstone, faintly shimmering.

At colony's edge, she prayed.

"We will shield and guide Odyr, the seeker," God said. "This day you will see the crystal fires of Tane, my friend."

Odyr, the brave, left her home for the core of Tane. She flew downward through the tightening voids of stone. She rounded bends of rusty gypsum. She sharply veered through crooks of shale.

When the tunnels narrowed and the hollows shrank too small, Odyr tucked her wings and glided slow.

Shard in mouth, she crawled through leanest cleft and crevice.

The Compassionate breathed cool mists against the scalding blasts of steam. I stretched myself upon the wings of Odyr, wrapped her sides, and split the winds against her. We passed through total darkness, steered by touch of mist.

When the flesh of Odyr could give no more, I lifted her by weightless airs.

When my own strength failed, the Fearsome carried.

A wide pit opened.

A crimson and silver light engulfed.

Odyr crept to the pit's edge, trembling through her wings.

I, too, trembled before the fire.

"What do you see, Crea?" God asked.

"I see an explosion of bloodred fire, swift and fierce as birth of star," I answered. "The untiring flames streak high. They strike for the upper world like noval lances. But silver works within the crimson. It courses through veins branched and bursting. A skin like mercury curls back; the sharp flames bend to rounded plume. I see the fluid harden, striate, cleave. Oh, God, the crystal shines - the sweep of multiplying prisms, the bright and splintered seas, the blinding facet turn. And the silver falls by leaden torrent back to crimson fire."

Never smaller, I stared into the crystal fires of Tane, transfixed by the clashing powers, stricken by the violent tearing. To the Hollow's filling, to the end of days, I might have stayed.

But the alder fly flew down.

Odyr plunged into the storming air.

Shard to chest, wings tucked, she fell as fast as the silver rain.

I rushed to shield her, but the Lord held me within the pit. "Watch," said God, "Odyr will be saved by slender shard."

The dim bloodstone against her chest burned with crimson light as she entered the heart of Tane.

The light surged silver.

Launched from the heart, Odyr sailed high.

In the wide pit mouth, she passed us by.

She headed for her home, her eyes bright lit by twin, reflected fire – crimson and silver.

"What have I seen, my God?" I asked in the narrow voids, following Odyr.

"The early ages of Tane were murderous and bleak," the Eternal said, "raw with tears and hunger, dark as any Blackstrom world. In the lizard wars, the killing pits were opened wide - enemies tortured, eyes blinded, limbs pulled slow. The fallen of Tane cried out to the sky.

"And the stars joined their cry.

"And Heaven shivered through her seas.

"Our holy rage burned against the cruelty. The wounded core of Tane boiled. The bloodfire seethed. Unrestrained, our anger would have melted every stone rib, every killer's claw. But blessed Daughter, Ana, tore herself from our side. She left the trees of Paradise for the barren voids of Tane. She shed her wind-jeweled cloak and train of prismed mist to take up silver lizard hide.

"By searing dream, the blessed were drawn to first colony. Ana opened the spinneret pore of the purple ant. She seeded lichen coves by spittle, stretched honeydew threads by lick of tongue, and pulled moss from the barest stone. She formed a common language from the sounds of every species. She led communal meal and song.

"When thieves and killers surrounded the first colony, Ana beamed like silver star. She fled to the killing pits, drawing the lower beasts, saving the blessed.

"And the killers, hating light, struck Ana down.

"And the thieves hurled my Daughter, piece by piece, into the fire.

"Our anger overflowed. Bloodfire launched for sky. The molten seas exploded.

"But Ana moved by climbing branch and vein, by fiercest love undying. Her cooling silver permeated the burning crimson. She quenched by multiplying crystal. She sated righteous anger.

"Ana reined the fiery deluge, but the tips of the highest flames embrittled, cracked, and flew. A glassy, slivered hail showered the thieves and killers of the pits. Bloodstone shards sunk deep into their sides.

"*The shards passed in rapid cycle between crimson and silver light, between scorching heat and numbing chill.*

"*The thieves and killers groaned from the agony of mind – their sweet relief so short, their returning pain so sure.*

"*The beasts climbed from the pits.*

"*They crawled in limping throng back to the first colony.*

"*Whimpering, they asked for mercy.*

"*And the blessed wept for Ana.*

"*And the blessed pulled the shards.*

"*The beasts tucked the shards to their chests. They ventured higher than the first colony. They built sanctuaries, coves, gardens, bridges.*"

The wings of Crea three times stretched to span then tucked against her blue-white flanks, their crater seas still drifting slow. Stones cracked loudly under her sapphire gauntlets as she rose to her feet; pebbles ground to powder.

It is time, my friend. You must now return to the island world.

"Crea, Crea," Dyraveen said, "your stories are half-told. Rest a little longer."

The worlds you have seen - the mysteries revealed - these are not enough?

"None will be forgotten," Dyraveen said, "each pondered and treasured. But please tell more, great Crea. You were changed just now in the telling of your story. Your eyes opened to new light."

Yes. By a truth wonderful. And terrible. An irony pathetic.

"My friend, what stirred inside you?"

Seven times the Life was torn for me, seven Sons and Daughters stripped - all to die upon my moons and suffer like bright Ana. And when the choice was made at Heaven's falls, God thought too much of my light pain and lesser grief. The Fool led me to the colonies of

Tane to comfort and distract; the Highest placed me higher, forgetting seven steep and looming roads.

Together, they climbed the rocky hillside.

They watched the crawling turn of the great planet, the weaving flow of vapor seas, pale green, gold, and violet.

Crea named each dotted moon that crossed the seas.

Dyraveen, skinned one, you must soon heal the world you took to war. Remember me long, my friend, my brother.

They left at dawn for the island world.

At saltland parting, Dyraveen could not look away. He stared into the shrinking star of Crea's trail, her shroud of blazing sapphire.

Dyraveen, blinded, alone, wandered the wasteland of Andara.

XIII. LLEVAR

The faint scent of smoke drew Dyraveen toward the sea. He stumbled through the saltland dunes, still blinded by the light of Crea. Weak and famished, he leaned helplessly into the headwind gales. Sideways gusts turned and spun him. In lulls of wind, he staggered forward.

He reached the shore at sunset, his vision cleared.

In a wind-sheltered cove, he found a boulder shattered into many pieces. The jagged cleavage of the fragments glowed like burning coals.

Near to the glow, Dyraveen felt no thirst, no hunger.

He knelt and touched the burning stone. A numbing chill poured through his flesh, an invigorating heat through his bones.

Savoring, he lay back. He gazed into the emerald moon, mouthing thankful prayer.

From the sea, a voice called out to him: "Why do you rest, Dyraveen? Why do you linger ashore?"

Dyraveen looked out to the sea. He saw a man of tattered, grey cloak standing upon the water, bobbing high with each new wave. "Who are you, Lord?" Dyraveen asked.

"I am Llevar. The slaughtered. The risen. Come to me, my friend."

Dyraveen ran into the sea.

His first step touched the sandy bottom, covering his feet with foam.

His second step sunk deeper, water rising to his knees.

His third step touched a solid spine. He looked down to see a ray, broad-winged and bright silver. Distracted, unbalanced, he stumbled.

The ray darted to catch the falling rider.

Dyraveen landed on his side. He stretched himself prone and gripped the wings' highest arch.

The ray sped forward with whipping twin tails. High to low, they rode the water's skin, crashing through the crests of waves, surging through the troughs.

The waves suddenly flattened; the sea abruptly calmed.

The silver rays of Dyraveen and Llevar circled one another slowly in the moonlit waters.

Dyraveen stood to face his God.

He saw familiar wounds under the skin of Llevar. The oldest scars of Ciralan's knife and branding iron glowed a fluid silver. The lined scars of fang and talon pulsed a vibrant green. The goring work of horns and tusks throbbed a veiny blue.

"Tonight, you will be privileged witness to a final wonder," Llevar said. "Tomorrow, your own labor will begin."

"And what will be my labor?" Dyraveen asked, "my great purpose in this world?"

"To watch and to listen. To follow and wait."

"I will serve like deadened stone?"

"In your old life, the commander led by fear and threat. But now you will follow humblest Teacher."

Llevar touched the chest of Dyraveen.

The lungs of Dyraveen filled. Then rested.

Llevar prayed with eyes to the deep and churning sea: "Hallowed Mother, Lavish Father, pull back the veil once more. Pour fresh blessing over Dyraveen, your servant. Reveal a final vision - a colony's birth - before his labor stretches long before him, before pain carves too deep."

Like sword of Obdiel, the flesh of Llevar glowed with flame.

He dove into the sea. Dyraveen followed.

The burning light of Llevar drove back the marine darkness.

They plunged together, deeper and deeper, scattering clouds of small fish and eel, long shadows fleeing from the fire.

As they descended, the flamelit waters passed around them, thin as aerie sky.

The depths parted with titan groan.

By a touch of shoulder, Llevar halted the fall of Dyraveen. "Come no closer," Llevar said.

While Dyraveen hung in the undersea void like a red-clouded moon, bright Llevar pierced the depths like wandering star.

The seabed emerged under his light.

A broad valley stretched to the edge of light's shadow.

Llevar called out loud warning to the creatures of the floor, his voice like a glacier cracking to ground.

By racing fin, tentacle flurry, and scampering shell, the valley cleared of all life.

The detritus settled still.

The star of Llevar crashed.

The seabed shook and howled.

The burning light passed from the flesh of Llevar. Chasms of fire spread from his feet. Widening rifts drew lava from mantle like knife-opened wounds. Red rivers branched through the valley. Geysers of steam shot through cracks.

Llevar worked.

His arms wove fierce circles.

The geysers were bent and brought low, the red rivers lifted.

Llevar collided counterspun streams, crashing lava and steam through the depths of cold sea. The steam-pored lava swelled. Then hardened.

From seabed to surface, Llevar crafted great spirals and arcs.

The quenched rock darkened; serpentine heat faded red to black.

Llevar walked the chasms.

His old wounds returned; his scars shined bright.

Light - silver, emerald, blue – poured out from the rifts, climbed the rocky arcs and spirals, throbbed the deadened stone.

Llevar again called out to the creatures of the sea, this time welcoming all.

As the creatures cautiously returned to the transformed valley, Llevar waved Dyraveen to join him.

Llevar touched the face of Dyraveen.

The future opened to his eyes.

Cyan algae thrived in the tunneled pores of the rock. On the surface sprouted thick-polyped seagrass, open-gilled fungi, tasseled moss, lichen wool.

The sea creatures feasted from surface to floor. They mated under spiral shadow, raised their young in nested pore.

When the living stone budded, stub-horned narwhals tended the branches, guided links from arc to arc.

Ribbon eel stretched vines of kelp and webs of bladdered ivy.

Sleek terrapin groomed floating wisteria gardens.

Lancelets raised the crowns of fern that reached for morning sun.

At pillars' base the nacre shells of fallen whelk and mussel were crushed under trains of tetrobite feet, the fragments stored in thorax sac, embedded in the rising pillars – long strings of iridescent pearl.

The waste of higher spiral creatures floated down to fertilize the crawling anemone forests, to nourish annelid, snail, and krill.

Lantern nettles ballooned over molten vents, riding thermals to higher waters and richer arcs, leaving trails of glittering amethyst, glowing ruby through their manes.

And from far seas the giants came - the dying, older races. The icthyan divers chased golden murrel from spiral tip to pillar base, catching few, collapsing hungry. Saurian dragons shredded the ivy webs to duel in open spaces, victims falling lifeless from the blood-inked clouds, dying victors soon to follow. The heavy-plated archelon, frustrated by meals of wispy vine, crashed against the rock pillars like axe to tree until their snouts bubbled red; their shells cracked and split. The scaled kronos sharks, eluded by terrapin and eel, ravenous, enraged, grinded their racks of teeth to nubs on jagged coral thorn.

"Back in Pheran homeland," Llevar asked, "would you return to ways of violence? to mind of war?"

"Could I betray great Crea, my teacher, my friend?" Dyraveen answered. "Her many worlds still sear my eyes with striking vision. Her hard words hurt me more than skinning."

"You know of higher ways? of paths to life?"

"I know that life burns fierce all throughout the Hollow. It gasps for breath. It crawls for light. It claws for every scrap of food and drop of water. And the Creator suffers with all creatures."

"But each is doomed to death and ash."

"Each must trust eternal Fire."

"Come with me, my friend. You must learn to sail."

On the back of goldleaf porpoise, they traveled by night to a chain of long-stretched islands over jagged seabed rift.

They slept on the beach of the largest isle, their backs to a thick-mossed boulder.

The morning sun revealed a warship off the isle, a wrecked Andaran vessel lodged upon a reef, its deck many times bombed and black-scorched, its hull wide split and filling with the tide.

They swam to the ship. They scavenged cables, ropes, tarps, tools.

Back on the isle, they gathered strongest driftwood planks and beams. For keel, they found a tall tree fallen into gully, arched by its own weight.

They worked through the day, sharing sweat and trading stories. They drank from stony pond, boiled shellfish over fire.

At dusk they gathered more moss to pad their bed between the boulders.

As the moons climbed high, Llevar prayed old poetry of the Cerrans.

Dyraveen listened, mournfully silent, his eyes on the bomb-blackened ship.

Day by day, their boat took shape.

The hull was formed by patchwork timber, rounded bow to stern.

The mast was set, the rudder fixed.

The sails were cut, stretched, tied.

When Dyraveen planned a wide and sheltering cabin, Llevar stopped him.

"Only one will make the long journey," Llevar said. "A single canvas will shield you from the wind and save you from the sun."

At nightly fire, the eyes of Dyraveen returned to the warship again and again.

"Let me gather the bones of the fallen Andarans," Dyraveen said. "Let me honor by pyre and shrine."

"You yearn for things beyond your power," Llevar answered. "We strive forward, child. Ever forward."

They launched their boat in the first heat of summer.

Llevar circled their isle. Then looped the island chain. Then traveled far into the sea.

"Tomorrow, I watch," Llevar said, "and you lead."

Dyraveen learned all summer from Teacher, patient and prodding. He learned the rhythm of the winds and tides, the reading of the clouds by color, shape, and turn. He learned the limits of his craft, the sounds of rising stress and strain, the creaking of each timber.

By summer's end, Dyraveen could sail alone on stormy, white-capped waters.

As the fall nights chilled and the sunlit hours shortened, Dyraveen slowed in his movements. Each morning he woke with swollen knees and elbows. His muscles cramped suddenly throughout the day; his heart fluttered weakly; his breathing stalled.

"The disease of my father," Dyraveen said. "I had hoped to outrun it to the end."

"We will wring strength from the sickness," Llevar said.

"But the illness cripples, Lord."

"The boy's adventures underground, the soldier's many wasteland marches, the man's long journey through Andaran jungle – Did these strengthen you or weaken? Were you forged or were you broken? My friend, you will learn great patience and compassion from this sickness. In moments of its waning, you will spring like uncaged beast."

Dyraveen dreamed one night of Cyadae and his mother. The two women walked together through starry fields of light. Their eyes blazed sapphire under bursting supernova. Across their skin rolled Aviet seas.

Dyraveen woke alone and set to sail.

MY DEEPEST THANKS

Heather
Mom and Dad
Jennifer Chikhani
Arik, Sam, and Ashley
Chris, Clint, and Hope
Allen, Rhonda, Lori, and Family
William English
Dustin Riedel
David Shord
Reid Gerken
Joseph Dove
Jesse Arriaga
Collin Hirano
Chad Demeyer
Dr David Hindman
Dr George R Wettach
Damaris Delmy Varela
Skye and Amy Bailey
Giovanni Disandro
William Rochefort
Heather Hatley
Dawn Ruskan
Scott Mitchell
Eric Hamblen
Devon Etter
Brett Dewey
Jeana Pillion

Eric Lopresti
Les Thomason
Marc Takeuichi
Krista Sandness
Maggie and Helena
Olivia, Lori, and Les
Kris Engelhardt Raley
Corrie Batishko Busch
Brian Smith McCallum
Michael and Eden Kidane
Matthew, Shanta, and Marvin Hill
Jeff, Chris, Lindsey, Katie, and Jill Troftgruben
Ruth, Joseph, Faven, Hermela, and Fisseha Assefa
Jhanzeib, Sanam, Saba, Kiran, Sana, and Kauser Dean

MY DEBTS OF MIND AND SPIRIT

Jesus
Hope Sandoval
David Roback
Mazzy Star
Ernest Becker
Dostoyevsky
Solzhenitsyn
Kafka
Melville
Cervantes
Milton
Caravaggio
Giacometti
Subcomandante Marcos
Rage Against the Machine
Zack de la Rocha
Noam Chomsky

ALSO BY
GARY DAVID SPRINGER

Phera (2009)
Gabriel (2007)
Fuegos (2006)
Coma Dreams (2005)

www.garyspringer.com

gary_springer@hotmail.com